D0851359

The Culai Heritage

by

Michael Scott

Meisha Merlin Publishing, Inc
Atlanta, GA

THE CULAI HERITAGE

An MM Publishing Book
Published by Meisha Merlin Publishing, Inc.
PO Box 7
Decatur, GA 30031

Editing & interior layout by Stephen Pagel
Copyediting & proofreading by Teddi Stransky and Kim Holec

ISBN: 1-892065-17-7

http://www.MeishaMerlin.com

First MM Publishing edition: January 2001
Printed in the United States of America
0 9 8 7 6 5 4 3 2 1
Library of Congress Cataloging-in-Publication Data

Scott, Michael, 1959-
    The Culai heritage / by Michael
    Scott.— 1st MM Pub. ed.
        p. cm.
"An MM Publishing book."
    ISBN 1-892065-17-7 (alk. paper)
    1. Bards and bardism—Fiction. 2.
Fantasy fiction, English. I. Title.
    PR6069.C5953 C85 2000
    823'.914—dc21
                        00-010860

Table of Contents

THE
CULAI
HERITAGE

List of the Gods

PANTHEON OF THE OLD FAITH

Lady Adur   Goddess of Nature; sister of Quilida
Alile   The Judge Impartial; Judger of Souls
Bainte   Winged messengers of Death, servants of Mannam
Baistigh   Lord of Thunder
Buiva   God of War and Warriors, the Warrior
Cam   God of Bridges
C'lte, Qua'lte and **Sa'lte**   The Triad of Life
Coulide Dream-Maker   God of Dreams
Lady Dannu   Prime female deity
Ectoraige   God of Learning and Knowledge
Faurm   Sea God; brother of Faurug
Faurug   The Nightwind
Feitigh   The Windlord, father of Faurm and Faurug
Fiarle   The Little God of Icy Spaces
Hanor and **Hara**   The first Great Gods
Huide   The Little God of Summer Rain
Luid   Fire Sprite
Lady Lussa   Goddess of the Moon
Maker and **User**   The Early Gods
Mannam of the Silent Wood   The Lord of the Dead
Maurug   The Destroyer
Nameless God   God of Madness and Delusion
Nusas   The Sun God
Ochrann   God of Medicine and Healing
Oigne and **Uide**   Gods of Cities
Quilida   Goddess of Growth
Shoan   The Smith
Sleed   The Maker of Mountains
Snaitle   The Cold God
The Stormlord   Unnamed God of Storms
Taisce   The Dewspreader
Tatocci   God of Fools
Uimfe   The Lord of Night
Visslea   The Spirit of the Mists

GODS OF THE NEW RELIGION

Aiaida   Lord of the Sea Wind
Hercosis   The Dreamlord; one of the twelve Trialdone
Hirwas   God of Far Seeing; one of the twelve Trialdone
Sheesarak   The Destroyer; one of the twelve Trialdone
Lady Asherat   The Taker of Souls; one of the twelve Trialdone
Ghede   Lord of the Beasts; one of the twelve Trialdone
Kishar Stormbrother   God of Storms
Kloor   God of War
Libellius   God of Death
Quatatal   Bronze Sun God
Tixs   Bat God; a minor godling
Trialos   The New God

OTHER GODS

Aonteketi
Six great birds that were once Gods of the Pantheon
   Scmall: The Spirit of the Clouds
   Kloca: Lord of Stone and Rock
   Aistigh: Lord of Subtle Harmonies; brother of Danta
   Danta; Lord of Verse
   Dore: Lord of Smiths (silver and goldsmiths)
   Fifhe: Lady of Beasts; daughter of Lady Adur
Bor   The Man God
Chriocht the Carpenter   Halfling carpenter of the Gods of
the Pantheon; brother of Toriocht
Lutann   Demon God
Quisleedor   Life Child of Sleed, the Maker of Mountains *(see*
Pantheon of the Old Faith)
Sinn   Mist Demon, Sun God
Toriocht the Smith   Halfling smith to the Gods of the
Pantheon

PRIMAL SPIRITS

Chrystallis The wind that blew through the soul of the One; The Soulwind

The One The first being

The Three Cords Disruption, Annihilation and Chaos

Duaite Collective name for evil spirits; Duaiteoiri (singular)

Auithe Collective name for good spirits; Auitheoiri (singular)

MAGICIAN'S LAW

Prologue

I have collected many versions of the life of Paedur the Bard in my travels, and since it is a tale which, with the embroidery of time, loses nothing in the telling, I have yet to hear two which match in every detail.

When I attempted to recreate the life and wanderings of the Bard, I went back to the original sources, and talked to the few who remained alive who had actually met him, or else read the accounts they had left behind. So, in many ways, this is really their account, their impressions of a remarkable man.

Some storytellers begin with his meeting with C'lte, the God of Life, while some others start with his encounter with Mannam, the Lord of Death. However, I have always thought that to understand the Bard, and why he accepted Death's quest, one must begin earlier—much earlier—and so I always start with a quote from Lilis' account of the last of the Nine Great Battles of Antiquity.

For a day and a night the great armies had fought, and when the mists of morning had cleared, nothing moved, save the tattered pennants on broken spears that fluttered in the rank breeze. Ten thousand men had given their lives in the last great battle between the Light and the Dark—but to no avail, for the Balance remained.

And the ravens and wolves gathered and fed.

Now in the afternoon of the third day after the battle, Lugas the Bard rode through the Vale of Anfuile and out on to the Plain of Goride—but which was thereafter known as the Bloodplain—and the carnage, the reeking dead, the butchered lives, and the senseless waste sickened him.

And as he rode away, he composed the Lay of Battle, and blessed it with the Old Magic, investing it with the power to quieten the most violent or maddened warriors.

And later generations came to know it as the Lament of Lugas, or the Dove's Cry...

The Bard wanted that magical lament. When he first took to the roads as a wandering bard, he used the opportunity to search through the libraries of the Tribes of the Seven Nations, the archives of the

monks and the Records of the Guild of Scribes—but to no avail.
When his fame became such that he was called to the Imperial Court,
many of his friends were surprised that he accepted—but he only
did so to gain access to the Emperor's huge library. Again, he was
disappointed.

The years passed and he eventually despaired of ever finding it.
When the situation at court changed, and his position became precarious, he retired to the solitude and silence of the forest, and he
almost forgot about the Lament of Lugas...

Life of Paedur, the Bard

1
The Quest

Mannam is the God of the Dead, and his guise is that of a withered and blasted tree...

C'lte is the third part of the Triad of Life; he often affects the appearance of a brightly clad effete youth...

Pantheon of the Old Faith

The amber ball of the sun sank down behind the mountains in the west, briefly touching them with fire, while the forest that nestled beneath them slipped into shadow. There was a long moment of twilight silence as the forest composed itself for night, and then the first rustlings began as the night creatures stirred from their burrows and nests.

Wood snapped, and silence fell again.

The tall shape of a man moved slowly through the trees, stooping now and again to pick up dead wood. His clothes had once been fine but were now patched and repaired, the ornate threadwork lost beneath a covering of filth and grime, and in the wan twilight only the bardic sigil high on his left shoulder took the light.

And it was difficult to recognise in the gaunt haggard face and sunken eyes Paedur the Bard, once Lore-Master to most of the kings of the Seven Nations.

A chill wind ruffled his long fine hair, and he turned his face into it; it was fresh with the tang of salt—a sign of rain. Paedur tossed his armful of rotten wood onto a rough oblong of cloth, stooped and gathered up the edges and then hoisted the bundle onto his back. He moved quickly through the thick undergrowth, leaves and dead branches crackling under his boots, heading back towards his shelter. Although it was only the afternoon of the year, the weather had already turned unseasonal, changing towards the Cold Months, and there had been sleet and snow showers for the past few days.

The tall man came into the clearing just as the first heavy drops of rain pattered against the leaves. He swore briefly and made a dash for the almost invisible stone cell which nestled beneath a huge oak tucked in one corner of the clearing. He had his head ducked into the wind and had almost reached the shelter before he saw the figure standing in amongst the trees. Without breaking stride, Paedur dropped the bundle of wood and threw himself away to one side, crashing into the bushes. He rolled to his feet and his right hand found the long knife tucked into his boot. His left arm came up and the razor-edged and pointed hook that took the place of his left hand carefully parted the leaves as he peered out across the clearing.

The bard squinted towards the spot where he thought he had seen the shape; he wasn't sure, but he imagined the shadows were thicker there. He tilted his head to one side, listening, but the sound of the rain on the leaves and wet turf blotted out all other sounds.

The shadows suddenly moved. Paedur slowly backed out of the bushes and moved off to one side, his eyes never leaving the spot. If he could work his way around behind...

A figure stepped out from beneath the trees—and the bard stopped in his tracks. The shape was man-like, a head taller than Paedur, as thin as a sword—and completely enveloped from head to foot in a cloak of seared and withered leaves.

"Bard, come forth; face me."

The voice was thin and high, a rasping whisper that set the bard's teeth on edge, and set the bats in the trees wheeling up into the darkening sky. The figure turned slowly, and then a skeletal arm rose and pointed into the trees directly towards the crouching man. "Come out bard, enough of these games."

Paedur waited a moment, his hard dark eyes scanning the trees and bushes, alert for others, and only when he was finally satisfied that the stranger was alone did he step out into the clearing to face the sinister figure.

"Who are you?" he asked, keeping his trained voice low but projecting it across the clearing with as much authority as he could manage. He deftly reversed the long knife in his hand, holding it by the blade, gauging the distance across the clearing.

"I am Mannam," the stranger whispered, his breathless voice whistling like the breeze through leafless trees.

"Mannam!" The bard felt his heart begin to pound, and he took a step backwards. Mannam, Lord of the Dead, Sovereign of the Silent Wood where the souls of the dead dwell until judged by Alile, the Judge Impartial. Mannam was Death.

The leaf-clad figure glided over the sodden ground until he stood before the bard. Paedur flipped the knife again and brought it up before the creature's face—if it had a face, for its head was mercifully shadowed beneath the cowl of its cloak.

"Put away your toy," the creature whispered. "It cannot harm me."

The bard thought about the idea of threatening Death and then he smiled. "Aye, perhaps not." He wiped the thin blade against his woollen leggings and then slipped the knife back into his boot.

"We will talk," Mannam whispered.

"What have I to talk to you about?" the bard asked. "I will not bargain with Duaite," he added quickly. He walked around the creature and strode over to his cell, calling back over his shoulder, "But if you do wish to talk, then I insist that we do it in slightly drier surroundings—before I catch my death," he grinned.

Lightning suddenly flashed across the heavy skies and it began to rain even harder. The bard ducked his head into the driving rain and ran for his cell. The Dark Lord turned and followed him, his cloak rustling like aged branches rasping against stone.

The circular stone cell was small and stark; a pallet of straw lay to one side of the warped wooden door; a small writing board resting against a wall and a deep studded wooden chest comprised the furniture. Surrounding the writing board were scores of parchment scrolls, some loose but the rest neatly piled up in their wooden tubes.

Paedur crossed the earthen floor and settled by the glowing embers of the fire and then waited until Mannam had settled in a darkened corner, as far away from the small stone-enclosed grate as possible. The wind coming in through numerous cracks in the stonework moaned as if in pain, the sound curiously human.

The bard looked into the shadows. "What is it you want?" he demanded, striking flint to stone, lighting a fire in the grate, for he knew the Duaite, the Dark Spirits, feared Luid, the Fire Sprite. He settled a bowl filled with a thick liquid on to the coals.

"I seek your aid," Mannam whispered.

"My…what!"

"I seek your aid," Mannam repeated softly, and then he added in the same sibilant whisper. "I seek the Mandlethorn."

"The Bush of Life, the Thorn of Death," Paedur murmured. "I have heard of it, of course, but I certainly do not have it." In the shadows, his teeth flashed in a grin. "Perhaps you should look somewhere else."

The Duaiteoiri moved, his cloak rustling. "Do not play with me, mortal—do not mock me. The Mandlethorn was stolen from me by C'lte the Undead. He burned the sacred bush which grew in the secret heart of the Silent Wood, but not before he had taken the twelve seeds from about the base of the bush. And beyond the Land of Mist, high in his kingdom, it flourishes—my Mandlethorn!" He gestured wildly, scattering leaves in all directions, some of them flaring and crisping in the small fire. His arm rose out of the shadows and he pointed at the bard. "I want you to return the seeds to me."

Paedur laughed; a rich melodious sound tinged with pity. "Me? Now surely you mock me?" He leaned forward across the fire and squinted into the darkness that had gathered about the Lord of the Dead. "Tell me," he said quietly, "are you Mannam, the Dark Lord?" He paused, and then added, "Or are you perhaps the Nameless God of Madness and Delusion, or Tatocci, the God of Fools?"

There was a dull snapping sound, like a rotten branch breaking, and the myriad night sounds fled into silence. Mannam's voice, when he spoke, was barely above a whisper. "You go too far, bard."

In the long silence that followed, Paedur sat back against the chill stone wall of his cell and slowly stirred his supper, now a thin vegetable broth in a bowl of beaten silver. The wavering firelight painted his lean face in shades of crimson and bronze, flickered along the length of the silver hook set into the bone of his wrist and struck fire from the bardic sigil on his left shoulder.

"So…" The bard leaned forward, wrapped a thick cloth about the bowl and lifted it off the fire. He looked across at Mannam, his eyes points of amber light. "Right then. You are…what you are. But why me?" he asked softly.

"You have been chosen," the Dark Lord whispered stiffly.

"Chosen? By whom?"

"You have been chosen," Mannam repeated.

Paedur brought the bowl to his lips, tilted his head back and drank deeply. A thin thread of liquid ran down his chin as he swallowed noisily. When he finished he wiped his chin and lips on his sleeve. He put the bowl down and looked into the darkened corner. "I think we have nothing to say to each other. You are wasting my time—and I yours, I think."

The Dark Lord shifted position, the brittle leaves of his cloak rustling sharply. "You are a difficult man, Paedur," he hissed.

"Tell me," Paedur said suddenly, "why do you have to deal with a mortal in the first place?" He leaned forward, shifting light dancing across his high cheekbones and forehead. "Why do you not seek the Mandleseeds yourself? Surely you have the power?"

The shadows about the Duaite seemed to shift and stir. "Your arrogance may be your blessing, but your stupidity will prove your undoing. C'lte is the Yellow God of Life, one of the Undead, the Undying. He is part of the Triad of Life, the least part of the three spirits created by Hanor and Hara. But on this plane, neither Sa'lte nor Qua'lte, his brothers, trouble themselves with the activities of mortals and only C'lte is concerned enough to watch over this world. He is my bane..." The whispering faded into the night and then the Lord of the Dead laughed with the sound of the wind soughing through rotting branches. "And the only reason that I cannot recover the seeds myself is that he is Life and I am Death. The very essence of the Undying would utterly destroy me, aye, and the Yellow God also. And without life and death, what would be left?"

"Nothing," the bard whispered, and he shivered in the chill of the night air, for Taisce the Dewspreader and Faurug the Nightwind were both abroad.

"Come mortal, your answer. Will you undertake to return the Mandleseeds to me or no? Your reward will be great," the Duaiteoiri added persuasively.

Paedur placed a lump of turf onto the fire and raked the embers with the point of his hook. "You want me to make my way through the haunted Wastelands, climb the Broken Mountain, outwit the Yellow God, and find and return the seeds to you...is that all?" he asked sarcastically.

"That is all," Mannam said quietly.

"But why me?" the bard persisted. "And don't tell me again that I have been chosen."

"Suffice it to say that you are a bard, familiar with the myths and legends of this plane, conversant with the mythos, the pantheons of the gods. Your knowledge of lore, your acceptance of the unacceptable will stand you in good stead."

"If I refuse...?

"Then there are others," the Dark Lord murmured.

Paedur remained silent, although somewhere deep within himself he had already made his decision. He relished the very thought of the quest—it was the stuff of myth and legend, and the bard dealt in myths. Finally, he raised his head and scratched the stubble on his cheek with his silver hook, the sound rasping loud in the silence. "And my reward?"

"I will give you the Lament of Lugas," Mannam said softly.

Paedur felt the sudden pounding of his heart, the constriction in his chest. "The Lay of Battle." His voice sounded numb in his ears. He swallowed hard. "You have it?"

The shadow in the corner rustled. "I have it; Lugas and his companion Auigne the Harper passed into my kingdom—as do all men."

The bard sat back, something approaching greed flickering in his dark eyes. "You have the Harp of Auigne also?"

"I have."

"I want it," he snapped. He leaned forward again. "Give me the Lament of Lugas and the Harp of Auigne and I will undertake to return the Mandleseeds to you."

The Duaiteoiri straightened in a blur of rustling darkness. "You are greedy, mortal, but you will have what you desire—if you bring me the twelve Mandleseeds."

Paedur stood and looked down at the shadowed figure. He wondered aloud, "and if I fail?"

"There is but one reward for failure," the shadow whispered.

"That is?"

The Dark Lord remained silent.

"I will not fail," Paedur murmured.

But Mannam, Lord of the Dead, was gone.

It was close to midday, and Nusas the Sun was high, blazing down upon the lonely figure of the man dwarfed by the huge bulk of the mountain which stretched upwards into the heavens. But at this height the sun did little to warm the man, it merely blinded him with raw, stone-reflected light. Icy fingers of wind plucked at his ragged clothing as he groped for a handhold on the slippery rock, threatening to tear him off. His silver hook—which he had worn for so long now that it was part of him—caught the light, splintering the pale sunbeams as he chipped rock and shale in an attempt to gain some purchase.

The bard slipped and his already lacerated palm was torn open again, streaks of blood staining the smooth stone. His scuffed and torn boots scrambled and found a toe-hold and he managed to snag his hook in a tiny crevice. His shoulder muscles cracked and threatened to tear with the strain. Summoning his last reserves of strength, he heaved himself upward, and his numb fingers brushed across a broad ledge. Paedur clung to the lip of the ledge, whilst his aching muscles bunched in a final effort to push himself up on to it. He prayed, warning Mannam that if he fell now he would never return the seeds, and then he pushed himself upwards. His hook screamed across the rock and then it caught, and then he was on to the ledge, feeling the stone smooth and cool beneath his forehead.

A month had passed since the visitation of Mannam. The bard had embarked on the quest immediately, setting out with a small bundle of provisions on his belt, along the abandoned King Road that led to the Wastelands.

Once through the western fringes of the Forest of Euarthe, the road had dwindled to a track, until it finally disappeared completely at the Bridge; a simple crude single-span bridge that crossed what was known throughout the Seven Nations simply as the Crevasse. This was an unfathomable gash that sliced through most of the western portions of the Nations from northern Thusal to southern Thusala without break. Beyond the Crevasse were the Wastelands, uncharted except in legends and myth, and uninhabited, except by the rumours that the gods of the Old Faith lived there.

Paedur had wandered through the Wastelands, using the myths as his guide; when he reached the fog-shrouded City of Souls, he knew he was on the right track. Although he avoided the city itself, his route led him along through the outskirts, and so he stopped his ears with beeswax against the beguiling cries and piteous wails that whispered and moaned through the tall hollow stones. The fog closed in then, and his only guide had been the warm fruit-scented breeze that blew through the ancient city from the Broken Mountain.

When he emerged from the mists several days later, he realised
he had passed beyond the known world into the Shadowland which
straddled the world of men and gods. Before him, the only feature
in a flat sandy expanse stretching from horizon to horizon, was the
Tulkaran Range, its once clean lines torn and shattered in the Demon
Wars, when the very planes of existence had heaved and bucked in
turmoil. Towering over the dark mountain range he recognised the
Broken Mountain, the legendary abode of C'lte, the Yellow God of
Life, the Undead, the Undying.

It had taken the bard ten days to cross the desolate barren landscape between the fog wall and the mountains: ten days with little
water and less food; ten days with almost no sleep.

The low rolling foothills of the Tulkaran Range quickly gave
way to slopes of broken shale and scree, dangerous, treacherous
ground where a foot or ankle could be easily trapped and broken in
the crevices. It was slow, tiring work and he had been exhausted
before he had even reached the first dark cliff faces of the Broken
Mountain.

Paedur had rested there for two days, camping in a small cave
by the side of a dried-up river bed at the foot of the first glass-like
wall. The first night passed without incident, but his dreams had
been troubled the second night. He had fallen into a light doze just
as twilight was purpling the mountain above his head, softening its
shadow on the plain that stretched out before him…and then the
mountain's shadow had twisted and shifted. Suddenly creatures without shape, beyond dimension, had risen up from the rocky plain.
He turned and ran, but they pursued him with claws of sharpened
thorns, and he had fled down a twisting maze which was filled with
the serpent-like hiss of dried leaves and the muted clacking of dead
branches. They reached for him—he turned and awoke exhausted,
trembling with fatigue and the pre-dawn chill; but, before the first
rays of the pale sun had touched the mountains with bronze, the
bard had begun his climb.

Time had little meaning on the mountain; he measured it by cliffs
and slopes, boulders and ledges—each one a conquest, each one a
mark of his progress. It had been relatively simple at first … but
that had been a long time ago, and now his breath came in pained
gasps and he was soaked in an icy sweat, his hair plastered to his

head, fever burning in his eyes. The rock swam before him, and tiny crystals in the stone sparkled and blinded him like miniature suns. He cursed the day he had agreed to attempt to return the Mandleseeds to the Dark Lord—but greed had decided him; the same greed that would be the cause of his death.

He spent the night on the small outcropping of stone barely half a length across which projected out over the chasm. Faurug the Night-wind howled and plucked at his torn clothing with icy fingers, and Fiarle, the Little God of Icy Spaces, caressed him with silken hands and razor talons.

And Paedur resigned himself to death.

It was in the darkest hour of night, that time when Uimfe, Lord of Night, hunted abroad, when the shade of Mannam came to the dying man. "How fares the bard?" he asked, his voice faint, whispering.

Paedur pushed himself into a sitting position; he had lost all feeling in his feet and legs, and his right hand was tingling painfully. Fever was burning in him—he knew it—and he accepted the Duaiteoiri's presence without question. "You've t-t-tricked me," he accused Mannam, his teeth chattering. "I will die here."

The shade drifted closer, floating half a span above the edge of the ledge, its leafy cloak blowing in some ethereal wind which did not touch the man. "No," Mannam whispered, "no, you will not die here upon this rock; your death, when it comes, will be both wondrous and tragic. I have come to succour you." The Dark Lord gestured with a hand that looked like twisted branches.

The outcropping was abruptly bathed in a coldly luminous foxfire. Tendrils of blue fire snaked along the stones and gathered in the darkened corners, until the entire ledge pulsed with the witch-light. The bard felt the painful return of circulation to his legs, and the leaden exhaustion that had claimed him fell away, leaving him alert and refreshed. Mannam provided food also—although, having looked closely at it, Paedur decided not to question its origin—and the last thing he saw before drifting off into a deep and dreamless sleep was the image of Mannam, his garments flapping wildly in the ghost-wind, drifting out across the empty night sky into the darkness.

He awoke as the first light of dawn was sweeping in from the east in long streaks of light, fully assured that the visitation was only the

product of a fevered dream. But he found that the ledge was blackened and the lichens and mosses were seared and crisped, and also
that his alertness and renewed strength were anything but natural.

So he pressed on. The weather changed; and Snaitle, the Cold
God, sent ice and snow whirling through the upper reaches of the
mountain and the temperature plummeted. The chill bit through the
bard's thin, worn clothing and his every breath burned in his throat
and lungs like liquid fire. But when the cold threatened to overwhelm
him, he found a cloak hanging on a diseased and leprous bush which,
he suddenly realised, was the only vegetation he had encountered since
he had left the foothills. The cloak covered him from neck to heel; it
had a high rounded collar and a deep cowl, and there was an ornate
silver clasp in the form of a snake swallowing its own tail set into the
stiff collar that would enable the cloak to be fastened across his throat.
It was woven of a smooth silken fur that rippled and flowed with his
touch, and the bard ran his fingers down its length trying to identify
the material. It felt like human hair. He shuddered; he was not squea-
mish, but the very touch of it against his skin repelled him. He sorted
through what his lore told him about the Silent Wood, Mannam's lair,
and he thought he knew where the Dark Lord had obtained the hair
to fashion the cloak. He suppressed the urge to fling it out over the
abyss; he knew he needed its warmth if he was to survive. And so he
wore it, and continued climbing.

Hanoresreth, the day set aside for the worship of the Pantheon,
dawned bright and clear with Nusas shining from a sky of liquid
azure and only a touch of the Cold God lingering in the air. Paedur
stood on a broad shelf of rock he had found the night before and
breathed deeply, savouring the sharp air. He ran his slim fingers
through his fine black hair and tilted his face to the sky, feeling the
warmth of the sun against his eyelids. And then he opened his eyes
and looked down. Below him, the cliff fell away, sheer and seemingly unbroken. He marvelled that he had even reached this far. On
an impulse he knelt and prayed, something he had not done for
many years, although he had always accepted the existence of the
gods—the evidence of his bardic lore confirming that. The words
and phrases came to him easily as he asked the Gods of the Pantheon to look down upon him and lend him their favour, and he
prayed also that C'lte would at least understand his motives, and
possibly even forgive what he was attempting to do.

C'lte, the Yellow God of Life, swore as the almost physical blow struck him. The saffron-coloured cloud he was riding fragmented and threatened to dissipate completely as his concentration lapsed. He threw up his mental shields and only allowed the merest whisper of the prayers and thoughts to trickle through to him—but the power and clarity were still tremendous.

The Undying urged his wind-borne chariot lower, riding the winds and currents that lashed against the smooth basalt walls of his kingdom like waves against the cliffs of some sea-shore. The rise and fall of the prayers grew in intensity until the Yellow God was forced to blank them from his consciousness lest they shatter his mind, but he could still feel them battering against his shields like a hammer of metal. He pinpointed the direction of the prayers and allowed his saffron cloud to be pulled apart by the wind; he dropped like a stone, his tight yellow leggings and short jacket of the same colour, moulding themselves to his slight form. He saw the figure below him—a mortal by his size and arrogant stance—and then he re-formed the cloud just above the creature's head. C'lte dropped onto it like a stone into a pond. The cloud rippled and bucked before settling.

The bard looked up, startled; he stepped back until his shoulder blades touched the cold stone wall, his knife slipped into his hand and his hook rose before his face.

The Yellow God surfaced from the depths of the cloud and smiled at the bard. "You are a curious one," he said in a high thin voice, like a boy's. "You have neither the visage nor form of those emaciated holy cringers who climb upon my mountain and make my life a misery with their whining. But then," he added, quietly noting the bard's strange cloak and sickle-like hook, "no one has ever reached this far before."

"I am not a holy man," Paedur said quietly, more startled and surprised than frightened by this foppish youthful-looking god.

"What are you then?"

"My name is Paedur, if it please my lord, and…"

"Your name is quite your own affair, and whether it pleases me or not matters very little." The Undead shook his head slowly and sighed.

"I have come seeking your aid," Paedur continued forcefully, suddenly annoyed at this effete creature whom men worshipped as a god. He rubbed the blade of the knife in his hand against the edge of his cloak and then returned it to his boot.

C'lte brushed back his corn-yellow hair with both hands. "We gods really don't care to aid you mortals," he said with a grin. "Oh, certainly an awe-inspiring demonstration of power is called for every century or so just to keep you mortals in line, you understand, but we do have our own worlds to rule and yours is but a minor plane of existence."

The bard was nonplused. He had expected many reactions from the god when he confronted him, surprise, anger, compassion, fear even—but certainly not indifference. "But the gods need men," he said almost absently.

And suddenly all the humour and boredom, the pretence, was gone from the Undying's lemon-yellow eyes. "The gods and men are bound together, they need each other," he snapped.

The bard smiled coldly, realising he had finally touched something in the creature. "I have heard it said that when man loses faith in his gods then the gods die, for without faith the gods have no substance."

The Yellow God stared at the man for what seemed like an eternity...and then he smiled. "I like you, mortal. Here you are, obviously exhausted after your climb, and yet in your first encounter with one of the gods, you find time to argue."

"I have not come this far to be put off."

"What have you come for then? What brought you here?"

"I followed a dream," Paedur said, dropping his voice almost to a whisper, looking away from the god.

The Yellow God nodded seriously. "I have found that men often do; and yours led you here?"

Paedur launched into the speech he had prepared during his climb. "I followed a dream planted in childhood, nurtured through youth, until it finally grew and came to flower with my maturity. It is a dream which has brought me across the Bridge, through the blasted City of Souls, across the barren Wastelands, up past the Shaled Slopes, past the Shattered Stones and even beyond the Little Pinnacle. My dream has brought me here."

"A pretty speech," C'lte smiled. "But now tell me why?"

"Because Lord C'lte, I am a bard—a poet also—and the tales and sagas I tell my listeners are full of the beauties of your domain, and I wish to fill my sight with images of life and beauty from your enchanted gardens…before I die."

"A bard and a poet," C'lte murmured, resting his pointed chin on his delicate long-fingered hands and leaning across the edge of the cloud. "But why have you come to me now; you are a young man with many years of life before you. Surely there are many beauties on your own plane waiting to be savoured before risking all on this climb?"

Paedur looked at the god and then sighed, slowly shaking his head. "Aaah, lord, I wish that were so." He dropped his gaze, his eyes refusing to meet the god's hard stare. "My lord, I have been informed that Mannam, Lord of the Dead, intends to call me from this world into the Silent Wood. I have a disease"—he rested his hook across his chest—"and my physician tells me that there is no cure. I have not long left in this life…" His voice trailed off into a defeated whisper.

The Undying regarded Paedur steadily for the space of a score of heartbeats, and the bard shivered as those sharp yellow eyes bored into him. Surely the god would discover the deception? But then C'lte smiled bitterly. "Ah yes, I know of the tiny life span of you Little Ones, and I have heard of disease, and, although it occurs in many of the prayers I hear, yet I fear there is little I can do about it since it is an absolute mystery to me." The Yellow God of Life shook his head slowly. "I cannot cure what I do not know." He suddenly reached out his hand. "Come then, come and I will guest you in my kingdom, and thus when you enter Mannam's dark lair, your memories will be of life and light."

Paedur stepped forward to the edge of the outcropping and C'lte gripped his wrist and lifted him effortlessly across the divide that separated the ledge from the saffron cloud. The bard floundered as he sank into the billowing softness, but the god held him.

"Believe in it," he said, "have faith." Then he added with a smile, "Faith lends Substance."

Paedur nodded dumbly, closed his eyes and imagined a sturdy fishing smack of heavy tar-daubed wood beneath his feet…and slowly the cloud took on the solidity and almost the shape of the vessel.

"You are a strange man, bard," C'lte said quietly, observing the changes in the cloud. "I did not think it was possible for a mortal to mould the *elementalis.*"

The bard grinned, feeling a tide of exhilaration surge through him. "You forget my lord that I am a bard; if I cannot visualise strongly then my audience will find their tales and myths lacking and shallow."

"Of course," the Yellow God nodded, but his eyes remained hooded. "Let us go then…"

They rose slowly until they were above the lower reaches of the mountain, and it was only then that the bard began to appreciate how vast it actually was. The endless wall drifted down before them; and when Paedur looked down he found that the base of the mountain was lost beneath a covering of cloud, while above them the pinnacle was still invisible in the dim and distant heavens. They passed huge gullies running in jagged rents across the slopes, ugly slashes and tears in the very fabric of the mountain opening out into giant craters and immense fields of shattered and broken rock.

C'lte nodded. "That is why it's called the Broken Mountain."

Paedur shaded his eyes, sure that he saw something moving in the blasted landscape. "How did it happen?" he asked quietly.

The Yellow God shrugged. "Oh, once long ago, in the war between the Usurpers, and their allies the Demons, against the Gods, the battle spilled over from Ab-Apsalom, the Battleground of the Gods, and its fury destroyed the lush green fields and wild forests that covered the slopes. And even now, many years after that battle, I will not touch it, for it is tainted and it taints all who come into contact with it." The god laughed mirthlessly. "Even if you had made it that far, you would not have come out of the Broken Fields a man."

They rose further, the mountain flowing grey and monotonously before them, and then the bard suddenly took a shivering fit. Something cold slithered down his spine and nestled there. His vision blurred and he pressed the heel of his right hand into his eyes. He blinked, squeezing his eyes shut, and when he opened them again he found he could see—although his eyes still felt gritty and everything was blurred…

They rose past the Glass Cliffs, and the bard smiled ruefully when he saw them: he would never have been able to scale those glacial heights. As they slid past, he thought he could make out shapes: buildings, towers, walls entombed within the crystal ice, but it was gone so fast he could not be sure. They rose past the huge circular nests of the Giant Eagles—empty now—cousins to the Roc and the Aonteketi, and as savage as the Gryphon...past the flimsy shelters of the Shepherds, who were once of the Culai, the First Race, demi-men, quasi-gods who ruled the world in the First Age...but those that now walked the heights were little more than brutes. But the gods used them in many ways, mainly to shepherd the thoughts and prayers of men, which by the time they had reached this far had assumed an almost identifiable form. The Shepherds gathered them together into neat bundles of desires... and then tossed them into the Gorge! Those garnished with the smoke of sacrifice and the blood of animals they put to one side and passed them on to the gods—if they remembered; but their memories are short.

And now the landscape changed, and the bard found it became even harder to distinguish between what he was actually seeing and what he thought he was seeing. His eyes were stinging again, and he found it easier to close them and listen to the Yellow God's voice as it rose and fell in a low drone as he listed the various sights. The bard found himself drifting into a light doze...

...They soared past the Eternal Fields where Youth and Childhood play hand in hand with Happiness and Joy, for there is no Sorrow in the Eternal Fields. They floated past the Gate of Years that leads to the Fields, and they rose over the Rainbow which hangs eternally over it, and the Road, of time-yellowed brick, which also leads to the Eternal Fields of Childhood...

Paedur struggled to free himself from the leaden exhaustion that now gripped him; his limbs trembled and ached and he could no longer feel his heartbeat or hear his breathing. And still they rose, and the Yellow God's voice continued remorselessly.

...They came to the Greater Pinnacle, where man's dreams gathered and howled defiance at a sneering Fate, and laugh and gibber through the small hours of the morning, for Coulide Dream-Maker stalks the minds of men then, weaving the Past with Present and Present with Future, granting desires a life and imbuing them with Joy or sometimes Terror, for his is a terrible power...

Paedur attempted to squeeze his eyes shut, but the images he saw and experienced lived within him, fired and fuelled by the Yellow God. The god's words, his descriptions of the Broken Mountain, were familiar, very familiar. The bard attempted to recognise the text the Undying was mouthing; he almost knew it; was it an ancient account of a man's journey to the heavens?

...They rose on the Silent Winds that sometimes blow through the soul with a soundless keening, and the saffron cloud tattered and frayed, but the Undying grasped the bard around the waist and, carrying him as if he weighed no more than a babe, soared above those mundane things which men hold important and which had gathered in ugly pools below the level of Dreams, while the cloud re-formed.

Up, ever upwards, past the Citadel of Man's Ambition which he builds in the Realm of Imagination; past the heights which he ever aspires to. A huge wall of roughly-hewn stones rushed past: the Wall of Ignorance which few men ever breach, but which must be surmounted if one wishes to attain life eternal...

"Benedictus!" Paedur suddenly shouted. *"The Vision of Saint Benedictus."* And, as abruptly as it had started, the hazy visions and sights disappeared and revealed the barren slopes of the mountain beneath. He shook his head, attempting to clear the muzziness which still clouded his thinking. "What did you do to me?" he demanded, raising his hook threateningly.

The Yellow God smiled and shrugged his slim shoulders. "Well, it's such a boring journey up here, nothing to see but ugly grey rock and black stone, and I thought it might add a little...interest." He bowed slightly. "You are correct of course; in the main I took the 'journey' from the *Vision of Saint Benedictus.*" He leaned forward and added confidently. "A most arrogant man—a coward also—he spent nearly twenty days living just inside the fringes of the City of Souls, which were not nearly so bad then as they are now, before he returned and proclaimed to all who would listen that he had visited my kingdom." The god shook his head, smiling coldly. "I detest liars and fools—and he was both."

"Had you anything to do with his curious death?" the bard asked, finding it difficult to remain angry for long with this boy-god.

"Who—me?" The god raised his hands in astonishment and then he grinned. "Well, a little. He was very fond of his drink, you know?" He paused when the bard shook his head.

"I thought he detested alcohol."

C'lte laughed. "The only alcohol he detested were the drops he spilt on opening a bottle. However, to continue; it so happened that a tiny seed found its way into his cup. He swallowed it and unfortunately it seems it took root in his stomach." The god shrugged. "A bush growing in his stomach; it was a miracle—and it gave him his greatest wish: it made him a martyr."

Paedur smiled tightly, but inwardly he shuddered: C'lte was capable of exacting a terrible revenge on those who crossed him. And suddenly Mannam's words came back to him: *You will not die here upon this rock; your death, when it comes, will be both wondrous and tragic.* Benedictus' death had been both *wondrous and tragic*—a fully formed bush bursting out from his stomach—and the bard wondered if this was what Death had in mind.

They continued rising, and then they suddenly passed through a band of cloud, tinted billowing strands of differing colours which hid the cold, bare rock, cloaking it beneath a fiery mantle. The bard squinted into the shifting colours; he could see other multi-hued clouds nearby, and it looked as if all of them were joined by a thin silver thread.

Suddenly they were out of the coloured mist and C'lte's yellow cloud slowed and stopped. "This way." The god reached out his hand and took the bard's arm. He stepped over the edge of the fragmenting cloud—and onto a bridge: a bridge woven of gold and silver thread, rising and falling, joining the rainbow-hued clouds together. The Yellow God gestured with a translucent hand.

"The Bridge of Twilight," he said simply, but Paedur detected a touch of pride in his voice. "Here Dawn marches forth and Dusk stalks in silence. The bridge is composed of the stuff of sunrise and morning, of light trapped undecided between night and day..." His voice trailed off, and then he added, "I will compose a poem in celebration of it one of these days."

The bard shook his head in wonder as he walked out onto the delicate-seeming bridge. "It is very beautiful."

Something of sunset and evening was in the composition of the bridge, of light shafting through purple clouds, of the close silence that tells that the day is almost done. The bridge looked insubstantial, almost wraith-like, but it was hard and unyielding beneath his feet, and when he stamped his foot, he almost imagined he heard a dull echoing boom.

The bard walked side by side with the Yellow God across the bridge; they paused once and stood to one side as the Grey Lights—

the semi-sentient creatures which are the precursors of the dawn—
flitted by on wings of smoke. Paedur looked over the twisting rail
and down to the tiny pockets floating in the mist on the multi-hued
clouds: the domain of C'lte, the Lands of Life Eternal. For a moment, he forgot he had come here to steal from the god, he forgot
the lies and the treachery and the greed that had brought him this far;
now, he was just a man, staring at something which had never been
seen by mortal man before.

The bard looked across at the Undying and there were tears in
his eyes. "We know nothing of all this," he said simply. He gestured broadly, taking in the bridge, the clouds, the islands. "Man is
blind to the beauty, the complexity of it all." He pointed back to
where the Grey Lights drifted across the edge of the bridge. "To
us, dawn is just the beginning of a new day, dusk the ending." He
shook his head sadly. "Few can appreciate the beauty of it all. We
are blind."

The Yellow God nodded agreement. "You Little Ones barely
live, inhabiting that zone between life and death where all is blurred
and shadowed. All your colours are pastel shades, all your sounds
are dull; and your lives are akin to that, they too are dull and muted.
You strive and strive and in the end what do you achieve…? Naught.
And why?" The Yellow God shrugged. "Because you have no
vision, no sight. You look ahead in spans of hours, days, weeks,
and sometimes years—but never centuries, millennia." The god's
voice rose, taking on a harsher note, and suddenly he didn't look
so young. "And yet in your arrogance you say, 'That is the sun, an
orb of fire, it has nothing to do with me.' But without Nusas to
light and heat and protect you, where would man be?

"You see the Broken Mountain in the tales and drawings of
your fathers and you say, 'God once lived atop that mountain,'
and then you laugh and mock the faith of your fathers, and yet
without that faith, and the Life that burns atop the mountain,
man would not—could not—exist. Man cannot see greatness,
for he is petty-minded and ignorant. Ignorant!" C'lte laughed
bitterly.

"But we believe," Paedur said forcefully. "We—I—had the faith
to climb up the mountainside, fully expecting, knowing that I would
find the God of Life. I know the gods are real, and there are many
like me who also believe."

"Aye, but there are also many who do not believe," C'lte interrupted, "they mock the faithful, revile the sacrifices, offend the priests; some even worship false gods."

"But that is your fault," the bard snapped. "The gods have not come forth in strength since my father's father was a young man, and even then it was but the momentary appearances of Oigne and Uide to bless a new city."

The Yellow God was silent for a while, and when he eventually spoke, his voice was soft and distant. "There are gods upon your plane even now; they come unexpected and go unheeded, but they are there. There is a change abroad upon your world, this we know; while some men openly question the Old Faith and are content with leaving it at that, there are others who are creating new, false gods. Human gods devoid of mystery and lacking in power—for the moment." C'lte gazed into the distance and his yellow-gold eyes narrowed as if he were gazing into a future, a future the bard could not even guess at, but a future which he feared he might live to see.

"But surely a false, base god cannot harm one such as you?" he asked quietly.

"Faith is a prerequisite for Substance," the Yellow God said softly, "and man is now playing with forces beyond his understanding, for he is creating gods in man's own image, and that is the most dangerous game of all." His long slender fingers brushed the bard's shoulder and he pointed beyond the Lands of Life to a region of twisting shadow. "There are many creatures lurking beyond the Threshold of Life who have not yet entered the gateway of the Silent Wood and who could provide a semblance of godhood to a gullible mankind. And, believe me, some have already been called!"

Paedur shivered suddenly, for there was a note almost of fear in the god's voice.

They crossed the remainder of the bridge in silence until they came to a series of broad shallow steps leading down into the clouds. The god gestured. "But come bard, enter into my kingdom: the Lands of Life Eternal."

Paedur stood on the top step and looked back along the Bridge of Twilight which was now tinged with amber as Dawn prepared to cross on dewed feet. And then he turned and looked down onto the fields of eternal youth, those unattainable, mystical lands sometimes glimpsed in fevered sickness or drug-induced delirium. From this height, they looked like tiny islands in a sea of coloured cloud, obscured and hazy in the distance. These were the islands of myth and legend, of faith and fancy. As the Yellow God led the bard down the steps which had been hewn from a white, almost translucent stone, he pointed out the various isles. Here was Tir na nOg, the Isle of the Blessed, and rocky Circondel; wooded Beliessa and beyond them haunted and sunken Lyonesse; golden tZlanta-tLeoto and Mu, twin islands with their similar tall bastions of glittering crystal stone. And there were more, many more, each one strange and different, and yet each one united in one thing—these were the lands where Death held no sway, basking forever in the reflected glory of the Yellow God of Life.

"My kingdom," C'lte said proudly.

Paedur shook his head in wonder. "I never realised that it was so...large."

The god smiled. "Oh, my kingdom expands, it will never fill. It is said that each man carries his own immortality within him...all I know is that some men create their own immortality. However, you may wander here for a while," he said in a different tone, "here you may fill your poet's mind with images and your bard's imagination with tales and sagas. But a warning," his hand brushed against the bard's shoulder and he pointed beyond the fields once again to the region of shadow. "Do not stray beyond the Lands of Life Eternal, do not approach the region of the shadow, the Netherworld."

Paedur squinted into the distance, but the black cloud wall was in constant motion and he suddenly felt dizzy and light-headed. His eyes watered and he blinked back tears as he turned back to the god.

"It is the Netherworld; it is neither mine nor Mannam's, belonging neither to life nor death. But it is inhabited by...creatures, the souls of men—and others—which have been cast out of the planes of existence to mouth and cry in silence for all eternity. And you would prove a tasty morsel for them, and it would not be just your corpse they would devour," he added with a grin.

2
The Geasa

He walked the Lands of Life Eternal, planning deceit.
The Life of Paedur, the Bard

Paedur walked slowly along the bone-white sands bordering the Aman, the White River, that flowed through the Yellow God's kingdom. It was, he reckoned, early morning, since he had lately seen the Bridge of Twilight blaze salmon and gold with the dawn. A heavy silence hung over the scores of islands—even the river on his right-hand side flowed without a sound and the crunch of his booted feet on the sands sounded almost unnaturally loud.

Several days had passed—exactly how many, he had no way of knowing, but he had watched the Bridge blaze and burn with sunrise and sunset at least five or six times. In that time he had travelled through most of the Lands of Life Eternal, crossing from field to field, island to island, ferried by an ageless creature in rags who acted as boatman. His sense of wonder had quickly dulled as he conversed with the heroes of legend who had been granted eternal life by the grateful gods; with the sages who had delved deep into the hidden lore and therein found the path to the Lands; and with the great kings of old who had attained immortality of a kind through the power of their sorcerer-physicians.

He had learned many of the secrets of the past as the procession of characters told their stories of the battles and migrations, of the building of cities and the rise of empires, and of the races that walked the world with men.

But although he learned much and discovered more, he learned nothing of the Mandlethorn.

Paedur sat down on a smooth rounded boulder set deep into the white sands. He felt as if time were running out; C'lte would not allow him to stay very much longer in the Lands of Life Eternal. He needed more time...

"Time is meaningless here."

Paedur looked up into the god's smiling face. C'lte was still dressed in yellow leggings and a short jacket, and today he wore a pair of soft velvet sandals embossed with gold thread. The Undying sank down onto his haunches by the bard's side and stared out across the broad slow river. He deliberately turned to look at the bard, and when he turned back to the river he continued on, his voice unusually solemn. "But although Time's encompassing hand does not fall over my kingdom, he still holds sway on your planc."

"You sound almost as if you fear Time," Paedur said quietly, tossing a handful of white sand into the turgid water.

"Time," C'lte said seriously, "is greater than us all, even greater than the gods—and we can only maintain pockets of timelessness with great difficulty. Were you to remain a little longer in my domain, then you would find your world much changed when you finally returned, for the world as you knew it would be lost in the past." The god stood and dusted off his hands. "So, I fear you must go now. I trust you have seen everything…?"

The bard stood up and nodded silently.

The Yellow God led the bard along the banks of the Aman River, the white particles of sand rising and swirling in the still air before falling back onto the beach, erasing their footsteps.

C'lte prattled on in his high, thin, musical voice, pointing out some of the furthest, most distant isles: silent Zotichal and Parandale, wherein it is always morn; tUse-tUse, inhabited only by lovers; Valsengard with its icy cliffs and eternal covering of snow; Nsu, the paradoxical Land of Waves…

"My lord," Paedur said suddenly, as they came in sight of the broad shallow steps leading upwards into the clouds.

The god paused and turned, and the bard thought he saw something like amusement in his yellow eyes.

"My lord, there is one thing I would like to see before I leave."

"And that is?" C'lte whispered.

"The Mandlethorn," Paedur began, and then hurried on when he saw the god's expression harden. "It is said that you stole it from Mannam himself…"

The god smiled bleakly, and when he spoke his voice was cold and distant. "Aaah, yes, the Mandlethorn, you must see that. You will want to construct a poem or tale from its history and my part in its theft…" He paused and smiled with something of his usual good humour. "Something suitable; something flattering and yet praising...and of course subtle, perhaps hinting at deeper mysteries." He laughed briefly. "But of course you bards are very good at that sort of thing, and I presume to teach you your craft. I will leave the Epic of the Mandlethorn to your own discretion. This way." He stopped, looking at the bard, his strange yellow eyes dancing with some private amusement. "There is something we have to do first, before we see the Mandlethorn; something important...indeed, crucial almost. You will bear with me—I'm sure you will find the diversion interesting." He nodded quickly, "Yes, very interesting, I'm sure." C'lte touched the bard's shoulder and led him away from the banks of the river and along a thin, winding pathway that led up into the rocky highlands which, although they were part of the god's kingdom, were not a portion of the Lands of Life Eternal. The bard had attempted to explore them some days ago, but had been politely—but firmly—turned away by two warriors still wearing the ancient wood-and-leather armour of the Shemmatae. He had been told then that this was the god's own private garden.

Paedur walked behind the slight form of the god. He could feel the small hairs on the back of his neck rising: something was amiss, there was something about C'lte's attitude...something he just couldn't put a finger on. Did he know or guess? He was a god— Paedur didn't even presume to guess at his abilities or powers—yet for all his bluster, the bard hadn't actually seen any demonstration of power that was unusually startling. There had been the cloud, of course, but levitation was possible—he himself had seen some of the Shemmat fakirs levitate themselves some several lengths into the air. The spell the god had cast over him to make him see the visions on the barren mountainside was not that difficult either: every trained bard possessed it to some degree; it was the ability to make an audience see what was not, and imagine what had been, to translate the speaker's words into pictures. So just how powerful was this boy-god, and just what did he know?

"How did you steal the Mandlethorn?" Paedur asked boldly. "I came across a mention of the feat in an ancient manuscript, but it didn't give any details," he added hastily.

C'lte glanced over his shoulder, and Paedur shivered at the look in his eyes. "Oh, it was very easy," he said quietly. He took a turning off the track to the left and almost immediately the ground began to slope down, and smooth walls of polished stone rose on either side. The Undying's voice echoed off and was distorted by the stone, and Paedur had to strain to catch every word.

"It was many years ago when I took the Mandlethorn, bard. Of course, the people's belief in Life was much stronger then, and I too was strong." His shoulders slumped. "In these times man seems to live only for death and I am not as strong as I once was. However," he continued, "I disguised myself as a corpse..." The bard blinked as he thought he saw the Yellow God's form flicker and take on the shape of a bloody and battered warrior from a bygone age. "...And I managed to creep past the wooded sentinels and the stone-bound guardians into the Silent Wood." The god's shape flickered and wavered again, and he reassumed his own youthful form. "I was accompanied by Luid, the Fire Sprite, and for several days we wandered the length of the Silent Wood, avoiding the savage beasts that Mannam keeps as pets and the bands of men—warriors who have died together but who find it difficult to accept their deaths and thus continue on as if they were still alive."

The track branched and C'lte took the right-hand fork that continued to lead downwards into the shadows. The walls on either side rose higher and almost joined overhead. "However, we eventually found the Woodsheart and the Secret Grove that runs the length of it, and there, growing on a small island, surrounded by filthy water, we found the Mandlethorn, the Bush of Life, the Thorn of Death."

The track swung to the left and the bard saw a long oblong of light on the wall ahead. "I took the twelve seeds that grew between the roots and I gave the rest of the bush to Luid..." He smiled grimly. "It was a brief fire." He paused, remembering, and then hurried on. "I took the seeds back here with me where I had created a suitable...garden...for them. I then called together Quilida, the Goddess of Growth, and Huide, the Little God of Summer Rain; they both blessed the seeds—and the bush has flourished."

C'lte led the bard out into a hollow and then into a grove of trees which blazed with liquid light. Paedur groaned aloud as the light burned his eyes and seemed to pierce right through to his skull. C'lte murmured an apology and the light abruptly dimmed. Paedur rubbed his streaming eyes with the corner of his cloak; and when he looked at the trees again he found that they were not wooden, but rather had been constructed of rare metals: gold, whele, silver, orchilium and *juste*. The leaves shivered slightly in a breeze the bard couldn't feel, and their delicate, haunting music hung—almost vibrating—on the air. He moved, and he suddenly found himself reflected on every side, glittering and scintillating in countless shades and hues. The Undying cast no reflection.

C'lte led him through the metallic forest along a winding track that led out into a perfectly circular clearing. In the exact centre of the circle stood a tree, a tree of natural wood which looked almost drab in comparison with its metallic copies. And it was surrounded by a carpet of shifting, pulsing, coloured light.

The god stepped forward and the light on the ground swirled and eddied, pulsing and throbbing like a living thing; Paedur hesitated a moment, and then followed closely behind. He found it was like walking through water; there was a slight resistance but it was gentle and comfortable, and as they neared the tree, the drag lessened, and it became obvious that the light was seeping out from the ground about the base of the tree itself.

C'lte stood beneath the spreading branches and bowed low, and the bard saw his lips move slightly, in salutation or prayer, the bard was unsure which. The Undying then reached up and, bending a low branch, plucked a small red-gold fruit from beneath the leaves and handed it to the bard. "Eat," he commanded.

Paedur examined the fruit carefully: it was small and soft, the skin slightly furred. He looked warily at the god.

C'lte smiled gently. "Eat it—it won't harm you—indeed, it has been known to grant men their heart's desire."

The bard lifted his hook, preparing to cut into the soft skin, but the god's fingers closed on his arm, pushing it down. "Eat it," he commanded.

"Not until I know what I'm eating," Paedur objected.

"This," C'lte said coldly, "is the Tree of Knowledge, and what is Life but Knowledge?"

"I don't understand," Paedur said, truly puzzled now. The god looked surprised and then he said, "No, I really believe you don't. Trust me," he said, taking the fruit from the bard's hand and biting into it, and then handing it back. The same look of sly amusement the bard had glimpsed earlier in the god's eyes was back once again. "It will help you to appreciate the Mandlethorn all the more."

The bard nodded doubtfully but bit into the fruit, immediately tasting the bitter-sweet tang on his tongue. He coughed and his eyes watered; the Yellow God, the tree, the metallic wood, dissolved into an artist's palette of colours constantly moving, constantly changing. He swallowed the fruit, and fire and lightning coursed through his body; his muscles locked and trembled as if he were fever-ridden, he felt his heart slow...slow...slow stop—and then start again. And his left hand—his missing left hand—ached with an agonising pain.

Paedur opened his eyes. For a moment he thought his vision was still blurred and he brushed his hand across his eye—and then he saw the flickering aura that outlined his fingers. It took him a few moments to recognise it for what it was; and then he realised that he was actually seeing his own life force. He looked about: everything had changed.

The trees and bushes, the blades of silvered grass, the golden rocks, the artificial stones, the shifting clouds overhead and even the very rivers and streams now throbbed and quivered with a burning aura of life. And the Tree of Knowledge—which had at first seemed so drab and colourless—now threw off streamers of fire which trembled on the still air, and the individual leaves now sparkled like gemstones.

The bard turned and looked towards the god, but C'lte raised his hand, his long fingers closing over the bard's face. "Do not look directly at me," the god warned. "You can now see the visible aura of Life that surrounds every living thing. I am the very essence of Life...the sight of me would blast your senses." The god moved around behind the bard and instructed him to close his eyes, and then Paedur felt a feather-light touch against his temples. "Perhaps it would be better if I were to dull that part of your new-found perception at least for the moment, until you have learned to control it yourself. You may look at me now," the god said.

Paedur turned, half expecting to see a pillar of flaming life forces, but the god appeared unchanged. C'lte spread his hands and smiled. "Don't look so disappointed," he said. He put a hand on the bard's shoulder, and led him deeper into the mirrored wood.

The god led him down into a small stone-enclosed hollow and then stopped before a slight mound. Even before he saw it, Paedur felt his skin crawling and the hair on his head beginning to rise in long wavering streamers.

"Behold the Mandlethorn!"

The bard blinked—and then cried out in pain at the vision that lanced his eyes: a vision of Life and Death inextricably entwined.

The Mandlethorn was a small stunted bush nestling against a huge boulder on the top of a tiny artificial mound…and it was familiar. Paedur could have named a score—or more—of bushes that it resembled—and yet it did differ from them, but only in small subtle ways. With his heightened senses he could see the very essence of life and growth covering the patina of death and decay, and the sweet smell of corruption mingled with the bitter perfume of growth.

"I can see the Life in it," the bard whispered, awed, "and at the same time the Death: both are present."

"In all Life there is Death," C'lte quoted, "but of course here," he encompassed his domain with a sweeping motion of his arm, "here Death can gain no foothold, and only in the Mandlethorn are we reminded of Mannam and his drear kingdom."

"Are there then creatures of life in the Silent Wood, reminders of this place?" the bard asked softly, still staring at the bush.

"There are some who shamble in a semblance of half-life in the Dark Lord's kingdom; a spark of life still burns within them, but it burns low, and they do not live in a way that you would comprehend."

Paedur moved closer to the bush and gently stroked the long drooping leaves which were shaped like flattened spearheads. They felt like human skin, soft and sensuous, warm and smooth, trembling slightly. Then he swore and withdrew his hand, pain and puzzlement in his eyes, a bead of liquid crimson nestling delicately on his fingertips. He brought his fingers to his mouth, but the god stopped him.

"No, do not swallow the poisoned blood." He took the bard's hand in his, breathed on the cut, and then gently brushed the blood from the wound…and, beneath, the jagged puncture had healed.

"Look," C'lte said and, kneeling beside the bush, carefully pulled aside the quivering leaves revealing the thorns: long thin evil spikes which pulsed regularly. They were both hooked and barbed and each barb glistened with a tiny spot of dark liquid. They recoiled like writhing serpents from the Undead's hand. The god smiled. "See how they cannot bear the touch of Life, for these are the Thorns of Death. It was a thorn from this bush which sent Artre the White

King to his death and put Erta his brother on the throne." He shook his head slowly, and then a sly smile spread across his thin face. "But Alile the Judge Impartial sent Coulide Dream-Maker to haunt the murderer with memories from the Eternal Fields of Childhood, and the usurper never again slept without Nightmare and Terror, Coulide's pets, stalking his dreams." The god's smile faded. "And in the end Erta took his own life—and that was a terrible crime for which we are solely responsible—and you might learn from it, bard: though the gods are all-powerful, they are not wholly omnipotent. And now the soul of the suicide cries beyond the realm of Life and before that of Death in the Netherworld..."

"My lord," Paedur said abruptly, "there is something I have to tell you."

C'lte rose to his feet and looked up into the bard's dark eyes and for the first time Paedur realised how small the god was. "You are going to tell me of the bargain you made with Mannam for the Lament of Lugas and the Harp of Auigne?"

C'lte laughed at the bard's expression, and taking him by the arm led him back through the wood and into a grove of trees which guarded a small black-and-gold marble pool. The Yellow God peered into the flat waters and moved his hand across the surface. Immediately the pool clouded and swirled with unseen currents, and as it settled fragments of images rippled across the surface. Suddenly the bard stiffened, for the pool had cleared and there, reflected in the waters, was not C'lte and the bard but rather the Dark Lord and the bard in his stone cell in the Forest of Euarthe, and he could hear with the sound of trickling water his conversation with Mannam.

"How long have you known?" he asked the Yellow God quietly.

"I suspected you were not all you purported to be from the very beginning, but I knew for certain shortly after I brought you here." The god dipped his yellow-tinged hand in the placid pool and gently moved his fingers to and fro, creating fleeting patterns of sparkling colours that danced in the evening light. "Faurug and Taisce came to me with a tale of conspiracy between man and Duaite, and the Dewspreader had recorded everything within his liquid pearls, and some he cast into this pool..."

Paedur looked over at the god. "And if you knew that, did you also know that I intended to try and trick you into granting me eternal life?"

C'lte smiled. "I guessed you might—and when you told me on the mountain that you were ill, and I could see that your aura burned bright and unblemished—that's when I began to suspect that something was amiss." He paused and shook glistening water droplets from his long gold-tipped fingers. "And so rather than allowing myself to be tricked, I took the precaution of giving it to you," he added, almost in a whisper.

It took a moment for the god's words to sink in...and then comprehension dawned. "The fruit of the Tree of Knowledge!"

C'lte nodded. "The Fruit of Life. You now have Life Eternal, Paedur—may you live long enough to enjoy it."

"But why?" Paedur demanded. "You knew I had lied to you; you knew I was coming up here to try and steal the Mandleseeds... and yet you gift me with...with..." he stammered, something he had not done since he had been a child.

The Yellow God smiled distantly. "Do not thank me for your gift yet; perhaps there will come a day when you will curse me for it."

"But why did you give it to me?" Paedur demanded.

"It is...necessary."

"Necessary? I don't understand."

"You will in time; suffice it to say that it is necessary to grant you Life Eternal." He pulled a small satin purse from his belt and handed it to the bard. "It is also necessary to give you these."

Paedur pulled the drawstrings and opened the bag. The contents tumbled out onto the palm of his hand where they lay pulsing like six clots of fresh blood. They could only be one thing...

"The Mandleseeds," C'lte said. "There are only six there, but those you may bring to Mannam, and henceforth let there be peace between us, for are not the Spirits of Life and Death equal, opposite and yet alike?"

"My lord," the bard protested, "I cannot accept these."

The god smiled grimly. "You have no choice. You are oathbound to return the seeds to Mannam, and now you are also oathbound to repay me for my gifts to you..." he said, his voice hardening.

Paedur went ice-cold. "Why do I suddenly feel as if I've just walked into a very well-laid web?"

C'lte shook his head. "You have not been trapped; we are not about to force you to do anything against your will. Yes, you have been…persuaded to come here, but I think you have little to complain about. You have been well treated and have even obtained your heart's desire."

"Granted; but you might also bear in mind that I almost died on your mountain."

"*Nonsense!* Mannam watched over you the whole time. You might have suffered some discomfort but you were never in any danger."

Paedur wiped the blade of his hook across his leggings. He controlled the sudden impulse to lunge at the god, use the sharpened edge and point of his hook to tear out his throat. "Would you like to tell me why you have gone to all this trouble to bring me here then?" he asked tightly.

"You are angry," C'lte said, surprised, "but you have no reason to be."

"I think, Lord C'lte, you will find that no human likes to be tricked, to be moved about like a piece on a game-board. Now just what is it that you want?" he demanded coldly.

C'lte sat on the edge of the pool and stared up at the bard. He found it difficult to accept the other's ill-humour, but then, man had always been difficult to comprehend. He looked away down the grove to where the last of the metallic trees blazed golden with the evening sunlight.

"You are aware," he said, without turning his head, "of the sudden resurgence of interest in the New Religion, that blasphemous, scurrilous, obscene travesty of a belief? It is not new, but lately it has grown in strength, and there has been an unprecedented increase in its followers."

"I know of it," Paedur said quietly, "but I don't see what this has to do…"

"Bard, for many generations of man the Gods of the Pantheon and the Old Faith have held sway throughout the Seven Nations and beyond. The great faith and belief of the people has lent us substance and their worship has made us strong. But now the people are beginning to drift away and follow the New Religion. They have created a god in their own image…and now a being has come forth from the Netherworld, a creature that was once a man—we think!—a being called Trialos, and he has assumed the mantle of godhood, and such is the people's belief in him—misguided belief it is true, but still powerful—that the New Religion, and especially their god, Trialos, now threatens the Old Faith." He paused and his eyes grew clouded. "Some of the older, wilder gods have already retreated to the more distant planes of existence where the faith of their followers still remains strong." C'lte turned and stared up into the bard's dark eyes. "Should the people cease to worship us, then we will return to the Void from whence we came."

Paedur breathed deeply, unaware that he had been holding his breath. Fragments of the old myths and legends came back to him, the tales of men and women called by the gods in times of great danger and confusion. He felt his whole world slide and shift; perceptions changed, plans were abandoned, and he felt something die within him. "What do you want me to do?" he asked numbly.

The Yellow God stood up. He placed his right hand on the bard's shoulder, and Paedur felt the tingling transference of power. He looked deep into the god's flat, cat-like eyes and saw something like pity mirrored there.

"This is your *geasa*. I charge you to wander the roads of the Nations and to uphold the Faith against the evil of the New Religion. And I charge you never to waver in your task." The god's voice boomed and echoed about the little grove. The smooth water in the pool vibrated and thrashed, and leaves broke from the branches overhead and floated down over the pair.

"Paedur, I charge you to be the Champion of the Old Faith!"

The bard opened his mouth, but the Yellow God smiled, and his aura expanded, dazzling Paedur with painful brilliance. Spots of exploding colour shattered on his retinas and ran in rainbow hues, dancing, whirling and fading in a glittering kaleidoscope of confusion...

...When he could see again, the bard found he was standing outside his cell of wood and stone in the Forest of Euarthe—with the six tiny clots of blood pulsing in the palm of his hand. He had the Mandleseeds.

In the days that followed, Paedur lived partly in a dream world as he tried, with quill and parchment, to fashion a record of his experiences in the Lands of Life Eternal. It would, he reasoned, be his monument. It would survive down through the ages: a true saga of the gods and their relationship with man, the true stories of the heroes and heroines and the first complete history of man...if he lived long enough to finish it

If he had been chosen as the Champion of the Old Faith, then it was highly likely that the followers of the New Religion would soon get to know of it and it wouldn't take them long to find him. He could of course flee now, but he had never run away from anything in his life. Let them come, he was ready.

His small stone cell had been encircled and warded with the old High Magic, and the one direct track that led to his grove had been touched with a spell of misdirection and delusion. A knowledge of the arcane arts was not common to every bard, but Bard Masters— in their further researches and delvings into the lost lore—almost unconsciously picked up a smattering of the rituals and incantations.

The season changed and so did the weather, and the bard began to think that the gods had forgotten him, or at least temporarily passed over him. The Forest of Euarthe remained quiet; his traps had not been sprung and his spells remained unbroken, and as the Month of the Wolf drew to a close, Paedur relaxed and began to consider gathering in supplies for the coming winter months.

The morning of the last day of the month—market day— dawned dull and overcast, with Faurug the Nightwind still lingering and the world covered beneath a mantle of white, evidence that Snaitle had been abroad during the night. Paedur abandoned his thoughts of going into the nearby town to the market and spent the day wrapped in his long dark cloak huddled over a small fire, attempting to finish the tale of Kutter Kin-Slayer which he had heard from Yuann the Wood Sprite in the Yellow God's kingdom. Yuann had been dead and had passed into legend almost five hundred years before the bard had been born.

The day remained dark and towards mid-afternoon it began to snow again. The only sound in the small cell was the muted crackling of the fire and the scratching of the bard's quill across the thick parchment.

"Bard!"

Paedur started and threw himself backwards, his hook flashing redly as it lashed out at the sudden sound. It struck something solid and the bard felt pain, quickly followed by numbness, shoot up his left arm. The shadow in the doorway moved...and Mannam stepped into the firelight.

Paedur struggled to his feet, nursing his trembling arm; it felt as if he had struck a tree-trunk. He swore when he saw the condition of his parchment, now sodden with ink where he had upset the inkhorn when he had fallen. He held up the curling square and allowed the ink to run off. "Ruined...ruined," he groaned.

"It is a parchment," Mannam whispered, "it is nothing."

"To me everything," Paedur snapped, and angrily crumpled the stiff skin and tossed it into the fire. It caught immediately and blazed, the still-wet ink hissing loudly. The Dark Lord retreated back into the shadows.

"I am surprised you have returned," Paedur snarled. "After all, you tricked me..."

"I never forced you to go," Mannam breathed. "I did my best to persuade you...but it was your own greed that decided you in the end."

Paedur changed the subject. "Have you got the Lament and the Harp?"

"Have you got the seeds?"

"I have—but let me see my reward first," Paedur demanded.

The Duaiteoiri moved, the sound like withered leaves being crushed underfoot, and produced the relics bundled together in a twig-woven basket. The Dark Lord handed them across the fire and then withdrew into the deepest shadows.

Paedur gently lifted them out of the basket and unrolled the covering, bringing the ancient talismans to light. The Lament of Lugas was tightly sealed within a tube of engraved time-yellowed ivory, etched with the glyphs of the Culai, the First Race. It was stopped at both ends with caps of delicate white-gold, and it exuded an aura of peace and silence that was almost visible. He placed it carefully on his writing desk and then unwrapped the Harp of Auigne.

The dark polished wood of the instrument ran with liquid highlights from the flames. It was sidhe wood, wood from the Sidhe Forest of the Far Isles of Ogygia, and it would neither rot nor warp, burn nor crack. Its strings were twined sun-wire, impossibly strong; once tuned, they would keep a note for all eternity. The soundbox was plain and unadorned save for a single black stone set flush with the wood: the *Clocauigne*, Auigne's stone, sometimes called the Heart of the Black Ibix. The air about the harp tingled with barely suppressed elemental forces; and the bard with his heightened senses knew, although he did not know how he knew, that it had been blessed by both Maker and User, two of the earliest gods.

"The seeds, bard." Mannam's voice jolted Paedur back to reality. He reluctantly put down the harp and produced a small carved quill box. With the point of his hook he pulled back the sliding lid and instantly the small cell was bathed in a pulsating blood-light which painted everything in shades of liquid crimson.

"You know of course that there are only six here," Paedur said quietly, trying to make out the Duaite's shape in the corner.

"Of course," Mannam whispered, "and for that reason I will take the Harp and Lament back." A skeletal stick-like hand reached out from the shadows.

The bard grinned wolfishly. "You still owe me for the six seeds," he reminded Mannam.

"C'lte has already gifted you," the Dark Lord snapped.

Paedur nodded. "He gifted me—you owe me payment for what I have brought back to you."

The Lord of the Dead rustled angrily. "I can see now why you have been chosen." Leaves and dead wood rustled. "Choose then."

Without hesitation Paedur chose the Lament of Lugas; with only one hand, the Harp was useless to him.

Mannam's stick-like hand swept out and the crimson light was swallowed up within it. Abruptly the Duaiteoiri laughed and the bard shivered with the sound. "And thus is our bargain completed. And now your wandering begins. You must flee from here, bard; the followers of Trialos are almost upon you." The god's voice faded to a muted whispering.

"Now you must begin the revival of the Old Faith. Use your tales, they are your greatest weapon. Take the road northwards; follow the King Road beyond Karfondal, and there seek an inn called the Coined Sword...the Faith is strong there...you must strengthen it even further..."

The wind moaned in through the cracks in the stonework and carried with them the last words of C'lte, the God of Life: *You are the Champion of the Old Faith.*

3
The Beginning

...This day: a bard, by name Paedur, tall of stature, sharp-visaged, and with but one hand...

Register of the Coined Sword Tavern

Something was wrong. Carp, ex-mercenary and proprietor of the Coined Sword, immediately sensed the change in atmosphere as he climbed up from the cellar with another barrel of rofion. The long, low-ceilinged room was unusually quiet, the crackling of the log fire at the gable end of the house unnaturally loud and intrusive. At this hour, with the men heading home from the fields and forests, the tavern should be humming with conversation and laughter and the clink of glasses and tankards.

The huge innkeeper paused at the top of the stairs and shifted the cold sweating barrel into a more comfortable position; and then, before stepping out into the room, he loosened the knife he carried in a sheath in the small of his back. Silence in a tavern could only mean trouble. It could be bandits; there had been some trouble in the district recently, and only a month past four men had attempted to rob the customers and his day's meagre takings.

Carp smiled at the memory. Two of them had held the door with drawn swords while the others demanded coin and valuables. The old soldier had hesitated; it had been a long time since he had seen battle with the infamous Coined Sword Regiment, fighting the savage Chopts in the northern ice-fields, but he still knew how to fight.

Carp had impaled one of the bandits to the door frame with a crossbow bolt and almost severed another's head from his shoulders with a thrown axe. It had all happened so quickly that the others had had no time to react. One managed to shout a warning before the ex-mercenary dropped him with a thrown barrel. The last man turned to flee and had almost reached the door before another crossbow bolt split his spine. There had been no trouble since.

But there was certainly something amiss now.

The huge innkeeper squeezed up through the door from the cellar, the barrel of rofion held before him like a shield, and stepped out into the room. He stopped, poised on the balls of his feet, ready to run or fall as the situation demanded. The smoky atmosphere stung his eyes and he quickly blinked away the tears, and then frowned: everything seemed in order. The customers—most of them regulars, and nearly all farmers, woodcutters or charcoal-burners from the nearby forest towns—were all sitting quietly at their usual tables and chairs.

And then Carp realised what was wrong; they were sitting far too quietly. There was no shouting, no laughter, no coarse jesting. He padded across to the long wooden counter, moving surprisingly quietly for so large a man, but no-one was looking in his direction— all heads were turned towards the far end of the room.

He was reaching under the counter for the loaded crossbow he kept there when Bale, the pot-boy, suddenly emerged from the shadows and almost ran across to the wooden bar. His small dark eyes were wide and there was a pulse throbbing visibly in his throat.

"Did you see him?" Bale whispered urgently.

"Who? What's happened up here, boy?" Carp demanded.

"Him. The bard." The boy glanced nervously over his shoulder towards the gable end of the room and the blazing fire.

Carp looked down the length of the smoky room. His eyes were not as sharp as they used to be and while the worn flagstones directly before the fireplace were bathed in warm red-gold light, and he could make out Amblad, one of the oldest men in the province, sitting in his usual seat beside the carved log-box, he could see no-one else.

"What bard?" he hissed.

"There!" the boy said, pointing, and his voice quavered and almost broke.

Carp squinted into the shadowy corners on either side of the fire, and then he started; there was someone there! And suddenly all his old warrior senses flared, as they had during his fighting days whenever they camped near one of the ancient Culai settlements. He was no sorcerer, no wizard, but he had a feel for Power. He had sensed the Power in some men before, but never so strongly as now; something was badly wrong.

He eased himself out from behind the counter and started down the room, squinting against the light from the fire, vainly attempting to make out the figure sitting back in the shadows to the right of the hearth.

"Now sir," he blustered, walking into the circle of the firelight, "what can I do for you?" He moved directly in front of the figure. "A tankard of rofion perhaps?" he asked, edging closer to the shape, puzzled. It was a man certainly, but it was difficult, almost impossible, to make out the features clearly.

"Yes, that would be very welcome." The voice was strong, clear and vibrant, and, as the man raised his head, Carp saw the distinctive triangular bardic sigil high on his left shoulder. The bard stood up and the innkeeper stepped back unconsciously as the darkness seemed to ripple and flow with him. The bard's right hand came up and the enveloping darkness rippled again, and then it fell away; and Carp suddenly realised that it was nothing more than a long furred travelling cloak. He was tall and thin, almost unnaturally so; his face was angular, with high cheekbones and deep-sunk eyes. Carp was about to turn away when he caught a glimpse of the silver hook that took the place of the bard's left hand.

"I'm going to need your name for the register," he said quietly, strangely disturbed by the gleaming half-circle. In his fighting days, he had come across many men who wore artificial claws or walked on wooden stumps, but he had never seen anything quite like the bard's hook. It was flat, shaped like a sickle, with a vicious-looking point and a blade that looked as if it had been recently sharpened; there also seemed to be script of some description etched into the flat of the blade.

"My name is Paedur."

"I'm sorry," he started, realising the bard was looking at him expectantly.

"I said, my name is Paedur," the stranger repeated with a smile.

Paedur. A bard, Paedur. Now where had he heard that name before? He fitted a spigot to the new barrel of the strong dark beer he brewed himself and poured a foaming tankard for the bard. He didn't frighten easily, but there was something about the stranger which chilled him to the bone. He had once fought the *quai*—soulless warriors—and he remembered feeling exactly the same.

He called Bale and gave him the drink, and in the unnatural silence in the tavern he could even hear the pad of the boy's bare feet on the sawdust-covered earthen floor. He waited until the boy gave the tankard to the bard and saw him drink before he stepped into the back room. There was something about that bard...

Before Carp had purchased the run-down way-station which he had transformed into the Coined Sword, he had scratched a living collecting the bounties on escaped prisoners and slaves. And now, during the winter months, when trade was poor, he usually travelled south into Karfondal and collected the crude "Wanted" posters: it didn't hurt to have them just in case someone wandered in...

He found it close to the end of the pile. There was no illustration and the print was dark and blotchy, even cruder than usual. Carp spelled slowly through the heavy black letters: *A Bard Paedur ...single hand...blasphemy against the New Religion!*

The reward was substantial—far more so than simple blasphemy would have merited. Carp smiled. Well, if the bard followed the Old Faith, then he would find himself amongst friends here. He tore the thin yellow paper in half, crumpled it into a ball and threw it into the corner of the room.

"We have not seen a bard hereabouts for many years," old Amblad was saying when Carp returned to the bar. "Your kind are usually to be found in the palaces of kings now and not on the roads—where they belong."

"Some of us still wander the roads," Paedur said quietly. "Not many, it is true, but don't forget, there are not as many of us as there used to be. The old ways are dying; young men are no longer interested in training to become bards and lore-masters."

"Who will preserve the old ways then, the old tales, the legends?" Amblad wondered, his small, strangely smooth face creasing in a frown.

"The old ways are dying," Paedur repeated, very softly, "there is a new order rising."

"An order in which there will be no place for you or your kin," the old man said. His eyes were sharp and blue, watching the bard carefully, judging his every word and movement.

Carp came up behind the old man and touched his shoulder gently, almost respectfully. Amblad lifted his head, but his eyes never left the bard's face while the innkeeper whispered urgently to him. Amblad nodded and then turned back to Paedur, his gnarled hands playing with a small amulet on a leather thong about his neck. "It seems you are a follower of the Old Faith," he said, his voice dropping to a whisper.

"We worship the same gods, *Datar,*" Paedur said, using the title for a priest of the Faith. He glanced over at the innkeeper who had moved back to the wooden bar. "But how did he know?"

Amblad shrugged. "Carp makes it his business to…to keep in touch with persons wanted by the Imperials. Your name and description was on their last list."

The bard sat forward suddenly, red firelight glancing off his hook, reflecting back onto his chest. "I'm on the lists? Since when?"

"Since before the season turned; Carp would be able to tell you exactly when. You are wanted for blasphemy against the New Religion."

The bard sat back into the shadows. "But I've been on the road for most of the Cold Months—I haven't had the opportunity to blaspheme against the New Religion. I've stuck mainly to the back roads and avoided contact with men"—he raised his hook briefly—"I am rather distinctive."

"Be that as it may, there is still a price on your head."

"Is the Religion that powerful already?" Paedur asked. "I've been a little out of touch lately."

"It grows stronger every day; in some towns the Faith is already openly frowned upon, and the Religion has found many converts in the palace, and Geillard has spoken with the priests, and has even received the High Priest, Thanos. And you know what will happen if they convert him…"

Paedur nodded, startled. If the Emperor was converted, the New Religion would become the accepted belief and that would in effect prohibit the worshipping of the Old Faith. "How does the Faith fare here?" he asked the old man, nodding to the rest of the tavern.

"My congregation shrinks almost daily. Most of the people here are of the Faith, but there are some with serious doubts…" The old man paused and added quietly, "That is why you are here, isn't it?"

"How do you know?"

The old man smiled toothlessly. "I have been a Datar of the Faith since my youth; I believe in the gods, I have spoken with them, asking for their help. I have known someone was coming since before the season changed."

"That's even before I knew," Paedur said wryly. He glanced around the room and then back to the old man. "What would you have me do?"

"You must speak to them," Amblad began. He paused as Carp came up and stood by his chair.

"The doors are locked, *Datar.*"

"Good." He looked up at the innkeeper. "You will ensure that we are not disturbed."

"Of course." Carp bowed slightly and disappeared back down the tavern. He stopped by the bar to lift a heavy hunting crossbow from beneath the counter, and then went to stand by the door.

Paedur shook his head. "I'm not sure I know what to say to these people."

"You are a bard, a storyteller; tell them a story."

"But which story?"

The priest sat back in his high-backed chair, and his red-rimmed eyes turned towards the fire. "A question which I am often asked concerns the Great Beginning of the Faith." His sharp eyes darted back to the bard. "You see, the Religion, its gods and their beginnings are well documented. If a people know where their gods come from, they somehow find them easier to worship. However, many do not know the Birthing of the Gods of the Pantheon, and so they are that much more remote, that much more distant, and that much harder to worship. The priests of the Religion use this, exploit it to their own ends." The old man paused and his voice dropped to a whisper. "Tell them of the Great Beginning."

Paedur paused to consider and then he nodded. Amblad raised his head and then he spoke loudly in the formal speech. "Would you honour us with a tale, bard?"

"What would you have?"

There was silence in the tavern; several people moved uncomfortably, but no one attempted to leave. To do so would be to invite the stranger's attention.

Paedur repeated the question.

"A tale of the Pantheon," Amblad cackled finally, "something we are not likely to have heard before."

Heads nodded in agreement and there was a quick murmur of assent.

The bard nodded. "Very well, and I'll make it short enough; I will tell of the Great Beginning," he said in his strong commanding voice. "I will tell of Creation." He sipped some of the strong rofion and then placed the empty flagon on the floor beside his feet. His dark eyes closed and he sat back against the cold stone wall, and began his tale...

In the Beginning, before all things, there was the One and the Void and the Chrystallis, which was the wind that blew through the soul of the One into the Void.

And the One slept, for there was naught to do in the Beginning, and he dreamt—but his dreams were troubled.

Now the One was without presence and beyond imagining, and thus his dreams—although the One was without gender— were curious and novel. And in the swirling chaos that was the stuff of his dreams, there arose concepts strange and images alien, for he dreamt that he had Form and Shape and Substance, and these dreams were both exciting and bizarre to the One, for he had no Form and was without Shape or Substance. And thus he stored these dreams in his soul to ponder and comfort him in his boredom, for he was often bored.

But the Chrystallis, the wind that blows through the soul of the One, grasped the dreams in aeolian paws and scattered them out into the Void.

And thus Form and Shape and Substance came into being.

But still the One slept—and his sleep was not akin to that of mortal man, being of a duration beyond time, and his dreams lasted aeons. And as the Void gradually took on a Form and assumed a Shape and Substance, the One dreamed again, and now his dreams thrilled him, for he dreamed of an Essence. This too he stored within his soul to comfort him, but once again the Chrystallis swept through his soul and carried it out into the Void and the Essence joined the other three and fused into their core.

And now the sleep of the One was troubled and he grew restless and his dreams were no longer pleasing nor exciting for he was haunted by Identity, and this displeased him and he cast it out, and it went forth into the Void and henceforth Form and Shape and Substance had an Identity and the Essence was at the core of all.

Thus it was for a timeless while.

And Chrystallis the Soulwind grew bolder still, and gathering together the dreams of the One, which it had brought forth into the Void, it mixed them together in the cauldron of the soul of the One. And there the dreams boiled and seethed and there was created that which was akin to Life, but which was puny and weakling, and the Chrystallis was displeased with it and cast it out into the further reaches of the Void.

Still the One slept and still his dreams were disturbed by that which gibbered and jibed beyond his comprehension, and these were the Passions, and they were anathema to the One and he cast them out; and thus the Greater Passions of Love and Hate and their brood of Lesser Passions joined with Form and Shape and Substance and took on an Identity, and were linked together by the mysterious Essence.

And again the Chrystallis swept through the Void gathering together all the elements of the dreams of the One and again it mixed them in the cauldron of the soul—with one addition—the merest drop of the Life of the One.

And when the heaving and rolling had ceased there had been created Life. It was strong and viable, with a form and a shape and created out of a substance; it was infused with the greater and lesser passions and it had an identity. And at the heart, the core of the newly-created Life, was that Essence akin to the One.

Then the Soulwind blew through the forgotten corners of the soul of the One, unearthing the old dreams and unrecalled nightmares, bringing them all out into the Void. Light there was and Darkness also; Chaos and Order and—greatest of all—Knowledge. And these settled into the Void and were infused into the Life.

And the One awoke.

And now a Lesser Passion held sway and grew, and this was Fear, and the Life attempted to hide. But when the One looked about, what he saw pleased him, and though he was unused to Creation, he delighted in it, and it amused him.

Thus he set about creating the very fabric of the Universe, fashioning it from the stuff of the Void. But it was empty and so he created the Galaxies and Suns, and Planets to circle the Suns and Moons to circle the Planets; and he scattered meteors and asteroids freely throughout the Universe. Now, onto some of the Planets he set the newly-created Life, and in places it thrived albeit in strange and grotesque forms—and in others it did not flourish and died.

The One soon tired of Creation and wished to sleep again, but still desired to keep that which had been created, and he pondered on how that might be. And so he took part of himself and enwrapped it with a Shape and gave it a Form and Substance and infused it with Identity and then he broke it in half and set one part to rule Order and the other part to watch over Chaos, and he called his creations Hanor and Hara, and then he slept and sleeps still.

And Hanor and Hara were the first Great Gods.

Now Hanor and Hara were full of the spirit of the One, and were powerful, but like all the gods, prone to boredom and, furthermore, were envious of the One's Creation, and thus in their envy and boredom they sought to emulate him. But they found that there was little left to create.

And so they found they must content themselves with Shadowworlds created on planes other than the one already in existence. And these new planes were like and yet unlike the Prime Plane in many respects. So the first Great Gods set Life upon these planes and it thrived.

But now Hanor and Hara had the Universe of the Prime Plane, created by the One, and their own multi-planed universe to rule, and they found it was vast—and they were but two, and thus they resolved to create others like themselves to ease the load of godhood.

Hanor and Hara then worked with the stuff of Chaos and Order, and brought forth the Old Gods, and these in turn tried their hands at creation and brought forth the lesser gods, the spirits and sprites, the demons and elementals, and set them up as the servants of the gods.

And in the Elder Days the gods walked upon the planes of existence and communed with the Life that swarmed upon it and finally brought forth their ultimate creation, the Culai, the First Race.

But that is a tale unto itself.

Thus endeth the tale of the Great Beginning, of the Creation of Life, of the fashioning of the Prime Plane and the lesser planes of existence, and of the greater and lesser gods...

The tavern remained silent long after the bard finished, drinks forgotten on the stained tables, the untended fire burned down to glowing embers. Paedur's dark eyes blinked and opened and a smile touched his lips as he looked around the darkened room. It was a great tribute to his storytelling. He dropped his voice to little more than a whisper and continued.

"In these days—modern, cultured days—there are those who no longer worship the Old Faith, nor call upon the Pantheon...and then they wonder why the gods do not answer their prayers. There is a magic in names—call upon the old gods by their true names and they will listen to your prayers." He paused and added, "In the naming of the New Gods, for example, there is little magic."

"But the New Gods come," a small, defiant voice muttered from a darkened corner of the room, "the Old Gods no longer heed the people's pleas: they are dead, but the gods of the Religion live!"

Paedur leaned forward, his hard eyes piercing the gloom. "Aye, and when you call a dog it comes. Are the gods of the New Religion lackeys to be called at your beck and whim? And when you call are you really sure you know what comes?" The bard's silver hook flashed redly in the glowing firelight. "Do you really know what you're worshipping?" he demanded.

The question hung on the still warm air, but no one moved to reply.

The bard sat back into the darkness and continued quietly. "I know there are those who argue that the Old Gods—ever fickle, ever wilful and disdainful—have deserted man; some will say that they have been overthrown by the New Gods. But know this," and suddenly the bard's voice rose on a commanding note, "the gods— your fathers' gods and their fathers' before them—are ever with us, and though they are often forgetful and heed not the prayers of man, they are there, and they will come again in power and glory. They will come again."

And once again silence settled over the tavern and encompassed all within its heavy warmth.

A figure moved along the wall, the sound of cloth against the cold stones loud in the silence. The bard sat forward, his head tilted to one side, listening. "Come out where I can see you," he commanded. He leaned across and tossed a log onto the fire. Sparks shot upwards as the resin-rich wood burst into crackling flame. Shadows writhed across the floor and up the stone walls, nestling in the smoke-blackened rafters.

A young man stepped boldly out into the circle of light. He was tall and thin, his eyes sunken and burning feverishly in an almost chalk-white face. He was shivering as he stepped up close to the seated figure of the bard. "Blasphemy," he hissed. "There is no god but Trialos, the True God." He pointed accusingly at Paedur. *"Blasphemer!"*

The bard didn't move, and the young man turned and gestured to the crowd. "Do not listen to this man; he is evil, a spreader of lies. The priests will deal with you," he added, turning back to the bard, "I will make sure of it."

"You have to leave here first, boy," Carp said, stepping up behind the young man, the crossbow cradled loosely in his arms.

"My gods will protect me," he said with absolute confidence.

"From this?" Carp held up the weapon, shifting it so that the firelight ran like blood down the polished wood and the iron tip of the bolt which projected almost a finger-length beyond the crossbow.

"You cannot kill me; I an Xanazius, acolyte and soon to be priest in the New Religion." The young man rubbed both hands briskly together and laughed mockingly. "Unless you reconsider your foolish beliefs you will all burn in the fires of the unbelievers. Count Karfondal has embraced the True Faith, and in a very few days it will become the official belief. Of course, you will all have the chance to repent..." Xanazius' voice rose higher and higher, verging on hysteria, but suddenly it dropped and he turned to the bard. "But you, of course, must die," he said casually.

He was moving even before he had finished speaking, the stiletto in his hand almost invisible as he lunged for the bard's chest. Paedur's hook flashed, metal rang on metal, and the finger-slim blade snapped as it buried itself in the hard floor. Although disarmed, Xanazius' momentum carried him forward, and instinctively his fingers hooked and reached for Paedur's eyes. There was a thump, and then he suddenly stiffened as the bard's left arm came up and the metal hook bit deeply into the flesh of his jaw and cheek. Xanazius slumped to the ground—and then the bard saw the bolt protruding from his left shoulder.

Carp stepped forward, smiling ruefully. "Sorry, I was aiming for his neck; I must be losing my touch."

Amblad leaned forward in his chair. "Will he live?" he asked quietly.

The bard knelt by the young man's side. He pulled the long, thick-bodied bolt from his shoulder and tossed it back to the inn-keeper, and then rolled Xanazius over and pulled open his jerkin. Blood welled from the ragged tear in the flesh. The half-circle which the bard's hook had cut into his face was also pumping blood and, if possible, the young man's skin was now even paler than before. Paedur sat back on his heels and slowly moved his left arm down the length of the youth's body. Shadows abruptly shivered along the length of the metal hook and tiny blue sparks danced in the runes. He paused when the hook rested over the wound in Xanazius' shoulder; a thin high-pitched humming trembled on the air, and the bleeding slowed to a trickle and then the wound visibly clotted. The bard moved his hand upwards and covered the facial wound with his hook; again the bleeding visibly clotted and stopped.

Paedur eased himself to his feet. His hook sparked and crackled as he moved, and the runes seemed to etch themselves into the semi-darkness. He nudged the unconscious man with his foot. "Take him far from here and release him; by the time he finds his way back, I shall be long gone."

"But he can recognise you," Carp protested. The firelight danced across the flesh of his face as he smiled. "I doubt if he will ever forget you—he'll bear your mark to his grave." And then the inn-keeper sobered. "He can also bring the guards and priests here."

"It will be his word against yours," Paedur said reasonably.

"They usually ask their questions with a rack and hot irons," Carp said quietly. "However, we will do what we can. But perhaps it would be better if you left now."

The bard nodded, and gathered up his cloak.

"Must you leave?" Amblad asked. "With you by my side, with your tales and knowledge, I could make the Faith strong again."

"I must go, I have work to do."

"Then is there nothing else you can tell us? I know we have a lot to thank you for already. You have reminded us of our youth, when we had gods we trusted, and a tradition followed by our fathers and their fathers before them back to the First Age of Man." There was a low murmur of agreement from the tavern. "You have awakened that which has slept: our Faith. For that we thank you again."

Paedur swung his cloak on to his shoulders and bowed deeply. Even if the Old Faith had regained only one of its former adherents, then he was pleased. And then he looked at the young man lying in a pool of his own blood, and he realised that the first blow in his battle against the New Religion had been struck.

The bard Paedur bowed once again to the old priest and the innkeeper; and then he slipped out into the night.

4
Kutter Kin-Slayer

And the bard took the north road to Baddalaur, the College of Bards.
Life of Paedur, the Bard

This day returned to us a brother, by name Paedur, called the Hookhand.
Register of Baddalaur, the College of Bards

There was a flash of crimson and gold as the riders in Count Karfondal's livery broke out from the shelter of the trees and into the wan sunlight. Tendrils of early morning mist eddied about their mounts' hooves, and the riders' leathern cloaks were slick with moisture.

The leader raised his hand and reined his mount to a halt, pulling it off the worn stone road onto the soft muddy margin. While he waited for his small group to gather around him, he allowed his eyes to wander back along the road to where it disappeared amongst the trees and then reappeared further up as a thin grey-white line that led to the sprawling pile of Baddalaur, the College of Bards. It had been a natural assumption that the renegade bard would return to his old school—especially since he seemed to be travelling north-wards along the King Road.

And they should have caught him there! He was a man afoot, and seemingly in no hurry, and damnably distinctive with that butcher's hook in place of his left hand. But they had somehow missed him. It had been the same story for the past three months. In every tiny hamlet and village they passed, they had heard talk of him, and saw the renewed signs of the Old Faith springing up again—but no sign of the bard.

Keshian was a warrior, and he had been in the employ of Count Karfondal for close on twelve summers now, a fighting man with little time for religion or the affairs of gods. But the way this man stirred up the people's faith in the Old Gods and turned them against the New Religion was frightening. And, unless he was stopped, Keshian could see the province erupting into a holy war.

"Again?" He turned, suddenly aware that one of his officers was talking to him.

"I asked what your orders were, sir?"

Keshian dropped his reins and stood in the stirrups, pressing his hands into the small of his back. He was a short, rather stout man, muscles beginning to run to fat—and getting far too old for this sort of thing. He sat back into the saddle gingerly. "We have two choices," he began slowly. "We can return to the count, with the news that we have somehow missed this bard..."

"But I still can't see how—he is afoot."

Keshian pushed back his mail hood and shook his head. "I don't know. We've been told that he is afoot, but we don't know that for certain."

"We found no horse tracks," his sergeant reminded him.

"Nor did we find any man tracks," Keshian snapped, "and you also know that he was in Lechfair, although the town was cut off by floods for most of the time he was there. No one answering his description came through Badaur, and yet we find traces of him in Baddalaur, which, you may recall, is accessible only through the town."

Keshian and his troops had missed the bard by what must have been barely an hour in the College of Bards. He couldn't understand it—he had had men stationed at the gates day and night, checking the description of everyone entering or leaving. Baddalaur was Culai-built, one of the ancient artifacts that littered the Nations of Man, relics of their god-like ancestors. It was a sprawling building, surrounded by a wall of solid stone, with neither seam nor crack in it, and the only entrance was through a massive teel-wood, iron-studded gate. Since time out of legend, the bards, scribes, scholars and poets had occupied the massive rooms, and thus it was one of the better-preserved Culai sites.

Over the years a small but thriving township had grown up, actually around the college's gates. The town housed mainly scholars, historians, priests, or magicians who had come to use Baddalaur's enormous library, and it also helped to cater in some part towards the needs of those bards and scribes living and training within the college. The main street of Badaur ended up at the college gates and it was thus impossible to enter the college except by passing through the town.

"Our second choice is to continue on into the Northlands," Keshian continued. "From the little we know of this Paedur, he seems intent on pushing northwards all the time. The college records last place him south in the Forest of Euarthe. We next hear of him in the Coined Sword, close to Karfondal, and then in almost every village running north after that." The captain pulled a short thick parchment tube from his saddle-bags and, giving one edge to his sergeant, pulled it open. His blunt fingernail traced the bard's route. "If he continues on this road, he will eventually reach Castle Nevin along the Mion River, and the next stop after that is Thusal—which has a bardhouse!"

The sergeant grunted in satisfaction. "His eventual destination perhaps..."

"Perhaps..." Keshian allowed the parchment chart to roll closed of its own accord, and slipped it back into his saddle bag. "We travel north then." He urged his mount back on to the road, and waited for his small company to fall in behind him. "We're heading north," he said gruffly. "Our next stop will be Castle Nevin, which we'll try to make before nightfall since I'm sure none of you want to spend a night in the Wastelands. And remember, between Baddalaur and Castle Nevin, there is nothing but open country, inhabited only by beasts and bandits—so stay alert."

Keshian urged his roan mount to a trot and, with his company strung out single file behind him, they continued down the King Road in search of the bard.

Behind them and beneath the trees, a tall cloaked figure watched them ride away. On his left shoulder gleamed the eye and triangle of the bardic college, and in place of his left hand was a gleaming silver hook.

There was a shrill keening sound and then a crossbow bolt sank up to its feathers in the scout's chest, punching through a hauberk of banded mail and leather and driving him up and out of the saddle.

Keshian was already dropping to the ground when the sudden screaming flurry of bolts scythed through his men. No, not men, he realised bitterly, boys; most of them had never seen any actual combat...most of them never would now.

He lay on the ground, unmoving, listening to the death-shrill of the quarrels as they spun through the air. He recognised the sound of old; Wastelanders cut tiny holes in the heads of their crossbow bolts so that the air, passing through them, shrilled like a cat in agony.

A horse bolted past him, its iron-shod hooves sparking from the hard road barely a handspan from his head; there was another brief flurry of whistles and then the horse crashed to the ground with a human-like scream. There was no movement from the rider.

The scarred battle-captain lay on the road listening to the pounding of his own heartbeat. The sun was warm on his face and beads of sweat were gathering just under his hairline and running down the back of his neck. There was a long burning scrape along one cheek, and blood from a split lip dripped on to the ground.

If the Wastelanders followed their usual procedure they would pillage the dead, stripping them of everything, clothing, armour and weapons, and leave the naked corpses to rot in the sun or as food for the scavengers.

There was a sudden scrape of metal off stone and then the slow rasp of a sword being withdrawn. Booted feet walked the pitted road off to one side, and there was more movement ahead of him.

"Karfondal's colours." The voice was rough, and strongly accented.

"Aye, and I wonder what they were doing this far north." The second voice came from behind Keshian; it was softer and the accent was cultured.

"Eight men," the first voice remarked, "travelling light. Chain and banded mail, no heavy armour, pressed provisions."

The voices came closer and a pair of scuffed leather boots stopped barely a finger's breadth from the captain's face. "Are there any message tubes?"

There was a brief pause, and then the first voice called back. "None."

"Then they must have been hunting someone," the second voice, which carried an unmistakable air of authority, said quietly, almost to himself.

"We cannot linger, sir."

"Aye. Call the men down and let them take what they will. Are there any left alive?"

"Just one!"

Metal rasped on metal and then a long slender dagger bit deeply into Keshian's leather-gauntleted hand. He winced and then his head was pulled back while a foot was pressed into the small of his back. His back arched and his spine threatened to snap. A cold sliver of steel touched his outstretched throat.

"This one still lives...for the moment."

Keshian found himself looking up into the broad smiling face of the leader of the Wastelands brigands.

"Let him up."

The foot was removed from the captain's back and he was roughly hauled to his feet, but the dagger never left his throat.

"Kutor the Renegade," he gasped, suddenly recognising the man before him.

The man bowed slightly. "At your service." He was a short, rather stocky man, slightly smaller than the captain. His hair—although he could not have yet reached his thirtieth winter—was iron grey, matching his sharp eyes. His features were broad, and there were tiny wrinkles around his eyes and mouth. He smiled and the wrinkles deepened into folds. "Tell me now, where were you going and in such a hurry?"

Keshian stiffened, his eyes gazing straight ahead, over Kutor's right shoulder at the group of bandits stripping the bodies of his men and their mounts. He watched two men, wearing stained leather aprons, move from horse to horse and cut free the crossbow bolts. In the Wastelands, nothing was wasted.

"I asked you a question." The voice was still mild, and the smile was still in place, but the eyes had turned hard and cold.

The captain knew a little of Kutor the Renegade, Kutor the Bastard, Kutor the Pretender. He was rumoured to be the Emperor's half brother, by Geillard's father and a country wench, and he often used the title of Prince. Some years ago, he had been persuaded by some disaffected nobles to attempt to enforce his claim to the throne by force of arms. With an army of mercenaries at his back, he had marched on the capital. His army had been welcomed as liberators in every village they passed through, and by the time he had come in sight of the capital, its numbers had doubled and redoubled. But they faced one of the most highly trained and well-equipped armies in the known world. The battle itself was brief—and his mismatched and ragged following had been slaughtered. Kutor and his few remaining followers had fled to the Wastelands, where they now preyed upon unwary travellers. It was a long way from attacking the capital, Keshian thought. He suddenly realised that they would not usually have attacked a group as heavily armed as his...

A blow to the back of the head sent him sprawling at Kutor's feet. The cut on his face began to bleed again and he tasted the copper tang of blood in his mouth. A hand caught in his hair and hauled him to his feet.

"So, tell me."

Keshian spat, spraying bloody saliva into Kutor's face.

Kutor smiled. "We could have talked, you and I. We could have talked. You could have told me where you were going, and perhaps I would have let you go. But now..." he smiled almost sadly and shrugged, "now, you will tell me and then I will have to kill you."

There was a sharp whistle and Kutor's head snapped around. Keshian heard booted feet running across the cracked road-stones behind him and then pound onto the grass verge. The brigand looked at the captain and then at the man standing behind him. "Take him, I'll deal with him later." And then he turned and vanished into the undergrowth that lined the road. Keshian twisted around—in time to see a rounded dagger pommel flash down into his face...

There was meat roasting and the pine-fresh evening air was rich with its odours. Fire crackled, and resin popped and spat, also lending its particular odours to the twilight. Keshian came awake with a pounding headache and no feeling in his hands or feet. There was also water running down onto his face, and when he looked up there was a coarse-featured peasant woman standing before him with a dripping bucket in her hands. She laughed when she saw he was awake and then walked away. Keshian shook his head, shaking out as much of the ice-cold water as he could, and then attempted to take stock of his surroundings.

He was sitting on one side of a small clearing of low, thick-boled trees. There was water bubbling behind him and a small muddy streamlet twisted by his side and across the encampment. He guessed that he must be in one of the small oases that dotted the Wastelands: small, fertile patches where life proliferated whilst all around the rocky Wastelands lay barren.

Centuries ago, when the Culai first built the King Road, they had chosen the small sheltered hollows as the sites for their Way Stations. These were long, low, strongly built buildings that served as resting posts for travellers. They were equipped with supplies of blankets and wood, dried provisions and simple medications, and travellers were expected to replace whatever they used. But as the years passed, inns had taken over from the Way Stations, and the routeways had changed, leaving many of the buildings isolated and abandoned. And then, of course, there were rumours that many of the Culai-built ruins were haunted. However, the Way Stations—safe on account of their isolation and the stories surrounding them—were often used by bandits both as a base and a refuge.

Keshian twisted around and stared into the gloom, looking for the station. At first he could see nothing, but as his eyes adjusted to the twilight that had already gathered in the hollow, he could make out the outline of the small square building against the scrubby undergrowth and stunted trees.

The battle-captain shivered. The Wastelands brigands had stripped him of everything except his breeches, and the cold wind that ruffled the trees and bushes prickled his skin and bit into his bones. Keshian was into his fortieth year now, a tough warrior once but grown soft with city living. The only action he had seen in the past twelve years in Count Karfondal's guard had been hunting brigands—such as these—or doing escort duty on the taxes into the capital.

Time had changed him, weakened and softened him. In his youth he would have never thrown himself to the ground when Kutor and his brigands had attacked; he would have fought them, charging into their midst with a swinging sword—and would probably have been shot down. Age had taught him caution; but then, who ever heard of an old hero? These people would question him, and if they didn't get the answers they wanted, they would torture and then kill him. In fact, even if he did tell them what they wanted to know, they would probably kill him anyway—but at least it might be quick and painless. And when a man reached Keshian's age in his particular profession, the best he could hope for was a quick death.

It was close to midnight when they came for him. He had fallen into a fitful doze earlier on that night, although he had awoken briefly some time later to watch the stars beginning their slow dance across the clear skies, and tried to gauge his location.

The agony of returning circulation brought him awake again. Someone had cut the bonds on his legs, and his ankles and feet were afire with stabbing pains and cramps. Still only half-conscious, he was hauled to his feet and dragged across the clearing towards the Way Station.

The light inside the long, low, rectangular room was sharp and painful, driving slim daggers of pain into his throbbing head. The air was harsh and dry, foul with the stench of unwashed bodies, urine, vomit and burnt food, and he had to swallow hard to keep his gorge down. But it was warm; he was grateful for that. All conversation died to a dull murmur as he was dragged across the room towards the huge open fire to where Kutor sat alone and apart from the others.

The prince was seated before a small ornate table of polished wood, its delicate filigree work inset with flecks of dark gold and winking gemstones. The remains of a meal were still on the table and, although the fare might have been rough, the tableware was of the finest worked gold.

Keshian's stomach rumbled hungrily.

Kutor patted his lips with a white napkin and looked up into the captain's eyes. He remained silent for a long time, and then slowly and deliberately he poured a measure of deep red wine into a tall fluted glass. He held the glass in the fingers of both hands under his sharp nose and stared deep into the swirling depths. "You are a very foolish man," he said finally, without taking his eyes from the glass.

Behind him, Keshian was aware that the entire room had grown quiet; he could almost feel the malicious smiles.

Kutor glanced up and smiled briefly. "We can talk, you and I," he said. "You can tell me who you are, where you were going, and why."

"And if I don't?" the older man asked quietly.

The younger man's smile deepened, and he shrugged. "I can wait while my men…question…you, and then we can speak again. You will tell me then," he said confidently.

Keshian nodded wearily, and his shoulders slumped. "Aye, so you could." He nodded at the vacant seat, and then at the wine. "May I sit, and drink?"

News of the slaughtered scouting party was carried back to Baddalaur by an itinerant poet returning to the College. Custom and tradition decreed that those poets and bards who had received their training in the College of Bards must, at least once in every five-year cycle, return to the College and record their tales and epics in the library, so that the lore of the Seven Nations might never again be lost as it so nearly had in the past.

The scholars in Baddalaur relayed the message back to Karfondal through one of their number who had the power of Speech, and that same night, while Kutor was questioning Keshian, word was being relayed back to the capital that the bard Paedur had slaughtered a band of Karfondal's men with his Old Faith sorcery.

No mention was made of the crossbow wounds on either man or beast, nor was the fact that they had been stripped of their arms and armour even discussed.

"My name is Keshian, son of Keshen, a smith, and I am a captain in Count Karfondal's army," the old warrior began, carefully sipping the heady ruby wine. He was sitting in a chair across the ornate table from Kutor, his hands unbound and a rough woollen cloak thrown across his shoulders. "Some days ago, word came in that a dangerous criminal was on the loose, a bard by the name of Paedur..."

"What was his crime?" Kutor asked.

"Sedition against the New Religion."

"Sedition against the New Religion!" Kutor spat into the fire. "That's hardly a crime."

"Aye, but the count has been received into that faith and he is enforcing his will on his court and subjects," Keshian protested. "The New Religion is now the official belief of this province."

"The people will never follow the Religion," the young man snapped, "but continue."

"This bard is immediately recognisable by the fact that he has but one hand and wears a silver hook in place of his left. The only other description we had was that he was tall and thin, sharp-featured and dark-eyed. I was told to bring him back to the count—alive."

"And all because he was preaching against the New Religion?" Kutor asked with derision. "It seems unlikely."

"I am a soldier sir, I follow my orders." Keshian paused and sipped his drink. "Perhaps, sir, I might add that this Paedur does not exactly preach against the Religion; he is a bard, and by all accounts a master of his craft, and so by using his tales he insidiously turns people back to the Old Faith."

"But to what end?"

Keshian shrugged. "I don't know."

"I don't believe him," one of the bandits, a huge ill-kempt southerner said, his accent thick, slurred from too much wine, his eyes bright and dangerous. "Eight men to follow one bard..."

"There was some talk that he is not wholly a man," the captain said quickly.

"You seem to know a little more about him now," Kutor snapped. "Perhaps if we were to pry a little more, we might find out what else you know about this bard, eh?"

"That's all I know..."

"Why don't you ask me?"

The voice was sharp and penetrating and cut through the thick atmosphere like a chill breeze.

In the stunned silence that followed, the crackling of the fire seemed unnaturally loud, and even the wind hissing against the thick stones of the walls was audible. A shadow moved at the back of the room, and then a figure stepped out into the light.

Steel rasped as weapons were drawn.

The figure was that of a man, clad in a long dark cloak of fine hair that covered him from head to foot. His features were shadowed beneath the cloak's deep cowl, leaving only his eyes glowing in the reflected firelight.

One of the bandits stepped in front of the man, bringing a thick-bladed sabre up before the figure's face. "Let's have a look at you, eh?"

There was a blur of silver, and metal sang—and the sabre was entrapped in a gleaming half-circle, a hook, that the figure was holding. The brigand attempted to pull his weapon free, but it was firmly lodged.

"The bard," Keshian breathed, recognising the hook.

"You know this man?" Kutor snapped.

"It can only be the bard...the man we were sent to follow," Keshian said quietly. "But, how did he come here...?"

The bard twisted his arm, and then the sabre blade snapped with a sharp ringing sound, leaving its owner looking stupidly at the stump of metal he held in his hand. "Perhaps there was a flaw in the metal," Paedur said quietly, his long-fingered right hand coming up and brushing back the hood of his cloak.

The bandits drew away from the bard then, touching amulets and relics, for there was something strange about him, something about the way his sharp eyes seemed to linger just a moment too long on each person that lent him an almost inhuman air.

He indicated the drawn swords and knives with a wave of his hand. "Do you defy the King's Privilege, and draw steel on a bard?"

"We do no honour to any King's Privilege," Kutor snapped.

The bard rounded on him, and the look in his eyes stopped anything else the prince might have been going to say. "If you intend to rule some day," Paedur said gently, as if speaking to a child, "you must base your rule upon solid ground, a background founded in history and folklore. People trust what they know."

Kutor stood up and moved away from the table, his hand falling to the knife in his belt. He took a step closer to the bard. "What do you mean," he hissed, "'if I intend to rule?'"

The stranger smiled and, with his right hand, undid the ornate ouroborus clasp near the throat of his cloak and swung it off his shoulders. He was clad in a black shirt of fine mail over a shirt of cotton dyed a deep purple. His leggings were a deep brown and he wore high black boots that had obviously seen much use. High on his left shoulder, the triangular bardic sigil winked blood-red in the firelight.

He tossed his cloak over Kutor's chair and sat back into it with a sigh of contentment. He looked up at the brigand, who was still standing, and indicated the chair opposite him. "Please sit."

Keshian scrambled up out of the seat and Kutor sat down slowly, his eyes never once leaving the bard's.

Paedur sat back in the chair and lowered his head into his shirt's high collar, until only his slightly prominent cheekbones and his burning eyes were visible.

"You want to rule," he began quietly, his voice certainly not above a normal conversational tone and yet carrying to everyone in the room, "you feel—and perhaps rightly so—that you have some claim on Geillard's throne."

"I am the Emperor's son—albeit on the wrong side of the blanket. In the past, men have come to power who have had as little claim to the throne," Kutor said almost defiantly.

The bard inclined his head slightly. "Indeed, that is so. But to continue. Your attempt to take the crown by force of arms failed and so now you are forced to live out your days here in the Wastelands. You have harried the Emperor's forces, robbed the merchants, slain or held to ransom the unwary and unlucky travellers who have fallen into your hands. You have made your name a curse on men's lips and turned the Wastelands into a feared place."

Kutor nodded, smiling slightly.

"And how long do you think you can continue?" Paedur asked mildly. He leaned forward and tapped the table with the point of his hook. "There is a change abroad at court. So far, Geillard has left you alone—the gods themselves know why, but perhaps he does feel something for you, his…his half-brother." The bard shrugged and sat back into the chair. Above him on the wall a torch guttered and died, oily black smoke wending slowly upwards against the stained and blackened beams. No one made any move to replace it, and the area below the torch was touched with heavier shadows which rendered the bard almost invisible, only the gleaming half circle of his hook and the bardic sigil visible. "If Geillard moves against you, he will crush you—totally."

"But he won't move against us," Kutor protested. "He would be stretching his resources too far; Count Karfondal would never lend him the support needed for any lengthy campaign in the Wastelands." He glanced up at the captain standing by his side, "Is that not so?"

"My lord Karfondal does not see eye to eye with the Emperor in many things," Keshian said carefully.

"Aye, but has not your lord been acting strangely of late?" the bard asked.

Keshian shifted uncomfortably from foot to foot. He shrugged. "Perhaps he has not been himself recently…" he agreed cautiously.

"Perhaps since he adopted the New Religion?" the bard persisted, leaning forward, his eyes catching the firelight and blazing like red coals.

"Perhaps."

"I don't see…" Kutor began.

The bard's hook rose. "Wait; listen." He turned back to Keshian. "And what is his attitude towards Geillard now?"

The captain rolled his cup in his large hands, looking down into the swirling depths. When he looked up his eyes were troubled. "He has changed towards the Emperor. In the past few moons many messengers have come and gone—and indeed, more so since we were ordered to seek you out. And Karfondal has even announced his intention to visit the Imperial Court in the near future— something which he has never done before, not since Geillard had his uncle put to death for treason."

The bard turned back to Kutor. "And tell me, what would happen if Karfondal were to make his peace with Geillard; how would that affect your position here in the Wastelands?"

Kutor shifted uncomfortably in his seat. "If...and I say 'if', mind, the Emperor decided to move against us, and he had the count's support, then it would make things difficult for us," he agreed cautiously.

"They would wipe us out," one of the men behind him suddenly shouted. "The Wastelands are our refuge, but they would also make a fine trap."

Keshian nodded. "It would be an easy matter to bring in troops to encircle the south, west and eastward sides of the Wastelands, and then draw them in—driving you northwards at the same time. Soon you would be trapped between the encircling troops and the Seven Bastions along the River Mion. And even if you did manage to cross the river—which in the Cold Months is possible across the ice—the Chopts would surely get you."

"Thank you," Kutor said grimly. He turned back to the bard after a moment's consideration. "But tell me, bard, why should the count suddenly resolve his differences with the Emperor?"

"You have heard no doubt about the New Religion that is sweeping across the land?"

"Rumours have trickled through to me—but I have little time for gods and their ilk; I pay them no heed."

Paedur shook his head. "Foolish, very foolish. A good leader ignores no rumours, no whispered tales, no scandal that might affect the higher echelons of power." He sat forward suddenly and impaled Kutor with his hard dark stare. "This New Religion is not just another fad, not just another passing fancy. It is a very real and dangerous threat to the Seven Nations."

"I don't see how any religion..." the brigand began.

"But it is not just any religion," Paedur snapped, his voice cracking through the room like a whip. "It is a man-made and inspired faith, and its believers are dedicated to it with a frightening passion. And it is that faith alone which gives it strength and substance. But—and this is where it affects you—old enemies have now become friends, old rivalries forgotten, old feuds mended. Groups such as yours—bandits, thieves and brigands—have already been slaughtered in the south and east. There is a move abroad to wipe out anyone—*anyone*—who does not conform to the standards of the New Religion and worship its gods."

"But why?" Kutor whispered.

Paedur shrugged. "I don't know," he confessed. "But perhaps you represent a freedom of sorts, and the New Religion is not too keen on freedom."

"And what is your part in all this?" Kutor asked suddenly.

"I have no part," the bard said, smiling. "I am merely a storyteller—in the traditional way," he added, with a sly smile.

"Do many listen to your stories?"

"More and more."

And what do your tales accomplish?"

"They help to remind the people of the past, of the traditional ways, the old beliefs, the old gods. A lot of people out there believe; indeed, they find it easy to believe. But they need someone to form around, someone who will focus their energy—they need a leader."

"What sort of a leader?" Kutor asked cautiously.

"Someone to rally behind." He paused. "My stories remind them of the past; I stress the importance of tradition and order. They need someone who would also stress the traditional ways; someone with an honourable ancestry, someone with a name. Perhaps someone with at least some sort of claim to the throne."

There was silence in the Way Station for a long time then. The implications behind the bard's words were not lost on any of those present, and it was as if a chill breeze had blown through the room. And even though nothing had happened, everyone there felt as if something had changed. It was an invitation—and a challenge. In the course of a few heartbeats their lives might take on a new direction. But the final decision would be Kutor's.

"What are you, bard?" Kutor asked softly.

"A storyteller."

"What else?"

The bard smiled easily, and shrugged. "As I've said, nothing else."

"Then tell me, storyteller," the prince asked quietly, "what would you do if our situations were reversed?"

"I don't have to make that decision, thank the gods."

"But if you had...if the decision were yours to make?"

Paedur sat back into the chair and seemed to consider. "I would move fast and by night, heading west to one of the ancient Culai settlements. Beyond the Wastelands many of the old forts are still in good order. With a little work they could be rendered inhabitable and virtually impregnable. As you know, they are usually well situated, solidly built, with their own water supply and often on a branch of the King Road. If I were going to conduct a campaign against the Imperial forces, I would certainly consider using one of the old forts."

Kutor nodded slowly. "And what then?"

"Then if a bard, let us say, were to continue on his travels and send anyone interested in the restoration of the old ways, the Old Faith, westwards to you, you would soon have a formidable force under your command."

"But to what end?"

The bard tapped his silver hook against the wooden table, emphasising his points. "Overthrow the current court, which has degenerated into a cesspit, and overthrow the New Religion. The Old Faith must be restored to its former position as the Empire's official religion—is that understood?" he demanded fiercely.

The brigand nodded, taken aback by the bard's vehemence. "You talk as if it's a foregone conclusion."

The bard smiled again. "Ah, but I'm only a storyteller, I've no gift for prophecy."

Kutor leaned back in the chair. "So you say," he mused. "What you've said is interesting, but you've got to let me think on it..."

"You don't have much time left," Paedur said quietly. Kutor nodded. "Aye, well...let me think." What this bard was proposing was...incredible. A few years ago he would have said yes immediately, and bedamn the consequences, but now...but now he had to think. Once he had started on this course, there was no turning back. He had to think.

He looked around the room, at the ragged men and women, brigands, outlaws, thieves, a few ex-soldiers. They would follow him, he knew, but had he any right to lead them away from here into what might be almost certain death? But if what this bard said were true, then their days here in the Wastelands were numbered. He needed to buy some time to think.

Kutor turned back to Paedur. "Well, sir bard, why don't you give us an example of your craft; why don't you let us have a tale, eh?" Behind him, the company shouted their approval, tension evaporating like the morning dew under the sun. "Aye, a tale."

The bard ran his hook down along his jaw, his face serious but his eyes were bright with amusement. "A tale. Well then, what would you have?" He looked across at Kutor. "Choose..."

The brigand smiled. "Give us a tale of my namesake: Kutter Kin-Slayer. It was a story I learned at my mother's knee. Give me your version."

Paedur nodded. "A strange choice..."

"Do you know it?"

The bard smiled. "I know all the tales and legends of our land." He tucked his hook into his sleeve and leaned back in the chair, and the shadows clustered about him, leaving only his eyes burning in the paleness of his face. There was a brief pause as he looked around the room, claiming everyone's attention, and then he began...

In the time of Churon the Onelord and Deslirda his lady, there was peace over the land for the first time in many years.

But it had not always been so, for when the invaders had come, the first decade of the Onelord's reign had been one of war and famine. But Churon had sworn to free his land, and to this end had cunningly oathbound the Brothers, the six kings of the neighbouring lands, and, gathering his allies together on the Sand Plain close to where the invaders from the Land of the Sun had beached their metal craft, he waged war upon them. And in a great battle lasting a day and a night, his army utterly vanquished the Shemmatae. From that time he ruled with an iron hand from his place in the Silver City of Shansalow, acknowledged by the Brothers as their overlord, the Onelord.

But the land was vast and still untamed, and there were large tracts which were claimed only by the beasts. Thus the Onelord, recognising that he could not rule alone, and, realising the dangers of even attempting to do so, therefore appointed his most trusted retainers to oversee the provinces on his behalf. The Onelord remained in the capital and his regents were answerable only to him.

And Churon ordered his loyal and trusted friend Kutor the Strong to invest the Castle of Oakin, and from there to rule the western seaboard on his behalf.

Thus Kutor, called the Strong, for he was a man of great physical strength, made preparations for the journey. And when his servants, warriors, and retainers had gathered together their belongings and possessions, they set out along the King Road to the West, and Gallowan Province.

For many days Kutor and his retainers rode, travelling westwards all the while. The year was drawing to a close, and the days were long and heavy with time losing all meaning. They rode past the Twin Cities of Foara and Faora upon the Heights, past ancient Palsaor, and then on to Broar where they stopped with Prince Huiet, feasting and making merry with their jovial host.

They continued on, and the Lady Lussa rode in her full finery thrice across the skies. And then, on that morning dedicated to Cam, the God of Bridges, they came to the Gluaddon Wood, and they rode through the ancient wood with their arms and accouterments clattering and twinkling in the dappled sunlight, and their voices were raised in song and laughter.

And thus Kutor, in his haste to reach his new domain, failed to pay tribute to the Wood Folk that abode deep in the leafy fastness, and furthermore, did not preserve the Wood Silence, that ancient law which enjoined all travellers to *"raise not a voice in joy nor anger, nor carry sparkling metal within the fields of the Crinnfaoich, the Wood Folk."*

And the Wood Folk were greatly angered, but decided to grant unto the new Lord of Oakin the opportunity to redress his omission, and thus they sent to him Yuann, the Wood Sprite.

Fair she was to look upon; her hair dark as the moss upon the bark, soft and shining; her skin tanned as dark as the great toor trees. Her features were delicate, yet sharp, and her eyes were naught but dappled pools of light amidst shadow. She flitted amongst the trees clad in a shift of feathery mostle leaves which clung glovelike to her skin.

She came to Kutor in the evening twilight as he sat beneath a gnarled toor tree looking down upon his camp which lay spread out over the Dale of Duil. When she spoke, her voice was like a summer breeze whispering through soft leaves.

"Lord Kutor...Lord Kutor," she called, "why dost thou not pay tribute to the Old Folk who have lived amidst these trees since time immemorial, and why dost thou not honour the Wood Silence?"

Kutor started and his hand reached for his great broadsword before he realised that the maid who had crept up so silently upon him was alone and unarmed. "Fair maid," the lord replied quietly, although he was nigh struck dumb with wonderment at the sight of such beauty and grace, "I know not what you mean."

"You have not acknowledged the Crinnfaoich as Lords of the Forest, my lord," said the maid.

"Child of the Woods," Kutor said roughly, "you must know that I am called Kutor the Strong, and I acknowledge no man my lord, saving my lord Churon." He paused and added in a gentler voice, "So you see, I will acknowledge no tree dwellers my superior, be they either gods or men."

The Wood Sprite fell silent, for the man's fearlessness—and foolishness—appalled her. "Surely you must acknowledge your gods as your superiors?" she wondered.

"Why should I?" Kutor demanded. "The gods have little respect for a snivelling man; they have fought to reach their present position in the Pantheon, and thus they respect a fighter. I am a fighter, and I therefore acknowledge the gods as my equals." He paused and added quietly, "Of course, the followers of Churon are expected to pay homage to the Pantheon, it is part of Churon's attempt to unify the Seven Nations: One Faith, One Land, One People." Kutor shook his head and laughed bitterly. "Aye, well, he'll never see it, nor will I."

"A godless man," the Wood Sprite whispered, "surely thou art lonely and afraid?"

But Kutor misunderstood her question. "I have friends in plenty. I am alone only in that I have no wife." The warrior's meaning was clear.

"Then you will not honour the Crinnfaoich?" the blushing
maid said quickly.

"No, I will not; I cannot, for honour's sake," Kutor said harshly.

"Then I prophesy that there will be little peace between you
and yours and the Wood Folk...and I would wish that it were not
so." A single tear slipped down her cheek, but Kutor brushed it
aside with a gentle hand and drew the maid close to him.

"I do not even know your name," he murmured softly, brushing the maid's green-tinged silken hair.

"I am Yuann, a Wood Maid, a *fraoicht,* in the Slé tongue."

And Yuann and Kutor walked into the wood and spoke of
many things, and when night drew on they lay together in a little
bower beside a clear pool and took pleasure in each other's bodies.
But in the morning, Yuann was gone, leaving Kutor puzzled and
frightened, although he did not know what he feared; and as the
day wore on he came to believe that perhaps he had dreamt of the
fraoicht.

But she came again that night, and every night thereafter while
the Lord of Oakin passed through the ancient wood, and she always vanished with the advent of morning.

Now on the last day of their passage through the Gluaddon
Wood, when the crenellated turrets of Castle Oakin rose tall and
misty above the greenery, the Wood Sprite did not come. And
though Kutor searched the deep forests and silent woods all that
day and for many days thereafter, he never again found Yuann the
fraoicht.

And the Wood Folk never forgave Kutor, and thereafter neither wood nor anything fashioned thereof survived in the Castle
of Oakin. Doors warped, tables and chairs collapsed, storm shutters split and cracked, wooden platforms and fencing rotted overnight, and neither bows nor arrows could be fashioned from the
wood of the forest. Even the usually indestructible brukwood
rotted and powdered once within the castle walls.

And thus all men knew that the Lord of Oakin had been
cursed by the Crinnfaoich.

That first winter of Kutor's rule was a hard one, and the castle
was cut off from the surrounding countryside by deep drifts of
snow and packed ice. Even the castle's well had frozen over and fuel
was running dangerously low.

One night, nigh on one year since he had invested the castle, Kutor found he could not sleep and walked the battlements as night's midnight hour was drawing on. It was in the very depths of the year, when Faurug the Nightwind with Fiarle and Snaitle the Cold God were abroad and dark clouds scudded across the face of the Lady Lussa, the Moon Goddess, like clumsy beast-like paws attempting to grasp a single pearl. The wind howled through the leafless trees, rent by the sentinel branches, and Kutor shivered, for he fancied he heard voices whispering and conspiring together within the cloaking darkness of the forest.

Then a sudden movement below stopped the lord in his tracks. A shadow had slipped from the mocking darkness and flitted swiftly along the ground, ominous and furtive, seeking every clump of darkened shelter and gradually drawing nearer to the castle. Then the night creature had reached the walls and crept along them to the postern gate. It hesitated a moment before stooping down and slipping a bulky object in the shadow of the gate; then the creature turned and vanished back into the hard chill night.

Kutor followed its movements until he could see it no more, then raced down the battlements to the small gate, calling forth the watch as he did so.

And upon the step, deep in the shadows, they found a blanket woven from the branches of the toor tree and lined with mostle leaves…and lying wrapped within, they found a baby, a boy-child and not yet one hour old.

Now the years passed and the babe grew into boyhood and thence to manhood and he was called Kutter. He was tall and strong like his father, but unlike Kutor, his looks were somewhat sharp and pointed, and his skin was smooth like a woman's. He was wise in the ways of the wood and the lore of the forests, and he had great skill in the working of wood.

But of his birth and finding Kutor told his son nothing, and instilled into the boy a deep and burning hatred for the Crinnfaoich, for the Lord of Oakin held the Wood Folk responsible for the loss of his love.

Now as Kutor reached middle years he became more and more distracted, and often disappeared for many days into the fastness of the woods, obsessed with his search for Yuann, the *fraoicht*.

His followers wondered at this, and they feared, and their fear turned to anger, for the Lord was neglecting his duties; and at last, in desperation, they made representation to Churon the Onelord.

When Churon heard of the matter, he was greatly troubled and saddened, for he counted Kutor a good and loyal friend, and it pained him to lose a friend to the Nameless God of Delusion and Madness.

But if the lord were unfit to rule…

So Churon pondered on the matter, seeking someone to replace Kutor even though he was loath to dishonour his friend by passing the regency of the province on to a stranger. And so, to settle the matter, he made Kutter vice-regent of Gallowan.

And thus it was for many years.

Now, when Kutor reached his eightieth year he grew ill, having contracted marsh fever while wandering through the damp woods. And age, which heretofore had but lightly touched the lord, now lay heavily upon him, shortening his breath, enfeebling his gait, dimming his sight, and dulling his hearing.

And he knew he was dying.

So on the evening of the fourteenth day of his illness and his last in this life, he dismissed his servants and called his son to him. His old eyes filled with tears when Kutter came and knelt by the bed, for he saw in him a shadow of his own youth. Tall and proud he stood with great strength of limb; his hair was a burnished copper and his skin deeply tanned; but even if one had not guessed it from his features, his eyes told of his mixed parentage, for they were pools of deep unreadable mystery.

And it suddenly saddened the old man that his son knew nothing of his mother, whom he so closely resembled.

They talked late into the night on many subjects, for the lord knew his end was near and wished to advise his son, and Kutter listened and remembered.

But one promise Kutor extracted from his son, a promise born out of a terrible anger: a promise that he would search out the woods and forests of Gallowan for the Crinnfaoich and put them to the sword, and the old man convinced his son that they were evil and had sought to usurp his rule and conquer the land.

But Kutter demurred, for although he feared the Wood Folk with a superstitious awe, he did not hate them with his father's violence.

But Kutor bound him with a thrice-sworn oath and sealed it with a *geasa*…and Kutter had no choice but to swear.

And as the dawn rose over the tree tops that were turning ochre and bronze with the turning of the year, and Nusas flooded the room with a fragile light, the old lord passed into the Silent Wood, the domain of Mannam, the Lord of the Dead.

On the morning of the following day—once called Ellamas Day, but thereafter called Kutormas—the lord was laid to rest with all due pomp in a simple grave which stood in sight of the forest— for that had been one of his last wishes.

And many came to pay homage to Kutor, for he had been a good ruler in his prime: his justice had been stern and swift, but fair also, he had laboured hard for his province and left behind a legacy of roads, bridges and aqueducts.

Now some weeks after the death of Kutor, an emissary came from the Onelord, for Churon, having heard of the death of his friend, had sent his son Chural to Gallowan, to place on the grave of the dead lord a broken spear, inscribed with the runes of the Onelord and hung with tattered pennants. It was the highest military honour, and a sign that Churon had lost a loyal and true friend who had served him faithfully to the end.

On the morning following the prince's arrival, Kutter and Chural, with a small company of guards, rode out towards Gluaddon Wood and Kutor's grave.

As they drew near to the spot they noticed a young woman kneeling by the graveside and there was an air of strangeness—of wildness—about her. Kutter was puzzled, for he had never seen her before and he was familiar with all the maids in the nearby villages and surrounding countryside. They were almost upon her before she stood up and faced them—and both Kutter and Chural were amazed, for hers was an almost frightening beauty. Though not above middle height, she exuded a presence, an aura, that lent her stature. Her hair was long and dark and rustled in a silken wave down her back, so dark indeed that it seemed to gleam darkly green and moss-like in the morning light. Her skin was clear and deeply tanned as if she had spent all her days in the open under the sun and her eyes…her eyes were deep and mysterious, and Kutter somehow found them almost frighteningly familiar. But as he dismounted, he saw that she was clad in a shift of feathery mostle leaves, and that there was dirt on her hands…

Fear and anger flashed through his brain with blinding comprehension, his sight darkened and his head began to pound. Here was a Crinnfaoich, a Duaiteoiri, come to despoil his father's grave!

Mindful of his oath and now filled with a loathing of this beautiful creature, he pulled his sword free with a cry of rage and in one movement plunged it into the woman's breast.

Prince Chural leaped from his horse with a cry of horror and ran to the stricken maid, clasping her in his arms as he tried to staunch the blood that flowed from her wound and dropped onto the heaped earth of the grave.

"Kutter, what have you done?" he demanded.

"She...she is of the Crinnfaoich," shouted Kutter, "come to torment my father's shade and befoul his grave." The young lord turned away, for now the anger and hatred had drained away and he was sickened and shamed and repented his hasty action.

But had he not sworn an oath to his dying father, and was she not of the Wood Folk and...? Slowly he returned to the graveside and crouched by the prince and the dying woman. "Forgive me," he whispered, "forgive me."

The woman shuddered in Chural's arms and her head lifted and her eyes looked up into his...looking at him...through him... with eyes that reminded him of...

And then he fell back, understanding coursing through him like a levin bolt, shattering the night of ignorance. But as he reached for the small, delicate figure, she shivered and passed unto Mannam, to Death.

Chural turned to look at the stricken lord, and there were tears in his eyes. "She said she was called Yuann," he whispered. "Yuann, beloved of...Kutor the Strong..."

The bard's voice trailed off to a whisper that seemed to linger on the heavy air of the Way Station long after it should. Even when the last tendrils of sound had disappeared, no-one moved or spoke, still enwrapped as they were within the bard's tale. Some of the bandits' drabs were weeping openly, and even the men's eyes were suspiciously bright and glittering.

A taper guttered and died, and the oily smoke coiled around the room, and the rancid bitter-sweet odour made someone sneeze, and suddenly the spell was broken. People moved, conscious of numb feet or hands, and reached for drinks that had grown warm and flat while the bard had worked his own particular magic.

Only Kutor remained unmoving in his chair, his eyes closed, his face curiously blank and almost childlike. When he opened his eyes, they seemed almost lost. "Tell me, bard, was there ever a Churon, a Kutor and Kutter?"

When Paedur began to speak again, the Way Station fell silent. "History confirms that there was a Chur'an, called the One or the Overlord, who ruled from Shansalow, some sixteen generations ago, and that he did appoint a Kutnor—who was called the Strong— Lord of the Province of Gallowan. There is also some evidence that Kutnor's successor was his bastard son, Kuttear."

Another taper failed and died and Paedur paused until the smoke had dispersed. "Kutnor died insane; and indeed Kuttear did pursue a policy of land reclamation and cleared many forest tracts and woodland areas, putting those inhabitants who refused to leave the forest and quit their hereditary occupations—char- coal-burners, wood-bearers, moss-gatherers—to the sword. The land was then settled with refugees from the decimated Whale Coast."

"What happened there?" someone asked from the heavily shad- owed room.

"A series of natural disasters which culminated with either the rising of the sea or the sinking of the land. It was probably a tidal wave," Paedur added, and then continued. "However, some years later, all settlement ceased in Gallowan, and there was mass emigra- tion from the region. Those fleeing the province told of unnatural growth; of trees sprouting overnight, and growing into horrific shapes, of cleared fields suddenly sprouting rank weeds and shrubs in a matter of hours, of pathways and roads abruptly covered in impassable growth.

"The whole region quickly returned to forest, and this area may correspond with the present location of the Great Guadne Forest, which lies to the north and west of here," he finished.

"And Kutter," Kutor said quietly, "how did he die, do you know?"

The bard shook his head, the movement almost lost in the shad- ows. "Not for certain, but Cambris, in his *Heraldic Genealogies*, states that a Kuttear, Lord of the Province of Gallowan, ruled for seven years following the death of his father Kutnor, son of Katar, son of

Kata. Kuttear himself died when he fell from his horse and was impaled through the chest by a branch of a toor tree."

Kutor nodded. "So I've heard, bard; so I've heard."

Another taper sputtered and died—for they had not been attended to while the bard told his tale—leaving only one smoking sconce lighting the room from above the door.

When the prince opened his eyes again, there was a look of absolute weariness in them. "So Kutor did not act soon enough, and Kutter acted too soon. What should I do, bard?" he asked simply.

"But, remember, Kutor did not heed the advice of the *fraoicht*. However, if you want my advice, head west; take one of the old Culai fortresses; gather together an army—a proper army this time—and prepare yourself for the coming battle."

"And I?" Keshian spoke for the first time, startling Kutor, who had almost forgotten him.

"Perhaps Prince Kutor will have need for a good officer, familiar with the Imperial Forces," came the bard's voice from the shadows. "I will send others of a similar mind to you, Kutor; in time you will have your army."

"How will I know them?"

"They will carry my mark—the sign of the hook."

"And what now, bard?" Kutor asked.

But there was no reply; the bard had gone.

5
The Weapon Master

And the bard met many on the road to the north and swayed them to his mission.

Life of Paedur, the Bard

*A Man without Soul; a Man without Heart; a Man without Conscience.
He seemed to me a man not of this world; he seemed to me a dead man.
from...The Warrior, the Life of Owen, Weapon Master*

Owen spent the winter in Palentian Province that year, resting and recovering from his wounds which, although many, were not serious. When he was fit, he took employment with Count Palent, instructing his son in matters of weapon-craft and the Way of the Warrior.

However, as the days lengthened, the Master grew restless and longed to be on his way, but he found it difficult to extract payment from the count, for the old man maintained that his son's education was as yet incomplete. But the boy was slow, and far too fond of his cups and his cronies to pay the Master much heed, and seemed to forget everything he learned almost immediately.

So, one evening, close to the Yearchange, as the sun was sinking below the castle walls and the night chill was closing in, Owen came for me. I was seated in my room in the small outhouse behind the stables, cleaning his shield with fine sand. It was dim and dark and smelt of horses, but a room in the castle had not been considered proper for the Weapon Master's servant.

Owen entered the small room suddenly. He pushed the door shut behind him and moved to the hide-covered window and peered out into the gathering night. Although the Master was dressed in his stained travelling cloak and the guttering taper on the straw beside me did not shed much light across the room, I immediately noticed that he seemed bulkier than usual.

I guessed what was happening and was already bundling my gear together when he moved across the room and knelt beside me, gathering up his longsword and shield. In the light I could see that he was wearing his battle gear beneath his cloak: a hauberk of thick yet supple leather and mail designed to turn an arrow or knife blade. He strapped his longsword across his back, with the hilt projecting above the left shoulder, and slipped his small shield high up on his left arm. He tossed a cloth-wrapped bundle onto the straw pallet.

"We're going, Tien, leave nothing behind." He moved about the room gathering up his few pieces of body armour while I arranged a bundle of straw beneath a blanket on the pallet. To the casual observer, it would look as if I still slept there. I then strapped my two axes onto my belt and slung my gear across my arm and I was ready.

The Master extinguished the taper, and then we waited until our eyes had adjusted to the darkness; it was with such precautions that we had survived as long as we did in our dangerous trade. And then we silently slipped from the outhouse, Owen in the lead, his left hand cupped in such a way that I knew he carried a blade hidden up his sleeve.

We moved from shadow to shadow, neither hurrying nor acting furtively, doing nothing that would attract the attention of the patrolling guards on the rooftops above our heads. We encountered no-one until we reached the postern gate. A single guard stood watch, leaning back against the wall, head nodding, a halberd cradled in his arms. He started awake as Owen drew out of the shadows, fumbled for his weapon and then levelled it at the Master's chest.

"Who goes there?" he called, but his voice was low and soft; he was young, inexperienced and tired. He stood uneasily, off-balance, the point of his halberd wavering between the Master's chest and throat.

"Who goes there?" he repeated, his voice rising slightly, and then cracking, his wide eyes darting from side to side.

"There is no cause for alarm," Owen said, stepping forward into the light, and as the guard recognised him and relaxed, the Master grabbed the halberd behind its hooked and pointed head, jerking the man forward. He stumbled and Owen deftly cut his throat as he fell; he died without a sound.

I then drove the halberd point first into the soft earth and held him while the Master tied the body by the hair and belt to the staff. From the distance, it looked as if the guard had dozed limply at his post; it was a ruse we had used on several occasions, buying time. While Owen put the finishing touches to the guard, I probed the lock on the gate. It was old and heavy, of the double key type, but I had served a locksmith in my youth and had picked up much of the trade, and so with a little probing with the point of my dagger, I soon had it open. Owen made me lock the door after us; it would help delay and confuse any pursuit.

We travelled hard and fast that night, until we struck the Seme which we followed upriver until it was bridged by the old King Road. We camped for what remained of the night on the fishing ledge under the bridge; and there Owen explained why we had fled Count Palent's castle in such a hasty fashion.

"It seems the count had no intention of ever paying our wage," he said, drawing his cloak tighter about his shoulders. "I had served my purpose and trained his son to a degree of weaponmanship he would never otherwise have attained—although, Tien," he added, "he lacks all feeling for his weapons, they are mere killing tools. He will always remain a butcher, he will never be a killer."

"How did you learn of their plans?" I wondered.

"I overheard him boasting that the good count wished his son and a company of guards to try some of their new-found skills on me," he laughed softly, shaking his head.

It was not the first time this had happened and undoubtedly it would happen again. The services of a Weapon Master do not come cheap, and the better they are, the more expensive they become—and Owen was one of the best. Thrice before he had been hired by unscrupulous lords who thought that they might have him disposed of before they actually had to pay him.

But it is difficult to kill a Weapon Master.

We took to the road as the first grey tinges of dawn lightened the eastern horizon. We made good time, for the King Road was in a fair condition even after the recent flooding and storms, although in places the ground tended to be soft and muddy beneath a thin covering of ice.

About mid-morning we passed through the town of Badaur which lies under the shadow of Baddalaur, the College of Bards, an ancient pile of time-worn masonry built, Owen told me, by the Culai, the First Race of Men. For generations the bards and minstrels, poets, and scribes who roam the Nations have been trained there; all knowledge passes through Baddalaur, for its pupils are everywhere.

The town was buzzing with the news that a crack battalion of Count Karfondal's troops had been found slaughtered either by bandits or a hideous hooded demon—there were two versions—just inside the Wastelands. The small town was packed with the count's men in their red and gold, and as we arrived some Imperial troops in their more sombre blue and black rode in, so we hurried on.

We ate our midday meal as we marched—luckily we hadn't stopped for any reason, because the gates were closed shortly after we left, and the soldiers began systematically to search and question everyone there. We continued pushing northwards, for we wished to put as much distance between ourselves and Count Palent as possible.

Once beyond the town, the character of the landscape—which was rough at the best of times—became even more desolate, and the King Road knifed arrow-straight and coal-black through it, rising and falling in long slow waves with nothing but grey, barren rock on either side. The road was deserted, no one braving the crisp weather and roving wolves and the recent bandit atrocity. But we were in good spirits, and chanted a soldier's marching song as we trekked northwards, heading for one of the Seven Bastions of the North, where a warrior was sure to find work.

Owen was in high good humour. Earlier I had remarked that the count had cheated us of our wage, but the Master had laughed gently and tapped the bundle he had given me back in the castle. When I opened it I found it contained cloth-wrapped gold plate stamped with the count's crest, which he had taken in lieu of payment. "He would have cheated me, slain us, but I was too quick for him, and struck first. Remember that, Tien, always strike first."

About mid-afternoon the sky clouded over and we began to think about seeking shelter for the coming night, for a blizzard was brewing and to be caught in the open would almost certainly mean death.

However, the ground on either side of the King Road was flat and unbroken, and we continued on, looking out for a suitable hollow, or windbreak. As we crested a slight rise in the road we spotted a lone figure in the distance, moving northwards. We immediately grew wary, for in these wild lands a single traveller was often used as a decoy, live bait for the marauding outlaws, escaped slaves, prisoners and the like who have made the Wastelands their home. What further increased our suspicions was the fact that the figure didn't seem to be moving at any great speed. No one lingers on the King Road after dark, and though it was but mid-afternoon, night comes early to the Wastelands this far north.

I saw Owen unsheathing his short curved sword, and I carefully unhitched my belt-axe, but kept it concealed beneath my cloak. As far as we could see, the figure was alone, and the ground seemed far too flat and barren to afford shelter to anyone or anything, but...

We hurried on, and soon caught up with the lone traveller and, although dusk had not yet fallen, the figure—a man by his height and build—remained strangely shadowed. I shivered, for who knew what strange creatures roamed abroad in this desolate land? Owen too, was disturbed by this strange apparition which glided silently and seemingly unconcerned before us.

Now, there is no one who can dispute my Master's bravery—no one alive that is—but I thought I heard his voice quaver as he called out to the figure. "Hold! You there, stop!" His voice sounded shockingly loud in the silence, and his sword came up threateningly, the burnished metal glowing wanly in the fast-fading light, and I could see that his thumb rested on the bone relic set into the hilt.

The figure stopped and turned slowly, eyeing us seemingly without surprise. He was tall, very tall, topping even Owen who was accounted a tall man, and he was thin, and his height made him seem skeletal. His face—from what I could see of it—was long and thin, and his eyes large and dominating, but most of his head and the fine details of his features were shadowed by the cowl of a long travelling cloak he wore.

He spoke, his voice soft, controlled and cultured. "Yes, what do you want?" His coolness surprised us, for he had displayed no emotion upon being confronted by us...and I must admit we did not present a comforting spectacle. Owen, tall and well-built, his harsh features scarred and tanned, brandishing a wickedly curved short-sword; myself, short, fur-clad, and—why should I not be truthful?—my features and yellow-tinged skin must surely have seemed sinister and alien to him.

"Tien, a light!" The Master's voice was harsh, a trifle high, as it was when he was unsure of himself. I knelt down and struggled with flint and tinder as the stranger approached Owen.

"You have no need of your sword," he said to the Master, and then he laughed, and it was the most frightening sound I have ever heard, "I will not harm you." And truly, I could not tell whether he jested or not. The flint sparked and the tinder caught; I uncovered the small travel-lantern, lit the oiled wick and slid the polished metal plate behind the flame, bathing the stranger in a ghostly milk-light. In the light he seemed even larger and more disturbing, for night had swiftly fallen, absorbing him into the blackness, and it was as if a disembodied face floated in the night before us.

"Who are you?" Owen snapped, waving his sword past the stranger's face in a move designed to draw his gaze, but the sinister figure never even blinked.

"I am Paedur," he replied, and then a glowing silver hook flashed in the light and a corner of his cloak was pulled back, revealing a sparkling eye and triangle device high on his left shoulder. "I am a bard."

"A bard! I...I beg your forgiveness, bard." The Master had been taken off guard and was disturbed and shaken, for no one accosts or draws a weapon on a bard, for they, like minstrels, priests and pilgrims, are accorded the King's Privilege and it is death to harm or obstruct them in any way. "I did not know, I feared..." he finished lamely.

The bard smiled then, and I have yet to see a smile so change a man. Although he still radiated an air of power and assurance, the aura of menace fell away. "I know and I understand, and you are right to be wary, for this is a wild and dangerous place, inhabited by men who are little better than beasts, and beasts which are in turn imbued with the intelligence of men. Aye, a dangerous land." He turned and stared into the moonless, starless night as if he could penetrate that utter darkness. His unnerving gaze returned to Owen. "But not too dangerous for one such as you..." His voice was gentle and held just a trace of amusement.

The Master swelled with pride. "No, I think not. I am Owen, Weapon Master, and this is Tien tZo, my slave-companion."

The bard bowed slightly to us both. "Your name, Owen Weapon Master, is of course familiar to me; the south is full of your glories and deeds and you are hero and villain both."

The Master laughed, pleased, for though he was a great man, vanity was always one of his failings.

The bard then turned and addressed me directly. "You I have not heard of...but then few remember slaves. What land do you hail from, Tien tZo?"

It is a question I have often been asked, for my yellow skin and jade-green up-tilted eyes attract attention wherever I go. "I am descended from the Shemmatae, who are called the Invaders by your historians," I replied. "My forebears were taken as slaves on the Sand Plain, but I am of pure blood and can trace my lineage back to there and beyond to my homeland, and thus it might be said that I hail from the Land of the Sun, to the east."

The bard nodded. "Strange...strange," he murmured, almost to himself, "I can see the hand of the gods in this." He glanced back to me. "I have but lately recounted the tale of Churon and his vassal Kutor; Churon defeated the Shemmat Invaders on the Sand Plain, and it is curious coincidence to meet one of their descendants."

It was now getting on for the forenight, and a sharp breeze had struck up, whipping across the Wastelands and carrying flurries of snow and ice. Paedur adjusted his cloak about his shoulders. "We must find shelter soon; Faurug, Fiarle and Snaitle are abroad tonight." I didn't understand the references, but I noticed the Master's startled look.

"And where are we going to find shelter around here?" Owen asked.

"This way." The enigmatic figure turned around and headed off the road. We hesitated a few moments before finally following him. We struck off due east from our original path, cutting away from the road and on to a thin, barely visible animal run. The ground was soft at first, for the day had been mild and the earth had thawed somewhat, but it was now beginning to freeze again. Pools of ice cracked and splintered beneath our boots and we found ourselves sinking up to our ankles in freezing mud. We stumbled through patches of irongrass, frozen as solid as its name, and it rattled and clacked horribly together, sounding like the finger-bones that the shamans of the south use for divination.

I had been counting—almost unconsciously—and we had walked perhaps a thousand or more paces when suddenly the path crumbled beneath my feet and I fell and crashed headlong down a slight incline into a copse of withered bushes. They collapsed around me with a noise like that of a score of sap-filled logs burning and sparking. I dropped the lantern as I fell and the light died and the night closed in, swallowing everything in its maw. I thrashed about, scattering branches and twigs in an effort to free myself, but I only succeeded in becoming thoroughly entangled in the claw-like core of the bush. I could not even cry out, for my face was pressed into the chill damp earth.

Suddenly something cold and sharp and metallic touched my cheek. My heart almost stopped. A voice hissed close to my ear. "Don't move; I will free you." It was the bard.

I couldn't move, even if I had wanted to, but with the bard's chill warning ringing in my head even my breathing stilled. Then above the gathering wind, I heard whistling—such as a sword makes upon the downward stroke—followed by a deep crackling report beside me. Again and again the bard chopped into the tough dry wood, cutting me free from the entangling branches. A hand gripped my collar and then I was pulled out and hauled to my feet. Something cold and metallic was pressed back into my hand almost making me scream with fright, but I recognised the shape as the lantern.

And only then did I realise that the bard had cut me free in absolute darkness.

Paedur's hand then sought mine. It felt cool and dry, the skin rough and hard; it felt like the skin of a reptile. "This way," he said, and led me up the incline and back onto the path. He then took my hand and put it on Owen's shoulder and he placed the Master's hand on his own, and thus we marched along behind him, blind-beggar fashion.

We continued on for what seemed like an eternity, when Owen suddenly stopped; I stumbled into him and I heard the bard walk on a few steps before stopping. "Where are you taking us?" Owen demanded. "There doesn't seem to be anything in this direction."

"There is shelter," Paedur replied shortly.

"Where—and when?"

"Nearby—and soon. Come now, we daren't linger; some of the night creatures will soon be abroad."

He must have reached out and taken the Master's arm, because I felt the Master stiffen and then his hand caught mine and placed it on his own shoulder. We trudged on a while longer, heads tucked down into our cloaks, for the wind had quickened and it was snowing heavily now—great soft, silent flakes that touched like chill fingers. A wisp of moon showed through the racing clouds and I could suddenly see Owen in front of me. He was silhouetted against the night as the snowflakes painted his left side white, whilst his right remained in darkness, and I could just make out the ghostly image of the bard ahead of him.

"I think you'd better tell us where this shelter is now, bard," Owen said loudly above the wind, and his voice was harsh with suspicion.

The bard stopped. "There!" He raised his arm and pointed, his hook flashing ice-silver.

I peered into the darkness, but I could see nothing save the dimly phosphorescent flakes whirling and dancing before my eyes. And I wondered then—and not for the first time—how this Paedur could see in the absolute night, how he could move so confidently, how he could point out a direction with such assurance and wield a blade with such certainty. It was unnatural—and terrifying—and if I had not been bonded to Owen, I would have turned and fled and taken my chances that night in the Wastelands.

"Let's go," Paedur said, and then we were moving again, this time slightly north of our previous direction, and we must have topped a rise for we were now descending, slipping and sliding on loose rocks and hard, dry earth. Once we found ourselves below ground level the wind immediately dropped, and the night became still and silent.

"Perhaps you should light your lantern now," the bard said quietly. For a moment I didn't understand what he was talking about, and then I realised I was still clutching the travel-lantern in my frozen hand. I knelt on the ground and fumbled with my flint box, but my fingers were numb and it took several attempts to even open the box. I stooped low over the lantern, covering the wick with my cloak, striking the flint, blinking as the sparks flashed and exploded in the darkness. The oiled wick caught and the dim half-light soaked into the air.

We were standing in a deep round hollow, one of many hundreds which pock part of the northlands. Above us the snow-laden wind whipped along in a white sheet, but very little actually drifted into the hollow and we were almost totally protected from the wind, and even the ground underfoot was dry.

The bard walked forward a few steps and we hurried after him, more fearful now, I think, of becoming lost than of him. Again the silver hook flashed and pointed and I lifted the lantern in that direction. Owen grunted in surprise and the light shook in my hand: there was a building in front of us. And in the north—and especially in the Wastelands—every building was inhabited, and not always by men.

But the bard moved forward without hesitation, and there was little we could do but follow him. As we drew near to the building, I could see that it was a Way Station, one of the countless that litter the countryside along the length of the King Road...except that this station was nowhere near the road and had obviously not been used for many seasons. The moon slipped free from the racing clouds and briefly washed the building in stark bone-white light. It was long and low, seeming smaller than usual, little more than a squat rectangle built into the ground in a style long out of fashion.

And with the shadows edging in around it, it resembled nothing so much as a great beast about to spring.

The closer we came to the station, the more conscious I became of an air of great age that hung about the place. I have stayed in Way Stations in many lands, and whilst they have always been spartan, comfortless places, none of them seemed as old and as forbidding as this. I remembered stories I had heard about the creatures that inhabited the more isolated stations, that preyed on unwary travellers, feeding on their blood.

"I can't say I've ever seen a Way Station like this one," Owen said loudly, and I could tell that he too was disturbed.

"It was one of the original Way Stations, said to have been built by the Culai themselves," Paedur said quietly. "Most of the stations you would be familiar with are usually modern copies."

"How modern?" the Master wondered.

"A thousand years old, perhaps younger."

We stopped and I held the lantern high, looking cautiously at the building. The stones were smooth and rounded, polished and shaped by countless seasons of wind and rain, ice and heat. The door leaned drunkenly to one side, held to the rotted frame by encrusted hinges; the shutter on the window nearest me was cracked and blackened where it had once been set afire; and a large rounded hole gaped under the window, with the bricks and stones pressing outwards as if they had been struck from within by some great force or power. I wondered what had happened here—and then I decided I didn't want to know.

I looked from the station to the Master; surely he, with all his superstitions, would see that this deserted and ruined Way Station, so far from any track or road, was a place of ill omen.

The bard descended the few steps that led down to the shattered door, and then he stopped and listened. He then silently retraced his steps and whispered softly to Owen, "I do not think anyone or anything is within, but…" he paused, his lips pulled back from his teeth in a smile that I found disturbing, almost mocking.

The Master nodded. He pulled off his heavy cloak and tossed it to the bard and then slipped both sword and dagger from their scabbards. I passed the lantern to the bard and unhitched both belt-axes, and then I took up my position behind and to the left of the Master.

The bard lifted the lantern, and the pale oval of light threw the doorway into sharp relief. Owen raised the tip of his sword slightly, the signal to prepare, and then he dipped it…

We leaped into the darkness, Owen moving to the right, I to the left. We stood poised, ready to move in any direction, but all was quiet, save for the drip-drip-drip of water somewhere to my left. We stood in silence, holding our breaths, almost half expecting to hear the scuffle of feet or the click of claws on the hard-packed earth. But nothing moved. Finally, when it became clear that the Way Station was indeed empty, Owen's sword clicked into its scabbard and then a softer metallic whisper told me that his knife had followed. Slowly, I relaxed.

I heard Owen move across the littered floor towards the doorway. "Bard, you may enter."

There was no reply.

The Master waited and then he tried again, now sliding his sword free. I pressed back against the chill stone wall, staring towards the paler rectangle of the doorway against the utter blackness of the interior of the station.

And then something sparked behind me!

I whirled about, one axe snapping out on its leather thong towards the sound. There was a sparking flash of metal on metal, a sharp high-pitched ringing and my arm went numb as the axe was

deflected to one side. I swung around my other axe, and then I was
suddenly blinded by a light that ripped through the station. I dropped
to the floor and rolled away to one side, eyes streaming, allowing the
Master a clear field of vision.

But there was no flurry of combat, no shouts or screams, and
only Owen's voice asking a question. "How?"

For a moment I thought he was questioning me, but when I had
brushed away the streaming tears and was able to see again, I found
the bard standing before me!

"How did you get in? No one entered through that door."
Owen's voice was tight and controlled, and I could see that he was
angry and confused. "You couldn't have got past me."

Paedur just smiled and shook his head. "But there is only one
way in."

The light that had blinded me turned out to come from two
small battered light-bowls that still hung from the ceiling, which the
bard had lit, thus throwing the room—and everyone in it—into
sharp relief. Even in the harsh light the bard lost none of his mystery. Indeed, his dark fine-haired travelling cloak seemed to absorb
the light and, save for his face and silver hook, he resembled nothing
so much as a shadow, animated by some foul sorcery.

Owen turned from the bard, and I thought I saw him shudder
slightly. He reached out and pulled me to my feet. "You had better
bring our things in."

I nodded and slipped outside to where our cloaks and few
belongings lay piled beside the door. It was snowing again, more
heavily this time, and the world was gradually losing all shape and
definition. With one last glance into the night, I re-entered the ruined
Way Station.

Later that night—or it might have been early the following morning—after a tasteless meal of hard bread and dried meat, washed
down with sour wine, we sat around the fire I had built in the shattered grate, staring into the glowing embers, listening to the wind
howl around the building.

For all its great age, the station was in surprisingly good repair,
except for the damage to the upper end of the building. The single
room was on two levels, with the lower end cut deep into the ground,
windowless and with but a single door. In the past travellers used

the lower section, while their mounts were stabled above them, both for protection and for the heat they provided. The room was bare, except for a single stout wooden chest set into a niche close by the fire. In the past it would have held dried food and blankets, but the box was empty now, except for twigs and a score of tiny feathers, the remains of a bird's nest.

Thinking of the Way Station brought me back to the bard, this Paedur.

He exerted a curious fascination for me, his mystery, aloofness, detachment and...power. He radiated an aura of almost tangible force, of power, although I doubted that he actually was a sorcerer or magician. I was inclined to believe that he was in truth, a bard, and I had little doubt that he would prove to be a terrifying storyteller.

Owen once said my curiosity would prove my undoing. But I wanted to know about this man, this creature, who professed to be a bard. Did bards usually wander the lonely and dangerous wild northern roads? Where were his students, his servants, his possessions? Where did he come from, and more important, where was he going? There was little to attract a storyteller in the Wastelands.

His hook also intrigued me. It was of exquisite workmanship; I wondered who had crafted it—no ordinary silversmith, I'd wager. It seemed to be of solid silver, inlaid with a delicate filigree of angular etchings that resembled nothing so much as some of the barbarous scripts I have seen in the Seven Nations. I don't know how it was joined to his wrist, but I got the impression that it was set directly into the bone. Along the edge of the hook, a thin band of darker metal ran from point to wrist. It would make a fearsome weapon—and then I realised just how the bard had cut me free from the bush earlier on.

I glanced across at the Master, and found that he too was watching the bard while trying not to appear to. Unconsciously, his left hand fingered the hilt of his dagger.

A burning log fell out of the grate and rolled on to the flagstones, scattering sparks and blackened chips across the earthen floor. Owen reached out and grabbed it at one end and flipped it back into the fire. As he did so, the sleeve of his jerkin slipped back, revealing the Iron Band of Kloor which covered his forearm.

Suddenly the bard's hook flashed in the firelight and encircled the thick iron bracelet in its silver grip. "Kloor?" he whispered, his eyebrows raised in question.

Owen angrily pulled his arm free.

"Kloor," repeated the bard, "I didn't think a Weapon Master would honour such."

Owen tensed. "Surely it is of little interest to you whom I worship? But yes, I worship Kloor, the Warrior's God. I am a warrior, he suffices."

Paedur was silent for a moment, and when he spoke again his voice held a trace of puzzlement. "You are a Weapon Master, therefore your father must have been a Weapon Master..." It was a statement rather than a question, but Owen nodded. "But surely your father would have honoured Buiva, the Old God of War and Warriors and not..."

"What are you getting at, bard?" Owen snapped.

"I am merely wondering why one who once worshipped Buiva now wears the Band of Kloor," Paedur said softly, curiously.

Anger flared in the Master's eyes, and I saw his face tighten. A muscle began to twitch in his clenched jaw. But when he spoke, his voice was soft and controlled. "I drew a weapon on you earlier, but that was in ignorance for I did not know your status. But unless you want to find my knife in your belly you will leave off this questioning. Here, bard, no one will find your corpse, and when they do it will be assumed that you were slain by bandits. My religion, aye, and my father's also, are none of your concern."

The bard laughed gently, almost mockingly. "You would not kill me, Weapon Master; you could not, you are too honourable for cold-blooded murder." He paused, and then added in a different tone, "and I think you would fear the retribution that would follow it if you did, eh? Consider what would happen when Mannam brought me before Alile the Judge Impartial to plead my case; surely he would send Coulide Dream-Maker to haunt you. Consider, Weapon Master, never to know a night's sleep again... to have the Nameless God hovering by your bedside..."

"STOP!" the Master shouted pressing both hands to his ears and beginning to rock to and fro like a child. "Stop—no more. Stop!"

It had happened so suddenly; I wasn't sure how this Duaiteoiri had reduced my Master to this state with just a few words, but it could only be one thing—sorcery.

The Master had been ensorcelled. But how? Those who think a mage can weave a spell without the usual trappings of the craft know little of how such things work. No, the bard had said something to frighten—no, to terrify the Master. I would stop it—even if I had to kill the bard. Unhooking an axe, I rose to my feet.

I allowed the heavy war axe to slip down low into my hand, until I was holding it by the thong. I spun it around once, twice, preparing to throw it at the creature—and at this range I could not miss. But then he looked up and his eyes caught mine—and held them. They took the light from the fire and began to burn with something like an inner fire of their own; it was as if something behind them now gazed out at me. They looked at me, through me, beyond me. I was caught in a whirling pool of exploding dust motes, of blackened stars in lighted darkness…falling, falling, revolving, spinning faster and faster.

"S-S-S-i-i-i-T-T-T." The shout—or was it a whisper?—blossomed and exploded within my skull and I lost all control of my body. My legs jerked and twitched of their own accord, my axe fell ringingly to the floor from nerveless fingers…and I was sitting frozen and paralysed—useless, although aware.

"You would kill me," the bard repeated, turning back to the Master as if nothing had happened. Owen still rocked to and fro, now crooning softly to himself, lost within some inner recesses of his mind. It was as if something had snapped, or a gate had suddenly opened and released…released what?

But whatever it was, whatever had happened—the bard was to blame, and I swore I would be revenged on him for it.

He spoke again, his voice rising and falling as if he spoke to a child. "Peace, peace. Do not upset yourself. No, you need not tell me of your faith, nor of your father's either. I know. I know." He paused and said, very gently, "He worshipped the Old Gods, did he not?"

The Master nodded silently.

"And you follow the New?"

Again that silent nod.

"You must have disappointed him greatly when you converted."

Owen stopped his rocking and raised his head; and his eyes were sparkling with moisture. "He never forgave me," he whispered.

"Tell me," Paedur continued, "when were you converted? You must have been very young, impressionable...?

"In my seventeenth year, in the last month of my training," the Master said, and then he suddenly sobbed, and there was nothing but pure anguish in his eyes. "But they tricked me," he suddenly shouted. "Tricked me. They entangled me in webs of words, confused and confounded me until I did not know what to believe; and then they pushed and pushed...and lied...but I believed them. They extracted an oath from me, thrice-sworn and *geasa*-bound, and then what could I do? I had sworn, I was trapped," he added bitterly.

The bard leaned forward, and the firelight took his face, deepening the shadows, aging it. "Aaah, gently, gently, Owen. You are greatly troubled, and you have been deeply hurt. But now let us see what can be done to salve that pain."

"I am not in pain," Owen muttered.

"There are wounds that are not of the body," Paedur said.

"There is nothing you can do. There is nothing anyone can do," the Master said fiercely, his eyes beginning to sparkle with tears again.

It shamed me to see Owen reduced to this, and I wondered just how this bard had frightened him. And yet I could also see that it was not the bard who had frightened the Master, but in some strange way, himself. There was something buried deep within him, something which the bard had consciously or unconsciously—I wasn't sure—triggered off. And then, dimly, I felt that here might be the answer to something which had troubled me for many years: the Master's belief in the supernatural.

Owen was a brave warrior, fearless and cunning in battle, usually victorious and always generous in defeat, and there was neither man nor beast that troubled him in the least. In many respects he was the perfect warrior. But if there were omens on the morning of the battle, or signs in the night sky, or if there had been foretellings and forecastings that had proved inauspicious, or if his dreams had been troubled—then he would not fight, and no amount of threats or bribes could force him against his will. He shunned the ruins that men said had been Culai-built, and wherein the gods of his people once lived.

He detoured around bridges blessed in the name of Cam, and often cut across fields to avoid an unlucky gallows-road. He fought with his sword in his right hand and his knife in his left, for he held to the belief that a knife was an assassin's tool and thus not worthy of the right hand. He favoured amulets and talismans, and he even had a relic, the finger-bone of some ancient seer, set into the hilt of his sword.

There were times when I even believed that he kept me because he thought I was lucky.

I have never made the Weapon Master out to be perfect, and he had many failings, and of those failings superstition was his worst, and now it seemed the bard had—accidentally, deliberately?—invoked the core of that fault, bringing it to the surface, terrifying the man.

Paedur reached out and touched Owen on the shoulder; then I suddenly felt the almost palpable aura of peace and tranquillity that emanated from him and enfolded the Master, soothing him, calming his fears.

"Come now, you are a Weapon Master, a warrior. It is not fitting that you should fear this. If you would exorcise this demon, then face it. Now begin your tale, and who knows, perhaps I can help...?"

"I don't know..." the Master said uncertainly. The lines on his broad, rather ugly face had softened, the muscles relaxed, so that he looked like a young man once more. Even when he spoke, his voice lacked the harshness, the authority, it usually carried.

Paedur leaned back, moving away from the firelight. "Start thus," he said. "You worshipped the Old Gods, you and your family. You had brothers...sisters?"

The Master ran his fingers through his hair and then sat back against the wall, his head tilted forward and almost resting on his knees, which he had drawn up to his chest. "Yes, yes, my family worshipped the Old Gods. My father was an Elder of the Faith, and my mother had served in the Temple in her youth. Thus ever since we—my brother and sister—could talk and understand, we were so deeply infused with the Faith and it was such a part of our lives, that we knew nothing else.

"We could recite the entire Pantheon before we could walk; we could list the Roll of Minor Spirits before we had learned our letters and could enumerate the Virtues of the Gods before we could count." He grinned mirthlessly. "We never missed a Sabbath, and always kept the Purification prior to the Holy Days or Hallowed Nights. The Four Great Eves were always days and nights of feasting and merrymaking in our home. The fattest bothe was always slaughtered, the tenderest *cuine* sacrificed, and the purest wool, the strongest crops, and the clearest water were always dedicated to the gods.

"We couldn't be stronger in our faith.

"As we grew older, my father decided our futures. I, as the eldest son would, like himself, become a Weapon Master; my brother would be trained for the religious life, and my sister would be dedicated to the Order of the Lady Lussa, where she would become a priestess of the Moon and versed in the magic of the tides of life and growth, birth and motherhood.

"And we were all satisfied. Including me.

"However, as I approached manhood, I began to question my faith." He shook his head, his eyes dim and distant as he looked into the past. "My father spoke of the gods as if they existed in a corporeal body; and while they might have been real to him, to me they became little more than abstractions. All the pomp and ceremony of the Faith's festivals suddenly seemed shallow and worthless.

"Like a fool, I kept my doubts to myself, and they, like a hideous disease, grew dark and monstrous. Should I have discussed them with my father? Should I?" He looked across at the bard like a lost child, but Paedur gave him no answer.

"In the last year of my training these fears and doubts came to a head, and in the last month of my training in weapon-craft, a priest of Trialos came to our town. He was not unlike you, bard; he was tall and thin and his very dedication to his beliefs was almost frightening. He spoke of the New Religion in a field outside the town, for the town fathers would not allow him to preach within the walls. We were, of course, forbidden to attend.

"But I attended. And as I listened to the preacher, I found that he made sense and his words had meaning. Perhaps I wanted to find a meaning in his words—I don't know; I was searching for something, and the Religion seemed to give me what I was looking for. When he was finished speaking, he walked through the small crowd that had gathered to listen, stopping now and again, speaking quietly with a man here, a woman there…and then he came to me. He stood before me and said nothing, and then he took my arm and led me to one side. Perhaps he sensed my uncertainty and doubts, I don't know. He talked long and cleverly, oh, so cleverly; I know that now. He told me how his belief was the One True Religion; of how the Old Gods had been defeated by the New, and how the Old Faith was dying. Most of the Old Gods were dead, he said, and this was why they no longer appeared to man as they had in times past. But the New Gods came and inhabited the bodies of their priests and thus were ever with us.

"And then the preacher told me of Kloor, the Warrior's God, and how he had defeated Buiva, the Old God of War and Warriors, in single combat, thus symbolising the defeat of the entire Pantheon of the Old Faith…

"And I believed him. I believed him, and then and there I foreswore the Old Faith and embraced the New. My word, my bond, was given and the bargain—for my soul—was sealed with a thrice-sworn oath, and thus unbreakable.

"That same day I was initiated into the band of Kloor, a select group of warriors dedicated to the War God and whose function was to fight and die in defence of the New Religion. And this," — he touched the iron band on his forearm— "was locked onto my wrist, sealed there by a light which burned without heat and which the priests said was a sign of my acceptance by Kloor…and of course, Trialos, Lord of the New Religion." He looked at the iron wristlet with dead eyes. "It is a band proclaiming my allegiance to the New Religion." The Master sighed and remained silent for a long time then.

"Your father," prompted the bard, "what did he say?"

"He was angry, terribly angry." Owen continued, his voice wooden. "I thought he would kill me—and he would have too, had not my mother intervened, crying and begging him to spare me, her first son. And then my brother and sister entered, he in his robes of a Guardian of the Faith, and she in the gown of the priestess. They were shocked and sickened by what my brother called my foul desertion. And then there were words spoken—angry words, violent words, words I regretted even as I spoke them; words I regret now.

"But now it is too late."

"What happened?" Paedur asked.

"They challenged me to prove that my new-found gods even existed; they mocked them, but I said my gods would be revenged for their blasphemies." His face tightened and his voice dropped to a dull whisper. "And they laughed. They laughed.

"Two days later, a strange fever raged through the town. My brother and sister died, and it crippled my father.

"I fled then; I have never returned." Owen buried his head in his hands, and his shoulders shook. He raised a frightened face and gazed imploringly at the bard. "I wasn't responsible for their deaths—was I?"

Paedur smiled gently, and placed his hand on Owen's shoulder, his long fingers biting into the flesh. "No, no, of course not. Their time—foredained beyond the reckoning of man—had come. Mannam, the Dark Lord, had taken them to himself. But you must not believe that they were taken through any intercession of the New Religion and its feeble deities." The bard's voice fell and he stared into Owen's eyes and began to whisper urgently to him. "You were tricked, you know that; tricked by those more versed in oratory than in religion."

The Master shook his head and squeezed his eyes shut, but Paedur gripped his chin, and forced him to look into his terrifying eyes. "You were tricked by clever, merciless men. Merciless, yes, merciless. Consider: they took a boy who, though strong in his faith, nevertheless wavered and questioned as the young are wont to do. They tricked and trapped him with webs of words, and bound him in threads of invisible honour, and turned him into a guilt-haunted man, doomed to search for the truth, and forced to regret his decision."

Owen pulled himself free from the bard's grip. He sat back against the chill wall and stared deep into the fire. "They said Kloor was the stronger god, and that he had defeated Buiva," he said, his voice almost defiant, "I didn't know...I still don't know." He looked over at the bard, "What is the truth?" he cried.

"Truth. Truth," the bard's voice rose on a commanding note. "Let me tell you the truth; let me tell you of the battle between Buiva and Kloor, the Old and the New, the Faith and the Religion. Let me tell you that part of the Battles of the Gods..."

The bard sat back into the shadows and folded his arms into his long sleeves and then, bowing his head, he began...

In the third hour of battle—though it was no common time-piece that measured the aeon-long hours—Buiva, the aged God of War and Warriors, blood-stained and weary, for he had fought long and hard, came upon Kloor the Usurper and self-styled god as he skulked behind the battle-lines directing his minions.

And when Kloor saw Buiva he felt the wind of fear blow across him and called forth his legion of *quai*—which are those souls claimed neither by C'lte nor Mannam and thus are neither of Life nor Death. The legion of *quai* positioned themselves before their lord, protecting him from the single ancient warrior.

But Buiva remained dauntless, and called out for Kloor to attend him in single combat to decide the day. And Kloor heeded him not and directed his *quai* to attack the lone god, and his laughter was terrible, for he felt assured of victory.

Now as the *quai* legion advanced upon Buiva, their lacquered armour rasping, swords gleaming in the light of no known star, the tramp of their booted feet heavy upon the chequered plain, the War God raised his nocked and blood-stained broadsword and cried aloud in the language of the gods, *"A w'Mhannaimm 'a w'bainte."* Immediately the air about him darkened and there was a sound like that of a thousand leafless trees rustling and clattering together, and suddenly the air was filled with a myriad of furred, winged, and taloned creatures.

And these were the *bainte,* the messengers of Mannam, the Dark Lord.

They circled above the chequered plain in heedless confusion, and then as one they wheeled and settled in a vast ebon blanket about the feet of the Warrior God. Now each *bainte* clutched within its razor talons a tiny spark of indeterminate hue, and each spark throbbed and pulsed with an independent life, now flaring into an eye-searing brilliance, now dying into slumbering quiescence.

And Buiva pointed with his sword and wordlessly commanded—and the *bainte* rose over the advancing *quai* and, hovering there, released their miniature cinders. The sparks floated downward in an intricate spiralling dance, and Kloor cried out a warning and tried to recall his undead legion—but it was too late. Each spark dropped atop a legionnaire, and instantly disappeared.

The legion of *quai* stopped.

Kloor, suddenly realising what was about to happen, retreated
and called forth his six great sheol, which are kin to those ice-en-
tombed feline remains which oft come to light in the frozen north.
And he ordered these cat-like monsters to guard him—from his
own *quai!*

And even Buiva, who feared neither God nor Duaite, man nor
beast, moved back, away from the *quai* and the sheol.

The vacant stare of the *quai* had now been replaced by the first
glimmerings of dawning intelligence; their mouths no longer hung
slack and open, and their gait—which had been shambling and beast-
like—was now erect in the manner of men. They looked around in
confusion, like dreamers awakening from a vivid nightmare.

And then realisation dawned, and the eyes of the former *quai*
glazed with sudden insanity—for this, all of this, was beyond their
comprehension. Had they not died? Were not their last memories
of death, some of violent deaths, in drunken brawls or
dishonourable battle, and some by their own hands? Had not their
souls been taken to the Silent Wood, and there been judged by Alile,
the Judge Impartial?

Did they not remember a time then, a time of terror and confusion, when they seemed to wander through an interminable gorge
or a crevasse with towering walls of slimed rock on either side? And
then...? And then...? And then what?

How came they here?

And what was this before them, spattered with gore and reeking blood, like the very personification of War? And behind them,
in armour of gleaming iridescent scales, armed with weapons of
gleaming light and surrounded by creatures out of their nightmare?
Where were they?

Was this the Afterlife?

And then their souls rebelled in shrieking terror—for that was
what the *bainte* had returned to the *quai*—their living souls. They
had been men before they had become *quai,* and they knew now that
this was *WRONG*—and who knows, perhaps the Nameless God
of Madness and Delusion had breathed upon the living sparks
before the *bainte* had returned them, and thus each man—for they
were men again—went totally insane.

They turned upon their companions, seeing in each one an
enemy, cutting and slashing, chopping through fine lacquered armour,

tearing chain-mail with sword and axe, mace and spear. Bloodless they fell, dismembered limbs twitching in a hideous semblance of life, bone glinting through ragged wounds, gaping mouths crying silently, wordlessly, and their eyes glazed in a second death with a terrible truth frozen therein.

Through the brief and bloody struggle Kloor raged and screamed, threatened and mouthed behind the six huge sheol. And the God of Warriors of the New Religion felt fear then, for he had seen his personal guard, his indestructible legion, destroyed by their own hand.

Once again he faced Buiva.

And once again the War God of the Old Faith called forth his challenge, but Kloor disdained to reply and released a sheol—a giant ebon cat-like creature.

Taller than the god it stood, thighs as thick as his waist and tipped with claws as long as his hand. Its eyes burned with a crimson fire, radiating pure hate, its one instinct to kill, to destroy. It opened its maw, revealing a double row of needle-pointed teeth, and it roared. Low that terrible cry began, almost inaudible, but it quickly rose to a skull-shattering scream that threatened to freeze Buiva where he stood.

The old man shook his head, angrily shrugging off the creeping numbness and gripped his great broadsword—the *Clef Fuin* of legend—and prepared to meet the sheol's charge. Carefully, he studied the play of muscles along the creature's haunches, watched them ripple and flow with every movement. Then the muscles bunched and the sheol was flying through the air, bristling claws and fur, its mouth agape in anticipation, dripping scalding saliva.

The warrior dived forward under the creature, slashing upwards with his sword, disembowelling the sheol in one swift movement. But still it lived. As it fell, Buiva came to his feet and chopped down onto its massive corded neck and almost severed the head. Again and again *Clef Fuin* bit into the still-living feline until it finally quivered and stiffened.

And now Kloor in a paroxysm of fury released the five remaining sheol, and Buiva despaired when he saw them, for he could not hope to defeat them all. So, in desperation he called upon the Lady Adur, the Goddess of Nature, sister to Quilida, the Goddess of Growth and cousin to the Triad of Life.

"A nAdur ea pl'ea," he cried forth in a strong voice that echoed across the battlefield. And the huge sheol slackened in their headlong run, for though their inner natures had been warped by Kloor, a part of them—a tiny part which all creatures of Life possess—recognised the name of Adur, their mistress.

But Kloor urged them on.

Suddenly a tiny insect fluttered before the Warrior God, spinning in the complicated rhythm of a dance, and as it weaved its pattern about the god, it grew, and then flickered in a startling metamorphosis, from an insect, black on gold, to a delicate patterned butterfly...a fragile rainbow-coloured hummingbird...a shining evil-eyed raven...a sharp-featured hawk...a golden-winged eagle... a monstrous harpy—and finally, a woman.

She was tall, taller even than Buiva, who looked down on most of the Gods of the Pantheon, and very beautiful in a strange haunting way that is almost beyond description. Her beauty was akin to that which is sometimes glimpsed in nature on a summer's eve across a mirrored lake.

And about her—as there is in nature—there was constant change; her hair and eyes flickering with multitudinous colours and varied hues and her skin rippling in ever-differing tints.

Now she was cold, hair white and snow soft, her eyes like blue chipped ice and her skin a translucent alabaster; and now her skin was a delicate russet with eyes of startling green; and then her skin became a darker hue, and her figure fuller. And now she smiled and there was the touch of summer in her smile, her eyes—sparkling brown—danced with merriment, her hair of rich ochre and skin deeply tanned.

And she was all shades, colours, moods, and seasons in between. She was Adur, the Goddess of Nature.

The sheol froze when she appeared, and their roars and savage cries turned to whimpers as they lay belly down on the chequered battlefield.

Buiva bowed to the Lady Adur, for he had a soldier's appreciation of nature, and then he pointed to the cowering creatures. The goddess turned, and anger flashed in her blue-green eyes, for were these felines not a travesty of nature? An abomination. They should not exist, they had no right to existence, and so...

Adur raised one pale white hand and pointed, her long ver-milion-tipped nails splayed. Her steel-grey eyes hardened as she began to close her hand.

The sheol began to turn and twist upon themselves; they ran in tight circles, snapping, clawing and tearing at each other in anger, confusion, and pain. And then they began to dwindle, to shrink in upon themselves…smaller…smaller and then…gone!

Adur closed her hand. In her domain there was no room, no place for the unnatural. She turned and bowed to the bloodied warrior, and then closed her eyes—and disappeared.

Buiva rested on his sword. "Face me now, Kloor, in single combat and let there be an end to this foolishness."

But Kloor was still afraid, for Buiva was the most powerful of the gods; had he not fought against many gods and godlets and the worship of many sects to reach his present position as the accepted God of War and Warriors?

But as Kloor looked at the Old God, something began to change his mind. "The Old God is tired," he murmured to himself, "he has fought long and hard and has put many to the sword this day. I am fresh, my weapons are sharp and well honed; he is set in his ways and is bound to fight with honour and courtesy, whilst I have many tricks and am not hidebound by such morals."

"I will fight you, Buiva," he called. "Soon, Old God, you will be a dead god."

But Buiva the Warrior laughed, and such is the mirth of the gods that, far beyond the Void in that place between the worlds, out where none will ever venture, elsewhere and otherwhen, a small planet winked fiery red in the heavens, and those who saw it, won-dered and accounted it a portent.

Then Kloor took the living sword *Sant,* and ran at Buiva, for he had a mind to take the Old God by surprise, and *Sant* keened and moaned with pleasure at the prospect of drinking blood.

And elsewhen and otherwhere, a tiny incandescent comet streaked its fiery trail across the night sky…and directly in its path lay the Red Planet; and astrologers nodded sagely and withdrew to consult their charts and make their calculations.

The *Clef Fuin* met the *Sant's* wild swing with a clangour that rippled through the Void, and the swords burned with a blinding light so that it was as if the two gods fought with staves of light. Back and forth across the chequered plain they fought, their weapons hissing and sparking with the violence of their battle.

And as the sparks from their weapons fell into the Void, they supplemented those numerous shapeless asteroids that were created by the One and which litter the heavens. And the blood of the gods—and it was spilt on both sides—became those crimson suns which glow on dead worlds.

Now, although Buiva was tired and weakened, he fought hard against the Usurper. And Kloor, young, untried and inexperienced, retreated before the Old God's onslaught. Buiva laughed aloud, for he could see that this would-be war-god was no warrior. And this was true, for Kloor had gained his position as the War God of the New Religion through cunning and the skilful manipulation of a weak and frightened priesthood, and he had once been but a minor spirit babbling beyond the Gorge until he had broken through the barriers of the mind of a heretic. The spirit that was Kloor had then used this heretic to spread his gospel of hate and violence, and then exhorted the people to pray for succour to the god Kloor, for even then, he had been styling himself a god.

Some folk prayed. And Faith lends Substance.

Soon the Cult of Kloor had taken hold, and the priests of Trialos had accepted the new god into their Pantheon of New Gods— a Usurper amongst Usurpers. They created the Band of Kloor, a group of warriors, all believers in the New Religion, and used them as the Guardians of their Religion. Then the priests of Kloor set forth on their mission: to entice more and more young warriors into the Band, and they chained these youths with an Iron Band, a physical reminder of their chains to the New God.

And this New God was now terrified, for should he be defeated, then that spark of soul which animates both Gods and men would be consigned back to the absolute depths of the Gorge for all eternity, never to rise again. So he fell back, further and yet further still, defenceless against Buiva's great sweeping blows. At last the Usurper reached the mound on which he had stood in the early stages of the Battle of the Gods, and then his questing hand gripped the haft of his great war spear—the *cle bor*—which stood there. It was a fearsome weapon, a relic even amongst the gods, which Kloor had stolen from the Tomb of Bor, the Man God. It was fashioned from the wood of the Sidhe Forest of the Far Isles by Hanor, the first of the Gods. Twice the height of Kloor it stood, its length engraved with glyphs of power, unutterable in any human tongue. Its massive head—as long as the god's arm— was of the purest diamond, and it had been honed and pointed in some unknown manner.

Kloor grasped the weapon desperately, and, leaping back, swung it around to face Buiva. To do this he had to turn to one side and drop *Sant* to grip the *cle bor,* and here the Old God's honour was almost to prove his undoing, for he did not strike the Usurper while he was momentarily defenceless.

But there is little doubt that the New God would not have acted in a like manner had the positions been reversed.

Kloor held the spear tightly in both hands and jabbed at Buiva. He was safe behind its prodigious length; and now strength poured into him—for such was the nature of the weapon—and he felt for the first time that he could even defeat Buiva.

He struck out with his new-found strength again and again, jabbing with the spear. But each time Buiva managed to turn the point with his sword, though each time by a narrower margin. Now it skimmed within a hair's breadth of his face, now actually brushing his throat, pricking his arm, nicking his side. His sword leapt and darted, turning the point here, deflecting it, now stopping it—but all at a price.

For each time the *cle bor* struck the *Clef Fuin* the sword became chipped and dented, even though it had been forged by Shoan the Smith using only the purest materials in his forge in the Woodsheart.

Suddenly the sword snapped; the battered blade shattering under the impact of the spear's diamond head, leaving Buiva defenceless against Kloor's attack. The New God immediately plunged the spear into the god's chest, driving him back and pinning him to the ground, the terrible wound spurting blood and ichor.

This ichor scattered into the Void and became that which men call the Core of the Universe, wherein there is but one light, and that is the light of a million million suns—drops of blood from the veins of the War God. And there are some that think that these suns are living, growing, expanding in an ever-increasing torrent— like blood seeping from some cut.

Kloor moved in to kill the stricken god, for though gravely wounded Buiva still lived. But he grasped the hilt of his shattered sword and flung it full in the face of the advancing, gloating usurper. The broken edge struck him across the bridge of his nose, and flakes of the enchanted metal entered his eyes, blinding him. Kloor screamed and screamed again, and great pools of empty dissolution opened in the Void as the very fabric of space was torn by his cries.

Then Kloor the Usurper turned and fled, and in the distant reaches of timelessness his cries are still heard, for there is none to succour him.

But in the temples and churches of the Old Faith there was a terrible emptiness and the priests felt as if their altars had been forsaken, as if all the Gods of the Pantheon had left this world. The sun disappeared below the horizon and didn't reappear, and even the Lady Lussa failed to ride across the night skies.

Thus it was for seven days. Then on the morning of the eighth day, Nusas shone forth with all his accustomed brilliance, and by this sign men knew that the gods had returned; and many wondered at their absence.

Now when Buiva had fallen, the shock of his wounding had torn through all creation and thus the entire Pantheon knew that their brother was sorely wounded. They quit their temples and palaces, gardens, dales and glades to come to render aid to the stricken god, and soon the chequered battlefield was dark with their glittering shadowless forms. Then from that gathering came forth an aged man, thin and stooped and with hair of purest silver, and he knelt by Buiva and ministered to him, for he was Ochrann, God of Medicine and Healing.

And for six days Buiva lay thus, and the assembled gods feared for their brother. Even Ochrann finally admitted that he could do nothing further, and so the gods—the great and little, the minor and major deities—took council together, but they could reach no decision and Buiva weakened further.

At last Huide—who is the Little God of Summer Rain—spoke. "My lords, it is my thought that there had been laid a Darkness upon us, for is not the solution to our problem plain for all to see? Let us send for the Triad of Life; for surely it is within their power to save the Warrior."

Thus the three Gods of Life were sent for, and Sa'lte, Qua'lte and C'lte came, riding on clouds of purest ebon, cobalt, and saffron, and they laid their hands upon the dying god and poured Life into him.

And he lived.

And when the gods would have rewarded Huide—for it had been his idea—he would have nothing. But thereafter, whenever Huide scattered his fine mist-like droplets upon the parched summer earth, there was seen emblazoned across the skies an arch of seven hues, in tribute and recognition to that tiny god's intelligence.

But the tale does not end here.

It was put about by the priests of Kloor and Trialos that the Usurper had defeated Buiva, and, to those who have the Hearing, they described the screams of the blind god as his cries of victory. Enough people still pray to Kloor to keep him in existence—but that existence is one of eternal torment.

But know this, Owen, Weapon Master—Buiva, God of War and Warriors, lives!"

The bard ended on a triumphant note. The Master's eyes were shining, but with what emotion I could not tell. What I do know is that, although it was a fanciful tale, it both moved and impressed me deeply, and to such an extent that although many events and happenings in my long life now fade and grow dim, the tale of the bard Paedur still burns bright in my memory.

"Then Buiva lives; he defeated Kloor, snatching his victory from defeat?" the Master asked quickly, stumbling over his words in excitement.

"Yes, he lives. You were tricked, lied to. And not only you, but others like you: all young, impressionable men. And the Religion is continuing to do the same today, continuing to corrupt your people." He paused and added softly, "And that is why it has to be stopped."

The Master nodded. "Aye, it has to be stopped," he agreed. "But how?"

Paedur leaned forward, the dying firelight washing his face in red. "The present order must be overthrown. There is a movement abroad to do just that."

"Revolution?"

The bard smiled thinly. "Call it a Holy War, if you will. South and west of here, Prince Kutor has just set off on a journey into the west, to one of the ancient Culai forts which he intends to use as a base to wage war on the Emperor's forces."

"Kutor—Geillard's bastard brother—but his last attempt on the throne ended in a bloody massacre."

Paedur smiled. "He hadn't a cause then, even he didn't really believe that he could win. He was defeated before he had even begun. Now, he has that cause; and he is putting together an army—a proper army—but they will need training and equipping, and for that he needs a man of experience." He paused and added, "I am advising those interested in fighting for the Faith to go to him…"

Owen smiled grimly. "Yes, it might be good to fight for a cause again."

"I don't think there'll be much coin in it—not unless it's successful," the bard warned.

"Oh, Tien and I have often worked for meagre wages," Owen nodded again, and then the smile faded and he held up his arm, looking at the ugly metal band.

"It will be a good cause," Paedur said, "you will be fighting for the Old Faith."

"An atonement," Owen said softly, fingering the metal band.

"Perhaps, but remember, you were tricked, lied to, and your promise was extracted under false pretenses, so you were never bound in fact. But now you can return to the Faith. You have obviously felt lost without it, and so you fell back on petty superstitions, pretty baubles and crude amulets as a crutch to ease your troubled mind."

The bard suddenly reached over and tapped Owen's wristlet with his silver hook. Immediately a tiny network of cracks ran along the band; they widened and thickened, covering the band in a darkening web. Then the Iron Band of Kloor dissolved in a fine powder which hung momentarily on the still air, then disappeared. It was gone and the only outward sign of its existence was a swath of pale skin encircling the Master's wrist and forearm.

"I thank you," Owen said simply, and then he tore the bone amulets from about his neck and prised the charm loose from the hilt of his sword. "We'll head south and west with the dawn," he said then, "and find this Prince Kutor."

"You'll need this then," the bard said, and, leaning forward, he slid Owen's knife free and etched a half circle onto the metal of the blade with the point of his hook. "This is how they will know you. It is the sign of the hook, the mark of the bard."

We slept then, and when we awoke the bard Paedur had gone. But of his going I could find no trace, for the snow piled high outside the door was clean and unmarked.

6
Gered and Leal

And he was master of all tales and had great skill in their telling.
Life of Paedur, the Bard

Aeal, the Captain of Bowmen, leaned over the edge of the walk-way and looked down into the courtyard. The smells of man and horseflesh mingled with the resinous torches, and other more pungent odours wafted up to him, and he felt his eyes sting and water.

Another carriage had arrived, and there was a brief flurry of confusion as the horses and men settled into the already overcrowded square. Steps were brought as the door of the carriage opened and a servant helped an ancient withered woman to the ground. Aeal was about to turn away, when he saw the second person alighting from the carriage; she was young, pretty and dressed in the latest court fashion that left the neck and shoulders bare. She stopped on the bottom step of the entrance hall and looked around, and the sharp-eyed bowman saw a flicker of disdain cross her heavily made-up, too-pretty face. He suddenly lost all interest in the woman; Castle Nevin might not be much to look at, but it was one of the Seven Bastions of the North, one of the forts which allowed the young woman to sleep peacefully in her bed without fear of being savaged and eaten by the Chopts.

Aeal turned back to the miserable-looking scribe standing on the battlements beside him. "Well?"

Danel consulted the parchment scroll in his hands and then nod-ded. "That was the Countess Devesci and her daughter; now all the invited guests have arrived—though some of their servants are still on the road."

"We'll keep the Waytorch burning awhile longer then." The bowman stared out across the moors. "There's a fog coming in— Chopt weather, we call it."

"Will they come?" The scribe looked anxiously across the Wastelands towards the black line that marked the Mion River.

The bowman saw the look and smiled, "For a learned man, you know remarkably little," he said.

"This is my first appointment as a professional scribe—and the first time I've ever been in the Northlands," Danel said quietly.

"It shows."

Danel was completely out of his depth—and he knew it. He was a third-degree apprentice, with another year's training to do before he had the experience, the etiquette and the knowledge to perform the duties of a scribe. But when Count Nevin had announced the betrothal of his daughter to Adare, the son of Count Adare, and had sent to Baddalaur for the services of a scribe, the only person available had been Danel, since most of the senior scribes had been called to the capital to assist in the recent census.

Danel didn't like Castle Nevin; it was small, cold and miserable. The people were distrustful of strangers, and the fact that he was an educated man only served to increase their suspicions and distrust. And Castle Nevin was far too close to the Chopts for Danel's comfort.

"There's no moon," Aeal said.

"I beg your pardon?" Danel asked, looking at the tall thin bowman in confusion.

"I said, there's no moon, and the Chopts will only attack when there's a moon. They believe that it guides their spirits to the Otherlife."

Danel nodded quickly in relief.

"It was one of the reasons the Betrothal was timed for the dark of the month" Aeal stopped abruptly and leaned across the merlons, staring down along the length of the broad road that led to the castle.

"What's wrong?" Danel asked, his voice rising and cracking.

The Captain of Bowmen waved him silent. "I thought I saw something on the road."

"Where? I saw nothing." The small, stout young man squinted over the edge of the battlements and down onto the road. He could just about make out the paler colour of the roadway itself, and the distant bulk of the Watchtower, but aside from that he could see nothing. "There's nothing there..." he began, but Aeal abruptly turned from the battlements, brushed past him and raced down the steps. A few moments later Danel saw two score men hurrying down along the road, with every second man carrying a travel-lantern.

The scribe watched the balls of light bob down the road, until they had passed the Watchtower. Then they stopped and milled around, and Danel thought he heard a muffled shout. With mounting excitement, he watched the lanterns form into two flanking lines— like that of a guard of honour—and then they turned and slowly began to retrace their way to the Castle.

But surely all the important guests had arrived? Obviously, someone of importance was arriving, and the scribe was just about to re-check his scroll of names when a young boy in a page's livery came panting up the steps and stopped before him. "My lord the count wishes to see you," he said breathlessly.

"Me?" Danel whispered.

The boy nodded silently, and then bowed and turned away. Danel followed him slowly.

Count Nevin was standing on the top step that led into the entrance hall waiting for the scribe. He was a tall, bulky warrior, looking very uncomfortable in court silks and satins, and the broad-bladed short-sword on his hip looked decidedly out of place. He glared at the young man as he paused on the bottom step and bowed.

"Who comes?" he demanded.

"I don't know, my lord." He held up the scroll of invited guests. "There are only servants left to arrive."

Count Nevin nodded. "That's what I thought," he murmured. He fingered the plain leather patch that covered his left eye-socket, and then, with a warrior's decisiveness, dismissed the matter. "Well, my guards seem to consider whoever it is to be someone of importance. Make ready for a new guest," he called out across the courtyard; and as the servants hurried to lay new rushes across the polished flagstones the old count turned back to the scribe. "You— stay by me until we find out who's coming."

Danel bowed and then stepped back away from the count, into the shadows, trying to become as inconspicuous as possible.

The wooden drawbridge thundered and roared as the squad returned, and the sound of their boots echoed off the high walls of the defensive entrance. Tension increased almost perceptibly in the courtyard, and the scribe saw movement high on the battlements as bowmen and archers moved into position.

The guards stamped to halt in the centre of the courtyard, facing the steps and Count Nevin. Aeal stepped out from their ranks and shouted a command and the men snapped to attention.

"Captain...?" Nevin asked.

"A guest, my lord..." Aeal began, and then stopped suddenly as a figure stepped out from amongst the warriors.

It was a man; a tall, thin, almost sinister figure clad from head to foot in a long dark travelling cloak. The figure walked to the foot of the steps and bowed slightly to the count. He pushed back the hood of his cloak, and the torchlight touched his long thin face with yellow light, giving it a faintly demonic cast. "My lord Nevin," he murmured softly, although his voice carried to everyone in the silent courtyard.

The count glanced from the stranger to Aeal, and frowned, his hand falling to his sword. He had opened his mouth to speak, when the stranger reached up and undid the ornate clasp that held his cloak at the throat. Nevin stared—first at the silver hook that took the place of the man's left hand and then at the eye and triangle symbol of a bard high on the man's left shoulder—and then the old warrior smiled.

"You are a bard?" Nevin said, a statement more than a question.

"I am Paedur, Bard Master, once of the Imperial Court at Karfondal, although now without position."

Nevin nodded. "Aye, I saw you once, and heard you speak there—but that was some years ago."

Paedur smiled slightly. "It would have been."

The old man walked down the few remaining steps and stood by the bard—although the count was by no means a small man, Paedur topped him by a head and more. The count's voice dropped to a whisper. "What brings you here—and now?"

"Chance," the bard murmured, "and the will of the gods."

"The will of the gods," the old man said, smiling. And then he threw back his head and laughed. "Aye, the will of the gods. But come bard, you must hunger and thirst after your journey. I will have a guesting room prepared and you may rest awhile, and then you will join us; this night my daughter is to be betrothed to one of my neighbour's sons. Perhaps you would do us the honour to speak for us..." Nevin threw his arm around the bard's shoulder and led him up the steps and into the hall.

The Captain of Bowmen was about to turn away, when he spotted the scribe in the shadows. He walked over to him. "Do you know this bard?" he asked, nodding up the steps.

Danel nodded. "I've heard of him," he said cautiously.

"What about him?"

"His name is almost legendary in Baddalaur. He threw away a fine position in the Imperial Court and went to settle in some forest so he could work without distractions."

"And what's wrong with that?" Aeal asked, hearing the disapproval in the scribe's voice.

"Well..." Danel said slowly.

"Well?"

"I did hear a rumour that he was wanted by the Imperial Court."

"On what charge?" Aeal asked quickly.

"Blasphemy against the New Religion," Danel said, a little breathlessly.

The bowman smiled. "Since when has that been an offence?"

"Since the Emperor Geillard began studying the Religion."

"Well, in the Wastelands we judge a man by more than the gods he worships," Aeal said, turning away.

The Great Hall of Castle Nevin had been newly decorated for the betrothal. The tall fluted pillars had been washed in shades of light brown and cream, making them look like trees, and the high vaulted ceiling had been painted a pale eggshell blue, giving it the appearance and effect of the sky.

Paedur the bard walked slowly down the empty hall. He looked around, nodding slightly, and then turned back to Count Nevin who had remained standing by the door. "Master Eldesan's work, I think."

Nevin folded his arms and began to rock back and forth on his heels. "Aye, I brought in craftsmen from the Outland Guilds, but they were under the direction of the Emperor's own master-craftsman."

Paedur nodded. "I recognise his touch." He wandered down to the end of the hall, running the fingers of his right hand against the golden-bronze of the long guesting table that took up most of the room. "This has a tale to tell, I shouldn't wonder," he murmured.

Nevin nodded, obviously pleased. "Aye; my ancestor, Nevin Ironhand, commissioned it on the occasion of his handfasting to

Maggan, the daughter of Thurle of the Two Forests. He was the ancestor of Adare—whose son my daughter is to be betrothed to this night. The legends say it was the source of the interbinding between the two families which continues to this day."

The bard rested the palm of his hand flat against the table and the old count imagined he saw something spark between the flesh and the polished wood. "It's carved from a single piece of wood," the bard said, almost in wonder.

Nevin stepped away from the doorway and walked to the table. He rested the tips of his fingers almost delicately against the wood. "It was carved by Chriocht the Carpenter, the Crinnfaoich."

Paedur glanced down the length of the table at the count and shook his head. "He was not pure-blooded Crinnfaoich; he was part human. He originally hailed from the Sidhe Forests of Ogygia, but he set out as a young man to wander the known world. His workmanship can still be found in the most surprising places."

"Well, this is my family's most prized possession. In all that time, it has neither cracked nor warped; and, although wood quickly rots in this cold and damp northern clime, this has remained as fresh today as it was when it was first hewn from the tree."

The bard nodded. "There is a little of the Old High Magic in it." He looked sharply at the old count. "Is there a wizard you trust...?"

Nevin was caught off guard by the sudden question. "Well , well yes, I suppose there is. Why?"

Paedur smiled. "Have him fire the table. Oh, don't look so alarmed—I don't mean burn it. He will know what you mean." He lifted his left arm with the hook and held it at chest height above the polished wood. A sudden bright blue spark leapt from one to the other. "There is Power in this wood; everything that has happened in this room is caught—trapped—by that Power. If your sorcerer fires that Power you will be able to see what happened here since the day Chriocht etched the final glyph into the wood when his work was complete."

"That...that might be interesting," Nevin said slowly, and then he added, "perhaps even more interesting following tonight's events."

Paedur walked to the head of the table and rested his hand and hook on the back of the ornate High Chair that Nevin would occupy later that night during the festivities. "Perhaps you would like to tell me why you've brought me here."

The count looked around and spread his hands. "Because it's the quietest room in the castle at the moment. We're not likely to be disturbed..." He glanced over at the thick-bodied red-ringed time-candle set in a tall holder in a corner, "...well, not for a little while longer." He turned back to the bard. "Your coming here is a gift, an answer to an old man's prayers. Tonight, I want you to tell the company here a story..." he stared down the length of the table at the bard. "I want you to tell a story that will terrify my daughter!"

The bard's long face remained expressionless, but he lowered his head, allowing the shadows to fall across his face, leaving only his mirror-bright eyes visible, reflecting the warm gold of the polished wood.

"My daughter Suila is a witch," Nevin said quickly, "not a full sorceress, nor bonded to any religion. We have a fine library here and she has used some of the ancient texts to...dabble. She has mastered a few of the minor incantations, but I'm terrified her meddling will soon come to the notice of...something powerful."

"I've seen it happen."

"I want you to tell her a tale that will warn her off from meddling with those forces." He paused, and then asked, "Can you do it?"

"Tell me why I should?" the bard said quietly.

"Because you are a bard, a follower of the traditional ways, and by your own laws you cannot refuse a request for a story." He stopped, looking into the crackling fire, and then added, "And because you might save a girl's soul."

The bard turned away from the chair and began the long walk down one side of the table. "I can tell the tale, but I cannot guarantee that she will listen, much less take heed."

The old count smiled broadly. "When a Bard Master tells a tale, then everyone listens."

The meal was a long slow affair, the food plentiful, and the wines, meads, ports, and beers even more so. There were some speeches, followed by entertainments: actors, jugglers, harlequins, tricksters, and dancers who had been brought in under special escort for the occasion.

Towards midnight, Count Nevin finally called for silence. He attempted to stand up, but he shifted and swayed and his speech was slurred and broken. "We...we are to be honoured on this... this happy occasion..." he began. He sat down suddenly, amidst a burst of drunken laughter, and continued his speech from his chair. "We are to be honoured by a bard—a wandering Bard Master in the grand tradition—who chanced upon the castle earlier this forenight, and he has agreed...he has agreed to tell us a tale of our choosing."

A sudden burst of applause drowned out the rest of the count's words, but they died just as quickly as the long room's double doors were thrown wide and the bard made his entrance in a gust of frigid air which guttered many of the candles and tapers.

Paedur walked the length of the hall in complete silence, all too conscious of the frightened stares he was receiving and aware of the half-concealed signs that were made as he passed. The northern folk were superstitious people, he reminded himself, and their fears and beliefs were a double-edged dagger—to be used either way.

He stopped before the tall main table and bowed slightly to the counts Nevin and Adare and their wives. He turned slightly and bowed to the young man and woman sitting apart in the brightly-flowered and wreath-decked chairs: Suila, daughter of Nevin, and Adare, son of Adare.

"A tale, bard," Nevin said quickly, glancing at his daughter, and then turning back to the bard.

"And what would you have?" Paedur asked, his voice low and soft and yet carrying to every corner of the hall.

Nevin smiled curiously over the rim of his goblet. "Why..." He paused, looking drunkenly down the table. "Well, this is my daughter's night. I think she should choose, don't you?"

The bard nodded slightly and then looked over at Suila. "And what is your pleasure?"

Suila looked from her father to the tall bard. As the head of the household, only the count had the right to ask a bard to speak, and now she instinctively felt that something was wrong. Suila was a tall, thin young woman, with copper-red hair and dull green eyes. Her face was long, and seemed almost flattened, and while she was no great beauty she was witty and intelligent, spoke four languages fluently, and could read almost as many more again. She looked at her betrothed, Adare. "What would you like to hear?" she murmured.

Adare was now more than a little drunk. He was a warrior, stationed in one of the border outposts beyond Thusal: a short, stocky man, a soldier in his ways and manners. Suila made him uncomfortable and, in some vague way, frightened him. He grunted, "Your choice."

Suila looked back at the bard. "My choice," she said, her hard eyes narrowing. "Can you tell me a tale of lovers," she asked slowly, "but yet, let it have a little spice to it, let there be war and death—and sorcery. Can you tell me a tale like that?"

"I can." The bard turned to Nevin. "With your permission then...?"

The count waved his hand. "Of course—but first, a chair." He half-turned and called back over his shoulder. "A chair for the bard."

While two pages struggled to manoeuvre a heavy chair up the hall to the centre of the floor, Paedur turned to look at Suila. She held his gaze—and then she shivered, for she felt as if he were looking through her, into her very soul. Finally, she blushed and looked away, busying herself with her goblet.

Paedur sat back in the high-backed ornate wooden chair and in the dim half-light of the hall the shadows seemed to cluster and gather thickly around him, leaving only the gleaming half-circle of his hook and the triangular bardic sigil visible.

Suddenly, he rapped his hook against the arm of the chair and a thin high musical note hung on the air, stilling all sounds. "This is the tale of Gered and Leal," he began...

Before the Cataclysm that destroyed the Second Age of Man, when the Southern Kingdoms were but a single continent, a new faith came into being—the unholy worship of Lutann, one of the Demon Gods. The Demon Lords were wholly alien creatures, not of this universe, but they gained access to it through the rents in the fabric of space which were created by the howling of Kloor, the defeated War God of the New Religion.

The worship of Lutann centred in the western city of Osteltos, the so-called White City. However, time and the smoke of countless sacrifices had blackened its squat marbled walls, and its ivory towers—which were literally sheathed in ivory—had tarnished and stained, giving the city a yellowed, diseased appearance from a distance.

Beton, the Blind King, ruled at this time, and he actively encouraged the worship of the Demon God.

Now to the north of Osteltos, although separated from it by the ancient Mathin Woods, rose Solestel, the City of Spires. It had been built in the centre of a broad, gently sloping plain, with one side to the sea, and its back to the Tirim Mountains. And, although it had been built using the same marble from the Mathin Quarries which had been used in the construction of Osteltos, while the latter had darkened, Solestel's walls still blazed golden with reflected sunlight on bright summer days.

Mechlor ruled in Solestel. He was Beton's twin brother, and they were the sons of Madran the Saviour who fell at Cellen Field, in battle with the Shemat, who were the ancestors of the Shemmatae, who were in turn defeated by Churon the Onelord in later generations.

Although they were twins and in their youth had been indistinguishable, time had changed that. Beton's strange worship had taken its toll and had warped his tall frame, scarring his flesh and robbing him of his sight. But Mechlor, who followed the Old Faith, retained his youth and vigour, and could almost have been taken for Beton's son.

But, although the two brothers were now separated by a divide that was greater than any ocean, their lives still followed a strangely similar pattern. And so at the time when Hanuiba, Beton's concubine, gave him a daughter, Mechlor's wife Iaiale bore him a son.

In the time of celebrations that followed, both kings swore to their differing gods to bring up their children according to their respective faiths. Beton named his daughter Leal, and she was dedicated to Lutann and, almost from the time she could talk, she was trained in the mysteries and workings of his magic.

And Mechlor, following the traditions of his race and family, named his son Gered, after his grandfather—Gered the White King—and he was raised in the Old Faith, and taught the ways of healing and kinghood.

Now many years passed, and the enmity between Osteltos and Solestel grew, and soon a bloody sectarian war raged between the two cities. And when the mortal armies had clashed again and again, but with little effect, the cities fought with magic and sorcery. Creatures and beings—some called from the furthest plains of

existence and others wholly created by the magicians—stalked the
Mathin Wood and the huge marble quarry which it enclosed. These
in turn disturbed some of the older forest dwellers and the quarry
stone folk, and in the skirmishes many of the magical creatures
native to this plane died.

Soon, the cities became isolated, while their creations roamed
the lands between, destroying everything in their path. And
Mannam claimed many—and they were the lucky ones—for there
were countless others who were slain by the creatures, and whose
spirits were claimed neither by Mannam of the Faith, Libellius of
the Religion, nor the Demon Lords, nor were they consigned beyond the Gorge, but continued to walk the land as spectres—but
spectres with a taste for blood.

The war dragged on, and neither side gained the advantage.
The priests and magicians on both sides began to research the elder
lore of their race, and they began to call up ever more terrifying
creations. Finally, in desperation, both sides, in their different ways,
turned to their gods for help.

The priests of Maker and User and the priestesses of the
Lady Dannu gathered in conclave in the holy place deep in the
heart of the Shining City, and prayed for guidance.

And the Lady Dannu, the Mother Goddess, attended by
her twelve handmaidens, appeared to the conclave and spoke
to them. She told them many things; of how the Demon
God's priests were even now attempting to grant Lutann a
physical form upon this plane and, if successful, the creature
would be almost invincible.

And she also told them that the Gods of the Pantheon would
not be able to assist their followers, for the gods themselves were
under attack. There were others—creatures of the Gorge—who
wished to usurp the gods of the Old Faith, and had thrown in
their lot with the Demons and now made war upon the chequered
fields of Ab-Apsalom, the Battleground of the Gods. The Lady
Dannu added that if the Old Gods were ever defeated then the
planes of existence would be divided between the Demons and
the Usurpers, and cleansed of the followers of the Faith. Lutann
must not be allowed to incarnate on this plane, for in time, by his
very nature, he would destroy all life, and not only on the Prime
Plane but on all the minor planes also.

But the Demon Lord had been summoned and was very near, hovering just beyond the Ghost Worlds, biding his time, awaiting a suitable host for his spirit. Also, his activities were restricted by the Old Gods, but they were hard pressed by the Usurpers.

The Lady Dannu reminded the priests and priestesses that a god's strength was in direct proportion to the number and faith of his followers, and thus, if the followers of Lutann and the Usurpers could be slain, then their gods would weaken and the Old Gods triumph.

Mechlor listened to his priests' report and called a full council, and after little argument they decided they had little choice but to carry the war to Osteltos and attempt to raze it to the ground. Only by destroying the city and its inhabitants and by wiping out the belief could they destroy the opposing gods and demons.

Raiding parties from Solestel attacked Osteltos, but with limited success. However, they did prevent the evil miasma that cloaked Osteltos from spreading; and the numbers of the creatures roaming the woods—which men said sometimes resembled lizards and sometimes great birds—did not increase.

Famine raged across the land and struck equally at the Twin Cities, and in a very short space of time killed almost twice as many as had died in the war. The cities gradually became isolated from the rest of the continent, and became almost completely independent, leaving the Mathin Woods to whatever were-creatures had survived.

And on Ab-Apsalom, the Battleground of the Gods, war raged unceasingly between the Gods of the Faith and the Usurpers, and there were many outward signs of the Great War. By day the skies were darkened with showers of meteors, which the philosophers said were the spirits of the defeated lesser gods and demons winging their way to the Gorge. Nusas the Sun was shadowed again and again as he battled with the Mist-Demon, and a great fiery ball of deepest bronze rode across the heavens and challenged Nusas. When this appeared, the priests of the New Religion and the Worshippers of the Demons rejoiced, for the Mist Demon was Sinn and the bronze sun Quatatal, the Sun God of the Religion.

By night the skies burned with leaden colours, and the light of the stars was befouled with rolling fogs and clouds that flickered with pulsating lights. The Lady Lussa bravely rode through the heavens, but even her pure light was trapped and dissipated by the Usurpers and coloured by the Demons.

And those both beloved and cursed by the Moon Lady—the fool and the changeling—screamed and writhed in invisible agony; coastal towns were swamped and none dared put to sea for the tides were treacherous and unpredictable. Children and animals were born before their time, unformed and dead; and there were those that were never born but lingered long past their term in the womb until mother and child died in torment.

Then there came a lull in the battle, when it seemed as if the Old Gods had triumphed and some semblance of normality returned, and the clouds of evil that had covered Osteltos dispersed, and the creatures that had haunted the fields and woods surrounding the town vanished as mysteriously as they had come...

Gered, son of Mechlor, was two-and-twenty when the Old Gods held sway in Ab-Apsalom. He was a strange youth, tall and thin like his mother, although with his father's darker colouring. There was probably some fey blood in him—his mother's people were not pure human—and he preferred the wilds of the domain of the Lady Adur to the restrictions of town and city. When the land became safe again, he spent much of his time roaming the Mathin Woods, wandering amongst the towering groves and hidden bowers and bathing in its secret streams. He developed an interest in the ancient healing and herbal lore, and when he returned each evening his saddle-bags were usually bulging with rare herbs and strange plants.

One day in late summer his wanderings through the wood took him farther than he had ever ventured before, almost to the southernmost edge. The blackened towers of Osteltos were visible through the trees, and evidence of the creatures that had once roamed this part of the wood was visible everywhere. There were great swatches cut deep into the heart of the forest, and most of the trees bore wounds and scars of some kind.

However, almost as if the forest were trying to make up for the damage that had been done to the trees, the floor was carpeted with scores of plants—many of them unseasonal, and most of which were very rare. It was a herbalist's paradise.

Gered swung his leg over the high cantle of his saddle and slid to the ground, pulling his satchel from his shoulder. He knelt on the soft spongy turf to pluck a herb of healing when he heard the metallic trickle of water and, looking up, spotted the glittering sparkle through the undergrowth. The sound suddenly made him realise just how hot and thirsty he was. He skirted the entangled trees and shrubs, and made his way around to what he realised must be a small pool. He was just about to pull apart the drooping branches of a Moss Maiden Tree when he stopped in astonishment, his heart beginning to pound; there was a naked young woman bathing in the pool!

From where he was standing Gered could see only her back, as she swam slowly across the pool. Her pale skin had been recently tanned by the sun, and he could see tiny spots of skin beginning to peel away, exposing the pink flesh underneath. And strangely, the sight of the young woman's sunburn made him forget his fear, and the fact that he was so near Osteltos' walls. He crouched behind the drooping branches of the tree and watched her. There was something about the dark-haired young woman swimming in a hidden pool in the depths of the wood that fascinated and attracted him.

The swimmer made her way to the far side of the pool and slowly emerged from the rippling water, her long-fingered hands squeezing out her thick black hair. She then bent for a towel—and spotted Gered. Colour rose to her cheeks but she made no attempt to cover her nakedness. She straightened up and pointed to the youth.

"And how long have you been there? Long enough, I'll wager. Well, shame on you. No honest man would spy on a lady as you have done."

Gered blushed in turn. He scrambled to his feet and bowed low. "My lady, I beg your pardon. I've only just arrived..." He glanced up to find the look of disbelief on her face. "It's true, I swear it..." He looked away, and he heard cloth rustle, and when he glanced up again he found she was now dressed in a shift of rich cloth, stiff with gold thread and heavy with lace.

"I believe you," she said finally. "But you still haven't explained what you're doing here in this part of the wood."

"I've been wandering in the woods since early morning," Gered said quickly, and then he shook his head and took a deep breath. He was all too aware that his hands were sweating and his heart was pounding painfully in his chest. "I am a herbalist," he said slowly, "and I range the forest in search of the rare and unusual herbs and flowers. Look!" He dug into the deep cloth satchel that hung around his neck and pulled out a tiny blue-petalled star-shaped flower. "I found this earlier this afternoon. It is commonly called 'Lover's Eye,' but it also has the singular property of healing head pains and muscular aches when it is properly prepared and applied."

The young woman rose on her toes and stared across the still water. "It is very lovely," she said, "I have never seen its like before."

"It is yours then," Gered said quickly. He stooped down and placed the blue star on a water pad, and then pushed it out across the pool. The maid leaned out and plucked the flower from the broad leaf and held it to her face. "Aaaah, it is beautiful and such a fragrance...delicate, familiar and yet strange."

"It will be stronger at night," Gered said, almost absently, staring at the young woman's face. "I am sorry..." he began again.

She raised a slim hand. "There's no need; I am convinced you meant no harm. Anyway," she laughed, "when I first saw you, there was a look on your face as if you had seen a vision."

"Oh, but I thought I had," Gered protested. "At first I thought you were a forest sprite, some creature of the Crinnfaoich, but now I see..." He paused and coloured.

"What do you see?" the young woman asked with a smile.

"I see a maiden of flesh and blood, and a very beautiful maiden at that."

And the Princess Leal, Beton's daughter, smiled and curtsied. "You are very kind, sir, what is your name?" she asked.

"I am..." Gered paused, and something made him hold back from giving his true identity. "I am Dereg, a wandering herbalist. And you?"

Leal smiled, and her inbred caution and sorcerous training prevented her from giving him her true name. "I am called Lean," she said, "I am a ladies' maid in the palace."

There was a pause while they looked—almost shyly—at each other. Then Leal glanced up at the darkening sky. "I must go. My ...mistress will be waiting for me."

"Will I see you again?" Gered asked.

"If you would like to."

"I would."

Leal smiled, her eyes softening. "Do you know the ruined Fane of Bleis the Unbeliever...?" Gered nodded, and she continued. "Tomorrow then, at noon."

"I'll be there," Gered promised.

On the chequered fields of Ab-Apsalom the war between the gods renewed, and once again the elements were thrown into turmoil and the sky—which is but the canvas of the gods—boiled with the fury of battle. But now war had turned in favour of the Old Gods and they began to prevail against the Usurpers and Demons, and so in desperation the priests of Lutann decided that it was now time to incarnate the Demon God on this plane. With his terrifying powers, they would defeat the city of Solestel and kill the followers of the Old Faith. With no worshippers to support them, the gods would soon be defeated. So they looked around for a suitable body for Lutann, for the Demon God was due only the best.

It was Andulin, High Priest of Lutann, who suggested that a Great Examination should be carried out to find that person most fitted to house the Demon's essence.

Weeks passed in the Great Examination, but in the end the priests had to admit that they had failed to find a suitable sacrifice— for the body of the host would have to be slain to allow the essence of the Demon to enter. So the priests of Lutann gathered together once again, and they performed the Rite of Questioning.

Andulin took seven night-black ravens and sacrificed them in the Demon God's name and their blood was collected in a white porcelain bowl. A sheet of whitest linen was spread upon the chill stone floor and the still-hot blood was cast upon it. As it struck the cloth it boiled and hissed as if it were molten, but the blood did not dry into the linen. It began to shift and twist about like a nest of serpents, while Andulin and his priests chanted to their Demon God for guidance.

There was a stirring in the air above the cloth and the liquid blood rose, as if straining to reach the disturbance. The air thickened, darkening all the while, and then suddenly something flickered from the darkness on to the cloth in a bolt of intense white light.

When the priests could see again, they found the linen cloth crisped and blackened, and the blood had dried to rusty streaks on the stone flags. Andulin bent over the marks, his thin lips moving as he spelled out a word in the Old Tongue, the word *Bleis.*

The High Priest returned to Beton and told him of their Questioning and the strange reply. The Blind King was silent for a time, his sightless eyes staring in the direction of the fire which, even in the heart of summer, was always blazing. When he spoke his voice was harsh and strange.

"My daughter Leal has taken to visiting the Temple of Bleis in the Mathin Wood lately. She says she feels a waxing of her powers in the ruined fane…" The Blind King fell silent again.

"Interesting," Andulin nodded slowly.

Beton nodded. "Yes, interesting." His scarred face turned up to the High Priests. "But I thought she was Examined?"

"She was—and found to be unsuitable."

"Well then, perhaps she goes there to meet someone—someone suitable."

"What time does she leave for the fane?" Andulin asked.

"About an hour before noon," the king said softly. "Perhaps, if you were to be there before her…?"

At first light, Andulin, accompanied by a decade of the King's Own, Beton's personal guard, set out for the Temple of Bleis. Now, little is known of Bleis, who is sometimes called the Unbeliever. He paid homage neither to god nor spirit, demon nor elemental, and furthermore he believed each man had the seeds of godhood within himself. He preached that each man should pay homage to himself and direct his devotions inwardly. And for this heresy his spirit is claimed neither by the Faith, the Religion, nor the Demon-worshippers, nor does it wander in the Gorge nor the Netherworld. And the spirit of Bleis the Unbeliever, forever outcast, wanders the planes in search of faith, in search of a god, in search of rest.

The temple was nothing more than a tall cylinder in a ragged clearing close to a tiny stream. Its door was long gone but Andulin noticed that the growth that had once obviously rioted its way across the entrance had been cleared away. The priest and guards entered, and following the scuffed footmarks on the dusty stone floor and steps, made their way to the top floor, where they found the remains of fruit and some empty wine casks. Then they waited.

It was almost exactly noon when there was movement in the woods below, and then footsteps were heard on the crumbling steps. The guards tensed as the sounds approached, and then— almost abruptly—the rotten trapdoor was thrown back and a figure climbed up onto the flat roof.

Two of the guards leaped forward, a weighted net in their hands. The struggle was brief, but in that time the man killed one with his knife and crippled another and had actually managed to cut himself free when he was struck unconscious. But only Andulin recognised Prince Gered, son of Mechlor, King of Solestel.

And to prevent a search for the missing prince, the High Priest sent a merchant to Solestel, with a tale of having found Prince Gered's clothing by the side of a pool in the heart of the Mathin Wood.

As the day of sacrifice drew near, there arose the problem of who would actually sacrifice the body of Gered to the Demon God. In its way, it would be a great honour, and advancement in the priesthood would be sure to follow. But then Andulin discovered that the young man was still a virgin and therefore could only be slain by a virgin...and it suddenly became much more difficult to find someone to kill the young man. However, there was one candidate...

On *Nathanaday,* which was the day of sacrifice, Gered was taken from his cell under the Temple of Lutann and brought in an enclosed cage to the Great Henge that nestled just beyond Osteltos' walls on the seaward side of the city. There he was stripped naked and chained upon the altar stone, there to await his executioner.

The stone gateways were ancient, dating back even beyond the First Age, back to the time when the gods had not yet perfected the creature that would become man. Nothing is known of its builders, for the Henge was old even when the Culai first walked this world. And in those elder days, when the gods walked this world, and the great lizards roamed free, the Culai worshipped within the gaunt and forbidding stone circle, invoking their dark deities with blood and sacrifices. So much evil had been done within the Great Henge that even the stones themselves seemed to have absorbed it into themselves. They were grimed and decayed, streaked with phosphorescent mosses which glittered dully, even in the light of day; although within the Henge it was always dusk, for the circle was forever shadowed within a twilight pall, and always—even on the warmest days—radiated a subtle chill.

Legend tells of other circles scattered through the planes, connected in some occult way, but their locations and use have been lost and the stones themselves have been tumbled and scattered.

And as they chained Gered to the flat slab, the sound of the wind moaning through the standing stones took on a different, almost human sound. Gered strained his neck upwards to look around, and for a single instant he thought he saw images of different times and strange alien places flicker between the Henge stones.

Then the worshippers began to arrive, singly and in small groups. Soon they thronged in a vast multitude beyond the stone circle, murmuring like the sound of the sea…and yet, even they, who were all too familiar with the horrors that haunted the streets of Osteltos, even they feared to approach too closely to the stones.

Then came the priests in their robes of grey, led by Andulin, who was clothed in white, and Leal, who wore the crimson executioner's garb. The priests stopped just inside the Henge and spread around it, until they encircled the altar stone, but even they were still some distance from it, and the sacrifice, lying flat against the stone, was barely distinguishable.

The King's Own arrived next, surrounding Beton's ornate litter, and he was seated in pride of place beyond the First Door Stone, and beside him sat Arak, the Eye of Beton, a small withered old shaman from the northern icelands, who reported all he saw to the blind king.

And the ceremony began.

The rituals were long and the day was hot, but Leal stood as if carved from stone, not moving a muscle, clasping the sacrificial knife—the Talon of Lutann—before her in both hands. The rites lasted throughout the day and it was evening, as the last rays of the sinking sun were striking through the perpetual twilight of the circle, bathing the altar stone and the sacrifice in dark ruddy hues, when Leal was called forward to consummate the ceremony.

She moved forward slowly, murmuring the Rite of the Talon, as she paced to the beating of a single throbbing drum, and then a pulse pounding in her temples took up the rhythm, lulling her into a daze.

Closer to the altar she moved…closer…closer still. She was only a few paces from the altar stone when she realised just who was chained there. She stopped, confused, and looked at Andulin who stood by Gered's head.

"Who…?" she murmured.

"Gered, son of Mechlor, a most fitting sacrifice," he said smugly.

"No," Leal whispered, shaking her head from side to side, "I cannot sacrifice this man. I love him."

"Aaah, but you must, you must," Andulin gloated, "you have very little choice now that you know he is the son of your father's most hated enemy, Mechlor of Solestel."

Gered raised his head from the chill stone and looked up into the woman's face. "You are Leal, the daughter of Beton?"

Leal nodded silently, not trusting herself to speak.

But Andulin continued. "Consider this; if your father, indeed, any of the people, should hear that you have violated your holy vows of chastity and consorted with this...this..." Words failed the priest. "They would tear you limb from limb."

"My vows remain intact," Leal protested. "I am still a virgin."

Andulin nodded. "Oh, I know that. But would they believe you?"

"But Dereg...Gered is my betrothed, I love him!" Leal pleaded.

"So? Consider this if you will. Sacrifice him, and in the sight of Lutann you will be doubly blessed. It would be as if you had given one of your own family to the god. He would reward you greatly for the gift."

"Leal, if you truly love me, lay down the knife and announce your love openly, and if we must die then let us die together. I do not fear death," Gered said suddenly.

"Remember, Leal, what power will be yours," whispered Andulin persuasively.

"Remember our vows, Leal, those promises we made together in the secret places of the wood, pledged beneath the noon sun."

"Remember the holy vows, Leal, which you made before you met this youth," Andulin urged. "You cannot throw your life away for this creature. Yes, you will feel the pain of parting, but you are young, you will soon recover from your loss. There will be many youths only too eager to help ease the pain. Yes, there will be many, I promise you." The priest's eyes glittered strangely, and his gaze drifted to where his own son stood amidst the ranks of the lesser priests. "But the choice is yours, and yours alone. And you would be wise to think carefully before answering, but choose now and, for your sake in this life and the next, choose correctly."

By now the dim rays of the diffused sun were slipping off the altar stone and the congregation were whispering urgently amongst themselves, wondering at the delay.

"The people grow agitated," the High Priest hissed. "The sun is sinking; you must give me your answer now. What is it to be? Your life and the power and glory that are yours by right of birth and acclaim, or the life of this wretch—who will die in any case?" he added with an icy smile.

Gered saw the distant look come into Leal's wide eyes, and it terrified him. "Leal, it is I, Gered, whom you knew and loved as Dereg...remember?"

"Be quiet," she snapped, "I must think." She was struck by strange and conflicting emotions, but there were two that bubbled to the top of this seething cauldron and cried out for attention. And truly the matter was simple. A simple choice; her love for Der ...Gered, balanced against her lust for power...and life.

Which was the stronger?

There had been little love in her life before Gered. Her father had been a distant terrifying figure; and, although she knew her mother's name and could point her out in the crowded harem, Leal had no feeling for her. She had been infused with the dictates and laws of Lutann almost before her birth, for she had been dedicated to the Demon God while still in her mother's womb. The priesthood was her life and it was a hard and brutal way of life, with little love or beauty about it.

And it has been said that those who traffic in evil sacrifice a little of the gentler emotions in return for the baser powers.

She glanced back over her shoulder at the people crowding beyond the Gates. She saw their empty staring faces, their slack mouths and dull eyes, panting in their blood lust. Did she want to rule this?

And the answer turned out to be, very simply, yes. Here, she would be worshipped as a goddess, with limitless and untold power to exercise. She would have wealth beyond her wildest imaginings, the coffers of one of the richest nations of the Southern Kingdoms would be hers to use as she would. She was born to rule. From earliest childhood this had been held up as her ultimate destiny. Would she—could she—toss this away for a youth?

And what of the youth?

She looked down at Gered lying bound upon the stained altar stone. He had lied to her—and she to him, but that was forgotten—he worshipped not her gods, nor she his. Could there ever be true love between them?

But somewhere deep, deep within her, a small voice, a voice almost smothered under fear and uncertainty, perhaps the voice of the Leal that might have been, murmured, *"You love him...you love him...you love...save him...save him...save ..."*

And then the voice of fear and ignorance spoke: "How? How can I save him and yet retain all that I possess, the power, wealth, position—and my life. How?"

"Save him...save him...his life...his life is in your hands."

"How?"

There was a moment in which she stood undecided, torn between the two voices, and then the crowd began to shout. And suddenly the decision was made. She stepped up to the altar, the black-handled knife in her hands burning like a single flame in the last rays of shadowed sunlight.

"Leal...?" Gered whispered.

"Silence, fool!"

"I thought we meant..."

"You meant nothing to me," and her voice was harsh and flat and strangely alien. "You were but an amusement."

She raised the knife high.

"I love you *Leaaaaaaa...*"

As Gered screamed his farewell, Leal plunged the Talon of Lutann up to the hilt in his breast, and as he died, with his blood upon the hands of his betrothed, he whispered softly, for her ears only, "I forgive you, my love..."

"Thus died Gered, son of Mechlor, King of Solestel, by the hand of Leal, daughter of Beton, King of Osteltos."

The bard's voice faded in the vastness of the hall, and in the silence that followed many turned to look at Suila. Colour rose to her cheeks but she couldn't ignore the hard stares. "Why do you look at me? I am neither witch nor sorceress. I am not like the Leal of the tale."

Adare, her betrothed, suddenly looked up from the goblet in his hand and turned towards Suila's father. "I think there was a reason in the telling of this tale, and I think its contents were not unknown to you. Would this be so?"

Count Nevin nodded solemnly. "It is so. I asked the bard to tell a tale such as you have heard." He looked from Adare to Suila.

"We all know my daughter has had leanings towards the darker knowledge of the ancients and I feared, not only for her spirit, but for those close to her. I didn't know what story Paedur would tell, but he has chosen uncannily well. Thus, for those with a mind to listen, there is a warning here."

The bard's voice suddenly cut across the count's. "There is a little more—my tale is not yet complete."

Nevin bowed. "My apologies…"

Paedur continued.

But the truth reached Solestel, for the spirit of Gered had been wrested from the grasp of Lutann by the Lady Dannu and her Maidens and now abode in the Silent Woods in peace and safety, though his body remained in unhallowed ground. And Coulide Dream-Maker visited Mechlor in a vivid nightmare to show him how his son had died.

And Mechlor, rallying his people behind him, overran Osteltos and razed it to the ground, killing everyone there, man, woman and child, for they were all tainted with the evil of the place.

Andulin, the High Priest, attempted to oppose Mechlor's army with spells and sendings, but the priests and priestesses of the Lady Dannu and the Old Faith successfully protected the army from sorcerous attack, and Mechlor's sendings came back on Osteltos. And it was Mechlor who plunged his sword into the priest, and took his head and set it up on a spire of the Temple of Lutann, where it gibbered and mewled with a hideous life of its own until the temple itself dissolved in flames.

Beton, the Blind King of Osteltos, fell to his death while trying to escape from the Solestelians, for his slaves had deserted him and he knew true blindness then for the first time. His body was taken and tossed to the dogs, but it is said that even they refused it.

And the Cult of Lutann died that day also, for its followers were completely destroyed, and without Faith there is no Substance, and the weakened Demons were defeated with ease by the Old Gods.

But of Leal little trace was found, save charred ashes and chipped bones in a tower by the outskirts of the city, where it was rumoured she practised her evil craft. It was said that she had tried to raise the shade of Gered and had been blasted by her own foul sorcery; or perhaps the Demon Gods took her because they had lost Gered to the Old Gods.

Although the Southern Kingdoms vanished beneath the seas in the Cataclysm that destroyed the Second Age of Man, the Great Henge survives on one of the Arrow Isles that are the last remnants of the once huge land.

But on winter nights, when the Wingstar shines in the north, it is said that shadow-creatures perform strange rites within the standing stones, and strange landscapes can be seen through the gates, and the shades of a hundred thousand sacrifices pace silently around the circle.

And on such occasions the wind whispers, Gereddddd... Leallll...

"Thus ends the tale of Gered the Prince who was destroyed by his love for the sorceress Leal." Paedur sat back into the chair, and was lost in the shadows.

The count turned to his daughter Suila, who was now weeping openly, while Adare tried uncomfortably to comfort her. "I asked for a tale such as this as a warning to you," he repeated. "Heed it."

The old man rose stiffly, thus signifying that the festivities were at an end. He walked around the ancient table and approached the bard's chair, pulling a heavy purse from his belt. He stopped in front of the heavily shadowed chair. "You have done me a great service..." he began softly and then suddenly stopped.

For the chair was empty. The bard was gone.

7
The Legend of the Shanaqui

The legend grew, making him a Duaiteoiri, a demon, a god, but in truth he was none of these things—he was still a man and, for all his powers, he was a puppet of the gods.

Life of Paedur, the Bard

There had been a time, when he was still fully human, when he slept and ate and his bodily functions were like those of normal men. He had feelings then, he knew love and hate, anger, rage, and pity. He had been able to weep.

All that was gone now.

He had lost that part of himself when the Old Gods had chosen him as their champion and gifted him with immortal life. Now, sleep was unnecessary, and he needed only the simplest food to survive. His emotions had also suffered; they had been dulled, muted, and he was no longer capable of the extremes of feeling, and love and hate had become almost abstractions. A dull satisfaction was all that was left to him. Even his tales, which had been his greatest joy and pleasure, were now little more than studies, picked and told for the greatest effect, chosen to excite a set of responses from his audience. Usually, it didn't bother him overmuch, but tonight...tonight had been different.

The bard leaned back against the tall pillar of rock and looked back down the long road, past the black line of the Mion River to where he could still see the lights of Castle Nevin. And he wondered at the morality of what he had just done. He didn't know Suila, nor did he owe anything to the old count, and yet, on Nevin's word, he had succeeded in ruining what should have been one of the happiest days of a girl's life.

Perhaps his tale would have some effect, and he might have deterred her from further delvings into the ancient lore, but somehow he doubted it. He had the Sight to a minor extent, and the only future he saw for Suila was a bloody fire-filled death. And he knew that she would remember the bard for the rest of her life...and hate him.

Shaking his head, Paedur the Bard turned around and continued on the road that led into the icy Northlands.

Paedur reached the coast in the still silent hour just before dawn. The darkness was absolute, with low clouds covering the stars and the Lady Lussa, but with his enhanced sight the night held no secrets from him. He allowed the rest of his senses to come to the fore, and the pre-dawn came vibrantly alive. The on-shore breeze was fresh and chill, carrying with it the promise of sleet from the Northlands, but he was also able to distinguish the odours of humanity nearby—smoke, cooked and burnt food, sweat and urine and fish. He wrinkled his nose in distaste; the stench of rotting fish was almost overpowering. He looked down the winding length of the road, and found it branched further on, one turning leading down towards the pebbled beach to a small fishing village, the other leading upwards towards an obviously ancient yet still formidable fortress perched on the clifftop almost directly across from his present position.

Paedur frowned, trying to place the spot, working out its position in relation to Castle Nevin and the River Mion, and then he realised he was looking at the northernmost community of the blue-robed monks of the Order of Ectoraige, the God of Learning and Teaching.

The monastery was built in two distinct parts and styles, with one higher than the other. The older building was constructed of rough-hewn blocks, cunningly set into each other without mortar, with a slightly sloping wood-and-lacquer roof. The two massive gates were solid brukwood, thick with characteristic square-headed rivets that were the trademark of the Culai carpenters and which were never known to rust. By contrast, the sprawling school, huddled at the foot of the monastery building, was built entirely of plain cordwood, and though it was an impressive structure in itself it seemed almost shabby and insubstantial against the older building.

Grey light flared far out to sea, startling the bard, but when he looked he found it was merely the dawn breaking over the horizon. He turned back to the monastery and school; it would be a good place to stop for a time, Paedur decided; it would give him time to make some plans and consider his future. It was sometimes difficult to remember that it had been barely half a year since he had left the Forest of Euarthe, and in that time he had walked almost half the length of the Nations, telling his tales, spreading the Old Faith. Yes, it would be good to rest.

His decision made, he was just about to move when he felt heat surge through the metal hook that was set into the bone of his left arm. He acted instinctively, dropping to the ground and rolling to one side into the twisted bushes that lined the track. He had been attacked on his journey on three previous occasions; twice by humans, and the last time by Tixs, the Bat God of the New Religion. And each time his hook had warmed and warned him.

He parted the bushes and looked around, now tasting a harsh metallic tartness in the air that overlay the salt tang of the sea. Light had seeped across the sky and in the twilight greyness he could see that a spot directly above the track he had been following was shimmering, sparkling with scores of tiny coloured dust-motes.

And then a tree appeared on the pathway. A tall thin blasted tree, with tendrils of leaves and ragged mosses clinging to it. The bard's metal hook turned ice-cold—it was a sending, and a powerful one at that.

Paedur pressed his hook to his lips, silently calling on the Pantheon for help, as he quickly ran through the gods and demons of the New Religion, trying to place the sending, trying to remember which one used a withered tree as a symbol...

The tree moved. It straightened, its branches twisting and curling, and what Paedur had at first taken to be leaves and mosses now formed and re-formed into a long cloak of withered leaves...and the bard suddenly recognised the figure.

"Mannam," he murmured.

The Lord of the Dead moved rustlingly forward and stopped, and then its head turned to where Paedur still lay. The figure bowed slightly, "Bard."

"Surely my time has not come yet?" Paedur asked quietly, standing up and brushing dirt from his cloak and tunic. He peered up at the Duaiteoiri. The last time he had seen the Lord of the Dead it had been dark, and the creature's features had been shadowed behind the long cowl of his cloak. However, even now, with his enhanced sight, he still couldn't make out the Dark Lord's features.

"Not yet, not yet," Mannam whispered sibilantly, "you have no need to see my features yet. When you do, you will have passed from this world, and will be in my domain."

"I thought you were one of the Religion's minions coming for me," Paedur said.

The Dark Lord nodded, his cloak whispering and hissing softly. "Aye, you must take great care now; their attention is fully on you, and I fear their attacks will become more frequent. But you have done well." Mannam drew a slightly gasping breath and continued, "Where you have been there is a swing back towards the Old Faith, people are beginning to question the New Religion openly and in some cases even defying its priests."

"There will be war," Paedur promised.

Mannam nodded, his leafed cloak rustling harshly together. "In all probability. Prince Kutor is already putting together a sizable army in the west, and the Weapon Master will soon join him. A little while longer and this army of the Old Faith will be a force to be reckoned with. Perhaps it might be wise to send you back to them, allow you to weave your own particular magic on them..." The god's sibilant, breathless voice died away. "But all that in time." The god paused, and the bard thought he heard a note of hesitancy creep into his voice. "But now there is something you must do for us, something important..."

"More! You want me to do more! Have I not done enough already?" the bard snapped, brushing past the Duaiteoiri and striding down the roadway.

"Your task has only just begun," Mannam whispered, falling into step beside him. "It will be complete only when the New Religion is destroyed."

"I may be dead then."

"If I do not take you, then you will not die," the Dark Lord said.

"And what will I become then? A *quai,* a mindless thing?" Paedur snapped.

"I will not allow that to happen," Mannam promised.

"That gives me little comfort."

Mannam glided around in front of the bard and stopped, forcing the bard to a halt. "Something is troubling you," the Duaiteoiri said.

"Tonight I told a story—the tale of Gered and Leal—to a young woman at her betrothal; I told the story with the sole intention to frighten her."

Mannam nodded. "I am aware of the circumstances."

Paedur ran his fingers through his hair, dragging it back from his face. "I told that story without stopping to think of the consequences; without thinking how the young woman would take it; I told the story because I was asked to." He stopped, and then added in a softer voice, "I'm beginning to wonder."

"About what?"

The bard shrugged. "If I'm doing the same thing. If my tales are only frightening people back to the Faith. Why am I doing this?"

"You are reminding people of their Faith, of the belief their fathers held and their fathers before them. And their belief makes the gods stronger, and in turn we protect them. When we asked you to be the Champion..."

"Asked?"

"Decided then, that you should be the Champion of the Old Faith, we did not lay down any rules for you. You were gifted with certain powers and then allowed to choose your own path. For reasons of your own, that path led northwards..."

"You told me to come north!"

"I merely suggested it," Mannam hissed, "but you chose it."

"I'm not even sure myself why I came north—perhaps I was just trying to stay out of trouble." With his single hand he pulled his cloak close around his throat. Although he was usually impervious to the weather, the Duaiteoiri radiated an insidious chill. "You know the Religion has offered a reward for my capture—dead or alive?" he asked.

Mannam nodded. "Yes; and a special arm of the Iron Band of Kloor have been assigned to track you down—their orders are not to return without your head and hook." The Dark Lord suddenly reached out and tapped the bard's chest with his long stick-like arm. "They fear you now—already the people speak of the *shanaqui*, the Tale-Spinner. You have become a symbol of the Old Faith—a symbol the priests of the New Religion must destroy if they are to keep the people's belief."

Paedur shrugged. "Well, I should be safe enough here..."

"If you continue into the Northlands they will find you. They are already watching the bardhouse at Thusal." The arm moved, pointing across to the monastery. "A scholar has recently joined the brothers to study in their library. He is one of the Iron Band."

"How do I know if you're telling me the truth?"

There was a sound of crackling, snapping branches that Paedur remembered as the Duaiteoiri's laughter. "You don't. You must trust me—I have no need to lie to you."

Paedur nodded and sighed. "What's this important task you want me to perform?"

Mannam turned to face the spreading dawn, and the bard who was looking up into the darkened cavern of Mannam's cowl suddenly caught a glimpse of the Duaiteoiri's face—a face like a slab of rotten wood, wormed and eaten with mould, with patches of scabrous moss clinging tightly to it. Paedur blinked—and the image faded.

"The gods of the New Religion have been busy of late, but to what ends we have been unable to fathom—until today. We knew for example that Hercosis the Dreamlord had visited most of the high-ranking priests and even the Emperor himself, and that Hirwas of the Far-Seeing, who is second only to Trialos himself, had ranged the length and breadth of this plane..."

"What were they looking for?" Paedur asked, interested now, for although he had lost much when he had gained immortal life he still retained his bard's curiosity and inquisitiveness.

"They were seeking a small sealed vessel, of the kind that are commonly found in the ruins of the Culai settlements."

"What's so special about this one?"

"It contains a fragment of the Soulwind," Mannam whispered.

It took a moment for the god's words to sink in. "The Soulwind," he asked, "the wind that blew through the soul of the One in the Beginning?"

Mannam rustled. "The same."

"But where is it, and what do they want it for?" Paedur asked quickly.

"It took us some time, but we finally located it; it lies beyond the Straits of Pinacloe, across the Sea of Galae, on the Blessed Isle of the Culai. The vessel itself is kept in the Inner City, enclosed within the Circle of Keys."

"What do they want it for?"

In the long silence that followed, the sound of wind rustling through leaves and shaking branches was clearly audible. "They intend to open it."

"But will that not destroy…" Paedur began.

"They believe that the Soulwind will sweep away the Old Gods into the nothingness from whence we came, leaving only the Gods of the New Religion."

"Will it?"

"The Soulwind will wipe everything clean. When they open it, this plane, and every other plane of existence, will vanish."

"And you want me to try and stop them?" Paedur asked incredulously.

Branches snapped and crackled. "You must stop them, bard."

8
The Taourg Pirates

This day: a merchantman taken and sunk off the coast of Adare, in sight of Mion Bay; a curious prisoner taken, a hookhanded warrior who professes to be a storyteller...

...from the log of the Taourg pirateman, Duneson

"Sink it—leave no trace." Duaize, Captain of the *Duneson,* a Taourg corsair, turned to his First Mate. "No trace, mind, we don't want the Imperial warships knowing we're in the area."

Tuan, the first mate, nodded briefly. "Of course," he said quietly, looking down on the captain, "of course." He was a tall mountain warrior, a native of Moghir, a province of Gallowan on the rocky north-western coastland, pale-haired and pale-eyed in the manner of his people, and completely in contrast to the short swarthy Taourg.

Duaize nodded and moved down the ship, leaving the first mate standing by the rail of the *Duneson* to supervise the rest of the crew as they systematically sacked the sinking merchantman.

Although the squat coastal trawler was hooked and grappled to the pirate ship's side, it was listing badly to port; and the storm that had driven the craft from its customary safe shore route was blowing up again. Both ships were rocking on the growing swell and Tuan glanced into the northern sky, his grey eyes reflecting the metal colour of the sky. "Hurry it up there! Storm coming!"

There was a shout from the merchantman and then the *Duneson's* cargo net was hauled across the short divide separating the two ships. Tuan watched the huge bundle thump to the deck, where it was opened and each item quickly recorded by two of the ship's officers under Duaize's greedy eye. As they worked they set apart a one-hundredth part of the spoils which would be weighted and cast overboard immediately, dedicated to Sewad, the Nasgociban Lord of the Waves.

Suo-Ti, the Shemmat navigator and tillerman, joined Tuan by the rail. The small man nodded to the growing pile which was destined to be cast overboard. "I have sailed with some strange crews in my time, but these Taourg are the most superstitious," he said softly, in his sibilant accent. "Such a waste."

Tuan nodded. "Aye, but if you've a mind to look closely, you'll find our captain's only disposing of the defective, spoiled, or damaged goods." He looked down at Suo-Ti and winked. "Profit before religion, eh?"

The sallow-skinned man laughed—and then turned it into a cough when he saw Duaize glaring at him. He turned around and leaned on the rail, looking over at the sinking ship. "I have decided to leave at the next sizable port," he said quietly to Tuan. "If you have any sense, you might think about doing the same."

Tuan ran his fingers through his salt-stiffened hair and beard. He glanced briefly at the Shemmat. "I have."

"Good; perhaps we will find a berth together. I find these Taourg disgust me." He spat into the water. "They should have stayed in their desert."

Still watching the captain sorting through the merchantman's cargo, Tuan asked, "How many dead?"

"We have lost six. We were lucky; the storm hid us, and the Taourg corsairs are not expected this far north."

"And the merchantman?"

The navigator shrugged. "They lost many before they even knew what was happening, the rest died in the fighting, and the wounded were despatched. There was one female on board, but she slew herself..."

"Rather that than be sold on the slave block at Londre," Tuan finished. He was about to continue when a shout from the merchantman made him turn. The pirates were finished, all the cargo had been transferred, and the pirates had begun to swing back aboard the *Duneson*. "There was a prisoner," he said suddenly, "what happened to him?"

"Below, and in chains; unconscious when I last saw him."

"I wonder why Duaize wants him alive," Tuan murmured. Suo-Ti spat into the water again. "Why wonder," he said, moving away from the rail, heading back towards the huge tiller.

With the crew back on board, the navigator set the men to the oars and manoeuvred the *Duneson* off the merchantman, using the motion of the waves to wrench free the metal-shod ram. She then stood off from the ship and sank it completely with a shot from her ballista. The first mate ordered the skiffs into the water to collect up as much of the broken wood and shattered spars as they could find, thus leaving no trace that the Taourg were in these waters. Even as they worked, the dark waters boiled with the frenzy of the *ise* and *rize*, the finger-sized scavengers of the northern waters; no bodies would be washed ashore.

Suo-Ti then brought the *Duneson* around into the wind, and the Taourg corsairs headed south, running before the storm, seeking a safe harbour for the night.

Tuan joined Duaize amidships. The captain was examining part of the cache of weapons the merchantman had been carrying. Duaize was a small swarthy man, with coal-black eyes and a sharply hooked nose. When Tuan had first sailed with him, a little more than three years previously, he had been going bald, but lately he had taken to shaving his head completely. His beard was thin and sparse. He looked up as Tuan stopped before him. "What do you make of this?" He tossed the mate a long, broad-bladed knife.

The sudden weight of the weapon surprised him and he almost dropped it. It was heavy, far heavier than a knife should be, but then the blade was almost twice the normal width of a knife and as long as his arm. "It's a Chopt knife I'll wager. Aye, look at the hilt." The broad flat hilt was a dull, slightly furred, brownish colour. "That's Snowbeast horn. It's a Chopt knife right enough."

Duaize smiled nervously, rubbing his hand on his bald head. "I have never seen one of these Chopts."

"In my homeland, there is a saying which goes, 'The only Chopt you ever see is the one which kills you.'"

Duaize reached for the knife, and Tuan passed it down to him, hilt first. "If this is the knife, what then must the sword be like?"

Tuan smiled broadly. "Big," he said.

The captain looked up, his dark eyes sparkling. "And what would a merchantman, carrying nothing else but ales, and cloth, and some fancy metal-work, want with a cargo of knives? Eh?"

"Smuggling?" Tuan suggested.

Duaize looked almost insulted. "Unlikely. However, we can find out. Bring the prisoner," he called. He slammed the lid of the weapons chest and then stood on it.

Tuan covered a smile with his hand; the captain—like most of the Taourg—was a small man, and the mate noticed that he was always careful to position himself where he could look down on those he was dealing with.

Two of the corsairs hustled the prisoner up from the hold and pushed him over to the captain. The crew formed a semi-circle around him, while Tuan folded his arms and took up position behind and to the left of the captain. Suo-Ti sidled up beside the mate. "What is he?" Tuan murmured.

The navigator shrugged, shaking his head slightly.

The prisoner was tall, though not so tall as Tuan, and though thin was well muscled. He was clean-shaven and unscarred, and his limbs were sound save for his left hand which was missing and had been replaced by a hook. Tuan frowned; he had seen many mariners with hooks or claws in place of hands, but this was not a common sailor's hook: it was a broad, rune-etched half-moon, seemingly of silver though edged with some darker metal. Its sheen was dulled and darkened with rust-brown stains. He was wearing a shabby black-and-purple leather jerkin and close-fitting leather breeches. His boots were scuffed and worn and had obviously seen much travel. When he had been captured he had been wearing a long hooded cloak of fur.

The prisoner had not entered the fighting until it became obvious that the Taourg intended killing all on board the merchantman; and even then he had not sought combat, but rather had waited until it had come to him. He had slain six of the Taourg before he had been taken. Three had died with their throats opened as neatly as a priest guts a sacrifice. The almost casual killings had brought two more of the corsairs and they had attacked together, but he had pulled one into the other and then deftly cut open both their leathern jerkins in one smooth fluid movement. Another had attempted to spit him with a short harpoon, but he had easily eluded the barbed head and, pulling the man forward and down, had driven the point of his hook into his eye.

With his back to the mast, he had faced the ever-growing circle of Taourg without flinching, and when the archers would have cut him down Duaize had intervened. With a score of spears and harpoons at his throat, he had been netted, struck unconscious, chained, and dragged to the *Duneson*.

"You fought well, Hookhand," Duaize said suddenly. "Killed six of my men; good men, too."

The prisoner didn't react.

"What is your name?" Duaize snapped.

"I am called Paedur," the prisoner said quietly, looking up at the captain for the first time. His voice was soft and cultured, and without fear.

"You are a warrior?" Duaize asked, "I have need of warriors, particularly now with six of my best dead," he added with a grin, some of the crew joining him.

"I am a bard."

There was silence. Some of the crew began to edge away from the man; and those of the Seven Nations and the Old Faith made the Horned Sign of protection, for they all knew the penalties exacted by the gods for drawing a weapon on a bard. But the captain was a Nasgociban and cared little for the superstitions of the effete northern nations.

"I do not think you are a bard, Hookhand. I think you are a warrior, a Weapon Master perhaps? In the employ of some northern noble, heading south on a secret mission?" He hefted one of the heavy Chopt knives in his hand. "Yes, a spy. Now just why are you travelling on a merchantman at this time of year, eh, with a cargo of weapons? Your mission must be of great importance," he added.

"I am a bard, nothing more."

"Your destination then, where is your destination?" Duaize demanded.

"The Sea of Galae, and ultimately, the Blessed Isle."

There was a quick murmur of surprise and superstition that rippled through the crew. They moved away from the prisoner, touching amulets and relics. The Blessed Isle was a myth, one of the universal legends common to every religion and faith. The very name was a mockery. Every belief described the Isle with loathing as the last home of the Culai, the First Race. It was a haunted place, close to the Abyss, the Gorge and the Netherworld, and where the damned roamed freely. It was said that beneath its sculpted glass cliffs lurked the sea deities of every belief, forever warring for the supremacy of the seas. The very mention of the Isle aboard a ship at sea was forbidden lest one of the gods—Sewad, Vorance, Paisod, Truil, Vi, Doge or one of the lesser sealords—be angered, and rise to vent that anger.

"No lies now—I asked you your destination," Duaize said quickly, visibly shaken by the bard's reply.

Paedur stared at him, his eyes hard. "You have my answer, and my destination."

Duaize dismissed the answer with a wave of the Chopt knife, and then he changed the subject. "You are on a mission then, something of great importance I'll wager."

"Something of great importance, I'll grant you that," Paedur agreed, with a thin smile.

"*HAH!* I thought so. What is it, eh?"

"That is not your concern," the bard said quietly, looking around at the crew. He glanced back up at Duaize. "And now, if you have finished…"

In the sudden silence that followed, the slapping of the waves against the tarred sides of the ship seemed very loud indeed.

Tuan's admiration for the bard increased. For a man facing torture and certain death, he was cool enough. Suo-Ti caught his eye. "He's either crazed or dangerous," the Shemmat whispered.

The first mate shook his head slightly. "Not crazed, no, definitely, not crazed."

Duaize jumped down from the weapons chest. Standing, the difference in height between the two men became very obvious. "I have not yet finished with you, though there will come a time when you wish I were. You should watch your tongue, Hookhand—lest you lose it. And," Duaize continued, stepping closer to the bard, his deeply tanned face flushed, "everything— everything—on board this craft is my concern. Now, answer me. What are you seeking?"

Paedur folded his arms, the chains about his wrists rattling, and smiled down at Duaize.

The captain suddenly struck at him, but before his open hand could connect, it stopped, frozen in mid-air, not a finger's length from the bard's jaw. Paedur smiled curiously, but with his mouth only; his eyes remained pitiless. "You will now order these chains removed," he said softly, staring into Duaize's startled eyes. "Release me."

The captain tried to stab upwards with the Chopt knife in his left hand—but the broad thick blade snapped before it touched Paedur's stomach.

Duaize suddenly screamed as his right hand twitched and convulsed and then leaped to his own throat, fingers digging deeply into the soft flesh.

Suo-Ti reached for his dagger but Tuan gripped his shoulder, his fingers digging deep into the muscle, numbing the navigator's arm. "Let it be."

Duaize fell to his knees as his face began to darken, his eyes bulging, his tongue protruding. Saliva began to trickle in bloody lines down his jaw where he had bitten through his lips and the soft flesh of his cheeks. He dropped the hilt of the shattered knife and the fingers of his left hand tore bloody strips of flesh from the right in an effort to pull it from his throat.

The bard turned to the crew, his gaze seeming to linger on each one in turn, chilling them. "Release me now, or he will surely die."

"Do it," Tuan said, turning away.

The atmosphere aboard the *Duneson* was tense and uneasy in the days following the bard's release. The Taourg avoided him, and he, in turn, seemed to prefer his own company, spending most of his time leaning against the ship's figurehead, a teel-wood carving of Sewad in the Third Aspect, the Water Seeker.

Duaize stamped about the decks in a foul temper, fingering his throwing axe and closely watching the bard, who was neither prisoner nor passenger. The entire crew had seen him humiliated and the presence of the bard was a constant reminder of that humiliation. Yet he could not dispose of the Hookhand, for the crew would surely mutiny; the bard having taken on an almost supernatural aspect, and even Duaize himself wondered whether the black-and-purple-clad stranger was a *deiz*, a spirit creature from the sands beyond the Fire Hills of his native Nasgociba.

The *Duneson* continued on its southward course, and though the weather became warmer and the days longer, the seas grew progressively heavier and the wind stiffer. Seven days after the sinking of the merchantman, they hove in sight of the first of the Arrow Rocks, the chain of islands which run compass-straight from north to south off the eastern shores of the Seven Nations. On Suo-Ti's advice, Duaize decided that they should lie up off the first island they came to and wait out the growing storm that loomed dark and menacing on their port side. It would be the third storm in as many days, and the *Duneson,* already in need of repair, might not survive another.

They dropped anchor in the small natural harbour of a barren clump of rock inhabited by birds that rose in raucous demonstration at the ship's appearance. The harbour, however, was in the lee of the island's jagged cliffs and they were sheltered from the gale that gusted now with ever increasing frequency across the waves.

The evening meal was prepared while Tuan and Suo-Ti listed the most urgent repairs. Spirits were low, the presence of the bard having cast a shadow over the usually good-humoured crew, and Duaize ordered a ration of rofion to be dealt out. A fire-bowl was lit and the pirates huddled around it in their cloaks, warming their hands about the steaming mugs, for a thick, chill sea-fog was rising, carpeting the waves with billowing white banks that brought with them the icy breath of the northern seas.

As the night drew on, the men grew sullen and quiet and the half-hearted attempts at songs or chanties fell flat. Now and again, eyes would flicker across to the stranger as he leaned against the rigging, almost invisible save for the silver hook shining like a new moon in the lantern's wan light. If any eyes caught the bard's cold gaze, they were quickly averted and an amulet clutched or a Warding Sign made.

At last Duaize spoke, realising that if this situation were to continue then his authority would be irreparably undermined; a ship's crew should fear only the ship's captain. "What is it you want, Hookha ...bard?" he called, his voice louder than was necessary. "Let us have an end to this waiting. Name what you want and if it is within our power to grant it then it is yours, yes, and gladly too."

The bard stepped into the wavering circle of light, although his dark clothes, and particularly the hooded cloak he wore, almost seemed to absorb the light. "Take me south," he said in his strong quiet voice, "south to Maante at the tip of the Aangle Peninsula, that is all I ask. I cannot pay for this journey with coin, but I am a Bard Master and well versed in the ancient lore of the sea, in the tales of the great mariners and in information—both ancient and modern," he added, with a thin smile.

"Information," Duaize mused, and then, grasping an opportunity to regain some of his self-respect, said, "Yes, that might be payment enough—if the information were of the proper quality.

Perhaps we can work something out." He laughed and rubbed his hands quickly together. "Come—sit by me." He patted the deck and moved a little to one side, nodding to Tuan and Suo-Ti to join him. The rest of the crew quickly moved away, giving the four men a semblance of privacy.

"This is Tuan, my first mate," he said, "and this is Suo-Ti, my navigator." The three men sat cross-legged, facing the bard. "Now," the captain continued, "bear with me awhile. You are a learned man; name for me the towns upon the Arrow Rocks, north to south."

Paedur smiled briefly. "You still doubt me, eh? But you must know that a bard is also a trained cartographer—it is a relic of the days when this world was first mapped by the wandering bards. However, the larger towns are Smos, Torg, Cossi, Vosge, Musen and Forme. These are also the names of the larger islands, but there are of course countless fishing villages along the Arrows. Indeed, it is unusual to find an uninhabited isle." He inclined his head slightly in the direction of the night-hidden island across the bay.

"Now," Duaize said slowly, "of these islands, which is the wealthiest?"

The bard did not answer immediately, and Tuan glanced across at the captain, wondering where this line of questioning was leading. Musen was the wealthiest of the islands, and the Musensi silver mines were renowned throughout the Seven Nations and beyond for the quality and purity of their metal.

"You already know the answer to that, captain," Paedur said softly.

Duaize nodded. "Yes, I know. But I want to hear your answer. You may take it that the information that you supply will pay your passage in part—for no man, be he bard or mage, warrior or merchant, takes passage aboard my ship without first having paid. You may pay your way with information and news."

"But why information, why news?" the bard persisted. "What need have you for such?"

Duaize smiled broadly, showing his gold teeth, and then shrugged. "We have been at sea this half year and more, and in that time we have stopped at no port—no civilised port, that is. Many years ago I learned the value of fresh news. Even now, the merest snippet can lead me to a fat cargo. Now I have heard rumours—little more than whispers—concerning the Arrows. Mysterious comings and goings by unlicensed slavers, the disappearance of ships in calm weather, one isle raiding another, or cutting off contact with the outside world...but only whispers, whispers." Duaize shrugged again. "But even such whispers are interesting. In my land we have a saying: 'the cloud on the horizon forewarns the wise.' It is obvious that something is happening on the Arrows. Perhaps plague has destroyed Forme's harvest, or Musen's silver mines have failed?" He smiled. "So, I listen to these whispers and I say to myself perhaps these whispers might have some basis in fact, and if they were true, what do they mean? And then, when I find a bard-warrior coming south on a merchantman, I wonder afresh."

Paedur laughed softly. "I see now what you're leading up to; you're wondering whether I was making my way to the Arrows, but I've already told you my destination—believe it, if you will. I leave the Arrows to you. However...as to information, and your question as to the richest of the isles, well then, Musen is accounted the richest of the islands, the Silver Rock it is sometimes called." He paused and added with a sly smile, "But..."

"But what?" Duaize whispered, leaning forward.

Paedur leaned back, out of the light. He brought his hook to his lips and said, almost absently, "I could make you take me to Maante," and then he smiled, "but that is not my way and it would probably leave me drained..." He suddenly pointed with his hook at Duaize, who drew back. "Attend me then. On Vosge—which has always been one of the poorest of the islands, with a small population of stoneworkers, weavers and fishermen—great pools of stinking black water have burst forth from the earth, as they once did in ages past.

"Now this is not an ordinary liquid, for when placed on water it floats..." he caught Tuan's startled look and nodded, "Aye, it is lighter than water, and furthermore, it burns—even on water. Now the Vosgeans have been purchasing slaves by the score, and paying for them with small glittering black stones, the like of which exist only in the most ancient relics."

"All this is very interesting; the black water could prove to be of some value..." Duaize said doubtfully, "and the black stones of course, if they are precious..."

"To continue," Paedur said, ignoring the interruption, "and if I may digress for a moment," he added. "Ramm, the city atop the

Wailing Cliffs, and not many leagues north of Maante—my destination—is besieged by a Count Palent with an army of mercenaries."

"I have not heard of this Palent," Duaize said. "Has he campaigned before?"

"No, the count has but lately ridden forth from the marshes of Palentian, where he had his son trained in all manner of weaponcraft, and no doubt the count wishes to make some use of his son's new-found skills.

"However, Ramm is, as I have said, atop the Wailing Cliffs, and furthermore, it is built on a spur, which means it is unapproachable on the landward side save along a narrow road which winds its way up the cavernous cliffs, with a sheer drop to the crags below on one side, and the sheer wall of the cliffs on the other. This road is held by a small force of the Rammans, and thus the count, try as he might, cannot reach the city, and he has lost many men on the cliff road. But the count and his son hold the lower reaches of the road, and while he cannot get in, the Rammans cannot get out."

"Then starve them out," Duaize said quickly.

Paedur nodded. "That is the obvious course, but Ramm has a reasonable supply of foodstuffs and is blessed with a freshwater lake in the caverns beneath the city."

"It would seem it cannot be taken," Suo-Ti said quietly. "The Rammans have but to wait for the coming of the Cold Months, and then this count will be forced to flee with his tail between his legs."

The bard shook his head slightly. "Ramm, remember, is a stone city atop a barren cliff..."

"Fuel!" Tuan interrupted.

Paedur nodded again. "Yes, fuel is certain to be in short supply, and the seasons are beginning to change. Surely the Rammans would pay good coin for..."

"The black water!" the captain shouted, rubbing his hands together. "Bard," he continued sincerely, "sail with us, forget this mythical isle you seek, sail with us and your fortune, aye and several more besides, shall be made. You have that ability, rare even in the most seasoned commanders on land or sea, the ability to connect seemingly unconnected information, and weld it into a coherent whole."

"The work of a bard is often to collect seemingly disparate tales and weave them into an ordered mythos," Paedur said, unmoved by the captain's wild enthusiasm.

"Aye," Duaize murmured, "it must be so." He turned to the mate. "Tuan, rouse the crew, inform them that the bard has conceived a plan that will make our fortunes. Tell them to prepare for a raid on the morrow. Now, where are my charts? We need a small fishing village. My charts," he suddenly roared, "bring me my charts!"

"I will bring them." Suo-Ti rose smoothly to his feet and moved silently down the craft. When he reappeared, he was holding a pile of ill-cured vellum charts against his thin chest.

Duaize snatched them eagerly, his hands trembling as he unrolled them, spreading them on the deck and moving the light-bowl closer. "Now, where are we...?" Suo-Ti tapped the chart with a long-nailed finger. Duaize nodded and continued. "Here. Now we will raid...Tobb! Aye, Tobb," he went on, seeing the bard's inquisitive look. "For barrels, casks, skins, urns, containers of every description. Then on to Vosge, the black water, and wealth."

"A warning," Paedur advised, "the Vosgeans guard their black lakes jealously, for they worship them as being formed from the blood of Sleed, the Maker of Mountains. They call the black water Sleedor, and furthermore, I have heard tell that not all their guardians are human."

"*HAH!*" Duaize roared, afire with visions of wealth, "be they human or demon, beast or sprite, they will not stand between us and fortune, eh, Tuan?"

"No, captain," Tuan said quietly, although his lack of enthusiasm was evident.

"And then," Duaize continued, "when we have filled as many containers—even the cooking pots if need be—with this Sleedor, then on to Ramm." He stopped and looked across at Paedur. "Is Ramm a rich city, bard?"

"It is built of common white smoat stone, but it is faced with red-veined black marble, and its temples are of rare red smoat and faced with ivory, and the roof of the Temple of Dannu is said to be made from thin sheets of worked gold."

"Good, good." The captain rubbed his small hands together furiously. "The nights grow cold in these waters, do they not? That too is good, for a cold Ramm will pay more for the magic black fuel, eh, bard? The rich cold Ramm will soon be a poor, warm Ramm," he laughed loudly, almost drunkenly. "Go now, go leave me. I have work to do. Navigator, stay awhile."

Tuan bid the bard good rest as they both rose and moved away from Duaize who was now rocking back and forth on his heels, still studying the charts. "I can't say I like this," the first mate said quietly, glancing across at the bard.

Paedur looked back at Duaize and nodded. "It's a risky enough venture."

"But profitable?" Tuan asked with a smile.

"'There is no gain without loss, and oft much loss without gain,'" Paedur quoted.

The Taourg raided the island designated on the charts as Tobb just before dawn two days later. But, although they entered the natural harbour under cover of darkness, with oars shipped and all lights doused, merely drifting in on the morning tide, the village which clustered around a crude freshwater well just off the shore was deserted.

Duaize ordered the island searched, but the scouting parties that were sent into the interior all returned empty-handed. It was as if the villagers had disappeared, and Duaize had to content himself with ordering the entire village to be levelled, but not burnt, for he did not wish a tell-tale plume of smoke rising to the heavens and perhaps attracting the curious.

Also, the village was not particularly rich in barrels and casks, and the Taourg had to content themselves with four large wooden barrels, which smelt strongly of fish, and two score small clay jars, which reeked of vinegar, sour wine, and cheese.

Back on board the *Duneson,* the captain had raged and threatened to raid another island on the morrow, and another the day following that—as many as he needed to until they had gathered enough containers for the Sleedor.

However, Paedur had pointed out that the more islands they raided the more certain it was that the presence of the Taourg would be made known, with the result that Imperial warships would soon infest these waters. The bard suggested that the ship's main hold, which ran almost the entire length of the *Duneson,* be emptied, and its interior tarred, turning it into one huge watertight container. Thus the Sleedor could be carried from Vosge in whatever containers they already had and emptied into the hold. He added that they were almost certain to find more casks on Vosge itself.

Duaize had grudgingly agreed, and the *Duneson* put in off one of the smaller Arrows for two days while the hold was emptied, the contents taken inland and concealed in a large cave, and the cave mouth sealed. When the Taourg had completed their business with Vosge and Ramm, they would return for their cargo.

Tarring the *Duneson* was a dirty, messy job, and soon the entire crew reeked of sulphur and pitch, and few escaped burns and scalds. However, when the mammoth task was complete, even Tuan, who had thought the idea unworkable, had to agree that it was the ideal solution to their problem, and that perhaps it just might work.

The *Duneson* then crept down the Arrows under cover of darkness; by day, they lay up in the sheltered bays of the smaller islets. Now that they were so close to their target, Duaize feared that a chance sighting of the distinctive Taourg ship with its triangular sail and snarling figurehead would bring the Imperial warships down on their heads.

And so, seventeen days after the sinking of the merchantman and the capture of the bard, the *Duneson* hove in sight of Vosge.

Dawn was breaking as the longboat beached on the rough Vosgean shore. The *Duneson* bobbed offshore, almost invisible against the night-dark sea and sky, stars still winking over its masts. Paedur, sitting in the bow of the longboat, gazed at the heavens where night was reluctantly giving way to day; the distinction was so sharp, he could almost trace the dividing line between the two. To the east the sky was ochre and gold, and the day promised to be both hot and dry.

There was a scraping of sand and gravel and the longboat shuddered. The four Taourg who had accompanied Tuan and himself jumped into the shallows and dragged the light craft up the shingle beach, stones and grit echoing against its sides, the sound shockingly loud in the dawn silence. Two of the Taourg then moved silently about the thin strip of beach, obliterating their own tracks and the gouge marks left by the boat in the shingle, while the others cut fronds from the encroaching forest to drape across their craft.

Paedur walked to the forest's edge and stared into the darkness. Dawn might be breaking behind them, but night still lingered within the fastness of the trees, and he doubted if the forest floor ever saw the full light of day.

The vegetation was subtropical for the most part, for the southern Arrows benefited from the 'sLanda Drift out of the Itican Gulf.
The two great islands further south, the Arrow Gates, Musen and
Forme, the Silver Rock and the Grain Bowl, were completely tropical both in climate and vegetation. However, the middle and upper
Arrows grew progressively temperate the farther north they went.

The forest growth stopped barely one man-length from the
water's edge, and consisted mainly of the small thick alm trees, which
clustered about the perimeter of the beach, while behind them were
the great laide trees that towered scores and sometimes hundreds of
man-lengths into the sky, their thin stick-like trunks suddenly sprouting thick fluffy heads as they broke into the sunlight.

Dense matted undergrowth grew throughout the alm trees, an
almost impassable barrier growing thickly back into the forest for
about one man-length, with wire-thin blood-vines and finger blossoms to the fore where they could catch the rays of the life-giving
sun that penetrated the forest edge. Farther in, however, the forest
floor was devoid of vegetation save for the faded albino creepers
that struggled upwards along the laide trunks and looped across
from tree to tree, creating a vast network of criss-crossing vines,
web-like in its complexity.

Tuan joined the bard at the forest's edge. He was swinging one
of the large-bladed Chopt knives. "I thought this might be handy,"
he said. "Which way?"

The bard pointed with his hook. "Straight on; the going gets
easier a little farther in."

Once they had hacked their way through the undergrowth with
the Chopt knives, and the forest floor opened out, Tuan became
aware of the absolute silence that hung over the forest. No birds
sang, nor were there any of the red-furred apes that usually infested
the southern Arrows. All the normal cries of the life and death hunt
of the forest beasts were absent, and even the crashing of the waves
was muted, as if they had passed through some veil that deadened
all sound.

The Taourg, too, sensed the unnatural silence and grew restive
and nervous, whispering uneasily amongst themselves, drawing closer
together, fingering their short-swords and crossbows. When they
reached a clearing, they stopped and looked to Tuan for direction,
and he in turn looked to the bard.

Paedur silently raised his left arm and, hook flashing dully in the light, pointed to the ground. "There's a track here; it's an animal run, but an old one."

The track meandered through the forest, but kept roughly to a northerly direction. Once, they sank to their ankles in soft green-brown muck that lay over the forest floor. It sucked noisily at their feet, exuding a foul choking miasma with each step they took. The muck clung to their boots, drying and hardening swiftly to a rock-like compound that weighted down each step, until they finally stopped and scraped it off. But, ominously, the thousands of miniature insects that should have fed on this rotting soup were absent.

It was as if the entire forest was dead.

Suddenly, the vague trail they had been following broke out into a broad uncluttered track—a road almost—that crossed their present route at right angles. Gesturing to the Taourg to remain where they were, Paedur stepped onto the road, and then knelt to examine the surface. Tuan joined him. "What is it?" he asked, gesturing to the flat almost glass-like smoothness of the surface of the trail.

The bard tapped it with his hook. "It's compressed earth. Look, you can make out the leaves and twigs—it's as if some great weight had passed over it. And see here, where the road curves upwards at the edge of the forest..." He pointed upwards. "There also..." The trees on either side of the pathway curved away from the road, interlocking branches overhead cut through with the same cylindrical design. Those closest to the road looked unhealthy, bare of both bark and leaves. The bard stood and gazed down the roadway, and he suddenly got the impression of a great tunnel. He beckoned to Tuan. "What do you think?" He nodded to the strange roadway.

The first mate looked down the length of the road and turned to look back along it, and then he called over Shode, who had been born and raised in the jungles of Rrank.

"Do you know what made this?" he asked, and was troubled to find his voice shook as he spoke.

The small pale-haired Rrankish tribesman swelled with his own importance, and began to bob back and forth on his heels. "I like it not, sir, I'll tell you straight. To me—and I am experienced in these matters, as much as you are or the captain is in matters of the sea—well, to me this has the look of a beast run. And I'll tell you further, I've yet to see the beast that could make a run that allows three men to stand abreast on it. And I'll tell you further, I don't think I'd like to meet that beast." He shook his head violently. "No sir, I would not."

"Say nothing of this to the others," Tuan warned the strutting Shode as he dismissed him, and then he turned back to the bard, his eyebrows raised in question. But Paedur just shrugged and no word passed between them. Tuan called the Taourg from the forest and put them in formation along the track, two men on either side, close to the forest, with himself and the bard in the lead, in the centre of the trail.

The mate joined the bard at the head of the group and then waited until they had moved a little away from the Taourg. "Is it wise to follow this path? We could not hope to combat the beast that made this."

"I do not think it is a beast," the bard said quietly. "There is no beast odour."

"I can only smell the rotting vegetation," Tuan spat, "Ach, I can taste the filth."

"It's strange," Paedur mused; "there is...there is not only an absence of odour, but also of vibration, there is no lingering aura as there normally would be."

Tuan looked askance at the bard, his finger and thumb automatically meeting in a circle to ward off evil.

Paedur laughed softly. "You need not fear me, I am not evil; you fear me because I am not as you, because I am different. Perhaps you hate me; 'Hate and Fear are brothers in blood,' as the proverb goes. But know this, Tuan, I am not the Duaiteoiri you think me, nor am I *quai* either. It is true that I am not fully of the world of man, but nor am I yet fully beyond the call of man..."

"What are you then?" Tuan whispered, feeling the chill sweat trickle down the back of his neck, even though it was stifling in the forest.

"I truly don't know," Paedur said, sounding almost surprised. "I inhabit the twilight world between god and man; I am a little of both, and yet I am neither."

"Why do you tell me this?" Tuan asked.

The bard smiled slightly. "Because...because I feel you will understand, because I think you are not fully in accord with the Taourg, and because I urge you to consider what you are now, and what you might become."

Tuan nodded slowly. "I have already considered that, but I will think about what you have said. And you can see what men cannot?" he asked, pointing to the trees.

"Aye, I can see beyond the physical," the bard explained. "All my senses are more highly attuned than those of man. You see—but I perceive."

Tuan nodded slowly. He was unsure just how far to trust the bard, how much to believe what he said. They knew not what awaited them on the island, they were facing the unknown, but Paedur was an unknown quantity also. And he wondered which was the more dangerous: the island or the bard.

"What do you see here?" he asked finally.

"I see nothing. No, that's not true. I can see a lack of life. This is a dead area; furthermore, it has but lately died. Something passed by, probably that which created the pathway and leached the life from this part of the forest. And not only the life but the very essence of life, therefore preventing any hope of further growth. Nothing will ever grow upon this path, the forest will never reclaim this wound through its heart."

Paedur stooped suddenly and, with his hook, cut a thin sliver of the compressed leaves and twigs that composed their path. He crumbled the hard earth between the finger and thumb of his right hand, and then licked the dry, gritty dust.

Tuan stared, appalled.

"This land is poisoned," Paedur spat, "doubtless the rivers also. In time the entire island will die and become a barren waste. Warn your men not to eat any fruit they may find nor drink from any stream; should they be wounded, or even be scratched by a thorn for that matter, ensure that the wound is cleaned immediately, and that no dirt enters the cut." He brushed his hand on his cloak and then, as if chilled, drew the cloak in around his shoulders. "The sooner we leave this island, the better."

As the mate passed on the bard's instructions, Paedur continued on down the trail, pausing every hundred paces or so to test the soil, still seeking some tiny pulse of life. But there was none.

The trail abruptly opened into a small circular clearing, surrounded on three sides by the forest and on the fourth by a slight rocky incline leading up to the slopes of the smouldering volcano that dominated the centre of the island.

Deserted tumbledown reed huts and the remnants of a log palisade littered the clearing. The forest had made some effort to reclaim the clearing, and the huts on its periphery were little more than
shapeless mounds of dried grass pierced through by thin shoots of
a dull leprous yellow growth. The huts in the centre of the clearing,
that clustered about the blackened remains of what must once have
been the communal fire, were larger and in better condition.

The pathway they were following cleaved right through the village, through two of the huts and out again into the forest beyond in
a straight line. The two huts were flattened into the ground, the only
evidence of their existence were the gaps in the circle of huts and the
lighter coloration of the ground beneath where the pale straw had
been crushed.

Tuan called Shode over. "How long ago was this village abandoned?"

The Rrankish tribesman bobbed back and forth on his heels,
twirling his long moustaches. "Well now, I really couldn't be sure.
Six moons certainly but no more, I'll wager. And I wouldn't say it
was abandoned, no, not abandoned. More likely deserted, suddenly
like. You see those stakes," he pointed to the listing palisade that at
one time had encircled the village, "stakes like those; now they're not
easy to come by. Blunt plenty of knives and axes in the sharpening
of them. Now back home, when we moved camp, we took our
stakes with us; when we got to a new place—rich pasture and the
like—we just banged them down. These folk, though, they were in
a hurry, else they would have been sure to take them with them.
Strange, now I come to think of it," he added, looking around,
"strange they didn't come back for them. Unless, of course, there
were none left alive to come back."

Tuan nodded. "Aye, my thoughts too. Remember, say nothing to the men," the mate's voice was flat and emotionless. He
turned to the bard. "I don't think we should go any further, Paedur.
I fear neither man nor beast, but we've no idea what sort of creature we're chasing."

The bard stared across the island, his eyes dark and hooded. "I
don't know either," he murmured, "but whatever it is, it is destroying this island." He looked over his shoulder at Tuan. "And when
Vosge can no longer support it, where will it go then? No," he
shook his head, "it must be destroyed."

"How?" Tuan protested. "It must be enormous, but beyond that we know nothing at all about it."

"I think it must be connected in some way with the Sleedor pools. There are traces of Sleedor along this track; perhaps if the pools were destroyed, then the creature would die also."

"Did you know about this creature when you suggested that we come here?" the mate asked suddenly, "did you come here for a purpose...?"

Paedur smiled. "No. But the gods move men such as myself to their bidding, as you would move the stones on a gaming board. It may be that they ordained that the *Duneson* should sink that merchantman, and thus capture me, therefore precipitating this venture."

Tuan looked uncomfortable. "I don't know," he said finally, "but it's true that I've never known the captain to spare an obviously poor prisoner before—no male prisoner, that is. If we're not within a day's sail of a slave market then they're usually slain out of hand. And he went along with your plan with little objection; a plan which, in my opinion, is foolhardy in the extreme." He suddenly shivered. "It chills me to think that, even now, the gods may be watching us, directing our actions, and all to some obscure purpose of their own."

But the bard shook his head. "No, never to their own purpose—but man's. Their duty is to us, their worshippers. Should we cease to exist, so too would they. For remember the old commandment, *'Faith lends Substance.'* So, you can rest assured, our mission on this island can only be for the greater good of man."

Two crewmen who had scouted the deserted village returned and stood before Paedur and the mate. "What did you find?" Tuan asked.

"The pathway continues off into the forest and thence downwards into a depression. We did not follow it there," one said, and then the second man took up the report in the same expressionless monotone. "There is another path leading upwards, there," he pointed back towards the incline. "It is overgrown and has not seen recent use. It leads to the mountain."

Tuan looked to the bard. "Which way?"

Without hesitation, Paedur chose the left-hand path, leading upwards.

The track wound up through entangled undergrowth, interwoven with stout vines, and Tuan had to caution the men against using their knives on the creepers, after the bard had severed one with a swing of his hook only to result in the earth beneath shifting and crumbling away. It seemed as if the creepers were actually holding the dry flaking rocks and soil together. Farther up the slope, the vegetation thinned out and the going became easier. Soon they found themselves on a rocky trail winding up the mountainside. The forest on their right-hand side gradually fell away, until they were level with the heads of the feathery laide trees, and even these in time fell below them. To their left, the black volcanic mountain rose dark and threatening, pitted and scored with thousands of tiny cracks and rough-edged holes. Here and there hardy rock plants struggled for existence in some soil-covered corner.

The trail they were following gradually thinned down to a cinder ledge which crumbled in places, and this gave way to a thin strip of soft cinder rock and gravel barely a handspan across. Ahead, the ledge narrowed and rounded a bend in the rock.

They could go no further.

Paedur, who was leading, turned back to Tuan. "I will go on. Around that bend the path broadens out on to a ledge from which I can look down onto the Sleedor pools."

"How do you kno...No," he raised one hand, "I believe you. Will the path support my weight?" he asked, looking doubtfully at the crumbling strip of blackened cinders.

"I think not. However you might climb around to the ledge." He pointed. "Up there and across. It would be difficult, but I think Duaize would like to have one of his own men report back to him. I am sure it would be better received than just my word." Paedur looked up along the rough rockface, sparkling with many-faceted crystals. "It would be a difficult climb; would you make it?"

"Bard," Tuan laughed, "I was born in Moghir, to the north and west of here, in Gallowan. I climbed cliffs like these before I was weaned."

"Aye, perhaps." The bard sounded doubtful. "Well, I will meet you on the ledge on the far side. Try to make as little noise as possible. Although this forest looks dead and deserted, I'm sure our presence here has already been noted. Be careful."

Paedur turned and moved forward, swiftly, almost carelessly, cinders of blackened rock crumbling under his boots to fall hundreds of man-lengths into the trees below. The ledge almost disappeared as it rounded the corner onto the far side. Paedur placed one foot onto the path, sliding it gently along the strip, his long fingers almost delicately seeking a hold in the gritty rockface. He edged forward, pressed flat against the cliff, his face turned away from Tuan.

There was a crack, and then suddenly the ledge crumbled into fine black dust. Tuan cried a warning but it was drowned in the echoing roar of the rockslide as a whole section of the cliff face fell. The Taourg cowered back, coughing and choking on the fine grit. The bard had disappeared into a maelstrom of flying rocks and billowing dust. Boulders tore down into the forest below, crushing through the trees to bury themselves in the soft ground beneath.

As swiftly as it had begun, the rockslide stopped, the final rocks seeming to take forever to clatter off into the distance.

The black volcanic cinders gradually settled back onto the remains of the ledge, but the thin path on which the bard had been standing had disappeared.

And of the bard Paedur there was no sign.

9
Quisleedor

Daily this cursed hookhanded bard grows more dangerous. The crew fear him or respect him—it is one and the same. I would kill him, if I could afford to, but we need him for a little while longer...
Journal of Duaize, Captain of the Duneson, Taourg Corsai

The bard was dead!

Tuan breathed deeply, consciously loosening his grip which had tightened in shock on the rockface. He blinked dust from his eyes and spat, clearing his mouth and throat of the sharp gritty cinders. Looking down over the edge of the track, he could see a billowing cloud of dust in the forest below, marking the bard's grave.

The bard was gone—no one could have survived that rockslide—and though he regretted his passing, Tuan had long ago learned not to mourn the dead. He would, however, send his men into the forest below to search for the body and give it a proper burial. He felt in some way as if he owed the enigmatic bard that much.

The small Rrankish tribesman stepped up beside him. He was brushing dust from his hair and there was a swelling under his right eye.

Tuan glanced at him, and then nodded to the bruise. "Anyone else hurt?"

"Cuts and bruises, sir, cuts and bruises. Nothing serious. The bard...?"

Tuan shook his head.

"What do we do now?" Shode asked.

Tuan ran his fingers through his hair and beard. "Duaize will want a report," he said, tilting his head back and looking up along the cliff, "and the bard did say that there was a ledge on the other side which looked down on the black pools..."

Shode looked up, and then glanced down into the forest below. "It's a long climb—and an even longer fall," he remarked.

"I know. Shode, take the men back down the trail and search the forest there," he pointed to where the pall of dust still hung in the air, "and try to find the body of the bard. Bury it and then wait for me in that deserted village. Conceal yourselves and make no contact with the islanders. I will go back up the path and attempt to climb over to the ledge mentioned by the bard."

"How long should I wait?"

"Until nightfall; if I'm not back by then, well then…then head back for the *Duneson,* and tell Duaize what happened here."

Tuan waited on the path while the Rrankish tribesman led the three Taourg back down into the forest, and then he turned to face the black volcanic mountain once again. He shivered, for though it was drawing on for mid-morning and the sun rode high in a cloudless sky, this side of the mountain was still in shadow and harboured the early morning chill, and the bleak face of the volcano only served to enforce that chill.

He started back up the path to the point where the bard had disappeared. He would have to climb up two or three lengths, and then crawl across the rockface for another three lengths; then he would have to manoeuvre around the sharp angle to bring himself out on to the far side. Shaking his head slightly, Tuan spat onto his hands, found footholds and fingerholds and levered himself up.

Though he had boasted to the bard of his climbing prowess, his ascent up the rockface proved more difficult than he had imagined. The volcanic rock should have presented no difficulty to an experienced climber; the countless fissures and breaks in the cliff face were ideal handholds and footholds. However, the rock was, for the most part, blanketed beneath a thick layer of powdered black ash that soon coated his hands and boots with a slippery gritty skin that prevented a sure grip. The rock was also diamond sharp in places, and fire-hardened splinters of stone gouged and tore at his fingers and hands. Several times the rock crumbled beneath his feet, leaving him pressed desperately against the jagged cliff face while dust and rocks rained down all around him. By the time he reached the bend in the cliff, he was coated in ash and blood, his shoulders and arms ached, and the open wounds on his hands stung with every hold he took. Tuan dimly recalled Paedur's warning about getting dirt or dust in a wound. He looked at his hands, and then at the streaks of thickened blood that marked his path up and across the cliff face. "Too bloody late now," he muttered.

As he rounded the bend in the cliff, the sun's rays struck him full in the face, blinding him. Desperately he squeezed his eyes shut, still seeing the orange disc through his clenched lids. And then the rock shifted. He froze to the cliff face, knowing that any movement could send him flying back off the mountainside to the forest below.

When the dancing lights in his skull dimmed, he opened his eyes, blinking away the tears, and taking care only to look at the rocks under his lacerated hands he began to move again. He shifted his handholds to chunks of the darker, harder rock, wincing as they cut into his raw flesh, and then he gently eased his way over the bend in the rock. Every movement sent stones and gravel rattling off the rockface beneath his feet. With the sun now warming his back, he climbed down the remaining man-length on to the broad ledge below. His questing foot found the reassuring width of rock and he collapsed exhausted onto the ledge, gently cradling his torn hands across his body, sobbing with relief.

But he knew he would never be able to make the climb back over to the other side.

He cursed the bard then for a fool, a madman, a crazed tale-spinner. He cursed the captain for listening to such crazed advice; he cursed himself for following it. They must have been bewitched, ensorcelled by that bard, that Duaiteoiri...Tuan's head began to nod and, as his vision darkened, his thoughts became more and more confused, dream and nightmare running together, with the bard flickering wildly in and out of both...he was a creature of Alile the Judge Impartial, come to pass judgment on the Taourg in general and himself in particular...was he a minion of the Destroyer, Maurug, or was he just Mannam, Death, in one of his many guises...? Finally, he drifted off into a feverish troubled sleep.

Tuan felt the shadow that fell over him while still sleeping. The nightmares shifted and twisted, and now an immense furred black creature swung a huge scythe closer and closer to his face...

He awoke, his heart pounding raggedly, echoing the pulse in his throat and at his temples...and he focused on a pair of scuffed boots before his face. His heart almost stopped. Forcing himself to remain still, he took stock of his situation. He was alone on a broad shelf of rock, facing an unknown number of potential foes. He was armed with short-sword—no, he had left that behind in a cleft in the rock on the far side of the cliff, as it had proved too cumbersome. He was armed then only with one of the broad-bladed Chopt knives. Against that, his hands were cut and torn, and they had now stiffened; he doubted he would be able even to hold a knife. His shoulder muscles had locked and there was no feeling in his legs, for he had fallen asleep with them tucked under him. He wasn't sure if they would support him...perhaps he could suddenly push the figure off the ledge, but even if he rolled against the legs...

He stopped, realising he was contemplating suicide.

He opened his eyes a fraction again and peered between gummed lashes. Black boots, scuffed and torn as if they had climbed rock; brown trousers tucked into the boots, and a purple-lined furred cloak fluttering between the legs...

And Tuan knew of only one...

Abruptly he pushed himself to his feet and found he was staring into Paedur's hooded face! And then with a cry he pitched forward as his numbed legs refused to support him. The bard caught him under the arms and eased him to the ground.

"Gently, gently now," he murmured, "you've been hurt."

Tuan shook his head, trying to clear it, then groaned aloud as pain lanced about his eyes and into his skull.

"I'll wager you never climbed a mountain like that before you were weaned," Paedur said with a sly smile, taking both the mate's torn hands in his right hand and examining them closely.

Tuan groaned again and licked his dried lips with a tongue that felt twice its normal size and was coated with foul grit. "I thought you were dead," he croaked.

"Aaah, no," Paedur smiled wistfully, "the god-sought, god-bought do not die so easily. Besides, Mannam and I do not care overmuch for each other's company."

The mate shivered. Paedur spoke of the gods with an all too easy familiarity, as if they were real and he had met them. And what was even more frightening was that it was very easy to believe he had. Perhaps he was mad, but if he were mad and touched by the Nameless God of Madness, then surely that self-same god was even now enfolding the mate within his gelatinous paws.

"You're cold?" Paedur asked, unclasping his cloak.

Tuan shook his head vigorously, even though he felt as if his skull were about to burst with each movement. He didn't want the bard to bring his furred cloak anywhere near him; his nightmare image of a furred, scythe-wielding creature was still fresh.

Paedur looked from the man to the cloak and laughed softly, almost chidingly. "You still fear me, you think me either devil or madman, or both. But I am neither." His voice dropped and he seemed to look beyond the man lying on the rock. "At one stage I feared that I was both; but I little realised what I had become then and what I was destined to become." He shook his head, dismissing the memories. "Now, your hands." He took Tuan's right hand in his and stared intently at the wounds. There was a stab of pain and the mate tried to jerk his hand back, but the bard's long fingers tightened, holding it firm, his strength surprising. "No, leave it." His hard gaze caught and held Tuan's eyes. "If your hand is not cleaned and healed, you will not make it back to the *Duneson.*" Tuan looked at his lacerated hands, encrusted with grit and volcanic ash. Already a pale fluid was seeping along the edges of the wounds.

"Do whatever you have to," he muttered.

Paedur produced a handful of leaves, plucked from the few bushes that clustered about the sun-warmed ledge, and proceeded to wipe off the encrusted blood and dirt that covered the mate's hands.

He then spat on to the edge of his cloak and cleaned the wounds themselves, forcing them to bleed, wiping off the blood and dirt with his cloak. Then, holding the mate's right hand in his, he gently ran his hook over the open cuts. As the tip of the silver half-moon scraped along the wounds the skin burned, and then it seemed to flow, to melt. Tuan squeezed his eyes shut and clenched his teeth to keep from crying aloud as cold slivers of pain shot through his arm and chest. With an effort he forced his hand to remain in the bard's. Then the pain began to lessen, gradually dying off to a dull throbbing. When he opened his eyes, he found that the skin of his palm was criss-crossed with thick white lines, like half-healed scars.

"You must brace yourself now," Paedur said calmly, placing his hook flat across the mate's open palm. Tuan nodded, and then felt the hook grow warm, pleasantly so at first, and then gradually becoming hotter and hotter, until it was almost unbearable. Sweat ran down his face, and he tasted blood in his mouth where he had bitten into the soft skin of his inner cheek. Suddenly the hook blazed intolerably, and he almost screamed aloud with the pain.

He took a shuddering breath, almost expecting to taste scorched flesh on the air, and opened his eyes, expecting to see his skin seared and crisped. But the air remained clean; and when he looked at his hand again, it was whole, complete even down to the callouses that ridged the base of his fingers and the ball of his thumb. All traces of his wounds were gone.

Silently, Paedur took Tuan's left hand, and began the process again, first cleansing the wounds, then drawing the skin together and healing the scars. But this time, Tuan thought the hook didn't burn his flesh so strongly. Even so, it was agonisingly painful. But once again his hand was whole. His breathing was ragged and he wiped sweat from his face, but when he began to thank the bard, Paedur raised his hook, stopping him.

"You have seen a measure of my power—word of which I would not like to have bandied about this ship. You will say nothing of this..." It could have been a plea or a threat.

Tuan nodded, holding both hands up to his face, examining the flesh, and he assured Paedur of his silence. He was about to stand up when Paedur pushed him back. "We will remain here for a short while. Stay alert; watch the skies for anything unusual. A cloud, a bird, aught that you consider...unnatural."

"What am I looking for?" Tuan asked.

"I'm not sure."

"What...what could come?" Tuan persisted, "and where would it come from?"

Paedur stared out over the forest, looking into the sky. "It would be one of the Trialdone, a sending of Trialos, the Usurper. They might come, if they caught the disturbance."

"Disturbance?"

"I healed your hands by using the natural power from the place-between-the-planes, the Shadowlands, the Ghost Worlds. Any use of the Power, even such a minor draining of the Ghost Worlds, disturbs them with ripples, like a stone dropped into a pool. For those of human-kind with the Sight and Hearing, such uses of Power are noticeable, recognisable as a momentary chill, a shudder, or an overwhelming sensation that someone is looking over your shoulder. However, the non-humans, the gods and demons, lesser gods and spirits are very sensitive to the changes in the Shadowlands, and if they are curious, they might decide to investigate." He rose on one knee and scanned the skies. "I hope not. A Sending might warn whatever lurks below of our presence."

"You mean because you used your power to heal me, that could have warned these others of our presence here?" Tuan asked.

"Yes."

"But what are these others, these Trialdone, and why should they seek you out?"

"Oh, they would investigate any major use of Power, but it would be an added bonus for them if they could find me."

"What would they do?" Tuan asked quietly.

"Kill me—or try to."

"I'll fight for you," Tuan said quickly.

Paedur laughed. "Well, let's hope it doesn't come to that. What power I drew off was small, it would barely register in the Ghost Worlds, and hardly worth the effort on their part to trace it."

"But how would they go about doing that?"

"First they would have to assure themselves that it is not one of their own people working; then they would have to quest through the rough and shifting greyness of the Shadowlands to track the disturbance to its source. Then they would have to open a window to this place and only then might they act."

"What will we do if something comes?" Tuan asked anxiously.

"If something should come..." he shrugged. "Well, although I might be put to defend myself, I should survive, I think. But you..." he shook his head slowly, "I think not."

Tuan drew his knife. "Any lizard-winged Duaiteoiri that tries..." He stopped as Paedur began laughing.

"Sit, Tuan, sit. If they send anything, then rest assured that it will not try to take us by force of arms. You will not find yourself fighting a creature of flesh and blood. Probably the volcano will erupt, or this ledge will disappear in a landslide into the forest below; a storm will sweep us off the ledge, or we shall be struck by lightning—or something equally unlikely."

"That's not very reassuring," Tuan said, with a wry smile.

"But it's the truth," Paedur said gravely.

Tuan crouched down again, looking up at the cone above their heads, watching the sky for any hint of cloud and the sea for any creature or disturbance—anything that might herald the coming of the Trialdone.

But the volcano remained quiet and the sky retained its bleached metallic white-blue appearance, completely devoid of cloud, and the sea was calm, the waves broken by nothing other than the reflection of the sun's rays.

Gradually, he relaxed. "Will anything come?"

Paedur shook his head. "Not now. If they were coming, they would have been here by now. Perhaps the Trialdone have other things to think of, and tracking through the Ghost Worlds is exhausting, both mentally and physically," he added, almost to himself.

They sat in silence for a while, the bard with his back to the warm stone, his head bent, while Tuan knelt and examined his healed hands in fascination. Finally Paedur, rousing himself from his reverie, looked up, catching the mate's eye, and nodded to the edge of the cliff. He dropped down flat and crawled to the edge of the outcropping of stone. Lying full length on the rock, he parted the stunted thorn bushes that grew in the soft earth at the edge and pointed to the forest below. Tuan joined him.

"The Sleedor pools of Vosge," the bard whispered.

There was a dry withered scrubland at the base of the cliff; diseased leprous bushes and trees that had rotted where they stood ringed a long deep bowl-shaped depression. In the centre of this bowl lay a vast shimmering black pool, surrounded by four smaller pools. Strange lights glinted within the pools and rainbow colours swirled lazily in wide swaths through the blackness. Otherwise, there was no movement, and the pools neither eddied nor rippled in the stiff offshore breeze. A strange vapour, like a heat shimmer, hung over the main pool, and this, too, seemed to be unaffected by the breeze. It was visible only in its distortion of the forest beyond. The four minor pools were connected to the larger pool by thin tendrils of the black Sleedor, which ran like shadows across the ground in short thin canals. The sun, now at its zenith, burned almost at the centre of the main pool, reflecting back in a strange, blue-green-white colour that dazzled the eyes—and lent the pool the appearance of a huge staring eye.

Grouped about the black pools were the ruins of a once sizable town, built in what must have been a series of concentric circles. With the main pool at the centre, the lines of the streets and remains of the encircling buildings were still clearly visible. In places whole sections of houses and streets remained standing, which managed to convey an impression of its former grandeur. As far as Tuan could see there were no signs that the town had been either attacked or sacked, and he got the impression that it had just been allowed to fall into ruin.

One building, however, larger than the rest, appeared to be in better repair. It stood almost on the edge of the main pool, a tall greenstone building, its massive blocks and mortar-less construction betraying its Culai origin, unlike the rest of the buildings which had been built some time later. However, it was surmounted by an elegant spiral, the top of which had been sheared off. That must have been a later addition, Tuan reflected, since the architecture of the First Race had no room for useless ornamentation. He also noted that a rough door and two equally crude windows had been broken into the side of the building, which led him to speculate whether the building—a temple obviously—was occupied or not.

The bard gestured with his hook towards the building. "See there; that was once Culai-hewn, but the additions were made by the Vosgeans. The spire, that was never Culai-built…but even so, it is old, crafted when the pools first made their appearance in the distant past, back when there were still craftsmen in the world. The Cult of Sleed were the first to settle on the island when they heard of the pools; they commissioned the spire from the native islanders."

"The door and windows are even more recent," Tuan said. "There are still blocks of greenstone about the pools. But one thing is puzzling me. Where are the original doors and windows?"

Paedur parted the bushes and pointed to a cube of blank stonework. "Look closely. Almost at ground level you can just about see the top of the lintel. See where the blocks are shaped…"

The mate nodded. "The buildings are sinking!"

"Aye, and the main temple more swiftly than the others because of its proximity to the pool. The Vosgeans have broken open the doors and windows for whoever plays priests to the…to that which lives in the pools."

Tuan pointed to the blackened streaks that covered the green-stone walls of the buildings. "It looks as if the pools covered the building at one stage," he said.

The bard nodded. "Perhaps; and there is something rather unusual about this place—the buildings are older than the island."

"That's impossible!"

Paedur smiled. "Not really. You will find examples of Culai architecture on nearly every one of the Arrows. And if you should examine the seas about some of the larger islands, you may be able to see the outline of stone walls and roads on the sea bed. What is now sea was once dry land. The Culai built on it; then the land sank and was covered by the seas. Then, some thousands of years ago, during the Upheaval caused by the Demon Wars in the Southern Kingdoms, the shock waves rippled through the planes of life. On most planes there was wholesale destruction, but on others the land rose—such as it did here, creating the Arrow Isles. Some of them still had the Culai-built temples and roads which went down with them in the Cataclysm. Indeed, I have heard it said that the Arrows run along the site of an ancient road, the remains of which can be seen from the Musen Causeway. When the islands were settled by the fanatics, the fools and the gutter-scrapings of the Seven Nations, they either used the ancient buildings themselves, or took the dressed stones to build dwellings of their own."

"I've often wondered about the massive stone temples and fortresses that stand isolated and forlorn on islands scattered among the oceans of the world," Tuan mused, "and of those mariners' tales which tell of cities and lights beneath the waves, and of bells that toll in the night far out at sea."

"Aye," Paedur said, "the Culai left us many strange and terrible relics of their time. 'The Culai Heritage,' I've heard it called by some..."

"Their day is done, their time is passed, let none mourn their passing," quoted Tuan from an ancient proverb of his homeland.

"No," Paedur whispered, "It is not finished yet; the age of the Culai still lingers. But soon...soon, it will end," he prophesied. His eyes suddenly blazed and the air about him seemed to chill. He looked at Tuan, and his expression was hard and frightening, and he opened his mouth as if he were about to speak, but then he turned away in silence. He pointed down to the temple by the pool. "See there, they worship dangerously."

Tuan looked over the ledge. Above the rough wooden door of the temple, set into a rusted sword scabbard, a reed torch burned, the flame sputtering smokily, yellow, blue and green, glowing sparks spiralling to the heavens. "What's wrong?" he wondered out loud.

"On no account bring fire near to the pools." He gripped the mate's arm for emphasis. "The liquid burns far stronger than fish-oil." Tuan nodded and rubbed his arm where the bard's iron-hard fingers had bitten into it, bruising the flesh.

Then, faint in the distance, a low murmuring began, rising and falling like the waves on the seashore, an ebb and flow of sound. It had the cadence of a chant, such as is sometimes sung in the great cathedrals of the Nations, but it was wordless, a mere droning on two levels. It drew nearer, and Tuan and the bard were able to make out other sounds—low whistles and guttural cries—that ran through the chant.

"It's coming from over there," Tuan said, pointing off to the right, the east, to where the diseased scrub had been pushed back to form a path. He loosened his knife in its sheath.

There was a hoarse shout, and the chanting suddenly stopped, and silence once more fell over the forest. Paedur gripped the mate's arm again and whispered. "No matter what happens, remain hidden. They must not know they are being watched."

There was movement along the track, and then four white-robed figures stepped into the clearing. They were small dark-skinned men, and although their features were almost indistinguishable from that distance, Tuan thought they were Formenai, from the southernmost Arrows. Their robes had once been white, but were now soiled, encrusted with thick deposits of matted filth, and streaked with what looked like Sleedor stains. They moved slowly through the ruins of the Culai settlement, threading their way around the shattered remnants of the once massive palaces and temples along a pillar-lined route. When they reached the main building with its shattered spire, they stopped and bowed thrice to the guttering flame, and bowed again as they faced each of the four smaller pools, before turning back to the great pool in front of the large building.

Behind the priests came a small band of warriors. These were native Vosgeans, being taller, more robust than the priests, with lighter skin and straight hair. They were heavily armed with short spears and throwing clubs, and some had metal knives and axes. They wore armour of overlapping scales of lacquered wood, which gleamed with the same shimmer as the pools. Tuan quickly counted six of the warriors, and wondered why they needed weapons in this seemingly deserted place.

Then another larger group came down the withered track. Tuan suddenly swore and had begun to move when the bard pressed him flat, holding him down seemingly with no effort. "Stay down," he hissed, and then Tuan felt a strange dizziness sweep over him, and a tingling in his limbs. When the bard released him, Tuan attempted to rise, but he found his arms and legs were numb and useless. He could only watch in anguish as the four Taourg from the *Duneson* were dragged forward. They must have been captured in the village, he realised, and by trickery, too, since they seemed uninjured. He should have sent Shode and the others back to the ship; but it was too late now.

The Taourg were herded forward by six more warriors. They had been shackled with manacles of what looked like stone, and were led forward by leashes of heavy metal links about their necks. Like *cuine* to the slaughter, Tuan thought, and shivered. They were separated when they reached the periphery of the pools, where the twelve guards broke up into four groups of three, each group taking one of the Taourg pirates to stand by the edge of the smaller pools.

When the prisoners were positioned before the Sleedor pools, the robed priests moved forward and, with arms raised high, began to chant in a shrill whistling tongue, totally unlike their earlier chanting. Simultaneously, one warrior from each of the four groups stepped up to the black water and dipped a spear into its glittering, glistening depths. They moved the spears back and forth in a deliberate weaving pattern, setting up a spectacular display of shifting lights beneath the surface. When they lifted their spears, they held them poised over the pools until the priests hurried over to them, each with a curiously worked metallic vessel, which they held under the spear points in order to catch the droplets of the precious liquid.

The four priests then turned and faced the temple, bowing deeply, the metal bowls held high in both hands. Something moved in the darkness of the crude doorway. The flame in the scabbard above the door flickered wildly as if torn by a strong breeze. Then a figure stepped out. He was tall, inhumanly so, and had to stoop almost double coming through the door. His skin was black, though not with the warm browns or soft blacks of the southern Arrows, nor with the deeper shades of the Teouteuchalai further south, but in a deep matte black almost the same colour as the Sleedor. His features were indistinguishable, though Tuan had the impression that they were sharp and angular; and when he opened his mouth to speak his teeth shone long and glistening white in the blackness of his face. His voice was slightly sibilant but sharp and piercing, the tongue that of the priests. When he raised his arms, his robe—a long white garment interwoven with black, silver and gold thread— slipped down his forearms, revealing a series of long sinuous tattooed curves that winked and sparkled in the sun, as if they had been worked in metal rather than ink. His fingers were tipped with long pointed nails, painted like a courtesan's with a black lacquer.

While the High Priest had been reciting, an absolute stillness had fallen over the priests, warriors and prisoners alike. They stood as if carved from stone, and Tuan wondered if they had been frozen by some magic, similar to that which the bard had worked on him.

The bard glanced over at him. "Our power is similar, and yet dissimilar," he whispered, "for his aura is etched with evil. He controls a far darker power than mine, in keeping with his Gorge-spawned gods. Watch!" he hissed.

Below, the High Priest had finished his incantation.

Almost at once the pools became agitated, the disturbance starting with the main pool, and spreading outwards in slow languid waves. Large rainbow-hued bubbles rose to the surface of the pools, bursting with a noxious rotting odour. It was as if some great creature stirred and awoke in the depths.

And then the High Priest screamed a single word, bringing his hands together in an explosive clap. Immediately, those warriors whose spears still glistened with steaming Sleedor, stepped forward, bowed to the High Priest, then stabbed the four Taourg through the back, pushing until the spear-points protruded through their breasts. Then the Taourg, still impaled on the spears, were pushed into the pools.

The black liquid boiled furiously, the disturbance flowing in towards the main pool this time. Light exploded in cascading streamers within the pools, flaring and then dying slowly, and there was the sudden stench of charred meat. The slow waves gradually subsided as they rolled inwards, swirling as they entered the larger pool, as if caught in a whirlpool—but then, this too, quietened.

The priests and warriors bowed to the smiling High Priest, and began to make their way through the ruins back into the forest. The High Priest remained in the doorway for a while longer, his head bent as if in prayer, then he turned and ducked into his tumbledown temple. Curls of weed and leaves gusted across the surface of the pools, but there was no other movement.

And silence returned to the island.

The fish-oil lamp swayed gently to and fro, illuminating the captain's cabin with moving shadows that leapt from wall to wall, giving them an eerie semblance of life. Tuan recited the day's events tiredly, reporting only what he had seen and omitting any mention of his own injuries or the bard's magic.

He drank deeply from a mug of rofion, and his speech was slurred, though not with drunkenness. He was exhausted, a mind-numbing physical exhaustion that stemmed from what he had seen and experienced that day.

Following the sacrifice of the Taourg, and the disappearance of the priests and warriors, Paedur and the mate had remained on the ledge until the shadows had lengthened across the ruins below. The bard had held Tuan bound with his magic for a long time, fearing that the mate would have run amok below; Tuan couldn't forget the almost casual sacrifice of the Taourg and the delighted smile of the High Priest. He had raged at the bard, cursing him in every tongue he knew, damning him to the Netherworld, Gorge and Abyss and every torment he could think of. But through it all, Paedur had merely smiled, until finally a mocking voice had spoken deep within the mate's head, commanding sleep. When Tuan had awakened, it was already mid-afternoon and a chill breeze blew across the ledge, bringing with it the promise of rain. The bard had at some time pulled him back from the bushes until he was in the shadow of the cliffs and had lifted the binding spell, so he was able to move again.

The climb back over the rough jagged cliffs had not been as difficult as the mate had expected. He was refreshed by his enforced sleep, and the bard had the knack of finding natural hand-holds and footholds in the cliff face, and at times it seemed as if they almost walked over to the other side. When they started the climb, Tuan wondered how Paedur would fare with only one hand, but the bard used his hook adroitly, cutting handholds in the sharp cinder rocks with great skill. "You're good with that," Tuan said at one stage, when Paedur had stopped on a tiny outcropping to allow the mate to catch up. "And you've climbed before, I'll wager."

The bard held up his left arm and allowed the half-moon to catch the light. "Aye, I've grown accustomed to it—it's part of me now. And yes—I've climbed mountains before," he added, with a faintly mocking smile.

However, it was a hard exhausting climb, and when they had reached the other side Tuan's strength left him and he would have fallen had not the bard caught him. Paedur had supported him down the barren track through the village back to the beach.

They had been met on the shore by a boatload of Taourg that had sailed with orders from Duaize to search the island and bring back the crew of the first boat—or their bodies. Tuan had fallen into a fitful sleep as the Taourg rowed back to the *Duneson* through roughening seas. His mind had wandered in that half world between sleep and wakefulness, and he cried out more than once in terror at some waking nightmare that stalked him across the waves, until the bard had gently touched his forehead with his hook, and he had fallen into a deep dreamless sleep.

When the boat reached the *Duneson,* Tuan had awoken feeling refreshed, though he guessed that the bard had somehow bolstered his exhaustion with some reserves of strength, and he guessed he would pay for it later with complete collapse.

Duaize had been silent upon seeing only the two return, but had ordered them to be taken to his cabin, and food and drink brought. As Tuan gave his report, Duaize only broke the mate's monotone with the occasional questions; and though the captain drank a great deal from a delicately spun crystal goblet, he betrayed no dulling of his awareness, and his questions were always succinct and to the point.

When Tuan finished, Duaize remained silent for a time, and the mate dozed off in the heat of the cabin. At length the captain raised his head and looked at the bard, who had remained still and silent, neither drinking nor eating, sitting swathed in his hooded cloak, as one with the shadows.

"You're costing me dearly in men, bard. What happened on that island?" he said almost gently, though his eyes were hard.

"Something that has not occurred on this island for a long time. A blood-sacrifice to Quisleedor, the Life Child of Sleed."

The captain's knuckles whitened on the stem of his glass. "Explain yourself, bard."

"Quisleedor is the creature of the black pools, perhaps it even is the black water. It demands blood sacrifice, else it rises from the pools to ravage...*Aaah,*" he hissed in satisfaction, "that would account for the lifeless track through the forest. So, the creature has already risen..." his voice trailed off in contemplation.

"Bard, if I thought you knew of this Quis...Quis, Quisleedor, and did not tell me..." The stem of the goblet snapped between the captain's fingers.

"I knew of the pools, but not of the creature."

"Then how do you know of this Life Child?" Duaize snapped triumphantly.

"I am a bard," Paedur said simply. "And the creation of the Life Child is recounted in many of my tales. Listen, and I will tell you of the birthing of Quisleedor."

"Be brief then, for dawn fast approaches, and I intend to raid that island with first light, no matter what tale you tell, if for no other reason than to avenge my men. Sacrificed!" he spat. "No pirate will be sacrificed and lie unavenged while the Taourg still sail."

"Briefly then," Paedur said, "the tale of Quisleedor. A thousand years ago, in the Southern Kingdoms, there were those who contrived to worship neither the Old Faith nor the New Religion, but rather took as their gods those we call today the Demon Gods. Now these were not of this plane of existence, and their fashioning was neither by the One, nor the first Great Gods." He looked from under his cowl at the captain. "You understand these references?"

"Many men sail with the Taourg; many men and many faiths. I have sailed with the Taourg for almost thirty years, bard, and though I do not question a man's faith, as captain I must know a little of my crew's beliefs, for if they have served with honour, then, when their time comes, they should be hastened to their gods with all due ceremony. Aye, I know the legend of the Beginning and the creation of the Gods of the Pantheon. Continue."

Paedur nodded.

"The Demon Wars were fought on two levels, that of gods and men. And the fields of Ab-Apsalom ran with the ichor of the gods as the fields of men ran with blood. Now there was one of the Elder Gods of the Old Faith, by name Sleed, and he was the Maker of Mountains, and his day was done, for nearly all his work had been carried out in the early days of this plane.

"And so now he rested.

"Now there came a time when the battle went against the Pantheon, and they called upon all the Elder Gods for aid, and Sleed was one of these. But in the battle that followed, Sleed took a mortal wound and even the ministrations of Ochrann could not heal his wound, for the blade had been poisoned.

"Thus the dying Sleed came to the Arrows, which had risen up during the Upheavals, and spent the rest of his days in solitude before he died here. And when men came to Vosge they saw that his blood had poured forth over a rocky wasteland in large black pools—for the blood of the gods is not like that of men and differs in texture and colour.

"And those pools came to be worshipped as the blood of Sleed.

"However, there came a time, not long after the island was settled, when a beast roamed Vosge, destroying all in its wake, and where it had been was marked by total desolation and naught would grow there until the area had been cleansed with fire, and the soil replaced.

"And the Vosgeans traced the beast back to the Sleedor pools, and thus they reasoned that whatever lived in the black water must be the Child of Sleed, a child perhaps created by the death of the god, thus the Life Child of Sleed: Quisleedor.

"Furthermore, they found that if a sacrifice, a blood sacrifice, was offered regularly to the creature, it did not rise. And so the priesthood of Quisleedor came into being, but the High Priest was invariably of the Susuru, for they are not wholly of the race of man and can commune with the beasts without harm to themselves, and their special gift is the taming of all creatures, be they flesh and blood—or otherwise."

"The tall one, with the blackened skin and tattoos; he is of the Susuru?" Duaize interrupted.

"Aye," muttered the bard, and his voice sounded troubled. "He is Susurun; I had not thought any of that cursed race still lived. But to continue. Five or six generations ago the Sleedor pools disappeared almost overnight, and with them the Life Child also. The Cult of Sleed went the way of all godless faiths, and the native Vosgeans returned to their primitive animalistic beliefs. Now, during the time of Quisleedor, the priests had not allowed anyone to leave the island but only those duly approved by the High Priest, and even then they were chained to the island by the priests with bonds of *geasa* far stronger than iron. Thus the island regressed and the people inbred almost to barbarism and imbecility."

"And nothing more was heard of this Quisleedor?"

"Nothing. It was as if he had never been. But now it seems, with the re-emergence of the pools, the Life Child has awoken and with it the Cult..." the bard's voice trailed off. "But there is one thing I would like to know. Where did the Susurun come from?"

Duaize shrugged. "Who knows? Perhaps he is somehow linked to the creature in the pools. When it sleeps, he sleeps. Maybe we'll find out later." He paused and breathed deeply. "So, it seems there is a creature in the pool with a liking for flesh and blood that leaves a trail of desolation in its wake whenever it emerges from its hold, and all this is watched over by an inhuman High Priest?" Duaize summed up.

Paedur nodded absently.

"Somehow, bard, I do not think draining the pool is such a good idea. Ramm can wait a while longer. We must withdraw and draw up a plan. The creature must be lured from the pools. We'll need a...a...a net of some sort. No, not a net, a great cave perhaps ...aye, and we'll coat the insides with pitch, and we'll trap the creature, and then toss a torch inside." He nodded. "Aye, we'll sail for..."

"No!" The bard rose to his full height and glared down at the captain. "I have wasted enough time on this affair for you. I have but one moon to reach Maante, I cannot afford to delay any longer. Either you raid Vosge on the morrow or you sail for the Aangle Peninsula. It's a simple choice."

"Damn you," Duaize shouted, leaping to his feet and hurling the glass goblet at the bard. "No one tells me what I do on my ship."

The glass shattered on the bard's hook, the sound bringing Tuan awake. Still not fully conscious, he seemed to hear the bard's voice rumble around the room like distantly heard thunder, echoing within his head, powerful and commanding. "You, captain, will do as I say. And you will raid that island on the morrow because I wish to get another look at those pools, and the Susurun—particularly the Susurun. Then you will take me to Maante, and then—and only then—will you return to Ramm where you may sell your Sleedor— if you get any in the first place. Whether you get the black liquid tomorrow or not matters little to me; we are to sail from here on the evening tide. My mission is of the utmost importance. And should I fail, well then, Ramm will never need its fuel and you will have lost nothing. Have I made myself clear?" he demanded.

"We will raid Vosge for the Sleedor on the morrow, and we will sail for Maante with the late tide," Duaize replied woodenly.

"Just so," Paedur smiled, "just so."

10
The Burning of Vosge

*Four more men dead; perhaps the bard is a deiz—what the westerners call
a Duaiteoiri...*
                    Journal of Duaize, Captain of the Duneson, Taourg Corsair

Paedur parted the dead undergrowth and pointed across towards
the ruins surrounding the shimmering black pools. "That is the main
temple and as such is to be avoided. The guards will enter along the
path yonder and then take up positions about the four smaller pools.
So if you..."

"You need not tell me my job, Hookhand," the captain snapped,
though he was careful not to meet the bard's eyes. He felt uncomfortable being so close to the bard; his memories of the previous
night were hazy and indistinct, and their very unreality made him
nervous, convincing him that he had been spellbound. He could
recall talking with the bard following Tuan's report, but then...

When he had awoken the following morning, he had apparently given orders that Vosge was to be raided with the full complement of the *Duneson*'s fighting men. He had also given Suo-Ti
instructions to plot a course to Maante, following the raid—no
matter how it turned out. He could not, however, remember
giving those orders.

What could he do? He could not say he had been ensorcelled
by the bard again. No crew would respect a weak-willed man, and
a strong will, he imagined, should be able to resist any spell, so he
was trapped into following his own orders...

Duaize turned to Tuan. "Divide the men into five groups, one
to each of the four smaller pools, the other to guard this trail. Conceal the barrels and skins in the ruins, and then wait for my command." Tuan nodded briefly and disappeared back along the track.

The *Duneson* had beached under cover of darkness and Duaize
had led the crew ashore; carrying the casks and barrels with them.
Tuan and the bard had then led them along the path they had cut
through the forest the previous morning. When they reached the

strange dead track they paused while Paedur tested the ground. He looked up at the captain. "Men have passed this way late last night."

Duaize nodded silently, feeling the hairs at the base of his neck rising. He didn't know how the bard knew—nor did he want to.

When they came to the village, the captain had ordered the tumbledown huts searched. They were all empty, save one. It held the skeletons of two children; in both cases the skull had been shattered and the spine snapped across. The bones gleamed as if they had been polished, displaying not the yellow ivory of age but rather a bleached almost chalk-like appearance; like chalk, also, they crumbled at a touch.

The bard had then led them down the second of the two tracks leading out of the village, the right-hand path, following it to a curve in the forest, where the vegetation began to sicken and die. Soon the great trees were gone, and those that remained were spindly and diseased. The undergrowth paled, the rich greens of the deeper forest giving way to a pale yellow-green, and thence to a dried and seared grass-like weed that waved gently above their heads.

Soon they came to the first half-buried blocks of the Culai buildings that even in ruin towered above their heads. At one time the forest must have completely claimed them, hiding them beneath a thick carpet; but the vines and creepers were now dead and hung like old ropes from the walls. As they walked through the dead ruins, Paedur took Tuan by the arm and pointed to the side of one massive edifice. "Remember what I told you yesterday..." he said softly. Along one mortar-less seam clustered the rocklike remains of barnacles and sea urchins—proof that these buildings had once rested beneath the waves.

They continued on deeper into the ruins, moving towards the shattered spire of the temple.

The vegetation finally gave out as they neared the Sleedor pools, and now even the stones began to take on a scaled, flaky appearance, as if they too were rotting away. And while those buildings closest to the forest were still recognisable as having once been dwellings, those bordering the pools were merely chunks of ragged, misshapen stone.

Duaize began to mutter orders, and his men slipped away singly and in groups, taking up position around the pools. Paedur and the mate crept nearer to the main temple, seeking shelter where they

could behind the great huge tumbled blocks, flitting from shadow
to shadow across the open spaces, until they were almost directly
opposite the temple door.

"Will the Susurun not sense us?" Tuan asked, peering over the
rim of a shattered column of dressed stone.

Paedur pulled him back and the mate heard something like anger touch his usually calm voice. "Stay low; we cannot afford to be
caught now." He looked back across the desolate ruins, seeking any
sign of the concealed men. "No," he replied finally, "the priest will
not know we are here. He should still be concentrating on the creature and yesterday's sacrifices. Aye," he continued, seeing the mate's
puzzled stare, "he draws on the departing life essence of the sacrificed, taking it to himself, and thus prolonging his own life."

"Undead!" Tuan shuddered. *"Vampire;* we have them in my
homeland."

"Undead, yes, but not *vampire* of the blood-sucking type. He
feeds upon emotional energy."

"I'll kill him," Tuan spat, "leeching the living like a damned
parasite."

The bard laughed softly, almost mockingly. "You? Impossible!"

Tuan opened his mouth to reply, but the bard raised his hand.
"No, Tuan, don't even think of it. The Susurun would blast you
before you had even neared him. And," he continued ominously,
"he would feed upon your essence, your emotions, your soul, if you
will. You would then be condemned to the Gorge to wander and
howl with the damned." His eyes caught and held the mate's. "No,
don't even think of it. The Susurun, I think, is beyond even my
power, for we are evenly matched, and neither he nor I could defeat
the other. His doom is yet to come, and the doom of a Duaiteoiri
is not pleasant to contemplate," he shook his head slowly.

"He is a Duaiteoiri then, a minion of the Duaite, the Evil Ones?"
Tuan asked.

"Aye, those of the Auithe do not pervert their powers. We do
not need to steal the life essence of others to prolong our lives."

"What of his gods...?"

The bard grinned mirthlessly. "His gods are long since dead.
When the Susuru died out, their gods died with them. There is a
saying in the Northlands, *'There is no Substance without Faith'*—you
must have heard it?" Tuan nodded. "Gods need the worship of

man; should the faith be questioned and the worship slacken, then the gods weaken and will eventually die. Thus it was with the gods of the Susuru; with no one to worship them, they died out. No; I think the priest worships some of the primeval gods that still roam the darker corners of man's faith. Perhaps he worships even Quisleedor itself," he added softly.

Tuan shivered although the sun was already baking the stones; this talk of gods and devils chilled him. The bard spoke so convincingly of their existence...

"Forever doubting," Paedur chided, "yet fearful of the truth."

The mate said nothing.

They waited in silence while the sun slowly crept towards its zenith. The air was thick and heavy, redolent of the sharp odour from the pools that caught at the throat and stung the eyes. The rock basin, trapped between the cliff and surrounded on three sides by the forest, contained the heat, the stones soaking up the sunshine until they were almost unbearable to the touch, radiating it forth in wave upon suffocating wave until even the Taourg, accustomed as they were to heat, were bathed in sweat and every water skin was empty.

Tuan awoke from his doze with a start. How long had he slept? Where was the bard? The crunch of gravel made him turn suddenly, whipping out his knife.

It was the bard. "You're awake then. I've just been rousing several of your crewmates," he answered the mate's unasked question. "Hah! The fearsome Taourg pirates sleeping on a raid." His eyes twinkled with mischief.

Tuan grinned. "We're not all demi-gods. Some of us need to eat and sleep; you know—the normal things of life."

Paedur was suddenly very serious. "Aye, the normal things of life." He glanced up into the sky, and then peered over the edge of the stone, towards the temple. "It's almost time."

Even as he was speaking the murmuring became audible, thrumming faint in the distance. The deep silence that blanketed the island seemed to thicken with the sound, as if the noise added an extra dimension to the silence. The chanting grew, deepened, assuming an almost pulse-like beat, broken by the same deep-chanted growl and raucous cries that they had heard yesterday. As it grew nearer, the cries became clearer, beginning to sound almost bestial.

Tuan felt the bard stiffen by his side. "What are they saying?" he asked.

"They are calling upon the Duaite of a thousand faiths, bidding them come forth to serve Quisleedor," the bard whispered, aghast. "Careful now, the priests are coming!"

The priests emerged from the forest into the ruins.

Tuan flattened himself against the rock, his knife slipping in his sweat-dampened hands, his heart pounding like a youth on his first raid. The bard had pulled his cloak tighter about himself, and even in the full light of the blistering sun overhead, he resembled no more than a shadow.

The mate briefly glimpsed the four Formenai priests winding their way through the ruins following an obviously ritual path, their harsh shouts contrasting with the low mumbled chant of their followers. Abruptly all sound ceased, and Tuan guessed that they had reached the pools. The bard had stood up and was crouching over the stone, peering across the open square. Tuan slowly raised himself up and joined the bard.

To their right stood the main temple, the scabbard-held torchlight flickering wildly although the air was still. Before them lay the four Sleedor pools, arranged in a rough circle about the main pool, and before each pool a dark priest stood and bowed repeatedly to the main temple. The Vosgean guards stood behind them, staring blankly ahead, their eyes dead in their heads. And chained and manacled by the pools were the sacrifices—four young women.

Tuan gripped the bard's arm. Paedur nodded slowly. "We have come just in time. They're virgins, I'll wager, and a virgin sacrifice would surely rouse the Life Child as nothing else would. The essence of the Unsullied would grant it power beyond imagining," he whispered urgently. "The sacrifice must not take place. Duaize must attack now."

"He will give the command as soon as the Susurun appears," the mate replied. "Where did they get those girls from?" he wondered, "They are neither Vosgean nor Formenai."

The four girls were tall and slender, taller than the Formenai priests, topping even their guards. Their skin was pale, almost translucent, and their white-gold hair reflected the black water. Their features were small and delicate, their eyes wide and blue, but they showed no fear. They faced the pools calmly, heads erect, proudly accepting their fate. Their robes had once been pale blue, though now they were soiled and torn; but the girls wore them as if they were robes of ceremony. About the neck of each hung an intricate amulet depicting a stylised hand clutching a flame.

"Priestesses of the Mother Dannu!" Paedur whispered.

"From Thusal," Tuan added, "probably shipwrecked, though what they should be doing so far south is beyond me."

The bard's voice was cold. "I don't think they were shipwrecked; I imagine they were kidnapped for this very purpose. Taken from the Northlands and brought south so they could not mindcall their sisters. Probably held in thrall to prevent them calling on their mother, the Lady Dannu. Had they been unprofessed girls, it would have been bad enough, but these are trained priestesses of the Mother." He turned to Tuan, "I can see the hands of the gods in this."

"You see the hand of the gods in everything," Tuan snapped. Then he shook his head and sighed. "I can see that it would be too much of a coincidence," he agreed. "I don't think I like being manipulated, Paedur," he added.

"You get used to it," Paedur said with a tight humourless smile, "and it is for your own good."

"And that of the gods too, I'll wager."

"That, too, always that."

The chanting died and the priests in their soiled robes faced the door expectantly, awaiting their master. Suddenly the flame above the door leapt as if fed with some volatile liquid, drawing all eyes. When the flame had died down the Susurun High Priest stood in the doorway. Tuan could see him clearly now and he felt his blood run chill, for the Susurun was undoubtedly inhuman. He recalled tales he had heard of the strange races that lived beyond the Land of the Sun. Tales told by mariners who had sailed to the very rim of the world, and repeated in taverns for a jack of ale. Tales of the Starlorn, non-humans belonging neither to the seed of the gods nor the race of man, and belonging neither to the Star Folk, that are as gods but not gods, but rather of both. It is said that the Lorn inhabited the vast seas beyond Shemmat, sailing forever in ships of purest gold and silver, crafts the size of islands. They had come...

"He is not of the *frai-forde,* the Starlorn," Paedur whispered softly, breaking into his thoughts.

"How did you...? No! What then?" he demanded angrily. Was he to have no privacy? Were his thoughts to be open to this strange, frightening storyteller?

"I do not deliberately search for your thoughts, rather you send them about you in waves. I felt them because you were near me, and concentrating deeply upon the legends of the Lorn." Paedur broke off as the Susurun began to chant in a high-pitched shrill tongue, the Formenai priests chanting the replies.

"But the Susurun," he continued, "is not of their race. His is an older, darker folk. The Susuru were akin to the Culai—some say they were even created by the Culai, the results of the sorcerous mixing of the essence of both base humans and beasts. And while the Culai could be wilful and thoughtless, they were not totally evil—unlike their creations. The Susuru worshipped the darker aspects of the Faith and delighted in evil, taking pleasure from senseless killing and torture. And through their arts they lived on for a while after the Culai died, though many died in the various cataclysms that warped the planes of life when the gods cleansed them of evil. Their gods were the darker side of the Pantheon; the true Duaite, vile bloated things that fed on the blood and violated life essences of sacrifices. But the Susuru were a fickle race and worshipped only those who could grant them the power they craved. When the Duaite's powers seemed to wane, they turned to other, wilder gods. It is said that behind every foul belief can be found the hand of a Susurun," he finished bitterly.

"They are not human?" Tuan asked.

"No. Once perhaps, but over the centuries they have bred with the Gorge-spawn. Look!" he hissed.

The High Priest had moved out from the wall of the temple and was now standing not six manlengths from the mate and the bard. His great height was added to by his extreme thinness, and his black skin—pure pitch in colour—seemed to absorb the light. He was completely hairless and his features were thin and angular, his nose sharp and jutting, eyes slanted like those of the Shemmatae and seemingly colourless, and his ears were without lobes. His teeth were filed sharp, like those of the island cannibals to the south or the northern Chopts. When he raised his hands in exhortation to whatever foul gods he now worshipped, his sleeves slid down his arms, revealing the strange metallic tattoos on his forearms. His long thin hands opened, his nails clawed the air, and he opened his lipless mouth to speak...

There was a sudden shrill piercing whistle and then the Taourg appeared in groups of twos from the ruins, bows and crossbows ready. There was another whistle—and they fired. Arrows and crossbow bolts screamed through the air, their iron tips and barbs punching through the guards' lacquered wooden armour. Some fell forward into the pools and were pulled down by the weight of their armour and weapons, sinking with neither ripple nor bubble in the viscous liquid.

One of the Taourg dashed from cover across the shattered court-yard and grabbed the nearest priestess. She struggled until the realisation of what had happened sank in, and then the four women turned and fled towards the forest.

Abruptly the minor pools erupted upwards in a huge gelatinous mass, their shapes vaguely bearlike. They seemed to claw the air; and then the four waving black pools suddenly fell in towards the main pool, splashing across the ground. They fell short and imme-diately began to heave snail-like across the barren soil, trailing a shim-mering rainbow-hued ichor. They slid—almost simultaneously—into the larger pool without a ripple. Initially nothing happened, and then, just below the surface, lights and spots of colour began to dance and shift. A ripple disturbed the surface of the pool, the thick, glutinous liquid shuddering like flesh.

The Susurun screamed, a single bone-chilling mind-numbing word that trembled on the air. Arrows buzzed about him, bursting into flame when they came too close, but he ignored them, his atten-tion caught between the fleeing priestesses and the troubled Sleedor.

And then the pool rose.

It lurched up in a vast sinuous curve, resembling nothing so much as a giant serpent. Light and colour rippled down its length, pulsing and throbbing like internal organs. Its body was as thick as the *Duneson,* tapering slightly towards the 'head', but there were no features. It swayed above the pits that had once held it, then dipped down and nudged the bodies of the fallen Vosgean guards and Formenai priests alike; and when it had passed the bodies had been stripped of all flesh, leaving naught but gleaming polished bones in its wake.

"Quisleedor!" Paedur gasped.

The Taourg commenced firing on the creature, but their arrows had no effect—merely passing through its skin to hang, still clearly visible, within the body of the Life Child. Several of the pirates, who had run forward intent on filling their containers with the black water, now stood frozen in shock. Duaize, standing at the edge of the ruins, with the four priestesses about him, shouted for his men to return.

But too late. The great head of the creature swung down, seemingly to merely brush the men, but when it had passed the Taourg were little more than skeletons, their flesh stripped off the bone. Tuan saw one man, his arm nothing more than bones and strings of muscle but otherwise untouched, scream and scream again, until someone mercifully put an arrow into his throat.

The Susurun began to chant again, his voice rising and falling urgently. A pale white fire began to flicker about his head and extended arms, pulsing in rhythm with the light within the Life Child.

Paedur suddenly gripped Tuan by the arm. "We can destroy the Susurun now, while his attention is elsewhere. Come!" He leaped from his hiding place and ran swiftly towards the High Priest. Tuan was up and running after him almost before he knew what he was doing. When he understood what he had done, he suddenly realised that he had just made a commitment to the bard in this and in all things—should he survive.

A ripple ran through Quisleedor and the Susurun began to tremble visibly; the creature's "head" shifted towards the High Priest, and slowly he began to turn to face his attackers. The bard was nearer now, his long black cloak flapping behind him like wings, his feet seeming barely to touch the rocky ground, neither stumbling nor slipping on the loose soil.

And then the High Priest's eyes flickered open and he smiled hideously. The white fire suddenly blazed about his head, lending it a skull-like appearance. He extended one arm and the white fire snaked along it, trembling at the tips of his long black nails. A bolt of light spat towards the bard. Paedur allowed himself to fall to the ground, and the light sizzled over his head. It narrowly missed Tuan, but the heat alone as it passed was enough to singe his hair and beard. It finally splashed against a listing wall which immediately collapsed, and the fire continued to burn on the bare stones for a long time afterwards.

The Susurun raised his arm again, this time holding his palm cupped. A ball of white fire began to form there. Then the fire wavered, suddenly becoming veined with bright blue threads. The Susurun screamed as the white fire about his head was shot through with blue sparks; then long tendrils of the blue fire suddenly engulfed the white, turning it a pale blue colour. Now the fire no longer burned about his head, it was actually stuck to his skin, burning. The High Priest opened his mouth to scream, but then Paedur was on him. Seemingly oblivious to the heat, the bard raised his hook, shouted at Tuan to go, and then brought his silver hook down upon the Susurun. The hook sparked on making contact with the blue-fire, but the fire was abruptly extinguished in the blood of the last of the Susuru.

With the death of the High Priest, Quisleedor was masterless. It hovered about the vast bottomless pits that it had inhabited, nosing the bodies of the slain. Then, as if it had made a decision, it lurched in the direction of the captain and the four priestesses. They turned and ran.

Paedur turned and grabbed Tuan by the arm, dragging him in the direction of the forest, calling on the Taourg nearest him to follow. They plunged through the seared undergrowth, the bard leading the way, angling away towards where the captain, the priestesses and the remainder of the crew must emerge. They burst on to the path used by the creature just in time to meet Duaize and the others coming round the bend in the path.

"To the shore," Duaize gasped.

"We must leave this path," Paedur said urgently. "This is its run." Without waiting for a reply, the bard led them across the path and into the depths of the forest, his hook flashing in the twilight, clearing the vines and creepers that barred their way. Without question the four priestesses of the Mother followed him; Tuan paused a moment, then he too followed the bard. The remaining crew looked at the captain. A tearing crash back along the track decided them, and they followed the bard into the forest.

Just as the last man dived off the track, the creature lurched into view, a vast undulating black column gliding swiftly along the track. It paused when it reached the point where the bard had led the others off the track, and swayed to and fro indecisively. A violent shudder ran down its body, and then it fluidly divided in two, one column continuing on down the track, the other smashing into the forest, following the fleeing Taourg.

Duaize called for a halt when they reached a small sun-dappled clearing in the woods. He was breathing heavily, as were the rest of the crew, and the priestesses looked close to collapse. The bard alone remained untroubled, his breathing even. "We must continue. Quisleedor will come."

Tuan began to count the stragglers as they came in.

"We can go no further, bard," Duaize gasped, "we must rest."

"Nearly two thirds missing," Tuan reported to the bard. "They may turn up on the beach, but…" He left the sentence unfinished. They both knew the missing men would not be turning up on the beach.

Duaize rounded angrily on the bard. The Taourg was pale and shivering, and there was a bloody froth on his lips where he had bitten into the soft flesh of his cheeks. "I hold you responsible," he screamed. "My crew lost, and all for what? Nothing…" A high-pitched scream—abruptly silenced—suddenly tore through the forest. In the silence that followed, Paedur turned to the priestesses. "We must go. I know you're exhausted, but Quisleedor approaches, and you must call upon the Mother for strength." He called Tuan over. "We'll move again; we'll try and circle around to the beach. I am entrusting the priestesses to your care. Should any one of them fall behind, then you must kill her." He caught the mate's jaw in his right hand and turned his head, so Tuan was staring directly into the bard's eyes, and continued, "You must. They cannot be allowed to fall into the hands of the Life Child."

"I cannot," Tuan whispered.

"You must," the eldest priestess said. "For our sakes, do not let the creature take us. Promise me this."

Tuan looked from the four young women to the bard. "I have learned to trust you, Paedur," he said. "If you say this must be done, then I will do it." He bowed to the priestess.

Paedur turned and ran into the forest, followed by the priestesses and Tuan. Without waiting for any command, the Taourg followed him.

The captain pulled his sword free. "Come back; we'll fight it here. Come back. This is mutiny. I'll kill you, Paedur!"

And then, with a crash, the Life Child broke into the clearing, its head reared high, its underside stained crimson. Duaize took one look, then he too turned and ran.

The forest began to thin out as their path led them uphill. Soon they were stumbling over small rocks and boulders set into the undergrowth, and a sea breeze began to ruffle the leaves. After the cloying stench of the Sleedor pools and the thick forest odour, it smelt like incense. The crash of the surf grew louder and the tang of the salt sharper, while the incline became steeper, the climbing more difficult, though they were still in the forest and the ground underfoot was soft.

The forest ended abruptly, and the ground levelled out in a wide green swath of gently waving grass. But the grassy area was barely four man-lengths wide—for they were on a clifftop overlooking the sea.

Tuan looked helplessly at the bard. He had come to think of him as almost godlike, and now he had led them here to the cliff edge where there was no way down, and no way back save through the forest in which Quisleedor roamed.

They were trapped.

Paedur began to arrange the men in a semi-circle about the four priestesses, placing them as far away from the forest as possible. The Taourg were pitifully few, Tuan realised, too few to stand against the Life Child, but he doubted even if the full complement of the ship's crew would stop the creature. He walked to the edge of the cliff and looked down. It was at least sixty man-lengths—and more—down to the sea. To his left, the *Duneson* bobbed gently at anchor, toy-like in the distance. Directly below, the shore was broken with jagged remnants of a rockslide. The waves foamed and crashed about spears of rock which rose like pointing fingers, and numerous eddies swirled about sunken rocks. Anyone jumping off the cliff would be dashed to pieces; there was no escape.

There was movement in the forest behind them, and then trees began swaying and falling, crushed by the weight of the creature, stripped down to the pith where its flesh touched them. A shadow moved within the cover of the trees where Quisleedor, smaller now, waited...

Duaize panted up to them and collapsed on the ground. Then he suddenly jumped to his feet and pointed. "Look!" His voice was a shriek. In the distance, trees were swaying and falling in a long snaking trail that was headed in the direction of the gleaming blackness of the serpent creature below.

Paedur nodded. "I see it," he said softly, sounding almost pleased. He glanced around as Tuan joined him. "The creature divided, it will soon re-join," the bard said, and Tuan once again realised his question had been anticipated.

The rending crash of falling trees grew nearer as the second creature closed in. Then the trees at the periphery of the forest fell and the second Life Child appeared briefly. Within the cover of the forest, the two shudderingly melted into one. Quisleedor was complete once more.

Paedur passed from archer to archer, giving instructions.

The captain shouted at him. "What's the use? Arrows have no effect on it. Better to leap from the cliff than to die by that." He pointed a trembling hand at the shape within the forest. Suddenly he turned and began to run towards the cliff. One of the priestesses screamed and Tuan turned, striking out at him as he passed, catching him in the small of the back. Duaize fell moaning to the ground. One of the young women knelt by his side. "Do not waste your life thus. Better for you that a shipmate slay you than you take your own life."

Duaize looked up at the mate standing over him. "Kill me, Tuan. Please kill me. Don't let that thing take me," he pleaded.

Tuan looked helplessly at the bard, but Paedur shook his head briefly. The mate looked down at the captain. "I'm sorry. I cannot kill you." He walked over to the bard. "I think he may be right; better we all leap off the cliff," he muttered.

"All is not quite finished," Paedur smiled. "Wait."

Quisleedor burst from the forest, branches and leaves showering off its back, some of them sinking into its flesh. It began to undulate up the slope. Behind it vegetation rotted and blackened, rocks crumbled to fine powder, and a foul miasma floated up the slope.

The first row of archers fired and immediately pulled back. Although their arrows struck home they had no effect. The second line of archers also fired, and then they too pulled back. The third line was level with the bard. "Fire on my command only," Paedur ordered. The bard then took a flint from his belt pouch and kneeling, struck sparks from it with his hook on to a small pile of leaves. The leaves began to smoulder; gently, he blew on them, coaxing them to a flame.

And Quisleedor approached.

Suddenly the leaves burst into flame. The archer nearest the bard stooped and snapped the iron head off his arrow, dipped the wooden end of the shaft into the flame, gently coaxing the broken head to burn.

Quisleedor reared, huge and black in the sunlight.

The rest of the archers turned and ran back up the slope, surrounding the four priestesses. Tuan loosened his knife in its sheath and wondered whether he would be able to kill the four young women. Duaize cowered, whimpering, on the ground.

The massive head began to descend.

Paedur touched the archer's shoulder and the young man raised his bow, the arrow tip sparking brightly, a thin tendril of smoke drifting almost lazily up from it.

Paedur looked back over his shoulder. "Everyone down," he roared. And the archer fired.

Those who didn't fall to the ground quickly enough were thrown down by the sudden blast that ripped across the clifftop. Three men were swept off the cliff with the force of the explosion, down onto the rocks below.

Flames swept back into the forest in a vast sinuous curve; trees exploded as their bark cracked and their sap boiled. The creature was gone, consumed in a vast conflagration of oily black smoke and blue-white flames. Where it had once been an inferno now raged, even the rocks bubbling with the heat. Quisleedor was no more. The forest, however, was only beginning to burn.

"Come," Paedur shouted, "we must make for the ship now. Soon the entire island will be ablaze." Obediently, the Taourg arose and, skirting the edge of the blaze, made their way down through the forest to the beach and the ship. All save one. Duaize, captain of the *Duneson,* remained on the clifftop, his face contorted in death, blood trickling from his mouth and nose. He had died of fright.

The four priestesses stood by the rail of the *Duneson* gazing back at the high plume of smoke that rose to the heavens, marking the site of the isle of Vosge.

"Will the entire island burn?" one asked.

"Aye," Tuan muttered, as he and the bard joined them. "Soon Vosge will be no more than a blackened ruin."

"There is a lot we still don't know," the priestesses said, turning to face the bard.

Paedur looked at the four young women and smiled. "Perhaps it's just as well. There was an evil on the island. It is gone; that is enough for you to know. But I thank you; you saved me from the Susurun. May the blue fire of the Mother burn brightly within you all."

The four women bowed slightly. "But where did you come from?" one persisted.

The bard glanced briefly at Tuan. "I imagine the gods had a hand in it somewhere," he smiled.

"By the Mother?"

"Perhaps," Paedur smiled, "aye, perhaps by the Lady Dannu."

"And where do you go now?"

"South," Paedur said shortly.

"To the Sea of Galae, to the Blessed Isle," the youngest of the four whispered, her voice sounding lost and frightened.

"You are Sighted," Paedur said, looking into her pale distant gaze.

"You are one of the god-sought, god-taught," she whispered, "I pity you."

"Spare me your pity—I don't need that—but rather grant me your prayers. Pray that the Lady Dannu will aid me in the coming battle with the evil ones."

"Our prayers will be for you," the oldest woman said.

"The priests of Trialos seek to open the vessel of the Chrystallis," the youngest one said, her eyes wide with fear. "But there is another danger—a far greater danger." Her voice cracked and became harsher, sounding almost masculine. "You will use the Magician's Law—the force of equals."

"Can you see an ending...?" Paedur asked softly.

Her voice changed again, returning to normal. "I can see the sun, hot and blinding...I see you...you approaching one who holds the vessel high...he raises it...All is blackness." She crumpled over and began sobbing bitterly.

11
The Priestess

And in the early days of his travels there were two companions.

Life of Paedur, the Bard

...a seafarer late of the sea, and a sorceress, both priestess and witch—these were the companions of the bard.

Tales of the Bard

Smoke coiled about the massive pillars in the ruined temple; grasping tendrils snaked about the scattered congregation, catching the torch lights, flickering in pale shades that hinted at deeper colours within. The torches spat and hissed as droplets of rain began to fall through the broken roof. Shadows wavered and writhed upon the lichened walls, disclosing the chipped remnants of once glorious murals now defaced by time, the elements, and vandals. Sparks, spiralling to the ceiling, died against the fire-blackened crossbeams that had once lain concealed above a canopy of azure plaster.

A sudden gust of wind scattered the coals in the large censer in the middle of the floor, blowing them into flames which illuminated the pitifully few believers come to pay homage to the Old Faith this chill night. Without exception they were aged, for almost all the younger generation had been enticed away to the revels that had come to pass for the worship of the gods of the New Religion in recent years. Nor were they wealthy, for the rich would not risk being caught at such a service. The poor had nothing to lose save their lives, and those were of little value.

Beside the shattered remnants of the altar stone the High Priestess intoned the litany. With arms upraised and head bowed she invoked the Gods of the Pantheon to come and have pity upon "your people, a people strong in faith and devotion; a people who have honoured the traditions and kept the holy days and who but await the return of the gods of their youth; the gods of their fathers and grandfathers." Softly the congregation muttered the responses, "We await your return...we have remained faithful...we will remain faithful..."

The responses lingered on the still air in the ruined temple, while beyond the shattered walls the storm that had been threatening all day broke over the ruined city. Lightning briefly lit up the interior of the fane, illuminating the High Priestess in bone-white light. Her jet-black hair burned almost indigo in the harsh light, and her eyes were bottomless pits in the starkness of her delicate fine-boned face. The simple, ceremonial robes of office ruffled about her slender form as the breeze began to howl outside the temple, darting quick icy fingers through the gaping walls and tumbled doors.

The High Priestess raised her arms once again, her long slender fingers splayed, drawing from the Mother the strength necessary to continue and complete the service. She opened her mouth to speak, and lightning flared again. And then her breath caught in her throat in a strangled scream. Something had moved in the doorway. Something large and shapeless. Lightning flared again, but there was nothing there now. The congregation began to move restlessly, and she slowly raised her arms for the invocation once again...perhaps it had just been a trick of the light...

The priestess began to call upon the Pantheon to "...enlighten and protect and direct and govern us this day in the name..." The sky was rent as night was turned into day with the next levin bolt.

She screamed.

All heads turned towards the door. There were muffled shouts and curses and the rasp of steel as swords and knives were drawn. A creature stood framed in the doorway. Tall, thin and shapeless, it radiated an aura of power that was almost palpable. Then the light was gone and they were in darkness, save for the sputtering torches and the censer's smoky hissing.

The priestess was calmer now. She called the people to her and had them sit in a circle about the cracked altar stone. She took a deep breath and set about concentrating on constructing a protective circle. Then, taking a long peeled wand from the bundle that was to be used in the final sacrifice, she began to trace a circle about the huddled people. She knew not what lurked without the door; if it were men, then they were caught and she would soon be dead, but if it was a Duaiteoiri or some creature of the Gorge, the circle would at least afford her small congregation some measure of protection against it. The torches sputtered once again, and then died as rain began to fall steadily through the roof. The censer lasted a few heartbeats longer, but then, with a final hiss, it too died. In the darkness the unseen terror immediately magnified, and the temple that had once seemed so restful and secure now throbbed with unseen menace.

Lightning flared once again and all eyes turned towards the entrance, but the doorway was empty, and the brief light had only served to re-double the priestess's fears, for the shadows about the walls were darker, more intense in the harsh storm light. Any-one—or anything—could be lurking there.

Grasping the wand in both hands she began to concentrate, calling on Dannu and her daughter Lussa to grant her strength and the power to accomplish what she willed. The wand in her hands began to grow warm, and the faintest nimbus of blue light flickered along the staff. So intent was her concentration that she failed to hear the soft footsteps which crunched up the dusty aisle to the altar.

"Dannu, aid me now," she gasped, straining to make the staff burn.

"Let me help you." The voice was masculine, though soft and gentle, and came from almost directly before her. Something rubbed against the staff and it suddenly blazed with the cold blue fox-fire of the goddess. The congregation cried out, and one or two swords were raised to strike at the figure revealed in the eerie light.

"No," the priestess gasped, raising her hand, pushing down the swords by her side. She looked over her shoulder at her congrega-tion, using the opportunity to regain her composure. "No, he must be one of us."

She turned back and coolly appraised the stranger. It was a man, of that she was certain, although the long, black, hooded trav-elling cloak almost completely concealed his face and most of his body. He was tall, for he topped her by a head and she was standing on the altar steps; and though the wand blazed with stark light the stranger was still partially in shadow, almost as if he absorbed the luminescence. And she knew that it was he who had activated the wand. She looked down at the rod she still held in one hand and gasped: there wasn't another hand above hers on the length of wood, but rather a flat silver hook, intricate runes and delicate tracery wink-ing in the pulsing light.

"Who are you?" she asked finally.

"I am Paedur, a bard," the stranger replied softly. "You?"

"I am Cliona, High Priestess of the Old Faith," she replied proudly. "You are of the Old Faith," she said, more a statement than a question.

"If he is truly the bard Paedur, then he is of the Faith," an old man stepped up to Cliona's side and murmured, peering over at the tall figure. He looked at the hook and nodded. "This is the bard. You are of the east, Cliona, perhaps the tales of the bard have not reached the Isles of Monatome."

Cliona shook her head, but then the bard spoke from beneath his cowl. "I am of the Old Faith, priestess."

"What are you doing here," she asked, "and how did you find us?" The cowled figure bowed slightly. "I am but passing through the city on my way…south. Earlier this evening, I felt a disturbance rippling through the Ghost Worlds, and knew that the Old Gods were being invoked, and I found I was curious." He gently disengaged his hook from the wand, and it slowly dimmed, until only the faintest glimmerings of the blue fire lingered about its tip.

"Are you the one called the *shanaqui?*" a voice from the darkness behind the High Priestess asked.

The bard laughed gently and said, almost shyly, "I am."

Hurried whispers ran through the congregation, and Cliona could feel the sudden tension and excitement.

"I was about to invoke the Pantheon and beg their blessing." she said, conscious that the night was drawing on and the service was still uncompleted. "Will you join us?"

"I would be honoured."

The congregation quickly found their places as Cliona relit the tall censer and then took up her position by the altar stone. She could just about make out the kneeling figure of the bard in the foreground, though in the flickering light he resembled some night-spawned wight.

Cliona raised her arms and crossed her wrists, palms outward. "By the power and mercy of Hanor and Hara, and with the blessing of the Lady Dannu, I call upon the Pantheon to enlighten and protect, direct and govern us this day; to grant us the physical, mental, and spiritual strength to bear our burdens lightly, to labour cheerfully and toil diligently. I ask this for my charges in the name of…of…" she faltered. Then another voice took up the chant, the powerful trained voice of a professional storyteller, a bard.

"In the name of the One who may not be worshipped, and of the Children of the One, Hanor and Hara, and of the Triad that are of Life, and Mannam that is of Death, for there should be a balance. Be with us."

"Be ever with us."

The priestess took up the chant again. "I ask of the Mother, the Lady Dannu, to send her daughters to our succour; may the Ladies Lussa and Quilida and Adur be ever above and below and about us. Be with us."

"Be ever with us."

And again the bard spoke, his powerful voice echoing off the chill walls. "In the names of Maker and User, who were amongst the First, and of Huide who is amongst the least, and of Nusas who is Master of the Day, and Uimfe who has the Night for his domain, may the Lords of the Pantheon be ever with us."

And now the voice of the priestess joined with that of the bard's, "Be with us."

"Be with us now and always."

As the final response settled over the ruined temple, the storm which had lulled throughout the ceremony finally broke in full fury. Icy rain gusted through the broken roof and walls on to the shivering congregation. Grit hissed against the stone walls, for the wind sweeping off from the sea was contained by the high cliffs surrounding the city and so re-doubled in force. Lightning cracked once more, and a long jagged spear leapt from the heavens down into the city. Close upon the lightning came the thunder, long booming rolls upon some heavenly drum.

Cliona felt a presence by her side, and a voice spoke in her ear, making her jump. "We must be going; Uimfe plays host to the Stormlord this night. Come, let us go before the revels begin in earnest…"

"And this is Tuan, late of the Taourg; he has recently decided to accompany me."

Tuan stood, his head almost brushing the low ceiling of the inn on the outskirts of the New City. He bowed slightly, showing the shivering priestess to one of the three chairs in the curtained alcove he had hired earlier that night.

"Tuan, will you get the priestess something to drink; and bring a firepot also, the chill of the night still lingers." Paedur slipped off his cloak as the mate pushed through the leather curtain into the inn proper. He gently draped it around Cliona's shoulders, drawing her away from the curtain and the ears of any listeners. "Here, sit here. Tuan will return soon, we can talk then."

Paedur leaned against the rough stone wall, arms folded, and watched the priestess with hooded eyes. She was tall and slender, her face oval, the bones rounded, her cheekbones prominent. Her eyes were large, slightly tilted, a pale green in colour, and perhaps set too far apart to be called beautiful. Her most attractive feature was her hair, which flowed in a thick ebon mane down her back to the small of her knees. She wore a simple tunic, sandals, and no jewellery.

She, in turn, watched the bard, seeing him for the first time without the enveloping, concealing cloak. She already knew that he was tall, perhaps a head taller than herself, and finely featured, clean shaven, unscarred and unblemished. His hair was fine and dark, almost invisible in the light of the flickering taper, and his eyes were just shadowed pits. Indeed, with his dark clothing it was difficult to make out details in the dull light. High atop his left shoulder a bardic sigil gleamed and his silver hook shone like a new moon across the night of his chest. She then lowered her gaze and allowed her eyes to unfocus, staring at her hands until she saw the warm gold outline of her own aura. When it was clearly visible, she looked back to the bard...

Two fingers touched her eyelids, closing her eyes. "Do not look at me in that way," Paedur whispered, "it would blast your sight."

And she, who had once dabbled in the darker arts, knew that he was not wholly of the race of man, although neither was he a god. Nor was he evil, for only those untainted with the essence of evil could invoke the Dannu-fire.

And if not Duaite, what then? Surely not Auithe; for the Auithe were of light, and the bard was undoubtedly of the night and darkness.

The heavy curtain rustled and Tuan re-entered carrying two steaming mugs of potent rofion, and cradling a firepot in his arms. He put the mugs on the small knife-scarred table and then unstoppered the pot and blew gently on the red coals. A small flame flickered, then flared, as he dropped some rofion on to the coal. The warm glow that suffused the tiny cubicle immediately warmed the priestess.

Cliona and Tuan sipped the bitter brew and huddled about the firepot, while the bard sat back in the shadows, neither needing the drink nor the warmth of the fire.

The priestess watched the mate across the rim of her mug. His dark weathered skin and pale bleached hair reminded her that the bard had said he had lately sailed with the Taourg. But he had not the looks of one of the fearsome pirates. Indeed, his features were almost soft and his eyes and smile were gentle. However, she did not doubt he would prove to be an awesome opponent. For all his height, he seemed almost squat; muscles rippled and corded with his every movement. The earthenware mug of rofion was almost lost in his large hands, which, she imagined, could easily crush it to powder.

"There is something I must know," the priestess said, turning to the bard. "How did you find me tonight? Outside the few that still pay homage to the Pantheon, no one knows the location of the Temple of the Mother in the Old City. And the route to the Temple is guarded with many cunning traps. And yet you found us without tripping any of the alarms or snares. How?" she wondered.

"I told you how I found you; I followed the ripples set up by your devotions in the fabric of the Ghost Worlds. And as for your traps...well, I didn't see them," Paedur said almost absently.

"And what do you want?" she asked, looking from the bard to Tuan.

The mate caught her worried stare and turned to Paedur. "I will go..."

"No, my friend, stay with us. What do I want? I want nothing. and yet..." he paused. "Tell me, do you believe in the will of the gods, that the gods use and move men like pieces on a board?" Cliona nodded and nodded again.

"It is central to my belief," she said, frowning, wondering where the bard was leading.

Paedur was silent for a moment, the fingers of his right hand rubbing against the runes cut into his hook, and then he said, "Tell me a little about yourself—you are not native to Maante...?"

The sudden question caught her unawares. "Well...but why do you want to know about me...?"

"I too believe that the gods move men, and I'm curious to discover why we have encountered one another. Why have the gods brought us together, eh? Answer me that! No, there was a reason, I'm sure of it. So..." he sat forward, moving into the light, his smile warm and encouraging. "Tell me a little about yourself," he repeated, "how are you called...?"

The priestess smiled shyly. "That depends who is calling me. My full name is Cliona Ravenshair Duringlaid, but in this city I am called priestess by those who know me. I come from the Isles of Monatome, in the east. Why I came here, I cannot say, save that I think I was called. I dreamt..." She shook her head abruptly; the heavy fumes of the rofion were making her drowsy. "I dreamt that the Mother called me, called me as if from a height and pointed out the headland of Aangle, and the town of Maante. And in my dream she said, *Wait, you will be needed.*" Cliona looked into the bard's shadowed eyes. "But you should know that I am not worthy to serve the Mother; I am not pure, I cannot invoke the Dannufire."

"Why?" Paedur whispered.

"I...my mother was of the Nightfolk, the dwellers in caves that come forth during the night to work their magics across the Islands. They shun the light of day, and it is said that the light of Nusas is deadly to them.

"My father was one of the princes of Monatome, and although third in line for the throne he only ruled a minor province on one of the lesser isles, for it was rumoured that the blood of the Duringlaid clan was not pure. Mayhap it was so, for my father liked to hunt by night, to work after dark; he was uncomfortable in the light of the sun. He made a point to conduct all his business with outsiders during the twilight.

"It was my father's passion to hunt the white stags that run by the light of the moon, for it is said that they are the steeds of the Lady Lussa, though I doubt that, for my father once brought one home and it dripped blood and was of flesh as any mortal beast. He said it was merely an albino strain, and was probably sensitive to the harsh sunlight.

"But one summer night, and this was before I was born, while he hunted as usual, he disappeared. The servants scoured the forests for days thereafter, but they found no trace save for a scrap of cloth, the colour of which matched my father's cloak, not far from the Night Gates; the cave entrance to the dwellings of the Night-folk.

"My father re-appeared one morning the following spring, wandering alone through the forests, dressed in that same clothing he had worn before he went missing, and armed with the same weapons. He was paler and his sight, which had never been good during the day, was now much worse, so that he stumbled almost blind along the forest tracks.

"He was shivering with a marsh fever, and he raved during the first few days of his return, and those who visited him came away disturbed with what they had heard. In time, his sense returned and, save for a strange air that seemed to cling to him, he was much the same as before. But he never said where he had been for over half a year, although everyone supposed he had been with the Nightfolk.

"Then one morning, quite suddenly, he announced that arrangements were to be made for his wedding, but he did not name his bride; and although there were several suitable maidens of noble birth on the neighbouring isles, no representations had been made to their fathers. Speculation was rife as the day neared, but on the eve of the wedding there was still no sign of the bride's name. The guests muttered and said that his brain had turned; he had obviously been ensorcelled by the Nightfolk.

"The day of the wedding came and went, and still no bride appeared; but as dusk hung across the skies and night was falling, there came forth from the forest one clothed in rock hues of grey and slate. It was a maiden, fairer than even the fabled Caia. She boldly walked to the altar stone of the fane of the Pantheon and announced herself my father's bride-to-he. In the silence that followed some of the guests left, refusing to attend the ceremony, some because she was of the Nightfolk and others because she was heavy with child.

"And she was Uaidara, my mother.

"I was born not long afterwards and named Cliona Ravenshair Duringlaid. 'Ravenshair' because even at birth my hair was as black as you see it now.

"My father was of the Old Faith and worshipped regularly at the temples of the gods, but my mother worshipped darker gods than those of the Pantheon and was versed in the Ancient Lore that is part of the Culai learning that still survives. And often, on those nights when the moon hid her face and even the stars seemed to shine less brightly, my mother would call me to her, and we would walk in the rock garden that my father had had made for my mother, and there she would instruct me in the dark magic of her people.

"I was enrolled in the Temple of the Mother when I reached my twelfth year and there I remained until I was professed. But on account of my dark knowledge I was told I would never attain the Higher Mysteries, and would never be more than a priestess. Although," she added with a wry smile, "the people here call me High Priestess.

"Then, as I have said, I dreamt that the Mother called me to her. In my dream she was seated upon the Throne of Heaven, she was all aspects of woman, yet none: maiden, mother, crone—ever-changing. And it was as if the land was spread out like a vast tapestry, rolling gently beneath my feet. And here was Aangle and here Maante, and the Mother rose from her throne and pointed out this town, and then it was as if a voice spoke from within my head. *'Go; wait; you will be needed.'* Then she was gone and I awoke cold and shivering in the dawn.

"And thus I came here on the first available ship," she finished.

"Why do you conduct your services in secret?" Paedur asked. "Surely the Faith is not banned in Maante?"

"No," she said, her eyes heavy with sleep. "No, the Faith is not banned here; Maante is very tolerant. There are temples and fanes to a hundred gods and spirits here; though I have noticed that the scholars and learned men who flock here to use the libraries have little time for religion or gods." She laughed bitterly. "They are too busy denying the very existence of god; why, some even doubt the existence of man."

"But you still haven't told me why you hold your services in secret," the bard persisted.

She sipped cautiously. "When I came here some four or five moons ago, the Pantheon was worshipped in the Great Temple of Hanor and Hara in the main square of the New City. A flourishing priesthood served the gods and the services were well attended. Since then I have seen all the priests die in mysterious circumstances— accidents—and the most prominent worshippers attacked, reviled and slandered, and in two cases, killed. It did not take long for the message to sink in, and the congregation soon dwindled almost as fast as the priests." She coughed as the rofion took her breath away. "Hah, but the Faith does not need those who flee at the first sign of trouble!"

"Where do you come in?" Tuan asked suddenly.

"There is an Order House of the Mother here in Maante..." Cliona began.

"We know," Tuan grinned, "we escorted four of your sisters there not three days ago."

Paedur waved him silent and turned back to the puzzled priestess. "Please continue."

"I had heard of the death of the priests, and slowly the realisation began to dawn that perhaps this was why I had been called to Maante. When I learned that there were no more priests left to carry on the Faith, I went to the Mother Abbess and asked her if I might be granted special dispensation to minister amongst the people. The Abbess knew I was unhappy in the confines of the House: knew that I longed to be doing something—anything—except waiting. She knew that the Mother had guided me to Maante, and she too wondered whether I had been called here for this very purpose."

"So you went amongst the people, knowing that your predecessors had all met their deaths. Was that not a foolish thing to do?" Paedur asked, curiously.

"I knew the Mother would protect me," the priestess said simply. "I was not afraid."

"You were tonight," the bard said softly.

"I panicked," Cliona snapped. "It will not happen again." She drank deeply and then continued. "I have been watched these past few days; my rooms have been searched; I did everything I could this evening to lose the men who were following me; I knew if they found the ruined temple, there would be a massacre. When I saw the shape in the doorway I thought you..."

"Have you any idea who is behind all this?" Tuan wondered.

"The priests of Trialos are in Maante," she said softly.

"Aaah," Paedur breathed. "How many? Have they been here long?" he asked urgently.

"They are many," Cliona said slowly, "and though they have not been here these many moons they have gained many converts, for their doctrine is attractive and welcoming, and gives the people quick and easy answers. But..." she paused indecisively.

"But…" the bard prompted.

"I don't think that's the real reason all the priests of Trialos are here."

"What are they here for, then?" Paedur asked.

"They seem to be waiting."

"Waiting?"

"There is always a priest on the road by the Towers, yet he never accosts any of the travellers with offers of money or food, as is their custom. And there is always a priest by the harbour and yet again he never stops the mariners; and they are usually easy fodder for the smooth-talking priests." She shook her long dark hair. "No, I think they are waiting for something—or someone."

"But for whom, I wonder," the bard mused, "someone important, I'll wager."

"Important enough for them to pass over possible converts," Tuan added.

Cliona put down her glass and, placing her hands flat on the stained wood, she stared over at the bard. "Now, I have answered all your questions. Tell me, what are you doing in Maante?"

Paedur replied slowly. "I am but passing through the city, nothing more."

"Where are you going?"

"The Sea of Galae, the Blessed Isle," Paedur said, almost absently, ignoring the priestess's sudden pallor.

"Why…why there?" she whispered, slowly rising to her feet.

Tuan stood and gently pushed the priestess back into her chair. He cupped her chin in one of his hands and said softly, "The priests of Trialos seek to open a vessel holding a fragment of the Chrystallis; we are trying to stop them."

Cliona sat still, only the sudden pounding of her heart audible in her head, though whether from the shock of the revelation or from the drink she couldn't tell.

Paedur moved suddenly, pulling back the leathern curtain. The thick yellow light of the inn spilled into the darkened alcove. One or two faces raised themselves from their flagons and looked curiously at the tall commanding figure who glared about the room; when they met his eyes they looked away. Tuan was behind him, the broad-bladed Chopt knife gleaming redly in the reflected glow of the firepot. "What is it?" he murmured.

"There was someone outside, listening; I'm sure of it," Paedur replied. He turned back to the priestess. "Come, we must leave here. Where are you staying?"

"I have the old priest's quarters behind the Temple of Hanor and Hara," she said, looking bemused. "What's happened?"

Paedur slipped his cloak from Cliona and swung it about his shoulders, pulling the cowl up over his head. In the shadows, he was almost invisible.

Tuan pulled his heavy woollen jerkin over his head and made the priestess put it on. The thick wool enveloped her from throat to knee, disguising her female figure in its folds. Beneath his jerkin, Tuan wore a vest of blackened ring mail. He loosened his knife in its sheath and looked at the bard.

"What's happening?" Cliona asked again, a note of desperation creeping into her voice.

"We're leaving," Paedur said shortly. "You are coming with us."

He turned to the mate. "You go first and ensure that our way is clear; Cliona—you and I will follow. We will return to our quarters; yours are, in all probability, a death-trap."

He nodded to Tuan, who slipped quickly through the curtain. Paedur moved to the thick leather and, with his hook, carefully nicked a piece from it. He put his eye to the hole and followed the mate's progress through the crowded inn. Several heads turned to follow him and, as he closed the thick studded door behind him, two men rose and wove their way—seemingly drunkenly—after him. Paedur turned to the priestess. "He was followed."

"What will we do?" she asked, her voice cracking.

The bard smiled thinly, and the glow from the firepot turned it bloody. "We will wait for Tuan to clear our way…"

"But you said that there were two of them," she whispered; "should we not help him, call for help or something?" she finished lamely.

"Tuan can take care of himself; there are only two of them."

The bard capped the firepot and they waited in the darkness. Paedur watched the inn through the tiny hole in the leathern curtain; everyone had resumed drinking and no one seemed to be paying undue attention to the curtained alcove.

"Ready now?"

The priestess nodded in the darkness.

Paedur gripped Cliona by the arm and pulled her through the curtain. He led her quickly through the maze of tables. One or two coarse jests were flung in their wake, but they ignored them, concentrating on reaching the door. The bard's senses were tingling, alert to every movement in the room. Cliona stared straight ahead, looking neither right nor left, concentrating on the door, half expecting a knife in the back. Two men, the bard had said. Had they come to kill her, as they had the others? The Mother would protect her... wouldn't she?

The raw night air streamed in through the open door and she suddenly realised they were out into the street. She breathed deeply, cleansing her lungs of the smoke and stench of the inn with the sharp sea breeze that swept up from the harbour.

The mate. Where was Tuan? The street was deserted and in utter darkness. In the distance a pale spark bobbed as some late reveller made his way homeward, preceded by his lantern-bearer and no doubt surrounded by his guards.

Paedur took Cliona's arm again and pulled her off down the street to their left, moving confidently through the blackness. He suddenly stopped and hissed softly. Something moved in the darkness, and Cliona almost screamed as someone took hold of her other hand.

"One outside, two following," came the mate's low whisper.

"And?"

"They sleep; one will not wake in this world, I think."

Cliona shuddered as she realised that Tuan had just killed a man. She vainly attempted to pull her hand free from his, but he gripped her more firmly and muttered angrily, "Be still, girl, or all is lost."

They made their way through the darkened streets, cutting through echoing alleyways and across four plazas, each one more foul-smelling than the last. Once they climbed steps and Cliona guessed that they were climbing past the Quarter Wall into the Upper City. They stopped twice and waited in the shadows while the Watch made their rounds, stamping past with a jingling of mail, their lanterns held high, casting yellow pools of light about their bearers. They hurried on, splashing through pools of noisome liquid that leaked from the sewers which ran down the centre of the streets. Then the bard led them off the main streets and down a dank filth-strewn lane. They paused while the mate struck a light from his tinder pouch, transferring the flame to a single candle enclosed behind thin slivers of horn. A pale yellow-white glow lit up the dripping alley walls. They were outside a door set deeply into the wall; the door was stained and scorched, and its base was rotten and reeked of urine and vomit.

Tuan stooped and put the guttering flame close to the lock. Tiny points of light winked back at them from the rusted keyhole and handle. He bent and ran the light over the ground under the keyhole. Spots of rust littered the rotted wooden step. Tuan turned to the bard and silently drew his knife from its sheath. No word passed between them, but Cliona knew that there was someone inside.

Tuan blew the candle out while the bard carefully slipped the long key into the lock, pushing Cliona behind him. Tuan pushed the door open. It squeaked, the slight noise like a scream in the night silence. The mate stood to one side while the bard preceded him into the blackness. There was a brief—almost noiseless—scuffle, then silence.

Paedur re-appeared as Tuan relit the candle, and in the yellow light they could see that the tip of his hook was dark and dripping.

"Just one," he said.

Tuan pushed the priestess into the small hallway, then pulled the door closed. The flickering lantern shone wetly on the long black stain that trickled slowly down the wall. Under the stain a figure slumped, head tilted back to reveal the gaping slash across the throat that was still pumping blood. A long stiletto lay buried point-first in the hard-packed floor where it had dropped from his hand; blood pooled about it. Tuan nudged the corpse with his boot, and then he stooped down and pushed back his sleeve; a thick metal band encircled his wrist.

"The Iron Band of Kloor,." Paedur muttered.

"You know it?" Tuan asked.

"Aye, I know of it; and of how youths are tricked into joining it, forswearing their gods, their families, heritage, past … everything. For what? Nothing!" He looked down at the corpse; it was a boy of no more than eight and ten summers. Suddenly he knelt by the body and placed his hook across forehead, then breast. "Rest in peace," he whispered. "Mannam, accept his spirit; Alile have mercy on him and do not judge him harshly." He looked up at the priestess who was staring at him in sick horror. "Do not condemn me, nor this youth either. We each have our reasons for doing what we do." He seemed about to say more, but then he stood up abruptly and walked up the corridor, feet gliding noiselessly over the earthen floor.

"I think we should leave here," Tuan said as they entered the tiny room at the back of the building.

"Aye, you're right; the priests of Trialos move swiftly."

"I'm sorry I got you into this," Cliona said quietly.

Tuan was swiftly by her side. "Priestess, we were in this long before we came here. The bard has been sought by the priests of Trialos and the Trialdone across the Seven Nations. This is not new to him."

"What will we do?" she asked.

"My destination is the Blessed Isle," the bard said. "But first, I would like to know more about the priests of Trialos and, more particularly, why they're waiting here. Consider," he said, holding up his hand, "to open the vessel containing the Chrystallis is not a task given to any ordinary priest. Therefore it must be someone powerful, someone well versed in the lore of both the Old Faith and the New Religion." His hand closed into a fist. "Thanos," he whispered. "Thanos."

Cliona shuddered. "Thanos, the Hand of God."

"Trialos' High Priest?" Tuan asked. "Surely not."

"He's the only one it could be. No one else has the power to open the vessel. And he will not come alone; half the High Priests of the false gods will accompany him."

"And you would go against him alone?" Cliona asked.

"I have to," Paedur said simply.

"There's movement outside," Tuan said, peering through a slit in the warped wooden shutters barring the windows.

"This way." The bard prised the shutters off the rear window that looked out into a squalid courtyard. A short drop below the window, a neighbouring roof jutted out until it was only half a span from the wall of their building. The mate went first, landing easily and coming to his feet in one smooth roll. He stood and stretched full length to receive the priestess as the bard lowered her down. "I've got her," Tuan hissed, "now come on!"

"A moment," Paedur snapped, and then he ducked back into the room. Cliona and Tuan stood and waited for the bard to reappear, faces raised anxiously to the gaping window.

Paedur meanwhile was slashing the rough mattress, his razor sharp hook cutting through the thin fabric to expose the straw beneath. He doused it with the remainder of a flagon of raw mountain spirit which Tuan had been drinking earlier, then he quickly spread the straw out around the door. He placed the lighted candle just inside the door—which opened inwards.

He ran to the window and leapt out, cloak flapping like wings, and landed noiselessly beside the startled pair. In the room above there was a crash, followed by a dull *whoomp,* and the window lit up with flames.

Paedur allowed himself a slight smile. "Shall we go?"

12
The Hand of God

And Thanos, the Hand of God, the High Priest of the New Religion, sent his finest warriors to slay them...

Life of Paedur, the Bard

They reached the Old City as the dawn was breaking in the east. The sun rose shortly afterwards, the ruined buildings etching long shadows about them. Cliona led them through the mazy paths, overgrown and sprouting small shrubs in the cracks in the stonework, past columns which had once supported vaulted roofs or held stairways which were now only shattered steps. The long snaking lines of walls were everywhere, gaps showing where the dressed stone had been taken down through the ages by the city dwellers for their own dwellings.

As the morning brightened and they saw movement on the outskirts of the ruins, they sought shelter in a squat two-storied ruin that had once been a massive sprawling house. The ruins of the outer wings had been torched at some stage and surrounded the main building in a crude and seemingly unbroken wall, looking harsh and ugly in the morning light. But the priestess led them through the tumbled stones and fire-blackened spars to the central rooms of the building—which were in surprisingly good repair. "This was once the house of the Chief Magistrate," she said, pointing to the crest depicting two crossed swords and a length of chain above the doorway.

"What happened?" Tuan asked, looking around at the desolation.

"I asked myself the same question, but all I could find out was that he hanged two fishermen for fishing without a licence. At the hanging there was a scene involving one of the men's wives, and she attacked the magistrate with a fish hook. She was cut down before she even got close to the man. The magistrate then ordered the families of the two fishermen all slain—as a warning I suppose." She indicated the tumbled walls. "Before the order could be carried out, the townspeople attacked his house...They killed everyone. Since then, the house has been more or less avoided,"

"Why?" Tuan wondered.

Cliona smiled. "It's supposed to be haunted."

"Well, it's empty enough now," Paedur said, squeezing through the half-open door. Tuan and the priestess followed him inside. "I'm going to go back to the New City," the bard said, his voice echoing slightly in the dim hallway. "I want to see about hiring a boat, and I'll bring some food back with me." He turned back to the door, and then stopped and looked over at the priestess. "I can contact the Abbess of the Order House and have them come and pick you up..."

The priestess shook her head, the strands of her long hair whispering sibilantly together. "There's no need. I'm sure the Order House is being watched; you daren't go there..." The bard silently nodded and then left, disappearing rapidly into the ruins.

Tuan looked at the priestess—and then he yawned hugely. "I think we should try and get some sleep; it looks like it's going to be a long day."

Tuan awoke suddenly, not knowing what had disturbed him. The house was deathly silent, the noonday stillness the Taourg called it. Without moving he opened his eyes—and then squeezed them shut again as the sunlight reflected off the white rock and dressed stone of the hallway. But in that single instant he had noted that the priestess was missing.

He had fallen asleep in a niche behind the main door, and he was confident that nothing could have come past without awakening him. He had left her sleeping in a small room just below the main staircase, where he had been able to see her, but now the thin sheet she had wrapped herself in lay balled by the foot of the pallet. He quickly checked through the lower rooms, but they were all empty and the dust on the floor was unmarked. Panic gripped him now, and he ran up the crumbling stairs, taking them two at a time. He began systematically checking the rooms on the second floor but they too were all empty, and caution prevented him from calling her name.

Tuan came back to the landing and stood by the stairs, looking around. He felt Cliona was still within the house; anyone leaving—

or entering for that matter—would have had to step over him. He was about to take the small staircase that led up to the third floor when he heard a small noise, the clink of metal on stone. It came from a room he had just passed; a room devoid of furnishing and with no possible place of concealment. He moved quietly down the hall, his knife gripped tightly in his left hand, his breath coming short and fast. He was conscious that he was more frightened now than he could ever remember being—even on his first raid, or even when Quisleedor had chased them through the forest.

He peered in through the open door. The room was still empty. The shutters were open and the sunlight, reflecting off the stones of the neighbouring buildings, painted the cracked walls in harsh colours that only served to highlight its bareness. Tuan eased the door futher open with his right hand. It protested loudly on rusted hinges. He suddenly pushed himself through the opening, diving to the left, rolling to his feet with his knife upraised and his back against the cracked wall.

And again he heard the noise. It came from outside and a shadow moved across the sunlight behind the shutter. Tuan threw himself across the room and hit the rotting shutters at a run, sending them crashing over the waist-high wall that encircled the balcony beyond.

And Cliona screamed. She had been standing by the wall.

"Where in the God's holy name were you?" Tuan demanded, fear and anger thickening his voice. He slammed his knife into its sheath, and then winced as darts of pain shot through his arm muscle. Long splinters of wood from the shutters had stuck into his left arm. Clumsily, he began to pluck them out.

"Here, let me," Cliona said, taking Tuan's arm in her cool hands and gently plucking the long slivers of wood from his forearm and shoulder. "That was a stupid thing to do," she snapped. "You could have been badly hurt; suppose you got a splinter in your eye?"

"I thought you were in danger," Tuan muttered in embarrassment.

Cliona bent her head, seemingly concentrating on her task, but her long thick hair hid the deep blush that burned her cheeks. "Thank you; but I was in no danger. I awoke a little while ago and…well you were sleeping and I didn't want to wake you. I came up here to get a breath of fresh air…and to think."

"What about?" Tuan asked absently.

"Myself...the bard...you," she replied shyly.

"Me!" He laughed. "I'm nothing. A farmer's son who ran away from home because I couldn't bear the thought of being a farmer. Since then I've been a wandering warrior and a sailor by trade. I've sailed with the Taourg these past years; and you know what the Taourg are," he stated flatly.

"I know. The scum of the seas: killers, thieves, cannibals and...other things." She blushed again. "Why did you leave them?"

"Paedur talked to me one day, gave me a glimpse of what I was and what I might become; told me a little of his mission— and saved my life."

"He is a strange man, he frightens me," Cliona said, leaning against the balustrade, staring out over the ruined city.

Tuan joined her, uncomfortably aware of her presence. "You need have no fear of the bard; he is not evil."

"No, he is not evil, but he seems so...so inhuman."

"Perhaps he is. He is more—and less—than a man. He speaks with a frightening familiarity of the gods, and he also said that he was one of the *'god-sought, god-taught.'*" He turned to face the priestess. "What are they?"

"They are human souls, chosen by the gods to perform a task. Gifted by them, they wander through the land almost as living extensions of the gods' will. Sometimes a god will actually inhabit the body, then the host becomes a *quai*, a mindless thing directed solely by the gods' will. That is the way of Trialos. The Gods of the Pantheon merely direct their servants, sometimes subtly and on occasion with an order. But the bard seems to be neither directed nor ordered..." Cliona shook her head slightly, the wind coming in off the bay whipping her raven locks about her face. "He is a mystery. Black and purple...are they the traditional colours of the bards?" she asked suddenly.

Tuan thought for a moment, then shook his head in puzzlement. "I haven't seen many bards; and although they all wore dark colours, purples, browns, greys, I've never known them to wear black. Why do you ask?"

She frowned. "In my land, black is the traditional colour of the dead. What of your land?"

"Aye, in Moghir we clothe our dead in black winding sheets, for we associate the colour with Mannam, the Dark Lord."

They stood in silence, immersed in their own thoughts, gazing out over the Old City. Far off in the distance, the New City gleamed white against the blue of the ocean.

Cliona shivered suddenly. "It's grown cold."

Tuan nodded glancing at the sky. "Aye, and it's not much past midday; there's a storm brewing." He stepped closer to the priestess and slipped his arm about her shoulders. He felt her tense and then relax.

"What about you and the bard," she asked, keeping her voice light and casual, "will you continue on with him?"

"I will, I have to." He shook his head. "It's hard to explain, but I feel I must."

"But you don't even know what he is!" Cliona protested.

"No," Tuan agreed, "but I know he is not evil. You know what he seeks to prevent; and I will aid him, if I can."

"I, too," the priestess murmured.

"What!"

Cliona smiled. "Don't you see, this was what I was called to Maante for? When you sail the haunted Galae Sea to the Blessed Isle, I will be with you."

Tuan gripped her shoulders with both hands and turned to stare down into her face. "There will be danger. The priests of Trialos and the Trialdone are the least of our worries. The Blessed Isle is reputed to be...inhabited with much that no longer exists. The bard calls it a place out of time, between the planes of man. It may be death for us just to land there..." He stopped; Cliona was smiling at him. "We may die," he almost shouted.

"I do not fear death; do you?"

"No...yes! Yes, I fear death; only a fool does not fear death, but I have faced it often; we are no strangers."

"I am still going," she said firmly.

"Priestess ... Cliona, I do not fear for myself. I fear for you. I would not see you slain—or worse—on the Isle."

Cliona raised one finger and placed it across his lips, silencing him. "And what if we are to die, then we will die together, in the cause of the Old Faith."

"Much good will that do us," Tuan said bitterly.

The priestess shook her head, her eyes bright and mocking. "Why, shall we not enter the Silent Wood together, to wander hand in hand through the still graves..."

Abruptly, Tuan tightened his grip on her shoulders, and then he fell to one side, pulling her to the ground, his hand pressed over her mouth, bruising her lips, smothering her horrified cries. She bit his finger, and as he snatched his hand away she screamed, "What do you think you're doing...you filthy Taourg! Take your hands off me lest I blast you..."

Tuan gripped Cliona's slender white throat and squeezed. The priestess choked and began to claw at his eyes. "Quiet," he hissed, "there's someone moving in the ruins below."

Cliona went limp beneath him and ceased struggling, the loathing in her eyes replaced with fear. Tuan rolled off her, and carefully raised his head above the edge of the balcony, his eyes seeking the spot of movement he had caught from the corner of his eye a moment earlier. The gathering wind moaned through the desolate remains of the once proud city; dust whirled and leaves circled in a smoothly intricate dance and tumbleweed rolled quickly down the deserted streets.

There!

He froze, his eyes never leaving the spot a little to his left, beside a shattered column. It could have been a shadow...and yet. It moved again. A figure ran from one clump of stone to another. Sunlight glinted off armour and a broad-bladed boar-sword. And then a second figure slipped from a doorway and joined the first. He raised his arm and several more figures appeared, running crouched from cover to cover, working their way steadily towards the magistrate's building. The leader raised his arm again, calling in more men, and Tuan stiffened and swore: a broad metal band encircled the man's wrist. He looked down at the priestess. "The Iron Band of Kloor," he mouthed.

Tuan pushed Cliona before him into the shelter of the empty room, then dragged her to her feet and hurried out on to the landing. They had to be out of the house before it was completely surrounded and they were trapped by the Band. They ran down the decaying stairs, sending chunks of rotten wood crashing to the floor below. At the foot of the stairs, Tuan paused, indecisively. To leave through the main door was out of the question, and he felt sure that any back exit was also watched.

A shadow crossed the half-open door. Quickly, he pulled the priestess into the darkened alcove under the stairs, pressing her back against the mouldering wall. Again the shadow crossed the doorway, and an armoured figure darted through the opening, light flashing off the short-sword he held poised across his body. The warrior stood just inside the door, silhouetted against the light. He was close enough for Tuan to see the whites of his eyes as they darted about, seeking movement, and he could hear the soft quick hiss of his breath. He gave a short sharp whistle and several more of the Band joined him. No words were spoken, but they separated and systematically began a thorough search of the ground-floor rooms. However, one remained blocking the door and another guarded the bottom of the stairs, so close that Tuan could have reached out and touched him. There were sounds from above and a door slammed, the noise echoing and re-echoing throughout the house. The search ended, the warriors returned and reported to the officer waiting at the foot of the stairs. He listened to their reports in silence, then, leaving one warrior to guard the door, ordered the rest to follow him upstairs. The Captain of the Band had decided that the fugitives must be hiding on the top floor.

Now, Tuan realised, was the best—and possibly the only—chance they would have to make good their escape. Once the Band realised that they were not in the upper rooms, they would conduct a more thorough search, or possibly even fire the building. He measured the distance between himself and the guard at the door. It was too great a distance for a rush; the warrior would have cried out before Tuan had even taken a few paces.

Tuan weighed the Chopt knife in his hand. It was not a throwing knife and the weight and balance were wrong, but...

He reversed the knife until he was holding it almost at the point, drew his arm back, calculated the distance, allowing for the weight and balance of the blade—and threw!

He was moving even before the knife struck home, counting on his speed and reflexes to evade the guard's sword should the heavy hunting knife miss. The warrior opened his mouth to cry out—and then the knife struck him in the throat, pinning him momentarily to the door, and then he pitched forward, his eyes forever frozen in that last astonishment. The mate caught him as he fell, easing him gently to the ground, retrieving his knife and taking the guard's sword. Blood pooled about his feet and he cursed silently as he attempted to wipe the thick stickiness from his heels on the warrior's leggings. He beckoned to the priestess.

Cliona paused by the fallen guard and her fingers fluttered briefly in the Sign of Peace above his head…and then Tuan, all too aware how horribly exposed they were in the hall, grabbed her arm and pulled her through the door into the blinding sunlight—straight into one of the Band of Kloor standing in their path!

Tuan slashed out blindly with the sword in his right hand, his knife stabbing upwards at the same time. He heard the sword deflected with a dull metallic clang as his knife arm was wrenched to one side. He became aware that Cliona was screaming at him, and got a look at his attacker before something flowed up his arms striking him hard in the chest…It was the bard. And then his weapons fell from his nerveless fingers and he began to shake uncontrollably, his lungs and heart contracting in spasms. A deep pit opened up beneath his feet and he fell forward into it, unconscious. Paedur caught him as he slowly folded. He slipped one arm about the stricken mate and hurried him into the shelter of the ruins. Cliona stooped to pick up the knife and sword and ran after them.

But a shout followed them from the balcony of the house; they had been seen.

The bard led them down seemingly impassable streets; streets clotted with tumbled masonry, rank with rotting vegetation, strewn with the debris of ages. Cliona helped Paedur guide the semi-conscious mate over the more difficult stretches. They ran for what seemed like an eternity to the priestess, until she begged the bard to stop. "Soon," was all he said. They continued on, down streets, across alleys and lanes, until she reckoned they must have crossed over half the Old City. She was just about to ask the bard to stop again, when he led them down a lane and into a plaza, in the centre of which was a tumbled street shrine. Paedur stopped and eased Tuan to the ground. "We can rest here," he said quietly.

Cliona nodded dumbly and fell down by Tuan's side, exhausted. She looked up at the bard, but he showed no sign of fatigue.

It was now mid-afternoon and the desolate city was silent, even the moaning wind having died during their flight. They had left the warriors of Kloor far behind, puzzling over the fugitives' disappearance down a seemingly blind alley.

The bard knelt by Tuan's side and began to slap his face, at first gently, then, when there was no reaction, he began striking him more forcefully until his head was rocking from side to side with the force of the blows. Cliona grabbed his arm and begged Paedur to stop.

Suddenly Tuan opened his eyes. "Stop...it is...I thought..." he mumbled, shaking his head. Paedur produced a flask from within the folds of his cloak and forced the mate to sip from it. He passed the flask to the priestess and, when she shook her head, he ordered her to drink also. She sipped the dark liquid, feeling it burn down her throat; it was foul and bitter, but she felt her fatigue-numbed brain begin to clear almost immediately. She looked across at the mate; he met her eyes and nodded, smiling.

"What happened?" Paedur demanded, returning the flask to his cloak.

"I thought you were..." Tuan began.

"Before that!"

"We were...we were standing on the balcony looking out over the ruins when I saw movement below. It was the Band of Kloor; we must have been followed..." He sat up suddenly. "Followed? But how; how did the Band know where to find us?"

The bard waved the question aside. "You forget that Thanos is a powerful magician. Continue."

Tuan pressed his throbbing head against the cool stone. "We hid beneath the stairs while the warriors searched the ground floor. Then they went upstairs, leaving one on guard. I knifed him, took his sword, then...then we..." He shook his head. "Where did you come from? I thought you were one of the Band. I could have sworn you were garbed in the fashion of the warriors. But..." He looked at the bard's travel-stained cloak, and shook his head again. "Then you were there ... and I had almost killed you."

The bard laughed softly. "Don't trouble yourself with that—it wasn't your fault. I had used a *glamour*, a spell, call it what you will, to assume the outward appearance of one of the Band. I had to get close to you. And then when you struck out, I had to defend myself..." He raised his hook slightly, "...but I only dazed you." He stood and listened carefully. "Come, we must seek shelter, there is a storm coming." He pulled Tuan up and then helped Cliona to her feet.

"Which way?" Tuan asked, swaying slightly. The priestess looped one arm around his waist and caught hold of his thick belt with the other.

Paedur nodded. "This way; it leads down to the oldest part of the city…"

Tuan looked up at the square blocky buildings that surrounded the plaza, noting their obvious great age. "Was Maante not the first city in the world?" he asked as they moved off.

The bard nodded. "One of the first. I would tell you its tale, but I only know fragments, and I never tell a broken or half-finished story."

"I know it," Cliona put in; "before I came here, I did some research on it."

"Tell us then," Tuan said eagerly.

"Many thousands of years ago, before the Demon Wars, even before the Isles of Monatome had risen from the sea, this was the original city of Maante, a flourishing, thriving sea-port. Where the New City now stands was once part of the Sea Lords' domain. The bay was so wide and deep that even such Culai warships as still survived and which were capable of holding a thousand fighting men could berth and dock safely here. Some say the city was Culai-built, but I do not think so. It lacks the solid grandeur of the Culai-built relics that dot even far-off Monatome."

"It was built by the hand of man, but designed by the last of the Culai architects, a link between the two worlds and times," the bard said unexpectedly.

Cliona paused uncertainly, then, at a sign from Tuan, continued. "Then came the Demon Wars and the Cataclysm, when the very surface of the earth was rent and the Southern Continent sank beneath the waves. New lands rose and others fell; islands appeared where there had been none before; whole chains of islands sank without trace. There were three days of absolute night, when many believed the Time of Reckoning was at hand. And when the sun shone again, it was found that the Bay of Maante had receded, and the sea-bed risen, and that there were now almost three leagues of beach between the wharves and the sea—and thus the Old City became useless almost overnight." She laughed suddenly. "Of course, the Cataclysm, that ruined the Old City of Maante, created the Isles of Monatome, my home."

"And how did the New City come to be divided into two parts, the Upper and Lower; who built the Quarter Wall which divides them?" Tuan asked.

Cliona shook her head. "I don't know; I never thought to check."

The bard spoke again, his voice seemingly lost in thought. "The citizens of Maante feared the sea would one day return, and the wall was intended to act as a breakwater. But as the population grew, so too did the need for space, and the land beyond the wall was utilised, thus creating the Upper and Lower sections of the city."

"There are some who hold that the sea is still retreating," Cliona said softly.

"That may be so. Our world is still a new world. These past ages are but its childhood. The land and the sea will have to settle, to shift and shape themselves. The land is constantly changing, but slowly... slowly, you could not see it unless you lived a hundred lifetimes. Even the sea is working towards this change; it is forever expanding, slowly eating away at the coastline, until...who knows? Perhaps some day when even Nusas the Sun grows old, perhaps then there will only be water on this world, a vast seething ocean." He turned and smiled thinly at Tuan and the priestess. "But not in your lifetimes."

"But in yours?" the mate asked in a whisper.

Paedur smiled, but said nothing.

They continued winding their way through the ruins late into the afternoon until the light was fading. Paedur at last stopped outside a high-walled building, in better repair than most. "We'll stop the night here."

And Cliona suddenly realised it was her own Temple of the Mother.

There was a hint of incense from the night before still in the air, overlying the dry odour of must which permeated even the very stones of the walls. Cliona shivered suddenly as they passed into the darkness and Tuan put his arm around her and drew her closer. This time she didn't shrink from his embrace. They paused just inside the door while their eyes became accustomed to the dimness.

Paedur meanwhile had wandered on into the desolate fane, his restless eyes noting the signs of the night's events: the scuffed prints of boots about the altar stone where the people had gathered around the priestess when he had entered. He smiled a little bitterly. Would he always be feared? He shook his head and then grinned ruefully— as long as man feared the unknown, the unnatural, they would fear, and even hate, him and his kind.

Cliona had left the wand Paedur had ignited with the Dannu-fire on the altar stone. He reached across and picked it up. It still felt warm to his touch and he felt the residue of power trickle along it and into the metal of his hook. He twirled it once about his head, spinning it with his fingers, bringing it to a brilliant blazing life, tremors of blue fire bathing the temple in azure light.

Tuan and the priestess came running, stumbling over the rubble littering the floor. They stood back and watched the bard in silence.

He raised the wand high, holding it by one end, and the streamers of fire slowly died until the bard was left holding a brilliant blue rod. Then the light began to pulse, and Tuan imagined he could see rings of blue fire travel slowly up the wand to gather about its tip.

A small circle of light surrounded the bard, radiating from the rod; slowly it began to expand until it encompassed the trio in a ring of pulsing blue-white light. And then Paedur suddenly reversed the wand, extinguishing it. But, although it was now nothing more than a wooden branch, the light encircling the companions remained, bathing them in waves of shifting azure. "Now, we are joined in the Fire of the Goddess," the bard said; "we are Companions in the old—and full—sense of the word."

Paedur handed the wand to Cliona. She accepted it gingerly and then almost cried aloud when she held it, for it was hot and it throbbed warmly, pulse-like—heart-like.

Paedur sat at the foot of the altar, resting his back and shoulders against the altar stone, watching them from beneath the shadow of his cowl. Cliona looked at Tuan and then turned back to the bard. And then she suddenly noticed that while the mate was clearly visible in the cold revolving Dannu-fire, the bard remained in shadow. It was as if he absorbed the light, or as if he could not be lit by the fire of the Mother. Did that not make him a Duaiteoiri?

"No," he said coldly, "I am not a Duaite, but neither am I Auithe."

Cliona started and opened her mouth to speak, but Tuan laid his hand on her arm, pulling her down beside him. "I think it's time we talked," he said slowly, softly, looking at the bard.

Paedur nodded. "It is time." He looked at Cliona, "You have decided to accompany us to the Blessed Isles." It was a statement more than a question.

The priestess was silent for a moment, then she looked from the bard to Tuan. "Yes, I have decided." She turned back to the bard. "This was why I was called to Maante..."

"You were brought here for a purpose; to aid me on the Culai Isle. But a choice was left you, for we would not force you against your will."

"*We?*" Tuan asked, sitting forward.

"We," Paedur repeated. "You know, Tuan, I am not alone: '*The Gods of the Pantheon on my right hand, the Duaite on my left,*'" he said with a thin smile, quoting the old proverb.

"I don't like to think I've been manipulated," Cliona said sharply.

"You get used to it," Tuan said, glaring at the bard.

"Be quiet," snapped the bard; "you're acting like children. Now attend me. The priests of Trialos seek to open the vessel that holds a fragment of the Chrystallis; the result would be to wipe out everything that has been created by the Soulwind; that includes this plane and every other plane of existence. It even includes the gods. Now, it appears the gods themselves cannot act directly to stop the priests and, similarly, Trialos and the Trialdone cannot aid their followers, for the Culai isle is a Place Apart, where time and the gods have no sway. Thus while the gods of both Faith and Religion look on helpless, we, their instruments, shall do their will; Thanos on the one hand will attempt to open the vessel, while I, on the other," he smiled and pressed his hook to his chest, "will try to ensure that the vessel remains sealed.

"Now Thanos and the priests of Trialos know that I am in Maante, and because of my reputation, he has brought a legion of the Band of Kloor, the Fist of God, with him. Their task is to guard the High Priest—and to slay us." He looked at Tuan and Cliona, "What do you know of Thanos?" he asked suddenly.

"He is the High Priest of Trialos," Cliona said, closing her fist in a Sign, "he is called the Hand of God."

"Anything else?" Paedur asked.

"He is reputed to be an evil man," Cliona said slowly, but Tuan shook his head. "No, I've heard he is a good, holy man, but influenced by evil men." He looked from the priestess to the bard. "Is he?"

Paedur laughed gently, humourlessly. "See his cunning? Your facts disagree even upon such information as you have."

"What do you know of him?" Tuan asked.

"I knew Thanos as a boy," Paedur began, "and I would say that I knew him better than any man alive. His was not an auspicious birth, for he was born in death. His mother died before he was delivered, and he would have perished also had not his father torn him from his mother's womb. His father was a blacksmith, a hugely muscled man, strong in mind and body, strong in the Faith. Yet he questioned the Faith thereafter. Why had his wife died? Why had the child lived? And in time he spurned the Faith and grew to hate the child. In time also his mind went and he took to wandering about the town, talking and laughing to himself, imagining his dead wife was with him. He was found dead one morning in his forge; he had cut his belly open in much the same way as he had delivered his son from his wife.

"Thanos was a strange boy, and some people said that he carried the shadow of his mother's death over him; that Mannam had set a *bainte* to watch him; that he was already dead and his spirit claimed by the Dark Lord."

The circle of blue light revolving about the trio suddenly quivered, rippling like a stone-disturbed pool. "Hah, they search," Paedur said softly, "and they're closing in. We must hurry. But to continue...

"Thanos and I played together as children. Folk would laugh to see us together, for he was as pale as I am dark; he was—*is*—albino. We were as brothers until the time came for me to enter Baddalaur, the bardic college. We wept together to be parted and swore we would be re-united one day. I never saw him again.

"When my mother died I was allowed home for her burial." His voice grew soft, and his eyes saw another time, a time past.

"Aaah, her death was a great ending in more ways than one. It was the last time every member of my family would be gathered together in one place. Even when my father died there were not so many present. And they have all gone now...all gone. I am the last..." His voice suddenly changed and his head snapped up. Whatever he had briefly experienced had vanished just as quickly. "Thanos wasn't there, though, and yet my mother had treated him like another son. And, although I tried to find out what had happened to him, no one knew—or at least no one admitted to knowing—except for one, my great-uncle Gahred, who was bard of the Ordivian line that ruled the western lands."

"I heard of him," Tuan said suddenly. "Did he not compose the *Lay of the Reiver?*"

Paedur smiled. "Aye, he did:

The Reivers return,
with blood and death,
and fire and storm,
 the Reivers return. "

Tuan's strong voice broke in:

"Their swords are singing,
bright and keen,
fearing neither god,
nor man nor beast,
the Reivers return. "

He stopped. "I didn't know Gahred was related to you."

"I did not know the lay was still remembered," Paedur said gently.

"All the Taourg know the *Reiver's Return.* "

"That would have pleased Gahred."

"Does he live still?" Tuan wondered.

 Paedur shook his head. "No, his bones rest in the grounds of Baddalaur." The bard continued on in a voice grown harsh with some emotion. "Time, time, there is little enough left. Gahred told me that Thanos had left the village the previous year…to study in Maante. Aye, here in Maante. He is returning, returning to the place of his beginning as it were. For it was here that he first came into contact with the priests of Trialos. They were not as active then as they are now, but they took the youth and schooled him. Perhaps they were aware of his potential, for Thanos received training above and beyond that of the ordinary novice.

"Something attracted him to Trialos and the New Religion; the power, the wealth, or a combination of both. Who can tell? He advanced quickly through the ranks of the older, more experienced priests. Some resented this, but they met with accidents. Eventually there was no one standing in his way, except Sutar, the High Priest."

"He died horribly," Cliona said with a shudder.

Paedur bowed his head slightly. "Aye, he died horribly. Someone—something—attacked him as he lay sleeping. A beast, it was said. But what beast could scale the glass-smooth walls of a sheer tower, enter through a slit window, decapitate, disembowel and dismember a man—and do all this silently?"

"A demon?" Tuan asked.

The encircling light flickered once more. Paedur glanced at it, then hurried on. "Perhaps it was a demon. But who invoked that demon? In any case, it left the way open for Thanos to assume the role of High Priest."

"Is he not supposed to be a recluse?" Tuan asked.

Paedur nodded. "That is an image he has worked hard to create. He has always stayed very much in the background, preferring to work through intermediaries, thus fostering his image as a simple man of prayer. Yet he is the real power behind the strength and resurgence of the New Religion today."

"And he is here in Maante?" Cliona asked.

"Aye, he is here. Thanos, his new acolyte Xanazius—whom I fancy I have come across before—and a full legion of the Band of Kloor. And tomorrow they sail for the Sea of Galae and the Blessed Isle—the Culai Isle."

"When do we go?" Tuan asked.

And for the first time, the mate saw indecision on the bard's face. "I suppose it must be soon," he said slowly.

In the silence that followed the Dannu-fire flickered and died. Then high above, where the ceiling should have been, a small cerulean clot of fire began to throb. It expanded, pulsing outwards, in ever-widening concentric circles. Cliona, gazing at the blue whirling cloud, felt as if she were falling up into the centre of the maelstrom. Abruptly the light swooped and expanded and was all about them, enfolding them within its warm embrace. They were blind and deaf, totally unaware of the ruined temple in which they had been scant moments before; totally unaware of one another, they were enrapt, encircled by the whirling, throbbing, gently susurrant, sapphire cloud all around them.

Light, vast streamers of vari-coloured belts of liquid light floated past their blind eyes, felt more than seen. Rainbow-hued fireflies danced intricate patterns across their skins, the touch of the tiny creatures needle-sharp and painful.

Then a voice—a female voice—spoke from within the colours; the clouds trembled, the delicate notes of the whispered voice sending ripples of colour through the cloud: azure, violet, turquoise, beryl, and aquamarine chasing one another in flowing patterns about the solid cloud of light. And now the rainbow colours were gone, just the pale and dancing shades of blue remaining.

"You have served us well, Paedur-*shanaqui*-Hookhand. And yet there is the one final task to be completed, but still you linger...linger. Your companions are at hand, why do you linger ...linger...?"

Paedur spoke, his usually mellow voice now harsh and raw, sending crashing waves of discordant non-colour through the delicate shades. "I would know what the future holds before I act."

And as the patterns gradually settled, the voice whispered gently once more, in reply to the bard's question. "There is no future... future. There is a darkness...darkness. Only you have the power to change the future..."

"Is that future not fixed?" Paedur demanded.

"It is what may be, not what will be...will be."

Again the crashing wave of white non-colour. "What help can you render me—us?"

"There is a boat ready...ready. A favourable sea and winds have been arranged...arranged. But our power does not extend on to the Sea of Gala...Galae. For there all mortal time ends and timelessness rules...rules." The voice slowly faded and the shades of blue began to pale, revealing the three figures. It continued to lighten until a thin film, almost a mist, surrounded the trio. Suddenly the mist was shattered as Paedur stood up, breaking the spell surrounding them. Cliona slumped forward and would have fallen had not the mate caught her. He looked at the bard. "What was that?"

"The Goddess," he said, but he refused to be drawn further.

"What now?" Tuan asked then.

Paedur shrugged and sighed. "You heard. To the shore, and then...?"

The door suddenly crashed inwards and the Band of Kloor poured in, weapons ready. "Kill them!"

Tuan counted ten of them as his knife came clear of its sheath. It was the only weapon he had; the sword he had taken from the slain warrior had been lost as they fled through the ruins. He began to pray, silently, desperately. Two against ten. He looked about for something to use as a weapon, something to give him extra reach; his short knife would be little use against a sword.

The wand the bard had fired earlier lay on the altar. He reached down to pick it up, but a slim white hand stopped him. He looked into Cliona's deep eyes, seeing himself reflected in the pools of light.

"No, this is mine," she said desperately.

The mate had no time to argue as the first of the Religion's warriors came upon him.

The Band had divided into two groups, five men to a group. They were attempting to encircle the two men. One man broke ranks and ran swiftly towards Tuan, his sword held high, poised for a downward swing that would decapitate its target.

Tuan threw himself forwards and down, coming up directly in front of the startled youth, the sword whistling past Tuan's head, moaning almost regretfully as it parted only air. The mate grabbed the youth by the throat and plunged his dagger into the extended jugular. Blood spurted over Tuan as the body fell forward, pushing him down onto his knees. Using the body as a shield, Tuan prised the sword from the dead man's locked fingers. Two more were coming at him; he pushed the body in his arms at them, felt it twitch and jerk as they hacked at it in a vain attempt to reach him. He stabbed upwards, blindly, with the sword, felt it connect, grate along bone, heard the shrill animal-like scream; he heaved the bloody burden away from him, into the faces of two others, stepped back to Cliona's side, parried a thrust with his knife, slashed with the sword, felt it tremble in contact with metal, then bite into flesh.

In the lull that followed, he found he had slain three.

However, the warriors treated the bard with a little more respect. They didn't know what to expect from this black-clad figure of whom they had heard so much. But Thanos had said that he was human enough to be killed by a blade, and a fortune to the first man who brought in his head and hook, a kingdom to the one who brought the bard back alive. The five warriors surrounded Paedur,

ringing him with steel. One probed with his sword, then was abruptly
wrenched forward as the bard caught and trapped the blade with
his hook, using it to pull the man in. Instinct made him retain his
grip, his free hand clawing for a dagger. The bard struck out with
the palm of his hand, catching the warrior beneath his nose, just
above the lip, striking upwards. The warrior felt his head explode as
jagged splinters of bone and cartilage were driven up into his brain.
He was dead before he hit the ground.

A shrill scream coming from his right distracted another of
Paedur's attackers. He glanced aside for a heartbeat—a fatal heartbeat. The bard's hook flashed out, a gleaming silvery blur, catching
the warrior under the chin, cutting upwards, opening his throat like
sliced fruit. Another warrior struck out, only to find his target was
no longer there but rather behind him; he felt the hook cut deeply
into his throat, pull, tear…then no more. Three down.

As the rest of the warriors fell back, the bard joined Cliona and
Tuan by the altar stone.

The four surviving warriors of the Band of Kloor rejoined and
looked about in amazement and horror. Six men, slain in no more
than a score of heartbeats. By two men. And one of them with
only one hand.

"I think they will try to rush us from both sides," the mate whispered. "They're going to be more careful this time." Paedur nodded silently.

The four warriors whispered amongst themselves and then divided into two groups, taking up positions on either side of the
altar, their swords and knives held ready. This time there would be
no mistake.

Tuan and Paedur placed Cliona between them, and then they
turned to face the remaining warriors.

Tuan found himself facing two youths, their eyes wild, jaws
clenched. Their faces were sheened with sweat. Tuan was gambling
that they were not seasoned warriors, gambling with his life. He
feinted to his left, then suddenly fell at the feet of the two young
men. One stumbled against his companion, putting them both off
balance; Tuan's sword ripped upwards striking one in the groin, his
knife slashing at the back of the other's knee. Both fell heavily on
top of him, but he was trapped, pinned to the ground by the weight
of their armour.

Paedur was not facing youths but seasoned warriors. They approached cautiously, one from either side. Almost impercepti- bly a signal passed between the two, and they attacked together. The bard, however, had caught the signal and threw himself for- ward between the two men, rolling easily to his feet and coming up behind them. One screamed a warning and spun around in time to receive the bard's hook across the mouth, severing his jaw, cutting almost back into the spine. The other stabbed with his sword, and Paedur felt the blade grate off his belt buckle. He grabbed the warrior's extended sword arm and squeezed. He felt the bones pop beneath his grasp. The warrior threw his head back to scream, and Paedur sliced his throat, ear to ear.

Tuan was in trouble. Both of his attackers were still alive and conscious, although one was severely wounded and the other ham- strung, but the mate lay helpless beneath the one he had stabbed through the groin. The mortally wounded warrior grinned at him, a ghastly rictus of his facial muscles, blood dribbling from his mouth where the mate's blade had pierced upwards into the base of his lungs.

"You...will die...for the greater...gl...glory of...Kloor!" he screamed as he died and then his hamstrung companion raised him- self on one arm, his knife held high. There was a sudden keening in the air, then a sickening thud as if rotten fruit were being crushed. The warrior stiffened and fell forward, the back of his head crushed. Cliona dropped the shattered wand and fumbled desperately at the two bodies on top of Tuan's, vainly attempting to pull the armoured bodies off him. She was weeping and laughing at the same time.

"I had to... he would have killed you...to desecrate the wand ...and such a good wand too. A powerful wand...one of the best ...but I had to."

Paedur gently lifted her by the arms and led the shaking priestess to the foot of the altar, catching her face, forcing her to look up into his eyes. "Sleep," he commanded. Her eyes abruptly glazed and she slumped, unconscious.

Tuan meanwhile had succeeded in freeing himself from beneath the two dead bodies. He stood with the bard and surveyed the carnage. Ten bodies, ten unknown warriors, some no more than youths, their spirits abruptly torn free of their bodies, their sprawled bodies looking almost alien, and some hideously comical.

Paedur looked at the mate's gore-splattered form. Tuan was covered from head to foot in drying blood; it clotted in his hair, encrusted his clothing, even smeared his teeth. He grinned ruefully. "I must look a sight, eh? Well, you're no beauty either." Suddenly all the humour left him. He dropped the sword and cleaned his knife on the corner of his shirt before slipping it back into its sheath. "Come on, let's get out of here." He bent down and lifted Cliona in his broad arms, his hands leaving bloody prints along the white and blue samite of her dress.

Paedur nodded absently. "We had better find someplace to clean up. Then..."

"Then...?" Tuan asked.

Paedur looked over at him and smiled thinly, without humour. "Then we'd better see about that boat."

13
The Sea of Galae

*And the bard and his companions sailed the Sea of Galae in search of the
Blessed Isle.*

Life of Paedur, the Bard

*The Blessed Isle is marked on many charts, but none have ever come to it, for
no one has yet navigated the Sea of Galae.*

Lilis' Geographica

Tuan shaded his eyes against Nusas' glare and nodded at the bulging
sail. "Why is our craft the only one that seems to be moving? Everything else is becalmed."

Paedur, who was kneeling in the prow of the small frail-seeming fishing smack, looked back over his shoulder. "Feitigh, one of
the Windlords, aids us now."

"And we're not the only ones moving," Cliona said, pointing aft
to where a long sleek coastal cruiser moved away from Maante's
harbour walls.

The bard stood up and shaded his eyes. "Thanos," he muttered.
"Aiaida, the Religion's Lord of the Sea Wind, must be helping him."

"Can we outrun him?" Tuan asked.

"No," Paedur smiled thinly, "but neither can he catch us. The
two windlords are fairly evenly matched. If they do battle..." he
hesitated and then shrugged, "well, the only winners will be Mannam
and Libellius, the Dark Lords of the Faith and Religion."

"What about magic; could he not attempt to sink us that
way?"

"No. Even I would not attempt a sending—or indeed, even a
minor working—so close to the Grey Wall."

"Why not?" Cliona wondered.

"The wall is Culai-fashioned, but to maintain itself it draws upon
the magic of this and the many other planes of existence. Every
time a spell of any nature is worked, a tiny fraction of it is drawn to
the wall. However, it also distorts any spells that might be worked

in its vicinity." He smiled at Cliona. "How many magicians did you know in Maante?"

She thought about it for a moment, then shook her head. "None; some minor spell-makers, and most of those were charlatans."

The crafts were swept out of Maante Harbour and on to the Aangle Sea by their respective windgods, with neither gaining on the other. This part of the coast was completely devoid of islands, and the sea stretched flat and unbroken to the horizon where it met the Grey Wall.

Cliona moved down the craft to stand beside Tuan, who had the tiller. "What is it?" she asked, pointing to the horizon.

Tuan smiled. "Fog."

The bard, who was standing in the prow, staring straight ahead, glanced back over his shoulder and smiled. "A little more than fog, surely?"

Tuan nodded. "A little. How long before we reach it?" he asked then.

"We should have reached the wall by nightfall." And what then, Paedur wondered, staring towards the distant wall, what happens when we reach the wall? He knew of it from his tales and legends; he had read the factual accounts of travellers and mariners who had sailed—either by accident or design—too close, or even into the fringes of the shifting fog banks. But no one knew what lay within the heart of the Grey Wall. Even the Culai Isle—which he had visited once before very briefly—did not hold as much fear for him as the Sea of Galae which lay behind the wall.

Their craft reached the Grey Wall just as the sun was sinking, tinting the shifting cloud a dull, bloody pink. It towered above them like a great bastion, its height lost in the clouds, and it dwindled away on both sides seemingly to infinity, curving with the distance. From afar it had the appearance of a solid wall, yet as they neared the Culai-fashioned barrier, the silent watchers could see that the wall floated above the waves at about the height of a tall man and was in constant motion, weaving and twisting, shifting as if blown by winds not of this world. Strange shadows slid past behind the grey veil, but the silhouettes were not of any animal either Tuan or Cliona knew. As night fell, there were a series of animal and bird cries and snarls and screams that floated across the still air, and again neither of them could recognise the sounds. With the onset of night the wall brightened and then gleamed with a strange milky opalescence, as if the Lady Lussa bestrode the heavens; but it was not the time for the Moon Goddess to ride out in her swan-drawn chariot.

And then the wind died, leaving their craft bobbing on the oily swell half a league from the fringes of the Grey Wall. Tuan turned to Paedur, "What happens now?"

"The gods' power must fade here." His hook gleamed silver in the light from the wall as he pointed aft, "The Religion's power also. Sleep, if you can; I don't imagine you will find much sleep once we are on the Sea of Galae."

Tuan glanced at the priestess. "I don't think I could sleep with that thing looming over me; the gods only know what might creep out under cover of dark..."

Paedur pressed the blade of his hook against his lips, covering a smile. "I don't think anything will come out. Even so, I think I'll remain awake..." He looked down at Cliona. "You could try to sleep though..."

The priestess shook her head. "No, I don't think so..."

Paedur inclined his head slightly. "As you wish then..."

A score of heartbeats later, she and Tuan were both asleep.

Tuan awoke, his mariner's instincts telling him that they were moving again. He found the bard in the stern, his hook curved around the tiller. "We're moving," he said, unnecessarily.

"A current came up just before dawn and began pulling us in; we have been picking up speed." Paedur nodded to the priestess. "Wake her up, and then hold her—I'm not sure what will happen when we hit the wall."

Tuan kissed the priestess, bringing her awake with a whimper. "Hang on," he murmured, "we're moving in to the wall." Even as he was speaking the craft began to pick up speed, a double wake of churning white spreading out behind them. Tuan crouched over the priestess holding her with one hand, the other wrapped around the mast, and then the tiny boat struck the shifting, misty wall, and shuddered to a standstill. Grey tendrils of freezing fog reached out and enveloped them. The fog thickened, and soon they could barely make out each other.

"What now?" Tuan asked, his breath pluming whitely on the air.

Cliona shivered. "We're going to freeze to death," she said, her teeth chattering, every breath she took searing her throat and lungs.

The bard shook his head, "No, we're just passing through the Place Between the Worlds; the chill will soon abate."

The banks of fog abruptly lightened, and the chill was soon replaced by a thick cloying heat. Tuan felt the rime that had formed in his hair and beard melt, and he looked down the craft at the bard to find his heavy cloak steaming. "We have passed through the wall; this is the Sea of Galae," Paedur said with a rare genuine smile.

The fog remained, although it was not as thick as before, but it served to muffle all sounds and a deathly silence hung over the sea. Even the normal sounds aboard ship were muted, and when someone spoke their voice was faint as if heard through thick glass or from a distance. They had no idea whether Thanos and the Band of Kloor had made it through to the Sea of Galae, although the bard felt they must have. Even here, on the haunted sea, he would have known if someone as powerful and malign as the Hand of God had died.

Time became meaningless within the wall; there was neither night nor day, and the grey half-light, not unlike the northern winter twilight, persisted. But the bard seemed to he able to keep track of the hours, for he would indicate whcn a meal should be prepared, or advise Cliona when her devotions to Dannu were due. However, Paedur seemed disinclined to speak and the constant, oppressive sameness of the sea depressed both Cliona and Tuan, and so they spent much of the time sleeping.

It was the morning of the fourth day on the sea, by Tuan's reckoning, when he noticed a change in their surroundings; the fog had lightened in colour and thinned considerably. He was about to speak to the bard when Paedur handed him a blindfold; Cliona was already holding one in her small hands, examining the eye-patches which had coins sewn into them to ensure that no trace of light seeped through.

The mate held up the length of cloth. "I assume this has something to do with the change?" he said.

Paedur nodded. "As you can see the fog has begun to lighten and soon it will seem as though it is about to dissipate completely—however, I'm afraid it is but part of the sea's defences. Shadow-figures will then appear—drawn from your own minds and hereditary memories—and they will be of people close to you, your mother or father, brothers or lovers, but they are only shadows. You will also feel touches and caresses; and they will also speak, enticing you, talking in terms of love and endearment. Again, you must not heed them; the voices—like the images—are only those of your own memories animated by the magic of the Grey Wall, and the caresses will be nothing more than tendrils of mist drifting across your face and arms."

"What do we need these for, then?" Cliona asked.

"I think you might find it easier not to listen to the voices, if you cannot see the wraiths."

"There are only two blindfolds," she added.

"I won't need one," the bard said, with a wry smile.

"Just where are we?" Tuan asked. "I have sailed across the oceans and seas of this world, but where are we now in relation to Maante, or the Aangle Peninsula, for example?"

Paedur glanced up into the lightening sky, judging how much time he had left. "This sea is not in your world," he replied. "We have sailed through the space between the planes—the Ghost Worlds, where we experienced the chill—and now we are sailing the fringes of the Sea of Galae, which belong to the Prime Plane but which touches the edges of all the others."

"I'm not sure I understand," Cliona said.

Tuan nodded, agreeing with her. "How can this place be on the charts of our world and yet not in our world?"

"You know the legend that the Culai still abide on the Blessed Isle, and although this isle is positioned on the charts of mariners, few sailors—if any—have ever succeeded in reaching it. How can I explain it...?" He looked around, at a loss for words, but then turned back and continued quickly. "What you see on the mariners' charts is but a reflection, the like of which you must surely have seen hovering above the dunes of Nasgociba if you ever visited there with Duaize." Tuan nodded and was about to speak, but the bard had pressed on. "From a distance they seem tangible, yet as one nears them the mirages fade, like the morning mist on a summer's day. Like the Culai Isle one may never reach them, no matter how close one approaches."

"And the Grey Wall?" Tuan asked.

"You might liken it to a doorway between the worlds."

"And is there traffic between the worlds...the planes?" the priestess wondered, for though she had been told the tale of the creation
of the Prime Plane and the lesser planes of existence, she had always
thought them nothing more than parables.

"There is some traffic," the bard said quickly, "though it is not as
frequent as it once was. But at one time the creatures that roam this
world—and even man—freely migrated through the Grey Walls."

"Walls?" Tuan wondered. "Are there more than one?"

"Many years ago, in my grandfather's time, there were many
walls and gates scattered across the Seven Nations, but now, alas,
they have all disappeared. This is one of the last, and it has survived
because it was the most powerful of all the walls, and the only one
which leads directly to the Prime Plane; although," he added, "I have
heard that there are still walls and gates standing in the strange hotlands
of the south."

"What happened to the gates?" Tuan asked.

"Neglect mainly; the gates thrived on use—they fed on a little
of each user's essence."

"Are they alive then?"

"Yes, they have life of a sort, but not as you would recognise it.
And now they are slowly dying, fading in the strong light of Nusas,
like mist burning away before sunrise. Even this wall is not as it once
was." He looked at them, his eyes flat and expressionless. "There is
an end coming to all things."

"And perhaps it is coming sooner that we think," Cliona whispered, but if either the bard or Tuan heard her they said nothing.

"Put your blindfolds on now," Paedur ordered them. "And
remember, ignore everything you hear or feel. I will not let any
harm come to you."

The priestess bowed her head and pulled back her hair and
Tuan slipped the blindfold around her head, settling the two coin-
filled patches over her eyes. He felt the tension in her neck and
shoulder muscles and he kissed her lightly on the forehead, whispering that she need have no fear—he was with her now. The mate
looked over at the bard, and Paedur nodded once, and then Tuan
pulled on his own blindfold and sat down with the priestess, with
his back to the mast.

Paedur looked down at the two huddled figures by his feet
and then he sketched a quick sigil of protection above their heads.

If the circumstances had been different, perhaps Cliona and Tuan might have had a life together, but then, Paedur realised, without the present circumstances it was unlikely that a priestess of the Old Faith and a Nasgociban pirate would ever have met. He felt his hook begin to warm, and he knew that something was approaching. He tugged his cloak close about his shoulders with his right hand and pulled up the hood; he was not afraid, but nor was he foolish enough to do anything rash. He glanced down at the priestess and the mate again and wondered would he be able to protect them, and then, in that instant—although he was not gifted with true foresight—he knew they would not be returning from the Culai Isle. A smile touched his thin lips; he had a feeling no one would be returning from the Culai Isle.

The muffled silence was disturbed by a faint moaning sound, like a summer breeze blowing through leafy copses. It began as a wordless drone but it soon broke up and single words and then fragments of conversation became distinguishable…and then the wraiths appeared.

They were fog-wraiths, creatures from coalesced mist and fog and drawn from the memories—both recent and hereditary—of Cliona and Tuan. Strangely, there were no memories generated from the bard's unconscious. Paedur watched the figures with interest. Some were recognisable, the resemblance to either the man or woman being marked, but as the figures continued to file past and the clothing, armour and weapons changed, belonging to earlier ages, the resemblances became less marked, except for the occasional feature which was definitely Cliona's or Tuan's. And the fog-wraiths reached forth with long misty fingers and stroked and caressed the cringing mate and enticed the terrified priestess. When there was no reaction to their caresses or blandishments, the figures moved on and vanished back into the fog.

Paedur suddenly stiffened as his arcane hook burned painfully into the bone of his wrist. He had thought the wraiths were gone, but there was another group gathering now; there were only four figures, and the bard realised that these must be the earliest memories of man—they were the Culai, the First Race.

They were tall and sharp-featured and they strode up to the small fishing smack with all the arrogance of gods. The Culai had often been worshipped as gods—and it was a title they had taken for themselves—but although they wielded their awesome powers with god-like negligence there was still something about them which marked them of the race of man. Perhaps it was in their eyes, which were hard and cruel—and only man can be cruel: the gods have no time to indulge themselves.

They paused and gathered about the craft, their great height dwarfing it. The bard's hook was blazing with the cold white fire that warned him of Power, but he didn't need his hook to tell him just how powerful these Culai-wraiths were. He could feel the awesome force radiating from them, and even the shivering pair became quiet and blindly turned their cloth-wrapped faces towards the Culai, like a blossom turning its head towards the sun. One stretched out his hand to the priestess, and though she could not see it she still reached instinctively for the long slim fingers.

"Come." His voice was strong and resonant, unmuffled by the mist, carrying with it the trace of an accent. As his hand approached the priestess it became more solid, taking on a definite shape and form, the veins becoming defined, the tendons rigid, the nails long and slightly curved. Suddenly the bard lunged forward, his hook glittering whitely, slicing through the outstretched arm. The wraith screamed, a high-pitched jarring sound that bit deep into Paedur's skull and set his hook vibrating. The hook blazed with a brilliant incandescence as it passed through the fog, and then long ribbon-like streamers broke away, and the entire shade tattered and was shredded as some ghostly wind pulled it apart.

Another tenuous hand slid across to grasp either the priestess or mate, but again the bard struck through it with his hook, the white fire coursing through his body, and again the Culai was torn apart by the unseen wind.

The two remaining Culai drifted away from the craft and hovered at about the height of the main mast, watching the two humans almost hungrily, Paedur thought. He wondered then what would have happened if they had actually managed to touch either of them. He sketched a sign in the air before them, and their forms wavered and then abruptly drew in on themselves and disappeared. "It is over," Paedur said, exhaustion settling over him; the Culai-wraiths had drained him.

As Cliona and Tuan peeled off their blindfolds, they plainly heard screams coming from the direction where they had last seen the boat carrying Thanos and the priests and warriors of Trialos and Kloor.

"What is it?" Tuan murmured.

"The sea's defences have attacked them."

"Perhaps those same defences will destroy the evil ones," Cliona whispered. She looked at the bard and found that his face was bone-white, his eyes sunken and dead in his head. "You are ill!"

Paedur shook his head. "Not ill, just tired. As for Thanos, well he may have lost some men, but Thanos is powerful and cunning and I have no doubt he will outwit the Cul...the defences." He looked over at the mate. "Take the tiller. Hold our course as best you can. I will try to rest."

Tuan and Cliona watched the bard sink into a cross-legged position with his back to the mast and settle his cloak about him, and almost immediately his head dropped forward and he was asleep.

"I've never seen him sleep before," Tuan whispered, more frightened now by the bard's exhaustion than by the danger of the Sea.

"I wonder what were the sea's defences?" Cliona said. "Something powerful and terrible if they were able to exhaust a creature like the bard."

"What do we do now?"

Cliona ran her fingers through her thick hair, dragging it back from her face. "We hold the course and wait for Paedur to awaken."

"How am I supposed to keep to a course with neither sun, moon, nor stars to guide me? And when will he awake?"

Cliona knelt by the bard's side and felt for a pulse in his wrist and then in his throat; she could find neither. And yet his chest rose and fell slightly. She lifted his head and peeled back an eyelid, but she could only see a white expanse of eyeball. She looked up at Tuan. "I'm not sure when he will awaken—I'm not even sure if he's alive!"

Paedur awoke two days later, just as the temperature began to fall and the fog wall was darkening. "We're nearly through," he said, coming smoothly to his feet, catching both the priestess and mate by surprise. "The Sea of Galae, the sea between the worlds, ends here, and now we're about to enter the Prime Plane."

"You're well again?" Cliona asked.

Paedur glanced over his shoulder. "Exhaustion, merely," he smiled.

"I don't suppose you want to say what you defended us from, do you?" Tuan asked.

"It's unimportant," Paedur said, turning away and making his way down the small craft to stand by the prow.

Although the temperature fell dramatically, it was not so cold as when they had entered upon the sea, nor was it as dark. The transition came quickly: one moment they were still within the mist and then it thickened—and vanished. They had passed through the last obstacle, they were upon the Prime Plane. They had come through the Sea of Galae unscathed, but the Blessed Isle lay before them, and neither man nor beast had ever returned from the Culai Isle.

They came out onto a wide, featureless ocean—whose waters were startlingly white, a bleached harsh absence of colour that pierced the eyes, the type which would surely bring a sudden blindness to those who stared too long into its alabaster depths.

"It reminds me of the deadly ice-fields beyond northern Thusal," Tuan said, his voice falling to a whisper, the white water bringing back terrifying memories of the haunted ice-lands where even the very elements conspire to wipe the land free of all living creatures, animal and vegetable.

"We're moving," Cliona said, turning to look at the Grey Wall that was now shrinking rapidly behind them, the featureless, almost colourless rolling fog stretching to the horizon, marking the boundary of their new world.

She suddenly swore, and as Paedur and Tuan turned they saw the sleek black craft that broke through the wall and they knew then that Thanos, too, had successfully navigated the Sea of Galae.

"I never expected otherwise," Paedur said quietly, turning away.

They sailed across the alabaster ocean for five long days, five days indistinguishable from each other, with no change in the bleached seascape. For five short nights also they sailed, pursued always by the black ship of Thanos. At night the bard would take the tiller and the mate and the priestess would lie sheltered in the lee of their craft's single sail, and they would gaze up at the strange stars that studded the cloth of heaven and the bard would name the stars for them and tell their histories and their attributes.

Here was the Sceptre and Orb, and these were the property of the Emperor, and they had been won from the Princeling, and in the battle he had been cast down and no longer occupied the Throne of Heaven. And there, faint behind the Empress, was the Emperor, for the Empress had come to usurp the Emperor much as he had done to the Princeling, and his light was already beginning to fade. These were of the House of Royal.

And Paedur also pointed out the Houses of Astrios, the Winged Ones; of Baaste, and of Wand, and finally as they rose late in the night, the Twilight House of the Culaithe, the Sign of the Culai.

On the morning of the sixth day, when the mate arose, he found the bard standing by the prow, staring intently ahead.

"What is it?"

The bard pointed with his hook, ahead and a little to port.

"What does it look like?"

Tuan shaded his pale eyes and squinted towards the smudge on the horizon. "Land," he said finally.

Paedur nodded, turning away. "The Blessed Isle."

As the blistering day wore on, the smudge resolved itself into an island, which rose up out of the ocean with an almost frightening speed. Around noon, it was still distant but so large that Tuan turned to the bard, shaking his head in astonishment. "That's not an island—it's a continent!"

Paedur smiled slightly and shook his head. "It's an island, I assure you."

As the afternoon moved into evening, the island rose up out of the water before them, and they could make out the high and lofty cliffs, carved from what looked like glass and worked with the effigies of men who were not truly men, and beasts that were not wholly beasts. And in the low afternoon sunlight it looked as if the figures were animate, for the shadows writhing and twisting across the glass cliffs gave them a semblance of life.

There was a wall on top of the cliff, but a wall the like of which even the giant builders of Necrosia could not have built. A wall that would have defied the abilities of the builders of the Tomb City of Ellian whose architects knew the secret of softening stone. Brick upon massive brick, it towered above the cliff, almost doubling its height.

"It's incredible," Tuan murmured.

"Each brick is as tall as a single-floored dwelling," Paedur remarked almost absently.

It took Cliona three attempts to count the number of blocks. "But it's eighty blocks high!"

A series of shifting cross-currents took their craft then, spinning them in beneath the cliffs, and then they rounded a promontory and found they were facing a broad shingly beach. The currents had died, and the natural pull of the sea swept them up into the shallows in a welter of creamy foam. Tuan was about to leap into the water to secure the craft farther up the beach when the bard stopped him. "On no account must you touch the beach with your bare flesh." His eyes were hard and cold, and the mate could see tiny white sparks running up and down the bard's hook, gathering in the etched runes, almost making them move. "Watch!" Paedur said.

The bard lifted a fruit from their supplies. It had been wrapped in its leaves to preserve it and was still firm and unblemished. He tossed it out onto the shingle beach. It had scarcely touched the smoothly polished stones when they began to move, sliding towards the fruit. They piled around the fruit, then they rolled over it, smothering it in a wave of shingle. With a spurt of juice it was crushed to pulp.

Tuan climbed back into the boat, rubbing his bare arms, smoothing down the small hairs which were standing upright. "What do we do now?" he asked, his voice trembling.

But the bard laughed shortly and leaped into the shallows, splashing up on to the shore. "The stones only scent living matter," he said. "If you're wearing shoes, you're safe."

The bard led them with an easy familiarity across the now quiescent stones, which however still moved threateningly, a tiny rattling off to their right, and now a rasp of stone to their left. They were halfway up the beach when the priestess began to shiver. Her lips turned blue and tiny particles of ice formed on her clothes and in her hair. Yet the mate and the bard were unaffected.

"T-t-t-uannnn..."

The mate spun around, his knife coming into his hand but he almost dropped it when he saw the state Cliona was in. She looked as if she had been caught in a blizzard. Her hair was frozen in long thick tresses and the frost had turned it white. Her skin was pinched blue and there was a thin coating of ice on her skin. Her clothing was solid. The mate reached out for her, but the bard's hook caught in his sleeve, pulling his hand back. "The cold is such that it would sear your own flesh—and hers if you touched her."

"But what's wrong with her?"

But the bard didn't answer, he merely used the point of his hook to direct the shivering priestess back onto the beach, almost to the water's edge. The ice melted almost immediately but left her soaking in freezing water. Tuan and the bard both threw their cloaks around her shoulders, but her teeth were still chattering as she told them what had happened.

"It was as if I had plunged into an icy pool, every breath was ice-fire in my lungs, and I felt as if my eyes were about to burst. I was going to die," she said, shivering now, not with the cold but with reaction.

Tuan looked over at Paedur. "What caused it—and why did it affect only Cliona?"

The bard shook his head slightly, staring up at the lifelike carvings. "I'm not sure…" He looked at Cliona. "Show me where you first felt the chill."

"About there," she pointed.

Paedur nodded, smiling thinly. "It's the shadow of the cliffs, I'll wager. Did you not tell us of your halfling blood—you're a child of human man and Nightfolk woman, are you not? And the Nightfolk are the last preservers of the Culai magic. So…" He pointed upwards with his hook. "These cliffs were not raised by the hand of mortal man…nor by the Culai, for in their last days on our world, when the infant kingdoms of man strove against the elder power of the Culai, there arose one amongst the First Race who was to change their world as never before. He was Kuallan, and was later called the Friend of Man.

"He saw his own race for what it was, and he had enough of the sight to realise that its days were numbered, and so he gathered together a group of Culai—visionaries, like himself—and he sent these out as missionaries to instruct man in that part of the Culai lore which might prove beneficial to the new race. When Kuallan knew that the Culai had very little time left, he devised a plan so that his race might not be totally annihilated. He travelled through the Grey Walls to the other planes of life and gathered together the greatest magicians and sorcerers on these worlds. Some were human-kind, but others had the likeness of beasts or demons and, although they were usually mortal enemies, Kuallan had bound them all together by extracting one promise from each of them. Until they fulfilled that promise they were his to command. And so he brought them here and they numbered one hundred and three, and should you care to count the effigies carved into the cliffs you will find the same number, for they left their likenesses carved here as the creators of the Isle.

"For that was their task; to build a home for the remaining Culai, an island safe and inviolate, unreachable and...inescapable. Thus they created the Blessed Isle. And these cliffs, carved from pure quartz, and the massive wall atop the cliff, and the strange and hidden city in the valley behind the wall, all of this is the creation of the Kuallan Oathbound, and it was the greatest single feat of magic in the myriad planes of life."

"But what has this got to do with the chill Cliona felt?" Tuan demanded.

"Because the Oathbound drew upon the stuff of the Void when they created the Isle. Kuallan had stipulated that they create a barrier to contain the First Race on the Isle; he knew they would attempt to escape once they had recouped their powers. And so the Oathbound wrought the essence of the Void into a wall—a barrier—which creatures of Power, and non-humans, may not pass. Cliona is sensitive to the chill of the Void because of her Nightfolk blood."

"What can we do'?" Tuan asked, looking up and down the beach, but he could see no way around the cliffs.

"You must leave me," the priestess said, "I must not hinder you."

Paedur shook his head slightly. "No, I won't leave you behind. Night will fall soon, so I suggest we return to the boat and wait and see what the morning brings. Perhaps by then I will have worked out a way to get you past the cliffs."

They reached the fishing smack just as the sudden night fell, the last rays of sunlight turning the white water to blood and sending shadows rippling up the cliff face, bringing the carvings to life. Sleep didn't come easily that night; they all felt the unseen eyes on them, and occasionally stones rattled on the beach and there were sounds of what might have been a furtive whispering on shore— or it might just have been the sound of the surf on the stones and sand. Once, quite close to midnight, the bard called out in a strange tongue and all sound ceased; and in the silence that followed they plainly heard something hurry up the beach, stones clicking and rattling under its feet.

But far more potent were their imaginations: the night was dark, and there were neither stars nor moon, and the white water gave no light.

In the darkness their imaginations populated the parasitic beach with all manner of strange beasts and men, creatures woven from what they had glimpsed of the carved cliff face. Only the bard seemed unperturbed; and he stood by the mast for most of the night, wrapped in his black furred cloak, his chin sunk on his chest.

Morning came with the same swiftness as night had fallen and, as the first tints of crimson dawn spilled across the horizon, he awoke his companions who had fallen into an exhausted sleep in the late hours of night.

"We must set out for the city this day," he said. "The Band of Kloor and Thanos cannot be far behind and we must reach the city before them at all costs."

"But how?" Cliona demanded. "I cannot pass beyond the shadow of the cliffs."

"There is a way," Paedur said, turning to look at the priestess. "It's dangerous, and it will mean revealing my presence here, but I can see no other way…"

"What do you want to do?" Cliona asked, something in the bard's carefully neutral expression sending shivers up her spine.

"I want to turn you into a *quai.*"

"No!"

"There's no other way," the bard said, turning away.

"But a *quai,*" Tuan protested, "a mindless thing. It's too dangerous."

"It is dangerous." Paedur agreed. "But a *quai* is completely under the control of its creator, and it neither feels pain, heat, nor cold. Cliona will be able to walk past the shadow of the cliffs, and once we've reached the other side I'll return her consciousness."

"And if something should happen to you in the meantime?" Tuan demanded.

"Then she would remain a *quai.*"

"Leave me behind. I can try to delay Thanos and his warriors when they arrive," Cliona insisted.

But the bard shook his head. "It's not as easy as that. I'm going to need you when we find the vessel of the Chrystallis…"

The priestess stared at him for a long time, then she turned away. "What choice do I have?" she said bitterly. "Do it."

"What choice do any of us have?" Paedur said softly.

"What happens now?" Tuan asked, putting his arm around the priestess, but she shrugged it off.

"We wait."

As the morning wore on, Tuan grew restive and suggested that he should scout the trail ahead. "There's no need; I already know the trail, and I need you here to watch for Thanos."

The second craft appeared about midday, coming in fast on the current. Tuan could see the warriors of the Band of Kloor lining the rail, and behind them the tall white-robed red-eyed figure standing up by the figurehead, one hand shading his eyes, staring across at the fishing vessel. "They're here," he said quietly, pulling his knife free.

The bard began to work his magic then, using his hook to reflect the wan sunlight into Cliona's eyes, his trained voice dulling her senses, robbing her of her will, turning her into a *quai*, a mindless creature controlled by himself.

Tuan saw Thanos stiffen and raise his head as if troubled by a distant sound or a strange odour. The bard's magic had disturbed the Ghost Worlds, sending ripples of power coursing through it. Thunder rumbled distantly, and a sudden swell rocked the crafts.

"Thanos will wonder what we're up to," Paedur explained as he took the priestess by the hand and helped her overboard into the shallows. "He may think I was attempting to attack him, or setting up a spell here. It will slow him down and, more importantly, it will confuse him." They were now up on to the beach, and with stones rattling, clicking, and sliding threateningly all around them they set off at a run for the path he knew. Cliona ran blindly by his side, untroubled now by the shadow of the cliffs, while the mate took up the rear.

Thanos' craft actually washed up onto the stones as the rising tide pushed them in. One of the Band, eager to bring back the head of the bard, leaped overboard. But his bare feet had scarcely touched the beach when the shingle began to move. Then it was as if a vast ripple ran across the stones and they flowed towards the stricken warrior, rolling in over his feet, crushing them beneath their stone embrace. He floundered helplessly, as his legs gave way and the weight of his armour bore him down, hacking at the stones with his sword; and then he fell and disappeared beneath a wave of pebbles. There was a single shriek and then the heaving mass of stone cracked and cracked again, and then spurted red liquid. The stones continued to rattle for a few moments more, but the cairn was still.

The bard led Cliona and Tuan along the mazy rock paths that wound about the base of the carven cliffs before they finally led upwards. The cliff sides were smooth and polished, the tracks slippery and treacherous and although Paedur and Cliona—who was still under his control—had little difficulty, Tuan was soon struggling. When they reached a broad natural ledge, the bard stopped and waited for the mate to join him. He flopped down onto the glass-like stone and took in great sobbing breaths. "I seem to remember the last time I climbed a cliff with you, it almost killed me," he gasped.

Paedur nodded briefly. "But the enemy then was not so dangerous," he said, and pointed downwards, his hook gleaming scythe-like in the early afternoon light. Tuan crawled out to the edge of the ledge and looked over. On the beach far below the Band of Kloor had disembarked, leaving Thanos standing tall and white in the prow of their craft, his garments fluttering on the light breeze. And then one of the Band pointed upwards, and all heads lifted up to where the bard stood outlined against the stark skyline, his hook burning silver against the dark night of his cloak.

Thanos pointed and Paedur and Tuan saw his mouth working. "We had better move," Paedur said, and the mate thought he detected a note of weariness in his voice. "We've a long journey ahead of us."

The cliff path soon gave out, and now their way sloped downwards through a long defile with the crystal wall of rock still rising up on either side, which at times also arched across the gully over their heads, so that it seemed as if they fled through a series of tunnels. Finally, as dusk was falling, Tuan called for the bard to stop awhile, for although he was a strong man he was now close to collapse.

"I'm sorry, I sometimes forget about the frailty of the human form. The defile finishes up ahead; we'll rest there."

The track opened out a hundred paces further onto a broad rocky plateau that was perched high above a forest. The bard called out to the priestess and she stopped obediently. "Rest awhile," he said to Tuan. "I will restore Cliona."

Tuan dropped down with his back to one of the glass walls and stretched his legs out in front of him, massaging the stiffening muscles. He looked over at the bard, watching him order the priestess to sit down, and then he saw the bard raise his hook, gathering together her essence which he had scattered about the Ghost Worlds and drawing it back to her body, restoring her to full life. Tuan knew it was a frightening and delicate business, for should the bard falter then Cliona would remain a *quai,* and her body might be inhabited by some creature from beyond the Gorge.

And so neither of them heard the stealthy approach of one of the Band of Kloor down the long defile. It was just one man, a tall blond-haired warrior, a native of the cold lands of Thusal, both swift and strong and accustomed to the rough trails of his home-land. The cliff face had presented him with no problems nor had the slippery trails—it was similar to walking on ice—and the bard and his companions were in too much of a hurry to disguise their trail, so he had caught up with them easily. The warrior paused in the mouth of the defile, feeling the power of his gods flow into him. He drew his sword and kissed the relic set into the hilt—his would be the honour of slaying the *shanaqui* bard.

He crept along the rough path noiselessly, moving nearer towards the *shanaqui* who was bending over one of his companions. He would kill them both together and carry their heads back to the Lord Thanos.

Yet even as he ran forward and leaped at the bard, his sword raised high, he was struck by a sudden thought—were there not two with the bard...?

He heard a hoarse shout off the rocks behind him. Aye, there was another—well, he too would die...but first he would take the *shanaqui*...

Something hard struck him in the back between the shoulder blades; it burned hot then cold—and he had taken enough knife wounds to know what it was. He could feel his blood flowing hot and warm down his back, but if he could take the *shanaqui* with him ...And then the bard was turning and his arm raised and his hook rang shrilly as it cleaved the air and...

And silence hung heavily over the stone maze of the carven cliffs of the Blessed Isle.

They camped that night in the fastness of the rocks' and of the three, only the priestess slept, for she was wearied and sickened by the *quai* transfer. The night was completely silent, and it even seemed to make the bard nervous, for he kept staring at his hook which glittered and sparkled as if it had been dusted with sand. In the early morning the silence was broken by the sound of sucking, which passed their sheltered spot, and the mate was thankful there was no moon to illuminate the desolate rockland— and what roamed abroad.

As the night moved on a mist drifted in from the sea, a thick rolling white fog that blanketed the rocky terrain with waves of shifting smoke. The fog clung to the ground and didn't rise above hip level, and the bard told Tuan to rouse Cliona and move as far back into the rocky niche as they could, for the mist was bound to bring out other night creatures to hunt and stalk.

And as the short night sped towards a bloody dawn, they heard screams behind and below them, echoing and re-echoing off the crystal walls, and they knew that another of the Band had fallen to the guardians of the Isle.

Dawn burned across the alien skies, but the fog did not lift; it merely deepened in colour to a bloody crimson, until even the air seemed to reek of the charnel odour of blood. The mist gathered on the cold stones and ran in twisting streams down the rocks, so that it looked as if they bled.

"It's nothing to fear," Paedur said, his voice calm and detached. "This fog is merely another of the island's defences. It is designed to terrify, but it has no other power." He looked at the terrified priestess, and noted Tuan's strained face, and realised what he was saying was having little effect. He knew what was causing the red fog; he knew it was merely an inanimate defence and he also realised that he was no longer human enough to fully comprehend the effect it was having on his companions. "Watch," he said simply. He stretched out his left arm, his hook a red scythe dripping blood, and then he began to whisper softly. The bloody fog began to lift almost immediately; it swirled away from Paedur's hook in concentric circles, moving away from them. The red liquid on the stones steamed and dried up into a fine rust-coloured dust, and then it scattered on a warm breeze that blew up from the valley below.

They set out for the City of the Culai. About mid-morning the rough winding paths they had been following through the crags changed and became a wide and carefully tended road. It continued to lead downwards, down to the level of the scattered clouds that hid the valley lying below them. Through the clouds they could just make out the tops of the tall trees, lush and almost painfully green after the starkness of the crystal rocks. The track wound down into a gully—and then the wall to their left fell away in a sheer sweep of rock, to the lush greenery of the valley, leaving them standing on a track that was barely a swordlength across. The track led sharply downwards, although the lower it went the broader the ledge became. The crystal rock also changed, becoming darker and cloudy, more like quartz, until it finally became a smoothly polished basalt. Further on, they began to notice markings in the rock that were too regular to be the work of nature.

Cliona ran her fingers along the notches, until she finally noticed a pattern. "They're glyphs," she said in surprise, looking more closely at them. Some were sharp, irregular notches that bit deeply into the rock, others were twisted spirals and helices, and there were blocks and half-finished squares that looked almost painted on the rock. In places pictograms and ideographs marched sedately along, whilst underneath long flowing lines of script swept past. She looked at the bard in wonder. "What are they?"

"What you see are the one hundred and three languages of the Oathbound," he said, looking back along the rock, frowning slightly.

"What do they say?" she wondered.

"The message is the same; it is a warning—a warning: '*Lifeless yet shall live, deathless ever be, ye who pass beyond.*'"

"But does it refer to any of the Culai who might be attempting to escape, or to someone—like ourselves—trying to get in?"

The bard shrugged. "I'm not sure."

The track rounded an outcropping and then opened out onto a broad ledge. Paedur stopped and pointed out over the broad forest below towards a massive walled and moated city.

"Ui Tyrin, the Last City of the Culai."

From their high vantage point, the city was a solid—almost featureless—mass of ochre sandstone, surrounded by a lush dense forest which encircled a broad golden plain around the walls. The city itself was in the bowl of the valley, running in strict lines of unwavering straightness within the precise geometric pentagon of its walls. Even from the distance they could see that it had been built from massively hewn blocks of stone that only the First Race knew how to work. If it followed the pattern of other Culai buildings, the stones would be laid mortarless, but such was the perfection of their craft that a knife blade could not be placed within the seams between the blocks. Unadorned in the manner of the Culai, it yet conveyed an aura of stark beauty and harsh simplicity. But it had one curious feature, for in the centre of the city was a single vast building built in the form of a goblet.

"That," Paedur said, pointing, "is the Inner City; it contains the Circle of Keys, and the Chrystallis."

Above its broad almost flat base rose a squat spire, as functional and as sombre as was the rest of the city, and atop this spire rested another flat-topped building—which completed the image of a cup. There were no windows as far as they could see; and from the distance the whole building looked as if it had been carved from a single piece of stone.

Tuan and Cliona stared at the city in wonder for awhile, and then the bard urged them on. Night was falling as they descended into the valley; and they then realised that there were neither lights nor evening fires from Ui Tyrin, giving it a deserted, haunted appearance.

They camped that night in a cleft in the rockface off the track and; at the bard's insistence, Tuan built a small wall across the opening, for they didn't know what creature might wander down from the heights or up from the valley below. "But I haven't seen any living thing here," he protested. "Where are the sea birds that should have circled above our heads as we came ashore; and what about the lizards and goats that we should have found living in and around the cliffs? We're coming down into a valley which is rich in forest and grassland; where are the *bothe,* the beasts of milk and meat, and what of the *cuine?* Is there anything living on this cursed isle?" he demanded, his voice becoming shrill.

The bard remained silent for a while. He was using his hook to prise flat rocks and stones from the ground to use in the wall. Finally, when Tuan was about to ask him again, he said, "There is life upon this island, though perhaps it is not recognisable as such. The life that lives here is not the life fashioned by Adur, for the

Old Gods hold no sway here upon the Culai Isle. There is a life of sorts here; for the Gorge and Abyss lie adjacent to this plane, and sometimes when the fabric of the world ruptures the damned escape here."

Cliona sat up and peered out through the gloom. "Are they here now? Why haven't we seen them?"

"They do not exist in your perception, but so, too, do you not exist in theirs. However, you both have life—and you both exist—and often in the same place at the same time."

"But how can two creatures exist in the one space?" Tuan asked. "It is inconceivable."

"Not so. For you are attuned to your plane of life in the same manner as they are attuned to theirs. You are like threads woven into a tapestry; each thread is separate and individual, yet each combines to make up a far greater pattern. The interweaving, intertwining threads do not break to allow another thread to pass through them; rather they bend and twist. Thus the isle is part of a pattern which uses many threads, for it stands at the hub of many planes, and no two threads will ever break upon one another, rather will they bend and twist…"

"And what is the pattern?" Cliona wondered.

"The pattern is creation, and its threads are invisible to all but a few."

"Can you see these threads?" Tuan asked, but Paedur smiled gently, and shook his head.

"I have been taught," Cliona said suddenly from the darkness behind them, "that Life is patterned like a tapestry, that its threads are destiny and its knots are choice. I've been told that there are some—and these may be the god-sought, god-taught—that can see the pattern and conceive its complexity." Paedur and Tuan heard her voice change, becoming almost accusing. "Strange that you should speak of the invisible life on the isle in terms of tapestry and threads."

The mate saw the bard incline his head towards the priestess. "You have learned correctly and remembered well. But I will tell you this: it is whispered in the darkened corners of man's mythos that the Spinners of the Tapestry were once Culai, but that they, unlike the majority of their kin, attained godhood."

"I'm not sure I understand. How did they become gods, for example?" Cliona wondered.

Paedur shrugged. "No one knows—all that is known is that they were rewarded by the Elder Gods, the First Gods, in return for some favour, and they were allowed to spin the threads of destiny for man, for remember—the Culai were once men. There is a lot on this isle that is unfitting and unsuitable for mortal sight, the merest glimpse of which might send you screaming into the domain of the Nameless God—and so I warn you, do not probe too deeply into the island's secrets."

"Why?" Tuan asked, looking around.

Paedur smiled, his teeth white in the gloom. "In case you might discover them."

14
The Fields of Knowledge

When the Culai left this world, they took with them the sum total of their knowledge, and they set it into the ground about their city...

Tales of the Bard

Tuan and Cliona were awakened by the bard as the first tinges of dawn were breaking across the distant horizon. They made a hasty meal of dried bread and drank a little from the mate's flask; and then they continued on down the valley towards the city of Ui Tyrin.

The track levelled out onto a rocky decline and then down into a broad and well-tended avenue which led directly into the forest they had seen from the mountains. The track was covered with a strange fine golden sand, in which, curiously, they left no footprints or marks.

"It is similar to the shingle on the beach," Paedur said suddenly, before Tuan could ask the question, "the grains of sand flow into our footprints and feed off the parasites and mud and silt deposited by our boots."

As they neared the forest they began to pass curious plants growing by the side of the track, mingling with other, more familiar plants. They were delicate, beautiful shrubs that looked almost like gossamer tendrils of spun glass, and they shone blood-red in the alien light. Tuan reached out to pluck one of the crystal buds for Cliona, but although they were web-thin and looked fragile they were incredibly strong, and he only succeeded in bruising his toughened fingers. He attacked it with his knife, but the blade screamed and screeched off the branch leaving it unmarked. He glanced over at the priestess with a wry smile. "I'm sorry..." he began, and then the bard's hook flashed out, its razor edge gliding easily through the hardened stem. He deftly caught the bud as it fell and handed it to Tuan with a slight smile. Tuan nodded his thanks and then, as the bard turned away, he quickly examined the stem Paedur had cut through—it was straight and perfectly smooth, with neither ragged edge, crack, nor split in the clear crystal.

When the priestess wove the translucent bud into her raven hair, it was as if it had disappeared, it was so clear and her hair was so dark, and yet occasionally the blood-red light would catch the crystal, looking as if a crimson teardrop glistened wetly on her head.

But the low delicate crystal shrubs soon gave way to strange distorted trees that writhed in ugly contortions, looking almost as if they were in pain. Their bark was rough pitted wood, covered in bloated pustules that leaked a black syrup, and their leaves were slim and edged with jagged serrations, like thorns. As the bard and his companions continued on down the track, the trees took on even more grotesque shapes—which strangely, Cliona thought, looked almost familiar. The track dipped into a hollow and entered a long grove that stretched arrow-straight into the distance. The trees changed again, and now it looked as if the road that ran through the grove was lined with the bodies of men and women frozen in aspects of terror.

Cliona stopped, feeling her heart hammering. The bard was unaffected, and Tuan during his voyages would surely have seen some gruesome sights, but this avenue of tortured bodies...

Tuan looked back over his shoulder, and then stopped, seeing her wide, frightened eyes. "What's wrong?"

"Look!" She pointed down the avenue and then gagged, pressing both hands to her mouth.

"What's wrong?"

"The bodies..."

Tuan looked around again. "What bodies?" he asked.

"Those..." she almost screamed, and then stopped and looked again: they were not corpses, but rather the blighted remains of trees, older and more worn than those they had just passed, whose shape and appearance was similar to man. And then she suddenly knew why the trees were familiar—they were giant mandrakes. It was impossible—and yet she had handled enough mandrake roots to recognise the shape now—but she had always thought that the mandrake was only found under marshy fens at certain phases of the moon, when the Lady Lussa hid her face from man.

She looked at Paedur and opened her mouth to ask him, when he said, "They are kin to the mandrake of your own plane. The mandrakes are the aborted children of the *Curiahe,* who are kin to the *Crinnfaoich,* the Wood Folk, and also kin to the dark and ancient trees of the Silent Wood, the abode of Mannam, the Dark Lord."

"Have they life?" Cliona asked, looking nervously at the tall misshapen trees.

"I feel as if they're looking at us," Tuan said nervously.

Paedur laughed softly. "Aye, they do have a life of a sort, and I would not doubt but that they are following our progress with their own strange senses. But, you needn't worry, we're safe for a time, for these have not yet reached full maturity and are still confined to the ground. They are also sluggish with the morning air, for the sun has not yet fired their sap."

The mate slid his knife free as he looked around. "Are you saying that these trees can move?"

The bard shook his head, smiling. "Not these but others of their kind, that are a little more mature." He nodded at the knife, "And that will be of little use against skins of toughened bark."

"Are they trees or men, then?"

"Both," Paedur said. "They are the *Curiahe*—and it is said that the *Crinnfaoich* are the sons of the *Curiahe,* much as man is the off-spring of the Culai." The bard stopped and pointed back along the path and then forwards into the hazy distance. "The evolution of the Woodfolk is laid out here—from the glass star-shrubs that legend tells once fell upon the world in uncounted crystal raindrops, thence to the grotesque trees that are neither bushes nor trees and thence to the mandrake that have the first glimmerings of sentient life in them…"

"And then?" Cliona asked.

But the bard just smiled and whispered, "wait and see."

As they continued on down the carefully tended path through the watching groves the mandrakes gradually became more man-like in appearance, their forms became straighter and taller, features became discernible, and as they moved deeper into the grove the features became finer and more delicate, and slowly the mandrakes regained something of the haunting beauty of the star-bushes.

Finally Paedur stopped. Ahead of them the grove ended and opened out onto a broad flat plain of rustling golden grain. He pointed to a series of broken craters that lined the track; soil still trickled into some of the holes as if the trees had just been up-rooted. There was no sign of the trees in the fields before them.

The bard pointed to the ugly pits by the roadside. "The most mature form of the mandrake must stand here."

"They can move?" Tuan asked, and when the bard nodded, he continued, "Then they must have risen very recently..."

The bard walked on. "Very recently," he agreed. "They must return to the soil by nightfall, else they rot and wither, for they are creatures of the day." His hook swept out, encompassing the fields of grain. "We may see them as they wander through the fields, but they are surprisingly shy creatures and avoid contact with others, particularly man."

Tuan shielded his eyes and looked out over the wavering fields. "I can see nothing."

"Count yourself lucky then, for though they are shy they will not tolerate trespassers in their domain. And they make fearsome—and almost invincible—foes." He glanced over his shoulder at Tuan and Cliona, and then nodded to the fields of rustling, whispering golden grain. The grain shifted and moved, bending its laden heads in sinuous waves as if some snake-like creature rippled through the crops. "These are the Fields of Knowledge; eat all the ears of grain here and you will become a god, for here is gathered all the knowledge and wisdom of the Culai and mankind." Something like bitterness crept into his voice. "But all this wisdom and knowledge is unsorted and uncategorised, and of course the grains of knowledge are unnamed, and so one could spend all eternity searching for a single fact. But, as you can see, the fields are far too big for any single person to assimilate. Of course, some have tried. On all the planes of existence there are growths like this, shadows or reflections of the Fields of Knowledge—they may be trees or bushes, pools or streams—but they all hold some faint glimmerings of the knowledge that these fields contain..." His voice trailed away, and his usually expressionless face tightened in pain.

"What causes the ripples in the grain?" the priestess asked. "There's no breeze."

"They are the ripples of man's seeking as he merely brushes the surface of knowledge—but it is rare for him to grasp the whole kernel. Look," the bard pointed with his hook to places around the field that were set apart from the rest, circles of stillness and tranquillity, and yet within these circles a single ear would waver and shudder as if a fieldmouse gnawed at its stem. "You can see there where man reaches out and grasps that which he cannot understand, taking isolated facets of useless information and dangerous knowledge—an ear here, a sheaf there—but he doesn't know what he's grasping, nor how he will use it."

"But there must be a plan," Cliona protested, "someone must harvest the fields."

The bard pointed to the dim and misty walls of Ui Tyrin in the distance. "It is said that a plan to the Fields of Knowledge is contained in the Inner City in the Circle of Keys. Legend also tells of a scythe, a scythe forged from part of the essence of man and the whispers of one of the very first emotions created by man: curiosity. Take that scythe and reap the fields with the plan in mind and you might reap the knowledge of the ages."

"But what about the dark lore?" Cliona asked.

"Use the plan and one could leave that part untouched. But one must take care, for knowledge—no matter how much it is intended for good—must be controlled, for knowledge is power and power is dangerous."

"Why has no man reaped and harvested the Fields of Knowledge before this?" Tuan asked. "Surely there are men of power who know about these fields and the scythe?"

Paedur laughed as he began to walk down the long path that cut through the high grasses. "Oh, men have tried in ages past, and some have even succeeded in reaching the Circle of Keys; and I know of one sorcerer who even succeeded in grasping the scythe, but he, like all the others, failed—betrayed by his curiosity about the Circle of Keys itself, and the need to explore it. All have failed," and there was a note of sadness in his voice. They walked in silence for a time along the strange path with its scratching, shifting, sandy covering, by the side of the Fields of Knowledge that towered above their heads and wavered in an ethereal wind that was the fumbling curiosity of man.

"I wonder why all those who came before us failed to reap the fields," Cliona remarked softly to Tuan, "I wonder, were they all evil men?"

The bard turned and looked into her eyes. "No, they were not all evil. Though there were some that would have used the knowledge they obtained for their own ends, most of them would have used their knowledge for the good of man. Some had found the fields through the shadowy reflections of knowledge on their own planes, and had used the knowledge they had found there to gain entry to the Blessed Isle and the Fields of Knowledge." He stopped speaking and continued walking, his head bent forward, the fingers of his right hand clenched. "These fields and their reflections might be likened to a poison; diluted they will cause little harm, yet in a pure state they are fatal. Most of the seekers did not know this. They thought the fields here were similar to the shadow-growths of their own planes, and they reasoned that they must eat the grain much as they had eaten the buds or fruits of the trees and drunk the water on their own planes. Some were lucky with the first few mouthfuls, because the knowledge they absorbed was not harmful, but sooner or later it killed them for they could not comprehend or encompass all that they had learned and their minds snapped under the sudden mass of knowledge."

"Why?"

"Because one must learn in steps, slowly, slowly, building upon a foundation of known facts, but they did not wish to build like that."

"But if one had the plan?" the priestess asked.

"Aye, if one had the plan of the fields, then it would be possible to learn and reap profitably and with proper care." The bard turned suddenly and rested his gleaming razor hook against the priestess's soft cheek. "Do you aspire to this knowledge and wisdom?" he asked softly.

"If I had the proper guidance..." Cliona said slowly, feeling the almost flesh-warm curve of the metal.

Paedur looked over at Tuan. "What about you; do you wish for this knowledge, bearing in mind its power for destruction as well as greatness?"

"I have sailed with the Taourg; I have known many lands, some of which men banish into legend, and many races which men speak of only in myth—and if I've learned anything, I've learned that man is happy only when he has a goal to attain. Take away this goal and you destroy the man. And this goal might be power or knowledge or conquest, but even so it is something to strive for. I think if you granted any man the wisdom and knowledge of the ages, then in one swift move you remove his very reason for existence." The mate suddenly laughed, and then coughed in embarrassment. "Listen to me, I must he going soft. Such thoughts are for the market-philosophers and roadside sages and not for honest warriors."

Paedur placed his hand on the mate's shoulder. "You have a wisdom beyond your years: treasure it, never mock it."

About mid-morning they passed an area of the Fields of Knowledge that was stricken with blight. Around it, the ground was seared and withered, and it looked as if a fire had raged here. The bard told his companions that here had once grown the most evil and dangerous knowledge. It had originally grown up out of the nightmares of the One, and had been compounded by the terrors of the First Men. It had lain for countless ages and festered and drawn into itself every abomination from the earliest ages of man and the twilight of the gods when they were wont to walk the worlds.

Then there arose a creature who had learned of the Primeval Lore and had striven to use it; and after many trials which damned his essence to the farthest howling chaos of the Gorge, he had finally reached the Fields of Knowledge and had eaten the dark grains of the Primeval Lore. Somehow, he had survived the terrible and shocking knowledge he had gained, for his Studies had prepared him somewhat for it. Then he had challenged the gods themselves to admit him into their company, but they had refused, and there had ensued a terrible battle in which even the very restraints of the Gorge were breached and the planes were flooded with the evil creatures that even now beset man. The would-be usurper had been defeated and cast into the Gorge, stripped of the form of man, and there it had writhed in unspeakable agony until, one day, man in his stupidity had called upon the usurper by name and released him."

"What happened to him?" Cliona asked.

"That creature was Trialos!"

The bard then pointed out the burnt stems of corn within the blasted area, which were writhing and swaying as if a gale blew upon them, but which was man's seeking the knowledge. "The Dark Lore always attracts man, much as the bait lures the unsuspecting fish, and like the bait for the fish it too often proves fatal."

Suddenly the bard stopped and raised his face to the alien sky, tilting his head to one side as if he were listening. "Move!" he hissed, and grabbed Cliona and Tuan and pulled them into the tall grasses. "Listen," he said, "listen."

"I can't hear anything..."

Cliona began, and then Tuan's hard fingers bit into her shoulder muscle. "I can."

"What is it?"

"It sounds like something crying..." Tuan said slowly.

And then the priestess heard it also. The sound was faint, a doleful crying that echoed and re-echoed across the fields. Then they heard a deep, throbbing booming, and at first Tuan and Cliona thought it was Baistigh, the Lord of Thunder, riding across the heavens on his clouds of sombre grey—but the sky was clear and cloudless...

And then above them flew six huge birds—the first living creatures they had seen on the island.

The birds were huge—larger even than the fabled roc—and Tuan guessed that from beak to tail they would have measured greater than a Taourg pirate ship. Their plumage was a pure white, save for their eyes and beaks and the tips of their tail feathers, and these were black but of a shade so intense that it appeared almost purple. They flew in a perfectly regular diamond formation, and the sound the three companions had heard was their singing. It was a bitter-sweet sound, lovely and pathetic, and Cliona felt tears well up in her eyes. She looked up at Tuan and found that his eyes were glistening. The six birds circled above the Fields of Knowledge and then they swooped down back along the trail, and now a new note entered their songs, one of rage and defiance.

There were shouts and screams from behind as the birds dropped even lower. "Thanos," Paedur muttered, and then the birds folded their wings and swooped, their claws extended. One disappeared into the grain for a moment, and when it rose up again there was something hanging limply from its ebon beak. The birds rose cawing and screaming into the air, and then they circled once above the fields before setting off towards Ui Tyrin, leaving the grasses rustling angrily in their wake.

Paedur dragged Tuan and Cliona to their feet and urged them back onto the path. "Hurry, now, hurry." He set off towards the city at an easy run. Tuan dropped into place beside him easily enough, although Cliona began to feel the pace very quickly. More to slow him down she asked about the six huge birds.

Paedur glanced back over his shoulder. "They were the *Aonteketi*..."

She frowned, "The name is familiar, but..."

"They were once gods of men, but are now the servants of the Culai."

"What turned gods into servants?" Tuan wondered.

"Briefly, then," Paedur murmured, and then his voice changed, taking on its professional tone.

"In the latter days of the First Race, when they had mastered the science that almost made them equal to the gods, there arose amongst them a group of savants and philosophers who believed that, since they had now equalled the gods, then in time it should be possible for the Culai race to become greater than the gods themselves. But there were some amongst them lacking the patience to wait for that future day and they sought to attain godhood without delay. Thus they devised a plot to steal from the gods the essence of their knowledge. Therefore they set out to capture six of the lesser gods, and when they did the Culai tortured and abused them for seven days, until they revealed what little they knew of the essence of godhood.

"But the Culai were not satisfied with what they had learned, and resolved to capture one of the Great Gods to wrest from him the secret of godhood. But the gods had become aware of the plan and sent Mannam, the Dark Lord, and Maurug, the Destroyer, to the Culai, and the Silent Wood was rent with the wailing of the damned, and Alile the Judge Impartial was drawn from his cavernous chamber and remained in judgement for many days thereafter. But when the gods had dealt with the Culai, they refused to take back the six who had betrayed them, banishing them to those they had been forced to serve—the last of the Culai. And thus when Kuallan, Friend of Man, had the Blessed Isle built, he brought the six gods with him and commanded them to watch over the enchanted island. They were transformed into the shape of great birds—the *Aonteketi*—by the power of the First Race. Thus they watch...and wait; for it is written that when the last of the Culai have gone into the Gorge then the huge birds will regain their rightful form and take their place once more in the Pantheon.

"On occasion they travel through the Grey Wall to our plane and the other planes of existence, and thus have given rise to the legends of the great and mystical birds that are said to haunt the lands of fable."

The bard suddenly stopped and then pointed off to one side, striking out along a thin, barely visible path that cut through the tall grasses. "This way." He led them to a squat standing stone that sat in the middle of a neat circle deep in the midst of the fields.

"This," Paedur said, patting the smoothly polished rock, "is the foundation stone upon which all of man's knowledge is built. It was a gift from the First of the Elder Gods to the First Race, and it was with such basic knowledge that the Culai survived their earliest days on the harsh world."

They camped about the Foundation Rock that night while the grain whispered and sighed all around them. There were other noises too, less distinct but even more frightening, and at one stage during the night Tuan surged to his feet, his knife in his hand, almost expecting to find himself facing…he wasn't sure what he could be facing.

The night wore on, but neither the priestess nor Tuan could sleep, and so Cliona asked the bard again about the *Aonteketi*. "Who were the six minor gods who were taken by the Culai and later renounced by the Pantheon?"

The bard remained silent for such a long time that the priestess thought he had not heard her question and was about to ask him again, when she saw Tuan shake his head.

When the bard spoke, his voice was low and seemed almost weary. "Aye, I know the six lost gods of the Pantheon, and I could never understand why the Old Gods did not show greater kindness and forgiveness.

"But the gods were these: Scmall, the Spirit of the Clouds, who ruled the misty wastes and cloudfields of heaven. When he disappeared the clouds became the property of all the Pantheon and are now used by many of the gods, such as C'lte and Baistigh.

"Kloca, the Lord of Stone and Rock, was lost also, and thus was lost the great art of fashioning in rock and the dressing of stone. His loss is one of the reasons why no great stone monuments are raised today, for the Culai took from him the secret skill of working stone—that is how they raised their cities and roads which still endure.

"The Culai captured Aistigh, the Lord of Subtle Harmonies, and that is why if you listen carefully you will find the elder songs and chants more delicate, haunting, and subtle than their modern counterparts. You've both heard it said that there are no great song-smiths alive today, but that's not true—their songs are as good, even better, but Aistigh is not there to breathe life into their tunes." Paedur's head dipped slightly. "Aye, we lost much when the Pantheon refused to recognise and accept the six.

"Danta, Lord of Verse, was captured, and a great beauty was lost when the Verse-Maker was taken, though I suppose there are few alive today that know that. But ask yourself; why is it that the old tales are always welcomed and the old lays always chanted; why is it that a bard is never refused a welcome? Why? Because the old tales were touched by Danta and, like Aistigh, he breathed a subtle life and fire into them, a haunting resonance, a depth of feeling that one doesn't find in the verse-makers of today." He paused and added quietly, "And those two, Aistigh and Danta, were brothers.

"Now," he continued, "you should ask the workers in gold and silver why their craft lacks the delicacy and beauty of the works of their forefathers, Of course they will deny it, and claim that their craft is greater now than ever before, and that it has improved down through the ages. But compare the old and the new and it is very obvious that the modern works lack…a something. You probably wouldn't be able to say just what this something is, but you would be able to tell the difference."

"Aye," Tuan said suddenly, "and the antique work fetches higher prices, even for pieces which, by today's standards, would be considered crude. I've seen the Taourg cast aside satchels of gold and silver ware for a piece or two of antique work."

Paedur nodded. "That is my point; people can tell that there is a difference—though they may not know what it is—and they find the earlier pieces more pleasing to the eye. The reason for the difference is simple, for the Culai captured Dore, the Lord of the Smiths, and so man lost the art of working metal. Even the workers in base metal lost the secrets of their craft." He looked up at Tuan, his face a dim oval in the night. "Why are the few antique swords and armour that still survive so much sought after?"

"Because of their strength and durability—which cannot be found in today's weapons."

Paedur nodded, the cloth of his cloak rasping softly together. "When the six were taken, some said it was no great loss and that they would not be missed. HAH! Little did the fools know."

"That's five gods; who was the sixth…?" Cliona asked.

"Aye there was one other, but a goddess rather than a god. She was Fifhe, Lady of the Beasts, the daughter of Lady Adur; and while she was with the Pantheon there was peace between man and beast and also between beast and beast. That peace was shattered when she was taken, and now man hunts not only for food but also for sport. Even the nature of the beasts has changed, and there are some now that hunt and kill but don't eat their prey. The old harmony between man and beast is lost. Once the beasts worked freely alongside man, but now they are constrained by bit and bridle, spear and whip, to carry for their masters. Once man took only what he needed from the beasts for food or clothing, and only then with the permission of the Lady Fifhe, but now he takes what he wants and not what he needs." The bard's voice changed in timbre and faded into a whisper.

"Scmall, Kloca and Aistigh, Danta, Dore, and Fifhe," Cliona murmured; "henceforth, I will include them in my prayers, for surely they did not deserve their punishment."

Paedur smiled gently and shook his head. "They did not."

The remainder of the short night was spent in silence, and the three companions watched the dawn come up like blood from a wound.

They continued along the winding track, and by mid-morning the walls of Ui Tyrin, the City of the Culai, rose before them, and looming high above the massive city walls was the tall bowl of the goblet-shaped building, the Inner City. From the distance the walls seemed to float on a sea of grain; like a vast stone ship sailing the Seas of Knowledge, thought the priestess as she stood with Tuan gazing up at the city.

"The end is in sight," Tuan said softly, almost to himself.

Not quite, Paedur thought, staring up at the walls; the journey was only just beginning. His non-human senses felt the disturbance of Thanos and his warriors off to their right. They must have marched through the night, and he could sense the mingled auras of exhaustion and anger, overlaid with the sour stink of fear. "Let's go—it wouldn't do to he caught by Thanos now…would it?"

As they neared the walls the grain shrank back almost to normal size and the track began to broaden and wind erratically. The priestess noticed a new plant growing amongst the golden grains: a short thick-stemmed weed edged with wicked hooked barbs. The weed itself was a strangely baleful colour that was neither black nor the deepest purple but a curious mixture of both. She was reaching out to touch one of the broad flat leaves when the bard stopped her.

"Don't touch it—it's deadly."

"What is it?" Tuan asked.

"It is alien lore from the furthest planes, and it presents a far greater danger than even the Primeval Lore, for while man knows of that danger he knows nothing about this, nor what its effects on the user will be." He pointed with his hook. "And see how it is already shivering in the breeze of man's curiosity."

Tuan knelt and examined the plant. "It's an ugly thing, and I wonder why we've only come across it here, so close to the city…"

"It came from those who have passed this way before us— undoubtedly a new species of weed is already growing up in your wake, having absorbed what knowledge you have."

"Have there been many before us?" Cliona asked.

"Many have come to Ui Tyrin—no one has ever returned. It is said that Ui Tyrin's great beauty holds them enthralled," he added with a smile.

But the city itself was plain—almost ugly.

Paedur stopped and led them off the path once again, and then he pulled back a tall sheaf of grain, and they stepped out onto a broad close-cropped plain that led down to a moat surrounding the city of Ui Tyrin. "Let's wait awhile," Paedur said, moving deeper into the grain.

Tuan and Cliona followed Paedur into the heart of the grain and then settled down. From where they were they had a clear view of both the track and the city. Their first impression of Ui Tyrin was of size, of vast, overwhelming, impressive size. It sat upon the wide plain like a great beast slumped in noonday slumber. There was an aura of strength and durability about it; it had stood for a hundred generations, and it would last for another hundred, and even in that dim and distant future it would remain unchanged and untouched by time. Its high castellated walls dominated the skyline, and the sharp angles of the pentagonal walls jutted knife-like against the wide and ominously swirling moat. The huge double gates were neither wood nor metal but seemed carved from a single slab of stone, and were set well back into the walls and fronted by a thick portcullis of shining steel. And the gates and portcullis looked particularly new, almost as if they had just been furnished and erected. But there was no drawbridge to lower across the moat, and a small tree grew in the crack in the earth where the door joined the walls. Obviously the gate had not been opened in a long time, and with no drawbridge it looked as if it had never been designed to open.

Suddenly the turgid water of the moat was disturbed and something long and sinuous appeared briefly, then sank again, leaving the smallest of ripples in the milk-white water. Tuan was just about to speak when the water parted once again and the creature reappeared. It was a serpent, but covered with sleek black fur and with a long almost flat head. It heaved itself up out of the water, coil after rippling coil, and spread itself out on the soft margin, soaking up the warmth. Its head waved about, its long black tongue tasting the air before it settled down.

Cliona shuddered. "It's a nightmare."

"I have seen creatures similar to it in some of the islands far to the south," Tuan whispered, "though they were not so large, nor were they covered with fur."

"It is a creature from the earliest days of man," Paedur said quietly. "Beware: for there are many such beasts," and he nodded towards the slumbering monstrosity, "some of them a lot more hideous than that."

"But what is it?" Cliona asked.

"That is the seast; it is said to be the ancestor of the serpent and the rat and it has the characteristics of both. See the sinuous length of the serpent and the eyes and tongue of one, but see also the fur and chiselled teeth of the rat. In some of the earliest manuscripts, it is written that the Culai, in their stupidity, raised some of the seasti to knowledge, and that they were the Serpent Folk of legend who once ruled the Southern Kingdoms of Teouteuchal."

"I've heard that," Tuan said; and Cliona nodded also, "Aye, in Monatome…"

Paedur smiled slightly. "Like the tale of the Creation, the legend of the Serpent Folk is universal to all the planes of life."

The morning whispered on to the accompaniment of the grain, and the huge bloated sun crept higher in the sky, casting its lurid light across the plain and the walls of the city. The seast slept on, and even Tuan and Cliona dozed in the heat.

Shortly before midday Paedur shook them awake, and they heard something crashing through the grain off to their right, something large that was moving rapidly. There was a shout—a human cry— and then they saw Thanos and the remnants of the once proud Band of Kloor stumble out onto the beach before the moat.

The journey had taken its toll on them. The band of men that had once numbered upwards of twenty-five of the Religion's finest warriors had been decimated, and now no more than ten bedraggled youths remained. They were dirty and unshaven, their weapons and armour rusted and uncleaned, their eyes hollow in their heads, staring out in dull apathy. They bore little resemblance to the arrogant fighting men of Kloor.

Even Thanos, Hand of God, High Priest of Trialos, looked exhausted—even more so than his men—for he, like the bard, knew just how dangerous the Blessed Isle was, and how deadly an opponent the bard could be.

But now they had reached Ui Tyrin; their goal was in sight; soon, soon the bard, and all his foul gods, would be no more. Trialos would reign supreme. In sight of Ui Tyrin's walls Thanos gathered his men around him and explained to them for the first time what he knew of the City and their mission. In the afternoon silence, his voice drifted across to the three companions.

"I have told you before about the City of the First Race, and the great treasure it holds; and now I must tell you the nature of the treasure." He paused, searching the closed faces for any trace of interest but finding nothing more than apathy. "It is no material treasure of precious stones or metals you seek, neither is it cloth nor workings in stone nor clay nor metal, but something far greater. You have been chosen by the Lord Trialos to seek out and find this treasure for his use. Now—and attend me carefully, for there is a reward that far surpasses gold and silver for the finder." His exhausted warriors began to show some interest, and he paused and took a deep breath. "You are seeking a vessel, a delicate urn of metallic glass of a greenish hue, that is fluted somewhat in the manner of the minarets of Maroc. And there are runes carved about the rim of the vessel and these are like and yet unlike the glyphs of the Culai, for they are the sigil of the Chrystallis. Furthermore, the vessel is stoppered with a gem of the purest water, colourless unless one should look into its depths, and then it will gleam with a hundred changes of colour, and if you should put your ear to the glass, you will also hear a keening, dirge-like and soulful. Now," continued Thanos, "should one of you find the vessel, seek me out immediately and, as you value your very life, do not attempt to open the vessel of the Chrystallis. You must remember that you are bound to me and I am ordering you to guard the vessel with your very lives; it is very precious."

"My lord, what are we to do should we not be able to find you?" one youth asked. Unlike the others, he was clad in the remnants of a priest's robes and carried no weapons, and stood apart from the warriors close to Thanos. As he turned, the three companions saw he had a broad curving scar across his cheek.

Paedur stiffened. "I know him...!"

The albino remained silent for a moment, his pink eyes moving slowly from face to face before finally returning to the youth. "Should you be unable to find me, then you must capture one of the First Race, or better still, one of the companions of the bard, should they still live. Then pray—pray to the Lord God Trialos for strength—and sacrifice your prisoner in the old manner, tearing out the still pulsating heart. You must then bathe the vessel in the smoking blood, and then—only then—you may open the vessel..." His voice which had risen to a shriek, now fell back to a whisper. "Your reward will be great indeed."

The scarred youth spoke again, "My lord, what is in the vessel? It is very precious?"

"It has a value beyond value, a price beyond price. I have told you what the vessel holds: it is the container of the Chrystallis, the Soulwind." Now his voice took on a new note, a note of fanaticism, of madness. His pale eyes widened and became suffused with blood, until they looked as if they were about to burst. "It holds the Wind that Blew through the Soul of the One and created the four Old Gods. I will release the Soulwind upon the world, and I will wipe out the unbelievers. There is but one god, Trialos, and his servant is Thanos!"

"And the Lord Trialos is well served," the youth murmured, with a sly smile: "there is none to equal Thanos."

Paedur leaned close to Tuan and whispered softly. "I've met that young man before. I gave him that little memento on his cheek. His name is Xanazius..."

The mate grinned broadly. "Aye, I've heard of him," he said. "He is called the Fingers of the Hand and it is said he is more than servant to Thanos..."

"Now come, you have rested long enough. We must needs enter the City of the Culai," Thanos called.

"But my lord, the creature..." said one man, pointing to the slumbering seast. "We must pass it."

"Coward! Is this what the Band of Kloor has come to—snivelling cowards that flinch at a simple dozing serpent? You," he snapped, pointing to the man who had spoken, "do you doubt my leadership, do you question my commands?"

"N-N-no, not I, my lord." The suddenly terrified man moved back away from the advancing High Priest. The youth Xanazius slipped up behind the warrior and pinned his arms by his sides. Suddenly Thanos reached out and placed his right hand on the face of the terrified man. "Never doubt me," he hissed, and the warrior screamed, his body convulsed and stiffened, and he fell back, obviously dead.

Thanos silently gathered his men about him and pointed to the fallen body, slowly looking from face to face. The bard and his companions could feel, even from the distance, the chill of his stare, and the threat and warning were obvious. Without another word Thanos led the Band of Kloor off towards the city, bearing to the right, away from the seast-guarded gate, in search of another entrance.

As soon as they had disappeared, the bard leaped to his feet and ran to the body of the warrior, Cliona and Tuan close behind him. When they reached it, the priestess cried out, sickened, and even Tuan, inured as he was to the atrocities of the Taourg, looked away.

The man's face, where Thanos had touched it, was burned to the bone, the flesh peeling away in blackened strips in the shape of a human hand. "I've always wondered why he was called the Hand of God," Paedur murmured, composing the body. They stood still and silent while Cliona recited the prayer of the dead, although she doubted the soul of this creature would find rest here in the wastelands of the spirit, the abode of the godless.

Then the bard led them back into the grain again, striking deep into the heart of the great Fields of Knowledge, and though they pushed through the tall waving grass they never broke nor snapped the blades, and the grass they trod underfoot quickly rose upright behind them, and the bard pointed out that this was a reflection of the durability of knowledge. They were following no marked path— save that the city was always to their right—yet the bard led them unerringly to a wide dell, a perfect circle within the gently waving grasses. Here the grass was short, startlingly brilliant, and the whole circle exuded an almost physical aura of peace and solitude.

In the centre of the circle was a pillar, a broad cylinder of stone, marvellously worked in the manner of the Culai with the abstract representations of the Elder Gods carved into the sides of the flat square of jade that topped the cylinder. About the base of the pillar were carved the representations of the Culai, one figure for each of the nine races, for when the gods made man they suited him to the nine climates; but the First Race was unique in that, though they were nine separate branches, they remained united as a race.

And incised deeply into the jade was a pentagram.

As the companions neared the pillar, walking carefully across the circle, they could see the jade was inset with five tiny points of light that winked and sparkled in the wan light. Each of the points of light turned out to be a diamond, the size of a man's thumb, set into the five points of the pentacle. The centre of the star had been inset with quartz and ruby respectively, giving it the appearance of a staring eye.

Tuan and Cliona looked on it in wonder; it was solidly built but somehow it seemed almost fragile; but it was very beautiful. Paedur walked over to it, and leaned back against the tall stone.

"This is the Circle of Innocence, and in it is contained all the knowledge of the innocent; see how smooth and even the grass is, unruffled and untroubled by the inquiring mind of man. A child's questions have no malice, no hidden meaning to them; when they enquire, it is with a genuine curiosity." He patted the stone with his hand. "This is also called the Cylinder of the Covenant, as it was fashioned to celebrate the union of gods and man in the first days of the First Race, when the Culai were free and innocent—childlike, almost.

"The gods walked with man in that time, and there were many who could claim the blood of the gods ran in their veins, and some saw this as the beginning of a new age, an age of godlike men and manlike gods, and so they fashioned the Cylinder to celebrate that New Age.

"But it never happened; the First Age of Man was destined to fall. For the offspring of god and man thought themselves greater than mere men and sought to subjugate them. And this angered the gods, and thus the fields of Ab-Apsalom were made a battleground for the first time. The halflings lost and were cast out beyond the very edges of the universe, though they were to return generations later during the Demon wars."

"And the Cylinder?" Tuan asked.

"Aye, the Cylinder. Well, it remained as a symbol of the great age of peace." The bard shook his head sadly. "We shall not see its like again. When Kuallan and the Oathbound fashioned the Isle, the Elder Gods took the Cylinder and placed it in the Circle of Innocence in the Fields of Knowledge, and they set these fields about Ui Tyrin as a lesson to the Culai. For though the First Race may walk along the paths that lead through the fields, they may never leave the paths and they may never taste the grain—perhaps because they, in their arrogance, once thought themselves the masters of all knowledge—and now, although surrounded by wealth, they have nothing. That is why the Circle is placed within the fields; the Culai know of its existence but they can never reach it; they can never regain that lost innocence. The Cylinder is a symbol of what might have been…"

Paedur turned and pointed to the five glittering diamonds with his hook. "But it has another use."

As Tuan and Cliona watched, Paedur touched each of the shining points, starting with the topmost and moving anti-clockwise, striking them with the point of his hook.

Abruptly the eye of the quartz and ruby flickered and glowed, and the air above it began to shimmer as if the stone gave off heat. Then, at the edge of the circle of grass a faint tracery of lines appeared, as if etched by fire, but the grass didn't burn. And these lines formed into the shape of a pentacle with the Cylinder at their centre, and, at the points, fist-sized pools of light burned with a cold radiance. As Paedur ordered his companions to place their hands on the stone, these cold liquid lights began to shift and spin about themselves until they were nothing more than lines of white fire. And the lines began to expand round the circle of grass, and pulse along the rim of this circle until it seemed as if the circle was slowly starting to revolve. It seemed to spin faster and faster, and the Field of Knowledge dimmed and faded, and they were in utter darkness…

Cliona and Tuan screamed aloud, but there was no sound. There was nothing.

15
The Three Cords

No human ever penetrated Ui Tyrin and lived—except the bard, but the bard Paedur was not truly human.

Tales of the Bard

There was only the Cylinder. Tuan and Cliona clung to the sole remaining tangible form in the wheeling void, their minds shocked, their fingers frozen on the icy stone.

And then there was sound as the bard spoke. "Remain calm; there is nothing to fear, but you must hold fast to the stone...the stone..." His voice echoed as if they were in a vast chamber or tunnel, but it was calming, soothing the terror that was threatening to overwhelm them both. Sensing this, Paedur continued. "The City of the Culai has nine gateways. Some are situated in the walls in the normal manner but the others flicker through the Ghost Worlds and lead beyond the city walls. However, the gate through the Circle of Innocence is the one most rarely used, for many of those from the world of man who reach the Culai Isle have bartered the last vestiges of whatever innocence and humanity they possessed for the route through the Grey Wall to the City..."

As he was speaking the shifting darkness lightened and paled towards greyness, and then the white light at the points about the rim of the star flared brightly once again, and then they began to slow down, gradually fading. The cold fires separated into five distinct parts—and stopped; and abruptly the three companions found they were standing in a great hall that stretched to dusky infinity in all directions.

Paedur sighed and stepped away from the Cylinder, absently rubbing his hook against his cloak. Tuan and Cliona followed him, clinging tightly to each other, their heads still spinning. As they stepped across the traces of the outline of the pentacle on the stone floor, the hall abruptly contracted and dwindled in size until it was no more than a large square room. "A matter of perspective," was all the bard would say, refusing to elaborate further.

The room was much like those found in the ruined temples of the Culai on the mainland. It was stark, and bare of adornment, and there was a thick layer of dust upon the floor, unmarked and undisturbed as if it had lain there through the ages. The air was dry and acrid, and a complete silence enfolded the place.

There was no doorway in the room and the single murky window set high in the sheer wall was barred with a lattice grillework.

Paedur looked around in amusement. "There have been some improvements since I was last here," he murmured to Tuan, his voice sounding flat and dull in the silence, robbed of its usual resonance.

"There is no door," Cliona whispered.

"Aye, they have blocked the door—probably to prevent me returning," Paedur said, pointing to a spot on the wall where a rectangle of smaller, newer stones was faintly outlined against the older, darker stones of the rest of the walls.

"You never told me you had been here before," Tuan accused him.

"Did I not?" the bard murmured absently. "It was a brief—very brief—visit in…"

"We're trapped," the priestess said, a thin note of hysteria in her voice. Tuan went and held her, but his own expression was troubled as he turned back to the bard. "She is right…" he whispered.

Paedur slowly walked around the room, brushing the grey walls with the tips of his fingers, pausing when he reached the lighter shading of stone which had replaced the door. And then Tuan suddenly noticed something. Where he and the priestess had walked, the dust on the floor was scuffed and imprinted with the marks of their footwear—his thick-nailed, rib-soled mariner boots, and Cliona's smaller, sharp-toed sandals. But where the bard had walked there was no mark, no impression.

"Can we get out?" he said, looking up and catching the bard staring at him with a strange, almost feral, smile on his lips.

"Aye, there is little trouble in doing that and yet…" the bard turned back to the bricked-up doorway and paused indecisively.

"Yet?" Tuan persisted.

"Yet to do so I must use a little Power, and that will undoubtedly alert the Culai and Thanos. I wish to avoid a confrontation with both groups for the moment. The former outnumber us, and the latter, if he were to feel a ripple of Power, might overreact and do something rash if he thought, or even suspected, we were within the City."

"But can you get us out of here without calling on your Power?" Tuan asked.

Paedur shrugged, shaking his head slightly. "No, there seems little else we can do." He suddenly tapped the brickwork with his hook, the sound ringing sharp and musical. "Tuan, look at this ... what do you think..." The mate stepped away from the priestess, and squatted down to look at the wall. "Look...here," the bard said, and then his voice suddenly echoed cold and chill within Tuan's head, terrifying him. *"You must forgive me for this intrusion, but what I must say to you is for your ears alone..."* The voice was sharp and insistent, but there was also a slightly breathless quality to it. *"At all costs Cliona must be kept safe,"* the bard continued. *"She must not fall into the hands either of the Culai or Thanos. Do you understand me?"* he demanded, staring hard at the mate. *"At all costs. "*

Tuan nodded silently.

"I'll have to call upon some Power, then," the bard said aloud, glancing over at Cliona.

The mate nodded, "I can see no other way for us to get out."

"Move back," Paedur commanded. Then he laid his hook flat against the joining of the new and old brick, and he began to whisper in a strange lilting tongue. The runes on the curve of his hook darkened and then they began to sparkle. They turned black, rust-coloured, and then red, until they finally glowed with an intense white heat that Tuan and Cliona could feel even across the room, although the bard seemed unaffected. Then slowly, like a knife cutting through butter, the edge of the hook sank into the stone, biting deeper and deeper until it was almost up to the bard's wrist. Paedur began to move his arm up along the seam in the door; mortar and chippings spat and ran in molten globules down the stonework and the air reeked with sulphurous bitter fumes. Stretching to his full height, Paedur traced the outline of the door, from threshold to lintel and back again to the threshold.

There was a grinding sound and then suddenly a large section of the brickwork fell inwards, narrowly missing the bard, the sound echoing and re-echoing through the building in a long rolling thunderclap. The bard slumped back exhausted and waved Tuan and the priestess through the opening before him. "We must hurry," he panted, his thin face sheened with sweat.

They looked out into a long arrow-straight corridor, stretching into the dim distance. Tuan went first, his knife in his hand, moving quickly through the hole, straightening and pressing his back to the wall. But the corridor was deserted. He lifted Cliona across the tumbled bricks and then reached out to help the exhausted bard through the jagged rent in the wall, but Paedur shook his head, and almost visibly seemed to draw upon some inner store of strength. "Come on," he said.

The bard led them at a run down the echoing corridor, ignoring the iron-studded doors that were set into the wall at every score of paces. And then rolling down the corridor came the slow solemn booming of some great bell tolling out a warning, reverberating against the walls, raining grey gritty dust down on them. But the bard ignored the bell, only urging them on. He knew they were racing against time now; his use of Power had—as he had expected—alerted the island's almost sentient defences, and the Culai would soon rouse themselves to investigate.

The high, slit windows admitted little light, and Cliona and Tuan stumbled on the cracked and uneven flagstones; the lack of light didn't seem to affect the bard. The walls were stark and without ornament but, in contrast to what the bard called the "gate-room" whose walls had been dry, the walls in the corridor dripped with sluggish moisture, and deep channels set into the floor carried the water away to overflowing grills. The whole corridor had a desolate air of disuse about it.

And then the bell ceased its mournful tolling.

The bard stopped and raised his hand for silence. "What is it?" Tuan whispered, but the bard shook his head impatiently. The mate could hear nothing except the monotonous drip-drip-drip of moisture. He was turning to the priestess when she stiffened, and stifled a cry. "Listen," she whispered, and then Tuan heard it. He half turned, feeling the familiar burning in the back of his throat, and the deepening pounding of his heart. Faint in the distance a stealthy padding came whispering along the corridor.

"Let's go," Paedur said quietly, but now Tuan heard a new note of urgency in his voice.

They ran then—and a nightmare began for Tuan and Cliona. The corridor loomed endlessly ahead, the high windows and tall doors on either side never changing and no end in sight in either direction. They ran, but it was as if they stood still while the corridor just flowed endlessly past.

The padding behind them grew ever louder, and then its tempo changed, becoming swifter, as if whatever nightmare was pursuing them now also ran. They could even hear the click of claws on the stones, and the faintest suggestion of deep chuffing breathing.

Tuan suddenly grabbed the bard by the arm, hauling him to a stop. He was red-faced and bathed in sweat, and there was an agonising stitch in his side. He bent over double and placed both hands on his knees. "We must rest," he gasped.

"We cannot—there is no time, the beast will soon be upon us."

"Fight it!"

But the bard smiled almost sadly and shook his head. "I cannot."

"You … you go on then. I…I will stay and try…" he left the sentence unfinished, and merely tilted his knife slightly, but his meaning was clear.

The bard hesitated a moment and then nodded, seemingly almost unsurprised by the mate's decision. He placed his hand on Tuan's shoulder, and the mate immediately felt a new strength flow into him. But it was a false, dangerous strength—he recognised it from his Taourg days. It would be short-lived and ultimately debilitating. Cliona looked from one to the other in confusion. "Tuan…?" she asked.

But the mate only smiled and pressed a finger to her lips, and then he kissed her gently. "I love you," he whispered.

Then she understood. She turned to the bard and her dark eyes filled, shining silver in the wan light. "Paedur, you cannot leave him here. You cannot. Use your Power…please," she begged.

"Priestess, I would not *ask* Tuan to stay here; it is his decision. And I wish I could use my Power, but at this moment I am totally drained…I cannot."

"Then I will," Cliona said defiantly. "I will call on the Mother…"

"Priestess, you will need your strength soon enough; do not use your Power now. I do not ask this lightly."

Tuan pulled the priestess tightly against his chest, and she clung to him weeping bitterly. He gently brushed her long thick hair. "Do as the bard says," he whispered; "it's for the best, trust him—I do." Then Paedur took the priestess by the arm and half carried, half dragged her away from Tuan.

Tuan watched them in silence and, as they were gradually swallowed up in the dusk, he called out, "I'll re-join you soon."

But they all knew he lied.

The corridor suddenly turned and the bard paused and looked back. Tuan had half turned and was watching them, but in the dusky light it was difficult to make out details, and only the blade of the Chopt knife was clearly visible. The bard lifted his hook and Tuan raised his hand in a final salute, and then he turned and prepared to face whatever followed. But the bard, turning away, silently pledged himself to find the mate again, whether he be in the Gorge or the Silent Wood.

The corridor now widened and branched. The bard did not hesitate but led the sobbing priestess down the left-hand corridor, which seemed to be leading downwards. It was colder and more damp here, and the slit windows were so high as to be almost invisible. The bard reached out and caught Cliona's small hand in his, leading her over the broken flagstones. She was surprised to find his flesh warm and dry, and even more surprised to find sword callouses on the palm of his hand and about the base of his fingers.

As they neared the bottom of the corridor, a long shrill scream—chokingly silenced—echoed off the stone walls. The sound brought Cliona to a halt, and she half turned, as if waiting for another scream. "That…"

"It was Tuan," Paedur whispered, turning her face slightly, staring into her eyes. "There's nothing we can do for him in this life," he added, his grip tightening as she attempted to pull away. "All we can do now is to ensure that he did not die in vain."

Cliona struggled against the bard's grip for a few moments then she suddenly nodded, her face hardening and her eyes beginning to glitter dangerously. Tuan's death had given her a new strength and the determination to avenge him!

They continued on, moving slowly in the dim light, when the bard suddenly felt a faint plucking at the fringes of his consciousness, a touch that was at once alien and yet strangely familiar. Again and again it attempted to breach his guard, and each time he repulsed it. But the battle of wills was taking its toll and, exhausted as he was after his massive use of Power earlier, he could not continue on for much longer. He staggered and Cliona caught his arm—and felt the tingling residue of the assault flow up her arm. Recognising the mind-touch, she allowed a portion of her own strength to flow into the bard.

Paedur felt the warm rush of new strength and power and he savagely lashed out, using the remnants of his own strength, and felt the intruder's touch fall away, but in that instant he recognised it. He had felt that touch once before…it was the mind-touch of his boyhood companion: Thanos. The Hand of God was in the City.

The corridor now sloped steeply and dipped below ground level into total darkness. The priestess stopped in confusion, tightening the hold which she still had on Paedur's arm. The bard's enhanced senses flared, and what was now a tunnel became visible for him in shades of pale blue-green. He continued on, leading Cliona along the winding tunnel, warning her when the roof dipped, when the flagstones were broken, or when there was a step cut into the rock, The tunnel seemed endless, and she quickly lost all sense of time in the echoing lightless chamber of stone.

Finally Paedur stopped and his voice echoed whisperingly around the tunnel. "Ahead of us lies an obstacle. We have avoided the rest—pits, clawed traps and the like…"

"You didn't tell me," Cliona accused him, her voice falling to a murmur.

"I thought it best not to say anything. However, the next obstacle stretches right across our path; it is a growth of sharp-spined razor-leaved bushes. Now, I must ask you to draw upon your fire."

"In this place…?"

"If you so will it—you can," Paedur said.

And the priestess composed herself and, calling on the goddess, attempted to fire the unseen growth ahead of her. The effort left her shaking with emotion, but nothing happened!

Then the bard whispered to her, "Now you have seen that your magic will not work here, because the Old Gods have no sway on this isle. But you have been trained in the Lore of the Nightfolk, and their magic is akin to that of the Culai; draw upon the knowledge your mother taught you."

"That was a long time ago, Paedur, I'm not sure…"

"Some things are not easily forgotten. Try it."

The priestess composed herself and concentrated once again, recalling dim childhood memories of kneeling beside her strange mother
while the pale woman spoke in her whispering voice, and taught her
the legends and magical lore of her own race. She invoked the image
of fire, held it, and then she poured forth all her anger and hate and
pain, fuelling it. A green levin bolt spat across the tunnel, sending her
reeling backwards. The bramble bushes erupted in licking yellow-
green flames that quickly and silently consumed them.

Paedur took her hand and led her through the blackened branches
and snapping cinders into a narrow side tunnel that was so low she
had to bend double, and the deeper they went the narrower it became. And the priestess was suddenly gripped by a sudden fear, a
fear that the low ceiling might collapse or the walls close in on her.
She felt her chest tighten and her heart begin to pound, and she was
conscious of a pulse throbbing in her temples, pounding and pounding until it felt as if her head were about to explode. The sudden
heat was becoming unbearable, suffocating…

She stopped, her only thought to leave…to leave now, return to
the mouth of the tunnel…for now the walls really were closing in
…constricting…the ceiling was surely lower now…

Then the bard was beside her, quiet, reassuring, his voice ringing
through her confusion and turmoil. "Fight it, priestess. This is but
another of the tunnel's defences. Fight it, fight the fear. Fight it…"

And then his voice was swept away in a wave of suffocating
constriction, and then she could actually feel the walls moving, closing in on her, and the pressure of the roof on the top of her head…

"Fight it; if not for your sake, then for the memory of Tuan.
Do not let his death have been in vain; he fought to save you. He
died for you. You can fight. Fight!"

Cliona felt the cold anger of Tuan's death return and grip her,
and the soul-destroying fear receded. In those brief moments she
cleared her mind and recited the simple incantations she had been
taught as a child to ward against the ffis flowers of her native
Monatome that induce fear and then feed on the emotion. Gradually the simple repetition drove out the last vestiges of the claustro-
phobic fear and barricaded her mind against further assault. "I'm
fine now," she said simply.

In the darkness Paedur smiled slightly in admiration at her self-control, and he wondered what the priestess might have become had her destiny not been woven with his.

They rounded a curve in the tunnel and found an irregular circle outlined greyly ahead of them. It was the mouth of the tunnel—they stopped when they reached it, and looked out into the cavern beyond.

The cavern was of awesome dimensions, and the distant walls were lost in the dimness. The walls were slimed with a phosphorescent fungus that glowed with a pale milk-white light, creating figures and leering shadow faces within itself. Stumps of stalagmites were dotted along the floor close to the walls, but the centre of the cavern was smooth and flat, with the natural floor polished to an almost mirror-like brightness. High in the roof of the cavern was a tiny circular spot of a blood-red colour—which, the bard said softly, was an opening to the sky above.

Paedur waited, using his senses, both natural and enhanced, to ensure that the cavern was empty before he hurried the priestess across the floor, their footsteps ringing hollowly on the stones. Cliona slipped on the smoothly polished stones and begged him to slow down, but he pointed with his hook to the tiny red spot on the roof and then to the floor directly beneath it. "The sun shines through that opening directly into this cavern close to this time every day; aye, every day—this plane has no seasons, and every day when the sun is directly overhead the Culai gather here in this, the Cavern of Power, and who knows what rites they perform, what beings they invoke?"

"You fear them?" she asked, her voice beginning to shake with exhaustion.

The bard smiled gently. "Only a fool would not fear the First Race. Yet, I am somewhat protected, for I have been gifted by a god, but you..." He shook his head slowly, "You have no protection save your magic, and that would be of little use here in the inner sanctum of the Culai." His hard dark eyes caught and held hers. "There is something else you should know, priestess; I would rather see you slain—and by my own hand, if need be—than let you fall into their hands alive."

"Tuan knew that, didn't he?" she asked.

"Aye, he knew. He knew you were too important to our mission to be captured, and that was one of the reasons why he stayed behind. And he too would not have allowed you to be captured and used by the First Race. For they would not slay you, oh no, they would bend you to their will; then you would be mindless, a *quai*. Remember the warning carved into the sides of the mountain?"

"*Lifeless ye shall live, deathless ever be, all ye who pass beyond,*'" she whispered.

When they reached the far side of the cavern, they found that there were three tunnels leading out from the Cavern of Power. Paedur stopped and raised his hook, his head tilted to one side, listening.

"What...?" Cliona began, but the bard's fingers crushed her hand, silencing her.

And then, suddenly, the cavern was ablaze with blood-light, glittering, shining, reflecting from the luminous mosses, and winking with a thousand points of light. Paedur flung his cloak over the priestess, but too late—the sudden light had all but blinded her.

The tiny circle in the high roof blazed with a blistering light, for the sun was now directly overhead, and a bar of almost solid light shafted down into the cavern. Directly beneath the light was a pool of slate-coloured, viscous liquid, which reflected the alien sunlight about the cavern. Around the pool were set ten stones of varying colours, which had been polished so smooth that they too caught and reflected the light in different colours off the walls, the ceiling, and the polished floor.

A slow throbbing began, sounding as if a great heart were beating in some distant cavern—and then a slow susurration whispered across the emptiness, sounding almost like a breeze disturbing dead and dry autumnal leaves; but the throbbing gradually intensified and the whispering resolved into a sharp liquid twittering.

Then silence.

And the sudden silence was all the more terrifying. There was shadowy movement against the lichened walls, and tall figures began to file into the cavern from scores of darkened openings in the walls. Paedur pressed Cliona back against the wall, forcing her down as the Culai approached.

More and more of the Culai arrived; they all wore the metallic sheath-robes favoured by the First Race in their latter days, and which reflected the light like so many burning beacons. They were unnaturally tall and thin, beautiful after a fashion, but their fine, delicately pointed features were blotched and marred by the changing colours.

Most of them passed within an arm's length of the bard and priestess, the reflected light from their robes almost blinding them, but then a small group came towards them, their heads bent deep in conversation...

Paedur closed his mind to the sight-destroying light from their robes and began to weave a web of emptiness about himself and the priestess, attempting to slip them fractionally from the present plane into the grey Ghost Worlds that exist between the planes of existence. Normally, it was a simple enough manoeuvre, one he could achieve by merely willing it. But now nothing happened. He pulled Cliona closer to him and rested the point of his hook against her smooth throat, while desperately attempting to complete the spinning. But the Culai were too close...too close...he would never...Abruptly he felt the chill given off by the edge of the planes and he was in the Ghost Worlds, with the priestess still in his arms. He was still able to see into the Cavern of Power, and he jerked back automatically as the four Culai seemed to pass over and through them. Cliona was still wrapped within his cloak, her eyes streaming from the blinding burst of light earlier.

The Culai had gathered about the large pool in the centre of the floor in long straight lines, like spokes radiating from a circle. Paedur did a quick calculation and found that each line was made up of one hundred Culai, male and female alternating, and that there were one hundred lines. These ten thousand were the last of the First Race, a race that had once numbered tens of millions. But they had not bred for many generations, and these were the same Culai who had been settled on the Blessed Isle when it was first created. In all that time age had not touched them.

They bowed their heads and began to chant, and in their voices were the haunting resonances of Elder Days. The sounds chilled the bard, dredging up memories he had long thought forgotten; his uncle had used those cadences and his grandfather before him, for they were amongst the purest of the bardic forms. The voices soared, thin and high, seeming to venture into those regions inaudible to human ears.

While the bard was entranced, Cliona struggled free of his cloak and blinked her watering eyes...and felt vertigo and sickness grip her.

For about her was a swirling grey nothingness, an abstract void reminiscent of the Grey Walls, but before her she could see into the cavern and the lines of chanting Culai, almost as if she were looking through a window. She reached out and touched the bard's forearm and, when nothing happened, she shook him. He turned his head slowly, and stared at her with no trace of recognition, his face hard and closed, almost inhuman. "Paedur...?" she breathed. Something moved behind his eyes, and then he shook himself like a man awakening.

He smiled slightly, and then turned back to the window looking in at the Cavern of Power. *"Now is our opportunity, while the Culai are deep in their devotions."* His voice rang in her head, ice-cold and terrifying. He told her to hold on to him and she felt his body tense as he attempted to move them out of the Ghost Worlds.

But now the chanting of the First Race had taken on a new note, a higher, more insistent keening...a calling. It was another reason for leaving the safety of the half-world; he had no idea what might soon be coming through it.

And then he felt the tug, the tiny giving of the fabric of the planes, as both he and Cliona slid back into the cavern, but not before they were both abruptly chilled by a sudden gust of icy wind that had rippled through the Ghost Worlds.

And as they scrambled for the shelter of one of the tunnels ahead of them, there was a high exultant cry from the assembled Culai. Paedur glanced back over his shoulder and saw a thin wavering line appear above the pool, a snake, a cord of absolute blackness.

And as the line twisted and wove back and forth, it seemed to gain substance from the wan-coloured lights in the cavern, for the colours paled and dimmed...and then suddenly it flickered once and was gone...

It reappeared, and this time it was not alone. Now there were two wavering cords of darkness, pulsating, twisting, weaving together...and then they too disappeared. And reappeared. But now there were three.

As they spun and interwove, the bard felt his eyes drawn hypnotically towards the three cords, and the swirling after-image on his retina suggested something...something he could not name, except that he was sure he had seen it before. The image was familiar—frighteningly familiar—and the very sight of it chilled him to the bone.

With a start, he realised Cliona was pulling insistently at his arm. He looked around and found he had stopped in the mouth of one of the tunnels—in full view of the First Race, but he doubted if anyone had seen him. The Culai acted as if they had been drugged or entranced as they stared mindlessly up at the weaving cords.

He turned and ran up the tunnel behind the priestess, the image left by the serpents still burning in his brain, tantalisingly familiar. He had seen it long ago, of that he was sure. Three twisting black lines …there was a symbol, a sign as old as the gods themselves, a sign of three twisting lines…a sign…The Sign of the Three Cords!

And suddenly he remembered!

And the memory terrified him.

Perhaps he fell—he didn't know; the next thing he knew he was sitting with his back against the cold stone wall of the tunnel, with the priestess bending over him. He started up, but Cliona pressed both hands against his shoulders and pushed him down, and he felt so weak, he allowed her.

"What happened?" he mumbled.

The priestess shook her head slightly. "I'm not sure. One moment you were behind me, and when I looked again you were on your knees, not exactly unconscious but not fully awake." She paused. "Do you want to tell me what happened?" she asked.

"I'm not sure myself."

"Do you want to tell me what are the three cords?" she asked quietly, and then watched his face tighten in pain and beads of sweat begin to trickle from his hairline.

"How do you know about the Cords?" he asked.

"You spoke about them while you were unconscious," she said. "What are they?"

"I think they are the reason we were sent here," he murmured, almost to himself.

"I thought we were here to prevent Thanos gaining control of the Chrystallis," Cliona said.

"So did I."

"What are these cords?" Cliona demanded. "You've seen them before, haven't you?"

Paedur nodded.

"Tell me," Cliona almost screamed, shaking him by the shoulders. "Tell me!"

Paedur ran his fingers through his hair, pushing it back from his eyes, and when he spoke his voice was so low that Cliona had to stoop forward to hear him. "I was a boy at the time," he began, "no more than eight years, I think, younger possibly but certainly not older. I found a stone in the ancient ruins in the hills above my home, a stone etched with three curving lines. I can remember my fingers finding the lines and tracing them over and over again and, innocently, I carried it home in my left hand. My father saw it and asked what it was, and when I showed it to him he wouldn't touch it, but he sent my brother for Gahred, my great-uncle, who was staying with us at the time. When I showed it to him, Gahred silently took me to the mountain stream that gushed from the ice hills further north and ran through the gully close to my home. There, he ordered me to strip and bathe in the icy stream; I refused and then he struck me, and I think it was only then that I realised the old man was terribly frightened.

"While I was bathing, Gahred cut a branch from a Lady Tree. In that terrifyingly powerful voice of his, he called forth the Dannu-fire. I'll never forget it; it was the first time I had ever seen the blue-white cold fire of the goddess. Then Gahred ordered me to stand by the water's edge and stretch out my left hand, the hand in which I had carried the stone home. I did as I was told, although I remember it took an effort to hold my left arm steady; because my hand now stung as if it had been burned, and it twitched and trembled of its own accord. My great-uncle then cried aloud in the Old Tongue that had been suppressed a generation before, and the white fire on the branch frose in jagged ice-like streamers. I had never seen such magic before and, while I was mesmerised with that, Gahred brought the branch down on my arm, severing my hand at the wrist." The bard lifted his left arm, and looked unseeing at the silver hook, remembering the hand he once had. He took a deep sobbing breath and continued. "I can remember looking at the stump of my arm and feeling no pain, merely a soft warm glowing that rose up from my feet until it reached my head ...and then I remember no more. But, before I lost consciousness, I do remember noticing that the wound had not bled.

"And all on account of a stone with three wavering lines cut into it.

"The days thereafter were the stuff of nightmare, and there were further ritual purifications. Afterwards I learned that the door of the house had been torn down and burned because I had touched it, and all the clothes I had worn also.

"I can also recall a twisted little man—a dwarf—who was seemingly of great age, whom even Gahred called 'Heer' which is 'father' in the old speech. He fitted an oversized silver hook into the bone of my wrist, and although I know he cut and sawed into the bone, I don't remember feeling anything. I do know Gahred laid his gnarled hand on my head and whispered strange words that buzzed and vibrated like a thousand insects inside my skull before the old man started his work.

"And when the hook had been fitted, the old man—and now I suspect that the dwarf might have been Toriocht the Smith, brother to Chriocht the Carpenter, the halfling servants of the gods—carved runes into the length of the delicate curved blade. He thought I was asleep but I heard him explaining to Gahred that the hook would grow with me, so that when I reached manhood, the hook would be the full and proper size for a man. My uncle asked about honing, but the old man said that there was a thin band of metal running along the edge of the hook. This, he said, was forged from the head of one of the spears of the Stormlord, it was knife sharp and would never dull…" Paedur lifted his hook, and looked up into the priestess's eyes. "And all for the sake of a stone. A stone with three waving lines cut into it. The three lines of Disruption, Annihilation and Chaos. The first is slow, the second total and the third ultimate. The most ancient legends say that they co-existed with the One, but they also hint that they existed before all things, before the One and the Void and the Chrystallis."

"Are they more dangerous than the Soulwind?" Cliona wondered.

Paedur glanced back down the tunnel, and then he shook his head. "Thanos and his warriors are a threat, but they are minor—a mere irritation—when compared to the forces the Culai are invoking."

"But what can we do?" the priestess asked, desperation edging her voice.

The bard stood up, the fingers of his right hand tracing the runes etched into his hook. "I'm not sure," he said wearily, "I'm not sure the Three Cords can be destroyed."

"But which do we attempt first—the Chrystallis or the Cords?" Cliona asked.

Paedur turned to look at the woman, her words sparking something deep within him, nudging some fragment of his bardic lore. He allowed his mind to go blank for a moment, knowing that whatever he was looking for would come to the fore if he left it alone.

"Paedur...?" Cliona asked harshly, finding his silence disturbing.

The Magician's Law," Paedur breathed, and in that instant he conceived a plan, a desperate measure to attempt to save the planes of life from complete destruction. It would mean death—death on a scale never even imagined but tiny when compared to the potential destruction of either the Three Cords or the Chrystallis alone. It never occurred to him to wonder by what right he made that decision—he never even thought of it—but deep within him he knew that this was his destiny. The Magician's Law—the force of equals.

The priestess shrank back from him, seeing him change almost before her eyes, seeing his features harden and close, his eyes become hooded. He had sloughed off that part of him that was still human and what remained was...godlike—and terrifying.

When he spoke she found that even his voice had grown harsher. "Come. We must hurry; we are racing time, the knowledge of the Culai, the readiness of the Cords, and Thanos. We don't know how soon the First Race might release the Cords upon the planes of life—if indeed, the Culai still maintain any control over the Three, which I doubt."

"Where are we going?"

"To get what we came for—the vessel of the Chrystallis."

The tunnel wound upwards in a slow spiral, and once they had left the flickering light that burned around the entrance, they were in total darkness. Paedur held Cliona's hand and dragged her roughly along. She struggled to keep up, frightened of running into something in the dark, frightened of falling, or cracking her skull against the ceiling. Frightened also of the bard. He had changed; the man that she and Tuan had followed on this doomed mission was gone, and had been replaced by...by what? She wondered then, had they ever been following a man—or merely a creature that looked and walked like a man? Had the bard actually changed back there in the tunnel—or had he just shed his human skin and become his true self?

What was it Tuan had once said to her: *I feel my destiny lies with him; I am drawn to him.* She smiled bitterly; his destiny had lain with the bard, and his destiny had been death. And what of her own destiny—was she, too, doomed? The bard needed her, he had needed her to come through the tunnel; he needed her in some way to preserve the seal on the vessel of the Chrystallis. Did that not give her some bargaining power? Power to bargain with him for her own life...and the life of Tuan. She felt sudden hope swell within her. The bard had admitted before his dealings with the Dark Lord, Mannam; might he not be able to bring the mate back from the Silent Wood?

And then there was a sudden light ahead of her, an orange circle against the black throat of the tunnel. The bard was outlined against it, a tall, inhuman, shapeless figure. He slowed and released her hand as they neared the opening, finally stopping in the mouth of the tunnel. He stood, half in shadow, his hook resting against her right shoulder, and then he turned and looked down at her, his shadowed eyes burning with a strange fire. He did not seem to speak, but his voice was ice in her head.

"Your thoughts do you no honour, priestess, and you belittle the memory of Tuan. I did not ensorcel you, nor draw you here by force of my will, nor are you following a Duaiteoiri. You followed a man and your choice was a free one—for the followers of the Old Faith are not like the minions of Trialos, who seek to force their will on others. But...but we are all puppets; even the very gods themselves are used by forces far greater than they. I have always been a puppet of the gods, and Tuan knew this. But you should also know that I have always retained my free will. I was not forced to come here, no more than you were. I chose to come, and my decision was based on a sense of duty and what I felt was right, and now that I am here I will do what I feel is right.

"I do not know why Tuan came; he had his reasons, but he, too, made what he considered to he the right decision.

"And you. Why did you come? Because of your dream? And do you always heed your dreams? Or did you come because you felt it to be right?" He turned away and went to the mouth of the tunnel out into the lurid sunlight; behind him Cliona wept silently.

"But I will tell you this," Paedur said, without turning around, his voice ringing ice-cold and painful in her head. *"I have sworn to find Tuan, whether he be in this life or the next. And I took that oath by the Pantheon when I last saw him, as he prepared to face that which followed us."*

Suddenly he turned around and spoke to her. "I am going on now; to reach the vessel before Thanos has now become even more important. You may stay here in the tunnel and I will return presently   if I can. Or you may accompany me. The decision is yours and yours alone."

And in a voice that was barely above a whisper, Cliona said. "I will come with you."

She joined the bard outside the tunnel and looked around in amazement. They were on the roof of a building, a broad square of rough sandstone, unrelieved by ornament or decoration, and without chimney or balustrade. Behind her the roof rose to perhaps twice her height, forming a high wall, the mouth of the tunnel the only opening. The tunnel must have led upwards through the core of the building.

Paedur saw her astonishment and said, "It's common in Culai buildings." He pointed across the flat roofs of the city spread out before them, and in each case the roof was on two levels, each displaying the black circle of a tunnel mouth. "They lead down to the Cavern of Power; it is at the very centre of the Culai way of life, and thus at the same time each day, no matter where they are or what they're doing, they must retire below and worship."

"But that means we must have passed a door in the tunnel on the way up," Cliona exclaimed.

"We passed several, but they would not open to us."

"And where is the centre opening through which the light comes?"

Paedur turned and pointed with his hook. Cliona followed it and there, behind her, towering above the rest of the city, was the goblet-shaped building of the Inner City. Its size was enormous; its base alone, which from the distance had seemed almost flat, was huge and almost topped the building on which they stood, and the spire which rose from the base was colossal, taller than the lighthouses that dotted the coast of her homeland and at least three times as thick. And the spire melded into the base of the building that squatted atop it without trace of a join or crack. As Cliona looked at it, she realised that something was missing. She puzzled over it for a moment—and then she realised that there were no windows or doors in the building.

Paedur nodded towards it. "The vessel of the Chrystallis lies within the Circle of Keys in the Inner City," he said.

"There is no door," the priestess protested.

"There is always a door," Paedur said. He walked to the edge of the roof and looked down into the silent empty streets far below.

Cliona called over to him, desperation edging her voice. "How are we going to get off the roof, never mind getting into the Inner City?"

But the bard remained silent.

"Are we going to jump?" she asked bitterly, coming up to stand beside him and staring into the streets below.

"Aye, perhaps," he said, squinting up into the orange sun. "We have a little time, the light still burns below, and there are features of the Inner City I would point out. Come, sit here." He drew her back from the edge of the roof and made her sit on the warm stone.

"What does its shape remind you of?" he asked suddenly.

"A goblet," she said immediately, and the bard looked so surprised that she continued, "See there, a base, a stem, a bowl."

Paedur nodded absently. "I see it now, though I must admit I have never thought of it that way before. Do the philosophers not say that life is like a rare wine, to be sipped slowly and enjoyed to the full? If we take your comparison, then that bowl is full of some rare vintage, for it holds the keys not only to our survival but also to the continuance of Order and Life on all the planes of life.

"But look again. Is the shape not reminiscent of the *naekt,* the glyph for fulfilment, discovery, and completion in the Old Tongue?" He continued on as she nodded. "Within the Inner City lies what we seek, the vessel of the Chrystallis. It is kept within the Circle of Gates or Keys. That is our destination. Once we reach it, our task is almost complete..." His voice died to a whisper, and then he stood up and reached for her hand. "Come."

"But how do we get off the roof...?"

The bard walked over to the edge of the roof and pointed down with his hook. "This way."

Cliona went over and stood beside him and looked down into the street. but she could see neither ladder, steps nor rope. "How...?"

"Trust me," Paedur murmured, and then, before she could ask him what he meant, he gripped her arms, pinning them tightly to her side, and jumped!

She screamed—but there was no sound. Her eyes watered in the wind that streamed upwards past them; she squeezed them shut, cutting out the sliding blurring sandstone side of the building they were falling past. But she could not shut out the sensation of falling ...falling...falling into a limitless space and then there was...

16
The Vessel of the Chrystallis

Faith lends Substance.

Ancient proverb common to the Seven Nations

This day the gods themselves walked amongst us once more...

Song of the Teouteuchalai

Consciousness returned to Cliona as she lay in the shade of the tall square building, the bard bending over her, his ice-cold voice calling urgently deep in her head. *"Awaken ... Awaken...*

Her eyelids trembled and opened, and then closed again as everything shifted and spun. And then something bitterly cold was pressed against her cheek, bringing her fully awake. Paedur lifted his hook from her face, and smiled in apology. "Come, we must hurry. The sun has shifted and the light will have died out down below. The Culai will soon be coming up from the cavern." He pulled the priestess to her feet and propelled her across a wide street in the direction of the massive base of the Inner City. "Hurry!"

His touch suddenly repelled her and she roughly shook off his hand and, head still spinning, staggered towards the featureless block of stone and into the shadow of the huge spire and bowl. Once out of the sickening glare of the red sun her head cleared and she began to think more clearly. "There's no door..." she said thickly.

Paedur gripped her by the wrist and gestured with his hook to a portion of the wall. And though his lips didn't move, his voice cut through the remnants of the fog in her head. *"There! Visualise a door there. A door such as you have seen in the Order House of the Mother on the mainland. There the lintel, and now the posts..."*

Gradually he built up in her mind the image of a door, a door similar to the Houses of the Mother; her imagination and memory supplied the rest, filling in the details, until she could almost see a door there.

And suddenly a door was there! A door such as she had visualised. A door from her memory, and past. She reached out to touch it; the brukwood felt warm and oily and the iron studs rasped against her fingers as she pressed on it.

Paedur pressed his hand flat against the door, and it swung silently inwards. He pushed Cliona through the opening just as they heard the sounds of high, musical voices approaching. She caught a glimpse of the Culai as they rounded the corner of a building farther down the street, their heads bent in conversation; and then she was inside the building, and the door...had vanished.

The bard pressed her back against the smooth wall, his hand raised for silence as he listened. He took a few noiseless steps forward. "Stay here, don't move," he hissed.

Cliona nodded, glad of the opportunity to gather her wits and look around. They were in a huge chamber that was so vast the far walls were invisible in the dim light. It had been constructed in the manner of the First Race, with the massive blocks of stone welded together without trace of mortar or clay. The stones were ice-smooth and portions of them had been polished to a mirror-like sheen. The floor was of black marble, and was worked through with tiny threads of gold and silver in a pattern of some sort, but the design was so vast that she could make little sense of it. The impossibly high ceiling was also of the same black marble and the constellations and planets were picked out with tiny sparks of light, like the stars in the heavens on a sharp winter's night. Something caught her eye and she looked again—there was something vaguely wrong with the constellations...and then she realised that what she was seeing was a representation of the night-sky many generations ago when the Culai walked amongst man. There were no windows in the huge room, but a vague sepia light emanated from some of the wall stones, giving the place an almost twilight atmosphere.

Paedur materialised out of the dimness and took her hand. He led her across the floor, and then stopped before a section of the glass-like unadorned wall of the chamber. "I want you to visualise a stairway here." He tapped the wall ringingly with his hook. "A stairway built in the manner of the Culai, the ruins of which you will have seen surviving in the Nations and the islands off the coast."

Cliona nodded. "I've seen them."

"Imagine it here!" Paedur commanded.

The priestess closed her eyes, concentrating on the image of a Culai stairway. They were nearly always the same; single blocks of stone laid haphazardly one upon the other. The steps were usually of differing heights and thicknesses, and of varying sizes, jutting crazily at all angles. This chaotic arrangement was at complete variance with the stark symmetry of all other Culai architecture. Some scholars maintained that the Culai had no use for stairways but had built spiralling ramps that ran around the outside of their buildings. However, they explained all absence of such ramps from the many Culai ruins by pointing out that external ramps would have been the first things to succumb to the ravages of time and the elements. There was little evidence to support this theory except that the crude mismatched stairways were only found in the later buildings, when the time of the First Race was drawing to a close.

Keeping his voice low and using all his bard's powers, Paedur built up a vivid word picture of a typical Culai stairway and Cliona added to it, drawing upon her childhood memories, for Monatome, her homeland, was one of the great centres of Culai ruins.

And gradually the flickering image of a stairway began to imprint itself upon the blank wall, winking in and out of a shadowy existence. Cliona tensed, forcing her mind to accept the image she was seeing; like all magics, she knew she must believe in it. Faith, she must have faith in it, Faith lends Substance. But she knew she had neither the strength of mind nor spirit to bring the stairway to reality.

And then the bard stepped up beside her and rested his hook upon her shoulder. There was a tingling transference of power and suddenly she felt new strength flow into her. The image immediately hardened and solidified, the blank wall faded … and the stairway was there.

The stones felt solid and real under her feet as the bard urged her up them. She slipped and fell upon the angled irregular steps, barking both shins, and she knew then the steps were no illusion. They were real. The bard pulled her to her feet and continued on without speaking.

The stairs wound endlessly upwards, weaving back and forth erratically, with neither rail nor guard and with a fall that grew steeper with every step they took. Cliona clung to the bard's cloak, keeping her eyes fastened to the stairs, blanking her mind to the terror that gibbered at the edges of her consciousness and threatened to overwhelm her at any moment. At one point she had tried counting the number of steps, but had given up somewhere around twenty-two hundred. She reached the point of exhaustion and begged the bard to stop, but he ignored her, and only seemed to increase the pace. Her leg muscles cramped, but she forced herself to go on, realising that the bard would probably leave her behind if she stopped now. She stumbled on, exhausted, almost sleep-walking on leaden feet.

Paedur abruptly stopped and Cliona staggered into him, and then slid down to her knees on the rough stone steps, gasping for breath, the pounding of blood roaring in her ears. She dimly realised the bard was speaking, but she couldn't make out the words. She looked down at the steps, her whole body shivering, her leg muscles twitching of their own accord, and when she looked up again the bard was gone. Something like terror gripped her, leaving her breathless, and she staggered to her feet...and then she heard the clatter of metal on metal—ahead!

Fear lent her strength and she ran up a few steps, and suddenly found that the stairway had ended and led out on to a short broad corridor. Midway down the corridor the bard was bending over the body of a ragged man, his hook dripping thick blood onto the polished stones. He looked up when the priestess appeared, and then silently lifted the dead man's arm in the curve of his hook. There was an iron band encircling it.

"The Iron Band of Kloor," Cliona panted.

"Thanos has beaten us."

"But how?"

Paedur shook his head in frustration. "I don't know how. Just as there are several ways into Ui Tyrin, I suppose there must he more than one way into the Inner City also." He turned and walked to the end of the short corridor, stopping before a high glass door set flush into the wall. He examined it closely, running his fingers over the opaque crystal, tracing out the curious design that was etched deep into the glass. Cliona walked slowly down the corridor, avoiding the grotesque and still bleeding body, and joined him, steadying herself against the wall.

"Do you recognise the design?" Paedur asked, tracing the hourglass shape in the glass with his hook.

Cliona looked at it and then slowly shook her head.

"Look again," Paedur snapped.

She ran her finger over the shape and then she suddenly saw within the design the outline of the Inner City.

"The *naekt,*" she said wearily, "the symbol for fulfilling, finding, and answering."

Paedur smiled thinly. "Just so. And that is what we must do now. Find the answer to the puzzle." He deliberately struck the door with his hook, but the crystal remained unmarked.

"What puzzle?" the priestess asked, the bard's words slowly sinking into her fatigue-numbed brain.

"This design holds the key to this door; something about this tracery will open the way for us. And it cannot be too difficult either," he added, pointing back down the corridor to the still body of the warrior. "It was not beyond Thanos."

"I still can't work out how he got here before us; I thought we left him beyond the city gates."

"I would have thought all the gates on the far side of the city wall would be well guarded...but Thanos is cunning, and it is a dangerous—and usually deadly—mistake to underestimate him. One fact remains..." He tapped the glass door. "He is already within; we have to get inside soon."

Paedur turned back to the symbol etched into the glass. This was the key to the door; all he had to do was to charge it. Given time he would inevitably find the answer—but there was no more time left. Thanos and his men had already passed through the door—perhaps they already had the vessel and were even now preparing to open it. He pounded on the door with his fist in frustration; he had come so far—he would not be cheated by the Hand of God, not now, not so late in the game. He would not allow it! At any instant all creation might be swept away in a swirling chaos of the time before Life, the era of the One and the Void and the Chrystallis—and the Cords.

And what of the Three Cords? They posed an even greater threat than the Soulwind. Should the Chrystallis sweep all the planes back to the Void, it would mean an ending to everything, but it would not be a final, ultimate ending. The process of creation could begin again; there might be a future. However, if the Cords should scour the planes free of life, rending through the soft fabric of time and the wafers of fragile space, then Disruption, Annihilation and Chaos would render the Void lifeless for all eternity. Even the One might not survive the passage of the Three Cords. They had to be stopped, but what could a mortal—even a mortal gifted by the gods—do against Disruption, Annihilation and Chaos?

Cliona slumped at the bard's feet, too exhausted to even think, images of the last few days—was it only days?—chasing each other in ever decreasing circles around in her head. Numbly, almost emotionlessly, she felt the salt tears fall to her roughened hands and splash onto the dry stone floor. Idly her fingers moved in the wetness, tracing the symbol of the *naekt* on the stone.

The bard knelt beside her, hunched and silent, his eyes darting about the corridor, seeking; seeking anything that might suggest the key of the door. If the Culai used this door with any degree of regularity, then it must be something simple—magic of any sort, no matter how minor, was draining. Therefore it was something built into the door, a crude static spell which could be charged by a simple process. And all he had to do was to find it.

His eyes fell on the priestess, and he saw her trace the shape of the *naekt* repeatedly. He watched her finger move…left to right, then down to the left-hand corner again, then across to the right, then back up to the left-hand corner, making two stylised triangles, one atop the other.

And realisation blossomed in the bard, and suddenly he had the answer—he had the key to the door. "Reverse the process," he murmured, "reverse it…!"

Pulling the priestess to her feet and supporting her with one hand he began to trace the shape of the *naekt* on the door in reverse with the tip of his hook.

Almost imperceptibly the crystal door began to split, a tiny crack at first beginning at the top in the centre and widening out in a long wedge until it touched the floor. The long triangular split seemed almost to be painted on the gleaming crystal, black velvet on white silk. "Are you ready?" Paedur asked Cliona, but, without waiting for an answer, he pulled her through the opening … into a suffocating cloying blackness that was tangible, an absolute, featureless, sightless nothing that the mind refused to accept.

Cliona opened her mouth and screamed, but there was no sound, and then she choked on the gate's foul inky ichor that enfolded her. Her limbs began to tingle—at first almost pleasantly, but then they quickly turned numb. The blood pounding in her ears and temples threatened to explode with the violence of the throbbing. Her eyes opened and closed, straining to see something…anything!

And this is what it must be like to die, she thought; perhaps this is death, and I am on my way to be judged. "Is this death?" she screamed silently.

Something brushed her mind, a feather touch, a caress, and then she could almost feel the bard within her head, and not chill like the last time but solid, comforting...and real, something she could cling to.

"This is like the space between the planes," Paedur whispered, his voice echoing hollowly within her head. *"You have passed through it twice before and, though it was not as powerful or as pure a force then as it is now, you need not fear it."* Even as he was speaking the blackness had begun to lighten, and the utter darkness was replaced by a dull grey semi-light, something akin to a winter twilight, which was shot through with darting points of white light...

...They emerged into a large circular courtyard that at first glance seemed open to the sky, but the priestess immediately realised it couldn't be the sky of this world, for the sky was a delicate pastel blue, the clouds were smoky white, and the sun, low on the horizon, was an orange gold. The familiarity of it all brought sudden tears to her eyes. The ceiling—for that was what it was—had been created by a master-craftsman and artist from tiny flakes of differing marbles, white and blue, red and gold. It was very beautiful and yet it looked almost out of place—it did not belong here amongst the starkness of the Culai Isle.

The large circular room itself was featureless, except for a simple stone pedestal set into the centre of the floor. But set into the walls were doorposts and lintels, and these opened out on to different views: a snowscape, a seascape, summer fields rippling beneath a gentle breeze, a barren plain. Cliona first thought that they were pictures, tapestries perhaps, but the bard took her to the empty pedestal in the centre of the room and from there she could see each of the nine openings. "Look closer," Paedur said quickly.

She looked—and found that there was movement in the pictures: the seas crashed against high cliffs: the wind whirled tumbleweed across the dusty plains. "They're like windows to other worlds..." she whispered.

The bard laughed. "Priestess, do you not recognise them? They are openings to other lands...they are the keys to our plane, for we are now at the hub of the Inner City, the Circle of Keys.

Behold the Keys!" His hook swept around the room, encompassing the nine doorways.

"I have never seen anything like it," she whispered, looking in wonder from opening to opening.

Paedur went over to one of the gates, through which Cliona could see a swirling snowscene, with desolate ice-fields beneath a leaden sky and a wan sun burning low on the horizon. "Ah, but the gates were once quite common," Paedur continued. "They provided a magically swift method of transport between any two points on our world. They were similar to the Grey Walls in that respect, except that the walls shift the traveller through the planes, whereas the gates confine the journeyer to one plane. Did you know, priestess, that there are still working gates on our plane?" He laughed gently. "Can you tell me where?"

"It can only be the Great Henge," Cliona gasped.

Paedur nodded. "That is the last circle of gates on our plane," he said slowly, walking from gate to gate, looking out at the Seven Nations. "But now they may not be used. They were the focus for much evil upon the Southern Kingdoms down through the generations of man, and evil draws evil to itself..."

"But if the gates are simply used for moving people from place to place," Cliona asked, "what's the harm in that?"

"The gates proved to be unreliable, and before they came to be no longer used they sometimes lost people, and occasionally admitted shadow creatures from the Gorge which had grown tangible with man's belief."

"Are these doorways usable?" she asked.

Paedur nodded silently.

"And what about Thanos?" the priestess asked.

"He has escaped us—with the vessel!" Paedur nodded to the empty pedestal in the centre of the room. "He's gone through the gates—but which one, which one?" He stood beside the pedestal and slowly turned, looking at each gate in turn. A thought struck him, and he suddenly darted to an opening across from the priestess.

"What is it?"

But the bard silenced her with a wave of his hand and stared intently through the opening. Beyond the gate a crude stone and mud-bricked village shimmered beneath a blistering sun. The tiny dwellings were bleached colourless and the rough windows and doors looked dark and ominous in the harsh light. Even the sky seemed bleached, with a delicate metallic blue only showing close to the horizon; the world seemed lifeless.

"Where is it?" the priestess wondered.

Silently the bard pointed to a mound beyond the village. Cliona squinted into the harsh light, already feeling the heat on her face and hands. The mound was a crudely shaped pyramid with a levelled top and had countless steps inset in its side.

"Teouteuchal," Paedur said slowly, almost triumphantly, nodding to himself. "Aye, it would strike Thanos as fitting to open the vessel of the Chrystallis atop the pyramid."

"Why?"

"The pyramids of Teouteuchal are amongst the earliest symbols of man's devotion to the Gods of the Pantheon. The Teouteuchalai have always worshipped Nusas, the Lord of the Sun, and Thanos would take great delight in defiling the god's altar."

"But how can you be sure he is there?" She looked around at the other gates. "He could be anywhere," she said, a note of despair touching her voice.

"He is there, I know it," Paedur said confidently, stepping up to the gateway. "Come."

He reached for her hand but she flinched away, and he saw the fear in her eyes. "What are you frightened of?" he asked quietly, and then he added, "The passage between places on the same plane is not as traumatic nor as severe as travelling between the planes. Trust me," he said.

Cliona nodded doubtfully, and then Paedur stepped through the opening, taking her with him into the southern Kingdom of Teouteuchal. She clung tightly to his hand, squeezing her eyes shut, but all she experienced was a sudden chill, nothing more, and then the heat struck her, a heavy, dry, desiccating blast of leaden heat. The bard spoke softly by her side. "We are through."

It still took another moment or two for the priestess to muster her courage, and then she carefully opened her eyes, peering through slitted lids. The first thing she spotted was a cluster of small dwellings ahead and to her left. They looked almost like part of the ground, with the dried earth and baked walls burnt to the same shade of ochre. One house, slightly larger than the rest, had been thatched with wisps of straw that were so old they looked brittle enough to crumble.

The bard touched her gently on the arm, startling her. "We must make haste—Thanos is here, I can sense him." He set off through the huts, moving like a shadow personified, but Cliona noticed with a tingling chill that the bard himself cast no shadow.

She ran after him, glancing back once ... and stopped in sudden wonder. The gateway through which they had come was gone, but in its place stood two upright pillars, topped by a crossbeam, beautifully wrought in an unusual emerald-green stone. Countless tiny intricate pictograms were worked into the stone, and the square blocky carvings winked and sparkled as chippings of metal or crystal caught the light. Beside the two uprights stood two tall fluted urns of baked clay, both painted in soft flowing colours. Tall reeds drooped in the urns, their golden petals or leaves lying scattered on the brown earth at the base of the pillars. Cliona found it interesting to see that although the reeds were now wilting with the heat they were still reasonably fresh and therefore could only have been placed there earlier that day. The priestess felt the bard by her side. "It's a holy place for the Teouteuchalai. They worship it as the doorway of the gods."

"But I can see right through it," Cliona protested. "I cannot see the Circle of Keys; how then do they know it's a gateway?"

"Through tales passed down from generation to generation. The legends also prophesy that the gods themselves will one day come through that gate..." He stopped suddenly. "Of course..." he breathed.

Cliona shook her head. "I don't understand..." but the bard had already turned and was running towards the pyramid that rose beyond the town.

"Paedur, wait," Cliona called desperately after him. "What's wrong?" But the bard had gone, his shadow-figure seeming barely to touch the unyielding baked earth. The priestess struggled after him, the fear of being left alone lending her speed. As she ran from the pillars, she suddenly realised that Thanos and the remnants of his Band had come through the gate—and the Teouteuchalai people would have thought them the promised gods. They probably thought he was the Lord Nusas himself. And they had gone with Thanos... gone to the mound where the Hand of God would undoubtedly open the vessel of the Chrystallis with a blood sacrifice. The Teouteuchalai would refuse him nothing, not even one of their own number to be torn asunder atop the stepped pyramid.

She ran through the deserted village, heading down the single street towards the pyramid, which she could now see was swarming with tiny ant shapes. She wondered if she dared call upon the Mother's Power—and if she did, would she be answered? On the Culai isle the Old Gods had no power, but she was not on the isle now. But it would alert Thanos to their presence...

Still undecided, she followed the rough pitted track that led out of the village, stumbling over the ruts and potholes. The track wound through tall thorny scrub and then dipped down a sharp slope. At the bottom of the slope she sprawled across a ragged body lying in a pool of still-flowing blood. Dragging herself to her feet she noted the look of horror etched into the features of the dead man. His throat had been torn out. He still clutched a stiletto blade, and as Cliona bent to pull it from his fingers the thick metal band about his wrist caught the light—Thanos had lost another warrior.

She followed the track up out of the hollow and found that it opened out into a wide plaza lined with short pillars. Across the plaza the first steps of the pyramid began. The pyramid itself was not large, nor was it pretty—this was no king's burial mound, with gilded stones and delicate paintings. It was a squat, broad-stepped mound, six or possibly seven floors high. The workmanship was crude and looked unfinished, although the pyramid itself looked ancient. But it was nothing more than an elevated sacrificial slab.

She ran across the plaza, and then found that it dipped down on the far side, so that the pyramid actually began in a hollow, making it taller than she had thought at first. On the slope she came across two more bodies; they too bore evidence of the bard's sudden and violent passage. But, curiously, there was no sign of the Teouteuchalai. She hesitated, and then heard the soft, chanted murmuring. Following the sound she found that one side of the plaza dipped down to a broad lake, whose waters seemed impossibly blue and bright against the drabness of the rest of the landscape. The Teouteuchalai had gathered on the lakeside, and seemed to be engaged in a ritual purification. When the rite was complete, they would undoubtedly gather about the base of the pyramid to salute their god, but by that time, Cliona realised, she and the bard would have to be well away from it.

When she reached the first steps of the pyramid, she looked up and could just about make out the black shape of the bard ahead of her. She took a deep breath and began the long climb.

Atop the pyramid, a sacrifice was in progress. Two short brown bodies lay in pools of blood about the base of a stained flat slab, gaping wounds in their chests leaking blood across the flat roof. A third youth lay spreadeagled across the dripping slab, his eyes wide open in terror. His arms and legs were held by two of the Band of Kloor, while Xanazius, Thanos' acolyte, stood beside him, his arms caked in gore up to the elbows. At his feet two shapeless lumps of meat still quivered. Thanos stood behind the altar, a delicately carved, tall-necked jar clutched in his arms. In the sunlight, his pale skin and bleached hair were almost translucent, causing his eyes and lips to look startlingly red. And about them the priests of the Teouteuchalai worshipped in watchful silence.

Thanos raised the jar high. "Behold the vessel of the Chrystallis. It has lain too long on the Culai Isle, and now it hungers. Feed it!" He nodded to Xanazius, who raised his butcher's knife high...

And then the bard burst onto the top of the pyramid. In the eyes of the Teouteuchalai priests he appeared as a Duaiteoiri, a demon, with blazing eyes and a curved talon dripping blood on to the scoured flagstones. They saw him raise the bloody talon and describe a design that burned with a cold white fire on the still air before the God-Priest who had come through the Gate of the Gods. The white-haired, red-eyed priest snarled in a guttural tongue and held the delicate-looking gem-stoppered vessel close to his chest. Immediately two of the priest's seven acolytes advanced on the Duaiteoiri, knives glittering in their hands.

Cliona heard the shouts and clash of metal as she struggled up the countless worn wooden steps of the pyramid. Calling upon the Mother for strength she redoubled her efforts to reach the top and aid the bard. There was a short shrill scream that was choked off in a liquid gurgle above her head, and she looked up—just as a body flopped over the edge of the pyramid and began to slide down the steps, arms and legs flailing in a grotesque parody of life, trailing a stream of glistening red-black droplets. The priestess cowered to one side as the body crashed past her and lodged a few steps below her. A terrible fascination drew her eyes to the upraised face. A scream caught deep in her throat; the face had been torn from forehead to mouth, down the left side, obviously slashed by a blade...or a hook. Fear, and the sudden need to be away from those ghastly staring eyes, made her turn and run up the planks of wood that had once been brought from the far Northlands to serve as steps to the god's throne.

She eventually reached the top, but stopped before the steps ended and raised her head to peer over the edge of the broad platform. She noted the miserable huddle of natives, now terrified witless by the sudden violence which had erupted on their holy place. And then she spotted the bard, who was surrounded by the five remaining warriors of the Band of Kloor. Paedur was standing over the body of another, and his hook and left arm were thick with blood. Behind them Cliona could see the white-robed albino Thanos, his bloodless hands clutching what could only be the vessel of the Chrystallis. His eyes were wild with a burning madness as he hissed curses at the bard and urged his followers to attack.

The warriors hung back, however, for they knew the power of the bard; they had lost too many of their number to his razor hook and extraordinarily fast reflexes. They shifted continually, jabbing with their swords and knives, probing for an opening. And then one suddenly lunged, his curved knife plunging towards the bard's unprotected back. As if on signal the remaining four made their move, knives and short-swords darting towards the bard.

Cliona screamed. And the Dannu-fire blazed blue-white across the roof of the pyramid, lapping fluidly about the three nearest warriors, They fell, writhing in agony as the cold flames ate through them with startling swiftness, burning through flesh to expose the white bones beneath before they extinguished themselves. The bard caught a blade on his hook while another shattered on his cloak as if it had struck stone instead of cloth. His hook flickered and blurred and sliced through flesh as easily as a knife through cheese, opening a throat, severing another man's jugular—and the last of the Band of Kloor fell.

The bard bowed slightly to the priestess as she joined him, stepping over the charred remains. Together they faced Thanos. Behind them the moaning priests scrambled down the steps, and the sacrificial youth slipped off the altar stone and ran down the steps followed, a moment later, by Xanazius. Thanos watched him go without comment. A brittle silence settled over the pyramid and, although the noonday sun beat down directly overhead, the priestess was chill.

Paedur took a step forward, his hand outstretched. "Give me the vessel." His voice was level, completely emotionless.

Thanos laughed.

The bard took another step forward, but Thanos raised his hand. "Come no further, *shanaqui,* else I will cast this vessel to the ground below."

"That would not serve your masters," the bard said, measuring the distance that separated him from the wild-eyed priest. "Break it now and you have no control over it."

"You will never claim the vessel," Thanos spat. "I would rather destroy the planes than surrender the vessel to you."

"But it is of little use to you now. You have lost...again. As your faith has lost for a hundred generations. The Religion is but a wayward child compared to the parent Pantheon. How could you even hope to threaten the Faith armed only with the best elements from a score of lesser faiths and beliefs and aided by a Usurper from the Gorge?"

Thanos began to laugh wildly. "But you're wrong, bard, you're wrong! The Religion has been growing, and we have more converts now than ever before. We are growing. And as we grow, so the Faith weakens and dies. Like a child growing to maturity as the parent comes to senility."

Paedur began to speak again, but Cliona abruptly felt his ice-cold touch brush her mind. She couldn't make out what he was saying, all she received was the impression that she was to make a move now, to act while Paedur held the Hand of God distracted. "Your converts are tricked, your priests entice them into the Religion with false promises."

"It is for their own good," Thanos said passionately. "Once they have joined the ranks of the faithful, they will see the error of their past and recognise the Religion for what it is: the one true belief. Our gods are real, they are living..."

Cliona took a deep breath and began to move back away from the bard, keeping him between herself and the priest. She stopped when her heels moved off the edge of the flat roof. Her foot found the topmost step and she stepped down onto it. She moved down another ten or so, desperately wondering what the bard expected her to do. He obviously expected her to distract Thanos, while he grabbed the vessel of the Chrystallis. But how? She could attack him using the Dannu-fire—but what would happen to the metallic green jar? She couldn't allow it to be damaged. But if she managed to get around behind him...?

She looked up the dozen or so steps that led to the flat roof. The steps ran almost the width of the pyramid, long flat slabs of polished black wood, slightly curving in the centre with the passage of countless feet. She moved to the edge of the step on which she stood. It ended just short of the corner, and she had no idea whether the steps continued around on the far side. Wiping a trickle of sweat from her eyes, she carefully slid one hand around the angle where the two sides of the pyramid met, fingers groping for a handhold on the far side. Using the edge of the step as a base, she extended her right leg around the side. But she couldn't feel any steps. Finally, her foot found and rested on an irregular outcropping and, resting her whole weight on it, she pulled herself around the corner. There were no steps; this side of the pyramid was unfinished. Pressed flat against the baking earthen bricks, she began to edge her way along the rough-hewn stones, chippings of mud and stone crumbling beneath her torn fingers.

Above her head Thanos' voice rose to a hysterical shout, "There is no god but Trialos, and I, Thanos his Hand, I am his representative upon this plane. Trialos is the one true god..."

Cliona glanced down. Below her, she could see tiny insect figures running to and fro, yet always returning to gather at the foot of the pyramid. Light glinted off metal, and she could hear a muted angry buzzing, and the priestess realised the Teouteuchalai were arming themselves. They would storm the steps at any moment to avenge their god's priest. Desperation lent her strength, and she dug her tattered sandals into the crumbling side of the pyramid and pushed herself up. And her fingers brushed a rough fibrous root. She wrapped her fingers around it and pulled; it gave a little, displacing a long line of mud but also showing her just how far it ran across the side of the pyramid. She pulled on it again—harder this time—and it didn't move. Breathing a silent prayer to the Mother, she used the root as a guide-rope and moved swiftly across the slope, dislodging chunks of dried clay and mud from between the stones. She stopped when she heard Thanos speaking directly above her head.

But now the root had disappeared back into the mound, and there were only the sun-baked stones above her head. The stones here were of differing sizes, crude and ragged; obviously the better stones had been used for the front of the pyramid. She reached up and pulled one of the stones—it came away in her hands in a shower of dried clay. She tried again, and a huge chunk of the dried earthen covering came away, revealing the hard packed earth beneath. She could go no further.

Above her, the voices rose to a crescendo, the bard threatening to call down the power of the Old Gods and Thanos threatening to throw the vessel off the pyramid.

Cliona suddenly remembered the stiletto she had picked off the corpse on the track. She had stuck the long thin-bladed knife into the laces of her sandals, and then forgotten about it. Pressing herself flat against the slope, with her left hand closed firmly around a chunk of dirt, the priestess carefully felt for the blade with her right hand; her fingers slid down the dry clay, then gently crept inwards until they were poised above the top of her right sandal where the hilt of the knife protruded. She was reaching for it when the coal crumbled to powder in her white-knuckled grip. In one swift movement she snatched the knife from her sandal and, as she began to fall backwards, plunged the knife into the side of the pyramid, deep into the hard packed earth. The knife shook and the thin blade bent, but it held, leaving her hanging by one hand as her precarious footholds crumbled beneath her feet. Her left hand scrambled for a fingerhold, prising loose chunks of stone and mud, and she kicked into the brittle clay with her pointed sandles. She lay there, trembling violently, the blood pounding in her temples, feeling the slickness of her palms seep into the dry mud.

She also became aware of the silence above her head, and then the voices seemed to be reaching a conclusion; the hysterical shouting of the priest had a terrible ring of finality about it. She desperately began working the blade from side to side, loosening it, and when she eventually eased it free she clenched it between her teeth. The fingers of her left hand reached for and found a handhold, and she pulled herself up—and over the edge of the roof. She was behind Thanos.

Cliona rested a moment, then she rose to her feet—just as the priest turned!

The albino froze in shocked surprise, and backed away from her, then suddenly realising that the bard was behind him, he turned, raising the vessel in both hands. Cliona lunged, the thin warped blade of the stiletto held at arm's length. The priest opened his mouth to scream as the blade entered his chest but blood suddenly welled from his lips—and with one last convulsive effort he threw the vessel of the Chrystallis from him...

Cliona lay where she fell, unconscious of the priest's blood trickling down her arms, unconscious of the body that had fallen across her legs, conscious only that they had failed. She had seen Thanos throw the delicate vessel of blue-green metallic glass over her head; desperately, futilely, she had reached for it, but she had already been falling and her fingers only brushed the base as it arced over her head.

It had all been for nothing.

She wondered dimly about the bard as she waited for the vessel to shatter on the ground below; she waited for the howling winds of destruction to sweep across the planes of existence, returning them to the Void from whence they came...

She heard the winds then, an almost human sound of exultation, a triumphant howling. So the vessel had struck the ground and shattered, and now the Chrystallis was howling through the Void, descending upon the plane...

She waited another score of pounding heartbeats and then wondered where was it?

Cliona opened one eye. Beneath her face the grains of grit loomed large as boulders. Shakily the priestess pushed aside the body lying across her and sat up—and then an arm enfolded her waist and helped her to her feet. It was the bard. He laughed in genuine amusement at the look of astonishment on her face and then, with a dramatic flourish, he produced the vessel of the Chrystallis from beneath his cloak. The priestess reached out with trembling fingers and touched it. And then she wept.

Before they began the long climb down the wooden steps, Paedur sketched the Sign of the Dead over the body of Thanos, and bent his head in a brief silent prayer. "I'm sorry he's dead, in a way," he said suddenly, pausing on the top step and looking back at the pale corpse.

"I thought he was your enemy," Cliona said, surprised. "He would have destroyed everything in his mad lust to see the Pantheon overthrown."

Paedur nodded absently as he manoeuvred around the body of the man he had killed earlier, which was still lodged on the steps. "I know; but he was a worthy foe, cunning and resourceful. He reminded me of Mannam in many respects." He was silent for a moment. "But he did truly believe in his Religion. And I wonder were we so different in our devotion to our beliefs?" He shook his head. "Aye, well, he was mad of course, and towards the end his petty god finally deserted him."

"And the vessel...?" Cliona prompted.

"Aye, the vessel, the vessel..." He lifted the jar and ran his hook over the curious opaque glass, tapping it gently. It sang with a high musical note, the sound quivering on the still air. "The vessel of the Chrystallis. Before I saw you clamber over the edge—and I think it surprised me as much as Thanos—I had begun to call upon the Windlords, Faurm and Faurug, and their father, Feitigh. The pyramid is old in the service of the Pantheon and the very power that Thanos sought to defile finally worked to his own destruction. The Windlords came and gathered about the pyramid..." Paedur suddenly laughed and shook his head. "And when Thanos threw the vessel as he fell, it was caught by the Windlords and clung seemingly in mid-air, and all I had to do was to pluck it free."

"I heard the wind and I thought the vessel had fallen and shattered and that the Soulwind was coming," the priestess murmured, "and I cursed you then as I cursed myself for not catching it."

"I tried...I tried," he said gently, "for I must admit I feared the Windlords might not be able to hold it."

At the base of the pyramid, the Teouteuchalai were gathered in silence, their bronze and stone weapons burning in the afternoon light. They watched as Paedur and Cliona stepped off the last step and prepared to start back along the rough track to the village. Some of the natives moved in threateningly. The bard eyed them coldly, his gaze seeming to burn through the still air, and they shuffled back in confusion. Gradually, the ranks of the Teouteuchalai began to part like receding tide waters, until they lined the track in a parody of a guard of honour. Swiftly Paedur and Cliona made their way through the people, the eerie silence unbroken on either side. When they passed, the natives closed in behind and as the bard supported the priestess along the winding track and through the pitiful village the entire population followed the terrifying despoilers of their altar.

When they reached the twin pillars of stone, the bard turned and faced the people and his hook gleamed in the dull light as it sketched a glyph that burned silver in the still air. "Accept this as my payment," he said clearly.

And suddenly the clear afternoon sky began to darken rapidly with swift-moving billowing grey clouds. Soon the sun had disappeared behind a leaden shield, and the faces of the Teouteuchalai turned upwards in wonder and sudden hope. And as Paedur and the priestess stepped through the gate the first large and heavy drops of rain began to fall...

17
The Magician's Law

Life comes only through Death, and destruction is, in itself, merely the starting point for a new beginning...

Culai proverb

The Magician's Law, the force of equals, allows a balance to be maintained...

Grimoire Magnum

...And they stepped back into the circular gate-room in the Inner City.

The brief passage left Cliona dizzy and slightly sickened, and Paedur took her arm and led her to the centre of the room to the jade and gold pedestal that had once held the vessel of the Chrystallis. He returned the metallic jar to its place and then put his hands to her shoulders and made her sit down with her back to the smooth cold stone. "Rest a moment," he murmured. The bard then returned to the Gate of Teouteuchal and stood gazing out at the puzzled faces of the natives. Rain sluiced down, turning the baked earth into a mire, but the Teouteuchalai knelt before the gate, their heads bent, arms outstretched in prayer.

"Why?" Cliona asked suddenly.

Paedur turned to look at her, his face impassive.

"Why did it rain?"

The bard moved his hook across the opening and the gate behind him immediately darkened and the Teouteuchalai vanished. "Payment, I suppose, payment for our trespass, or for undedicated blood-letting on their altar, for invoking gods other than Nusas..." He shrugged. "And it has not rained there for many seasons." He began moving around the gates, drawing his hook across them, darkening them all in turn.

"What will we do now?" the priestess wondered, watching the bard.

The bard joined her at the pedestal, squatting down to stare into her eyes. "Now we must return to the Cavern of Power."

"But why?" she whispered. "We have what we came for."

"I know," he sighed. "But now we must face a far greater threat than Thanos ever posed." He saw her look of incomprehension. "We must face the Three Cords, the Cords of Disruption, Annihilation and Ultimate Chaos, before the Culai loose them upon the planes."

"But how do you know they will free the Cords?"

"I don't think they will have any choice in the matter—they will have to release the Cords soon before they become too powerful for even the Culai to control."

"I'm frightened," Cliona whispered, suddenly shivering, "more frightened now than at any other time."

"I know," Paedur said softly. His emotions had been blunted when he had been given eternal life, but he was still able to experience the most powerful emotion of all—fear. He stood up and lifted the vessel of the Chrystallis from its pedestal. He held it up to the light and watched as the gemstone stopper came alive with sparkling, shifting lights. Cliona, however, was looking at the way the green light of the metallic glass reflected back onto the bard's face, giving him an aged, dead look. And suddenly she was filled with a terrible foreboding, an abrupt chill fear, not only for herself but for the bard also.

"Why must you do this? We have prevented the vessel from falling into the hands of Trialos' followers. We have saved the planes of life. Thanos is dead, and the Religion has been dealt a mortal blow. Can you not rest now?"

The bard knelt by her side again and, placing the vessel on the floor, took both her hands in his single hand. "Priestess, I can never rest," he said softly. "It is a price I pay..."

"What price...?"

"For a 'gift' I received and a vow I took some time ago," he murmured, his voice lost in the mists of memory.

"But how can you fight the Three Cords?" she demanded.

Paedur shook his head. "I'm not sure I can," he said softly, "but I can try; I'm going to use the Magician's Law."

"What happens if it doesn't work?"

The bard smiled. "Then we'll never know."

The chilling benighted passage through the glass door was shorter than the priestess remembered it, the darkness not so complete nor as heavy and cloying. The stairs were as they had left them—the creation still held, although its edges were becoming ill-defined and hazy. They passed the body of the warrior the bard had killed in the corridor, but it stank now as if it had lain there for many days.

Paedur paused, looking at it. Cliona glanced briefly at it, and then turned back to him. "What's wrong?"

"Time," he said very quietly. "We've lost a few days. Come; we must make haste!" And then he turned and ran silently along the length of the corridor, and started down the steps. Cliona struggled along behind, hesitating only for the space of a single pounding heartbeat, before dashing down the stairs, her fear of losing him greater than her fear of falling. She ran with her left hand brushing the wall, her eyes fixed firmly on her feet or the few steps ahead of her. She knew that if she looked either up or down she was lost.

However, the lower she went, the more fragmented and un-real the steps became. After a while she realised that her feet were sinking slightly into the stone, and actual holes were beginning to appear in the steps. She finally caught up with the bard, only to find that he had stopped because the last stairs disappeared into a shifting, swirling fog.

"The illusion is fading. Come now, concentrate, create once again a Culai stairway." He stepped behind her and rested his right hand and hook on her shoulders and poured strength into her.

Cliona drew upon her own strength and the power of the bard, and set about creating the illusion of the stairs from the agitated fog. Gradually the angles and planes of the chaotic stairs, the differing sizes, the irregular shapes and mixed stonework began to appear. And solidify—and abruptly the stairway was complete.

The priestess was soon staggering with exhaustion, her move-ments automatic, her brain numbed. Eventually Paedur took her arm, fearing that she might actually reel off the edge of the stairway, and led her down the final few steps back into the great marbled hallway of the Inner City. Cliona slumped at the bard's feet as they stepped off the last step, and as she drifted into unconsciousness she was aware that the stairway was just dissolving back into mist. Her last conscious impression was of the bard lifting her up...

As Cliona awoke there were a few terrifying moments of disorien-tation, and then she became aware that she was in one of the small side tunnels that led into the vast Cavern of Power beneath the City of the Culai. The bard sat by her side wrapped in his enveloping furred cloak, the dimly glowing vessel between his feet, his hook touching the stopper, firing the gemstone, bringing it to life so that it glowed with a soft blue radiance. When he saw she was awake, he removed his hook from the glowing gem, and the light faded, leaving them in darkness.

Beyond the tunnel the Cavern of Power was empty and in silence, the phosphorescent fungi giving it a ghostly sub-aqueous appearance. This, she thought wildly, must be what the Netherworld, beyond the Silent Wood, must look like.

They did not speak; there was nothing to say. They each had their own thoughts; Cliona's were confused and sluggish, the events of the past few days—was it days?—crowding in, one atop the other. In contrast, the bard had but one thought, one fixed immutable idea—to destroy the Cords, if he could.

Cliona dozed again and was awakened by the bard's hand pressed over her mouth. His ice-cold voice echoed in her skull. *"Culai!"* She sat up; beyond the dark circle of the tunnel the Cavern blazed with liquid fire-colours, bringing tears to her eyes. Shadows moved before her streaming eyes, and when she brushed the tears away, she found that figures were passing across the mouth of the tunnel.

The Culai were arriving.

Their metallic, mirror-bright skin-sheaths reflected the burning light so that it looked as if the delicate elfin features of the First Race floated in a shifting sea of liquid colour. The Cavern of Power was filling swiftly and silently, the only sound the gentle susurration of the Culai's cloth slippers on the stone. They gathered about the light-burning pool of reflective liquid, looking up at the long beam of light stretching upwards to the tiny glowing eye in the roof through which the sun shone. They took their places, the lines radiating out from the pool, their shadows hard and sharp and black against the colours.

The chanting began then, a high, thin keening, their voices soaring aloft, the sound pure and fragile. Cliona strained, attempting to catch the words, some of which sounded almost familiar. It seemed to be a single sentence or phrase, repeated over and over again. The chant picked up in speed, becoming faster and faster until there was just one long continuous sound, wail-like in its intensity. The priestess didn't know the words, but she recognised the meaning—it was a call.

And then it stopped—almost as if the First Race had heard an answer.

The chant was taken up again. But now each line of Culai intoned the chant in turn, the other lines taking up the chant sequentially until a piercing crescendo was reached and the insistent calling was such that even the priestess felt the primeval pull of it, the sudden compulsion to move forward into the centre of the cavern. Cliona suddenly felt the bard stiffen, and simultaneously the air above the shimmering pool darkened and began to flicker. The Culai chant took on a new note, a note of triumph. And abruptly above the pool a long thin snake-like band appeared, writhing in convoluted circles.

The first of the Cords, Disruption.

The Culai had fallen silent with the appearance of the first of the Cords, gazing at the weaving strip of nothingness as if entranced. And then the Cord was gone, and for the space of a single heartbeat the grey swirling mists of the Ghost Worlds seeped into the cavern, only to be dispersed like wind-blown smoke.

And then two Cords winked into the Cavern of Power, and the second was Annihilation. Together they interwove and spun in silence, drawing substance from the colours and light and the faith of the Culai. Then they too were gone, and the air above the pool was suddenly flooded with rich, warm, vibrant colours to replace those leached out by the two Cords.

A third Cord winked into existence—Chaos.

And now the Cords began to swirl and twist with ever increasing speed, weaving pattern after pattern in the paling air, until they had assumed the shape of three interconnected black rings orbiting one another. The colours faded from the air above the pool, leaving a misty greyness in their wake, and then the circles began to thicken and grow in size. Immediately, the light in the vast cavern dimmed and a chill and bitter wind swept down the tunnels and howled about the gathered Culai.

Now the colours were almost totally gone; the rainbow-hued stones that had encircled the pool were now only slabs of black and grey, and the beam that shot down into the pool was nothing more than a milky grey sliver of light. The Cords were beginning to move

out above the Culai, spinning in flat circles, leaching the last vestiges
of colour that lingered about the assembled group, until only a gritty
black and white and grey remained. The three spinning bands now
came together with an audible crack that echoed and re-echoed about
the cavern, reverberating off the walls, shivering through the stones.
Loose rock and stalactites rained down on the Culai, felling some to
the floor, but the others paid no attention. They were enthralled by
the Cords.

The Cords had now melded to become one, and above the
First Race wheeled a flat disc of total darkness, darker than the
furthest reaches of the Gorge, colder than the Land of Muirad.
The high glittering roof of the cavern was lost behind it and the
distant walls began to waver and shred in a wispy darkness, for the
fabric of the plane was beginning to break down under the onslaught of the Cords. The vast circle of darkness began to descend
upon the heads of the Culai. The Cords would feed.

A cold blue radiance flared from beneath the bard's hand, and the
priestess realised Paedur had fired the gemstone in the mouth of the
vessel of the Chrystallis. The sudden colour attracted the Cords,
and sable tendrils began to snake towards the blue circle of light that
outlined the mouth of the tunnel.

The bard handed the delicate vessel to Cliona. "Open it!" His
voice was harsh and strained, belying his slow careful movements
and emotionless features.

For a moment, his words didn't register—and then the full enor-
mity of what the bard had asked her to do sank in. She looked at
him, slowly shaking her head, her eyes round with horror. She opened
her mouth to protest, but Paedur raised his hand, pressing his fingers
to her lips. Glancing desperately at the approaching darkness, he
shouted above the roar of disintegrating stone and the twisted rending of the fabric of space.

"Only you can open the vessel. The gem is merely another
aspect of the Dannu-fire; only a priestess of the Mother can open it.
But you must hurry, the cords are growing stronger…"

Cliona shook her head, struggling to make sense of what he
was saying. How could she open the vessel when all they had done
so far, all they had suffered, and Tuan's death, had been to prevent
that from happening? The bard's chill voice suddenly spoke in her

mind. *"You must open the vessel ... it is the only chance we have of wiping the Cords clean from this plane. Do it!"*

The Magician's Law, she suddenly realised, the force of equals, the Cords and the Chrystallis!

Her fingers fumbled at the gem, attempting to prise it free. She looked out into the greyness of the cavern—the snakelike streamers from the Cords were very close now, leaving in their wake a total absence of light. Frantically, she pulled at the gemstone, lacerating her fingers on the sharp points, but the gem wouldn't move.

The streamers of night coiled about the mouth of the tunnel. *"Priestess...!"* Paedur cried.

Praying desperately for strength, Cliona raised the vessel in both hands—and smashed it down into the mouth of the tunnel...

The gem splintered into minute flecks of blue light that winked and glittered like a myriad fireflies, then they too were lost as the encroaching darkness swept in. The bard turned, his face floating, disembodied, towards her, his mouth working, his eyes alien and completely terrifying. She was aware of a terrible soulless howling, a bass moaning that plucked at the consciousness with black insistence, and then—there was nothing...

The Chrystallis erupted from the tunnel in a burst of vivid blue light with an exultant—almost beast-like—roar that reverberated through the disintegrating cavern. The shock shattered slabs of stone, sent them tumbling from the ceiling where they were absorbed into the chaos of utter night that was the Cords. The Soulwind began to encircle the cavern in a whirling vortex that sucked everything in its path into a seething maelstrom of destruction.

Jagged rents ran along the wall, lumps of stone flying into the vortex of azure-touched wind, revealing not another wall of rock but the twisting grey mist of the Ghost Worlds. The fabric of the planes had been breached. Tendrils of the Cords venturing out to the edge of the cavern were shredded and torn in the gusting silent Chrystallis.

But in the centre of the cavern, the eye of the storm, nothing stirred.

And then the encircling Chrystallis began to close in, tightening like a closing fist. Some few of the Culai still left standing were whipped into its embrace. The flat disc of the Cords was rent along two irregular streamers and dispersed in the Soulwind. The circle of the Chrystallis grew smaller and smaller, strangling everything within its grasp.

The Cords—torn to shreds—separated with a crack that staggered the Chrystallis, and for a moment the Soulwind remained motionless, pulsing insistently. The Cords shot out tentacles of blackness deep into the semi-visible sheet of the wind.

The Chrystallis recovered, and began to move again—and the probing streamers were gone, lost in the whirling depths of the Soulwind.

With the spell of the Three Cords broken, the last of the Culai came to their senses. Terrified and dazed, some moved back to the pool in the centre of the cavern, huddling together, while others ran screaming into the wind—only to be torn to pieces in its grasp. A few attempted to defend themselves, calling down their magic, but even the most powerful sorcery was useless against the raw elemental power of the Cords and the Chrystallis. Worse, it only served as a focus for the shrinking Cords, calling them in...and then the last of the Culai race were absorbed into the blackness of the Cords.

The grey slabs of stone about the pool were ripped apart by the Cords, chunks of jagged rock exploding outwards, only to be pulverised into dust by the encircling wind.

The Cords were now confined to a small space above the pool. They compacted into a tight ball of pitch-like darkness and began to spin. Tendrils of night snaked from the ball, darting into the Chrystallis, and were instantly destroyed.

And now the nameless liquid in the pool boiled upwards and was absorbed into the Soulwind, giving it shape and form, so that it came to look as if a circle of liquid glass encircled a black sphere. The centre of the cavern was now a tightly compacted mass of pulverised rock and shattered stone, the torn and mutilated bodies of the Culai, and at the heart of it, the tiny ball that was the Three Cords of Disruption, Annihilation and Chaos. Tighter and tighter the Chrystallis closed, the black ball flickering wildly. Abruptly, a part of it had gone. And then another part. Now, only a tiny mote of darkness remained like a black star—then it too flickered and was gone.

And the Chrystallis crashed in upon itself with a roar that rippled through the myriad planes of life in a cataclysm much as there had been in Elder Days. Seas boiled and rose; lowlands were lost beneath the waves; islands sank without trace and others rose where none had been before. Mountains fell and rose again in new configurations and open-mouthed cones spewed forth burning filth, while the northern and southern ice-caps shifted, crashing into the warming seas and immediately beginning to melt.

And many went to Mannam that day to be judged by Alile the Judge Impartial.

But the Chrystallis and the Three Cords were no more.

They left behind in the cavern a seething cauldron of indescribable chaos. The Chrystallis and the Cords had ripped vast swatches of matter from the plane, and now jagged rents in the delicate fabric between the worlds caused the thin grey mist of the Ghost Worlds to leak into the plane—but the material impacted upon entry, slowly sealing the holes. However, had the Chrystallis or Cords been allowed to continue, they would have rapidly broken down the entire fabric of the plane, returning it to the Void or Chaos.

The remnants of the cavern rippled with the exploding matter, rebuilding the fabric of the shattered plane. Nothing could have lived through the passage of the Cords or the Chrystallis, both of which were the very antithesis of life. The imploding matter rained chunks of incandescent material about the cavern, destroying even the creatures of the halfworld which had come to investigate the disruption in the fabric of the planes.

Nothing human could have survived—but through it all wandered a tall figure, clad in a stained and worn cloak and hooded like a monk. His face was lined and pained, worn, but his eyes were expressionless. They were now flat and reflective, like mirrors. And once a curved silver hook rose to etch the Sign of the Pantheon on the turbulence, and a row of flickering figures, godlike and serene, appeared briefly to place their mark upon the newly fashioned place: *"This is the Ending; go now in peace for you have served us well…"*

The hooded bard turned away, shaking his head slowly, and when he looked back there was nothing human left in him. "No," he hissed, "you are wrong. This is not the Ending—it is merely the Beginning!"

DEMON'S LAW

Prologue

There are gaps in the life of Paedur the Bard, many gaps, and later bards and storytellers have made much of these, creating the most fantastical adventures for the Champion of the Old Faith.

The first major absence takes place almost at the beginning of his career, shortly after he returned from the Culai Isle. There are accounts of him in Maante, the seacoast town, and without exception they speak of this terrifying, awesome man, whose eyes were like polished mirrors and who radiated crackling power. And then one day he simply vanished.

It is important to remember that this was the Time of Cataclysm. The Chronicles speak of it as a time "...when the seas boiled and rose; lowlands were lost beneath the waves, islands sank without trace and others rose where none had been before. Mountains fell and rose again in new configurations and open-mouthed cones spewed forth burning filth while the northern and southern ice-caps shifted, crashing into the warming seas, melting, beginning the Flood.

"It was a time of Heroes, of Gods and Demons, when creatures out of myth, out of time, walked the world once again. It was a time when the world changed, a time of war and revolution, when Empires crumbled and were reborn, a time of death, disease and famine.

"History has left us some of the names of those who lived and died in those evil times, of those who helped sculpt the shaken world. Some were mortal men, others more than human..."

The first of the legends surrounding him began then, tales of demons and devils, of assassins and murder, but in truth no one really knew what had happened to the bard. Until now.

Life of Paedur, the Bard

1
The Silent Wood

Tradition tells us that the forest is now stone, but it has not always been so. In the days when the world was young it was a great forest, covering the land for leagues in every direction. But in that time when the Gods fought for control of the Planes of Existence, the trees had been warped and deformed by their magics and powers into grotesque and hideous shapes, and then the Gods and Goddesses of Life had abandoned them, revolted by their appearance, leaving them frozen. The place had become an abomination, and in an act of awesome destruction the ground had split and the frozen forest had been forever sundered from the world of Men by a Gorge of immeasurable depth. The forest was divided, the frozen trees marching to the very edge of the cliff, the last trees actually clinging to the lip, overlooking the Gorge, while on the far side, what remained unsullied and untouched grew normally.

No one knows the extent of the forest of stone, nor the length nor width of the Gorge, although there are stories which measure the length by several days' journey, but no man ever tells of having completed it. For the Gorge defines the limits of the Silent Wood, the abode of Death, and its dread denizens walk its borders.

No one has ever been foolish enough to attempt to build a bridge between the two worlds, that of Life and Death, for who knows what might walk from its grey domain to feed on the living. But there is a bridge of sorts— and perhaps it was the gods themselves that uprooted one of the great trees of stone and flung it across the Gorge, bridging the gap.

It was a temptation, and a temptation that proved too strong for many. They have walked the bridge of granite wood into Death's Domain—and never returned...

Lilis' Geographica

A figure crouched in the fringe of forest on the edge of the Gorge, still and silent, watching. The man touched one of the trees, the bark rough beneath his calloused hands, feeling the life coursing through the wood and swirling in eddies and circles around him as the forest hissed and whispered in the breeze. He drew a little of the life to himself, feeding on the sensation, the part of him that was still human taking a small pleasure from the richness of the air, and the myriad odours of the forest.

He allowed his senses to expand, taking in the sights and sounds, scents and hidden pulses of the living forest, becoming part of them, and then he deliberately closed his mind to the sounds of life and the creatures that swarmed in the earth and moved along the ground and nestled in the trees. Without their noisy, colourful intrusion on his senses he looked across the Gorge towards the petrified forest—and saw a shifting grey wall of fog!

With his human eyes he could see the grey pillars of stone, but with his enhanced senses he was blind. Paedur the Bard smiled grimly; it seemed everyone entered Death's Domain on equal terms. Pulling his furred cloak higher on his shoulders, the tall, thin man stepped out from the concealment of the trees and took the two steps necessary to stand on the fallen stone tree that acted as a bridge between the worlds.

If he had expected something—a tingling of power, an aura of arcane forces—then he was disappointed. There was nothing; it was merely stone beneath his booted feet. And so, slowly, carefully, checking every step on the stone-smooth bark, he moved out from the safety of the living forest and over the Gorge. The wind plucked at him then, ice-cold and tainted with the unmistakable fetor of death and decay, whipping his cloak around his legs, pulling at his long, fine hair, dragging it across his thin, sharp-boned face. With the hook that took the place of his left hand, he dragged it back and, although reason told him not to look down, he still retained the all-too human failing of curiosity.

The walls of the Gorge were glassy smooth, as if the earth and rock had been seared by some incredible heat, and they fell away below into an abyss that at first glance seemed bottomless. However, as his eyes adjusted to the gloom, Paedur spotted the fires—scores of huge, blazing bonfires on the floor of the pit. Although he knew it shouldn't be possible, he thought he saw movement around the flames, as if figures were dancing before the fires. The breeze wafting up from the pit was heavy with a thick, cloying, vaguely unpleasant odour, like rotting fruit, and carried on it a tremulous sighing, which might have been the wind, or the moaning of scores of souls in mortal torment. He had seen the damned.

He looked away, recognising the danger of staring too long or too deeply into the pit, and turned his attention to the petrified forest that lay ahead of him. It was only as he approached it that he realised that it was not, in the true sense of the word, a forest. A forest suggested trees with leaves and bushes, grasses, vines and weeds, while this place had none of that. Now only the stark columns of the trees remained, most without branches, all without leaves, and where there had once been grass and weeds there was now nothing more than grit and slates and a powdered grey dust that covered everything.

Paedur hesitated before stepping off the makeshift bridge, waiting, listening, watching. But there was no movement within the petrified forest, no sound.

And yet he knew that that appearance was a lie. For the Silent Wood was the abode of the dead, the Kingdom of Mannam, the Dark Lord, the Lord of the Dead, and it teemed with life—if it could be called life. But perhaps here, close to the edge of the world of Life, the dwellers of the Silent Wood didn't care to venture.

Before he took the final step off the bridge, Paedur stooped slightly and pulled a long-bladed knife from the sheath sewn into his high boot, but he kept it concealed beneath his cloak. Away from the Gorge, the gusting foul wind died and there was no sound now but the crunch of gravel beneath his booted feet. Now that his enhanced senses—the gifts of the god C'lte—had been numbed and he was once again relying on his purely human senses, he realised for the first time how much he had come to rely on and accept the advantages they gave him. Without them he felt naked. He knew again what it was like to be human, although he was still without a human's capacity for emotion—that had been the price of his god-touched arcane senses.

The frozen stone trees stretched without a break in every direction, distance turning them into a solid grey wall, menacing and formidable, with the knots and boles of the trees assuming vaguely human features when looked at quickly. The branches of most were gone, either lopped off for some unimaginable purpose by the forest dwellers or else fallen to the ground under their own weight. He looked at the mass of trees and realised that it would be all too easy for him to become disoriented and lost within the grey

sameness of the wood—then it would be only a matter of time
before he joined the dwellers in the wood in earnest. He reviewed
what he knew of the Silent Wood, what his myth and legend-lore
told him, and found it was precious little.

The Silent Wood was the place where the souls of the dead
dwelt until they had been adjudged by Alile, the Judge Impartial, and
sentenced either to the Broken Mountain to dwell with the Triad of
Life or cast down into damnation in the Gorge. But while they
remained unjudged within the confines of the Silent Wood, they
were under the command of Mannam, the Lord of the Dead, a
seared and withered creature who had assumed all the characteristics
of his dead trees.

Legend spoke of peoples of all races and times still carrying on
a semblance of life within the Silent Wood: kings and peasants, warriors and priests, all living out an eternal parody of their days in the
World of Men, perhaps even unaware that they were dead, their
kingdoms dust, their times long forgotten.

There was even a tale that Mannam deliberately kept the finest
the World of Men had to offer, the wisest kings, the bravest warriors, the most powerful magicians, the most knowledgeable bards,
and ruled them himself...

But no one knew for certain, for no one had ever returned
from the Land of the Dead to speak of its wonders. And the
bard wondered, would he too fail to return from Mannam's dead
kingdom?

He spotted the track almost immediately; it was a mere discoloration, a slight curvature of the ground, but he knew a track when
he saw one. He crossed to it, his feet crunching on the grit. It was
broad enough for a man-track too; animals usually travelled single-
file along an established run. Without hesitation he stepped onto it,
and had taken barely two steps when the creature stepped out from
behind a tree.

Paedur froze, dismayed that he hadn't sensed the presence of
the creature. It was his height, standing on two legs and vaguely
man-like, and covered in broad, shimmering, white scales that ran
the length of its body but left its arms and legs free, and these were
covered in a wrinkled pale hide. Its surprisingly slender feet ended
in a single spike and its paws were two spiked pincers. Its head was
huge and flat, with two sharply curving horns beginning alongside

the eyes and almost meeting above its head. The eyes were tiny amber beads, deep-sunk into its skull, and the rest of the features were lost behind a mask of fine grizzled hair.

They stared at one another for perhaps a score of pounding heartbeats and then the creature deliberately stepped away from the man, paused, and then suddenly darted forward, two curved blades appearing in its misshapen paws. Paedur held his ground, both arms still concealed beneath his cloak, and something that resembled a smile touched his lips—this was something he could deal with. When the two curved blades had begun their whistling descent, the longer of the two cutting horizontally, the shorter, vertically, the bard moved. His deeply curved hook shot out, catching the long blade, snapping it down, while he pivoted on his heel, spinning in a half circle, smashing his back into the creature and allowing his attacker's arm to snap across his shoulder, the force of the blow knocking the sword from its paw. Paedur then rammed the knife in his right hand into the creature's underbelly. The blade scraped, screamed and snapped!

The creature grunted and smashed its head into the base of Paedur's skull, throwing him forward and onto the stony ground, and Paedur remembered what pain was. He hadn't experienced such pain in a long time and its very intensity shocked him motionless. He was dimly aware that the creature was moving closer. His body reacted automatically, rolling him to one side as the long blade hissed through the air where his neck had been. He scrambled to his feet, his head pounding, tiny spots of colour dancing before his eyes, his left arm held up across his body, the wickedly curved hook dull metal in the wan light.

The creature was now holding the sword in both hands, weaving the blade to and fro in a move designed to draw the eye, cutting patterns on the air. It had lost its shortsword in their brief encounter but the very length of its longsword lent it a great advantage. The bard had broken his knife—he could see the scar across the creature's scales—and his only weapon now was the hook. The creature moved suddenly; emitting a terrifying scream it cut at the bard, the blade held high in both hands. Paedur immediately threw himself forward, rolling to his feet almost alongside the creature and inside the sword cut. His left arm punched up, catching the creature under the chin, the curved hook seeking a spot to sink into so as to rip and tear. The blade scraped and then caught.

Paedur twisted his hand, securing the hold and then pulled. And ripped the creature's head off!

Even while he retained all his human characteristics, Paedur had long considered himself to have lost the capacity for surprise, and he looked now in astonishment as the head spun slowly through the air, the eyes empty, the neck bloodless...

Once again only his extraordinary reflexes saved turn. He fell forward as the curved sword whistled over his head, so close he could feel the tug on his scalp as it cut through a lock of hair. He continued rolling, finally coming to his feet a score of paces away from the creature...and then he received his second shock. He was looking at a cold-eyed, snow-haired woman. From the neck down she was still the scaled creature, but her head was that of a woman.

She spat something at him, the accent strange and sibilant but the words vaguely familiar, and then she snapped the sword up, the blade horizontal, level with her amber-coloured eyes, both hands wrapped round the long hilt.

And Paedur suddenly realised what she was. She was Katan, a warrior-maid, a member of the legendary Guard of Churon the Onelord. The legends spoke of their fabulous terrifying armour, the cast-off skin of the ice-serpents of Thusal. But the last of the Katan had died defending their lord on the Sand Plain in the battle with the Shemmatae several hundred years previously.

The woman took a step forward, her eyes never leaving his face, the sword in her hand rigid and unwavering. Paedur desperately sorted through his lore, sifting the various tongues and variants he knew, trying to establish a language she would have been familiar with when she had lived.

"I mean you no harm," he attempted, watching her eyes for a flicker of comprehension, and then repeated the sentence again and again in a score of languages. Finally he tried it in the Shemmat tongue, the language of the invaders she had died defending the land from. Her reaction was immediate. She attacked furiously, the blade coming in fast and low, the move designed to disembowel. Again, Paedur caught the sword on his hook, sparks shivering along the blade, but the force of the blow almost tore the hook from the bone of his arm. She cut again, high this time, and then changed the move as the weapon darted in, dropping the blade, slashing across his chest. It struck his furred cloak—with the sound of metal on metal, the force of the blow ripping the weapon from her numbed hands. And then Paedur was behind her, his hook completely encircling her slender throat, the point resting coolly beneath her ear.

"Move," he hissed in Shemmat, "and I will rip your head off."

He felt her stiffen, but she remained still and unmoving. "Now, I am not of the Shemmatae," he continued evenly. "I merely chose their tongue because I thought you would understand it. If you give me your race, I may know that language."

She remained silent so long that Paedur had actually opened his mouth to speak again when the woman spat one word. "Lostrice!" Lostrice was the southernmost of the Seven Nations.

Her sibilant accent suddenly became comprehensible and Paedur was familiar enough with the three huge volumes of myths from the southern lands that had been collected by previous generations of wandering bards to know enough of the tongue to communicate.

"I am Paedur, a bard," he said in that language.

"A bard?" she said after another silence.

"A bard."

He carefully lifted away his hook and then quickly stepped away from the woman. When she turned to look at him, he lifted his cloak, revealing the triangular bardic sigil high on his left shoulder. He had no doubts but that the woman would be familiar with it; the sigil had remained unchanged for nearly two thousand years.

"Why did you attack me?" he asked finally.

"I guard the Way," she said simply.

Paedur hooked the toe of his scuffed boot under the woman's shortsword, which was by his feet, and flipped it towards her. She deftly caught it and then pulled out a short length of white linen, which she used to wipe the blade clean before smoothly sliding it back into its scabbard. Still facing the bard she looked around for her longsword.

Paedur smiled, the movement transforming his face. "Will you attack me again?"

"I guard the Way," she repeated.

"From what?" he asked.

"From the humankind of the World of Life," she said.

"I am from the World of Life," Paedur said with a wry smile, "but I am not wholly human."

The Katan stared at him for a few moments and then she turned and went to where her sword had fallen. She sank to the ground beside it, her legs folding gracefully beneath her, her oiled, supple armour settling noiselessly around her, and she began to wipe the blade. When she looked up at the bard again, there was something like humour in her amber eyes. "No, I suppose you're not. No single human would have been able to defeat me."

Paedur sat on the hard ground, not even feeling the grit and stones beneath him, well used to the rigours of the road by now. "You haven't told me your name," he said finally.

"What use are names in the Land of the Dead?" she said fiercely, and then lowered her gaze and continued polishing her sword.

"You realise you are dead, then?" Paedur asked.

"Of course," she said in surprise. "Whatever made you think I didn't?"

Paedur shrugged. "I thought you might still be carrying out the role you pursued in the World of Men, unaware of your death."

The warrior-maid slid her longsword home with a click. "No. There are some who cannot accept that they have passed into another world, but they are very few."

"You still haven't told me your name," Paedur reminded her.

The woman smiled. "I have told you that names are unimportant."

"But you had a name?" he persisted.

"Once."

He continued looking at her.

"You may call me Katani."

"I thought that was the title of your warrior-caste."

"It was, but I am all that is left now. The rest of my sisters accepted their judgment at Alile's hands and went their various ways. Only I remain."

"Why?" he wondered.

"Because when I have been judged by Alile, the Judge Impartial, then I will be truly dead. This way I still have a chance."

"A chance for what?" he asked.

"Why, for battle," she said, her amber eyes opening wide in surprise. "I was raised and trained for combat, I died in one of the most glorious battles the World of Men has ever known, and now I guard the borders of the Dead from intruders from the Living."

She looked quickly at the bard again. "You are a fine warrior, and fast. I don't think I have ever seen anyone as fast."

"I have some advantages."

"I noticed. I should have opened you from shoulder to shoulder but for your cloak. Wearing it, you have no need to fight."

"I wasn't sure if it would work," he confessed. "I thought that all the forces, properties and laws of the gods were negated in the Silent Wood."

Katani frowned slightly. "That I have heard also, but your cloak is obviously an exception."

"Perhaps because it was a gift from Mannam himself," Paedur said softly, watching her expression, wondering how she would react.

Her face remained expressionless, her eyes hard and cold, but the bard caught the tightening of the muscles and cords of her neck. "You have met the Dark Lord?" It was a question, rather than a statement.

"I performed a small service for him once," he said. "And not entirely through choice either," he added. "He gifted me with the cloak when it seemed as if I might fall prey to the elements before I had completed my mission." He ran his hook down the fine hair of the cloak, the rune-etched metal hissing slightly. "I have found that it has certain properties."

Katani relaxed again, the tautness leaving her face, and while she was not beautiful—her jaw was too strong, her nose too sharp, her eyes too cold—she was not unpretty.

"Why do you stare?"

Paedur shrugged apologetically. "Forgive me. I was unaware that I was staring. I find it difficult to accept that you have been dead for some hundreds of years."

Katani grinned, showing her small white teeth with the incisors filed to points, which had been customary with the Katan warriors. "Why do you find it so strange? You would accept the concept of journeying between the various Planes of Existence?"

"Yes. I have done so."

"That is all death is—another plane of existence. A different sort of existence, certainly, where the body is at last unfettered from the base needs of humankind, like food and drink and the desire to procreate."

"Can you die?"

Katani came fluidly to her feet and the bard rose with her. "We can be killed, but we will wake again. But if we have been injured in a battle here in the Silent Wood and have sustained a wound or lost a limb, then that loss will remain with us when we awaken, although the wound will be healed..."

They both heard the sound at the same time, a scraping, rasping of stone on stone. Katani's swords slid noiselessly from their sheaths and she moved out into the centre of the clearing. Paedur took up a position behind her, his left arm raised defensively across his body.

"What is it?"

She shook her head. "I'm not sure. It could be a score of different creatures, Mannam's pets. They won't be able to eat you, but they can inflict terrible wounds which will remain when you awaken."

A single pebble rattled onto the track and then the bard actually saw one of the petrified trees shake. They both turned to the sound, and a huge head rose up over the trees and stared down at them.

"Peist!" Katani hissed, fear thickening her accent. She immediately began to back away from the wavering head.

Paedur looked up at the creature, recognising it as something from the very earliest legends of man. When the Culai had first walked the world, they had done battle with the Fomori, demonkind created and then outcast by the gods, who had ridden upon the backs of the peist, primeval horned serpents. The tales told of a score of Formori riding upon a single creature.

"Move, bard," Katani murmured.

Paedur moved his left foot backwards and pulled away from the creature, his eyes never leaving it. The peist was huge, the width of its head easily the height of a tall man, its eyes wide-set and lambent yellow, its scales close-set and fine, looking as if they had been merely drawn onto its cream-coloured flesh. Two slightly curved and needle-pointed horns began above its eyes and there was a flat bar of hide above its broad mouth giving it a curiously comical appearance. The enormous mouth, which was easily the width of the head, was open, revealing that it was surprisingly toothless. Abruptly, the mouth closed in a firm straight line.

"Bard!" Katani screamed.

Paedur threw himself to one side as the creature's huge head lunged over the columns of stone and darted forward, striking hard into the ground where the bard had stood barely a heart-beat before. There was a solid jarring thump, and when the head twisted away there was a slight depression in the hard-packed grit.

The bard rolled to his feet as the creature's head snapped around again. He fell away as the broad, blunt head smashed into one of the petrified trees, pulverising the stone, cracking it in half.

"Bard!"

Paedur rolled towards the sound of Katani's voice, realising that the only way to avoid the creature was to delve deeper and deeper into the forest, weaving through the trees. He caught sight of Katani's extravagant armour and headed for it, not even daring to look back. He followed the woman, abstractedly admiring the skill with which she wove through the trees in the obviously heavy and bulky armour without even scraping the stone trunks. Behind them they could hear stone cracking and the grinding, tearing sounds of trees being uprooted.

They stopped running only when the petrified forest opened out onto a broad, gently sloping plain that led down to what the bard first took to be a black ribbon of road.

Katani stopped at the edge of the forest. She was breathing heavily and strands of her ice-white hair were plastered across her eyes. Behind them, but distantly, they could still hear the peist crashing through the forest.

"I have known them to track a person for days," she gasped.

"Why, if they cannot feed?" Paedur demanded, hauling himself up by his hook onto one of the granite limbs of a gnarled oak to try and locate the creature. In the distance he could see the tops of the trees wavering slightly, marking the peist's approach.

"Do the Hounds of Maurug still roam the World of Man?" Katani asked.

Paedur nodded. "Some, but the beasts are nearly extinct."

"The peist kills, as they do, for sport, not to feed. They too are Maurug's creatures."

The bard stared back into the forest. "I've faced the dogs," he murmured.

Another tree fell, the stone exploding with a roar. It was many years since the bard had stood against one of the huge slavering dogs; he had been a young man recently graduated from Baddalaur, the Bardic College. Only his razor-sharp hook had saved him, and only then because the creature had been so intent on killing him that it had sprung straight for his throat. He had instinctively raised his arm to protect himself and the dog had bitten down on the curved blade, completely severing its own jaw. But even though it had been mortally wounded, the hound had still worried at the man until it simply bled to death in the snow. The ferocious dogs had been named after the god Maurug, the Destroyer, and Paedur had reflected then that they had been well named.

Katani continued into the lengthening silence. "I saw a man once who had fallen to the peist. His body had been pulped, for the creature kills by constriction, but the man still was aware. Every bone in his body had been broken, parts of him were unrecognisable, he couldn't walk or speak or move, but he was still aware."

"What did you do?" Paedur asked, looking at her, his trained ear catching a subtle intonation in her voice.

"I killed him; a true death by the only means possible in this place—I burned his body, reducing it to ashes. He would not have suffered much."

"You knew him?"

Katani pointed to the distant black line that cut across the plain. "That is the River Naman, we'll be safe on the other side," she said, quickly checking the buckles and ties of her armour. And then she added, "He was a friend."

The bard nodded but said nothing. He had already guessed.

If the stone forest had once been wood, then the plain would have been grass, Paedur reasoned, but now it was grit and sand and small rounded pebbles that looked as if they belonged on a seashore. It was flat and featureless, with no stone bigger than a small rock and the only colours those of slate and shale. Against the monotones, Paedur realised that his purple-black cloak and Katani's ice-serpent armour would have stood out even if they weren't the only beings moving on the blighted landscape. He also knew that when the peist finally worked its way free of the stone forest, then it would quickly gain on them, the slope of the gradient lending it speed.

Later he realised that the odour must have been present for a long time, and again he was dismayed by the loss of his especially acute senses. The stench was primarily of blood, the thick, cloying, bitter-sweet, copper-tart stench of blood. He glanced sidelong at Katani, but she seemed unaware of it.

Stone exploded, and then every stone and pebble on the plain actually trembled. Paedur glanced back over his shoulder to find that the peist had finally broken free of the Silent Wood and that its horned head was now wavering above the tops of the petrified trees. The rumbling noise he had heard were two shattered tree-trunks rolling down the slight incline. As he watched the huge creature begin to undulate down the incline, Katani started to run.

"Will it cross the river?" he shouted.

The woman didn't even look back. "I don't know. I don't think so. I hope not."

They had almost reached the river now and the stench had become unbearable. Paedur gagged.

"It is the Naman, the Black River," Katani said.

The bard remembered his lore then, and recalled that he had seen its twin, the Aman, the milk-white river that flowed through the Fields of Eternal Life. It was Life and purity, while the Naman washed away all the blood that was spilt in the myriad worlds of men.

They stopped a few paces from the banks. The stench was unbearable, and even Katani, who was well used to the odours of Death, was pale, taking care to breath only through her mouth. The river flowed sluggishly, dark lumps of reeking matter moving within it; and whereas from the distance it had looked black, close to it was a deep reddish purple, streaked with thicker, darker lines of ichor.

"It's not wide," Paedur suggested.

"But if you fell in," Katani said slowly.

"You cannot drown," Paedur reminded her.

The woman shook her head. "No. You can drown, you can die. But you will awaken again in the morning…and I'm not sure I want to know where that river ends."

Paedur touched her arm with his hook. "I don't think we have any choice." The peist was undulating rapidly across the plain, dust and grit rising in its wake. "Come!" The bard pounded down towards the river, took a deep breath, and then he leapt at the last possible moment. It wasn't a long jump and he landed well clear on the far bank.

Katani hesitated a moment longer and then she followed his example. She was loath to approach the edge of the lapping river and she jumped just a fraction too early, miscalculating, failing to allow for the weight of her armour and weapons. She hit the edge of the opposite bank with a thump, her legs sinking into the river of flowing blood. She scrambled for fingerholds as the force of the water began to pull her away, but she could barely see what she was doing with the eye-watering stench. The river was warm and clinging; it gripped like a gentle hand and pulled.

And then iron-hard fingers wrapped themselves around her wrist, pulling her up and out of the water easily, and set her down on her feet. She began to thank him when he suddenly raised his hook and brought it flashing down against her arm...and sliced through a thin snake-like creature that had attached itself to the shoulder-plate of her armour. She looked down her body and discovered that there were scores of the eel-like creatures attached to her legs, sucking hungrily on her lacquered armour. Almost abstractedly she wondered what would have happened if one of them had managed to sink its teeth into her flesh.

The peist had stopped about a man's length from the river, its horned head twisting to and fro, its huge mouth opening and closing rapidly, pulsating ripples running the length of its armoured body.

"It seems reluctant to approach the river," Paedur said, storing the information away, adding it to his already vast store of knowledge. "Perhaps it is sensitive to the smell."

"Bard," Katani hissed through clenched teeth, "there is no creature living—or dead—that wouldn't be sensitive to this smell!"

Paedur grinned. "Of course." They both watched in silence as the peist curled up on the opposite bank, its horned head resting flat on the ground, and then it began to change colour, pulses rippling through its many segments, gradually assuming the stone and slate colours of the plain. Soon, except for the two curved horns and the glowing eyes, it was almost invisible.

"I didn't know they could change colour," the woman-warrior said quietly, "but it would explain how they can stalk and kill with such apparent ease."

"It is waiting for us," Paedur remarked.

"There's no way back," Katani nodded, "not at this place certainly. Further down the river widens, while upriver there is only the Mire, and that is infinitely more dangerous, where the outcasts—both human and otherwise—from Death's Kingdom congregate."

"That is of no account. I had no intention of going back—not just yet at any rate."

"Tell me, bard. Just why did you come to the Silent Wood?"

Paedur turned away and began to march across the plain. "I am looking for something."

"Something—or someone?" Katani asked shrewdly.

The bard glanced at her and smiled. "You're right. I'm looking for two people, companions, friends—dead now, but they died before their time, died needlessly." His voice changed slightly, becoming almost formal. "And I took an oath to look for them, return them to Life to allow them to live out their allotted span of years."

"I have never heard of Mannam giving up one of his subjects," Katani said slowly.

"Oh, he'll give them to me," Paedur promised, with a smile that had nothing of humour in it.

2
The Fortress

Although the Bard now walked the Silent Wood, the seeds he had planted in the World of Men were beginning to bear fruit...
Life of Paedur, the Bard

And so the Weapon Master returned to the way of the Faith...
from The Warrior, the Life of Owen, Weapon Master

The mountain had reclaimed the fortress, absorbing the massively hewn blocks, blanketing them beneath vines, creepers and clinging grasses. Now, only a vague regularity in the mountainside betrayed its presence, and the casual observer would have missed it all too easily.

But the two men standing in the lee of a tumbled cairn of stones hadn't missed the building; they had journeyed across half a continent deliberately seeking out the abandoned Culai-built fortresses. Their instructions and directions had been vague: they were seeking a group of wasteland outlaws who were heading into the west in search of a suitable base from which to conduct a campaign against the Imperials, and the only firm information they had was that the outlaws would settle for one of the Culai fortresses.

"What do you think?" the smaller of the two, a sallow-skinned, tilt-eyed Easterner, asked.

"No sign of life," the second man murmured. He was taller and broader than the Easterner and wore a warrior's light mail over a thick leather hauberk. "Tracks?"

"Nothing. But the recent rains would have seen to that."

"It will be dark soon. We'll wait until then before approaching the fortress."

"I'm not so sure I want to, after the last time," the small man said with a wry smile. The previous fortress had been occupied by a score of starving wolves, and both men had been lucky to escape with nothing more than scratched armour and torn cloaks.

Owen the Weapon Master and his servant-companion Tien tZo had been on the road for nearly four moons now, trekking farther and farther into the west, seeking out the abandoned Culai fortresses, searching for Kutor the Renegade and his followers. It was a foolish, foolhardy mission, with no thanks and almost certainly no coin in it, but Paedur the Bard had suggested it and the Weapon Master had been in no state of mind to refuse him anything at that time. And although he had never stated it directly, he had more than hinted that it might be a suitable way for Owen to redeem himself in the eyes of the Gods of the Old Faith.

When they had set off into the west trailing the bandits—from what they had gathered from the bard—the group had no more than a single moon's head start and two men travelling fast and light would easily make up that distance.

But then the Cataclysm struck. It lasted only a single day, but in that short day the entire eastern coastline of the Seven Nations changed forever. No coastal town or village escaped unscathed. Roads were swept away; bridges destroyed. Islands were swamped, some vanishing forever beneath the waves, while in other places new islands appeared, torn, raw and steaming, from the ocean floor.

It was impossible to estimate how many had died on that single day of Cataclysm, or how many more would die of famine and disease because of the destroyed crops and the rotting corpses of man and beast alike. Communications with Karfondal, the capital, were disrupted, but Geillard the Emperor had reacted swiftly: law and order were slowly but surely coming back to the outlying provinces, while cartographers and surveyors were charting the new coastline, and bards and scribes were working on a census.

But the loss of roads and the new configuration of the land had caused inevitable delays, delays which had lengthened as Owen and Tien tZo found work for their mercenary talents, defending small towns and villages from marauders, both human and animal, although in some cases the distinction was not so easy to make.

They stopped briefly at Baddalaur, the Bardic College, and while Owen made a few discreet inquiries into Paedur's background, Tien tZo paid a Scholar for a complete listing of all the ruined Culai fortresses in the westlands. However, the Weapon Master was unable to discover anything about the enigmatic figure of the bard, save that his name and the appellation "Hookhand" appeared on the Roll of Bards, with an index of all the tales he had contributed to the college library. And because most of the senior bards and scribes, who would have been of Paedur's generation, had been called to the capital to assist in the census, there was no one there who actually knew the bard personally. Equally, Tien tZo's task, which would have taken a competent Scholar a single day, took the apprentice he had employed four days.

Most of the Culai fortresses were on the King Road or a side road, and so their task was not difficult, merely tedious and often frustrating. The first two fortresses they had gone in search of were missing entirely, having been torn down and the stones used by the locals. The third was completely desolate, and the atmosphere of dread and the menace that clung to it so palpable that both men had left hurriedly, not even bothering to check the interior to see if it was occupied, knowing that nothing of human-kind could live in that blighted place. The fourth had been occupied by a pack of plains wolves. Before them now was the fifth, and after this one the fortresses became further apart, with the next a six-day march, and then a ten-day march after that to the one beyond.

Night fell with the same unaccustomed swiftness of the past few moons. Owen was of the opinion that the Gods were warring amongst themselves, hence the destruction and the sudden change in the seasons and weather. Tien tZo, whose education was far broader than his master's, decided that the sudden early nightfalls were due to an excess of dust in the atmosphere, but he wisely kept his opinions to himself. Since Owen's release from the Iron Band of Kloor, the normally superstitious warrior had become almost fanatically religious, sometimes frighteningly so, and would hear nothing ill spoken against the Old Faith, even in jest.

Tien tZo suddenly pointed, but Owen was already nodding, "I see it." A light had appeared briefly, high up on the cliff wall, a tiny eye of light. It vanished and then reappeared, only to vanish again just as quickly.

"A candle flame," Tien said quietly, his soft accent almost lost on the night air, "lighting a guard's way up turret stairs."

Owen nodded. "Aye, of course; and we're seeing it as he passes the arrow slots. Well, it proves there's someone there."

"It could be brigands," his servant suggested, loosening the two hand-axes that hung on either side of his belt.

"It's unlikely that they would post guards."

"Unlikely, but not unknown." Tien smiled.

"But a nervous renegade prince might…"

Tien nodded. "He might. How do we go in?"

"Through the main gate," Owen grinned.

Soan sleepily watched the spider busily encasing the struggling moth in thread, idly contemplating if it was worth his while cutting a few threads of the intricate web to make the spider's job just a little more difficult. A short time ago he wouldn't have had a second thought about it, but now, with all this talk of gods and powers, demons and forces, he found himself remembering his religion, and he had begun to murmur the prayers again—just in case. He looked at the spider and its struggling captive and wondered which of the Gods or Goddesses of the Pantheon had dominion over the creature: probably the Lady Adur, the Goddess of Nature, he decided.

The knife came slicing through the web and stopped, resting just below his nose on the top of his lip. "Don't even think about it," a cruel, emotionless voice hissed, and then the glittering edge of an axe touched the soft flesh under his jaw. Soan's wide eyes twitched, and looked into the leering face of a yellow-skinned, slant-eyed demon.

The dagger moved down, dropping off his top lip to rest on his fuller lower lip. "I have come to see Kutor the Renegade. Now, you can take me to him or I can kill you and find him myself. What is it to be?"

"I…t-t-take…"

"Try anything," the grinning demon hissed in Soan's ear, "and I'll cut your leg off. I haven't eaten in days."

Soan resisted the temptation to throw up.

The Culai fortresses had been built in the earliest Age of Man, but by a technology or magic that was beyond the finest builders or magicians in the Emperor's court today. This particular fortress had been carved out of the cliff face and then dug back into it. Whole floors of rooms had been cut into the mountainside and never saw the light of day, while the dungeons and cellars were far below ground. The front of the building, the battlements, turrets, and main gate were overhung by a huge outcrop of rock that effectively protected the occupants from attack from above, and from some of the sleet and rain storms that scoured this part of the continent. However, it also ensured that the fortress was in perpetual gloom, since the sun never shone directly onto it at any time during the day except briefly at sunrise.

The years had been kind to the fortress, softening its harsh edges, smoothing away the skeletal gauntness and then coating the entire building beneath a carpet of grasses and vines. No part of it had escaped, nor had it been discouraged by the scores of clans, tribes, and other groups that had lain claim to it down through the years. It helped disguise the building, and also provided a little insulation from the icy fingers of Snaitle, the Cold God, and Fiarle, the Little God of Icy Spaces. The thick covering also ensured that the entire fortress smelt of growth and damp.

A meal was in progress in the main hall when Owen stepped into the room followed a moment later by Tien tZo, with his axe at Soan's throat. The small grey-haired man at the head of the table spotted the intruders first and stopped, shocked and wide-eyed, with his glass raised halfway to his lips. Silence ran down the table like fluid as heads turned towards the door. Metal and wood scraped simultaneously as swords and knives were hurriedly unsheathed and chairs were pushed back from the table, and the Weapon Master and his servant found themselves facing over twenty armed men. Tien tZo pushed Soan away from him, sending him sprawling across the table, and then unclipped his second battle-axe, allowing it to swing loosely at the end of its thong.

Owen broke the startled silence. "I have come for Kutor," he said evenly.

A short, stout man near the end of the table suddenly produced a cocked and loaded crossbow and levelled it at Owen's chest, while the men standing beside the table immediately moved clear, allowing him a clear shot, and then they began to spread out and encircle the two.

"I take it you have come here for a reason?" The accent was cultured, the speaker a small, slender man at the end of the table. He raised his glass to his lips and drank. "What are you?" he asked.

"Killers, more than like," someone murmured.

"Killers don't usually announce themselves," the man said, lowering his glass, positioning it precisely on the scarred table.

"The very confident ones do," the stout man with the crossbow said quietly, his eyes never leaving the Weapon Master.

Owen bowed slightly. "You do me honour, sir."

"What do you want?" the man demanded, moving the crossbow slightly, positioning the broad-headed bolt on Owen's throat.

"We are seeking Kutor the Renegade."

"You've found him," the stout man said quickly.

Owen smiled. "No, I don't think so. But you, sir," he looked directly at the man at the head of the table, "you have more the mark of a leader about you."

The man smiled slightly. "I think now you do me honour. Yes, I am Kutor. Now, perhaps you would answer Keshian's question. Who are you? And perhaps if I could add one of my own, why are you here?"

"I am Owen, Weapon Master. This is Tien tZo, my slave-companion. We have come to join with Kutor the Renegade."

An uneasy laugh ran around the room, but then Keshian, the man with the crossbow, spoke suddenly. "I have heard of Owen, Weapon Master. He is a legend; everyone knows of his defence of Car'an'tual with less than a dozen men. I am curious, though, why one of the finest mercenary soldiers in the Seven Nations would want to join with us—and I become more curious and perhaps slightly suspicious when I remember that the same Owen swears fealty to Kloor, the God of War, and is a member of the select Iron Band."

Owen pushed back his sleeve, revealing the pale rectangle of skin which the metal band had once covered. "I left the Band and the Religion. I have returned to the Faith."

"No one leaves the Religion, and especially not the Band of Kloor," Kutor said quietly.

"Perhaps you're not even the real Weapon Master," Keshian said with a cold smile. "Perhaps you are a spy..."

"Oh, I am what I say I am," Owen whispered.

"We'll see." Without warning, he fired.

No one even saw Owen's sword leave its sheath. All they heard was the crack as it sliced through the crossbow bolt in mid-air, spinning the two pieces of wood away. One length fell into the fire and began to burn unheeded.

In the stunned silence that followed, Keshian dropped the cross-bow onto the table and placed two additional bolts beside it. "He's the Weapon Master," he said simply.

Kutor took a deep, shuddering breath. "Well, we've proven your identity. Tell us now, why are you here?"

For an answer, Owen unsheathed his knife and sent it sliding down the length of the table. Kutor picked it up, examining the heavy blade carefully, and then he silently passed it to Keshian. The old man looked at it for a long time and then he casually spun it through the air back to the warrior. "It bears the mark of the Hook," he said to the room, "the sign of the Bard."

The room was small and held nothing more than a simple bed that was merely a straw pallet thrown onto a low, raised, stone dais. There was a fireplace in the corner, the small, guttering fire there did little to dispel the stone chill of the place. Four chairs had been dragged into the room and Kutor and Keshian occupied two, while Owen sat astride a third, but with his back to the wall. Tien tZo remained standing by the door, his arms folded, fingertips touching the butts of his axes.

"The bard sent you to us?" Kutor began without preamble.

"He suggested that we might wish to fight in a worthy cause," Owen said slowly, looking at the Pretender to the throne of the Seven Nations.

"I doubt if there will be any money in it for a long time," Kutor added.

"You can pay me when you're on the throne."

The prince grinned almost shyly. "Whenever that may be."

"The bard supports your cause. That is enough for me," Owen said simply.

Keshian sat forward on the edge of the hard chair and looked from Owen to Tien tZo. "How well do you know the bard?" he asked.

"We met him once, spent a night in his company," the Weapon Master said slowly.

"He is not human," Tien tZo said abruptly, startling everyone. "Man, yes, but not wholly of this world."

"He has power," Owen agreed.

Keshian lifted a wooden flagon and filled the four glasses that had been left on a wooden tray by his feet. He passed a glass to Tien tZo, who put it to his lips and then, after a moment's hesitation, passed it on to Owen. The Weapon Master saw the flash of anger behind the old warrior's eyes. "He does it out of habit," he said quickly, "and means no insult by it."

Prince Kutor laid his hand on Keshian's arm. "The Weapon Master does not know us," he said reasonably. He deliberately lifted his own glass and drank deeply.

Keshian passed a second glass to the stone-faced servant and then lifted his own, but Tien still waited until the stout man had drunk first before he put his own glass to his lips.

"We have been on the road for nearly twenty summers," Owen explained, counting the years in summers in the manner of the southern peoples; the northern dwellers counted the winters. "One of the reasons we've survived so long and in relative safety is on account of the precautions we've adopted. Some"—he lifted his glass slightly and nodded at his servant—"have become second nature and we do them unthinkingly." The Weapon Master drank deeply and then looked directly at the prince. "And if you intend to rule, then I would suggest you should begin to take the same precautions."

Kutor grinned. "Why, there's hardly any need here in the Outlands..." he began.

"There is every need," Owen insisted. "When you take the throne you must be in a position to surround yourself with people you trust, and trust with your life. Begin the process now."

"Begin to live like a prince," Tien tZo hissed.

"Tien is right. At this moment you are nothing more than a bandit. You think of yourself as a bandit and your followers consider you to be a bandit. And the people coming to your banner will consider you nothing more than a bandit. Your enemies will consider you nothing more than a bandit, and they will begin with that great advantage over you."

"Think like a prince, an emperor," Tien added.

"I can see now why the bard sent you to us," Kutor smiled. "You will stay?"

"We haven't crossed half a continent to leave now." Owen grinned, passing his glass back to Keshian to be filled again "What numbers have you?"

"Keshian can best tell you that. He has become my sergeant-at-arms, captain of the guard, commander of my forces, armourer, quartermaster—everything, in fact, since he joined us. Amongst us, his military service is certainly the longest and without doubt the most distinguished."

"The prince does me too much honour," Keshian smiled. "I was merely a battle captain in Count Karfondal's guard before I joined the prince's band, and again the bard had a hand in that too. Before then I had seen some little service in the Island Wars and had patrolled the Fire Hills of Nasgociba with a band of mercenaries in the employ of the Taourg." He refilled Kutor's glass and then offered the jug to Tien; Tien shook his head—the glass in his hand was almost untouched.

"We have a little over forty men at present. We started out with nearly double that number, but the rest drifted away as we travelled into the west, or returned to look for families or loved ones when the Cataclysm struck. Forty men," Keshian repeated, "five of those are deserters, and so I suppose you could say that they had some military service. The rest are a mixture of farmers, servants, runaway slaves and escaped convicts."

"Women?"

"Ten women. Two are married, the rest just camp followers, and tend to drift from man to man."

"Children?"

"None; although one of the women is pregnant." When Keshian finished, Kutor leaned forward and watched the Weapon Master. "Well?" he asked.

Owen leaned back against the cold stone wall. "Well, you don't need me to tell you that you need more men."

"Professional soldiers?" the prince asked.

Owen shook his head. "The professional fights for coin—you have none—and he feels no loyalty to his employer. That is one of the reasons your last attempt for the throne failed so miserably. No, you need to get the ordinary people on your side..."

"But we tried that the last time," Kutor interrupted, "and it didn't work."

"They lacked a cause and they were untrained," Tien tZo said softly.

"Aye, and their enthusiasm probably caused more harm than good. No, this time we'll train them properly. Now, while I'm sure the bard will send you more men, I think you should go out and actually recruit..." He suddenly stopped, and looked from Kutor to Keshian. "I'm sorry. I didn't mean to dictate. I am only making suggestions, you understand; I've no wish to usurp Keshian's position."

"I would be honoured to serve under you," Keshian said immediately.

Kutor nodded. "And that is why Paedur sent you here, isn't it?" he asked.

Owen nodded. "Aye. Well then..." He drank quickly, finishing his wine and refusing Keshian's offer of more. "There are two things which must be attended to first; the fortress must be secured because—and you may be assured of this—you will be attacked by Imperial forces before this affair is closed; and we must begin stock-piling and constructing weapons." He glanced up at Tien. "If you will attend to that." The Shemmat nodded. "And if you, Keshian, will build up our defences." He nodded. "Good, then on the morrow, you and I, prince, will ride out in search of an army. Why do you smile?" he asked suddenly.

"From the moment the bard suggested that I might one day rule, everything seemed like a dream, everything seemed to happen so fast. And then we wound up here, and it was as if I had come back to reality: I was in a cold, dead fortress on the edge of civilisation, surrounded by a few dispirited men. And now you're here, and the dream is beginning again."

Owen smiled and rose smoothly to his feet. "This will be no dream, prince; this will be a nightmare!"

3
The Road to Manach

And he was god-like in the Worlds of Man, but human in Death's Realm...
Life of Paedur, the Bard

A warrior, whose race was not of the human kind, guarded the path.

"One of the frai-forde," Katani hissed, "the Star Lorn."

They had spotted it earlier, a solitary figure standing still in the centre of the thin band of road that ran arrow-straight across the plain. Caution had taken them off the track, and they had used what little natural cover the plain possessed to approach as close as possible to the figure. They had finally taken shelter in a shallow dip in the ground not twenty paces from it. Paedur peered over the lip of the depression and looked closely at the creature. His first impression was of height; it stood half again his own height and he was accounted a tall man. The frai-forde was also completely devoid of hair and this only served to emphasise the rigid lines of corded muscle. The head was almost completely round and sat directly on the broad shoulders. Its only discernible features were two small round eyes, and a round mouth. As it breathed, the mouth opened and closed, disclosing that it was ringed by a series of tiny needle-pointed teeth, like those of certain species of fish the bard had seen in some of the warmer climes. Its only garment was a long kirtle of banded metal plates that began low on its chest and ended just below the knees. It was unarmed.

"It seems to be asleep," Paedur said quietly, watching the rise and fall of the massively corded chest.

"They always do," Katani remarked wryly, "until you attempt to pass them."

"Is there any way to go around it?"

The woman-warrior shook her head slightly. "No, and even if you could, you're wasting your time. Just beyond the Star Lorn the road crests a rise and then it is downhill to Manach, the City of the

Dead. The city is completely surrounded by three circular rings of a river, which are only bridged at one particular point, and at the three bridges you will encounter more of the frai-forde."

"Perhaps it could be slain…" Paedur mused, almost to himself.

"When I was in the World of Men, the Katan fought one of these creatures—an assassin—who had been hired to slay the Lord Churon. We lost fourteen warriors before it was eventually slain. The Star Lorn are fast, bard. You have never seen a creature move so fast before. The Lord Churon formed the opinion that they lived according to a different timescale."

Paedur looked at the huge creature again, examining the enormous body, searching for weaknesses. With its almost featureless face, it was impossible to make any judgment as to its expression, whether it was even awake or asleep.

"What would happen if we were merely to stand up and approach it?" he wondered.

"It would attack us both," Katani said simply, "without question, without reason, and tear us literally limb from limb. We, or rather I, would awaken again, and I'm not sure I want to regain consciousness without the use of my limbs." Her eyes clouded. "I don't know what will happen if you are slain here; because you are living in the Land of Death, would you then truly die, or would you reanimate again?" She shook her head. "It is a paradox."

"Have you ever visited the city of Manach?" Paedur asked suddenly, not looking at her, still watching the frai-forde.

"Bard, I think you should understand that I have always kept to the borders of Death's Realm. You are heading deeper and deeper into his kingdom, and this is a country I know nothing about, nor indeed want to know anything about for that matter. Manach, the City of the Dead, is a legend—even here, in the land of the Dead. No-one has ever come out of Manach to tell of its mysteries or wonders, and no one has ever gone in, because no-one has ever managed to pass the guards."

Paedur nodded glumly. He came away from the lip of the depression and moved down beside Katani. The woman was lying on her back staring up at the pale blue sky, her matched swords in their lacquered scabbards lying by her hands. "What will you do?" she asked, without looking at him. "Attack?"

The bard rested his chin on his clenched fist and stared blankly at the woman, wondering what he was going to do this time, evaluating the possibilities.

When he had been a younger man, before he had been visited by Mannam and set out on his quest, and before he had been gifted by the Lord of Life, Paedur the bard had been a shy, almost frightened man, living a quiet hermit's existence by himself after a brief, artistically successful but politically disastrous spell in the Imperial Court. He had always been too direct, lacking tact and discretion, and had managed to insult far too many of the Emperor's cronies with his historically truthful tales—truthful was not how they wanted to hear them. Eventually he even succeeded in enraging the Emperor himself when, at the feast following the Imperial Games, Geillard had suggested he tell the tale of his own ancestor, Geillard the Great. The Emperor had expected to hear the accepted version of the tale, which told of a wise and benign sovereign freeing the land from the tyranny of the Court of Churon. Instead, Paedur told the story of a bloody courtier in the Onelord's court who had plotted and murdered his way into a position of authority, and then plunged the country into a bloody civil war which ravaged the countryside and laid waste enough fertile land to cause the Hunger, a twelve-season famine that had decimated the population of the nations and changed the political map forever.

Following that, the bard had wisely fled the court and retired to the solitude of the forests, where he had remained in obscurity until the Dark Lord, Mannam, had come to him.

But his stay at the Imperial Court had taught him many things. He had learned that men will listen only to what they want to hear, and that had taught him caution; and he had learned that there was no shame in subterfuge, and that a lie saved pain and hurt. And these were lessons which he considered to be as valuable as his training in Baddalaur.

And then he had been gifted by C'lte, the Lord of Life, and suddenly all the lessons he had learned were almost forgotten. His new-found power made him invulnerable, his knowledge, virtually omnipotent. He could now do what he wished without fear for his life, could say what he wanted, and tell his myths and tales whether men wanted to hear them or not. When he had fought the Three Cords on the Culai Isle, his powers had increased a hundredfold…and the cost had been the loss of whatever little humanity had remained in him.

And then he had entered Death's Kingdom—and found his god-gifted powers were negated. Paedur the Bard was a man once again, and now he had to re-learn the cautions of a frightened man. His only advantages once again were his knowledge and his lore.

"How did you kill the Star Lorn who attacked Churon?" he asked suddenly, looking at Katani.

Katani raised herself on her elbows, her face softening as she remembered. "He was detected as he came in over the wall, and the alarm was sounded. In the pursuit he killed two of the Katan Sisterhood, but then he was trapped in a narrow corridor, so we could only come at him one at a time. He was unarmed and naked except for their customary long mail kirtle and a pair of metal gauntlets. But his speed was as such that he would catch the sword blades and wrench them from my sisters' hands, and then throw them back like knives. Arrows were equally useless, he brushed them aside like insects or caught the shafts in mid-flight… He was an extraordinary opponent."

"But you overcame him…"

"He was finally slain with a thrown talon." Katani smiled as she remembered. "Funny. He didn't even seem to see it coming."

"What is a talon?" Paedur asked quietly.

"Ah…it is—was—one of the Katan warrior's secret weapons, and it was forbidden under pain of death to reveal it to one not of the sisterhood." She smiled broadly. "Under pain of death," she repeated. "but since I am dead, I suppose I can reveal it to you. A talon is a flat square of metal, the four edges sharpened to razor points. When thrown, the square naturally revolves at high speed and I've seen them actually cut through a piece of solid brukwood."

"How many of these talons were thrown at the creature?"

"Three. The first two just missed its head, the third ripped out its throat."

"And it didn't react when the first two talons missed?"

"Not at all."

The bard traced an arcane pattern in the soil with the tip of his hook. He glanced up at Katani. "I don't suppose you would have any of these talons?" She shook her head ruefully. "No, I suppose not," he answered his own question. "So we'll have to make do. Now tell me, how big are these talons?"

The stone, no bigger than a man's eyeball, struck the frai-forde right between the eyes with a solid crunch that was clearly audible to the bard and the woman crouching by the side of the road. The Star Lorn fell without a sound.

"How?" Katani asked.

Paedur folded the sling he had fashioned from a strip of cloth and tucked it into his belt. "I think their perception of movement is different to ours. You said it was fast, that it could pluck arrows out of the air, and yet it didn't even react to the talons. Perhaps simply because it couldn't see it, perhaps because it was too small."

"Like the stone."

"Just so. Hopefully, the same method will take us past the three guards on the bridges."

They climbed up onto the road and walked to the fallen creature. The front of the skull was crushed with the force of the blow, the black stone protruding like a third eye.

"Let us hope his brothers are not expecting us," Katani said quietly, nudging the creature with her foot.

"What do you mean?"

"I have heard that no one sleeps—dies, if you will—in the Land of the Dead without the Dark Lord's consent." She nodded to the frai-forde. "He knows we're coming now."

Paedur nodded seriously. "I would imagine that there are scores of deaths occurring both here and on the various Planes of Existence where Mannam reigns as Death at the same time, and while he may be aware of their occurrence, he cannot know the details of each and every one." He grinned. "Anyway, I think if he knew I was here, he would have made some move against me by now."

"What about me, the peist, and now the frai-forde?" Katani demanded. "Surely we all moved against you?"

"I prefer to think of you and them as part of the natural hazards of the Kingdom of the Dead." He smiled. "It will make a fine tale when I return to the World of Men. My journey through the Land of Death will admirably complement my stay in the Lands of Life Eternal." He sobered and then looked at Katani. "I think you should think very seriously about whether you want to remain with me or not. The nearer we come to the City of the Dead, the more dangerous it will become."

"And what is the worst that can happen to me?" the woman asked with a sly smile.

"You could be kill…" The bard suddenly laughed, realising what he had been about to say. "Have you ever died here?" he asked.

"Not here," Katani said, something shifting behind her eyes. "I have only died once, and that was enough."

Paedur, sensitive to the emotion he now recognised as pain and loss, bent and heaved the incredibly heavy corpse of the frai-forde off the road and down the incline into the hollow. He slid down after it and kicked grit and pebbles over it, hiding it from a casual observer. When he was finished he straightened and looked up at Katani, who had remained standing on the road.

"How does it look?"

Her head snapped up. "What?"

"I asked how it looked from up there."

"Oh. It looks like a body covered by grit," she said, smiling wanly.

Paedur clambered up the incline, using the point of his hook to pull himself up. He straightened beside the woman and looked into her deep amber-coloured eyes. "Something is troubling you."

"There is nothing."

"A bard is trained to be sensitive to the mood of his audience. Tell me."

She shook her head and turned away, settling her armour around her shoulders and adjusting her swords. When she looked back at Paedur, her face was completely devoid of expression. "I would suggest we hurry. There's no telling how long the Star Lorn will stay dead, and I don't want to be around when he awakes."

Paedur strode after her and the pair walked in silence for awhile. Finally the bard said softly, "Something about your own death is troubling you. There are memories which are painful, that is obvious."

Katani began to shake her head, but abruptly changed her mind and nodded.

"Do you want to tell me about it?"

"What good would that do?" she demanded, her voice sounding surprisingly bitter even to her own ears.

"It is said that naming something gives one power over it, and similarly, knowing the name of something or someone evil lessens their power to harm. Perhaps by naming your hurt, you will lessen its power to distress."

"I doubt that. You don't know what happened that day."

"I am a bard; I know all the tales of the Battle of the Sand Plain with the Shemmatae, and the gallant defence of Churon the Onelord and his Katan warriors, and their victory over the invaders from the Land of the Sun even though it cost them all their lives."

"You don't know the whole story, bard," Katani said, derision in her voice.

"I am a bard," Paedur said simply. "I tell what I have learned. If you know more, then teach me."

The road dipped, taking them down into a hollow where the walls on either side were a handspan and more taller than the bard. Their footsteps echoed in the defile, and they both instinctively fell silent, eyes and ears alert, aware that it was the perfect place for a trap. But they came up out of the long defile without incident and found the road now stretched away arrow-straight, sloping gently downhill to the horizon. Nothing moved on the flat expanse of grey stone and grit.

"Manach, the City of the Dead, lies just beyond the horizon," Katani said quietly.

"A day's march," Paedur estimated.

"There is no time here, bard, no day, no night. You will not tire, nor feel the need to sleep, but it would be best if you rest, lest your fatigued muscles suddenly betray you."

Paedur nodded obediently, unwilling to tell the woman that it had been a long time since he had slept the true sleep of the humankind.

"Tell me your tale of the Battle of the Sand Plain, bard," Katani said suddenly. "I'm curious to hear how history has treated us."

"It's a long story…" Paedur began.

"Just the battle will do. And then when you have done, I will tell you how that day went."

The bard nodded. "That would be interesting." He adjusted his cloak around his shoulders, pulling up the hood, allowing it to fall forward across his face, cutting himself off from his surroundings, and then he began…

They came in crafts of metal, impossible constructions that had no right to ride the sea, ships that were an affront to the Lord of the Sea, and yet they remained afloat. The invaders beached their metal crafts on the Sand Plain, turning the sea-going fortresses into land castles, and from there conducted their reign of terror across the Seven Nations.

Armies rode against the savage yellow-skinned invaders, who fought back on the small sturdy ponies they had brought with them in the bellies of their huge metal crafts. And the armies, for all their armour and weapons, numbers and supplies, perished. The invaders—the Shemmatae—were warriors for whom death was a state to be embraced, a joy, and they threw themselves willingly on the spears of the mainlanders to allow their brothers to triumph. And soon, while they did not completely rule the coast, a major portion of it was under their influence, and by controlling the ports, they controlled the movements of supplies of food and fuel. And the Seven Nations began to hunger.

But finally a man appeared, a slave who had fought his way up from the slave-market at Londre to freedom. To overthrow a monarch in those troubled times was a simple matter for a man who had appeared out of the wilderness with the most feared warriors in the known world at his back, the Katan. Once he was secure on the throne, he immediately set about organising the defence of the Nations. Realising that there was safety only in strength, he set about extracting an oath of fealty from the Brothers, the six kings of the neighbouring nations. But the kings were proud, haughty men who had no time for freed slaves, and so the man—by name Churon—had to trick the kings into giving him their oath before witnesses...and how he accomplished that would take a tale to itself.

And when he had their word and they had declared him the Onelord, he warred on the invaders. Over the next few moons, there were skirmishes and many died on both sides, but when Churon realised that the real victims were the common people, who were suffering not only the depredations of the Shemmatae but also from hunger and disease, the Onelord decided that there would be one last battle, a final effort to crush the invaders completely.

The battle on the Sand Plain lasted a day and a night, and when it was finally done and the dead counted and the wounded numbered, twenty thousand men had gone to their gods that day, and three times that number had suffered wounds. Over the next two days another six thousand men went into the Land of Death. The Shemmatae were completely crushed and the Onelord and his warriors took over fourteen thousand Shemmatae men, women, and children as slaves, and so even now it is possible to find pure-blooded Shemmatae still serving as slaves...

Paedur finished and looked at Katani. "That is the shortened version," he said carefully.

She looked at him in amazement. "But it tells nothing, where is the detail? What about the Shemmatae's secret weapon of cold fire? What about the Magician's War before the battle took place, when our mages fought theirs? And the attack by the Chopt-like creatures they kept as pets, when Kutor the Strong killed one with a single blow of his mailed fist? What about the death of the Katan?" she asked finally.

"We know nothing about such things," Paedur lied. The events surrounding the Battle of the Sand Plain were documented in great detail, but he wished to draw the woman out to discover what was troubling her. "Tell me," he said suddenly, "tell me about that day..."

Katani walked on slowly, her head bent, the knuckles of her left hand wrapped whitely around the hilt of her longsword. "In truth the battle began just before dawn," she said suddenly, "when their sorcerers attacked our camp with a plague of tiny flying creatures completely alien to the Nations," She shuddered, remembering. "They were similar in shape and form to a sewing needle, no bigger than one, and blood red in colour. They attacked the face, flying straight into the eyes, the open mouth, up nostrils, into ears...and then they fed. We lost many fine men to that disgusting death. It was an evil death conceived by an evil man.

"And our sorcerers retaliated. Praetens was Churon's magician then; he was of the Susuru..." Katani broke off and glanced at the bard. "You are familiar with the Susuru? I am not sure if they still survive in the World of Men; they were a dying race even in my own time."

"Their race became extinct only recently," Paedur said with an enigmatic smile, recalling the half-human creature that had controlled the Quisleedor.

"Praetens wove a spell which sent the creatures back on the Shemmatae, and soon the screams of their maimed mingled with ours. Praetens and his fellow magicians then retaliated by sending a wall of freezing fog down on the invaders. The wall was no thicker than a sword's length and no taller than a man, and it moved in a straight line down across the Sand Plain and onto the beach. Everything it touched was coated in a layer of hoar frost. The Shemmatae invaders were terrified, such intense cold being completely unknown in their own land, and some broke ranks, turned and fled back towards their ships, but these were calmly shot down by their own officers." Katani smiled. "Some of us even believed that the battle had been won then, but we were wrong. The invaders' magicians brought fire down from the heavens in the form of a cold rain, like sleet, that burned, eating through raw flesh like acid. Praetens called up a wind and blew the sleet down onto the invaders; the Shemmatae turned it back. Praetens sent scores of tiny bouncing balls of fire into the invader's camp; their magicians called them all together and sent a huge fireball screaming back. The Susuru stopped it in mid-air, holding it floating just above his head like a second sun. He seemed to fold it in onto itself, and then encased it in something black and hard. When it was the size of a man's head he held out his talon-like hand and the ball dropped into it. And then he threw it at the Shemmatae...at the same moment that they fired what looked like a tiny silver arrow at him.

"The black ball fell amongst the Shemmatae magicians and exploded in a massive fireball that reduced everything around it to cinders, completely destroying the invaders' magical forces, and a sizable portion of their supplies and foodstuffs. But the tiny arrow they had fired had grown and grown until it was a shaft as thick as a man's body. It pierced Praetens, pinning him to the ground—and the shock of his death killed his fellow magicians, blasting their minds, leaving their bodies nothing but empty husks. One was standing quite close to me when he died and it was as if ...as if a candle had been snuffed out. One moment he was a man and his eyes were alive, and the next there was nothing there but a body devoid of all intelligence. That was the beginning of the attack proper."

"When did the Katan enter the fighting?" Paedur asked, not wishing to hear a full blow-by-blow account of the battle.

"As the day wore on into evening," Katani said slowly, "the Shemmatae, perhaps sensing that they had lost, made one last desperate attempt. They concentrated everything on an assault on Churon's position on the hill overlooking the plain. Our forces were initially taken by surprise and forced back, and the Shemmatae drove a wedge straight through the heart of our lines to the foot of the hill. And there they encountered the Katan." Her voice changed, becoming proud. "They had saved their finest warriors, their elite Dragon Guard, for the attack, knowing that if they killed Churon, the alliance would fall apart—perhaps not immediately, but eventually—and even if they weren't victorious on the Sand Plain, then when the Brothers had gone their separate ways they could return.

"So the Katan fought the Dragon Guard, while the rest of our forces gradually forced the Shemmatae army back down to the shore, leaving the two elite forces fighting together. The Dragon Guard outnumbered the Katan by almost two to one, but we were the better warriors..."

The pause was so long that Paedur turned to look at her. Her face was pale and drawn and her eyes were distant. Her grip on the hilt of her sword was rigid, her knuckles white.

"What happened," he asked eventually.

"We died defending our lord," she said softly.

"All of you?"

"All of us."

"Do you want to tell me how you died?" he asked, wondering how she would react.

Katani shook her head defiantly. "I died defending my lord."

"There is a tale—a legend, surely—of a single Katan warrior who betrayed her lord and attacked him, and was very nearly responsible for killing Churon the Onelord. Did you ever hear that tale?"

Her sword made no sound leaving its scabbard—and the point of the bard's hook touched her throat. The woman was shivering with rage and spittle flecked her lips. "The sword..." Paedur said softly. Katani watched him, and for a single instant Paedur thought she might actually complete her move, draw the sword and attempt to disembowel him. He pressed the point of his hook against the soft flesh of her throat. "I'll kill you," he promised, "and by the time you wake up, I'll be long gone."

"You would?"

He nodded.

"I don't suppose your legend tells why the Katan attacked Churon?"

"I once read that she was in the pay of the Shemmatae," he said quietly.

"I can believe that." She pressed the blade back into its sheath and adjusted the catch that kept the blade locked in place.

"Tell me the real reason," he suggested, removing his hook from her throat and stepping away from her.

"Churon was not a sane man," Katani said slowly, watching him, gauging his reaction. "He was arrogant, suspicious, petty in many ways, fearful of everyone. But he had vision, a vision of a united land, the Seven Nations, with him as emperor. He ruthlessly removed every obstacle in his path; the Shemmatae were merely another obstacle and he disposed of them as he had disposed of kings, lords, barons, and beggars.

"When the Katan fought the Dragon Guard and died in doing so, he was, I think, secretly delighted. The Katan obeyed one basic tenet: loyalty to a cause of justice. Not loyalty to a man, but to an ideal, and in the beginning Churon upheld that ideal. But as he moved more and more away from it, so too did he lose the respect and loyalty of the Katan Sisterhood. Before the battle with the Shemmatae, the Katan had sent a request to the Onelord for an urgent meeting to discuss their future in his service. It is likely that we would have left, and more than likely that we would have been forced to do battle with his forces at some later date.

"But the Katan fought the Dragon Guard and died, though they killed all the Guard in doing so. Only one Katan, mortally wounded, survived the carnage long enough to hear the Onelord say, 'This saves me the trouble of poisoning them.' I was enraged and attacked him—and his archers cut me down," she finished simply.

They walked in silence for a while, and then the road began to slope upwards.

"And have you ever encountered him here?" Paedur asked.

"Not yet," Katani said ominously.

They crested the slight rise and before them stood Manach, the City of the Dead.

"Not yet?" the bard asked, "I would have thought you would have gone looking for him."

"Oh, I know where he is," she whispered.

"Where?"

Katani pointed. "He is Mannam's closest adviser, protected by him, surrounded by the frai-forde and Mannam's other pets. But this time..." she said, her voice trailing off.

"This time?

"This time I'll do it properly," she whispered, her voice a promise. "I owe it to my sisters and myself."

4
The Warning

If a cause is worthy, then it is worth dying for...
The Warrior, the Life of Owen, Weapon Master

The village was called Bridgetown, for no apparent reason since it possessed no bridge and the nearest river was half a day's ride away. It huddled in a valley around a freshwater spring, a miserable collection of stone and thatched huts, encircled only by a palisade of sharpened stakes.

Owen reined in his mount and let his eyes wander over the village, reading the signs of smoke, the dust of movement, the discoloration of the earth, looking for the flash of metal.

"What do you see? Kutor asked, standing in the stirrups and shading his eyes with his hand from the early morning sun.

"I see a village of fifteen recognisable houses, an elder's house, a forge, what might be a place of worship or perhaps a woman's house, and a well-house. I see it is surrounded by a flimsy wooden palisade, which is there obviously as a deterrent for animals, but no trench, and that tells me the village is too poor for bandits to bother with."

"They could be paying the bandits to leave them in peace," Kutor suggested.

"Did you do that often in the Wastelands?" Owen demanded abruptly, glancing sidelong at him.

Kutor looked away. "We had to live..." he said defensively.

"And what of the villagers who were paying you? Did they not have a right to live as well?" he snapped.

"That is in the past," Kutor mumbled.

Owen glared at him, and then he suddenly nodded and turned away. "I'm sorry...I had no right. We have all done...well, we have done things which time has coloured and tinted." He looked back. "When I was a boy, my village was forced to pay tribute to a band of outlaws. It was a fierce winter and we lost many of the old, the children, and the sick because we had less food and fuel. It has always been something that can raise me to anger." He finished suddenly, regretting his outburst, and urged his mount down the gritty track that led towards the village.

"Was that why you decided to defend Car'an'tual?" Kutor asked, coming up alongside.

The Weapon Master thought about it for a moment, and then he grinned with rare good humour. "Partially. The Brugh were attempting to extract tribute from the city fathers. And if they weren't paid, the Brugh were going to sack the city, level it to the ground, kill the adults and sell all the children into slavery at Londre." He shrugged. "I had very little choice in the matter."

"And you stopped the Brugh on the city walls?" Kutor said in wonder. "It is the stuff of legend."

The Weapon Master smiled in something like embarrassment. "Get the bard to tell you the tale. If we ever see him again," he added.

"Oh, I'm sure we will."

A small party was waiting for the two riders at the gate: two old men, obviously village elders, three large men behind them, farmers or shepherds more likely, and a little to one side a small, sharp-faced, barrel-chested man wearing a blacksmith's full-length leather apron.

Kutor reined in his mount and immediately dismounted, careful to show no discourtesy to these people. He bowed cautiously to the two older men, noting the wariness in their eyes and the open defiance and anger in the faces of the others. These people were afraid.

"A blessing on your hearths and families," he said gravely, deciding on the standard Northland greeting.

"A blessing received and returned." One of the old men bowed slightly. "You are not Cormac's men?" he asked immediately.

"We know of no Cormac," Kutor answered, glancing up at Owen, who had remained mounted and shook his head slightly.

"You are newly come to the Outlands, then?" the second man asked.

"Recently. Should we know of this Cormac?" Kutor asked quickly.

"He calls himself the King of the Outlands." The old man almost spat the name.

"Hush, now. These could be in Cormac's employ," his companion advised.

"I care not. I've had enough of them," the old man continued. He stepped up to Owen's mount and glared up into his face and then he tapped a long swollen-jointed finger against the warrior's high boot. "Tell your master that. Tell him that Alun of Bridgetown has had enough…"

The second elder touched his arm and almost dragged him away. He looked up at Owen's impassive face. "He does not know what he says. He is old and his wits are addled."

Owen raised his hand, silencing him. "I don't know this Cormac, and I am not in his service. I am Owen, a Weapon Master, currently in the employ of Prince Kutor." To the villagers' obvious surprise, he indicated the small man standing before them. While their attention was on him, Kutor said, "I take it this Cormac is extracting tribute from you?"

Alun, the old man, shook off the restraining hand. "Aye, and every month his demands grow more extravagant. We're a poor village; a few shepherds, some quarrying, a little iron work. We have nothing…certainly nothing to spare."

"I can see that," Owen murmured.

Kutor stepped up to the old man and stared deep into his tired faded eyes. "Would you be free of this Cormac, self-styled king of the Outlands?" he asked quietly.

"How?" The voice was a rasp, the accent thick and guttural.

Kutor turned towards the voice, and found himself facing a dwarf, the blacksmith. He was tall for one of the Stone Folk, standing just a little shorter than the prince, although his barrel chest and overdeveloped arms lent him an almost animal-like appearance, which was emphasised by his broad, flat face and thick unruly mop of hair.

"How?" he demanded again.

"I am Prince Kutor, half-brother to Geillard, the Emperor."

"You are the Renegade," the blacksmith stated flatly.

"So called," Kutor admitted, "but only by my enemies. My forces have recently invested the old Culai fortress just beyond the ridge under the mountains. I will have them wipe out this Cormac for you."

"And the price?" the dwarf demanded.

"Join me."

"Then we only exchange one slavery for another," Alun said simply.

Owen said quickly, "The prince was merely suggesting that if we defeat Cormac's forces some of you might wish to join us."

"Another assault on the throne?" the dwarf sneered.

"Just so," Kutor agreed, smiling pleasantly.

"And if we do not wish to join forces with you," Alun asked, "what will you do to us then?"

"Nothing!" Kutor sounded surprised. "We are not bandits to force our will on others." He was aware of Owen's impassive stare on his back. "Tell us where this Cormac may be found and when we have dealt with him, then make your decision."

"Prince," the dwarf growled, "how many men have you?"

"Enough."

"Experience has shown me that enough usually means too few." He grinned, showing his solid horse-like teeth. "Cormac controls a legion of men." He saw Kutor and Owen's look of disbelief and continued maliciously. "Yes, a legion, a hundred decades, all armed, all armoured and half of them mounted."

"And where can we find this Cormac?" Kutor asked.

The blacksmith shrugged his massive shoulders. "Don't even look. He'll find you."

"We had a visitor," Keshian said, hurrying down the cracked steps to meet the horsemen. Behind them the two huge gates boomed closed and Owen nodded in approval as a newly trimmed tree-trunk slid home, barring it.

"One of the King Cormac's men?" Kutor asked, dismounting.

Keshian stopped in amazement. "You met him?" he asked finally.

"We were told about him," Owen said. "Where's Tien?"

"Here." The Shemmat appeared alongside Keshian, a double-recurve horn bow around his shoulder, a quiver of broad-head arrows on his belt.

As the four men strode down the musty corridor, Owen and the prince listened intently to Keshian's and Tien tZo's account of what had occurred earlier that afternoon.

"There were three men," Keshian began, "mounted and armed."

"Professional warriors," Tien added, "carrying weapons of choice rather than issue."

"Experienced too, and although only three came forward, I'll wager there were more watching us."

Tien nodded agreement.

"I've never seen warriors like them before. Tall men, dark, weathered skins but not black—oiled and curled beards, divided in the middle..."

"Gallowglas," Owen said decisively. "They carried swords almost as tall as themselves?"

Keshian and Tien both nodded.

"Gallowglas," Owen repeated, nodding. "Professional soldiers from the tribe of Gallowglas, which borders the Northlands. They have more than a touch of Chopt blood in them. They were said to be cannibal, like their savage cousins, but now they only eat human flesh on special ceremonial occasions. What did they say?"

"Very little," Keshian continued. "They demanded to speak to the lord of the fortress. When they learned he was not here, they said they were the men of Cormac, King of the Outlands, and would return to speak with you at dawn on the morrow."

They had reached the rooms that had been set aside for the prince, but when Kutor would have strode straight in, Owen laid a hand on his arm and Tien moved ahead, an axe in his left hand. When he reappeared moments later, the Weapon Master allowed the prince to enter. "Get used to it," he said, smiling.

The prince's suite was a series of three interconnecting rooms—caves—cut into the heart of the stone. Each room was separated by a snugly fitting solid brukwood door and Kutor had, at Owen's insistence, chosen the last as his bedchamber. Owen had also insisted that later, when they had enough men to spare, they would position guards at each of the doors. They passed through the first room and into the second, which was almost identical except that it had a large, rough, wooden table and a score of chairs of various types scattered around the room. The room itself, like most of the others in the fortress, was almost completely bare except for a series of fading pictures that had once been painted directly onto the wall and which Kutor thought might have been there to give the impression of windows.

The four men arranged themselves around the table and then, briefly and succinctly, Owen related what they had learned from the villagers.

"A legion," Keshian whispered, "one thousand…" He stopped as a sudden thought struck him. "Surely not one thousand of the Gallowglas!"

Owen smiled and shook his head. "No. I'm afraid there just aren't that many to go round. You saw three this morning…"

"There were more," Tien interrupted.

"Even so, assuming there were another two in hiding, that gives us five…" He paused. "I would guess this king has a decade at his command. But remember, each Gallowglas is worth…four, five ordinary warriors."

"What do we do?" Kutor whispered. "They'll be here in the morning."

"Pay, fight or run," Tien tZo said firmly.

Owen nodded. "Aye, it's a simple enough choice: pay, fight or run." He looked at the prince. "Do you want to pay?"

Kutor shook his head. "And we've nowhere to run to," he added.

"So we fight." The Weapon Master looked at Keshian. "Can we defend the fortress?"

"Yes…and no." He spread his short, stubby fingers and began touching off points. "We are not enough to man the walls, so we will lose the battlements, the courtyards, the well there, the provisions for the animals, and possibly the animals themselves. However, the fortress itself is accessible only through one reasonably solid door. Four men standing abreast could hold that door. But I discovered a mechanism earlier which allows an iron grill to fall from the ceiling into slots in the flagstones; it effectively seals the opening while allowing arrows or spears to be fired through. Should that gate fall, there is the door to the fortress itself, and that too has the iron grill behind it; but even without the grill, a single man could hold the door for days. There is also another lever just beyond the last gate which I think precipitates some sort of rock fall to seal off that entire corridor, but it also traps the defenders inside the fortress. There is food enough for all of us for just under a moon in here, and with the two freshwater wells, water presents no problem."

"But we would be trapped?" Kutor asked.

"I have not yet found a way out, although I imagine there must be one."

The Weapon Master nodded his thanks and turned to Tien. "What weapons do we have?"

The sallow-skinned man pulled a disgusted face. "Swords mostly, of every race and shape, and with hardly an edge on any of them. Some spears, axes, maces, morningstars, a few bows, not enough arrows, three crossbows, none of which are working properly, and we've few enough bolts for them in any case."

"Well, we're not going to hold off an army with that," Owen sighed. He looked from Keshian to Tien. "We'll need arrows for the bows, and we'll need them soon. If you can get the crossbows working then so much the better."

"That may be possible," Tien agreed.

"We'll want broad-head arrows and bolts—flesh-shredders— and also some armour-piercing..." He stopped as Tien shook his head.

"That may not be possible. I have neither the facilities nor the materials for forging armour-piercing heads here."

"We'll need something to punch through the Gallowglas armour," Owen said, looking at Kutor and Keshian for suggestions.

"Darts," Keshian said slowly, raising his eyebrows.

Owen's face broke into a rare grin. "Darts!" He looked at his servant. "Darts and pipes?"

Tien smiled slightly. "It is possible. I saw some suitable reeds beyond the fortress walls. You would want them poisoned?"

"Yes."

"No!"

Everyone turned to look at the prince. "I will not, cannot, allow my campaign to be tainted by the use of such things. It is hardly chivalrous."

"Prince," Owen said very softly, "I came here to win you a throne. Now, if I am to do so, I must be given a free and full hand to wage this war in whatever way I see fit. You talk to me of chivalry now...now, after years of banditry in the wastelands, when you robbed and killed, raped and ransomed." Kutor opened his mouth to protest, but the look on the Weapon Master's face quelled him. "Do you think your enemies will fight by a code of chivalry? Do you? Did they fight by any such code in the past? Did you?" he asked savagely. "Now, we will shortly be going up against one of the most feared clans of warriors in the Nations since the Katan.

We need, desperately, to reduce their numbers, and I will do that by any and every means at my disposal."

To break the growing silence Keshian said finally, "Owen is right."

Kutor sighed and nodded. "I know. I just wish it were otherwise." He looked at Owen. "You are the Weapon Master. Do as you feel necessary." He smiled hesitantly. "I suppose when I am Emperor you will want to become the commander of my armies?"

Owen shook his head and laughed humourlessly. "I am merely an adviser. Keshian is your commander, not I. And when you become Emperor, Kutor, you will not want to know me, or else will probably arrange to have me killed. Oh, don't look so shocked. It is a practice that has been hallowed by history." He stood up suddenly. "Come, Tien, we'll look over the fortress's defences." He nodded to the prince and Keshian. "We will see you shortly before dawn."

When the door closed and the footsteps had disappeared down the corridor, Keshian looked at the prince and poured him another drink. "Was there any truth in what he said?" he asked softly.

"In what?"

"That you might order his death when you have gained the crown."

Kutor lifted the glass and downed the fiery liquid in one swallow. "Probably," he gasped.

Owen and Tien walked the battlements, their greatcloaks wrapped around them against the chill of the night. They had made a cursory round of the fortress, only confirming what they already knew: in its present state the fortress was indefensible against a concentrated attack. It needed several moons' work on the walls and complete refurbishment by skilled craftsmen to make it even halfway habitable. They stopped just above the main gate and leaned on the chill gritty stone, looking over the dimly visible plain, their eyes and ears alert for anything untoward. Experience taught them that the fortress was being watched and they both knew there was a possibility, albeit a slim one, that there would be a night attack.

"We could leave," Tien suggested quietly, his soft voice almost lost on the wind. "We could be far away by dawn. Our gear is still packed."

"I have never run from a fight before, Tien," Owen said coldly.

"No," the Shemmat agreed, "but you have made strategic retreats before, and returned to do battle when the odds were more in your favour. Even you cannot do battle with a decade of Gallowglas warriors."

"But I cannot just leave."

"Why not?" Tien asked in surprise.

"Because...because the bard sent me to them. And I owe him, old friend, I owe him more than you can ever comprehend."

"We spent but a single night with the bard," Tien reminded him.

"It changed my life!" He unconsciously rubbed the wrist that had been recently covered by the Iron Band of Kloor. "We may have spent just a single night with him, but I felt it was longer. I feel I've known him all my life."

"And where is he now?" Tien demanded.

"I don't know," the Weapon Master said feelingly, "but I wish he was here!"

5
Manach

The city thrived and yet no life walked its cobbled streets...
Life of Paedur, the Bard

From the distance they could see that the three bridges that led into Manach, the City of the Dead, were unguarded.

"Where are the frai-forde?" Paedur asked quietly.

Katani shook her head slightly. "I don't know, but I have heard that they never leave their posts. In the way that I chose to guard the way from the World of Men, the Star Lorn are doomed to guard the bridges into the city."

"And yet you left your post," Paedur reminded her softly.

"Because of you," she said with a smile, "you broke the spell."

Paedur turned back to the blasted landscape, looking for signs of movement, unable to shake off the feeling that they were under observation by someone or something just out of sight.

"Were you in fact under a spell—a proper spell, that is—that kept you at the entrance to this place or was it more like a vague compulsion to remain there?" he asked suddenly.

Katani thought about the question and then shook her head. "I'm not sure. I wandered through the Silent Wood for a long time before I came to that place, and when I reached it, I felt no desire to leave. It seemed only natural that I should stay and guard the way."

"A *geasa*—compulsion," Paedur grunted without looking at her. The feeling of being watched had grown, and he had to resist the temptation to look over his shoulder once again. And once again he longed for his enhanced senses, realising how much he had come to depend on them.

"What do we do?" Katani asked.

"We've come this far..." Paedur said softly. He adjusted his cloak and strode off down the track.

They walked up to the first bridge—the Bridge of Wood—and then stopped, looking across its broad width. The bridge had been constructed of broad lengths of black wood which had been worn to a soft greyness in the centre with the passing of generations of the dead. There was no rail on either side.

Paedur walked onto the bridge, his boot-heels echoing thunderously, and strode into the middle before moving to the edge to stare down into the black water below. The river was surprisingly close to the underside of the bridge, less than one man length—but because it was completely black, it was impossible to gauge any impression of its depth.

Katani joined him, looking in disgust at the sluggish, foul seeming liquid. "It is part of the Naman," she spat, "the Black River."

Paedur nodded. "I know. Did I tell you I saw its counterpart, the Aman, in the Yellow God's kingdom?"

"You told me." She nodded towards the river. "It's not water. Have you any idea what it is?" she asked, tossing a stone into the liquid; it disappeared without a sound, without leaving a ripple in the tar-like surface.

"It is the River of Death," the bard said, glancing at her, "supposedly the tears of the One, from whose essence the Planes of Existence and the very first gods were created. When the One awoke from his slumber and saw what the Great Gods Hanor and Hara had wrought, he supposedly wept, tears of joy and tears of sorrow at the creation. And C'lte, the Lord of Life, gathered up the milk-white pearls of his tears of joy and set them in a river in his kingdom, and Mannam gathered the ink jewels of his tears of sorrow and caused them to flow around the city he was only then building for himself—Manach, the City of the Dead—protecting it."

"And that brings us back to the Star Lorn," Katani said. "Where are the three guards? The first should be here, guarding the Bridge of Wood; the next, just beyond, standing before the Bridge of Stone; and the third, off over there, holding the Bridge of Crystal."

"Wood for his body, stone for his heart, crystal for his eyes," Paedur said softly, and then added, "an ancient description the Lord of the Dead. No," he continued, "I think it's obvious. The guards have been removed as an invitation."

"I think there are some invitations best left unanswered."

"Ah, but this is an invitation from Death," Paedur smiled delightedly, "and some invitations you just don't ignore."

"So you're just going to march in?"

"Through the main gate," Paedur stated, and crossed the bridge. From the distance Manach, the City of the Dead, had looked white—startlingly so against the stone-greyness of the landscape and the leaden sky—but as the bard and warrior-maid neared it, the colour altered subtly, turning from cold white to a soft yellow and then to a faded ivory, the colour of old bones. The second bridge was of stone, each block incised with lines from the Book of the Dead, and, crossing that, they began to gain an impression of the actual monumental size of the city. The third and final bridge was of crystal which was so pure and clear that although it had been visible from the distance, close up it was little more than a vague outline, only the lines of script in the ancient language of the Culai, that had been cut into the crystal stones and which now hung solid and unmoving on the air, giving it solidity. But it was firm and solid under their feet. They stepped off the final bridge and stopped to stare in wonder at Manach. It appeared to have been constructed of a single stone: there were no seams in the blocks of stone, no trace of the mortar that held them together. The only opening in the ivory walls was the main gate, a huge arch that was without doors. A dozen towers rose up over the battlements, regularly spaced and so thin and narrow that they couldn't possibly be habitable, with the exception of one that was larger and broader than the rest.

When they walked into the shadow of the walls, the temperature plummeted, and even Katani, whose senses had been blunted by the process of death, shivered. Katani settled her horned helmet on her head and adjusted the mail coif and neck-scarf with a practised shake of her head. She pulled her heavy leathern gloves sewn with metal plates from her belt and dragged them on. Paedur pulled up his hood and settled his arms into his wide sleeves. He heard a curious hissing sound and it took him a moment or two to realise that the woman was laughing.

"What's so amusing?"

"I had forgotten what it is like to be cold," she said. "It almost makes me feel alive again."

There was a wide metal grid set into the ground at the entrance to the city and they both stopped before stepping onto it. About a single man-length below the grid they heard the slow gurgling movement of a river.

Katani leaned over and then just as suddenly recoiled, gagging. "The Naman. But what's it doing here, and what is the purpose of this grid?" She looked at the bard.

Paedur shrugged, the movement dislodging his hood. "I don't know," he admitted.

"It is to ensure that you bring nothing from the Silent Woods into the city!"

Katani fell into a fighting crouch, both swords sliding free of their scabbards with a venomous hiss. Paedur remained unmoving, staring towards the slight figure that had stepped out into the shadows beneath the archway but who still remained shadowed. "Who are you?" the bard asked calmly.

The figure shrugged, a movement that lifted its shoulders unnaturally high. "A name is something left in the world of Men; in Manach all are known to one another and our Lord, and there is no need of names."

"I am..." Paedur began.

"You, and your companion, are known," the figure continued.

Katani described a circle with both swords, bringing them around until they touched, the metal singing, the sound taken up beneath the archway and magnified, leaving it shivering on the air long after she had sheathed her weapons. "What do we call you, then? What are you?" she demanded, her accent turning the question into a growl.

"You may call me what I am, and I am but a servant."

"A servant?" Paedur said, the question implicit.

"A servant of Mannam." The figure moved towards them with a stiff-legged, unnatural gait. And it was only when it stepped into the light that they saw the wings.

"Bainte," Paedur breathed. "Mannam's winged messengers of death," he explained to Katani, who was still staring curiously at the creature. The bainte was naked and about the size of a child on the threshold of adulthood, thin and gangling, and possessing the characteristics of both sexes. Its skin was completely hairless and milk white, and its large red-rimmed eyes and round open mouth gave it a skull-like appearance. Its arms were thin and straight with no elbow joints and hung loosely by its sides. Beginning just above the shoulder joints were the wings. They were folded now and it was impossible to gauge their size, but they were taller than the bainte and judging from the wedges and knots of muscle, they were incredibly powerful.

"Scrape the dirt from your boots and follow me," the creature commanded, its voice clear and unaccented.

Paedur strode straight across the grill without stopping. The creature hunched and suddenly unfolded one of its wings, and a talon that was as long as the bard's arm and just as thick touched the centre of his chest. "Your boots," the bainte said emotionlessly, "clean them."

"Why?" Paedur demanded, unmoving.

"Because it is the law of this place. Nothing from the Silent Wood may come into the City of the Dead."

"Why?" Paedur persisted.

"Ask Mannam," the bainte said reasonably.

The bard stared at the creature, unsure if it was playing with him but unable to form any decision from its bland wide-eyed expression. He scraped his boots on the grill, knocking off the grit and stones clinging to the soles down into the glutinous water.

Katani joined him on the grill. "Why the ritual?" she asked softly, tapping her boots together, watching the grit tumble into the water below.

With his eyes still on the bainte, he shook his head. "I don't know. I have an idea, though."

The bainte suddenly turned away and headed down the broad statue-lined avenue that led away from the gate. Paedur and Katani hurried after it, looking in wonder at the statues that lined the broad cobbled street. There were hundreds of them, all completely life-like, of men and women from a score of lands and from all ages, on tall plinths which usually bore a single line legend. Some, history had awarded some recognition—kings, priests, leaders, warriors—but in the main they were of unknowns, or at least unknown to the bard's vast lore. There were non-humans scattered amongst them—Star Lorn, Susuru, and Chopts—and some that looked close cousins to the Culai. Paedur attempted to read the script, but the language was strange and even he, for all his learning, couldn't decipher it.

"They're too real to be statues," Katani murmured, looking at one particularly vivid representation of a Katan which was complete even down to the nicks in the scales of the lacquered armour.

"I thought that too, but what need would Mannam have for this type of sorcery?"

"Mannam is a vain creature," Katani reminded him "It might please him to have these beings immobile here—living statues, as it were."

"Living?" Paedur asked, smiling at her use of the word. "But I agree, it is curious."

"Something else we must ask Death," the woman murmured to herself.

The avenue ran arrow-straight for a thousand paces and then it dipped gently down into a huge hollow and opened out, and here the first buildings began.

"It looks like any other city," Katani said softly, looking from side to side, her left hand still resting on the cloth-wrapped hilt of her sword.

"Except for the people," Paedur murmured.

"What people?"

The bard glanced at her and smiled enigmatically. There were no people.

"Did you ever visit Bannoche?" she remarked a little later, when they had walked deeper into the city and the buildings had become taller.

Paedur shook his head. "In my time it had long vanished, the creeping sands having finally claimed it."

"That was already happening in my day," Katani said softly. "And this place reminds me of it."

"Because it is so empty?"

Surprisingly the warrior shook her head. "Bannoche was already called the City of Ghosts in my time; it was dead during the day, but at night it came alive with the shades of a score of centuries, all going about their tasks as if they were still in the World of Men."

"There is no night here," Paedur said reasonably, but aware of what Katani was suggesting, recalling what he knew of the legends of the City of Ghosts. "I wonder if the houses are really empty?" he murmured.

"Why don't you look?"

"No look! No stray from the path!" The bainte's words were clipped and harsh, and although it didn't turn around, its round head swivelled through a complete half-circle to stare back at them.

"Extraordinary hearing," Paedur remarked with a grin. He turned back to Katani. "Tell me about Bannoche. I think I would have liked to visit it."

"My experience of the place is limited," she said, "and from what I now know, I am inclined to believe that it may be an outpost of Mannam's kingdom, a place where the fabrics of the various Planes of Existence meet."

"What were you doing there?"

Katani smiled, remembering. "We were chasing bandits, three of my sisters and I, and their trail led to the City of Ghosts. Of course, we had heard rumours about the city, but we thought them nothing more than the usual legends that always grow up around deserted villages or cities, and we chose to ignore them. What we didn't know then was that Bannoche was used as a bandit camp during the day, although they always left as the sun was setting and spent the night in a series of fortified caves close to the walls. And so we four rode unsuspecting into the city and promptly found ourselves in the midst of a bandit camp. We contemplated a struggle, but they had archers and crossbow-men and we knew it would only be suicide, so we surrendered."

"I thought the Katan warriors never surrendered," Paedur said.

"Being a warrior means not only acknowledging victory but accepting defeat," Katani quoted.

"Fand," Paedur said, "the foundress of the Katan Sisterhood."

"How do you know that?" she asked, surprised.

"I am familiar with her monumental work on the Path of the Warrior. Surprisingly, it is required reading for those studying to be a bard, and I know some of the warrior schools still use it as a textbook. But I interrupted you; please continue."

"There's little enough to tell. The bandits captured us and abused us somewhat, in the way of such creatures, although they didn't manage to take our virginity, which was their aim. They stopped because night was drawing on and their fear of the place was far greater than their lust. They promptly gathered up their belongings and rode out of the city to huddle in their caves like beasts. But they left us behind," she said slowly, her voice falling to a whisper. Her eyes closed briefly, and when they opened again, they were clear, the grief and pain hidden once again. "I am dead now, bard, dead these many years, and I am familiar enough with the ways of the Silent Wood and its occupants to know that we have little interest in the living, and even less interest in interfering with them. Oh, there are some, of course, who spend more time in the World of Men than is proper, and their motives may not always be good, but in the main, fear is their only weapon. However, at that time I didn't know that, and you can imagine how terrifying it was for the four of us to be suddenly confronted with the shades of the dead.

"We had been tied to a pillar in the centre of a square, and before our eyes the city slowly came alive—if that is the right word—and a market was set up around us. In the early twilight the shades were tenuous and from Bannoche's recent past, but as the night drew on we found ourselves able to distinguish the different ages and cultures of the city, until towards dawn we were looking at the earliest age of Bannoche.

"It would have been bad enough if the dead had merely walked around us, but some seemed to be able to see us, and examined us curiously like specimens in a glass phial." She shrugged. "Again, I understand that now, but at the time..."

"It must have been terrifying," Paedur said absently, not looking at her, watching the buildings on either side. He had the impression that they were not as empty as they seemed.

"It was," she whispered.

"It says much for you that you survived with your sanity intact," Paedur continued.

"We retreated into the lore of our Order, repeating the lessons again and again, meditating on Fand's teachings."

"And the bandits?"

"They never returned to Bannoche," Katani smiled. "They were ambushed by a party of our sisters as they rode back towards the city the following morning. None of them survived, especially when they admitted what they had done to the four of us..."

Paedur suddenly reached over and touched her arm. He said nothing but his eyes moved towards an open doorway ahead of them. Katani continued to chatter, but nodded almost imperceptibly, following his gaze. She nodded briefly again; she too had seen the movement in the darkened doorway.

The bainte had now led them into what was obviously a fairly prosperous part of the city. The buildings were tall and imposing, and temples, fine houses, merchants' stores and brothels lined both sides of the streets, the frescoes above each doorway proclaiming the trade or occupation. The street itself narrowed and then narrowed again, until it was little more than a broad alleyway, and the

only thing that distinguished it from a street in any city or town in the
World of Men was the absence of awnings or stalls lining the walls.
And people.

Paedur started suddenly, something of his old awareness making him turn, but there was nothing behind him.

"You need not fear, bard," the bainte said abruptly, without
turning around. "Nothing will harm you here in the Drear God's
Kingdom."

"Oh, I know that," Paedur said with a grim smile. "I was merely
wondering where the inhabitants of this city were."

"Dead," the bainte remarked.

Mannam's palace was set on a low knoll in the middle of an
artificial lake in the centre of the city. The only access to it was by
a single drawbridge, which was raised. The palace itself was
long and low and sprawling, primitive and ugly in appearance—
but on second glance, artificially so. Its style was blocky and
massive, in the manner of the Culai builders, but unlike their
work, the huge square stones had been polished to a mirror brightness and some had been gilded. The windows, which were set
high into the wall just beneath the sloping, polished roof, were
surprisingly barred and the portcullis was down across the low
double gates.

A double line of trees ran around the edge of the island—the
first sign of vegetation the bard had seen since he had crossed into
the Silent Wood. But when he looked closely at the trees, he realised
that they were artificial; they had been cast from stone and then
painted in superbly realistic colours.

The bainte walked to the edge of the black waters of the lake
and hunched over. It then raised its two huge wings and brought
them together in a thunderous clap that rolled across the water, setting its blood-black surface vibrating. There was movement on the
walls and more bainte appeared, and then slowly and ponderously
the portcullis was lifted and a single span of wood was pushed
across the lake, barely a hand-breadth above the surface of the water. It thumped onto the land and without hesitation the bainte
walked out onto it and then its head described its unnatural half
turn. "The wood will only support one at a time." It turned back
and continued across the bridge.

"This...this is all wrong," Paedur whispered. "Something is amiss."

"You are wondering about the bars on the windows," Katani said.

Paedur nodded. "Aye, and the other precautions. Hardly the signs of a secure monarch."

"But surely nothing can threaten Death?" the warrior asked.

"Nothing," Paedur said slowly, "unless..."

"Unless?"

"Since you walked the World of Men, a new religion has grown up. It is a false belief, ruled by false, base gods with none of the qualities of godhood and all the vices of mankind. They constantly war with the Gods of the Old Faith, attempting to overthrow them, warring for control of all the Planes of Existence. There are times when the Gods of the Old Faith triumph, but the New Religion daily grows in strength and numbers and its gods grow arrogant. I wonder if the war has gone against the Old Faith?"

"Is that possible?"

"Mannam is afraid. He protects himself behind water, behind bars, in a closed city. Obviously he fears."

"But what would frighten Death?" Katani wondered.

"That only thing that could threaten Death is death itself!"

6
The King of the Outlands

"Any man with an army at his back can call himself king, but only the fool thinks he can rule."

Owen the Weapon Master

The dawn sunlight was lancing low across the plain when the first rider appeared on the crest of the rise, his shadow etched long and sharp onto the stony ground. He was followed, a moment later, by two more riders, but these were taller, broader men, riding huge southern shire-mounts, their size dwarfing the first rider between them.

"An emissary with his guards," Keshian said, squinting against the glare of the early morning sunlight.

"And the guards are for show," Owen murmured.

"Are they Gallowglas?" Prince Kutor asked, shading his eyes and staring at the guards. "A handsome addition to any army," he murmured.

The Weapon Master passed Kutor a wooden seeing-tube. "They are difficult to control, and it is foolishness bringing two or more together; when they are not fighting amongst themselves, they are plotting to overthrow their employer."

Kutor turned the wooden tube slightly, attempting to sharpen up the image, but the glass had been poorly blown and the image of the warriors and the emissary remained indistinct and fuzzy. "Perhaps if we were to offer to employ them," he suggested.

"With what?" Keshian snapped, fear sharpening his voice. "We have no coin and no comforts here, and even if we had, I'm not sure I or the men would want these flesh-eaters amongst us."

The two Gallowglas stopped and allowed the smaller, human rider to continue forward a score of paces. The man reined in his mount and plunged the spear with the black truce-ribbon tied to it into the ground. Then he threw back his head, contemptuously scanning the battlements.

"I am Diarmon, emissary of King Cormac, and I ride under a flag of truce." The man's voice was strong, well-modulated, and obviously cultured. He waited a few moments, and then added, "Do I speak to stones?"

"You do not speak to stones." Kutor climbed up and stood astride two of the merlons with his hands on his hips. "I am Kutor, a prince of the blood, half-brother to the Emperor. And I know of no King Cormac in the rolls of nobility."

The messenger grinned, revealing a smile that was all the more unusual for being perfect, and completely insincere. "I do not recall reading the name of Prince Kutor there either."

"Do not allow him to anger you," Owen snapped.

"State your business."

"My master, King Cormac, wishes to deal with you."

"I have no business with your master."

"But you have taken one of his castles. Tribute must be paid, a debt must be discharged." The messenger's face was a study in surprised innocence.

"Don't argue with him," Owen advised, his eyes on the two warriors sitting grim and impassive on their mounts behind the messenger, seemingly unconcerned with the proceedings.

"I have incurred no debt and there will be no tribute, no dealings," Kutor said flatly and climbed down from the merlons.

"My master commands a legion," Diarmon said proudly to the now-invisible figure, "and the Gallowglas honour us with their presence. Your paltry force cannot stand against us. Now, my master is a reasonable man and so he offers you the option of tribute rather than death." He stopped. No movements were visible on the battlements and he glanced around at his guard in frustration. They looked at him as if he were an animal, beneath contempt. "Then you will all die," he screamed to the stone walls and wheeled his mount round and galloped away, followed at a more leisurely pace by the warriors.

Tien tZo returned a little after noon, when the shadows were beginning to stretch again. Kutor, with Keshian and Owen, was in the process of poring over a hugely intricate chart they had discovered in a small room off one of the main corridors. The room had many shelves and the shelves had been lined with books and scrolls.

And while all of these turned out to be nothing more than the daily fortress history as recorded by a succession of bards, pinned to one wall had been a plan of the fortress itself, laid out floor by floor and indicating in faded coloured inks the various hidden entrances, including one which ran for almost three thousand paces and came out on the far side of the mountain.

"Well, at least we cannot be trapped," Keshian was saying when Tien tZo came into the room. He stopped when he noticed the Shemmat.

The three men looked at the small warrior expectantly. "Cormac is Gallowglas," he said simply.

Owen nodded. "I suspected as much. There was no other way for him to control so many Gallowglas."

Tien tZo sat in one of the high-backed wooden chairs and slowly and carefully made his report. "I followed the emissary to Cormac's camp, which lies in a guarded valley less than half a morning's ride from here. There is a town, but it has now been turned into an armed camp and fortifications are being built. I saw Cormac's legion, and they are conscripts to a man, with little training and in absolute fear of the Gallowglas. I saw a man being flogged, and there was a body on a gallows beside the main gate." The small man sipped the proffered wine, his sharp green eyes moving from face to face. "The Gallowglas are everywhere and they treat the legion soldiers badly. Free the legion from the Gallowglas and you will have recruits," he added shrewdly.

"And Cormac?" Keshian asked eagerly.

"I was coming to him. He is a big man, bigger than the Gallowglas riders who came with the emissary. There is much of the Chopt in him; he is beast-like and brutal. When I saw him he was devouring a lump of meat that looked suspiciously like a human arm."

Kutor looked at Owen. "I though you said the Gallowglas only ate human flesh on special ceremonial occasions."

"Obviously this Cormac is not an ordinary Gallowglas—if there is such a creature as an ordinary Gallowglas," the Weapon Master added wryly. He turned back to Tien tZo. "You say the legion fears the warriors."

"They are terrified."

"Then why do they not rise up and attack these creatures?" Kutor demanded. "Surely a thousand men are more than a match for... for how many Gallowglas?" he asked Tien tZo.

"It was impossible to estimate their numbers, but I counted two decades of shire-mounts."

Keshian sat forward. "I think you'll find the Gallowglas are holding hostages," he said quietly. "When I was a mercenary in Nasgociba, fifty of us once held a city of three thousand by simply taking as hostages the women and children of the likely trouble-makers."

Tien tZo bowed slightly. "I saw few women and equally few children."

Owen stood up suddenly. "We need a map of this district," he announced, "there may be one in the library."

"You have a plan?" Prince Kutor asked hopefully.

"Merely an idea."

There was no moon and the sky was obscured with thick, roiling clouds that had blown up just as the light was beginning to fade. Thunder boomed in the distance and there was the ghostly promise of lightning on the horizon.

Beneath the overhang of rock the fortress was in total darkness and, on Keshian's orders, no lights or fires had been lit in those rooms which had a window opening out onto the rocky plain. Almost certainly the fortress was under observation, and while it was possible for the guards on the battlements to just about make out the vague shapes of larger boulders and stones on the plain, it was hoped that any watchers would find it extremely difficult to distinguish the fortress from the rock face.

In the blackness a small arched side gate opened on thickly oiled hinges and ten men crept out. Keshian watched them melt into the plain and become invisible although they were no more than a handful of paces in front of him. The last one stopped briefly beside him. "We will be back," Tien promised, and then moved on.

"I hope so," Keshian murmured, locking the door and heading up the stairs for the battlements. It promised to be a long night.

Owen's idea had resolved into what Keshian had declared to be absolute folly: ten men, all volunteers, would be chosen to infiltrate Cormac's camp and kill as many of the Gallowglas as possible. If they could kill Cormac, then so much the better, but no one seriously expected to slay the king on their first raid; no one except Owen, that was.

There was no shortage of volunteers, and both Kutor and Keshian eventually ended up picking eight of the fiercest of their brigands. Tien tZo had then explained the mission to them and detailed the risks involved, and had given them the opportunity of stepping down with honour. Perhaps unsurprisingly, none of the men stepped down. Their clothing had been blackened with soot and their skins likewise covered in a mixture of soot and grease; even the blades of their weapons had been blackened with a mixture of candlewax and soot.

Shortly before the moment of departure, Kutor made his way to the Weapon Master's room. The door was locked and he had to knock before Tien finally opened it. The Shemmat smiled apologetically. "Habit," he said.

Owen was putting the finishing touches to the blacking on his sword; he was already completely black himself.

"You look like a shadow," Kutor said nervously.

"That is the idea."

Kutor nodded and moved around the room, stopping briefly at the door to watch Tien blackening his skin in the small side-room.

"What's wrong?" Owen asked suddenly.

"I want you to call off this mission," Kutor said, turning to face him.

"Why?"

"You are the only one amongst us with the knowledge and experience to raise and train a fighting army. Without you, we have nothing; we are nothing but a band of outlaws."

"We don't stand a chance against the Gallowglas on their own," Owen stated flatly, "never mind the legion forces. But if we should slay some of these 'invincible warriors' then we gain a twofold advantage: we reduce the numbers of the warriors and we demoralise the legion. There is also the added possibility that the legion will realise that they can throw off the shackle of the Gallowglas."

"And assume Keshian is correct and they have captives. They will do nothing while their wives or children are held as surety for their conduct," Kutor protested.

"Well, we'll have to see if we can do something about that, too."

"And if you are killed...?"

"I'll try not to be," Owen said wryly.

Against the rocky plain, the ten men were invisible. Owen led them, while Tien tZo ranged ahead to deal with any sentries. The Weapon Master was only too aware of the risk he was taking. Should they be captured, Prince Kutor's dream died with them. The eight men with him represented the best that Kutor had to offer, and his own and Tien's experience was invaluable to the Renegade's cause. However, it was not in Owen's nature even to consider defeat...

Hesht dug the heels of both palms into his eyes, watching the coloured lights explode against his eyelids, and yawned hugely. In his opinion, there was nothing more useless or soul-destroying than sentry duty. Who in their right mind would even consider attacking one Gallowglas, never mind two decades of the animals?

He never even saw the figure that rose up out of the ground and noiselessly opened his throat...

Dyfa raised the wooden tube to his eye and looked out across the plain, smiling a little self-consciously, knowing the device was almost useless during the day and more so on a cloudy night. But when the nights were clear and the Lady Lussa rode the heavens, then the far-seeing tube showed him the wonders of her unearthly chariot. Now all he could see was a vague circle of dull grey on black...with a tiny spot of silver in it.

Dyfa removed the tube from his eye and was wondering vaguely if he had seen a star when the arrow ripped into his eye, piercing his skull, killing him instantly.

The click of the bone dice was barely audible on the outspread cloak and the tiny stub of candle cast just enough light to read the cubes by. "Two horns! Mine!" The voice was young and excited. He had just won the equivalent of a night's pay with one roll of the dice.

"We're only starting," the second voice replied. He was older, more mature, and not unduly worried about losing; he had two loaded dice in the top of his boot and in this light he had no doubts but that he could substitute them when the young recruit grew greedy.

"Whose turn?" the youngster asked.

"Mine!" a third voice hissed, twin hand-axes whistling in the night air, striking flesh...

When Owen and the rest of the group joined Tien tZo moments later they found him carefully positioning the two dead men in such a way that to the casual observer they would seem to be still alert and on duty.

"How many?" the Weapon Master asked softly.

"Four."

"I thought there might be more," Owen remarked.

"I was expecting less. These are arrogant people with nothing to fear," Tien tZo said. "They have the Gallowglas."

There was a low ridge ahead of them, and while Kutor's eight warriors crouched in the small hollow, Owen and Tien tZo crawled to the lip and looked down. Cormac's camp lay spread out before them but, more importantly, directly below was the corral and, off to one side, a separate corral for the huge shire-mounts.

"Fire or poison?" Tien tZo asked, looking at the mounts. "Fire," Owen said without hesitation. "We'll drive them into the camp. That will create even more confusion."

"When? Now, or..."

"After we kill as many of the Gallowglas as we possibly can," Owen murmured.

"I'll fetch the men," the Shemmat said, moving silently back down the incline, rejoining the waiting men.

From Tien tZo's earlier reconnaissance of the camp they knew, albeit roughly, the placement of the Gallowglas' tents and the king's 'palace,' which was in reality nothing more than a rather crude wooden hut that had been daubed with a yellow paint, and the thatch roof replaced with one of slate and sods of black turf. The plan called for Owen himself to attend to the king, while Tien tZo led the rest in an attack on the tents. The element of surprise was essential, and Owen had ordered no actual contact with the enemy unless it was completely unavoidable. All the men had been issued with hollow tubes and Tien tZo had brewed a foul-smelling black tar-like substance which had been painted onto the overlong darts.

Three of the Gallowglas were standing outside the king's house, heads bent in conversation, when the lone man approached, weaving drunkenly down the main street that was little better than an open sewer. Their large dark eyes immediately fixed on him and, with a mercenary's true instinct, their hands found weapons. The man stopped and peered uncertainly at the three huge creatures, then he lifted a stone crock and swallowed long and hard. And then he wandered over to the three guards. A sword the length of a tall man tapped against his chest, stopping him. Smiling widely, he extended the stone jug. "Drink?" he slurred.

The guard with the sword shifted the ungainly weapon, resting the flat of the blade on his shoulder. He stepped forward and took the jug, sloshing it around, breathing in the fumes of raw rofion.

The drunken man swayed on his feet and then sank to his knees in the muck, hiccuping loudly.

The Gallowglas grinned broadly, showing his yellowed, pointed teeth, and then he threw back his head and tilted the jar back, noisily swallowing the fiery liquor...only to end up gagging on his own blood. He reached for his throat, aware of the chill and the bitter taste and then the pain. He touched the bone handle of the knife embedded in his throat and died as he attempted to pull it out. Owen's second knife took the second guard through the eye as he ambled forward to see what was amiss, and he had another knife in his hand and his arm back ready to throw when the third guard went down without a sound. He darted forward and rolled the man over; in the little light that came seeping through the ill-fitting door the Weapon Master saw the tufted dart that protruded from the man's jugular. He raised his hand to the shadows, silently acknowledging Tien tZo's handiwork. He eased the door open, calling on the Gods of the Pantheon that it wouldn't creak, and as he made his way through the palace, Owen wondered how his men were faring...

The Gallowglas were dying.

Two had been slain in their tents as they slept, the poison darts ensuring that they would never wake again. Another had died as he stood by the cesspit relieving himself; he had toppled forwards into the filth and had been immediately swallowed up by the seething muck. Two of the foul creatures had been taking their pleasure together when the darts had struck, joining them together in the final ultimate union. One of the Gallowglas had been in the process of slowly and methodically whipping a man who had been bound to the frame of a door. The man's back was now merely raw flesh and it was obvious that the Gallowglas had been at his work for some time; he had stripped to the waist, exposing his corded, muscled back, covered with a bristling reddish-black hair. Every now and then he stopped and stretched out, rubbing his coarse hands on the man's raw flesh and then licking his fingers with great enjoyment. He drew back his arm for another swing with the metal-tipped whip, and then he froze, feeling the insect nick on his broad bare back. There was a second and then a third sting and the huge mercenary turned—and there was another pinprick in the centre of his chest. He looked down to find a long feathered sliver of wood protruding from his flesh, and as he opened his mouth to cry out, he died.

Owen padded noiselessly down the length of the wooden corridor, his short sword in his left hand, held reversed, the blade flat against his sleeve, a throwing knife in his right hand. The hut—he could never think of it as a palace—was silent, unusually so, and it was only when he cracked open one of the doors that lined the corridor that he discovered that the floors, walls and even the ceilings had been covered with scores of rugs and carpets, which completely sealed the room and deadened all sound.

He stopped at the juncture of another corridor and, pressed flat against the warm wood, risked a quick peek around the corner. He spotted the two guards standing outside one of the doors—Cormac's room, or was it? He knew of several kings who posted guards outside empty or trapped rooms, while they themselves slept securely in small, unguarded bedchambers. He smiled tiredly. He had been in cities too long—here he was up against a primitive, barbarian Gallowglas tribesman, an arrogant braggart, unsuspecting and therefore vulnerable.

Owen pulled a blowpipe from his belt and slipped two darts out from the pouch sewn onto his sleeve. It was going to be a difficult shot; both guards would have to be taken out almost simultaneously. The furthest guard first, then—while the guard nearest to him was hopefully looking at his companion as he crumpled to the ground, Owen would be able to dart him. He forced a dart into the tube, took a deep breath and blew!

And missed.

The Gallowglas looked dumbly at the feathered sliver of sharpened wood that protruded from the door-frame beside his face. He had been drinking heavily earlier that evening and his reactions were slow. He opened his mouth to say something when a second dart took him through the mouth, and he died with a look of absolute amazement frozen onto his face.

The second guard was reaching for his huge sword when the thrown knife ripped out his throat. He reeled backwards, crashing against the door, partially tearing it off its leathern hinges. There was an almost animal-like roar in the darkened room and Owen saw a huge, pale shape moving in the darkness. He quickly spat two of the poisoned darts into the room, hoping for a lucky hit and then turned and ran...

Tien tZo waited until the eighth man had passed him and then he sank back into the shadows to await Owen. He reached into his pouch and touched the two remaining balls of Shemmat-fire he had prepared earlier. They were small earthen bottles filled with a mixture of powder and acid that were kept separate by a thin wafer of soft metal; when the acid ate through the metal, it mixed with the powder to produce a brief and fiery explosion. Usually he placed the bottles in puddles of lamp oil, but this night he had to content himself with tossing them onto the tents and into the animals' straw. While he was waiting for the first to explode—and they were unstable and temperamental—he strewed the beaten track with caltrops—spiked balls that lacerated the feet of men and animals alike.

The Weapon Master moved slowly and confidently through the men that were spilling out from the tents, alerted by the sudden commotion from the palace. The huge, bellowing, roaring sound was like that of a bear in heat, Owen mused. And then there were other shouts as the dead Gallowglas were discovered. Somewhere a gong began booming as a general alarm went up.

And then the first tiny bomb exploded. It had been placed under a fold in a tent and even when it burst it went completely unnoticed, even though two men were standing directly in front of it. The intense heat quickly melted through the heavy woollen fabric and it smouldered for a score of heartbeats before the entire side of the tent exploded into flames. And suddenly all across the camp the tents were beginning to burn.

The fires in the corrals terrified the animals, shire-mounts and horses alike, and as the stalls themselves began to burn, hissing sparks and stinging cinders, the animals surged away from them, lunging against the stout palisade, which immediately buckled beneath the weight of the enormous shire-mounts. Free, the animals raced down the track, straight onto the caltrops. Their screams were almost human. Completely maddened now, the crippled beasts thundered through the camp, flattening everything in their path, destroying the tents and the flimsy wooden shelters. Two of the shire-mounts blundered against Cormac's palace and actually managed to knock it from the support poles that lifted it up off the muck. One end of the building crashed to the ground, caving in the roof, leaving a jagged rent that almost split the building in two.

Owen stood back in the shadows and smiled triumphantly at the chaos and destruction. It was good to be working again.

King Cormac lost nearly two hundred of his legionaries that night, as well as fourteen of his Gallowglas mercenaries. Ten of them had been slain by the intruders and four had died beneath the flailing metal-shod hooves of the panicked horses. Of his twenty shire-mounts, all but one had to be slain, and over fifty of the horses had to be butchered also. The town was a shambles: not one building remained standing, everything had been trampled into the dust, and all their food and supplies for the coming Cold Months had been destroyed. But more dangerously, there was now a definite air of mutiny about the men. The Gallowglas had brought down the attack; they were to blame for it. And the men had learned a very valuable lesson: they had been taught that the feared mercenary warriors were not invincible.

Around noon a single rider approached the camp. He was challenged only when he reached the spiked palisade, which the men had worked all morning at re-erecting.

"What do you want?"

"I want to see this self-styled King of the Outlands."

The guard fitted an arrow to his bow. "The king will see no-one today," he called.

"He will see me," the stranger said mildly, sitting easily on his mount, not even looking at the guard, watching the men working on a section of the palisade.

The guard contemplated loosing an arrow into the smug stranger. "Why should he see you?" he asked contemptuously.

The stranger looked up and favoured him with a chilling smile. "Why, because I caused all this!"

7
The Lord of the Dead

*Mannam is the God of the Dead, and his guise is that of a withered and
blasted tree...*

Pantheon of the Old Faith

"You are impudent, bard, and your impudence will have you..."

"Slain?" Paedur suggested, stepping into the room. The bainte
had left them in a corridor of the palace, standing before a tall
golden-wood door that was worked with a design of leafless
branches and twigs. Paedur had touched the knot-like handle with
his hook and the door had swung open, and then the voice had
spoken from within.

As the bard turned to look at the creature, there was a sound of
snapping, crackling branches—a noise the bard had come to recognise
as the sound of Death's laughter. "I think I recall now why you
were chosen." The figure turned away from the low, arched window, a shadow in black, shapeless and menacing. "The Gods of the
Pantheon met in conclave—a rare event, I assure you—and tried to
decide upon a mortal man to carry our battle for us, a Champion.
Some called for bravery, others for intelligence, others for coward-
ice and cunning. I called for stupidity, maintaining that the line between a hero and a fool is very slender indeed." The voice was
sibilant, hissing like the wind through bare branches. "And now here
you are, boldly marching into the very heart of my kingdom, and
that, I think, proves my point."

Mannam glided silently across the room, his cloak of seared
and withered leaves noiseless now, although the bard could remember occasions when it had hissed like a nest of serpents. Katani had
encountered Death on only one previous occasion, and then their
meeting had been brief; she had been but one of many dead that
day. He was taller than the bard, thin, and covered from head to
foot in the long leafed cloak. A deep hood covered his head and the
warrior wasn't sure if she wanted to see what it hid.

In the centre of the room was a large triangular table of a black
and slightly leprous-looking wood, with three chairs around it, one
large and grotesquely ornate, the others simple and plain. Mannam
settled into the largest chair, his cloak rustling now like a leaf fall.
"Sit," he said, extending an arm, although no hand appeared. "Sit,
and tell me what you want."

Paedur glanced at Katani and then he crossed the dun-coloured
marbled floor and sat in one of the chairs. Katani remained standing, taking up a position behind and to his left, her left hand resting
on the hilt of her longsword, the fingers of her right hand touching
the slender throwing dagger that was strapped under her armour.

Paedur rested his hook on the coal-black table and then placed
his hand over it; almost automatically, the index finger began tracing
the runes cut into the metal. "Why do you assume I want something?" he asked, looking directly at the Dark Lord, remembering
the fleeting glimpse he had once had of the creature's face, vaguely
relieved that without his enhanced senses there was no chance that he
would be able to see it again.

Mannam gave what the bard assumed was a sign. "Paedur
Hookhand, do you know how many from the World of Men come
into my kingdom daily?"

The bard shook his head.

"And do you know how many come here willingly?"

Again he shook his head.

The Dark Lord leaned forward. "And do you know how many
of those who come here are alive?"

Paedur smiled.

Mannam hissed. "So, you want something, something which
only I can give, and that means someone dead."

The bard nodded seriously. "I want you to return two people
to me, two who died in the World of Men, but two whom I had
come to love and who had come to love one another. They died in
defence of the Old Faith. Their deaths were untimely," he added.

"No death is ever untimely, no matter how it looks at the time,"
Mannam hissed. His cowled head moved from side to side, and
then he suddenly stopped and looked at the bard. Paedur shivered,
feeling two dead, knowing eyes watching him, the sensation one of
a crawling, prickling insect, and he experienced a sudden moment
of ice-cold dread.

"What you are asking is impossible," Mannam said simply.

"No! You accepted their deaths then. You can refuse them now."

"I cannot."

Paedur brought his hook crashing down on the black table, the metal ringing through the huge room, but the table was unmarked. "You can do it. There is a precedent in the myths and legends of the Nations. The Gods have returned the dead to the World of Men."

"The circumstances were exceptional," Mannam said very slowly.

"These circumstances are exceptional. These people gave their lives for you and your kind. Refuse to help them now and you become nothing more than the Religion's petty godlets, cruel, blustering and powerless."

Wood snapped. In the almost physical silence of the room, Katani eased her sword a finger-length free of its scabbard, ready to move, to bring the long razor-edged blade around in a sweeping decapitating half-circle. By his very precautions, Death had shown himself to be vulnerable.

"You go too far, bard," Mannam hissed.

"They were my friends," Paedur said simply. "I owe it to them. Why won't you help them?"

"I will not..." Mannam began.

"Will not or cannot?" Paedur said coldly.

"You try my patience," Mannam said, and rose in a rustle of autumnal leaves plainly signifying that the audience was at an end.

"What are you afraid of?" the bard suddenly demanded. "Why do you hide in a closed city, behind walls, and bars, and water? What is it the great God of Death fears?"

Mannam turned away and strode rustling across the floor to stand before the window. The shadows danced as Paedur chased after him, but the Dark Lord cast no shadow.

"Tell me," he demanded, reaching out to grip the god's arm. The dry, faintly musty air of the room was suddenly charged with a sharp, acrid, faintly metallic odour. A mite of blue-white fire sparked from beneath Mannam's cowl and raced along the bard's hook, sizzling up his arm, twisting him around in soundless agony and flinging him across the room

"Never touch me, mortal," Mannam crackled.

Katani's swords hissed as she slid them free of their oiled scabbards. She brought both swords around and touched them gently together and assumed a fighting stance.

Mannam's left arm began to rise; a bony, stick-like finger and then a gnarled, knotted tree stump of a hand appeared. The finger pointed...

"No!"

Paedur pushed himself into a sitting position, his left arm pressed tightly against his pounding ribs. "No...no more. You forget we are on your side, god," he spat.

The Dark Lord turned slowly. "I do not know what side you are on, bard."

"I fought for you," Paedur said, coming to his feet, feeling the sting as he breathed in, knowing he had cracked one or more ribs. "Surely that entitles me to some trust?"

The silence between the two began to lengthen uncomfortably, but neither seemed inclined to break it. Finally, Katani brought both swords around in a complete circle and slid them home into their sheaths, the collars clicking solidly. The sound broke the tableau.

"I will tell you," Mannam said, and then immediately turned away and rustled across the floor towards a staircase.

Katani stretched out her hand and the bard grasped it. She hauled him to his feet with surprising ease, her eyes on the Dark Lord's retreating back. She turned back to Paedur, her eyes questioning. He shrugged and shook his head slightly; there was little they could do but follow him.

The Dark Lord led them up a steep, winding staircase that quickly had the bard gasping as his cracked and bruised ribs throbbed. After a score or more steps, what vestiges of light that had been seeping up the stairs from the long room disappeared and they were ascending in complete darkness. Once again Paedur was reminded of what he had lost when he had entered the Silent Wood. In the World of Men, his enhanced senses allowed him to see clearly in the dark; now he was like an ordinary man, sweating with pain and exertion and yet shivering with fear as he felt the ever-growing distance between himself and the floor far below, and no rail to keep him from plummeting down into the room below. It had been a long time since he had feared heights.

He stumbled once, clattering onto the worn stone steps. In the darkness Katani reached for him, touching his cloak, and then he felt her iron-hard fingers dig deep into the muscles of his arm, hauling him up. "I will carry you," she said seriously.

But the bard shook his head stubbornly. "No, no. I can manage," he gasped weakly, resisting the urge to vomit.

"Is it much further?" Katani demanded into the darkness ahead of them. "Where are you taking us?"

"To the tower," Mannam said shortly, his voice sounding surprisingly close.

Katani was half-carrying Paedur by the time they reached the top of the seemingly interminable staircase. Like the Dark Lord, the climb had no ill-effects on her in any way, but the bard was close to collapse. He cried out in pain as he stepped through a tall arched doorway and onto the roof of the tower. After the absolute darkness, the grey diffused twilight of the Silent Wood was painfully blinding and he sank to his knees and buried his head in his cloak, allowing his sensitive eyes to adjust. When he could see again, he found that Mannam had led them out onto a broad flat roof that overlooked his palace, the lake, and the town beyond. In the distance they could see the wall that surrounded the city, and beyond that the greyness of the Silent Wood, and the snaking black line of the Naman as it wound its way through the heart of the Land of the Dead.

"This is the Tower of Time," Mannam said suddenly, startling them, walking over to an ancient sundial and resting his stick-like hands on it.

Paedur limped over to the stone plinth and looked at the obviously Culai-wrought relic. It was marred by a jagged gash that split it in two. He traced the crack with the point of his hook. "I thought the sun never shone on the Silent Wood," he whispered.

"It doesn't."

Paedur touched the dial again and looked quizzically at the Dark Lord.

"There is no time in the Land of the Dead," Mannam said with one of his branch-snapping laughs.

"Why is the dial here, then?"

The edge of Mannam's cloak brushed across the crack. "It shows that here even Time is dead."

"Why have you brought us here?" Paedur was suddenly weary of the god's strange humour.

"Here we are assured that there are no listening ears," Mannam said. He turned and looked quickly at Katani. "And can you trust this warrior-maid?"

"I think I can. I think I already have."

"Can you trust her with your life, your soul?"

"There is no life in this place and the Pantheon holds my soul." He nodded. "I trust her."

Mannam nodded reluctantly. "On your head be it then, bard. You must know that there is something greater than the gods themselves," he said softly, almost to himself, the words whispered like rain on leaves, "and that is Fate. Even the gods must bow to their Fate. Perhaps Fate has brought you here," he said with sudden animation. "Yes, yes. Fate." He touched the blocky script of the Culai that was set into the outer ring of the sundial and the runes glowed briefly. "You asked what I feared, bard." He turned to look at Paedur and the man had the fleeting glimpse of a face beneath the cowl—a human face—but it was immediately replaced by the sickening image of the wormy skull. "I fear death, bard," he hissed.

"You are Death," Paedur said slowly.

"I am of the Old Faith. The Deathgod of the New Religion threatens me."

"Libellius? How?" Paedur demanded incredulously. "And here in your own kingdom? Surely it is not possible."

"What does Libellius promise to his followers in the World of Men?" Mannam asked harshly.

"A life after death."

"And what is my promise?"

"Just death."

"So you see that his promise is more attractive than mine. The people flock to him and why? Why? Because he refuses to accept the death of some of his followers—returns them to life, if you will. Rumours and stories of these miracles spread, and grow, and so do his followers, and as their numbers increase, so too does his power, and so mine weakens."

Paedur nodded. "Aye, I can appreciate that, and I will see what I can do about it when I return to the World of Men. But I still cannot see how this godlet can possibly threaten you in your own kingdom."

"Because he has had help."

Katani moved forward. "Help? What sort of help?"

"One of my captains made a pact with Libellius, and this man has been operating on his behalf within my domain."

"Someone close to you?" Paedur asked.

Mannam turned away and stared out over the city. "Close to me," he agreed reluctantly.

"Who?" Katani asked, and the bard turned to look at her, catching the undercurrent of excitement in her voice.

"A creature called Churon. In the World of Men he was called the..."

"Onelord," Katani hissed triumphantly.

Paedur settled himself against the cracked and useless sundial and looked at the tall, stooped figure of Death standing against the twilight sky. "I think you should tell us," he said simply.

"He came to me when he died, as all men do, but unlike some, he was not confused, nor was he troubled, nor fearful that he was now dead and in the Silent Wood. My bainte brought his essence here, and when he had taken the shape of man again, he was as a lord, tall and proud and vain, unbowed by his bloody demise.

"I watched him as he woke from the Sleep of the Dead. He woke not as some men, slowly and brokenly, but came alert and awake as if he had but closed his eyes a moment before. When he come to his feet, he checked his weapons and then touched his armour where he had taken his mortal wound, but the armour was whole again, and then he ran his gauntleted hands through his blond hair, brushing it away from his forehead, and then he threw back his head and laughed.

"And in the Land of the Dead, laughter is a strange and frightening thing.

"My bainte appeared as they always do with the new-dead, and he looked on them, not as some men do, as Duaite—as demons— but rather curiously, much as you looked on them earlier, bard, merely as strange creatures. And then he spoke to them. "Tell your master Churon the Onelord is here; he is expecting me."

"So came Churon to my kingdom.

"Death did not bother him; he had no regrets for the life he had left behind, no sadness at leaving his new bride, nor his children by his previous marriages, nor the huge treasure he had amassed in his lifetime.

"And let me say this to you now. Every man and woman who has ever lived in the World of Men and worshipped the Old Faith has, with few—very few—exceptions, passed through my domain. Emperors and kings, warriors, princes, murderers, bandits, thieves, artists, peasants—an endless list—they have all come here. But none of them ever interested me. Some I took, yes, keeping them here, but only as a collector amasses varieties of types to complete his collection, but Churon...ahhh, the Onelord was different.

"And now I must tell you something which no mortal has ever known, bard, and I tell you this so that your understanding of my tale will be clearer, but you must never repeat it. You see, bard, the task of Death is unlike the tasks of the other Gods of the Pantheon. From the earliest time, when the gods first ascended to their position as gods or godlets, spirits or sprites, they have remained unchanged to this day. But this is not true of the post of Death. The Lord of the Dead is set apart. Unlike the others, he alone is not dealing with the living, be they human or animal, vegetable or mineral or spirit; he alone deals with the dead, those who have left the World of Men, and are now but dust and rotting flesh and bone.

"And had I a soul, I would say it was soul-destroying. You smile, bard, but you lack understanding. It takes a special man, someone cold and unhuman, someone more than a little mad, to hold this post. Someone like you, Paedur Hookhand.

"I am the third to hold this post. I do not know where my predecessors went. The last merely cursed me with this shape and walked out of the Silent Wood, and even the gods do not know where he went.

"And now I am weary, so weary. I know how he must have felt. So when I saw Churon, saw him as a man apart, a special man, cold and unhuman and more than a little mad, I knew he would be my successor.

"So I took him and made him a captain in my army—and you have not seen my army, but it is huge—and I ensured that he wanted for nothing. He accepted it all—indeed, he almost expected it as a right. He was a wealthier, mightier, more powerful man here in the Silent Wood than he ever was in the World of Men.

"But he was greedy.

"As much as he had, he wanted more. He wanted it all. He wanted to rule the Silent Wood, to command the Host of the Dead. He wanted to be a god. He could have had it all with my blessing, but perhaps he did not believe me when I told him that it could be his, perhaps he was just not prepared to wait.

"He must have learned of the New Religion from one of the dead. I don't know, but he always questioned those newly come to this place. Nor do I know how he made contact with Libellius, except that he often disappeared for long stretches, 'riding the marches,' he would say on his return. But I suspect—in fact, I know now—that he was meeting with Libellius in one of the Shadowlands which border my kingdom.

"About this time too my power began to weaken, not dramatically so, not by much, and perhaps not even enough for me to notice. But then a plague swept through one of the southern towns in the World of Men. They are a common enough occurrence there and kill perhaps three-quarters of the population, but this time less than half arrived here. Libellius had claimed the rest. I took it as a measure of his growing power.

"And so it went on, with Libellius claiming more and more of the dead and in turn my power becoming weaker and weaker. And then finally, I was attacked. Attacked, here in the Silent Wood, my own domain!

"Very little can harm me, you know that, but because of the corporeal form I was cursed with, fire is one of the few things which can.

"I do not sleep…but you know that, bard. I think it has been a long time since the sleep of Man claimed you, and so it is with the gods. There is no night in this place, but on a whim I sometimes allow a darkness to fall over the land; the reactions of my subjects always afford me some innocent amusement. But as I walked the battlements, listening to the howling of the dead and the wailing of the damned—for their voices are always clearer at night—I saw something that had no right to exist in this place. A light, a star, a meteor…a fire!

"It lay out beyond the farthest reaches of the Naman in the Mire, which is a place not rightly of my kingdom nor truly of one of the myriad Worlds of Men, but it partakes something of each.

It is not a Shadowland, because a Shadowland is a separate place, something apart, while the Mire is of two or more worlds and exists completely in all of them. What I was looking at was a fire, a huge blazing conflagration, sparks spiralling like stars to the starless heavens, and the stench of smoke was as foul to me as that of offal is to you.

"And then the arrow came. It was more than an arrow; it was a spear, a huge blazing spear, streaking through the night sky like a thunderbolt. It screamed across the Mire and over the Naman and sped towards me...

"I was frozen, shocked, amazed, aye, and terrified if the truth were known. I watched it coming and there was nothing I could do. But it was low and shattered against the wall below me, exploding in a shower of metal and wood, pitch and sparks. I felt the cinders sting, and I realised then that the unthinkable was happening. Someone—or something—was attempting to destroy me, to destroy Death.

"There was a second spear of fire, and then a third, but my attackers had lost the advantage of surprise and those I deflected easily enough, throwing up a shield of power over the city. There have been three other attacks, and there was a recent attempt when a creature from the Silent Wood calmly walked into the palace and attempted to set fire to my cloak. Hence my precautions.

"And Churon? Churon disappeared after the first attack. I knew it was him and he in turn knew I would be aware of his treachery. But I think he momentarily forgot that I am a god and although I may not always be aware of what is happening in my kingdom, I am capable of finding out, even though it happened in time past.

"So Churon betrayed me. The plan was simple: he was to slay me and take my place as Lord of the Dead, and then he would lead an army of the dead back into the World of Men! Aye, Churon wished to be Onelord again, but lord not only of the World of Men but of the Silent Wood also, and who knows—for even the gods know not the future—perhaps he would even scale the Broken Mountain and attack C'lte, one of the Gods of Life, in his kingdom.

"And he must be stopped!

"Stop him for me, bard, and in return you will have what you came for, in as much as I can grant it to you. You must become the Champion of the Faith again, and you must stop the Onelord before it is too late, for this world and for yours!"

8
The Blood Price

"Always believe you can win, never doubt it in your own mind. If you believe strongly enough, you have already won."

Owen, the Weapon Master

"YOU!" King Cormac leaned over the edge of the palisade fence and glared at the man who had remained still and unperturbed on his coal-black gelding. "You caused all this? You attacked my palace, killed my men, crippled my animals?" He was almost incoherent with rage. The huge head disappeared and then the double gates were thrown back and the giant strode out, the long-spiked battle-hammer in his hands looking like nothing more than a child's toy. Cormac was a huge creature, his face level with Owen's—and he was still mounted—and he was broad in proportion. He was naked except for a long, blood-stained leather apron; he had been slaying the crippled horses and there was blood on his arms and across his furred belly. Matted, filthy, flame-red hair framed a flat, broad face which was more beast-like than human and his lips were drawn back exposing his cruelly pointed teeth.

He stopped in the shadow of the gates and looked at the mounted warrior, his small dark eyes assessing him, his mount and weapons. "You did all that?" he suddenly bellowed and ran towards the seated man.

"Stop!" A crossbow had appeared in the warrior's hand and a hollow-headed bolt screamed through the air to embed itself in the wooden haft of Cormac's battle-hammer. "No farther," the warrior warned.

The king reluctantly stopped. "I'll have the head off your shoulders while you're reloading that toy."

"Move towards me and my companion in the trees behind me will put an arrow through your head."

"And I am supposed to believe that you have more men in the trees?" Cormac sneered.

"Believe what you want," the rider said dismissively.

But to punctuate his reply a broad headed hunting arrow whistled out of the bushes and hammered into the soft earth between Cormac's feet. The king didn't even flinch, nor did he take his eyes off the rider. "Who are you?" he snarled.

"I am Owen, a Weapon Master."

"I don't know you."

"Your emissary visited my employer yesterday."

"Your employer?" The king frowned. "Your employer? The Renegade, Kutor?"

Owen nodded. "The same."

"And so you killed, destroyed, maimed, and mutilated because of my request for rent on the fort your employer stole from me!" From Cormac's tone, it was obvious that he thought himself to be dealing with a madman.

"No one has ownership of the Culai fortresses."

"This is my land," Cormac snapped.

"This is the Emperor's land—my employer's half-brother, you'll remember."

"This is my land by right of conquest."

"And you conquered it from farmers and herders?" Owen sneered.

"Push me and I'll kill you," Cormac warned.

"Threaten me again and I will come back and finish the job I started last night."

Cormac ran his fingers through his flame-red hair, unable to believe the audacity of the man. "Do you know how many of my men you slew last night? Do you know how many animals had to be slaughtered because of you?" Recognising that the questions were rhetorical, Owen remained silent. "There is a blood debt between us, Weapon Master, and this must be cleared."

"That is why I am here," Owen said mildly.

Startled, Cormac said, "You are familiar with the Gallowglas custom. You must pay coin or blood."

"We will pay blood."

"Single or multiple combat?" Cormac demanded eagerly, eyes flashing.

"Single."

"Weapons?"

"Of choice, with the exclusion of spears, bows or slings."

"Agreed." Cormac rubbed his hands together briskly. "And the stakes?"

"What remains of your legion!"

The king looked at him as if he hadn't heard him correctly.

"Your legion," Owen insisted.

"And what will you wager?" Cormac asked eventually.

"You can have Prince Kutor and what remains of his rebel band. The reward on them is high."

The king nodded slowly. "Your champion against mine?" he asked, his small eyes narrowing, calculating.

"Just so."

"Agreed!"

"When?" the Weapon Master asked, gathering up his reins, already turning his mount's head.

"On the morrow at noon."

"Where?"

"On the flat ground before the Culai fort."

"Agreed," Owen said, and then turned his back on the king and allowed his mount to canter away.

Cormac watched him go and then he began to shake. He drove the battle-hammer spike first into the earth and placed both hands on his hips and began to rock to and fro with uncontrollable laughter.

In the bushes Tien tZo pulled his recurve bow over his shoulder and found he could only agree with the king's sentiments. This was absolute folly of the worst kind. This was suicide.

"I think you'll be up against the king himself," Keshian said quietly, glancing sidelong at the Weapon Master.

Owen nodded non-committally. He was walking the battlements with the old soldier, inspecting the repairs and changes that had been made to the defences.

"I've had new mortar poured into the cracks along here," Keshian pointed, "and the men will be setting sharpened slivers of wood and nails into the tops of the merlons—which should surprise any climbers."

Owen nodded again, his eyes distant.

"This outer wall is indefensible, so I intend to booby-trap it," Keshian continued. "I'm going to saw through all the support struts on the walkways with the exception of one or two, which I'll keep intact. I'll attach a length of rope to these and we should be able to pull the walkways down from the windows opposite." He jerked his head in the direction of the building proper, but Owen didn't even look.

They continued walking in silence while the evening drew quickly on for night, the shadows already thickening in the mountain-wrapped fortress. "It will be the king," Keshian said then.

And the Weapon Master nodded. "I know. His honour demands it."

"He'll use a Gallowglas sword or a battle-axe," Keshian continued.

Owen leaned on one of the merlons and looked out across the flat stony plain in the direction of King Cormac's camp. There was a storm hanging low and purple on the horizon, whipping up distant dust clouds. "Would the sword not be too long and unwieldy in a confined place?" he wondered.

"Have you ever seen a Gallowglas use one of the longswords?" Keshian asked.

Owen shook his head.

"I did once. When I was a mercenary many years ago, one of them rode with us. In the beginning we all laughed at his sword, which was nearly as tall as himself and so heavy that even the strongest amongst us could barely lift it. But let me tell you, Weapon Master, the Gallowglas can wield them one-handed, using them as if they weighed nothing more than a knife. And I needn't tell you that a weapon that is as long as a tall man, with all the weight and strength of a powerful Gallowglas arm behind it, will cut a man clean in two. I've seen it happen," he added hoarsely, the suddenly lurid image flashing behind his eyes, and he saw again the explosion of flesh and blood and bone and matter against the searing golden sands of the Fire Hills of Nasgociba.

"I've heard tell that the blades are magically bonded to just one man at the moment of their construction and that only he can lift and wield it," Owen said, almost absently.

"I've heard that also," Keshian agreed. He nodded at the growing clouds. "Storm coming."

Owen ran his hands across his greying hair, which Tien had recently cropped close to his skull. "What weapon would you suggest I use?"

"I'm honoured you should ask me," Keshian began, "but surely you are the Weapon Master, surely that decision is best left to you."

"I am asking the advice of a fellow-warrior," Owen said with a smile, and in that moment whatever reservations the battle-captain may have had about the infamous mercenary vanished.

"I would suggest something like a mace. You can use a mace?" He caught Owen's disgusted look and hurried on. "Use a mace with an especially heavy head."

"Why the extra weight?"

"To batter aside or even trap the longsword, while you strike with a sword or thrown knife."

"Can I break the blade?" Owen asked.

"Impossible. You are talking about a bar of metal as tall as a man, which is a hand-span broad and as thick as two fingers from the guard almost to the tip. It is double-edged and sharp—but not unusually so—for most of its length, but at its tip, which is pointed, it is sharp enough to shave with. There is no possible way you can break a blade like that."

"Armour?"

The wind shifted, smelling of salt and spices and carrying dust and sand. Keshian spat grit over the battlements. "I would advise against it. You're going to need all the speed and agility you can get. If you're wearing armour, it'll just slow you down and if even one of the Gallowgla's blows strikes you, it will crush your bones to powder despite the protection."

Owen nodded. "Thank you, you've cleared my own thoughts on the subject."

"Have you made any decision as to how you're going to fight him?"

"Not yet. I'll speak to Tien tZo later when he returns."

"I didn't know he had gone out," Keshian said, surprised, automatically scanning the plain below, even though he realised the chances of seeing the Shemmat were almost nil.

"He had a little...job...to do," Owen smiled.

The Weapon Master sat in the small room he had taken close to Kutor's quarters and carefully cleaned and sorted his weapons. Usually, Tien tZo took care of this, but the small Shemmat warrior still hadn't returned. With his warrior's sense of time, Owen knew that full night had fallen outside, and even through the solid stone he could hear the distant hissing of the storm against the exterior walls. Tien tZo's absence had made him apprehensive, although he knew that the Shemmat was an extraordinary warrior in his own right, and the two men had been in each other's company now for so long that each had absorbed much of the other's fighting skills.

Owen glanced at the pale yellow candle sitting before a polished rectangle of metal in a niche high on the wall; it had perhaps half a finger's span left to burn. When it had guttered out he would go in search of his slave-companion.

The Weapon Master looked at the weapons laid out on the cot and once again realised that these were his only possessions, these tools of death, together with a few clothes, and they too were connected with death. It was little enough to show after over twenty years on the mercenary trail. He reached into his belt and spilled the contents of his pouch onto the cloth: a dozen copper coins, barely enough for a night's drinking in a reasonably clean inn. But then, he had never had a great head for money. A trained sword never lacked for hire, and he had been able to command a good wage, but that money was just as easily spent: there was always fine food and drink, and women ...always the women. It was the mercenary's disease; when the next day might be the last, every day had to be lived to the full. And when the money ran out, there were always more wars to replenish the coin, and after a while it became a wretched cycle from which there was no escape.

He had tried, though. He had moved out of the cities and practised his art in the provinces before moving on to the Outlands and then finally the Wastelands, training petty lordlings how to hold a sword or pull a bow. But these were men with little respect for the title of Weapon Master, and these were the people who attempted more often than not to cheat him.

He had been fleeing one such stupid lord when he had met up with the bard, and from that single meeting everything had undoubtedly changed. Suddenly he had his Faith again, and he had a course to follow. When the bard had suggested he join the Renegade's group, he had been more than a little doubtful, but recently he had begun to see Kutor's cause as a chance to change the direction of his own life, to earn a little wealth and settle down, perhaps even open that warrior's school he had dreamed about so often and begin training his successor. Throwing in his lot with the renegade prince was a chance—a desperate gamble—but if it paid off he would be able to realise that dream.

And that was one of the reasons why he was prepared to challenge one of the fearsome Gallowglas in single combat.

The candle in the niche guttered out and Owen stood up, reaching for his sword belt…and the door opened and Tien tZo stepped into the room, something like a smile playing about his lips. "It's done."

"You killed my men!" Cormac screamed as soon as Owen appeared on the battlements.

"I thought our contest was at noon," the Weapon Master shouted down, squinting against the glare of the early morning sun.

"You killed my tribesmen last night!" the king repeated, "all of them." He was wearing full armour and the square plates took the early morning sun and blazed, lending the huge Gallowglas an almost godlike appearance.

"Your men were slain?" Owen asked innocently.

"What happened?" Prince Kutor asked quietly, coming up behind the Weapon Master, a bow in his hands.

"My men were murdered last night!" Cormac raged, spittle flecking his chin.

"It seems his nine remaining Gallowglas brothers were killed last night," Owen smiled.

"And you had nothing to do with it?" the prince asked.

"I did not go out last night."

"Did I see Tien tZo coming back late?" Kutor wondered aloud.

"I think you might have." Owen smiled.

"We will fight now!" Cormac roared.

"I am not ready," Owen said mildly, spreading his arms wide.

"Then ready yourself!" Cormac screamed, the cords in his neck standing out, the veins writhing along his bare arms and temples.

Tien tZo touched Owen lightly on the arm. "Anger lends strength," he said softly, his eyes on the king.

"And angry men make mistakes," Owen replied.

"He is not like other men," Tien tZo said patiently. "He only needs to hit you once—just once, that's all."

The Weapon Master nodded. He leaned over the edge of the battlements, studying the king's armour. He was wearing a leather jerkin and kirtle, which had been sewn with crude overlapping squares and rectangles of metal. His head was uncovered and his arms and legs were bare although he wore thick, studded wristbands on either arm.

"Fight me now, man!"

"Wait, Gallowglas. Let me arm myself."

In the stillness of his room, he dressed himself for what might very well be the final battle. Jerkin and leggings of supple black leather, with the jerkin woven through with strands of wire, designed to turn a knife blade or arrowhead, while its high collar was stiffened and plated with metal to protect the back of his neck and head. High metal-toed and heeled boots, with a flatbladed throwing knife in each. He wore fighting gauntlets which had been banded around the knuckles with stiffened wire, and there were plates running along each finger, and disc-shaped metal plates on the back of the hands. He strapped his scabbard across his back with the hilt of his longsword projecting above his left shoulder, and there was a broad-bladed Chopt knife in his belt. He had followed Keshian's advice and had opted for the mace, but where he would have fought with mace and shortsword, Tien tZo had suggested two maces and had spent most of the night demonstrating the effectiveness of the unconventional weapons.

Owen slipped the leathern thongs around his wrists, loosely held the short leather-wrapped handles and allowed the spiked balls to dangle at the end of their chains, scraping the floor. He glanced at Tien tZo. "Well...?"

The Shemmat nodded. "It is how I imagine your god of war would look."

Owen nodded, pleased. "I know he often used the mace as his weapon of choice."

"But two of them?" Tien tZo asked.

Owen laughed and went out to face the Gallowglas.

"I am going to kill you, little man," Cormac snarled, his face turning into an animal's mask.

"You're going to try," the Weapon Master corrected him mildly.

"Before there is any killing done here," Keshian interrupted, "we must finalise the stakes and rules."

His opposite number, one of the captains of Cormac's legion, nodded in agreement.

Cormac spat between Owen's feet. "There are no rules."

The Weapon Master nodded.

"I will wager the loyalty of my legion to the victor," Cormac snapped, lifting his enormous sword with one hand and allowing it to drop into the palm of his other hand, his eyes on Owen's face.

"If you are defeated, the legion will swear loyalty to Prince Kutor," Keshian persisted.

"That is what I have said!"

The legion captain cleared his throat. "And you will wager the renegade prince and his followers?"

Keshian nodded. "Agreed. If our champion is defeated, they will surrender to you."

The legion captain nodded and then both men backed away, leaving Owen and Cormac standing alone on the rocky ground before the ruined Culai fortress.

Both men stared at each other for a score of pounding heart-beats, and then they attacked simultaneously.

Cormac brought up his sword, which was actually taller than Owen, as easily as if it were a rapier and brought it down in a fast scything blow that would have cut the Weapon Master in two had it connected. Owen threw himself forward and down, beneath the cut, and slashed at Cormac's legs with the mace in his right hand, but the range was too great and his blow fell short. Continuing to move, he rolled away just as the king brought the sword around and down, gouging deep into the ground where Owen had lain. The Weapon Master came to his feet, facing the Gallowglas, and began the complicated movement Tien tZo had taught him, working both hands together, the balls on the maces spinning in two lethal, humming circles.

Cormac slashed again, leaning back away from the spiked balls, using his great reach and the full length of the sword, and this time its tip ripped through Owen's jerkin, slicing the leather and expos-ing the silver wire beneath. The force of the glancing blow sent Owen sprawling back, just as he released the mace in his left hand. The solid ball struck the Gallowglas square in the chest, instead of the throat, punching him backwards, staggering the giant. Owen, from a prone position, spun the second mace in a tight arc and released it, but Cormac saw it coming and brought his sword up, and the chain wrapped itself harmlessly around the blade. The king roared triumphantly—he had the Weapon Master now—and the first knife took him through the throat, while the second merely glanced off his skull.

Mortally wounded, the Gallowglas raised his sword above the fallen warrior, determined to take him into the Silent Wood, when the broad blade of a Chopt knife almost tore the head off his shoulders. He was dead before he hit the ground.

In the confusion and uproar that followed a hand reached down and hauled the Weapon Master to his feet. Owen found himself looking into Kutor's eyes and the look on his face was one of extraordinary surprise.

"Now tell me why. And the truth this time," the prince murmured.

"Reasons..."

"Reasons?" Kutor persisted.

"It was a ready-made army," Owen said in a hoarse whisper.

9
The Onelord

And he was always the Champion of the Gods of the Pantheon...
Life of Paedur, the Bard

"There has been another attack on Mannam!"

Paedur looked up as Katani strode down the length of the library. "What happened?"

"I thought you would have heard the uproar above. I thought you would have been there."

Paedur shrugged. "I heard nothing."

"I should have known I would find you here," the warrior grumbled.

Mannam had lodged his visitors in rooms in the cellars close to the library. The bard's incredulity that there should even be a library in Manach had turned to absolute amazement when he saw it.

The library was enormous—bigger even than the fabulous library of Baddalaur, the Bardic College, which was reputed to contain all the knowledge in the known world. It was said that if the planes of Existence were to be destroyed, it would be possible to rebuild them from the records in the library at Baddalaur. But Mannam's library dwarfed it.

The shelves ran the entire length of the cellars, which the bard paced out at a thousand paces from end to end, and were four times the height of a tall man. And they were crammed from end to end with books, scrolls, manuscripts, folios, and charts. There was no order, no systematic collection of authors or subjects, and Paedur knew that it was a lifetime's task—no, two or more—just to prepare a catalogue of the enormous collection.

Mannam's library was unique in one other way: none of the books in it had ever been published; they were all posthumous works and they were all original. It had intrigued and delighted the bard, and Mannam had laughed his crackling laugh and said that every writer died with at least one work unfinished. His stick-like fingers had then indicated the shelves. "These are the finished works."

From that moment on, Paedur was lost, and it was all Katani or indeed Mannam could do to drag him away from the library.

Katani nervously strode around the book stacks and shelves. She had left off her horned helmet and her ice-white hair hung down her back, whispering off her lacquered armour like oiled silk. Her weapons were noiseless.

"One of the newly dead attacked him," she said abruptly. "Mannam had gone to inspect a batch of those newly come to his kingdom when a blacksmith from one of the border villages launched a vicious attack on him. I was directly behind the Dark Lord and could do nothing; I couldn't even reach him, the man was so fast, so berserk."

"And Death?" Paedur asked urgently.

"Unharmed, but frightened. The blacksmith's huge hammer shattered against Mannam's cloak, and by that time the bainte were on him and had removed the spark of his soul, leaving him "dead" again. He was chained and the spark returned to him, and then I...questioned him. And I know many ways to loosen a man's tongue."

Paedur laughed without humour. "I am sure you do. And what did you discover?"

Katani grinned savagely. "The man had been a follower of the New Religion in the World of Men, and had been a special devotee of Libellius's Cult of the Dead. It seems the leader of this cult had received a message from their god asking for a volunteer to go into the Silent Wood to assassinate Mannam; if he succeeded, then Libellius would come to power and the man would be returned to life with great glory and honour."

"I wonder bow many men would have volunteered for such a mission," Paedur remarked sourly. "Surely they knew it had no hope of succeeding."

"Obviously something must have encouraged them to think that there was a hope, because there were so many volunteers that the winner had to be chosen by lottery—and the blacksmith won."

"Well, he won little enough. Not one, but two quick deaths, followed by torture by a Katan."

"There will be more attempts," she said seriously. "If we're going to do something, we'll have to do it soon, before an attempt succeeds!"

Paedur nodded. "I know." He turned away and walked down along the untidy shelves, his fingers brushing the backs of the polished leather and vellum bindings. The warrior fell into step beside him. "Tell me about Churon," he asked suddenly.

Katani grinned humourlessly. "I would have thought that you as a bard would know more about him than any man."

"My knowledge is taken from my lore and the myths and legends of the Nations, but you met with him, spoke with him. I can tell you about the historical man; you can tell me about the real person."

Katani turned and swept clean a section of shelving, tumbling the books and manuscripts onto the floor, and then she heaved herself up onto it. "What do you want to know about him?" she asked, watching the bard carefully.

"Anything. Everything," he amended quickly, stooping down and beginning to gather the books Katani had tossed onto the floor. He quickly stacked them and straightened, leaning back against the shelves, facing the woman and folding his arms. "Describe him to me."

Katani closed her eyes, remembering. "He was tall—taller than you—and broad, and although the colour of his skin was black, his hair was white and his eyes were blue, so there was mixed blood in him." Her amber eyes flickered open and she smiled, almost shyly. "He was a handsome man, and he exuded an aura of absolute authority."

"And what were your impressions of him?"

"My first impressions were of a man of great strength and power, a man of vision. His virtues seemed to me—and not just to me—to be similar to those of the Katan Sisterhood: he was a warrior with honour, a man of courage and charity. But as I grew to know him, I formed a clearer impression of the man behind the mask, for believe me, it was a mask. It was an image he projected like some cheap fairground magician." Katani shook her head, smiling sadly. "The title Onelord was of his own choosing. And that was what he wanted to be—a Onelord, an Emperor—the ruler not only of the Seven Nations but of all the known lands. And I have a vague memory of hearing him say once that he would climb the Broken Mountain and trek the Silent Wood if he could free his homeland."

"And where was his homeland?" Paedur asked.

Katani shrugged. "No one knows. His colouring suggests the southern lands, but he had been sold off the slave-block at Londre when he was around twelve. He ended up in Thusal. But I never heard him call any one place home, unless it was Shansalow, his capital..."

"Was the city really built entirely from silver?"

Katani looked at him in disgust. "The palace roof was sheathed in silver. The city itself was of white brick—and it was a shabby, smelly, foul, and dangerous place. It was no fit place to live."

The bard nodded. He had walked the tumbled ruins of the Silver City and spent some time with the prospectors who dug in its ruined streets searching for the hoard of silver bricks that was reputed to lie buried in some cellar. "And what do you know of his family, his advisers?" he asked.

Katani shrugged. "He had no close advisers, except perhaps Praetens, his magician, and he was slain on the Sand Plain. Kutor the Strong would, I suppose, have been closest to him, but Churon grew mistrustful of his popularity and banished him to the west, to Gallowan, where he died mad and almost forgotten."

"I know," the bard said softly, remembering the legends. "And Churon's family?"

"There was Deslirda, his queen, and one legitimate son, Chural. There were stories, of course, of his many mistresses and catamites— for Churon was a man of large appetites in every respect—and he was reputed to have sired several bastards."

"Tell me about Deslirda," Paedur said. Before he went in search of the Onelord he needed to have as much information about the man as possible.

Katani surprisingly shook her head. "I know very little about her. She was a strange, shy woman, quite small, almost childlike, who rarely appeared in public and was surprisingly plain—not ugly, you understand, but just plain." She paused and added, in a tone almost of wonder. "And I really think he loved her."

Paedur looked up quickly. "Truly?"

Katani nodded. "Truly."

The bard tapped the wooden shelving gently with the flat of his hook, the delicate ringing hanging on the soft, musty air. "That might be a place to start. But first, tell me about Chural, the son."

The woman warrior smiled again, warmly this time. "He was his mother's son in every respect, quiet and gentle, not a fighter, but with enough knowledge of strategy and weaponcraft for him to gain his father's respect. I don't know what happened to him. Did he succeed Churon?"

Paedur shook his head. "It has always been accepted that Churon had him murdered for those very qualities you mentioned ... and also because he became an extraordinarily powerful magician when he reached his maturity, with special control over the elements. It was when the common people began calling him the Stormlord that Churon turned against him and had him killed."

Katani hissed through gritted teeth. "When I kill him, bard, I'll make sure it will be impossible for him to return to any semblance of a life."

"If I don't do it before you, or Mannam doesn't do it before either of us," Paedur smiled.

"If I don't do what?" The Dark Lord glided silently into the room, his cloak of seared and withered leaves making no sound on the polished wooden floor.

"I was merely saying that you would ensure that the Onelord never returned to any semblance of life—in this world or the next."

Mannam laughed, the sound snapping on the air. "I have Churon's future mapped out," he whispered, the sound ominous and shrill. "I can destroy his body, but I cannot destroy his soul. However, I can place it in the body of an animal, something suitable ...some crawling, slithering thing."

"Something edible," Katani suggested. "An inoffensive *cuine* that will be slain and eaten."

"Something foul," Mannam continued, almost gleefully, "something loathed and feared, something that will be hunted and slain by man."

"Or what about something defenceless?" Katani added, with a broad grin. "One of the creatures that is hunted by just about every predator..."

"If you can both contain yourselves," Paedur said quietly, "let us remember that we are dealing here with one of the most dangerous men ever to have walked the World of Men; a man of great strength of will, a man of vision and imagination, and with enough daring to carry his plans through. We are talking about a man who has not let death stand in the way of his plans of conquest. I do not think it will be too easy to kill this man, if indeed we can kill him." He turned to Mannam. "Is it going to be possible to knock him down, cut his throat, disembowel him, something—anything—and ensure that he stays that way for some time?"

"For how long?"

"As long as it takes to bring the corpse back here to you. Can that be arranged?"

Mannam shook his head rustlingly. "Not easily, no."

"Why not?" the bard demanded.

The Dark Lord shook his head impatiently, the movement curiously human, and Paedur once again had the fleeting impression of the face beneath the cowl. "When a human dies, bard, his essence leaves his body and is taken by one of my bainte and carried here, and here we replace it in a replica of the body. When someone in the Silent Wood is slain the essence, the soul, remains within the body, and therefore the body regenerates within a short period."

Paedur shook his head, brushing his fine hair back off his forehead. "You have not made yourself clear."

"If—when—you kill Churon, I or one of my bainte would have to be on hand to rip the essence from his body, and that can only happen at the traumatic moment of death. If that moment is missed, even by so much as an instant, then the body will regenerate. The timing is essential. To have even a slim hope of success, I would have to accompany you, and that, as you know, is impossible."

"If I totally destroyed Churon's body..."

"Have you ever tried to completely destroy a human body, bard?" Mannam hissed. "Obviously not! All the bones have to be reduced to powder and the dust scattered, the tissues, organs, and muscles have to be completely shredded, the hair and nails similarly disposed of. And even if you do that, then we cannot be certain that Churon's essence will not end up in another body..."

Paedur raised his hook, the runes sparkling slightly in the wan light. "Wait. You are saying that this man cannot be killed, and even if he could be killed then there is no point because he will return to life again. And even if we totally destroy his body, we cannot be sure that his essence will not regenerate in another body! Well then, god, with all due respects to you, you are asking me to do the impossible."

"Not impossible..."

Paedur suddenly smashed his hook into the shelving, the razor edge cutting deep into the hard wood. "Well, then, help me!" he demanded. "Suggest something!"

Katani slid off the shelving and crossed to rest her gloved hand gently on Paedur's arm. She looked at Mannam. "He is right. You are not helping us in any way. You must suggest something."

The Dark Lord glared at them both for a moment and then he suddenly turned away and swept down the length of the library, his cloak rustling loudly like leaves in a storm-shaken tree. When he reached the far end of the cellar, he abruptly turned and shouted, "I don't know what to do!" His anger and anguish sent something like forked lightning running along the floor, buzzing and crackling, sparking on the polished wood.

Paedur raised his left arm, holding his hook straight out from his body, the point downwards. The lightning hissed like serpents and then raced along the floor and leapt upwards towards the hook, where it spun and crackled, bringing the runes to sparkling life before disappearing into the dark metal.

Paedur looked at the Spirit of the Dead and shook his head. "You must not fear him," he said softly.

"He will kill me," Mannam whispered sibilantly, his voice echoing along the length of the room.

"If you allow him to."

"I don't see how I can stop him."

"You are Death," Paedur reminded him.

"Bard, in the World of Men, you are as a god, while here you are nothing more than a man. In the World of Men I am a god, but here in my own kingdom, my powers are limited."

"What about the other gods?" Katani asked softly, looking from Paedur to Mannam.

A smile touched the bard's thin lips and he looked up at the Dark Lord, now hunched still and silent like a blasted tree at the far end of the cellar. "Yes, what about them?" he asked, "surely they would help?"

Mannam remained silent for a long time, and when he finally spoke his voice was slow and cautious, "Few of my brethren in the Pantheon can enter my kingdom. They deal with life, I with death."

"But surely some of them can..." Paedur began.

"Yes, yes," Mannam said impatiently, "some can, some can."

He glided back to the pair, his movements now silent again, the leaves on his cloak quivering slightly. "Whom would you suggest?" He looked at Paedur.

"Buiva, the War God," the bard said immediately, and Katani nodded with a smile.

"And what of the Nameless God of Madness," the warrior suggested.

Mannam nodded, then there was the sound of a branch snapped in half, and then he spoke one word, "Maurug."

"Maurug?" Katani asked, frowning, trying to recall the Pantheon of the Old Faith.

"The Destroyer," Paedur smiled. "Maurug the Destroyer."

Mannam reached out to touch Paedur but drew his stick-like hand back when a spark shot from the bard's hook to coil around the twig-like fingers. "I am confident again," he said. "I will call them to us."

"I want you to call upon one other, if you can," Paedur said quickly, as the Dark Lord began to turn away.

"Name it?"

"I want you to call on Deslirda, Churon's lady!"

Paedur and Katani walked the streets of Manach and looked at the people. The bard had to keep reminding himself that he was looking at the dead, men and women who had left the World of Men, tens, hundreds and in some cases thousands of years ago. As in Bannoche, the City of Ghosts, the people from all ages existed now side by side, and none seemed to think the differing styles of dress, the customs or mannerisms to be strange or unnatural.

At one point, Paedur turned to Katani and asked, "Do you think they know they are dead?"

"Oh, they know, but like humankind—and I know because I did this myself—they forget, or at least prefer not to think on it. I think you will find that they have come to terms with their present existence."

They turned into a small, quietly beautiful plaza and stopped beside a fountain. A creature from one of the southern mythologies, a beast with curling tusks, carved from the same dirty grey stone as the city, spouted water from its tusks.

"How did you find your own acceptance?" Paedur asked, touching the surface of the water with the point of his hook and snagging up a long tendril of weed.

Katani sat on the low fountain wall and looked across the square at the merchants tending their stalls; no one bought anything, no one sold, but people still came to browse. And there was no food of any description, no fruit or meats, no eggs or fish for sale. She nodded and the bard followed her gaze. "I returned to my old profession, like them. They have nothing to sell, no-one buys, but they still go through the ritual of setting up their striped and colourful awnings and spreading the tables, setting out their wares. I returned to what I had been trained to do almost from my birth—I killed."

"Why?" Paedur asked very quietly, his voice a murmur.

"In the beginning I think I was a little mad. Any man that stood before me I slew. And when I realised that they would rise again, I maimed them, so that they would never walk again, or speak, or perform the act of a man with a woman." Her voice had become hoarse with the memory and she shook her head and fell silent.

"And?" he prompted.

"And then I suppose I realised what I had become."

"And what was that?"

"A berserk—a killing-machine without soul..." She smiled at that. "Without soul. But with that realisation came a form of acceptance, and it was as if the madness had been burned from me. I set about exploring my surroundings, learning more about where I was, going to the Fairs."

"The Fairs?"

"Yes, the Fairs. They are huge gatherings of the newly dead and those recently come to the Silent Wood. It is a place of meeting, where friends and relatives can be reunited, where the last barrier—death—no longer exists. There are bainte there; they explain what has happened and where you are and how to go to the Place of Judgment if you desire to be judged by Alile, the Judge Impartial. But they always add the warning that while we could walk the Silent Woods unjudged for all eternity, once we went to the Place of Judgment and Alile had passed judgment, then we would be bound to accept his decision, which was final."

"And what sort of decisions does he hand down?" Paedur wondered.

"No one knows. No one has ever returned." She pushed herself off the wall and walked away quickly, heading out of the plaza. Paedur followed more slowly.

"Is that why you have never gone for judgment?" he called after her.

Katani stopped and looked back over her shoulder. "What do you mean?"

"Is it because you are afraid?"

"I am of the Katan; I fear nothing. Not even death, not any more," she added.

"Then tell me why have you not gone to stand before Alile, the Judge Impartial?"

"Why do you ask?" Katani turned around to face him, her left hand resting on the wrapped hilt of her longsword. There was a chill edge to her voice.

Paedur walked across the cobbled stones to stand directly in front of her. And then he placed his right hand on her shoulder and looked deep into her hard amber eyes. "Because when I face Churon the Onelord, I will need to know, I will need to trust, the person standing by my side. Surely you can comprehend that?"

Katani nodded silently.

"I need to know why you have refused to face the last great mystery of this place: the Judgment of Alile."

Katani looked into his deep dark eyes and saw only sympathy there, no mockery. "Because I don't want to return to the World of Men," she said very softly.

The bard stared blankly at her.

"Don't you see? When you have been adjudged by Alile, you are returned to the World of Men in another life, another guise, to start again!"

"But you've just said no one knows what those judgments are?" Paedur protested.

"Bard, the finest necromancers, magicians and sorcerers have passed through this place. And I have always put the same question to all those I've met: what is Alile's judgment? And their reply is always the same. He passes judgment on one's life and then sends one back into the World of Men for another span of life."

"For how many spans?" Paedur asked, suddenly terrified by the very thought of it. In the World of Men he was virtually immortal. What would happen when he died and was adjudged? Was he to return as an ordinary man, ungifted and untalented?

"No one knows," Katani answered him, "except Alile, the Judge Impartial. And no one has ever been able to discover the truth."

"Oh, I will," Paedur promised, "I will."

10
A Cause

"A just cause does not automatically guarantee victory, but if a man believes his cause is just, then he will defend it all the more fiercely."

Owen, the Weapon Master

Sunlight the colour of smoke slanted in through the stained-glass windows and ran like coloured inks down the faces of the four people sitting around the ornately carved brukwood table. The warm light lent the room a slightly mysterious atmosphere, softening all the edges, and the delicately cut crystal goblets on the table had taken on an insubstantial, ethereal air, as if a reaching hand might pass right through them.

Conversation had lulled, the routine business of the day having been conducted, and by unspoken consent they took a few moments respite before moving on to more pressing matters. By their clothing and studied mannerisms they could have been taken for merchants or bankers, and they had that unmistakable air of those who were used to commanding rather than being commanded.

However, this small, dimly lit room was part of the Emperor's personal chambers and these four people represented the ultimate power in the Seven Nations.

Geillard XII sat with his back to the window. He was a tall, rather thin man, his features sharp and severe, his eyes deep-sunk behind prominent cheekbones, giving him a permanently morose expression. His hair, which had faded to a pale nondescript colour, was thinning and his bare scalp burned redly in the reflected light. His hands, which were unusually long-fingered, rested easily on the table, the tips barely touching his goblet of wine.

To his left sat Salier, his chief counsellor, magician, and personal attendant. There were rumours that Salier was more than just a servant to the Emperor, and it was widely recognised that he exerted a more than natural influence on the throne. He was a small, dark man, soft-spoken, quiet and evasive, with the manners of a cleric and the morals of an assassin.

Directly facing Salier sat Fodla, Geillard's Captain of the Guard. By tradition the Emperor's bodyguard was always female, a tradition that had begun when Churon ruled and kept the Katan as his personal guard. Her bravery and weaponcraft were legendary and it was considered a great honour for a young girl to be chosen to be trained under her command. She was a huge woman, tall and bulky, her green eyes perpetually wide, giving her an innocent and slightly lost expression, and the splash of freckles across her face lent her an almost girlish appearance. Her ancestry was shrouded in mystery, but rumours abounded which ranged from the fanciful to the outrageous. She had served with Geillard now for twelve years, and she was one of the few people he actually trusted and listened to. Her contempt for Salier was matched only by her respect for the man, whom she considered to be absolutely evil.

Facing the Emperor sat Barthus, the Hierophant, newly elected pope of the New Religion, which the Emperor recently had taken up and pronounced as the official religion of his empire. The Hierophant was a slender ascetic whose features were so indeterminate that he might easily have been taken for either sex. He seemed to deliberately accentuate his hermaphroditic appearance by his choice of extravagant clothing, and his movements and gestures were studied and precise. Of them all, he was the one the Emperor trusted the least, and he was equally loathed by both Salier and Fodla, but they were all forced to recognise the immense power he had at his command.

The Emperor touched his goblet with the tip of his finger and the crystal rang like a bell. "I will have your reports now, if you please," Geillard said softly, studying his hands.

In keeping with the tradition, Salier began. "Precise and verifiable information is difficult to obtain since the Cataclysm. All that is certain is that the New Religion has been dealt a serious blow, and that the Pantheon has consolidated its position. The Planes of Existence are in turmoil and the Void is wracked with spasms of such power that several of our magicians and sorcerers have been destroyed as they travelled in search of information."

"Does anyone know what brought on the Cataclysm?" The Emperor looked from Salier to Barthus.

The magician grimaced. "We have nothing definite at the moment, but my lord Barthus has suggested that it is in some way connected to this so-called Champion of the Old Faith."

"And have you discovered anything about this person or being?"

Salier nodded. "As far as we can determine, it is a bard, by name Paedur..."

Geillard started. "Was there not a bard at court by that name?"

The magician nodded again. "We believe it is the same man. This champion is described as a bard with a hook in place of his left hand."

The Emperor nodded. "The same," he breathed.

"He is also inciting revolution!" Fodla said abruptly, her deep masculine voice startling them all. The Captain of the Guard leaned forward and began tapping out her points on the table with a stubby finger. "Although hard information is difficult at this time, my spies have reported that Kutor the Renegade and his outlaws have vanished!" She saw the Emperor's startled expression and continued more slowly, her eyes now on his face alone. "A hook-handed man spent a single night with his band before their departure. I have further reports of them heading into the west." She paused and then added more slowly, "I also have reports of a Weapon Master accompanied by a Shemmat slave travelling into the west...

"Owen," Salier whispered, and Fodla nodded in agreement. "It can only be him."

The magician turned to Geillard. "You will recall him, Majesty. We hired him on two previous occasions through intermediaries, and his defence of Car'an'tual has made him a legend."

"I remember him," Geillard said, suddenly looking at Barthus. "He is one of the Iron Band of Kloor?"

Surprisingly, the Hierophant shook his head. "No more. The link was severed, the band shattered."

"That is impossible," Salier snapped.

"I have always believed so, but it has happened." He coughed delicately. "Our last Sighted image of Owen is of a silver hook striking the Iron Band and destroying it."

"The bard again," Fodla grunted. "I should have killed him when I had the chance. I would have, if it hadn't been for your meddling," she snapped, looking at Salier.

"The man was a genius, and useful too. It would have been such a waste."

The Captain snorted and opened her mouth to reply, but the Emperor raised a hand, the rings on his fingers taking the light, red reflecting from a large ruby darting across their faces like new scars. "What else do you have?"

"Cormac, the Gallowglas King, is dead!" she said simply, and allowed the sentence to hang on the still air.

"How?" Barthus whispered.

"When?" Salier demanded.

"Tell us what you know without dramatics," Geillard said tiredly.

"I know very little," Fodla confessed. "Cormac is dead, killed in a fair fight—if you can believe that—and his Gallowglas warriors slain to a man."

"And his legion?" Salier asked, his agile mind desperately working out all the possible implications.

"I don't know."

"Is it perhaps too much of a coincidence that both Kutor and Owen have headed into the west, and now Cormac, one of our creatures, is slain?" Barthus asked, forgetting for once his lisping, derisive tone.

"Barthus is right," Geillard said decisively. "Fodla, send your people into the west and have them seek news of Kutor and his people, the Weapon Master and the fate of Cormac's legion."

"It's my guess that we'll find them all together," Fodla said grimly.

"That's what I'm afraid of," Geillard admitted, reaching for his glass and draining it in one swallow.

Prince Kutor turned as someone noisily mounted the steps behind him. "I'm getting too old for this," Keshian moaned, leaning on the battlements to catch his breath.

Kutor smiled. "Strange. I thought I saw a man who looked just like you spend most of yesterday morning showing men the safest and quickest way to run up and down a ladder wearing full armour."

"That was yesterday," Keshian growled, "and some days are easier than others."

The prince nodded down into the courtyard below, where their new-found army was training. "How are they working out?"

His captain shrugged. "There's very little to do with them. When we got them a moon ago, they were a well-trained legion and now— well, now they're the finest fighting force I've ever worked with. Owen and Tien tZo have worked them hard—very hard—but some-how the men don't seem to resent it."

Kutor nodded. "I know. I think it's a matter of pride with them now, they feel honoured to be trained by the finest Weapon Master in the Nations, the man who defeated Cormac in single combat. How go the defences?"

"Almost complete. But that's what one thousand men can do. The outer walls have been completely repaired and the moat has been cleared and reset with spikes and stakes. We are redirecting the stream which once fed it back into its original course. The two wells we discovered within the fortress have been cleared and the escape tunnels have also been cleared of debris and shored up."

Kutor nodded. One thing he resented about the present state of affairs was that he was not as involved as he wanted to be, or felt he should be. "Has there been any more trouble?"

"None. Owen has seen to that."

Although the legion had been properly oath-bound to Kutor once the Weapon Master had slain the Gallowglas, he gave them the choice of joining him or moving on into the west if they desired. Some chose to move on, taking their chances in the westlands, but the majority of the legionaries, knowing no other life, accepted his invitation to join with him in his attempt on the throne. Naturally, there had been a certain amount of friction between the new arrivals and Kutor's men, and there had been several incidents, the last of which had ended in a vicious fight which had left two men dead and a dozen injured. Owen's justice had been swift and merciless; the two ringleaders, one from each side, had been taken out and challenged to a duel by the Weapon Master. And he had killed them, swiftly, easily and with no apparent effort. There had been no trouble since.

"Where is the Weapon Master now?"

"When I last saw him, he was setting out to check on the sentries. He's convinced the Empire will be sending a force here very soon now."

Kutor turned to look at the distant hills, wondering whether he would one day see them alive with the blue and black of the Imperial troops. "And what do you think?"

Keshian shrugged. "Even allowing for the breakdown in communications because of the Cataclysm, I'm sure some sort of rumour has reached them of Cormac's death. It's not every day a Gallowglas is slain in single combat."

"What will happen?"

The captain shrugged again. "I would imagine they'll send a raiding party rather than an army, looking for information: troop deployments, fortifications, leadership. Perhaps they'll even try to capture one of our leaders."

"Are the men ready to fight?"

"They're ready to fight; all they need is a cause."

The prince smiled. "I thought they were fighting for my cause?"

"They're grateful to you, or rather to the Weapon Master, for freeing them from Cormac's tyranny and returning their wives and children, but remember that most have joined you merely because you offer them security of a sort in this wild land. They need, they expect, to see some gain at the end of all this. You need to make them think that they're fighting for their freedom and faith and, more importantly, for their families."

"They need a cause," Kutor smiled.

"They need a cause."

The Weapon Master lay flat on the ground and watched the line of horsemen wind their way slowly up along the treacherous defile below. The afternoon had turned towards evening and the shadows were already beginning to thicken at the foot of the gully, and he knew if he was going to act, he would have to do it soon.

He watched the shadow of a tall silver-white tree grow along the ground, timing it, and he was actually rising to his feet when he heard the long, slow, grumbling rumble of falling rock off down at the far end of the defile. Tien's timing was as precise as usual. He immediately applied his weight to the long lever he had wedged beneath a boulder on the lip of the gully and pushed. The rock groaned and then moved—fractionally at first and then with a sudden give that almost precipitated him out over the edge. It thundered down the rockface, ripping smaller rocks and boulders from the cliffs and pulling them down with it. By the time it reached the canyon floor it was carrying enough debris to effectively block the mouth of the defile.

Owen almost reluctantly picked up one of his servant's recurve bows and prepared to do the methodical work of butchery. Away at the other end of the defile he heard an unholy agonised scream echoing off the rock walls and knew that Tien's first arrow had sent one of the Emperor's men to the Silent Wood.

Owen and Tien rode back into the fortress as dusk was drifting in like fog. They were both silent, but while Tien tZo's silence was one of exhaustion, the Weapon Master seemed almost angry. Kutor strode out to meet them, followed now by the guards Owen had picked and trained himself. Kutor had resented them at first, but gradually realised that they helped promote his image in the eyes of his men—and he was thinking of them as his men now—as a prince and future ruler. He watched the two men wearily dismount and then noted that although both men were carrying bows, their quivers were empty.

Owen stopped in front of him, his face tight, his eyes hooded. "We will speak later," he said, his voice cold and distant.

Kutor opened his mouth to protest, but caught Tien tZo's tiny shake of the head. The prince nodded. "Of course, later."

Owen nodded and then brushed past the prince, heading in the direction of his quarters, Kutor's guards and the guards on the door coming alert and saluting him as he passed. Uncharacteristically, he didn't return the salute. "What's wrong?" Kutor asked the Shemmat.

"He's tired. He has had a hard day."

"Doing what?"

"Killing," Tien smiled uneasily, and then hurried after his master.

Owen flung open the door and stormed into the room. The feelings that had been boiling up within him since the first killing earlier that afternoon now threatened to explode and he had to make a conscious effort to lower himself into a seat and clasp his hands together, interlacing the fingers, lest he suddenly grab a weapon and begin laying about him.

Behind him the door closed with a barely audible click, and although Tien tZo's footsteps were noiseless, Owen felt him approaching, and then his practised fingers began loosening his belts and ties.

"What's wrong with me, Tien?" Owen asked, his voice a harsh whisper.

"The killing bothers you?" the Shemmat asked.

"No—yes! I know it shouldn't have, but it did."

"We've slain in that fashion before," Tien remarked, removing Owen's broad leather belt with his scabbard and knife sheaths and laying them on the smooth stone floor. "You once killed two squads of conscripted youths without a qualm of..."

"Conscience," Owen finished. "That is what is bothering me about the killings today. They were all innocent men and women…"

Tien moved around the table and sat down opposite the Weapon Master. His eyes caught and held Owen's troubled gaze. "Can you honestly say that all those you killed were deserving of death?"

"No," Owen whispered.

"These were Imperial troops. Why are they different?"

"I don't know. I don't know!"

"The Gallowglas were evil, killers and murderers to a man. There was never any doubt but that they would be—must be—killed. That was a judgment you made; you judged them and found them guilty. Today you made a similar judgment and found the Emperor's men innocent, but still you killed them."

"What is the point?" Owen snapped.

"In the past," Tien tZo continued patiently, "you would have killed them all—good and bad alike—with no hesitation, no second thoughts."

"In the past?" Owen asked.

"Before you met the bard."

"While I was in the Iron Band you mean?"

"Just so."

Owen remained silent for a long time, and when he finally raised his head, the Shemmat was horrified to find moisture around his eyes. Instinctively he reached out, his long-fingered killer's hands gentle as they touched his master's face.

"What is happening to me?" Owen moaned.

"You are becoming human again," Tien said very softly, his voice awed. "It seems the bard gave you a far greater gift than you imagined."

"We killed forty warriors today," Owen said, looking at Kutor and Keshian. "They were the Emperor's people," he added, watching their reactions.

"Did you have to kill them?" the prince asked quietly.

"I felt it was necessary," Owen said quickly, surprised at his own defensiveness.

"Of course, and I abide by your decision. I was merely wondering why they had to be killed."

"We knew we would attract interest sooner or later. In fact we're lucky to have survived this long, but we've had the Cataclysm to thank for that. Undoubtedly word has trickled through to the capital that something is amiss here in the Wastelands, and they have decided to investigate. I would imagine we have a moon—certainly no more—to consolidate our defences here, or to attack."

"Attack!" Kutor started. "You mean begin...carry the fight to them? But surely it's too soon? We need men...weapons...food..." He felt suddenly breathless with the thought of it.

"The Cold Months will soon be here," Owen said reasonably, "and they are harsh in the Wastelands. We will undoubtedly be sealed within the fortress and almost certainly lose some men to desertion as boredom eats away at them. By the time the season changes, news of our strengths and numbers will have reached the Emperor."

"It seems so sudden," Kutor breathed.

Tien grinned. "Not so sudden. Even if we start tomorrow, it will be fully a moon or more before we are ready to move out."

Owen nodded. "Tien is right. But I think this is a decision which should be made now."

"We're not ready," the prince protested.

"We are," Owen said calmly.

Kutor looked to his captain for support, but surprisingly Keshian also nodded. "The men need to fight."

"A victory would be good for their morale," Tien agreed.

Kutor smiled tiredly. "I have a feeling this is not really my decision, is it?" He shook his head and folded his hands. "Fine, arrange my future between you. I will go along with whatever decision you make."

"Without you there are no reasons for decisions," Tien said quietly.

"Our decisions will make you an Emperor!" Owen grinned.

The Emperor Geillard awoke suddenly from a terrifying nightmare in which a vaguely humanlike creature loomed over him, drooling jaws wide and dripping scalding acid. His eyes snapped open to find Salier leaning over his bed, a long blood-coloured candle in his hand, hot wax dripping onto his bare chest. For a single instant, the dream creature and Salier's face superimposed and the Emperor resisted the impulse to scream and strike out at the were-beast.

"What...what is it?" he mumbled.

Salier suddenly threw back the covers, revealing one of the Emperor's concubines lying crouched in a bundle by Geillard's side. The woman's eyes were wide and terrified as she looked up at the magician.

"Begone," he hissed, and with a squeal like a trapped animal she rolled out of bed and darted for the door. Salier watched her naked form for a moment longer than necessary, letting her know that he was watching her.

"What is it?" the Emperor demanded.

"The patrol we sent into the Wastelands is no more, but never mind; their mission was successful," Salier said, a barely disguised note of triumph in his voice.

"What do you mean 'no more'?"

"They have been slain," Salier hissed.

"How do you know this?"

"One of them was my creature. Although its body went into the Wastelands, its essence remained with me. I won't bore you with the process, but when a body dies or is slain that essence is released into the Void, where, according to whatever belief you follow, it is seized by Mannam's bainte or floats on Libellius' river to its ultimate destination. To shorten the tale, a bainte came for the essence I still held, but I managed to trap it within a Circle of Power, where I was able to question it at length about the situation in the Wastelands."

"And?"

"You must prepare for war, Emperor. Your bastard half-brother is coming for your throne!"

11
The Gods

Maurug is the Destroyer, and his guise is that of a small and stunted man,
but his power is awesome...
Buiva is the God of War, an old and grizzled man, wise in the ways of war
and of Man, but weary...
The Nameless God of Madness, the Fool, the Innocent, a hermaphrodite,
whose touch can drive men mad...

Pantheon of the Old Faith

Buiva arrived first, a tired-looking old man in a simple suit of rusted chainmail. His face was gaunt, pinched, and lined, and there was a three-day growth of stubbly beard on his chin. Only his eyes were alive; they were bright, alert, and darting, and a deep luxurious brown in his weatherbeaten face. Indeed, it could have been the face of any nameless mercenary who had fought across the Seven Nations. There was a sword strapped to his shoulders, and a long-bladed dagger, and mace and chain on his belt.

He appeared on the top of the Tower of Time silently, and then, with a warrior's ingrained caution, paused in the darkened doorway before stepping out into the light. When he moved, he made no sound. His mail, though rusted on the surface, had obviously been kept oiled, and he had wrapped his huge gloved fist around the haft of the mace and chain to ensure its silence.

He stepped out onto the roof and immediately approached Paedur and Katani, ignoring Mannam. The bard was wrapped in his long dark-furred cloak but with the hood thrown back and the ties undone, allowing it to flap open, revealing the wicked hook in place of his left hand and the bardic sigil on his left shoulder. Katani was in her full grotesque armour but with the mask-helmet lying by her feet. War looked them both up and down and then stepped over to Mannam, who was standing by the cracked sundial.

"I trust you have a reason for all this, Death?" Buiva rasped, his voice raw and hoarse and inexpressibly weary.

Michael Scott 447

"I would not have asked you here if I had not," Mannam snapped.

Buiva nodded at the man and woman. "These?"

The Dark Lord raised his stick hand. "Allow me a moment, War. Two of our kind have yet to arrive. I will make the introductions then."

Buiva nodded grumpily and then stamped over to stand before the woman. "Katan warrior," he growled.

Katani nodded slowly, unsure whether it had been a question or a simple statement.

"What weapon?" Buiva asked suddenly.

"All," she said quietly, with just a touch of pride in her voice. Advancement in the Katan Sisterhood was measured by proficiency with weapons; the greater the warrior, the more weapons she had. There were few who could have said all.

"No weaknesses?"

Katani smiled at the fierce-seeming old man. "I'm sure there must be now; it has been long since I practised with more than sword, spear, knife and bow."

Buiva was about to say more when he suddenly turned, moments before a second figure appeared in the doorway.

"Maurug," Mannam and Buiva said simultaneously.

The Destroyer was a small, stunted man, squat and with a pot-belly. His face was round and fringed with a few remaining strands of snow-white hair that mingled with the similarly ragged threads of a beard. His eyes were cold, black, hard, piercing, and completely without compassion. He was wearing a courtier's robe of crimson silk that had been fashionable several centuries previously, high-necked, puff-sleeved, and ground length; the sleeves were wide and flowing and the small man's hands were lost in them.

He looked slowly from face to face, his eyes lingering on Paedur and Katani, his lip curling in something like disgust. "I smell intrigue." His voice was a whine. "Death and War together, an interesting and apt alliance."

"And now Destruction," Buiva added slowly. "The trinity is complete."

"Not quite," Mannam said, his rasping, cracked voice sounding weary. "There is one yet to come..."

"Who?" Maurug snapped.

"Me, perhaps?" The voice was high and lisping, sounding slightly breathless.

Paedur distinctly felt the atmosphere change and beside him Katani stiffened; whatever feelings the three gods of the Pantheon had for each other, they were at least tempered by something close to respect, but the bard, even without his enhanced senses, knew that this feeling did not extend to the Nameless God of Delusion and Madness.

The god was tall and thin, his build similar to the bard's, but fair where he was dark. His features were soft, almost gentle, with a definite effeminacy about them, until one looked at his eyes—and they were bronze. He was barefoot and wearing a simple peasant's garb of jerkin and breeches, which looked completely incongruous on such a soft-looking creature, for he seemed more suited to satins and silks than the rough woollens and worn leathers.

"Well, well, well," he lisped. "Death entertaining War and Destruction, how interesting. And two others, also…" He turned, the movement deliberately exaggerated, and stared at Paedur and Katani, and his glittering bronze-coloured eyes narrowed, and suddenly he didn't look quite so crazed, only infinitely cunning and dangerous. "What have we here, eh? A creature from the World of Men, but not wholly a man, and a woman of the Silent Wood, but not completely dead. What a truly interesting combination." He put his large and surprisingly rough hands on his hips and turned to look at Mannam. "You must explain."

"These two," Maurug growled, his thin voice querulous, turning his large head and glaring at the two silent figures. "Who? Why?"

"The woman is a warrior of the Katan," Mannam said slowly. "She has been within my domain for some time now. Her presence here is perhaps fated; she chose to accompany the man, and she has his and my trust. The man…well the man is Paedur, the…"

"Bard!" the Nameless God hissed in delight. Maurug merely grunted but turned to look at Paedur more closely, while Buiva remained silently watchful. "Why, this is becoming enthralling," Madness enthused. "You must know that I was entirely in your favour when we chose a champion," he said to Paedur. "I just knew you would be the most successful…"

Paedur raised his hook, the sudden movement silencing the god. "We have much to do, much to decide upon," he said quietly, using his trained voice to project a sense of urgency, "and while I know time holds no sway here, our time—or rather your time—is being measured on different planes, and slipping away."

Buiva shifted his grip on his mace and chain, the rattling sound shifting all attention onto him. "You should explain," the God of War said quietly. Madness opened his mouth to add something, but a glare from Maurug kept him silent.

Paedur went and sat on the edge of the low wall that surrounded the roof and looked down over the city. It was unnervingly quiet, Mannam having returned his subjects to their dwellings, where they stood in the shadows like statues, their senses active, their bodies immobile, and now the only movement was the turgid flowing of the Naman, the air bitter and foul with its stench. When the bard looked back, he found the gods had settled themselves in various attitudes of attentiveness; Madness was now leaning eagerly across the cracked sundial, Mannam had stepped back into the shadow of the doorway, while Buiva was sitting with his legs stretched out straight in front of him, his eyes closed, his back against the low wall. Maurug was crouched on his heels close to the God of War. Katani had taken up position beside the bard, her eyes alert, watching the city— and beyond—for any movement, any signs of an attack.

"I will speak," Paedur began, "and I must beg of you not to question me at this time; there will be time enough for questions later.

"Now, the situation is a simple one. Mannam is threatened with death. Aye, someone is attempting to kill the Dark Lord. But it is not just Death and the office of Death that is in danger here, but also all the Planes of Existence. We are facing an enemy who is not content with securing Death's somewhat dubious crown, but also seizing the various crowns of the differing kings of all the Planes of Life. And I would imagine he intends to do this with an army of dead.

"That man is Churon, who in the world of Men bore the title Onelord. Ah, you all smile. I see you know the name. Well, if you are familiar with the name then perhaps you will recall something of the man behind it. Yes, a man who secured the Nations from the Shemmatae and founded the Seven Nations as they are now, but also a man who butchered untold thousands because, he felt that in one way or another they stood in his way or opposed him.

"History has made much of this man, has made him what he was not, and the myths and legends that surround his name only add to the glamour. But you all knew him, and knew what he truly was—a warmonger, a destroyer and quite, quite mad." Paedur glanced at each god in turn and they all slowly nodded. "And now this man wants Mannam's place!

"He has already made some attempts on Death, and waiting in the wings is Libellius, the Deathgod of the New Religion. Now, we cannot imagine what dealings these two have had together; perhaps Churon will take the crown for Libellius, and the New Religion will rule this place, or perhaps Churon will rule as Death..." He shrugged. "We cannot tell. Personally, I imagine the Deathgod of the Religion would be only a figurehead; the real power would be Churon. I think it is plain that he wants to be Onelord again, lord of this place and all the Planes of Life." He stopped and then added slowly, looking at each face, noting their expressions. "And he must be stopped, not just for my sake and the sake of all those in the World of Men, but for yours, also. For if he triumphs here, how long do you think it will be before he sets his sights on your positions? We have to kill Churon," he finished.

"Impossible," Maurug snapped.

"Completely so," Madness agreed.

Buiva remained silent, but he nodded his head, an almost private movement.

"Why?" Paedur suddenly thundered, startling them. "You are Maurug, the Destroyer, a joyless creature whose only pleasure is destruction, and whom legends accuse of being almost entirely responsible for the fall of the Age of the Culai. Think of the challenge, think of the joy, it would be to destroy the greatest threat not only to this world but to all the worlds, a threat to the very gods themselves.

"And you, you are Madness, Delusion and Madness. Surely we have here one of your creatures, one of the god-touched. Tell me how difficult it would be for you to make further suggestions to this man, to drive him further over the brink into absolute raving insanity? If it is true that you feed on the essence of those whom you claim, think of the feast you would have on Churon's blighted essence.

"And what of War? What do you say? Churon has served your cause often and bloodily. With all your experience of the man, can you not tell me how I can defeat him?"

Buiva was the first to break the long silence that followed. "I can tell you what will defeat him," he said softly. "It is true that I sat with him often enough while he planned his campaigns, and so I can tell you that he is a brilliant man, with that depth of vision that is found only in the greatest of warriors. Defeating him is relatively simple—after all, he is but a man—but I think your greatest problem will be getting close to him." He sat forward, his rusted mail scraping off the stone. "Do you know that he always wears a suit of leather next to his skin? It encases him from neck to groin and is woven through with strands of supple iron wire, designed to turn a knife or even a sword thrust." He paused expectantly.

"A precaution for a man in his position. I know that there were several assassination attempts," Paedur said slowly.

Buiva smiled mirthlessly. "But that is not the reason. Do you know that Churon the Onelord has a fear, a simple dread?"

"I never knew him to fear anything," Katani interrupted, turning slightly to look at the War God.

"He fears spiders," the Nameless God lisped, "small, harmless, unobtrusive things, but he has a dread of the creatures. But then, he is mad, I suppose," he added with an innocent smile.

"I know of people who fear spiders," Paedur said in surprise, "and I would not have considered them mad."

"But do you know of someone who feared spiders enough to kill one by plunging a burning torch down onto it…when it was walking on his own leg!" the Nameless God lisped.

"Are you saying he fears them even to his own destruction?" Paedur asked, looking at the gods.

Buiva, Maurug and the Nameless God nodded in unison.

"Well then, surely here is a way to his destruction?" Paedur said slowly.

"I don't think the sight of a spider, no matter how big, will frighten him to death," Buiva said gruffly.

"I know that, but it might distract him long enough to lower his guard, and then he is just as open to a sword or knife blade as any man." He looked at Maurug. "Let us say I manage to kill this man. Can you destroy his body so that he cannot return to any semblance of life?"

Maurug nodded sharply. "Once Mannam or one of his creatures takes his essence, he could pass it to Madness, who will feed on it, and I can then feed on his body. Nothing will survive when we are done with him."

"That still brings you back to how are you going to slay him in the first place. How are you going to get close to him?" Buiva asked.

Paedur smiled grimly. "I intend to ask his lady those same questions."

"I am Paedur, a bard, and this is Katani, a warrior of the Katan Sisterhood. You are Deslirda, wife of Churon the Onelord."

"Once," the woman whispered very softly. "No more."

"You are comfortable, my lady?" Katani asked, stepping out of the shadows that clustered about the edges of the long cellar library.

The woman nodded, the movement quick and shy, her sky-blue eyes darting from man to woman and then dropping back to her hands, which were resting on the simple table she had been seated behind. "I am comfortable."

She was a small, delicate-seeming woman, with pale, almost translucent skin, and bright blue eyes that seemed far too large for her face. Her hair, which was the colour of old ivory, had been crudely chopped in a ragged line across her forehead and hung in untidy clumps down her back. She was wearing a simple peasant-woman's gown of rough sacking tied around the waist with a belt and she was barefoot. Her long-fingered hands were raw and chapped and her nails were broken and ragged.

The bard had watched her from the shadows when she had arrived. His legends had constructed him an image of a completely different person, and he found it hard to think of this simple, frightened peasant-woman as the Lady Deslirda, the Light of the Nations. A bainte had brought her and Paedur watched it bend its round head and whisper something to the shivering woman before it stepped away and pulled the library door closed behind him.

Katani touched his arm lightly. "What was that all about?" she murmured.

"Last minute instructions—what to tell us, or what to withhold. I cannot help feeling that Mannam is playing with us, using us to further some obscure end of his own."

The warrior nodded.

Paedur stepped out of the shadows, visibly startling Deslirda. He bowed deeply without speaking and escorted her to the far end of the library to where a small, ancient table and two chairs had been set up. He seated her and then sat down opposite the woman and introduced himself.

"My lady, I must apologise for bringing you here so abruptly and without so much as a by-your-leave..." Paedur began.

"Are you Death?" Deslirda asked suddenly.

"No, my lady," Paedur smiled, "I am not Death."

"You remind me of him." Her eyes drifted off his face and then slowly returned. "You are somehow connected to him?"

"No, my lady," the bard said softly, something in the woman's attitude and manner beginning to alarm him.

"I met him once," she breathed, her large eyes darting.

"Who?"

"Why, Death. I met Death, when I died." She smiled. "One of his winged creatures brought me to him, the same one that brought me to you. Or at least I think it was the same one; they all seem alike." Her eyes focused briefly. "You must have some influence with Death."

"I think I might have a little," Paedur smiled, his eyes never leaving her face. He was aware of Katani moving around behind the woman, knowing that she too was aware that something was desperately wrong with the woman.

"What did the bainte tell you before he left?" Paedur asked softly, projecting calmness and confidence, using his trained bardic voice to lull her suspicions.

"He brought me, as he once brought me to Death, and now he brings me to you, but he tells me not to speak to you of the Place of Judgment. Why is that, I wonder, if you are Death?"

"I am not Death," Paedur repeated patiently. "What is the Place of Judgment?"

"Where Alile sits," Katani said very quietly, "passing judgment on the dead. Obviously there is some *geasa* about speaking of the judgment."

The bard nodded, his eyes never leaving Deslirda's face. "I do not wish to speak to you about Death," he continued, calmly, softly, "nor do I wish to speak to you of the Place of Judgment. I want to speak to you about Churon."

Something moved behind Deslirda's eyes at the mention of the name, something fearful. "You are not from him, are you?" she asked, a thin, high note of desperation creeping into her voice.

"No," Paedur said forcefully, "we are not from your husband; we have no connection with the man, and we mean you no harm. Do you fear him?" he asked in the same tone of voice.

"No, not now. He can do nothing to me now; he is dead and I am not!"

"My lady," Katani said very gently, "you too are amongst the dead."

"No, no, no," Deslirda said quickly, "I have been judged, I am dead no longer." And then, suddenly realising she had said something she shouldn't, she clapped both hands to her mouth, her eyes wide and terrified. "Oh, I didn't say that! You didn't hear me say that!" she said fiercely, pleadingly.

"We heard nothing," Paedur said quickly, glancing at Katani.

"Nothing," she agreed.

"Tell us about Churon," Paedur said, watching her face closely, and once again he saw the reaction, saw the fear flicker in her eyes.

Abruptly the woman's shoulders slumped, and the tautness left her face. "Why do you want to know?" she asked tiredly, and suddenly the slightly mad and terrified woman was gone and in her place was a tired young woman in a shapeless, foul-smelling dress.

"We need to kill him," he said evenly.

Deslirda stared at him for a moment, and then she began to laugh, the sound shocking and terrifying in the still silent place. When the laughter grew towards hysteria, Paedur slipped his hook from beneath his cloak and touched the back of her hand with the ice-cool metal. The shock brought her back to her senses. "He is dead, bard, dead," she gasped, "and he cannot be slain now. You are too late, you and all the others who would, who should, have slain him during his life, cannot harm him now. Kill him and he will rise again and again..."

Paedur abruptly tapped the metal surface of the table with the point of his hook, scattering sparks, shocking her into silence.

"I intend to kill the man, my lady, and I intend to ensure that he does not rise again. When I am finished, Churon the Onelord will be no more."

"No more," Deslirda whispered. "No more," she nodded, liking the idea. "And how will you do this?" she asked.

"That is to be determined, but I will need your help," Paedur said cautiously.

"Freely and gladly given," Deslirda said quickly, something like animation coming back into her face.

"I need to know about the man," Paedur said, "and I am drawing an image of him from various sources. But you knew him best of all. You lived with him for what, twenty summers?"

"Closer to twenty-five," Deslirda said absently.

"How did you meet him?"

"I was sold to the Onelord when I was twelve summers old," Deslirda closed her eyes, remembering. "But I suppose the legends about him don't say that now, do they?" She opened her eyes and looked at the bard. He silently shook his head. In the myths, the fearless warrior Churon wooed and won the heart of the beautiful princess of Broar only after defeating several other claimants for her hand.

"I was twelve years old," she murmured, shaking her head slightly. She looked at Paedur and smiled. "Before I died I decided I would leave a record of my life with Churon, telling how we met and how I came to be his wife—for, you see, even in my own lifetime the myths were already growing up. But I never committed it to paper; I was afraid Churon or one of the servants—and they were all his spies—would find it. But I have it all written down here." A slender finger touched her head.

"Tell me," the bard said quietly.

She nodded, her expression now calm and composed, her earlier fear and nervousness forgotten as she remembered. When she spoke, her voice took on a sing-song quality, almost as if she were reading from a page of script.

Churon began his career as a slave, and then became a bandit, and he was ambitious even then. Unlike conventional bandits who contented themselves in the main with stealing from caravans and merchants, Churon and his gang would raid villages and, as they grew in numbers, towns, and finally cities.

My father was King of Broar, with his capital in the city on the road to the west, when it was attacked by Churon and his army of brigands. However, this time, instead of sacking the city and enslaving the inhabitants, as he had lately been wont to do, he demanded just one thing: the hand in rightful and lawful marriage of the Princess of Broar—me. His reasoning was simple: by marrying a princess of the line, he would become heir to the throne of Broar, which, although a small and rather unimportant kingdom, was of some strategic importance; but more importantly, it would enable him to pursue his claims to the throne of the Emperor—or the Onelord as it was known then—with a certain amount of respectability.

And respectability was something Churon always desperately wanted.

He was born a slave, the son of a noble woman who indulged her appetites for coupling with animals by mounting a Chopt. When she had finished with the creature, she cut its throat, and then when she found she was with child, she kept it. Even Churon himself was unsure of the reasons; perhaps she was unsure just who the father was, for she had many lovers, but she was also a cruel woman, and perhaps the idea amused her. When she was delivered of a black-skinned, white-haired babe, her secret was out, and it is a measure of the widespread knowledge and acceptance of her licentious extravagances that no one thought too much of it. The child was given to a servant to raise as her own, and he grew up thinking himself a slave.

But his mother was a strange and cruel woman, and when he was fourteen or fifteen winters, she seduced him. She slept with him a dozen times before she finally told him the truth. He said nothing to her then, but the next time they made love, he strangled her at the height of her passion with his bare hands.

So...

So, this man, this terrible, terrifying man, more beast than human, gave my father a choice: allow him to marry me or he would destroy Broar. And he was quite capable of doing it. So I was married to him.

He felt nothing for me, he knew nothing about me, didn't even know my name when he was demanding my hand in marriage from my father. All he knew at that time was that the King of Broar had one daughter and through her he might legitimately pursue a claim to the crown.

He took me with him into the countryside, but I was only so much extra baggage, and I felt that there were times when he thought about killing me—he would still retain the title to the city of Broar and the rights that went with it—but otherwise he ignored me. He killed and tortured, burned and pillaged and whored without any thought for me, and many a night I sat in the back of the tent and watched him take two or more women to his bed, some of whom were willing, others less so.

It was some two summers later before he consummated our marriage, and if the truth be told, he remained faithful to me for at least two moons after that, although we were making the beast with two backs every night for those two moons. And then he lost interest; there were other bodies to explore and he moved on. Oh, he still returned to me occasionally, much as a child will return to a favourite toy, or a storyteller will come back to a favourite tale, but it was always only briefly.

For Churon had one ambition: to rule. And he set about achieving that ambition with singleminded determination. Marrying me had been a step, deciding on a cause was the next. He wanted a cause which would unite the people behind him, something emotive. And he settled on the Shemmatae.

The Shemmatae had been in this land for a long time before Churon made them a cause. He accused them of being recent invaders, but in truth they had been trading with the Nations from the First Age of Man. They were never well liked but they were always respected. They were great traders and brought spices and rare herbs, furs, precious stones, fabulous armour and weapons and rare books from the Land of the Sun. They were wealthy—wealthy beyond belief in some cases; indeed, there was a story current then that the poorest of them was wealthier than the richest king.

To achieve his ends, Churon employed a group of wandering bards to campaign against the Shemmatae. He had them create myths and stories about them and their atrocities; if the truth were only known, some of the Shemmatae atrocities Churon had perpetrated himself, and then these bards took to the roads spreading the tales.

And you are only too aware of the power of the bard...

Public opinion turned against the Shemmatae—surprisingly quickly, too. Indeed, it happened almost too quickly for Churon, and he was forced to act swiftly to put his army together to achieve his great victory. But when he tallied his troops and those who owed him allegiance, he was honest enough with himself to admit that there was no possible way he could win; he needed more men.

So he set about extracting an oath of fealty from the Brothers, the Kings of the Nations. Some he tricked and some he threatened, but in the end they all gave him their armies, and with them ... well, he won the Battle of the Sand Plain and defeated the Shemmatae. And he was the hero of the nations. In return there was nothing left for the Brothers to do but to acknowledge him the Onelord.

And although he had achieved what he desired, he remained unsatisfied.

He sat about building his dream, the Silver City of Shansalow. But that was something he never saw completed. From the very start it was a shambles, and he was still naïve enough to be cheated. The silver with which he had ordered the palace roof sheathed turned out to be nothing more than polished and painted tin. The diamond wall he ordered built in our bed-chamber—that was a whole wall inset with diamonds—turned out to be base also, the diamonds were nothing more than quartz.

And what a rage he flew into when he discovered that. He had the gem merchant flayed alive and then had the quartz stones ground into powder and rubbed into the man's raw flesh. That was before he boiled him in oil.

I would not say his reign was successful. He was a man of great ambition and vision, but he was a bloody barbarian at heart. He lacked tact and was unable to see—except for a crude instinct—that he was being plotted against. He quickly attracted a huge crowd of hangers-on, and most of these he foolishly appointed to posts far beyond their abilities to control or indeed even comprehend in some cases. The Empire he had come to rule quickly began to fall into disarray, although that was not immediately apparent on the surface. There were wars aplenty, and this kept the people and the merchants happy, and for the first time in many years the Nations knew prosperity.

But it was all a lie, a lie...

Deslirda abruptly fell silent, and eventually Paedur leaned forward and touched the rough cloth of her sleeve. When she looked at him her eyes were wild and darting again.

"You see, bard, he destroyed the Empire, destroyed it—because of his ego and stupidity. Churon the Onelord was a fool."

"And you loved him!" Katani stated flatly.

Deslirda nodded briefly. "And I loved him."

"What did he fear?" Paedur asked quietly.

"He feared nothing."

"Every man has a secret fear, something which brings him awake in the dead hours of night, heart pounding."

Deslirda opened her eyes and stared at Paedur. "When he died, bard, I heard he stood up and demanded that he be taken to Mannam. Even death held no fears for him."

Paedur glanced quickly at Katani and then looked back to the woman. "I have been told that he had a morbid fear of spiders..." he said slowly, watching her reaction.

"Spiders," she whispered, a broad smile spreading over her wasted face, "ah yes, how he feared them. And yet snakes and lizards held no fears for him. Is that not strange?" She looked at the bard, her eyes wide and staring.

"Strange indeed," Paedur returned her smile. "What were his interests?" he asked gently, grasping for something, something which would give him an insight into the man.

"His only interest was himself—and his dream," Deslirda said bitterly.

"He took no special joy in something: good food, wine, art, jewellery, weapons?"

"He collected women, bard, briefly, and with the sole intention of impregnating them!"

"Why?" Katani blurted.

Deslirda half turned to look back over her shoulder at the warrior-woman standing in the shadows. "He had this idea of siring a child on a woman from every land, so that one day all the nations on this Plane of Existence would be ruled by his children."

"Did he like children?" Katani asked.

"You forget, lady, this was the man who burned the monastery school of Moise, but only after ringing it with his troops to ensure that no-one—and they were his orders, no-one—escaped. I don't know how many children and monks died that day."

"Half a thousand," Paedur said sombrely.

Deslirda turned back to the bard. "Now I have answered all your questions fairly, and I would have you answer just one of mine. Can you kill him—kill him so that he will never rise to walk again?"

"I intend to kill him," Paedur said simply. "I must!"

12
The First Battle

"I think perhaps it was the first cause he truly believed in."
Tien tZo, biographer of Owen, the Weapon Master

The first sightings were made just before the grey lights of dawn brightened the east. By sunrise the sightings had been confirmed: an Imperial army of three legions was marching into the wastelands.

Although the number was a surprise, their coming was not unexpected. Recently, the numbers of refugees coming in from the devastated coastlands, fleeing the erratic tides and unnatural weather into the more stable interior, had died to a trickle, and for the previous few days none had come through the mountain passes which Kutor's men held.

On Keshian's instructions, spies had been sent out into every village and town on the borders of the wastelands, but none of them had returned, and similarly a small foraging party had also vanished without trace.

Curiously, Keshian had been inclined to treat this as a good sign. With his experience of the Imperial forces, he explained that it was common policy to completely seal off a suspect town or area, allowing nothing in or out, and then gradually pick off the raiding parties or individuals who ventured out. The purpose was twofold: it served to reduce the numbers of defenders and instill a degree of fear and uncertainty. However, he added, it was a policy they pursued only when they were unsure of the numbers they were facing.

Kutor found Owen in one of the towers with his eyeglass in his hands, slowly and methodically scanning the horizon. He didn't move as the prince entered the small, chilly room. "You've heard?" he asked quietly.

"How many?" Kutor asked, strangely feeling nothing now that the moment of truth was fast approaching. Up to this point he had been entertaining the vague fantasy of just leaving, of just mounting up and riding away with his own men, heading south into the forest lands and taking up his old trade as a simple bandit. The prince was quickly coming to the conclusion that he was not cut out to be a leader—certainly not on the scale that Owen and Keshian were suggesting. And by acknowledging that, he knew that he was also in some vague way acknowledging the fact that they were in control. Owen and his slave-companion were organising the men, had turned simple, badly-trained and crudely organised farmers and shepherds into dedicated warriors; Keshian had turned a tumbledown fort into a fortress the Culai themselves would have been proud of. What place was there for him? "I'm sorry?" he said, realising that the Weapon Master was speaking to him.

"I said there are about three legions. I certainly counted three different standards, and that would confirm the earlier reports. I can see no siege weapons and certainly there are too few wagons for a sufficient quantity of either food or weapons."

"And?" Kutor asked.

The Weapon Master looked at him. "And what?"

"And what happens now?" the prince asked in exasperation.

"And now we wait for them to attack," Owen grinned.

"How can you be so sure they'll attack?"

Owen pointed and handed the prince the eyeglass. "Look. See there, and there. You can see the cavalry spreading out for a charge, and there, close to the front and centre, the huddled figures, you can just about make out a battering ram."

Kutor turned the wooden tube and a dim shape mistily resolved in the poor glass. "A tree trunk?" he asked.

Owen nodded. "A crude battering ram. They obviously brought no assault or siege weapons with them this time, but the next time they'll come prepared." He saw the grimace move across the prince's lips. "You don't approve?"

"Does it matter?" Kutor said, his voice sounding more bitter than he had anticipated, surprising him.

Owen took the glass from Kutor's hand and then turned the prince by the shoulders to face him. He looked deep into his dark eyes. "What's wrong?" he asked easily, almost gently.

"There is nothing wrong."

"There must be. Prince, we're on the eve of the first battle of your revolution. When we win this, the men will be a fighting force, confident and strong, able to face whatever the Imperials throw at us. This is important—vitally so. I would have expected

many reactions from you: fear possibly, eagerness, excitement—
but why the anger?"

"I've a feeling I'm not needed in this."

"But you're the reason we're doing this!" Owen said, surprised.

"No!" Kutor suddenly shouted, "No, I'm not the reason! I
may be the excuse, but I'm not the reason. You all have your own
reasons, for power or glory or coin or land. I don't know and I'm
not sure I care. But I know I'm only a figurehead, like a piece on a
gaming board which remains static while all the other pieces move
around it."

"I think you're making a mistake, prince," Owen said coldly.

"I wish I was," Kutor snapped. "Tell me, why are you doing
this, for what reason, for coin, land, favour, position?"

"But you can give me none of those," Owen reminded him,
"not now and possibly never. No," he shook his head, "I'm doing
this because the bard suggested that herein lay my destiny."

"And you generally follow the advice of someone you've never
met before?" Kutor sneered.

"Didn't you?" Owen asked mildly, turning back to the battlements and raising the glass again. "They're coming," he whispered,
and suddenly Kutor's anger vanished to be replaced by something
very close to fear.

"What do we do?"

"Do?" Owen turned to look at him, surprise on his face. "Do,
we do nothing. We let them come to us. This fortress will withstand
many moons of siege from a fully supplied and properly armed
siege-force. This force can do nothing against us. We'll let them
come, let the traps take their toll, and then I'll lead the men out and
they can finish off the rest."

"Do you intend to kill them all?"

Owen dropped the eyeglass into the pouch on his belt and
pressed the heels of both hands against his eyes. "It would be nice
to think we could, but that, of course, is impossible. What we must
do, however, is to kill the leaders. They must die. It is vitally important that we ensure than no officer or experienced soldier lives to
report back to camp."

"Why?"

"An experienced man will be able to give fairly accurate details
of the fortifications, our numbers, arms, and skill," Owen explained.

"However, an inexperienced, frightened soldier who has just seen his comrades butchered will tell hugely exaggerated tales of an impregnable fort and thousands of heavily armed and ferocious warriors."

"Surely that just means that the next time they will send a huge army against us?"

Owen grinned delightedly like a small child. "But we won't be here, prince. We will be knocking at Geillard's door while his army knocks on ours!"

The legion horsemen made their stately way down the incline towards the fortress, slow and confident in their numbers, expecting only a token resistance and a quick victory. According to their intelligence, the Culai fortress before them had lain empty for nearly a century and certainly from the distance it looked neglected and tumbledown. The company leaders drew their commands to a halt nearly three thousand paces from the open and rotted main gates of the fortress, and on order spears were levelled with all the precision that was the hallmark of the Imperial forces. And then, without any visible instruction, the legions started moving again, a trot that gradually gave way to a canter and then finally, with the open gates looming large and inviting, a gallop.

Less than a hundred paces from the fortress they hit the first of the pits. Those lucky enough to avoid the pits galloped directly into the small holes in the ground which were just deep enough to trap and snap a horse's hoof. Beyond the holes was another series of pits. Tien tZo and Keshian had dug the pits, staggering them to trap the greatest number of men and beasts, causing the most disruption. The screams of men and horses mingled together in an abominable cacophony. Those who rode into the pits died instantly on the poisoned stakes, but those who fell in on top of them were not so lucky. The warriors whose mounts had broken legs and hocks but had survived themselves were ridden down by their comrades in their headlong gallop, or the horses crashed into fallen mounts, sending their riders tumbling.

In a score of heartbeats the orderly, precise formation of the Imperial legions had been reduced to chaos. And while men and beasts milled around, archers appeared on the fortress walls and began pouring scores of poisoned shafts into the ragged lines.

Crossbowmen suddenly appeared then behind the disordered lines of the legions. Working in groups of two—one firing, one loading—these had been carefully chosen by Owen for the task of slaying the legion officers. They wore legion armour, and leathers, and worked slowly and methodically, relying on the confusion to cover their actions, picking out the captains, with their distinctive long straight-bladed swords, then the decade sergeants, with their shorter curved blades. The crossbowmen were using broad-headed, barbed quarrels, designed to punch through even the thickest metal-plate armour and inflict the greatest possible injury. And Tien tZo had coated the bolts with a virulent poison.

Ironically, the legion commander, whose weapon was tradition-ally a mace, had been killed in the first few moments of battle, his mount snapping its foreleg in a hole, sending its rider tumbling onto the ground and then crashing over on top of him, killing him in-stantly.

The three legion captains died in the first volley, and nearly two-thirds of the decade captains had fallen before someone realised that specific targets were being chosen. The remaining decade ser-geants attempted to rally the men together, but the signallers were dead, and when a man picked up one of the long curling horns to sound a command he suddenly sprouted bolts.

And then, into all the confusion, Kutor's forces marched out from the fortress.

The battle was brief.

Owen and Kutor walked the battlefield as night was drawing in. The sky was clear, and the heavens sparkled with the familiar con-stellations but also some of the new stars which had arrived with the Cataclysm and which were strangers to both men. The plain had been more or less cleared of all the usable arms and armour, and the dead had been stripped of everything, and in the fading light, the naked bodies looked like strange fungoid growths. In the distance the first tentative howlings of the wolves began, the blood and dead meat calling to them. With first light, Keshian and his men would build a score of funeral pyres and burn the bodies of men and beasts together.

"It seems I owe you an apology..." Kutor began.

"For what?"

"For doubting that you could do it."

"There was never any doubt of that," the Weapon Master smiled slightly.

Kutor detoured around the bodies of two men and a horse. They all bore the neat puncture wounds of arrows or quarrels, but the shafts had been removed, to be cleaned, refletched if necessary and reused. "I wasn't quite so sure," he admitted. "What happens now?"

Owen stopped by a corpse and turned the head slightly with the toe of his boot. "I knew him once; he was a captain in the legion," he remarked expressionlessly, and then continued on. "What happens now? In the morning we go through the prisoners, removing those whom we consider to be intelligent enough to give a coherent and informative report of what they have seen here."

"Remove?" the prince asked.

"Kill," Owen said, glancing at him. "Now is no time to be fainthearted," he warned, watching the prince's face change.

"I wish it were otherwise."

"You knew what you were getting into when this started," Owen reminded him.

"I'm not so sure I did," Kutor muttered. He pressed both hands to his throbbing temples and nodded. "Continue, please."

"We give the prisoners the opportunity to join us, and then we release those who wish to go."

The prince avoided a pit which was reeking with the stench of horse and human meat and waste. "Is that wise?" he asked.

"We want only those who want us. We need no conscripts. That was the mistake you made the last time you set your sights on the throne; your warriors either didn't want to fight in the first place or were simply paid to fight. I am giving you an army that want to fight for you. These men have a cause; they may not realise it yet, but they need to know that their cause is just, that when they die they can do so with honour. I wish to all the gods the bard was here; he could put it into words that would have them willing to die for you. But he is not and it's up to us, or rather to you, to do that." He paused and stooped down, examining the line of tattoos on a warrior-maid's upper arm. "Stone Clan from the Islands," he murmured, dusting off his hands and standing up, looking at the young woman's bloodsplotched face. "What a waste."

"How did we fare today?" the prince asked.

"Well," Owen said, sounding almost pleased. "We lost twenty men—only twenty—and there are another forty or so wounded, but none of them seriously, and Tien is attending to them with his salves and potions. We captured close on a thousand horses, good beasts too, strong, healthy and in excellent condition; and by my estimates there must be another thousand roaming the Wastelands by now, and I would be surprised if we didn't capture the vast majority of them within the next few days.

"The armoury has swelled to bursting, and I went through it earlier this evening with Keshian and Tien, sorting through the weapons, discarding those we considered unsuitable. As you know, we raided their camp late this afternoon, and as a result we have usable plate and chain armour for over half the men now, and we took enough scraps and bits to kit out the rest in some sort of body armour. Added to that, we have a huge quantity of clothing, beddings, cutlery, jewellery of all types, and coin. We also have the legion's supplies—mostly hard bread and dried meat, but it is just the fare we'll need when we march on the capital."

"You're serious about that, aren't you?" Kutor asked. "You seriously want to march on Karfondal?"

"Are you serious about ruling?" Owen snapped. He stopped and, taking Kutor's arm, turned him around, so that he was looking across the plain towards the dark bulk of the fortress. The plain was dotted with white corpses, like huge patches of moonflowers, their open faces turned towards the Lady Lussa. "We did this for you, prince," Owen hissed, "no matter what you might think, we did this for you. All of these souls went either to Mannam or Libellius this day. If you quit now, or consider this as less than deadly serious, then you do their honour and the honour of our own dead a great disservice."

Kutor nodded, looking across the battlefield, glad of the night and the enveloping darkness; he didn't want to know what creeping, crawling things were feeding now. He nodded abruptly. "What now?" he asked, suddenly decisive.

"Now, we consolidate our holdings here in the Wastelands, prepare camps and supply bases closer to the Nations, and set a series of guards on all the routes into this place." He walked down the slight incline and waited for the prince to join him, and then they walked side by side back towards the fortress. "And as soon as we have word of an approaching Imperial army, we head for the capital."

"And let us assume we manage to take Karfondal, then all that leaves us with is an Imperial Army at our back."

"Oh, I've a few surprises lined up for them," Owen said with a wicked grin.

Salier sat before the leather-topped wooden table and slowly and deliberately spread the cards before him, reading aloud their meanings to his scribe, who sat out of sight behind a screen by the door where his presence wouldn't offend his master. Salier himself was in a mild trance-like state and was almost completely unconscious of what he was saying, and it would be only later, when the scribe's notes had been written up, that the magician would attempt to put some order to them.

He turned each card with exaggerated slowness, allowing its full implications to sink into his bemused brain before pronouncing on it. "I see War...and Trickery, Knavery, a soldier trapped by knavery ... no, an army destroyed by trickery. I see a man...a man of the blood, a Prince...and another, a Soldier and another, a Hermit...a seeker of knowledge...these are all influencing the Wheel, but the Wheel is still turning and the future remains mutable...

"I see death and the fall of cities...and death again. And I can see a dangerous hidden foe who brings death or who carries the taint of death on him. Avoid him at all costs..."

Salier was silent for a long time then, turning card after card, his lips moving noiselessly, his eyes tiny in his head, pupils lost in the shadows. "I see the death of a king, the end of a cycle, and yet I can also see the beginning of the family's rule." He shook his head angrily. "It is unclear. Damn this means of divination," he suddenly shouted, his frustration breaking his trance. "Would that I could travel the Void again." The small man stood and stretched, and then strode over to his scribe, and snatched the notes from him. "I hope you got it all," he hissed.

"Every word, Lord Salier," the scribe promised.

Moments later the magician was on his way to the Emperor to inform him that his army had been slaughtered.

13
The Mire

He was destined to rule, and his one great boast was that he would continue his reign after his death...

The Onelord: The Barbarian Saviour

The Mire borders Death's Kingdom, but is not truly part of it, and extrudes into several Planes of Existence...

Lilis' Geographica

The Silent Wood had an odour, a dry, desiccated odour of something long dead that had mouldered into dust; but the Mire smelt of warm, fetid death and decay, overlain by the offal stench of the Naman.

The Mire bordered Death's Kingdom, a huge area blighted by seepage from a rupture in the fabric of the Ghost Worlds that separated the various Planes of Existence. The dead walked in the Mire, those who had come in from the Silent Wood, and they mingled with the living from a dozen Planes of Life.

The Mire was a refuge on the fringes of Life and Death; there was no law, and while death was commonplace, resurrection of those already dead was equally frequent. Consequently, the inhabitants of the Mire had refined torture to a very fine art. It had become a game of sorts, a game played to certain obscure rules, the principal one being to keep the victim alive for as long as possible; death was a release.

Whole towns had grown up in the Mire and there was a city of sorts; and because the Mire bordered the others Planes of Existence, time touched it somewhat and it had a recognisable night and day.

It was night when Paedur and Katani came to the Mire.

The atmosphere in the tavern was redolent of sweat, sour wine, smoke from a score of filthy oil lamps, urine, and the acrid odour of fear. No one even looked up as the tall, hooded figure and the rag-wrapped woman entered the long room; the inhabitants of the Mire paid no notice to any of the strange creatures, be they human or otherwise, that wandered through its crazy streets and twisted alleys.

The man pushed the woman into a rough wooden seat in a corner while he went to the bar, which was nothing more than a score of roughly planed planks on crudely shaped uprights. The barman glanced in his direction and the man tapped two fingers on the scarred wood; the barman immediately set up two small mugs of a bitter-smelling black liquid that obviously had too much of the River Naman in its making. The hooded man produced two of the flat bronze chips that were one of the accepted currencies in the Mire and then carried the mugs back his female companion. He set one down in front of her and raised his mug to his lips.

"I think you're taking your life in your hands drinking that stuff," Katani murmured, raising her own mug to cover her lip movement.

"I've no intention of allowing even a single drop to pass my lips," Paedur said earnestly.

"A nice place," Katani said, looking around.

"I've been in worse," Paedur said, pretending to concentrate on his drink whilst he took in his surroundings, noting the entrances and exits but more especially the tavern's extraordinary clientele.

Many were from the Silent Wood and were dead, their weapons and costumes dating them from nearly every age, with the exception of the First Age of Man. Others were Sons of Men from the various Planes of Existence that bordered the Mire, and then there were others that were only vaguely human—the Were-Folk, creatures with too much non-human blood in them. The group was almost evenly divided between males and females; however, the majority of them were warriors of some sort, the remainder thieves or harlots.

An uneasy truce prevailed in the bar, all the more extraordinary when there was such a mixture of races and clans, some of whom were inimical to the other and all of them heavily armed. It was only when Paedur looked up and discovered the score of hard-eyed crossbowmen standing on the first-floor balcony that he realised how the peace was kept.

Paedur and Katani had come to the Mire looking for Churon. Because of their lack of knowledge, it had proved almost impossible to formulate a plan of campaign except in the very vaguest terms, but their first priority was to get close to the Onelord, and join his forces if possible. If, as Mannam claimed, Churon was operating out of the warren of the Mire, then it followed that he was recruiting his army principally from there also.

As the night wore on, the bar became even more crowded, and although tempers often flared, a warning from the bowmen above was usually enough to finish the argument. However, one dispute went beyond words and, amidst much wagering, the two warriors decided to settle the argument in the street outside. The tavern fell silent, the sounds of metal on metal, the grunts of the men and the final scream were all clearly audible to the silent listeners. All heads turned towards the door and money was already beginning to change hands when a soul-chilling howl ripped through the tavern. In the breathless silence that followed, the sounds of an animal feeding were clearly, disgustingly audible. Even the hardened warriors looked vaguely uneasy and Paedur noticed that the crossbowmen had transferred their attention to the heavily barred windows and the solid iron-studded door. And even in this place, where the gods had few believers, amulets and talismans were touched and rubbed, and lips began to move in quick, silent prayers.

The sounds of feeding continued—bones snapping and cloth or flesh ripping—for what seemed like a very long time, and then the creature moved on, something metallic scraping along the cobbles and against the alley walls to eventually fade on the warm night air. Eventually, when nothing further happened, the buzz of conversation began again, but it was muted now, the drinkers listening, hands never straying from sword or knife hilt.

The door abruptly burst open; an almost visible ripple of shock ran through the crowded room and the rasp of steel being drawn was plainly heard in the sudden silence. It remained open and empty for a few long moments and then an old man with thinning grey hair and a lined weary face, a cloak of broad dark-patterned tartan over rusted, stained mail, staggered into the inn pulling a length of chain.

"Brought your pet, eh, Grandad?" someone called.

A ripple of laughter ran around the room, and abruptly died as the old man hauled in the chain and they found it was attached to a long serpentine head easily as tall as anyone there present. Flat plates of overlapping scales covered the snout and two long curved tusks as large as a man's hand protruded from its snout. Its eyes were closed, or rather one of its eyes was closed; there was a gaping hole where the second had been.

The old man straightened up and pressed both hands to the small of his back. "I found this piece of vermin down the alley. It looks like it had been feeding on some offal outside," he said pleasantly, looking around the room.

"You...you killed it?" A huge warrior with skin the colour of saffron and eyes of coal said incredulously, looking down on him and his bloody burden.

"Butchered it more like," the old man agreed.

"I don't believe it," the warrior said.

"Nothing to it."

"I don't believe it," the warrior repeated, shaking his head. He nudged the creature's head with the point of his boot.

The old man's deep brown eyes hardened as he looked up at the warrior. "Don't call me a liar again," he said, the warning plain in his voice.

The saffron-skinned warrior grinned hugely, displaying his teeth, which had been filed to points. "Why? Are you going to kill me, as you killed this?" he demanded, his hand going to a huge broadsword that stood propped against the bar beside him.

"Aye, I'll butcher you, as I butchered this," the old man agreed without raising his voice, but everyone in the room heard it.

The warrior looked over his shoulder at the barman. "Indulge me this one, let me fight him here. My honour is at stake."

"Threatened by an old man?" the barman asked with a leer. Nevertheless he looked up at the bowmen and nodded his head. "Let them fight." And then he turned back to the room. "I'm giving odds on Gutandard."

In the general laughter that followed, a cold, curious voice cut through the hubbub. "And what are the odds on the old man?"

All heads turned to the hooded man sitting in the corner. "You've got money to waste, eh?" the barman asked, rubbing his hands on his broad, much-stained apron.

"I only bet on sure things," the hooded man said with a laugh. "All I've heard from this one is talk, while the old one is hauling a dead mireworm."

The saffron-skinned warrior strode over to the table and dropped his sheathed broadsword onto the wood. "When I kill the old one, I'll kill you, but slowly...slowly."

The seated man threw back his hood and looked contemptuously at the huge warrior, his face flat and hard, his eyes expressionless. "And what will you do? Talk me to death?"

Gutandard snarled and reached for the hilt of his sword, and suddenly his hand was encircled by a gleaming half-circle of polished metal. He looked incredulously at the hook that took the place of the man's left hand.

"I can take your hand off as easily as plucking an apple," the hard-eyed man said very quietly. "Now, why don't you go and die at the hands of the old man?"

Something like doubt flickered behind the warrior's eyes as he carefully wriggled his hand free of the encircling hook. Abruptly, he grabbed his sword and strode into the centre of the room, pulling his sword free and tossing the stained leather sheath to one of his companions. "Come, Grandad, it is time to die."

The old man nodded wearily. "Yes, time to die." He dropped the chain he was holding and walked over to meet Gutandard, his hand closing around the haft of his mace and chain. He was within half a dozen paces of the bar when the huge warrior charged, his broadsword sweeping around in a high decapitating cut.

The old man ducked with a swiftness that belied his years, and the spiked iron ball at the end of the arm-length of chain snapped towards the warrior. It struck low, hitting him squarely in the belt buckle, but with enough force to wind him. Gutandard staggered back, one hand going to his midriff, expecting it to come away sticky with his blood and almost shocked it didn't.

"Let us end this," the old man said reasonably. "I have no wish to kill you."

Gutandard looked at the gouge marks in his thick leather belt and experienced an emotion he hadn't felt for a long time—that of fear. But he forced a sneer to his cruel lips. "A lucky blow, old man. But you are dead now."

He cut wide and low, the sword coming up in a move that should have split the old man from hip to shoulder, with all of Gutandard's broad shoulders behind it. But the old man merely stepped back and the blow went wide, leaving the warrior slightly off balance.

The spiked ball of the mace ripped most of Gutandard's face off, splattering bloody matter all across the walls and the gaping onlookers. The warrior stood swaying for a moment and then he sank to his knees before finally collapsing full-length on the dirt floor. The old man nodded and then he lifted the corner of his tartan cloak and began to methodically clean the gore from his mace. "Anyone else?" he asked very quietly. The occupants of the tavern turned to their drinks, the body on the floor unheeded and almost unnoticed when it was dragged away a few moments later.

The old man picked up Gutandard's drink at the bar and then sat down beside the bard and Katani, his back to the wall. He drank deeply and then wiped his sleeve across his mouth.

"I'm astonished," Paedur said softly.

"For what," Buiva asked in surprise. "He was an amateur." Paedur shook his head and smiled. "No, not for that—that's no more than I would have expected. I'm astonished you managed to drink that foul stuff."

Buiva smiled tightly. "Killing always makes me thirsty." He drank again, as if to emphasise his point.

"How long will it take?" Katani asked softly, directing her question to no one in particular.

"Not long, I expect," Buiva answered. "If Churon is as good as I believe him to be, then he will soon know what has happened here. I think he'll want to meet the man who slew a mireworm and then Gutandard, one of his captains."

"He might decide to send you an invitation on the end of a sword," Katani remarked.

Buiva shook his head. "No, he needs good men badly. He'll be curious enough to send for us."

"Or come here himself," Paedur said, stiffening as the sound of a horse-drawn cart rattled over the cobbles.

"Unlikely," Buiva said quietly.

The door of the tavern scraped open and a half dozen shabbily dressed men entered, rough peasant's clothing knotted around their waists with lengths of rope. They made their way to the bar and were immediately served by the tavernkeeper, who set up six cups of the dark foul-smelling drink that seemed to be the only beverage the tavern possessed.

"Warriors," Katani said decisively, watching them closely.

"Are you sure?" the bard asked.

"I'm sure."

"How do you know?" he asked, dropping his head to his drink but continuing to watch the group.

Katani shrugged. "The way they walk, the way they hold themselves."

"A weaponed man walks and holds himself differently to an unarmed man," Buiva said without turning around. "Beneath the rough tunics, I'll wager they're wearing leathers and carrying knives or shortswords, and almost certainly one will possess a crossbow."

"There is one stooped over almost double, like a hunchback," Paedur said.

"That's the one."

"One is coming over," Katani hissed, loosing her dagger in its sheath.

The man was tall and broad, and his face would have been handsome except for the scar that began just above the bridge of his nose and then traced its way through his eyebrow and disappeared into the thick, curling hair just above his ear. "You'll pardon me?" he asked, indicating the space beside Buiva.

The old man nodded. "Please."

"All the talk is about you," the newcomer said, bringing the chipped cup to his lips but not actually drinking.

"And what do they say?" Buiva asked with a smile.

"They say you killed a mireworm and then killed Gutandard because he laughed at you."

"They talk too much."

"Is it true?" the stranger asked with a smile that curled his lips but didn't reach his eyes.

Buiva turned to look at him. "I killed the last man because he doubted my word," he said very quietly.

"It's true," Paedur said from across the table. "Now, why don't you tell us what you want?"

The man spread both hands wide. "I'm just a simple peasant…"

Paedur's hook shot out, wrapping itself around his wrist, and then with his right hand he pushed up the rough woollen sleeve, exposing a broad metal-studded leather band. "Not many peasants wear a warrior's wristband," the bard smiled.

The man pulled his hand free, scraping the flesh of the back of his hand on the inside of the hook. "Just who are you?" he demanded, the voice now hard and arrogant, the tone one of command.

"Travellers," Buiva said slowly.

The man's five companions had now surrounded the table and the tavern had fallen ominously silent. Katani looked up and nudged Paedur's foot with hers. He followed the direction of her eyes and found that all the crossbowmen on the floor above had their weapons trained on them.

The seated man pulled open the ties of his tunic exposing the metal-plated leathern tunic beneath. On his chest was an emblem, a single white circle on a black field. "We are Churon's men."

"Then it is you we want to see, or rather your master," Buiva said quietly.

"I'm not sure I understand."

"The mireworm and the warrior were both slain to attract your attention," Buiva said without expression.

"But why not come directly into our camp? We are recruiting warriors every day."

"I am not just another warrior!" Buiva said coldly, turning his curiously soft, gentle-seeming brown eyes on the man.

"So what was the point?" the seated man demanded.

Paedur smiled tightly. "This was an example."

The warrior shifted his attention from the old man to the hookhand. "And just who are you?"

"I am Paedur, a bard, newly come into the Silent Wood in search of the greatest myth in the Seven Nations."

"A myth?"

"Churon the Onelord."

The soldier smiled, nodding his head. "A myth, aye. A myth-made man, a man-made myth." He glanced quickly at Katani. "And this?"

"My woman," both Paedur and Buiva said together.

The warrior looked from man to man and smiled knowingly, and then he turned back to Buiva. "And you, grey-hair. Who are you?"

"I am Bove, mercenary warrior in the World of Men, until I came into the Silent Wood."

"I'd like to meet the man who dispatched you," the soldier grinned.

"Eight of them came with me into Mannam's Kingdom, the other twelve even I couldn't account for."

"If any other man had told me that I'd say he was lying."

"But you won't say that about me, eh?" Buiva asked.

The warrior shook his head. "I won't." He stood up and pulled off his peasant's garb. His squad likewise stripped themselves of their guise. Both Buiva's and Katani's estimation had been correct: the stooped man had been holding a cocked and loaded crossbow.

"I am Rade, captain of Churon's personal guard," the man finally introduced himself. He looked at Buiva. "If the Onelord finds you acceptable, I'll take pains to have you placed in this unit. We could do with a man of your experience." He glanced at Paedur, obviously dismissing him. "I haven't seen you fight."

"Pray you never have to," the bard said with a smile.

Rade glared at him, attempting to size up the enigmatic man. He was not a warrior, but he didn't look like any bard he had ever seen. "I'm sure the Onelord will find some use for you," he said finally. "We are always in need of jesters."

"I am quick to avenge my friends' honour," Buiva said softly, looking at the man.

Rade ducked his head, his eyes avoiding Paedur's. "Come then, and I will take you to Churon the Onelord."

14
Tien tZo's Tale

Like most great men he saw things in stark shades, black or white, good or bad, right or wrong—there were no halfway measures for the Weapon Master...

The Warrior, the Life of Owen, Weapon Master

It was, if the truth were told, an easy victory, and not truly ours. The men were jubilant, and naturally so; for most of them it was their first battle of any scale. But there were a few amongst us who recognised that the Imperials had been defeated by the use of the pits, and so our victory couldn't be taken as an indication of our strength.

I watched the Master walk the battlefield with Kutor the Prince in the aftermath of the battle and I knew by both their expressions when they returned that their discussion had not gone well. They parted company without words at the gate, the prince following the sounds of revelry towards the main hall, while the Master headed in the direction of his rooms. I finished up with Keshian—we were in the process of sorting the weapons—and hurried after the Master.

"The man is afraid," Owen snapped as I fell into step beside him. "He wants and yet he does not want the crown. He would like someone to give it to him painlessly and bloodlessly; I dare say he'd like Geillard to abdicate and pass the crown on to him." He shook his head savagely. "I cannot understand him!"

"Is he frightened of winning the crown?" I asked, "or is it that he fears your way of achieving it?"

The Master sighed and shook his head, running his hands through his thinning hair. "I don't know, Tien. Truly, I don't. He had a reputation as a ruthless brigand, and yet here he is now and I find myself fighting for a man I'm beginning to think of as a coward."

"But he fears for the lives of others," I pointed out.

The Master grunted and said nothing further until we had reached the door of our cavern-room. He paused with his hand on the latch. "I wonder where the bard is now. We need him." He looked at me, his eyes wide and troubled. "We need a bard, someone to fire the men with ancient battles, someone to remind Kutor that the price of most kingships is paid in blood."

"Finding a bard may well be difficult," I reminded him, following him into the room, "you recall the trouble we had in Baddalaur. All the bards and scribes seem to be in Karfondal restoring the records."

Owen pulled off his sword-belt and flung it onto his sleeping pallet. "Not a trained and recognised bard then, but a storyteller or reasonably literate historian." He pressed the palms of his hands deep into his eyes, wiping away the fatigue. "Oh, I don't mean now, not immediately. But you might bear it in mind when we go on the road."

"And when will that be?" I asked.

"The sooner the better," Owen sighed, sinking down into a chair, resting his elbows on the table. "If Kutor is left to brood for too long, I think we might lose him."

I sat down facing the Weapon Master, watching him, clearly sensing his concern and the underlying fear that everything might indeed come to naught. For as long as I knew him—and I knew him for most of my life—I think I truly began to understand him more in those few minutes than I had at any other time in our association. "This campaign means more to you than it does to him," I suggested softly, watching his face. "He is right, isn't he? He is only a figurehead."

Owen stared at me for a few moments without replying and then he said very slowly and deliberately. "He will make a fine Emperor."

"That is not what I asked."

"I know."

"Why are you doing this? What makes this war so special? And don't tell me you owe the bard a debt," I snapped, my voice louder than I intended it to be.

"You forget yourself!"

"I apologise." I immediately stood up and stepped back away from the table and bowed.

Owen suddenly sighed and buried his head in his hands, covering his face. "Sit, sit...please." When he looked up his eyes were red-veined and looked bruised, and in that moment he looked all his years.

"How long have we been on the road, Tien?" It was a rhetorical question and I didn't even attempt to answer it. "For too long," Owen said. "And what have we achieved, what have we gained?

Lesser Weapon Masters are now wealthy men, whilst we have nothing except what we can carry on our backs."

"We have our honour and our reputations," I said quickly.

The Master nodded. "And there is a place for both, but we cannot live on honour and reputation; we cannot eat honour and our reputations will not keep us warm in the Cold Months." His voice fell to an awed whisper. "We are getting old, Tien my friend, old."

"And you think this great campaign will make up for everything you've missed, give us everything we need?" I asked, conscious of the bitterness in my voice.

"It might," he said defensively. "It should mean we will not spend our last years in misery, as guards on some borderland fort."

"Have you forgotten that it was you who said that Kutor might have you assassinated when you had achieved his aim?"

Owen smiled, but there was no humour in it. "I said he would try. But I intend to have our position secured by that time, making our removal impossible."

"How often have you said to me that if someone wants you dead badly enough…" I reminded him. "We have killed kings and princes who thought themselves secure."

He nodded, leaning back and sighing. "It's a risk," he agreed. He suddenly sat forward in the chair and clasped both hands together on the table before him—a gesture of rare trust, since one of his hands was usually on a weapon. "Now, your estimation of today?" he asked, the decisive warrior again.

"We were lucky," I said shortly.

"I know. But your estimation of the men in general."

I shook my head. "It will be very hard to make any decision about them until we have actually gone on the road. You're sure to lose a few then."

"And Keshian?" he persisted.

"A fine soldier A little staid and predictable perhaps, but solid and dependable."

"Do you think he could control this army alone?"

"Without us?" I asked, surprised.

Owen nodded silently.

I looked at his face, but he had schooled it into that impassive mask he usually wore when he was planning something audacious. I thought about it and then finally nodded. "Yes, I see no reason why he could not. He has both the will and the experience, and his natural caution will be no hindrance in this campaign. A minor problem perhaps is that you will have to ensure that the men respect him. Perhaps a ploy?"

Owen nodded impatiently. "Of course, make him a hero in their eyes. But you are agreed that he can do it."

"I've no doubt of it."

"Good," he hissed in satisfaction, my conclusion obviously agreeing with his. He closed his eyes and relaxed, and I could almost see the tension draining out of his body.

"Do you want to tell me why it will be necessary for him to command the army?" I asked eventually when he continued to remain silent.

Owen stood up and strode around the room, slowly and methodically removing his weapons and piling them on his sleeping pallet. "You agree we won today by the will of the Old Gods..." he began, but I interrupted him.

"I didn't say that," I protested.

"By chance then?"

"I'll agreed to that."

"Well, whatever," he said impatiently, "we are agreed that something worked in our favour and the traps worked to perfection."

"Granted," I nodded, wondering where all this was leading. It was not unusual for the Weapon Master to ask my advice on matters of warcraft, and we were friends and battle-companions in many ways, but there was always the constant, albeit unspoken, reminder in our dealings that we were Master and slave.

"I think you'll also agree that taking out the legion captains and decade sergeants worked to our advantage."

"It was a master stroke. It left the legion like a serpent without a head, coiling to and fro without direction."

Owen nodded triumphantly. "It is a ploy I intend to pursue!"

I shook my head. "I'm not sure I comprehend..."

His eyes blazing, Owen sank into the chair opposite me and began to talk in a low intense whisper, using a version of one of the Shemmat dialects he had picked up from me. The chances of anyone understanding the obscure language was very small indeed.

"We are both agreed that Keshian can command this army and so there is little need for us here. But we must carry on the fight, we must carry it to the capital. You and I, Tien, are heading back east to Karfondal!"

"What!"

Owen nodded, pleased.

"Our names and descriptions are known all across the Nations," I said, a little breathlessly. "I'm sure every mercenary knows you by sight, every bounty-hunter knows the price on our heads—and these are people who would burn down a house full of people just to ensure that we died."

"You exaggerate," Owen said mildly. I shook my head and opened my mouth to reply, but he held up both hands for silence and continued, "I don't intend to walk straight into Karfondal with you trailing alongside carrying an armload of weapons. We will have certain advantages, including the fact that by now we will have been placed with the rebel forces. The Imperials know that the rebels are many days away and so we will not be expected—and man does not see what he is not expecting to see."

I nodded, accepting his argument. "What are we doing in Karfondal?"

Owen smiled, showing his teeth in a feral grin. "We are going to kill Salier and Barthus, Fodla and, if possible, Geillard himself!"

Ignoring my appalled silence, he calmly went on. "Salier is the Emperor's magician, counsellor, friend, and some say his catamite. Remove him and Geillard immediately loses someone he depends on a great deal, as well as one of his principal sources of occult power. Barthus is the Hierophant, the temporal representative and spiritual leader of the New Religion. He backs Geillard fully by word and deed, and he has an army of warrior priests at his command. He is a powerful force behind the throne but if he is slain, then the priests of the Religion will be caught up fighting amongst themselves for control of the Religion, and the Emperor will lose what little control he has over the holy Warriors. We could gain much by that confusion. Fodla is Geillard's Captain of the Guard..."

"I have heard of her," I interrupted.

"Kill her and the Imperial legions fall apart." Owen persisted.

"Did you ever hear of a Battle-Captain called Loust?" I asked him suddenly.

He stopped, confused, wondering at the abrupt, seemingly irrelevant question. "No..." he said slowly.

"He was a warrior," I said, carefully keeping my tone neutral, "one of the finest natural killers I have ever seen. As good as—and I say this most respectfully—perhaps even better than you. He took a commission to assassinate Fodla. By dint of bribery and trickery, he managed to evade her guards and reach her bed-chamber, but instinct or chance saved her and Fodla awoke as he was poised to strike and rolled from her bed as he cut. The man was armed with shortsword and knife and wore leathers, while she was naked and defenceless except for a small metal hand-mirror and a solid silver comb, which she snatched from a bedside table. She could have cried out and her guards would have cut Loust to pieces, but she didn't; she attacked him! The noise eventually brought the guards running and when they burst into the room, they found the huge woman standing over the broken body of the assassin. She had beaten him to death, using nothing more than the metal mirror and comb to defend herself."

"You're telling me this as a warning?" Owen asked.

"An illumination," I smiled.

"Assuming I can kill this mountain of a woman, the next will be Geillard himself."

"I would advise against it," I said quickly.

"He too has beaten someone to death with a comb?" Owen asked derisively.

I shook my head. "For Kutor's claim to the throne to have any real validity, it would be better if Geillard retained the throne. He must then lose it to Kutor, and more importantly, be seen to lose it."

Owen considered for a moment and nodded. "Agreed. It seems to be a relatively simple matter." He rubbed his hands together and laughed aloud. "Why, we're practically giving Kutor the throne."

"You still have to take it from Geillard," I reminded him.

I went in search of Keshian later that night; I wanted his opinion of Owen's scheme. I had come to like the small, rotund, grey-haired battle-captain, and he in turn had, I think, formed a certain measure of respect for me. I had encountered his like before in many lands; men grown old in the service of war. They were never brave men—brave men die young—but they were always competent, and age and experience had taught them the skill of killing with the least effort. Their lives always seemed to be ones of missed opportunities, of backing the wrong side, not running when they should have, or perhaps even running too early and quitting an ultimately winning side. And now, as ageing warriors, perhaps with a commission in an Outlands or provincial lord's force, they had little to show for all their years of war and battle. They were invariably unmarried and their friends were few. But they were rarely discontented; they lived, when so many of their companions over the years were dead or maimed.

I found Keshian in one of the well-rooms, deep in the bowels of the mountain. When we had first discovered it, the room had been filthy, the well almost completely hidden beneath piles of debris, but it had been scoured, washed with a mixture of lime grit, and brightly lit. The well itself had been cleaned of the filth and muck of ages, the slime scraped from the walls, the ropes replaced, and large waterproof buckets fitted. In times of siege a room such as this was life or death to the occupants. The battle-captain was sitting on the step that surrounded the well, holding up a crystal glass of well-water to the light, and watching a thin, green thread slowly twist and weave through the water.

I joined him and stared into the glass. What I had first taken to be a solid thread turned out to be a darting spark of fire. I looked through the glass at Keshian.

The old man smiled almost shyly. "The only magic I know," he said softly, lifting the glass slightly, "is a small spell my father taught me when I was a child and used to creep into his forge to watch the sparks fly as he shaped white-hot metal. It's a spell of water purification and calls upon the Lady Adur, the Goddess of all natural things, to cleanse and purify." He smiled as the darting green light winked out. "I was just making sure." He lifted the glass and drank half of it in one swallow. "Aaah, cold, cold, from the very heart of the mountain, and tart too. I once knew a man who could tell what land the water flowed through just by drinking it. And my father could tell what water was good for ironwork just by touching it to his lips." He handed the glass to me. "Drink?"

I hesitated before touching it, attempting to interpret his gesture. Amongst my people to share a glass is to create a bond, but I did not think this man would be aware of it. I nodded my thanks and accepted the glass. The water was as he had said, ice-cold and slightly bitter, tasting of copper and mineral salts.

"Will your water purification spell work on the whole well, or just on small amounts of water?" I asked.

Keshian shrugged. "I don't know. I've only ever used it on small amounts, usually only my own personal drinking water, but I could certainly try it on a suspected poisoned well or water-hole." He paused and then said, "But we would need volunteers to drink the water."

"Volunteers?" I scoffed. "Have we no prisoners?"

"I thought there were to be no atrocities," the battle-captain said warily.

"I hardly think giving the prisoners water would be considered to be an atrocity."

"But poisoned water?"

"No one would know," I pointed out.

"I would."

I looked at him again, this short, grey man with his too-soft eyes and his quick concern. "A battle-captain with scruples."

He smiled easily. "That's why I'm still a battle-captain and not a commander."

I drank again and then to change the subject, explained Owen's plan.

"It is madness, absolute madness!"

I nodded silently.

"Has he no idea of what he is up against?" Keshian demanded. "It is suicide! Surely these are not the actions of a Weapon Master?"

I shook my head. "That too has troubled me. And I will admit he has been acting strangely since we encountered that cursed hook-handed bard."

One of the sconces guttered in the draught coming up from the well, plunging one corner of the room into shadow. The battle captain got up stiffly and crossed to the bundles of rushes, pulling one from its rusted holder and holding its pitch-daubed head against a lighted one. When it was burning again, he reset it but remained standing, with his back against the smooth white wall, his arms folded across his chest.

"The bard is the key to this," he said slowly, "he has influenced us all in one way or another, drawn us all here, and has done more than his share to precipitate this coming conflict. And where is he now?" He suddenly shivered and rubbed his hands quickly against his arms. "I sometimes wonder if he is indeed the Champion of the Old Gods, as people are claiming, or just another Duaite in disguise."

"A Duaite?"

"An evil one, a dark one."

"There was nothing comforting about his appearance," I offered.

Keshian smiled mirthlessly. "Though I should not talk about him so. He did save my life."

"It appears he saved all our lives, and what greater debt can a man owe than his own life?"

"A ploy to trap us perhaps?"

I nodded. "Perhaps."

"And now we have the Weapon Master, our prime hope, preparing to go off on a wild, misconceived, hasty plan to Karfondal."

I held up a hand, stopping him. "It may be wild, but I doubt if it has been hastily conceived. I've known the Weapon Master for many years and when he finally sets out a plan of this kind before me, he has usually been considering it for quite some time. However," I added slowly, "in this case I am forced to agree that it does seem particularly ill-considered. But his mind is set; he passes command to you and we set out for Karfondal." I shrugged.

Keshian crouched until his eyes were level with mine. "But we need you both," he said softly, and there was a note of genuine concern in his voice that truly touched me. "Both of you are keeping this legion together, not Kutor and the promise of kingship, not the vague promises of payment and position someday, but the honour of being trained and fighting alongside Owen the Weapon Master. That is what they want, that is what keeps them here. They will not fight for me. I don't command enough respect in their eyes."

"But if Geillard's advisers could be slain..." I persisted.

"We would win," he said simply.

"That is the conclusion the Master has reached. And he feels strongly enough in this cause to risk everything to achieve it."

"But it still comes back to the simple fact that the legion will follow neither Kutor nor me."

"If Owen tells them?"

Keshian shook his head. "Would you follow second-best?" he asked.

I was forced to agree. "Well then," I said, "we will have to give the legion a reason to follow you!"

15
Churon

He was the Onelord, a man who knew it was his god-given right to rule, and the obstacles in his way were merely trifles to be disposed of.
The Onelord: the Barbarian Saviour

One Faith, One Land, One People…and One Ruler.
motto of Churon, the Onelord

"You bring me from my bed to show me a grey-hair, a one-handed cripple, and a woman! Have you taken leave of your senses?" The voice echoed down the cold stone corridors, booming off the chill sweating stones. The shouts were clearly audible to the three companions, who had been left to wait in a small chamber in what had obviously once been a monastery but was now being used by Churon as his headquarters.

Rade had led Buiva, Paedur, and Katani to the monastery on foot by a long and winding route that doubled back on itself more than once. The ploy was to meant to confuse, but the bard knew that with his trained and near-perfect memory he would be able to retrace their steps back to the tavern, and thence to the monastery again if need be.

Katani started at the harsh voice. "Churon," she whispered.

"You're sure?" Paedur asked.

"Some voices you never forget, especially when it's the last voice you heard before you died."

Paedur nodded and was about to speak when Buiva raised a hand. "They're coming."

There was movement in the hallway outside and then Rade stepped into the doorway. He was white-faced and there was a sheen of sweat on his face. Before he could speak, he was roughly thrust aside and Churon the Onelord strode into the chamber.

Partially from Katani's description and partially because he had been expecting more, Paedur was disappointed with the

Onelord. He had formed an image of a tall, broad, perhaps even a Chopt-like man but what he saw was a man no taller than himself, broad-shouldered but not excessively muscled, and it was only his ebon skin, that contrasted sharply with his snow-white hair and eyebrows and startlingly blue eyes, that lent him a slightly unnatural appearance. He was naked except for a heavy woollen cloak thrown across his shoulders, and he carried a thick-bladed hunting knife. He stood in the doorway and looked at each in turn, beginning with Buiva and finishing with the woman. He turned to look at the bard again and then walked up to him. It was only when Churon stepped up close and fixed his ice-blue eyes on him that Paedur realised that here indeed was a man of great power. Even without his senses he could sense the aura that surrounded the man.

Churon looked at the bardic sigil on Paedur's shoulder and then turned his attention to the hook, his eyes narrowing. He looked up suddenly. "Rade tells me you are a bard?" His voice was deep, slightly harsh, as if his throat had been damaged at some time, and his accent was that of the Northlands.

"I am Paedur, a bard." He bowed slightly.

"Why have you come to me?"

Paedur heard the note of eagerness in his voice and hid a smile. This would be easier than he thought. "I am but newly come to the Silent Wood, lord, and when I heard of your existence here in the Mire, I knew I could not let the opportunity pass to see the great Onelord. In my time, lord, you are a legend."

"A legend," Churon said softly. He pulled his heavy woollen cloak tighter around his shoulders, for the night was chill and damp. "So, they still remember me."

"There is no greater hero in the mythology of the Seven Nations," the bard replied truthfully.

"You must speak to me of these legends, bard," Churon said slowly, a thin smile touching his lips. He turned away from the bard and looked into Buiva's deep, brown eyes. "I am told you killed a mireworm and then one of my warriors—and all just to attract my attention."

"The mireworm was to attract your attention; the man called me a liar."

"And you killed him for that?"

"He besmirched my honour, and a man without honour is not a man," Buiva said with a smile.

Churon grinned. "I believe I said that."

"I believe you did. I am Bove, a mercenary in the World of Men."

"And now?"

"Still a mercenary."

Churon half turned to Rade. "Perhaps you did not do so badly after all." He turned back and looked at Katani, staring into her eyes, the only part of her face that was visible. "And you, what are you?"

"She is nothing, she travels with us," Paedur said quickly. There was always the possibility, however distant, that the One-lord would recognise Katani, or that her hatred for the man would betray her.

Churon looked at the bard and then at Buiva. "If she stays with you, she is your responsibility. Women are few enough in this camp and my men are…well, men."

"I can take care of her," Buiva said quietly.

"I'm sure you can," Churon said easily. "Rade will find you quarters and we will speak again in the morning. I can best decide then what to do with you." He nodded briefly and then left the room, followed by Rade.

The three companions remained in the chamber until Rade returned. There was a smile on his broad face and his scar stood out white against his tanned flesh. "Welcome to the Onelord's army. The pay is lousy, the food inedible, but the prospects are excellent."

"What are the prospects?" Paedur asked lightly.

"Life for those who have died." He laughed at their obvious surprise and hurried on. "And we're going to rule the world—and not just this world, but every world, every Plane of Existence." His voice fell to a whisper and he leaned forward, as if imparting a secret. "Perhaps even the Realm of the Gods themselves."

Katani stood with her back to the door of the turret room, one side of her face pressed against the wood, the fingers of her left hand brushing the handle, her shortsword in her right hand. Paedur leaned against the room's only window, a tall, arched opening that had once held glass—but now only the rotted remains of a wooden frame remained. He was watching movement in the courtyard far below, but his attention was in the room behind him. Only Buiva was resting, lying full-length on one of the room's two straw pallets. The only other furniture in the circular room were two bowls: one held water, the other was stained and foul-smelling.

Rade had apologised when giving them the room, explaining that there were no others available as the earlier arrivals had claimed them, but suggesting that if they saw something they liked he would have no objections if they were to claim it for themselves.

"We could have killed him," Katani said softly, almost accusingly. "He was there in front of us, naked, unguarded. We could have gutted him, should have."

"I know. However, I must admit to a certain curiosity," Buiva said, lacing both hands behind his head and staring up at the filthy beams that supported the conical ceiling. "I want to know how they are going to go about attacking not only the Worlds of Men but also the Realm of the Gods."

"There is a sizeable army camped here," Paedur said, nodding down into the courtyard. "And I can see what looks like hundreds of campfires burning in the surrounding countryside."

"Campfires are no indication of an army's size," Buiva remarked absently. "But you miss my point, bard. No army, no matter how big, how well equipped and trained, could hope to stand against the Gods of the Pantheon. Your friend Mannam would reap as he has never reaped before. Men can stand against men, but men cannot stand against the gods." He shook his head, "No, there is something more here."

"Unless he intends to unleash his army of dead and undead on the planes of existence and slay the followers of the Old Faith. Without their faith, the gods would be sufficiently weakened to enable the Gods of the New Religion to successfully attack," Paedur suggested very quietly.

"I know. I had considered that."

Paedur turned from the window and looked at the god. "Then surely by killing Churon..."

"But we don't know his plan, and without it there is little point in killing him." The god settled himself on the mouldy straw. "But there is little point in speculation now. Try to rest. We will see what the morrow brings and plan our campaign then."

"Churon stumbled across the monastery when he first came to the Mire," Rade said, answering the bard's question as he led the trio down the spiralling stairs. "It was a ruin then, and almost exactly as you see it. We've fixed up the gates, repaired the rents in the walls and cleaned out the cellars, but that's all."

"And you found no artifacts, no inscriptions?" Paedur persisted.

"Nothing. And I know Praetens has conducted several ceremonies in an attempt to discover the identity of the religious order that worshipped here."

"Praetens is here?" Paedur asked, surprised, "I thought Churon's magician had been destroyed in the battle of the Sand Plain?"

Rade laughed, "Aye, so did Churon. You should have seen the look on his face when the mage wandered into the council chamber one morning."

Alarmed, Paedur glanced back over his shoulder at Buiva. The god nodded, silently. If Praetens was as powerful a magician as legend made him, then he would immediately recognise the god.

"I would like to meet Praetens," Paedur said to Rade, his voice echoing off the walls. "I have never met one of the Susuru folk."

"An ugly devil," Rade admitted, lowering his voice, "but I'm afraid you'll have to contain yourself for a while longer. He left some days ago. I heard he had gone deep into the Mire, almost to the edge of the Shadowlands, on a mission for Churon."

Paedur looked back at Buiva and the god smiled. Praetens would be the perfect intermediary between Churon and Libellius. "I look forward to meeting him," he said.

"I don't know when he'll return," the captain confessed. The captain led them out into a broad courtyard that had once been paved with countless tiny mosaic tiles. Many were missing now, grasses and clumps of bushes and in some places just patches of bare earth breaking up what must have been a hugely complicated pattern. Paedur promised himself that if he got the opportunity he would walk the battlements and attempt to make sense of the pattern.

The courtyard was still and silent at this early hour. Twisting wreaths of yellow mist coiled around the remains of a score of campfires and the huddled bodies of warriors from a dozen races and times as they slept, wrapped in blankets and hides.

"If these are Churon's personal guard then they leave a lot to be desired," Buiva remarked.

"They are not part of the Onelord's guard," Rade replied without turning round. "The Onelord needs no guard here in the Mire; he has no enemies in this place."

"What about all the Shemmatae he dispatched in the World of Men?" Paedur asked with a smile. "Churon was the most powerful man in the known world in his day, and a man like that does not come to the throne without making some enemies."

Rade looked back over his shoulder, his face expressionless. "But there are none in this place." He led them into what had obviously once been the chapel of the monastery, but only its shape and the remains of a huge slab of stone that had once served as an altar betrayed its previous purpose. The tall arched windows that were set deep into the thick walls had all been boarded up and hung with moth-eaten tapestries on the inside to cut down on the draughts. The floor had been cleared of pews and there had obviously been tiles set onto the floor; now only broken chips remained. The walls and the high, vaulted ceiling were flaking, and there were gangrenous stains creeping up the walls in the darker corners. An odour of decay, of rot and damp and hidden foulness pervaded the building.

The Onelord was alone in the chapel, sitting on a simple wooden stool and using the altar stone as his table. He was clad in silver-blue body armour with a white snowbeast fur cloak thrown across his shoulders, and their opulence and colour only served to emphasise the desolation of the place. A naked flame-edged dagger lay on the altar beside him.

Rade turned away at the door without a word and without announcing them, and hurried back across the courtyard, finally disappearing into the shifting mists.

Buiva and Paedur strode down the length of what had once been the aisle, leaving Katani behind them standing just inside the door in the shadows.

"Ah, you slept well, I trust?" Churon half turned and lifted a delicate bottle of green-tinged liquid, shaking it slightly. "Drink? No? Pity, you don't know what you're missing." He tilted his head back and drank deeply, a trickle of liquid finding its way down his chin and settling onto the breastplate of his armour. Paedur noted that the fine silver metal was already stained a deep emerald and seemed to be blistered.

"I take it you want to fight with me?" Churon said suddenly, looking at both in turn.

"I will fight if the price is right," Buiva said slowly. "I do not know about the bard. We met on the road and only later discovered that we shared a destination."

The Onelord nodded. "Ah. I wondered how two such odd characters should come to be keeping company. And the girl?" He looked up searching the shadows for her. "She is?"

"A camp-follower in the World of Men who carried her profession with her into the Silent Wood," Paedur said with a smile.

Churon grinned hugely. "Of course. Old habits die hard." He turned his attention to the bard. "And why have you come here, bard?"

"I told you last night, lord. To meet with a legend."

"Is that the only reason?"

"I am a bard," Paedur said slowly, "I did wonder if it would be possible for me to create a new version, the true version, of the Tale of Churon the Onelord."

"Tell me, man. What do they call me in the World of Men now?"

"The Barbarian Saviour."

Churon threw back his head and howled with laughter, slapping his hands down onto the hard altar stone. "The Barbarian Saviour, eh? And what of my city, is that still remembered?"

"Shansalow, the Silver City?" Paedur shrugged. "Like most other cities of its type, it is assumed that it was a legend, a myth—like the Culai Isle," he added, with a slight smile.

"What! Shansalow was real. It was eighteen years in the building, and even when I left the World of Men it was still expanding. It was the finest city in the world. Why, the bards of my day compared it to…to…" He shook his head in exasperation, searching for the word, "the Culai capital," he said eventually.

"Ui Tyrin," Paedur supplied.

Churon nodded. "That was the place." He grinned fondly, remembering. "I will speak to you of Shansalow sometime. It so happens," he continued slowly, "that I think I am in need of a bard. The legend of Churon did not end when I left the Planes of Existence. I have been labouring long and hard both in the Silent Wood and in this place. I should imagine I have enough material for you to fashion a score of ballads."

"I am a bard, lord. My material is not set to music," Paedur interrupted him.

"I think my lord Churon knows that, bard; I imagine he has been subtly testing you, determining if you are indeed a bard," Buiva said with a grin.

Churon stood up and came down the steps to stand in front of Paedur and Buiva. He was holding the long flame-edged dagger in his left hand, tapping it absently against the rings of his silver-blue body armour. "You are a clever man...eh?"

"Bove."

"Aye, Bove. But I am satisfied he is what he says he is. But you, tell me how I may test you. When I walked the World of Men, I never met a mercenary as old as you."

"Do not let my looks deceive you, lord," Buiva smiled.

"For a mercenary, you are remarkably unscarred. How sure am I that you were indeed a hireling blade in the World of Men?"

"A scarred man is usually unlucky or just slow; I like to think I am neither of those things. I was a mercenary on the Planes of Existence, just that. A professional soldier, my sword and skills for hire to the highest bidder. I have fought in every land and for more causes than I even remember. In the last few years, however, because of my experience, I've commanded others, and before I entered Mannam's kingdom it was enough for me to sell only my advice and not my weapon skill."

"You are that good?" Churon asked, the disbelief clearly audible in his voice.

"He is known as the Master Warrior in the World of Men," Paedur said. "His fame is widespread."

The Onelord walked back up the steps and sank down onto his simple wooden stool, one elbow resting on the altar stone, his head on his hand. "I have an enemy," he said slowly, "a powerful man commanding a very powerful army. I want control of that army. How do I go about it?"

"Are they loyal to the man or the office?" Buiva asked.

"The office, I believe."

The war god shrugged. "Replace or buy the man."

"He cannot be bought."

"Replace him."

"How?"

"Assassination, of course."

"No stranger can get close to him. He is protected by...by an elite force, and he is also a magus of some strength and surrounds himself with spells and wards."

"Attack from within. If you cannot get close to the man, work on someone close to him, perhaps even use his elite force against him. Either have one of them kill him or turn them against him."

"And when he is out of the way," Churon persisted, "what then?"

"Replace him with a man of your own. Someone you either trust or control. Preferably the latter."

The Onelord nodded. "Your judgment is sound."

"Was that a test case or a real situation?" Buiva asked.

"Why?"

He shrugged. "Just curious. But if it was a real case I might volunteer to dispose of this enemy for you."

"Just to prove yourself?"

"Something like that."

"I doubt if even you could dispose of this enemy," Churon laughed.

"And why not? I've slain magicians before. Counter their spells, negate their power, and you'll find they bleed like other men."

"Not this one. I see the disbelief in your eyes." Churon smiled humourlessly. "My enemy is Death, old man, the Lord of the Silent Wood, Mannam."

Buiva nodded wordlessly.

"A powerful enemy," Paedur said. "I know of no other man who has earned Death's personal enmity."

"I am not as other men," Churon said coldly.

"Death must have a foe. There must be someone or something inimical to him," Buiva said slowly, almost as if he were thinking aloud. He looked at Paedur. "With your bardic knowledge, can you tell me what Death fears?"

"Death has no enemies," Paedur said, lifting his hook and beginning to clean it on the end of his furred cloak. "C'lte, one of the Lords of Life, might be considered a natural foe, but their enmity is more in the way of a game than anything else. The only person—being—inimical to Mannam would be Libellius, the Deathlord of the New Religion..."

Buiva nodded decisively. "Then that's it. You must enlist this Libellius and use him against Mannam."

"Hah!" Churon crowed triumphantly. "I am ahead of you." He saw the puzzled looks and came down the steps to place a hand on both their shoulders. "Libellius is in my employ, and has been for some little time now. We are already plotting to overthrow Death. My magician meets with him and his cohorts this very day to plan the final assault on the Lord of the Silent Wood."

"And Libellius will take Mannam's place?" Paedur asked.

"Aye."

"And you can control this Libellius?" Buiva asked.

"This Death God of the New Religion was a man before he became a god, but he has taken his vices and habits of one life into another. He can be controlled." The Onelord threw back his head and the flaking monastery walls echoed with his laughter. "Nothing can stand in my way. First I will take Death's Domain, then the World of Man, and finally the Realm of the Gods. I will be the Onelord!"

Two thin needles of steel touched the Onelord's throat. "I think not!"

16
Plans

"Men believe only what they want to believe, even when all the evidence points to the contrary."

Tien tZo

Details emerged only later.

The assassins had come in over the cliff face that jutted out over the fortress's walls, dropping down onto the battlements on hempen ropes woven around wire. The men, six of them, had killed the guard and then made their way down through the main body of the building, seemingly finding their way by trial and error to Kutor's guarded room. What happened then was unclear, but it seemed that one or more of them had returned to the supply room, which they would have had to pass, and started a small fire there. It was obvious that the intention was to create a diversion which would draw the guards, leaving Kutor alone and unprotected. However, as the will of the Gods would have it, Keshian, on his way to his own chambers, spotted the fire and the masked assassin and, although he was unarmed, tackled and killed the assassin. Grabbing the dead man's weapons he had raced down the corridor to Kutor's room and had reached it just as the five remaining assassins were preparing to attack. Without hesitation he attacked them and although they were bigger, well-armed and more comfortable with their weapons, he killed them in the time it took for Kutor's guards to race down the corridor to join him. The two guards had stopped in amazement, looking at the five dead bodies with the small stout man standing in their midst, bleeding from a score of small cuts.

The realisation of what might have happened, combined with shock, brought a rictus that might have passed for a grin to one of the guard's lips. "Is that all?" he had asked hoarsely.

"There's another in the storeroom," Keshian had said without expression.

"I feel sullied."

"There was nothing else we could do," Owen said quietly, patiently, but he avoided Keshian's accusing eyes.

"It was wrong," the warrior protested.

"It was necessary!" Owen insisted.

Kutor tapped the base of his goblet on the polished wooden table. "And it was successful. I've heard the tale a score of times today and each time it grows in the telling." He looked across at his captain with a smile. "Do you know you slew a dozen Gallowglas?"

Even Keshian grinned, and then sobered. "But if they ever find out?"

"They won't," Owen said, "and as the prince said, it has achieved our aim, the men are now looking on you as a hero."

"But I'm not a hero!"

"Have you never done an heroic deed?" Tien tZo asked quietly. He was standing with his back to the door, his hands behind his back, the fingers of both hands resting lightly on the rough wood. If there was movement in the corridor outside, he would feel the vibrations through the wood.

Keshian looked at him and shrugged in embarrassment. "I don't know."

"You are too modest," the Shemmat said quickly. "If the honour the men pay you now sits uneasily with you, then consider it as nothing more than payment for your past deeds of honour."

"Tien is right," Owen said, his voice weary, "and now let us end it. Keshian is a hero, the men will accept him as their leader—and that is enough," he added warningly, seeing Keshian about to protest again. "Now let us turn to the real business of this meeting." He looked at both Kutor and Keshian and glanced across at Tien, and then turned back to the prince and his captain. "It is necessary to add one thing further to the plan. No-one must know where Tien and I have gone, no-one must know the reason. Put out whatever story you wish, even that we just upped and left because there was no possibility of pay. That should be believed. After all, I am a professional mercenary soldier..."

"Was," Tien corrected with a slight smile.

The Weapon Master nodded, acknowledging the jibe. He too had been coming to the realisation that his days as a professional mercenary were nearing an end; he was now a soldier in Kutor's

army. "Whatever story you decide upon regarding our disappearance must be kept up. In the next few days and in the moons
leading up to action, there will be desertions and volunteers. Treat all
newcomers as possible spies, for you can be certain some of them
will be Geillard's people, and I would suggest you deal with caught
deserters with the utmost severity to discourage others."

"I will not agree to barbarity," Kutor said immediately.

Owen looked at him in astonishment. "Is this not the man who
regularly cut off merchants' toes, one by one, returning them to his
family until a ransom was paid? Is this not the same man who
removed a distinctive birthmark from a woman's thigh by the simple
expedient of removing the skin of her leg, which was then sent back
to her family to encourage them to pay up quickly? Is this not the
man who paid the Chopts a bounty on the travellers' trains they
frightened off the main trade-routes and into his traps? Don't talk
to me about barbarity!" he spat.

"What's past is past," Kutor said smugly, "and cannot be undone. But my reign must not be achieved by excessive methods."

Owen's fist crashed onto the table. "We've just slaughtered the
best part of three legions and you speak to me of excessive methods? How do you want us to win this throne of yours? By soft
words and diplomacy, no doubt?" He made them sound like obscene acts. "Well, it is too late, princeling. You are committed, like it
or not. Let's just say it's your destiny," he added with a chill smile.
"The Gods themselves are now directing you."

Keshian cleared his throat into the long silence that followed.
"When will I start moving men back into the Nations?"

"Give us a moon's start. It will enable us to make our way into
the city and establish a base there. Tien has also suggested organising
the disaffected parties within Karfondal and inciting them to revolt,
and that may indeed be possible, although I think it will probably
happen of its own accord in any case once the city is attacked."

"Will a warrior and a Shemmat entering the city together not be
noted?" Keshian asked.

Tien tZo answered. "We will be entering by different gates on
different days at different times; ideally, close to the end of the shifts
when the guards are tired and careless. The Master will adopt the
guise of a wandering soldier, down on his luck—there will be many
such on the road—and I will be one of the Andam Brotherhood."

"When will we strike?" Kutor asked suddenly, his voice low and subdued.

"I would suggest you merely continue to press forward, bringing the battle to them, forcing them to fight you on your terms. As you approach the capital, you will be up against the pick of the Imperials, and by then all the odds will be in their favour. They will be fighting on their own ground and they will have the added impetus of desperation spurring them on. However, by that time you should have a sizable army at your back and the men you have now will be well trained in the art of war. Also, the sight of Karfondal's walls should spur them on. Listen to Keshian," he urged. "I know we set him up as a hero, but he has a wealth of knowledge; he knows the ground, he knows Imperial tactics and troops dispositions—and he has survived."

"But when should we strike?" the prince persisted.

"We will time our action to aid you; you are not there to aid us," Tien said softly, his gaze distant. "In every war there is a decisive battle, usually just one, which swings the balance of the whole course of the war. The Sand Plain was the one which destroyed my people..." His eyes re-focused and he looked at Kutor and Keshian again. "And so we will strike when we see your army preparing to march on Karfondal."

"Should I attempt to send men into the city beforehand?" Kutor asked.

Suddenly all three men were shaking their heads. Finally, both Owen and Tien looked at Keshian. The battle-captain turned to the prince. "Once news of our approach has been confirmed, the gate guards will be doubled and then re-doubled and their vigilance will be such that no-one unknown to them or to someone within the city walls will be able to get past them." He paused as a sudden thought struck him and he looked across at the Weapon Master. "And that of course means that you will be trapped in the city. If your attempt fails, you will not be able to flee."

"If our attempt fails there will be no need to," Owen said very softly, his voice no more than a whisper.

Barthus the Hierophant glared down at the shaven head bowed low before him. "Is this all?" He contemptuously tossed the rice-paper scroll into the low, smouldering fire.

"Yes, Holiness. Salier has re-doubled the guards around the Emperor, and Fodla herself inspects them at irregular intervals. She personally strangled a guard she caught drinking on duty."

Barthus glared at the terrified priest for a few moments longer and then abruptly dismissed him. "Continue with your work."

"Yes, Holiness. Thank you." The man scrabbled to touch the hem of the Hierophant's gown, but Barthus impatiently twitched it from his grasp and turned away. The man backed from the room and the door clicked shut behind him, and then Barthus heard the clink and jangle of metal as the warrior-priests outside his door settled themselves. Alone at last, the slender young man relaxed and allowed the haughty, arrogant pretence to fall away, revealing the fear beneath. He sat back into a high-backed, winged chair, massaging the tight skin around his eyes with his long, fine fingers, and stared deep into the fire, watching the edges of the intelligence report begin to twist and curl with flame. He rested his head against the polished brukwood and allowed his mind to wander, letting it find and settle into the soothing rhythms of his beliefs, taking comfort from their familiarity. And while on one level he was praying to the Gods of the New Religion, on another, deeper level, his mind was sorting through the various threads of information which he had in his grasp at the moment.

From what he could gather, the situation in the Outlands was worsening at a terrifying rate. What had started as an outlaw band had turned into an army, and an army on the move; and the small, independent townships, each with their own tiny militia forces were flocking to the Renegade's banner, swelling his numbers. The Emperor's expeditionary force had been decimated and there had been another equally brief and even more bloody struggle at the Line Bridge, the traditional place of demarcation between the Outlands and the Provinces. Two legions had attempted to stop Kutor's army by holding the bridge and the approach routes. The Renegades had simply hung back and laid down a devastating fire of poisoned arrows and crossbow bolts which massacred the Imperial forces as they camped on the open ground and bridge. That night what was left of the Imperial troops had been attacked by a raiding party from Kutor's army. From an estimated force of nearly two legions, less than two decades had survived. The way was now open for the rebel army to march directly into the western provinces.

There would be a decisive battle without any doubt, but where? How close to the capital would Geillard allow his bastard half-brother to come before he destroyed him? But, and more importantly, could this present situation be used to further Barthus' ambitions, and that of the New Religion too, of course?

He knew the Emperor was somewhat in awe of him, and that was something he wished to encourage, but he also knew that both Fodla and Salier distrusted him, hated what he represented. For what he represented was power, the like of which had not been seen in the Nations since the Gods and Culai had last walked the World of Men.

Barthus was no magician, no necromancer, no magus; he had neither sorcerous nor shapeshifting powers, but he could call on the Gods, and they visibly and tangibly answered his call. He was Hierophant of the New Religion and that entitled him to the respect and adulation of a vast number of people—including, in theory, the Emperor himself. If Barthus called on the followers of the Religion to rise up and fight, then they would do so; for example, if he called upon them to support the Renegade, Kutor, then they would do that...

The Hierophant sat up suddenly, an idea flitting around the edges of his consciousness. A piece of coal cracked and sparks fell in the large grate, and the idea crystallised. The followers of the Religion must follow the Hierophant's dictates, that was part of the accepted creed of the Religion, and if he ordered them—no, if he informed them that he was convinced of Kutor's right to the throne—then they were bound by their Religion to follow his command. Now, Barthus wondered, how much bargaining power did that lend him, not only with Geillard but also with his half-brother? Barthus would deal with either.

He sat back into the chair, his long fingers steepled before his face, working out the ramifications of his plan, the gains and possible losses. One of the advantages of dealing with Kutor, for example, would be that there was no Salier, no Fodla, to interfere with his plans. Something cold and inhuman settled down behind his eyes, and then Barthus began to quiver with suppressed humour; whatever happened in this coming war, he would ensure that neither the mage nor the warrior-maid would survive.

But first, Kutor must be acquainted with his plans. Barthus leaned forward and stared at the dancing flames and curling smoke of the fire. And then he called upon his Gods...

Fodla was entertaining Salier in her chambers, which was something she would rather not have been doing, and she had the vague idea that the very presence of the magus in her rather spartan chambers sullied them.

Salier had looked around in frank interest when he entered the rooms—this was his first, and for all he knew, his last invitation, and the magician was of the opinion that it was possible to learn more about a character from their rooms than from the person themselves. Look at the person and you saw an image; look at the room and you saw the personality. Fodla was the perfect example. Her image was of cold ruthlessness, a killer without conscience or care, and at times she accentuated her feminine characteristics almost as if to make her actions seem even more incomprehensible. She was called the Weapons-Maid, not only on account of her skills with the tools of death but also because of the huge number of weapons which she carried about herself; two matched swords rode on her back, there were knife sheaths sewn onto the sleeves of her uniform just above the wrists, which allowed the handles of the knives to fall easily into her hands, and there was another set of sheaths sewn into her boots. There was occasionally another longer sword on her belt, and she sometimes carried a small hand-axe or a mace.

So, Salier would have almost expected to find the walls hung with weapons, shields, and banners, perhaps captured colours, but instead they were bare, painted a dull oatmeal colour which matched the off-white *cuine*-skin rugs scattered across the chill stone floor. There was a long ironwood table beneath the window, glowing in the late afternoon light, and two matching chairs were placed at either end. A broad metal-bound travelling chest was tucked into a corner and a low, two-shelf bookcase completed the room's furnishings. However, he knew there was another, smaller room leading off this one—Fodla's bed-chamber, where her armour, clothing and weapons would be kept, no doubt.

The huge woman crossed to the ironwood table and took one of the chairs, plainly indicating that Salier should occupy the other, facing her down the length of the table. The mage sat easily, his hands folded on the polished grey wood table before him, looking at the woman and realising for the first time that she was actually quite lovely. Without the enveloping armour and the shapeless mail, her figure, although full, was firm, her skin smooth and unwrinkled, and her red hair had been swept back off her face leaving her bright green eyes staring out of a broad oval face.

"You're staring," she said coldly.

Salier attempted a short bow. "I apologise, my lady, but this is the first time I have seen you without your armour."

"And you have discovered I am a woman?" Fodla asked, the bitterness in her voice surprising even herself.

"I have discovered that you are a very beautiful woman," he said, a smile touching his thin lips.

Fodla grimaced. "You and I are too old for these games," she snapped.

The mage nodded. "Too old to play them, and that means my compliments are truthful observations and have no other intent."

The woman nodded stiffly. Compliments had been rare in her life and she had never learned to accept them easily.

"You asked me to come here?" Salier said, breaking the growing silence, settling into the high-backed chair.

Fodla nodded gratefully, glad to be back on safe ground. "We need to talk, you and I, and this is the only place within the palace where I know we will not be spied upon."

"There could be listeners, secret passages, listening tubes," Salier suggested with a wicked grin.

"There is nothing. I checked the room myself, and to ensure our privacy, I've invoked a small spell I know which should work."

"And what spell is that?" Salier asked, taking a professional interest, more than a little surprised that the captain knew any spellcraft.

She dismissed it with a wave of her hand. "It is nothing, a trifle I learned from my mother." Her tone indicated that the subject was at an end. "We need to talk about Geillard and Barthus, and this situation in the western provinces."

Salier nodded. He was about to speak when the door opened and a young woman entered, carrying a plain wooden tray holding two glasses and a crystal goblet worked in the blue glass of Lostrice. The woman was wearing the armour of Fodla's own regiment, the Emperor's Legion, the dagger crest indicating that she held the rank of captain. She put the tray down in front of Salier, her eyes on the mage, and then she went to the far end of the table and spoke briefly to her commander in a soft whisper before she left, moving almost noiselessly despite the heavy armour and weapons.

Fodla looked at Salier and smiled, and the magician, for all his powers, felt the skin at the back of his neck tingle and something cold move down his spine. For a single instant, the moment when her lips had curled in a smile, Fodla had ceased to be a woman and he had glimpsed something else behind the mask, something cold and merciless, bestial and slavering, and he wondered briefly if she had any beast blood in her. "It seems you disobeyed my command to bring no weapons with you," she said, her voice silk and ice-cold. She reached in under the table as she spoke and brought out a cocked and loaded hand-crossbow and pointed it squarely at Salier's chest.

"I brought no weapons," Salier protested, staring at the weapon held unwaveringly in the woman's large hands. The crossbow was a perfect miniature of the larger model and the broad-headed triangular bolt was perfectly capable of punching clean through him and into the chair he was sitting on at this short range.

"There is a knife in your sleeve and another in your boot," Fodla said, grinning mirthlessly.

Salier silently produced both weapons and placed them on the polished grey wood of the table. "I've carried them for so long now, I don't really consider them…" he began to explain, but Fodla waved his explanation aside.

"Business," she snapped. She placed the crossbow on the table by her left hand, but left it cocked and loaded and still pointing at Salier. "Let us begin with this Prince Kutor," she said. "His threat this time is much more serious than the last and his men are disciplined and trained. And what's more, they seem dedicated to their cause. This is no rabble helped along with a few score hired mercenaries, and I think we must both consider the very real possibility that Kutor will march to Karfondal's walls to enforce his claim to the throne."

"He is certainly showing unusual determination," Salier agreed.

"I need to know if he has any legitimate claim to the throne."

Surprisingly, the magician nodded. "He has. He is the present Emperor's half-brother, born on the wrong side of the blanket, it is true, but his claim is legitimate nonetheless. He is actually next in line to the throne after Geillard; he is the nearest living relative."

The woman grimaced. "I've seen men put on the throne with even less claim. It's a pity; I had rather hoped he was just another imposter."

"Does it matter?" Salier asked, surprised.

"It does. I could have convinced my people that we were fighting a renegade imposter, a commoner with ideas above his station, as it were. But if Kutor has a legitimate claim..."

He nodded. "It makes it a little more difficult," he agreed.

"My spies can tell me nothing about who is training this army. The Weapon Master, Owen, has been mentioned, but his name turns up everywhere these days."

"His name is mentioned in my reports," Salier interrupted.

"Then do you think there is any truth in these stories?"

He shook his head. "The Weapon Master always travels with a Shemmat, and they are a distinctive enough race in the Nations, but none of my reports mentions him."

Fodla nodded. "As I thought. The man is a legend amongst the common people, so it is almost natural that his name should come up. The only other name which appears is a Keshian or Kesian, but I know of no one of any calibre called Keshian or Kesian. Has his name appeared in your reports?"

"No."

Fodla ran a blunt nail down the polished wood of the hand-crossbow. "So we may assume he is an Outlander, with little or no experience, and therefore only a limited threat." She moved the crossbow again, shifting it slightly, so the bolt now tilted upwards, pointing at Salier's throat. Seeing his startled expression, it was only with some difficulty that she managed to keep her face straight. "And we must also consider the reports that King Cormac and his Gallowglas army have been slaughtered."

"I have a similar report, but can you see anyone killing Cormac or indeed even one of his Gallowglas, let alone an army of them?" Salier asked derisively.

"The Gallowglas are mainly reputation," Fodla remarked. "I once killed one of them."

"But you are an exceptional woman!"

The warrior smiled and hurried on. "They would have been difficult to kill by fair means," she admitted, "but treachery might account for it."

"One or two perhaps, but all of them?" Salier shook his head. "I don't think so."

"When was the last time you received a report from the King of the Outlands?"

The mage stared at the warrior for a few long moments without replying.

Fodla grinned mirthlessly. "Come, come now, magus, don't be so shy. I've known you were supporting the Gallowglas for a long time."

"And you're not interested in a reason?"

"Whatever opinions I hold about you, I've never considered you to be a traitor," she said with a tight smile, "and I can only assume that what you were doing was in the best interest of the Emperor."

Salier bowed, his estimation of the woman soaring. "I've heard nothing from Cormac," he said shortly.

"Then we must assume he is either dead or captured."

"Dead, I would think."

"And the Gallowglas?"

He shook his head. "Dead or scattered. I know it seems inconceivable, but I am left with no alternative."

"But where is the remainder of his army, his legion?" Fodla asked eagerly.

Salier nodded in understanding. "The core of Kutor's army?"

"Precisely."

"But what would have encouraged them to fight for Kutor, especially if he had killed Cormac?"

"I don't imagine the Gallowglas was a benign ruler," she shrugged. "Perhaps it was simply a better cause." She looked directly at Salier, noting with some surprise the worried frown on his face. Perhaps there was still something human in him after all.

"And we may have another problem," Salier said slowly, with the air of a man imparting something he would rather have kept to himself.

Fodla continued to watch him in silence.

"It is my belief," Salier continued, carefully picking his words, "that Barthus is not to be trusted. He will place his precious Religion above everything else, and if he thinks he will get a better deal from Kutor, then I have no doubts but that he will try. And if he does, then he will have no use for either of us."

Fodla nodded. "We should dispose of him," she agreed.

"Now!" Salier snapped.

"It is not an immediate worry and would cause more confusion while the church bickered amongst themselves. Right now we have to decide where and when to attack Kutor's forces."

The wind changed, scattering the flames, sending long shadows dancing up along the walls of the shallow cave Kutor had settled down in for the night. On the plain down and around him the hundreds of campfires of his army and followers winked like fallen stars. The wind gusted again and he lifted his face to it, smelling it, tasting it, realising that the wind was from the sea and that there was rain or possibly sleet to follow. Shivering, he leaned forward and dropped some long slivers of dried dung onto the flames. The fire hissed and crackled and thousands of tiny points of light spiralled heavenwards.

Kutor lay back against the rough stone wall, ironically aware that although the cave was cold, chill, and smelt of something long dead, he felt comfortable here. Owen's six hand-picked and trained guards were dotted around him—even he didn't know where—and he was surrounded on all sides by men, some of whom were devoted to his cause while others were honour-bound to follow him. There had been assassination attempts, both of them brief, botched affairs but they had brought home to him the need for guards. But here, in the middle of a windswept plain, he was safe; here there was no possibility of anyone attacking him. Here he could rest.

"K-K-Kutor-r-r."

The prince sat bolt upright, his knife coming to his hand. But there was no movement in the gritty darkness, no one around. Even his guards had remained invisible and they were usually on hand if he so much as turned over in his sleep.

"K-K-Kutor-r-r."

The sound was directly in front of him, coming from just beyond the fire in the mouth of the cave. Dragging his short-sword free, he crept towards it.

"K-K-Kutor-r-r."

The voice was sharp, brittle almost, the accent unnatural, as if the speaker was articulating with great difficulty. But he had identified its position now; it was coming from a point directly beyond and to the left of the fire.

Kutor crept up to the mouth of the shallow cave, gripped his sword tightly in both hands and then rolled through the opening, coming to his feet with his back to the wall, his sword extended—and found himself facing nothing more than a shadow.

But it was not his own.

The shadow on the wall was tall and thin, vaguely man-shaped with the edges decidedly indistinct. Even when the outline of the shadowshape was still, the image on the wall seemed to be writhing within itself.

"Who…what are you?" Kutor demanded, pleased at the steadiness of his voice.

"*I am Tinis, Firelord of the Gods of the New Religion and servant of Barthus, Hierophant of the True Belief.*" The voice was cracked and clicking, like burning wood, and came from the heart of the fire.

Kutor knelt and looked into the fire, but all he could see were the tiny dancing flames, nothing even remotely manlike about them.

"What do you want?" he demanded.

"*My master Barthus sends me to convey his greetings and to place his terms before you.*"

"What terms?" Kutor asked, intrigued although his heart was hammering.

The dancing shadow leaped into a paroxysm of activity. "*His full support and the support of all the followers of the New Religion.*"

"In return for what?" Kutor asked, immediately suspicious.

"*In return for your loyalty,*" the shadow crackled, "*in return for your support in turn for the cause of the New Religion.*" Another gust scattered the creature's shadow momentarily and Kutor had the impression of a man-shape flying apart, arms and legs all disappearing in different directions. "*Come, I need your answer. Barthus will support you, make you Emperor in effect, if you will support him. What say you?*"

Kutor took a moment to consider and then he said slowly and distinctly. "I have never had much in my life, but whatever else I lacked, I've always had my faith. It may have drifted sometimes, but it was always there, and the bard reminded me what I owed it and what it could do for me." He suddenly threw a handful of dust onto the flames, dousing many of them, destroying the creature. "I owe the Old Faith too much, and that is my answer!"

17
The God's Tale

All men die, few can kill.

Katan proverb

"Don't kill him!" Paedur hissed desperately, as blood began to trickle from the soft flesh just beneath Churon's ears.

"Why not?" Katani demanded. "He killed me."

"You can kill him, but not now," Buiva said reasonably.

"You're mad, all of you," Churon said tightly, his head rigid, unmoving with the two spikes against his flesh. "What do you hope to gain? You cannot kill me, not permanently in any case."

Katani moved one of the spikes up Churon's face, leaving a glistening red trail against his coal-black skin, stopping when it was touching the corner of his eye. "I can maim you, Onelord. I can ensure that when you walk again, it will be blind and deaf, dumb even, with severed tendons and mutilated nerves. How would you like that, Onelord?" she spat.

"There are those in the Mire to whom torture is an art, a fine delicate art, and each body a tapestry to be worked upon. I will ensure that you will be their masterpiece," Churon said coldly. He shifted the flame-edged dagger which he still held in his right hand, but Paedur leaned forward and knocked it from his grasp with his hook.

"I am of the Katan. Ah, I see you recall the name. Well then, you'll know your threats mean nothing to me. By killing you, I avenge my sisters and the honour of the Katan warriors."

With a scream of wood on stone, the chapel door scraped open, but only Paedur turned towards the sound; both Katani and Buiva kept watching their prisoner. Rade, Churon's captain, strode into the chapel carrying a tray holding a bottle and four crystal goblets. The bard was actually moving towards him before the man realised what was happening.

"Hey! Guards! Guards to Churon!"

Rade flung aside the tray and ran down the aisle, his sword in his hand, while behind him the doorway immediately began to fill with the Onelord's mercenary guards. Paedur met the captain's downward swing on his hook, catching and then snapping the blade in one smooth move, while his right hand shot up, the stiffened fingers catching the man in the throat, crushing his larynx, leaving him choking and dying.

Buiva raced to the bard's side and found himself facing two pikemen whose height, colouring and weapons suggested they came from the Whale Coast. The Whale warriors were fisher-folk and their preferred and traditional weapon was the long, barbed, and hooked fishing gaff. But while they had the reach on the war god, they lacked his speed. One jabbed, while the second brought his pike around in a long, low sweep. Buiva almost casually batted aside the first weapon and then hopped up as the pike came around and then dropped onto it. His weight slammed the weapon from the warrior's hands, and while he fumbled for it, Buiva's mace and chain ripped off the top of his head. His companion jabbed again and Buiva grabbed the weapon behind the barbed head and jerked forward, pulling the man off his feet. As he went down, Buiva drove the spiked haft of his mace into the base of his skull.

The bard meanwhile had dispatched another guard, opening the man from neck to groin through his thin leathers. "Let's go," he called, heading back towards the altar stone. "There's another door." He pulled a long, slim stiletto from his boot and placed it in the hollow of Churon's throat. Katani gratefully pulled off her peasant's dress, revealing her Katan armour beneath, and pulled both swords free with a blood-curdling shriek. And while a guard looked at her in astonishment, she took off his head with a single sweep of her longsword.

Paedur looked into the Onelord's wide blue eyes. "Now, I can kill you, Onelord, and carry your lifeless body until it revives, or you can run with me," he said simply. "The choice is yours."

"I'll run."

"A wise choice." He urged Churon around the altar and back towards the small wooden door he had noticed earlier. Katani and Buiva covered their rear, dissuading the Onelord's warriors from becoming too courageous. He sheathed his knife and gripped the ornate metal handle in his right hand and turned, or attempted to turn it, but the lock wouldn't move. "Open it," he commanded, pressing his hook to Churon's neck.

"It will not open," Churon said calmly. "The lock has rusted solid and the door has warped into its frame."

Paedur hit the door with his hook, the razor sharp metal biting deep into the wood above the lock. He struck again and a sliver of wood jumped out. He was about to cut again, when there was a sudden hiss of air and the spiked ball of Buiva's mace shattered the lock, almost ripping the stout door from its huge hinges, snapping it open. The bard pushed the Onelord through, his hook never leaving his back; Buiva followed, while Katani lingered in the doorway, the entrance being small enough for one person to defend.

They were in a long, low chamber lined with cross-shaped pieces of wood; long, filthy tatters of coloured cloth were hanging from the crosses. "A vestment chamber," Paedur said, looking around.

Buiva pushed past him seeking an exit.

"Can we kill him now?" Katani called back over her shoulder.

"No," Buiva snapped, "not here, not now." He reached the end of the chamber and swore loudly, slapping his gauntleted hand against the blank stone wall. There was no exit. He returned to Churon and, grasping the Onelord by the throat, lifted him off the ground. "Is there any way out of here?"

Churon choked and gagged but managed to shake his head. Buiva dropped him to the ground, and then allowed the ball of his mace to dangle before his eyes. "Is there?" he demanded.

"I don't think he knows," Paedur said softly. "This room has not been used for a long time..." He broke off as there was a sudden flurry of activity at the doorway and Katani's swords sang their whistling death song, accompanied by the warrior-maid's keening death psalm. The guard retreated, leaving two more of their number behind them. When they had moved back, the Katan warrior busied herself hamstringing the corpses, ensuring that even if they rose again, they would never walk properly.

Buiva turned back to the bard. "Use your bardic lore, find us a way out of this place."

"If this monastery follows the pattern of all the others I've been in, then yes, there should be. The priests or monks come in here, robe themselves and then make their way out to the altar to perform their ceremony. They would usually then return here, divest themselves of their robes, and then leave by the same door they entered by."

"Then there is a door. Find it!" Buiva commanded. He glared at Churon. "I'll take care of this."

Paedur made his way down the chamber, tapping his metal hook on the stones, listening for a change of sound, straining to hear a different tone above the clash of swords at the door. He finally thought he had detected a change, an echo, when he was near to the back of the room. He pushed aside two tall wooden crosses with their ragged remnants still on them and tapped the stonework again. The sound rang hollowly. He tapped on the wall again, moving to one side and then back again, judging the extent of the opening, and then he began to probe with the fingers of his right hand, seeking the lever, looking for an indentation, a crack, an irregularity in the stonework.

"Well?" Buiva demanded.

"It's here, behind a false wall. I just cannot find the mechanism for opening it."

"Try the corners."

"I've tried," Paedur said desperately, vainly wishing for his enhanced senses once again.

"They're bringing up archers!" Katani suddenly shouted.

"Bard!"

Paedur hissed in exasperation and then he felt something give. Abruptly the back section of the wall moved inwards—and something leaped forward onto the bard!

He shouted aloud, his left hand snapping up, catching the creature under the chin, slicing through bones, ripping the head clean off the body, shattering it against the stonework. The body fell to the ground, and when the bard looked down he found there was nothing more than the tumbled bones of a skeleton around his feet. The bones had been bleached by time to a pale ivory whiteness and were wearing the remnants of hideously ornate ceremonial robes. Still clutched in one hand was a small leather-bound book. Paedur stooped to lift the book, but the skeletal fingers were wrapped so tightly around it that he had to snap them off. Without even opening it he slipped the book into his inside pocket.

He heard the whistling scream of a hollow-headed crossbow bolt and then one shattered into the stonework over his head. He looked up and saw a second, large, triangular-headed bolt glance off Katani's ornate armour to clatter harmlessly onto the floor, but the force of the blow was enough to stagger her. A huge, bearded guard leaped into the doorway, a broad-headed axe that looked far too small in his hand raised over the Katan's head. The bard's thrown knife took him through the eye and he swayed on his feet before finally falling into the doorway, partially blocking it.

Katani scrambled to her feet and pulled the bard's knife from the dead man's face and raced back to Buiva, who was pushing Churon down the room towards the opening. Katani was first through the opening, followed by Churon, Buiva, and finally Paedur. As the bard was desperately looking for the lever which would swing the section of wall back into place, a score of guards finally managed to clear the door and pushed into the room, two archers in the lead. One fired blindly into the dark circle he could see at the far end of the room. The arrow hissed past the bard to shatter on the wall, while the second man, spotting the glint of Paedur's hook, loosed an arrow towards the shape. The bard desperately threw himself to one side as the bolt screamed towards him, and it struck sparks from the ground not a hand-span from his face. Then suddenly the slab of wood began to grind closed. As he climbed slowly to his feet, he realised the palm of his hand was resting on a smoothly rounded lump in the otherwise rough-hewn corridor.

The tunnel was high and surprisingly dry, although the throat-catching odour of dust and powder made him gag and there was the ever-present damp reek of the Mire about it. It wasn't completely lightless either; at some stage in its history the walls had been painted with a series of religious frescoes in what the ancients had called winterlight, a natural pigment that glowed in the dark, and enough remained on the walls to emit a dim, green-tinged glow.

He had taken no more than a score of paces when the smoothly curved wall of the tunnel was broken by an oblong opening which might have once held a door but which was now barred across with four wrist-thick metal bars. The bard glanced out, and was surprised to find that the opening was high off the ground and concealed behind a trailing screen of greenery. He found he was looking down on the courtyard they had crossed earlier, which was now alive with confusion, and he suddenly found himself wondering how, in the name of all the Gods of the Pantheon, he had come to find himself in such a hopeless situation. Well, he had no one to blame but himself, and the same Gods of the Pantheon, for that. Shrugging his thin shoulders, he hurried on. He found Buiva and

Katani further down the corridor standing before another barred opening; Churon was sitting with his back against the wall. Paedur silently joined them and peered through the bars. It seemed as if they were now around at the rear of the monastery and about one man-height up from the ground; if there had ever been steps or a rope, they were long gone now.

Buiva hit the bars with his mace, but they merely vibrated, the sound thrumming through the stones, and a shower of rust flaked away.

Behind them, something solid and metallic began a steady hammering on stone, the sound vibrating through the corridor, sending dust-motes shimmering. Patches of winterlight flaked off the walls, deepening the shadows.

Churon smiled broadly. "My men will be here soon and then this charade can end."

Katani moved her sword so that the tip rested on the Onelord's cheek. "Shut up," she advised.

Buiva hit the bars again with his mace, but with as little result.

"Let me try." The bard knelt before the opening and wrapped his hook around the centre of the three bars close to the floor. Then, holding his left wrist with his right hand, he pulled. There was a moment's resistance and then the hook slid silently through the rusted metal bar. He stood up, rubbing flakes of rust from the inner curve of his hook. "Hold the middle of the bar," he said to Buiva, and then he repeated the procedure, cutting into the bar at a little above eye level. Once again his hook slid through with ease. Buiva pulled the bar back out of the way and examined the cuts; they were clean and smooth.

Katani squeezed through the opening and dropped down, landing noiselessly on the soft boggy ground, moving quickly into the shade of a stunted, sickly-coloured tree. She scanned the monastery walls above them, but there was no movement. When she nodded, Buiva merely pushed Churon through the opening and when he hit the ground, Katani's swords immediately crossed against his throat. Buiva followed; he sank up to his ankles into the soggy mulch, his mail pulling him down. He swore softly and dragged his feet free, glaring at Churon as if it was all his fault. The bard was the last down, his black cloak flapping out behind him like wings. He landed lightly on his feet and darted into the bushes.

"Let's go," Buiva said.

Paedur grabbed the god by the arm. "Wait a moment, if you will. What is stopping us from killing Churon now?"

"We still do not have the information we need," Buiva explained patiently.

"And?" the bard persisted, something in the god's manner not quite ringing true.

"And the Gods of the Pantheon hold no sway here. Neither Mannam, Maurug, nor Madness would be able to come to this place," Buiva said, his voice weary. "I'm afraid we must take Churon out of the Mire and back into the Silent Wood for the gods to exact their vengeance on him."

"Mannam forgot to mention that," Paedur said grimly.

"Aye, well he would," Buiva smiled.

"You will never cross the Mire," Churon said with a smile. "My men control all the access routes to this place from all the Planes of Existence, including the road from the Silent Wood."

"Even you have not enough men to watch all the roads," Buiva said evenly.

"I have enough," he boasted.

"Well, if we cannot go around them, we'll just have to go through them," Katani said almost eagerly.

"Could we perhaps discuss this later?" Paedur asked. "Somewhere not so close to the Onelord's warriors."

Buiva grinned broadly, but when he turned to Churon the smile faded. "You have the choice again: you can walk or we can kill you and carry you with us. We'll still have you when you revive."

"I'll walk," Churon said, his eyes narrowing.

"Try to escape and I'll cut off your legs," Katani warned.

"I've no need to escape. My people will rescue me."

"Don't count on it," Paedur smiled, hauling him to his feet and pushing him through the bushes.

The ground was soft and boggy underfoot, low stunted trees and twisted scrub growing in patches on the little islands of dry soil in the marsh, and they made slow headway until before noon when they struck a rough hard-packed track. Without discussion or hesitation they struck to the east, heading back in the general direction of the Silent Wood. The track was deserted and there was no evidence that it had been used recently, with neither spoor nor droppings to indicate an animal run. Indeed, this part of the Mire, so close to the Silent Wood, was completely devoid of all animal, bird, and insect life, although the remainder of the Mire was inhabited not only by peoples and races from countless lands and times but also by the flora and fauna from those places.

They marched for the most part in silence, the atmosphere oppressive and the heat stultifying. Around noon the pale disc of the sun burned through the ever-present clouds that blanketed the Mire, and the marshlands began to bake, steaming in the abrupt heat, but the thick, foul-smelling fog only served to slow them down. Paedur shaded his eyes with his hand and stared at the orange disc and then shook his head, deciding it was not the sun he was familiar with.

They stopped only once, and that was to allow a score of Churon's warriors to gallop past on animals that had too much deer in them to be truly called horses. Katani ensured Churon's silence by placing a knife in his mouth: any sound would have ripped his tongue in two.

The misty, fog-bound forenoon slipped quickly into a deeply shadowed afternoon and then night fell with its usual swiftness. And even though the fog lifted, there were no stars and no moon visible. With the onset of night, they were forced to make camp. Although Paedur found that he could just about make out the shapes of his companions and prisoner, and Buiva moved with perfect ease, both Churon and Katani were almost completely blind. Buiva took the lead and struck off the track they had been following, heading for one of the tiny dry islands in the marsh; if they were discovered, their attackers would have to come at them through the marshy ground. The island was no more than an outcrop of dry land barely a score of lengths across and almost smothered beneath a thick covering of flourishing vegetation. Close to the centre of the island, they found a dry hollow almost completely surrounded by trees and bushes. Large chunks of polished and worked stone were scattered around the hollow and Paedur was just about able to make out the outline of a circular building on the hard-packed ground. Fire was impossible under the circumstances; even if the light remained invisible, the odour of smoke and fire would have been a beacon amidst the rancid odours of the Mire, and so they broke their day-long fast on strips of dried meat and stone-hard bread washed down by tepid water. Churon's legs were then staked to the ground and his arms and torso lashed to the bole of a tree. He was neither gagged nor blindfolded, but Katani positioned herself behind and to his right, her shortsword in her hand, the tip resting on the Onelord's shoulderblade.

Buiva and Paedur walked around their makeshift camp, closing off the openings, tying branches of trees and bushes together and lacing vines across the paths, ensuring that a noiseless entrance to the dry hollow would be impossible.

"I wonder what stood here," Paedur said, rubbing his hook over one of the large flat stones, scraping off the moss.

Buiva shook his head, his mail tinkling softly. "Too small for a house, the walls are not thick enough for either defence or a tower…"

"A shrine?" Paedur suggested.

"Possibly, but not to any god I know."

The two men sat down in the lee of the highest remaining wall. Against the stones which were shadowed from above by a twisted march-tree, they were invisible, but they had a clear view of the only large entrance to their camp. Across and to their right they could make out the shapes of Churon and Katani; the Onelord was slumped against his bonds, his head on his chest as if asleep.

"He doesn't sleep yet," Buiva remarked.

"I know. His breathing has not yet changed."

Buiva smiled, his teeth white against the shadows. "You are a remarkable man, bard. Here you are wandering through the Mire, the Borderlands, in the company of a murdered warrior, a dead tyrant, and a god, and you accept it so casually."

"What else can I do? Besides, I've grown used to gods. I spent time in the Kingdom of Life, remember. I walked the Culai Isle. I watched the destruction of the Cords. I saw the last of the First Race die. And after that…well, little surprises me now."

"I was not in favour of you, bard, when we were choosing a Champion. I thought a military man would be more suited, a man of action, and yet on reflection a man of action would perhaps have been too hidebound in his ways and thinking to accept all this."

"Show me a warrior who does not fear what he cannot kill."

Buiva nodded. "Aye, there's the rub." He turned to look at the bard, his eyes glittering slightly. "Why are you doing this? The gods wanted a Champion in the World of Men; they gifted him for the Planes of Existence. Here, you are a man again, and surely you knew that you would lose your powers once you entered Death's Kingdom?"

"I guessed."

"So, why did you throw it all away? What brought you into the Silent Wood in the first place?"

Paedur laughed. "I thought you would know that."

"I am War, a powerful but not a very intelligent god. There are others, the Weavers of Fate, the Judgers of Souls, aye, Death too, and even the mis-named God of Fools and Madness, who are far cleverer than I. It takes very little to bring men to War," he added ruefully.

"Have you always been War?" Paedur asked.

"I have been War since...since the time of the First Race of Man, when the Gods of the Pantheon were fully established."

"I thought all the gods were created by Hanor and Hara, the First Great Gods, who were in turn created by the One," Paedur murmured, attempting to keep the edge of excitement out of his voice.

Buiva nodded. "The major gods and forces, aye, they were, and they in turn created the others, the world gods, the plane-gods, the gods of bridges and winds, of night and the mists, and all the lesser gods, spirits and sprites."

"And War?"

"The creature Man had a hand in the fashioning of more than one god, but perhaps his greatest creation is War."

"You were created by Man?" Paedur whispered aghast.

Buiva nodded slightly. "In his own image."

"Were you human once?"

Buiva laughed shortly. "I suppose if I don't tell you, you will worry at me like a dog at a bone until you have your answer. But since you are our Champion...well, I will tell you, but only on condition that you never repeat it, never!" The warning was clear in his voice.

"You have my oath," Paedur said immediately.

"And how do you swear?" Buiva asked with a wry smile.

"Why, by the Pantheon, of course."

The god shook with silent laughter. "I think you and I will become friends," he said eventually when he caught his breath.

"Well then, listen, bard, and I will tell you a tale no other man knows, nor has ever heard. Now remember that I speak of the time in the shadow of the Culai race, when Culai and Men walked the worlds and mingled with those Gods that were already in existence, a time when there was no such thing as legend, for all the world was legend then…"

They had sat in council for a score of days, and when the High Chamber of the Culai ended, there was no announcement, and the First Race returned to their palaces and villas on the coast in covered carriages and with perhaps more haste than was seemly. And those who had waited at the foot of the white and gold marbled steps went away disappointed and vaguely troubled.

Rumours abounded in the City, for there was but one in this time of legend and with no need of a name, and the taverns were full that night and the stories told varied only in the vividness of the imagination of the tellers. One tale, however, was commonplace, and that was that the Culai race had come to the decision to subjugate the race of Man, as well as the Were-Folk, those with too much beast blood in them to be called fully human. Other tales suggested that the Culai folk had plans to enslave their fellow creatures, using them body and essence in their foul sorceries to prolong their already overlong lives.

But the truth was far simpler, but equally despicable: the Culai, who were the offspring of Man and God, had simply grown tired of its parent race of Man, with its petty squabbling, its arrogance and ignorance but more importantly, its independence and inventiveness, and had decided to destroy them.

And so while the more rational elements amongst the human-folk attempted to quell the growing tide of fear and mistrust, the Culai set about annihilating the race of Man, the race they had sprung from. And paradoxically, they instructed the elite Storm Warriors to begin the genocide. But the Storm Warriors were all drawn from the ranks of humankind…

The Battle-Captain crumpled the fragile rice-paper and dropped it to the intricately tiled floor of the roof garden. Then, deliberately, he ground the heel of his boot onto the ball. "That is what I think of your orders," he said, looking into the blank, slightly hooded eyes of the Culai.

The Culai nodded, his finely boned head bobbing on a neck that seemed far too slender to support it. "A predictable reaction and one which I was prepared for." His speech was clipped, as if speech was not his natural mode of communication, and indeed, when in company together, the First Race were never known to speak. "Those are your orders, Battle-Captain. I would suggest you obey them."

"I will not slay my own kind!"

"They are human, Battle-Captain," the Culai protested mildly, turning his face slightly to catch the warm breeze that was blowing in off the ocean.

"I am human! You were human once!" the warrior protested, his hands on his hips, the fingers of his right hand resting almost unconsciously against the haft of a mace and chain.

"I was never human!" the Culai snapped, a distinct glottal stop between each word.

"You had a human parent."

"There was a woman once," the creature acknowledged, "but there was a god, also." The Culai paused, turning its head slightly from side to side, light reflecting off its bald head. "You claim you are human too, but you spent many years in our service; there is nothing left for you in the World of Men, you have no ties, no relations...none of the Storm Warriors have. We own you."

"And when we have killed the human folk, will you then have the were-creatures kill us?"

"Why would we do that?" the Culai asked, sounding genuinely puzzled.

"And what will you do when the Race of Man has been destroyed?" the warrior continued without answering. "How will the First Race of Culai survive?"

The Culai's bland features creased in a puzzled frown. "Why should I discuss this with a Battle-Captain? What gives him the right to even ask?"

"Because you asked this Battle-Captain to butcher his own race."

"I asked a Battle-Captain to obey an order."

"I will not do it," the man said simply.

"Then I will have someone else do it, and you, of course..." The Culai never even saw the spiked ball of the mace which exploded against the side of his head, crushing the large skull. The force of the blow should have sent the creature reeling, but he remained standing, an expression of surprise etched onto his long face. The Battle-Captain brought his weapon around in a tight arc ready to strike again when the Culai merely toppled over. The Battle-Captain knelt beside the body and cleaned the spiked ball in the Culai's robes and then went to stand against the low wall that surrounded the flat roof, leaning both fists on the sun-warmed stone, his head bent, breathing deeply. When he finally looked up, he allowed his gaze to wander out over the City, past the carefully planned and flawlessly executed designs for houses, palaces, and theatres of the Culai to the more random, tumbled, jumbled human constructions. Scattered among the City buildings were a score of temples, each inhabited by its own god. Beyond the City, the intense blue of the ocean was shimmering like molten metal in the morning light, the harbours bright with the sails of a hundred ships from half as many places, with the scarlet sails of the Were-Folk predominating. At this hour of morning, the odours of cooking were beginning to waft up the hill which held the majority of the Culai dwellings and the Battle-Captain breathed deeply, savouring the rich smells, mentally identifying the peoples and races by their food. It was all so peaceful, so natural.

And then the Battle-Captain turned and looked again at the body of the Culai, his head now completely swathed in a thick, glutinous pool of blood, and knew that with this simple act he had changed the face of the world. This was the first of the Culai folk to die by the hand of a human and the Man's name was Buiva.

A lesser man would have turned and run then, fled the City, taken ship to another place and prayed that he would not be found. But Buiva was not as other men. He retrieved the paper he had so contemptuously ground underfoot and returned to his barracks. There he had called his men together and calmly read out their orders to them, and then quelled the uproar that followed; he had equally calmly and with no expression told them how he had killed the Culai. The stunned silence lasted only long enough for someone to draw his breath and begin to cheer. And without exception the Storm Warriors defected from their Culai paymasters to the leadership of Buiva.

Before the day was out, the entire City knew of the Culai plan and the death of one of the self-styled First Race and Buiva's name. He was hailed as a hero, the saviour of Humankind, and by nightfall the leaders of the various races and peoples and factions had come to him in the Storm Warriors' fort, pledging their oath and support.

And so the man found himself trapped in the position as the leader of all Humankind.

The war with the Culai was long and bloody, with the technology of the First Race ranged against the numbers and determination of the human folk, but that is another tale in itself. It was principally fought in and around the streets of the City and many of the battles were planned and commanded by Buiva himself; his name became the war-cry of the humans, and soon the Culai grew to loathe the buzzing of "BUIVA-BUIVA-BUIVA" as it came up from the City to their stark, white-walled houses.

The tide of war had swung in favour of the humankind when their commander died, not by treachery and not by violence. He died simply and peacefully in his sleep on the eve of what everyone, both human and Culai, knew would be a decisive battle. News of his death rippled through the human army like wind across a field of wheat, but paradoxically, instead of disheartening them, it only served to urge the people on to greater efforts, and before the battle all of those present—and they numbered many, many thousands—bowed their heads and prayed for Buiva to aid and guide them.

And Faith lends Substance.

And towards noon, when the battle seemed to be going against the human folk, a single warrior dropped on the battlefield, a thin sliver of metal buried in his chest, and called aloud for his old commander...

And Buiva returned.

In the midst of battle, a creature of fire and bronze, of death and destruction—of WAR—stalked, rallying the human kind, striking terror into the Culai. A new god had been born...

"So my advice to you is to be careful, Bard," Buiva finished with a smile. "I understand your name is already honoured and revered by the followers of the Old Faith. Be careful, lest you too might one day join the Pantheon's hallowed ranks. We have not had a new god for many, many years."

Paedur shivered and pulled his cloak tighter around his shoulders. "I prefer being a man," he said sincerely.

"Bard, you ceased to be a man a long time ago," Buiva said drily.

18
The Andam

"Men kill for reasons, for coin or honour, for duty or pleasure. The Master killed for all these reasons, but often he killed simply because it was necessary."

Tien tZo

They came into the city separately, using two different gates on successive days. The Weapon Master maintained his role as a warrior, merely adding some dirt to his clothing and allowing a rough growth of beard to cover the scars on his face and add to his disguise. Tien tZo adopted the loose, grey, ragged robes of an Andam, a holy man afflicted by the disease that touched many of the followers of the strange sect. Their temple was deep in the heart of the Southern Marshes; and eight out of ten that went to study this early and primitive version of the Old Faith came back afflicted by the terrifying disease which wasted the flesh and drew the skin so taut on the bones that it eventually cracked and split, leaving long, open sores and weeping scars.

The Master had no problems entering the city: mercenary soldiers were arriving from all across the Nations, news of the coming conflict having spread like a summer fire, and he wandered in through the open gates surrounded by a score of his ill-assorted brothers in the mercenary trade.

Tien tZo, however, did not find entrance to Karfondal so easy. It was market day when he arrived and although it lacked some time to sunrise already a long line of farmers and merchants was filling the great road that led up to the city walls. The Shemmat hung back from the end of the line, his long robes of filthy grey cotton wrapped around him, completely obscuring his body and face, leaving only one eye showing. There was a simple wooden begging bowl in his right hand and his cloth-wrapped left clutched a long metal-shod walking pole.

A coin clinked into his bowl.

"Blessings on you," he murmured, pitching his voice low, turning stiffly to look at his benefactor, and finding himself looking up at a man wearing the loose grey robes of the Andam. For a moment he thought he had been discovered and his grip tightened on the walking pole, preparing to bring it around in a crushing blow if the man seemed about to betray him.

"We must support our own," the taller, older man said wearily. "Give when we have a little to give."

Tien bowed. "Just so. And what is life, but giving of oneself to the creator?"

The Andam stopped, seemingly surprised, although like Tien most of his head was hidden within a deep hood and it was difficult to gauge his reactions. "Yes," he said finally, "that is good. A refreshing viewpoint. Good. Yours?" he asked, gasping slightly, as if the effort of speaking exhausted him.

Tien shook his head. "I have wandered far, brother, and spent many years in the Land of the Sun and have absorbed much of their culture. The saying is theirs, not mine."

"But it holds true nonetheless," the Andam priest said. He nodded towards the city. "You are going there?"

Tien nodded.

"Permit me to walk awhile with you?"

"I would be honoured."

"The honour is in the giving," the older man said, and Tien could almost imagine the smile.

"There is also honour in a gracious receipt," he said.

The two grey-robed men walked up past the line of carts and wagons, the stamping horses and the patient horned bothe with their cartloads of grains and fruit for the market. Those carrying slaughtered blood-meat were black with flies and the air around them fetid with the smells of offal and the metallic odour of blood.

The villagers and merchants signed themselves as the two figures walked slowly past. The Andam were both respected and feared, and in parts of the Nations they were considered almost as Duaite. The Andam belief in a single God or Being of creation ruling all things rather than in the Pantheon found little favour and much distrust with the common people, even though both the Andam and the Old Faith worshipped the One.

"Tell me about the Land of the Sun," the older man said suddenly as they began to climb the long, wide road that led up to the city gates.

Tien, who had been frantically trying to remember what he knew of the Andam and their beliefs, groaned inwardly. Although he was directly descended from the Shemmatae who had been defeated on the Sand Plain and knew of their lore and culture, he had never visited the Land of the Sun and his knowledge of it was very sketchy and composed mostly of hearsay and travellers' tales.

He coughed and drew the cloth even tighter across his mouth, hoping that at least a part of what he said would be muffled. "It is a land of beauty, rich in history and pomp, but poor in good land and forests. Their Gods are those of the Old Faith," he said, hurrying on to safer ground, "but with some additions: local deities who have assumed a rank all their own in the eastern lands, and naturally they are the ones most frequently called upon."

"Of course." The Andam walked on in silence for a few steps and then, without turning, he said, "And do our brothers hold much influence in the Land of the Sun?"

It was the question he had been waiting for, fearing. They were now too close to the gates for Tien to turn and run, and so he was forced to brazen it out. "I worked mainly in the highlands to the north of the country and I can honestly say I saw none of our brothers there."

The older man nodded, his breath coming in a long hissing sigh. "Ah, I had heard it was not going well there. Perhaps I should go."

"The journey is long and the way is hard."

"The One will protect," the Andam said quickly, ritually, almost in the form of a benediction.

"The One will protect," Tien repeated.

They walked on in silence, the shadow of the gate looming over them. Tien could see the guards stopping and checking each cart, and not a quick, cursory glance either, which would have been usual, but a thorough and detailed search by two men of the Gate Squadron while what looked like at least a decade stood guard beyond them. "There are more guards than usual," he said slowly.

"It is the trouble in the west," the Andam said quickly, glancing at him, his face barely visible behind the tattered grey cowl.

"Will they let us through?" Tien wondered aloud.

"They will not stop us," the priest said, and then he corrected himself. "Well, they will not stop me, but I am known to them."

He paused and then stated very softly, his voice so low that Tien was unsure at first if he had heard the man correctly. "You are not of the Brotherhood."

Tien didn't have many alternatives, and of the few he had none of them seemed particularly attractive. "What are you going to do?" he asked, determined that if the priest betrayed him, at least he would die first.

"My actions are, I would imagine, determined by yours. Why have you assumed the guise of an Andam to enter the city?"

"I intend to kill Salier and the Hierophant," the Shemmat said simply, surprising himself with his answer.

The Andam nodded. "And your companion?"

"What companion?"

"You have a companion. Who does he intend to kill?"

"Geillard and Fodla." Again, the answer was completely involuntary.

"You are agents of the Prince Kutor?"

Tien nodded.

"And what faith does he profess now?" the Andam asked, his voice silk and ice.

"The Old Faith!" Tien gasped against his will, his eyes locked on the gate and its guards now barely steps away.

"And you are?"

"Tien tZo, slave-companion of Owen, the Weapon Master." Tien was shivering now; he could feel the icy sweat trickle down the back of his neck beneath his robes. He knew what the Andam priest was doing, and yet there was no way he could fight it.

"I have heard of this Weapon Master," the priest said softly, his voice becoming distant. "He is of the Iron Band of Kloor, is he not?"

"He was, but no longer."

The Andam looked at him and the early morning light shafting over the city walls illuminated the interior of the priest's cowl. Two metal-grey eyes burned in a face that was little more than raw meat, a mass of blood and scar tissue. "I have never heard of a man leaving the Band of Kloor," the Andam said slowly, his teeth surprisingly white and strong behind bloodied lips.

"He did!" Tien snapped involuntarily.

"Oh, I believe you," the priest said. "I was merely curious as to how he achieved the feat."

"There was a bard."

"A bard!" The Andam stopped and reached out, his cloth-wrapped fingers tightening around Tien's forearm. "A bard with a single hand and a hook in place of his left?"

"The same."

The Andam hissed softly. "And all this is his doing?"

"He started it."

"And where is he now?"

Tien shrugged. "No one knows. He has not been seen in a long time." Realising the Andam was no longer exerting his insidious control over him, Tien managed to ask. "You know of him?"

"I know the bard. All the followers of the Faith know the bard." He reached out and took Tien's arm again, but gently this time. "Come, let us enter this city together. You have work to do."

Geillard XII, Emperor of the Seven Nations and the Island King-doms, was sitting beneath the carefully pruned and shaped branches of one of the oldest trees in the palace, his eyes blank, the scrolls in his hands lying unopened and unread. There was no reason to read them; he knew their contents by heart, for they were his father's diaries.

Geillard XI, his father, should never have been a ruler. He was a scholar and a historian, a minor magician, a necromancer of some power, a mediocre alchemist, superb herbalist and healer, but he was not a leader. He had neither a ruler's temperament nor patience, and was easily led and swayed by his advisers. They, in effect, had ruled the court, corrupting it, weakening it, ultimately destroying it. And that was one of the reasons why when Geillard XII, the present ruler, had come to power, he had had them all slain in a single bloody night; he had seen how they had destroyed his father by allowing, even encouraging, him to indulge himself.

Geillard XI had one other failing, which in other men, other rulers, was dismissed as a mere right of office but in the Emperor's case became something much more. His appetite for women was extraordinary and as Emperor of the Seven Nations he was able to indulge his appetites. Before his legitimate son had come to power, there were at a conservative estimate at least forty children who could claim Geillard XI as their father, and in other courts and other times, they would have been brought to court and given a minor title and some land—and watched. But the old man had always ignored them, and if they or their mothers became difficult or demanding, they were wont to disappear. When Geillard XII came to power, one of his first acts was to instruct his spies to seek out the remaining bastard sons of his father and slay them. More than thirty young men met mysterious and curious deaths. Some survived, naturally, and one of those was Kutor, self-styled Prince, the Renegade.

A shadow fell across him, breaking into his reverie. Salier bowed stiffly. "My lord, I did not mean to startle you."

"I was dreaming," the tall, gaunt man said, his dark eyes fixing on the darting colours of the fish in the extravagantly ornamental pond.

Salier's eyes glided across the rolled diary parchments and he concealed a smile. "The bastard again?"

Geillard nodded. "I have begun to fear him," he confessed. "He is beginning to haunt my dreams."

"Then it is time to act. Do you wish me to arrange his death?" Salier asked smoothly.

"Is it possible?" the Emperor asked without much enthusiasm.

"Everything is possible."

For a long time Geillard didn't react and his attention remained riveted on the darting splashes of colour in the pond. Salier was beginning to think he hadn't heard the question and was about to repeat it, when the Emperor suddenly nodded. "It is necessary. He has become a positive danger. His progress across the Nations has been too swift. Soon people will begin to think that the Gods are on his side."

"I have already heard that," Salier lied.

"Well then, arrange his death, but make it look like an accident, or the result of his own stupidity, if possible. We don't need a martyr with a cult growing up around the name."

Salier bowed.

"Don't use any of our own men. Hire mercenaries from the taverns. I've read the reports that hundreds are flocking in for the coming battle."

"Oh, there are mercenaries aplenty in town. We should have no difficulty finding a man to suit our needs."

The atmosphere in the tavern was thick with smoke and sweat, and something else—the tart odour of blood on the air. The tavern was called The Barracks; and in the capital it was the unofficial hiring station for the mercenary troops that periodically wandered through the city. Men looking for a hired sword, for defence or attack, sought them out at The Barracks. It was run by a man whose name had once been legendary throughout the Nations, Thome the Iron Man. Age had tarnished the iron man's image somewhat, but even now, at eighty and more summers—an unheard of age for a mercenary—he was still tall and straight, his eyes sharp and knowing, and he still commanded much of the respect that he had enjoyed in his youth.

Thome leaned against the polished wooden bar and idly watched the two knife fighters in the sunken pit in the centre of the room. They were competent fighters, both using two knives, but their footwork was wrong and their balance off. Both had shallow cuts across their chests and arms, and he was wagering that the taller of the two, a blond-haired youngster from Thusal or thereabouts, would tire first. His opponent, although a smaller, darker man of indeterminate origin, had conserved his energy, and the cut to his chest had stopped bleeding remarkably quickly, indicating some formal body training or perhaps a minor spell. It was enough, though, to give him the advantage, and this time it would probably save his life.

The old warrior allowed his gaze to wander across the motley mixture in the tavern. Most he knew—the professional mercenary trade was a small and select one—but there were one or two newcomers, noticeable by their too-bright eyes and nervous swagger. One of them was attempting to buy what he obviously thought was one of the tavern women for the night. Thome suppressed a grin as the tall, buxom woman almost casually struck the man in the groin with her mug of rofion. The blow doubled him up, smashing his face into the table, and then there was a knife at his throat and Thome saw the woman's lips move. He knew the woman and could guess what she was promising the man if he so much as came near her again. But the newcomer had learned a valuable lesson—neither judge quickly nor by appearance. And he had also been painfully reminded that the mercenary trade was staffed by as many female warriors as male.

The door opened and Thome, who was turning away from the bar, glanced up and then stopped. The old man had worn a weapon since the time he could walk; he was a warrior and the son of a warrior, and he could trace an unbroken lineage of freelance soldiers back through seven generations. And if there was one thing he knew, it was a warrior, a professional soldier. It showed in the way he stood, the way he moved, the way he wore his weapons, in the way his eyes took in the room, noting the exits first, and then fixing the principal groups and their leaders in his mind, and then the tavern guards.

Thome was already setting up two jugs of rofion when the man approached the bar. Without a word he pushed one across. The stranger looked at the grey-haired man and then silently nodded his thanks before taking it. Thome lifted the second jar and both men toasted one another.

"Life!"

"Death!"

It was the drinking toast of the mercenary.

"You are Thome." It was more a statement than a question. "I understand you could find employment for a man of skill."

"There is always work for a skilled man. But the level of skill is important."

"I have the skill."

Thome nodded non-committally. "And you are?"

"I am Owen, the Weapon Master."

"The Defender of Car'an'tual?" Thome asked, keeping his expression neutral.

"The same."

"There was a man in here recently claiming to be Owen, the Weapon Master, the same Defender."

"And?"

"He was killed in the ring."

"Hardly likely if he were the real Owen."

"Accidents happen," Thome remarked with a grin. He knew beyond any shadow of a doubt that this was indeed the real Owen, the Weapon Master. When he looked at him, Thome saw himself as he must have looked when he was a younger man, a lifetime—ten lifetimes—ago. He wondered if his eyes had looked so tired then, so weary.

"You wish to test me in the ring?" Owen asked, finishing the last of the drink.

"I must be certain."

"I understand."

"And if you are indeed the Weapon Master, then there is employment, lucrative employment, when you have done."

"Announce it then," Owen said softly. He had been expecting the test and knew it was the only way Thome would believe him. He also knew that Thome supplied the mercenary instructors to the Imperial army and had the monopoly for supplying professionals on demand; he usually guaranteed his choice, and took his cut from both the employer and the employee.

In the ring, as Thome had predicted, the blond young man was being dragged out by two of his friends. He wasn't dead, not yet anyway.

"A trial!" Thome suddenly shouted, his deep, resonant voice booming throughout the tavern and instantly silencing it. "This stranger challenges all comers."

There was a quick murmur of excitement and a general movement towards the bar, and Owen suddenly found himself being scrutinised by a hundred and more iron-hard, ice-cold, and pitiless eyes. Some recognised him for what he was, reading the same signs Thome had, and they turned away, but there were still some takers. "What's the wager?" someone shouted.

"The Imperials are looking for a man, high risk, high pay. The winner will be that man."

There was another surge towards the bar, and Thome suddenly found himself facing a score of knife hilts. Closing his eyes he stretched out his right hand, running his calloused fingertips along the handles, and suddenly closing around one. The warrior whooped with pleasure and spun around to face Owen.

"I am Brega of the Isles and you are going to die!"

"It will take more than your wind to kill me," Owen said quietly. "Your weapons?" he asked.

"Knives," the man announced gleefully. He was taller than Owen and broad, his skin dark and weathered, his eyes startlingly blue against the colour of his face. He turned away and headed towards the steps that led down into the ring, already pulling off his cloak and unbuckling his sword belt.

There was a general move away from the bar towards the ring, and someone began shouting odds, and coin and scrip were produced and exchanged.

Owen turned back to Thome and pulled off his cloak and tossed it across the bar. "Will you take care of these for me?" He unbuckled his shoulder straps and shrugged off his buckler, and passed the two matched fighting swords across the bar. He pulled a pair of gauntlets from his belt and pulled them on, and then stooped and pulled a knife from his right boot.

"May I?" Thome asked, nodding at the knife. Owen flipped it and silently passed it hilt first to him. The old mercenary lifted the knife, noting the balance, tilting it, allowing the light to run along the blade. The blade was not long but it was thick and broad, pointed and double-edged; the hilt had obviously been wrapped in soft resin, which had now assumed the shape of Owen's hand. Thome placed the weapon down on Owen's cloak. "A fine weapon."

Owen picked the knife up, rubbing the blade against his sleeve, polishing the blade to mirror brightness. "Do you want this swift or slow?" he asked.

"Brega is a good fighter, that choice may not be yours to make."

Brega of the Isles stood in the centre of the ring, confidently awaiting the stranger. He was wearing a hauberk of large-link mail over a cotton shirt, which left his muscular arms bare. He wore two studded wrist-bands, and he was casually twirling two broad-bladed Chopt knives when Owen climbed down into the ring.

"Are you ready to die?" he asked, noting Owen's single knife, the leather jerkin and the gloves. He would have to assume the jerkin would turn all but the most forceful of blows, but the single weapon puzzled him. Most professionals fought with two knives—one to parry, one to thrust.

"No man is ever ready to die," Owen said softly, watching the man move and the ease and dexterity with which he manipulated the heavy, ungainly knives. He might indeed be a dangerous opponent.

Brega went into a crouch, his right arm close to his body, his left outstretched, his wrist pointing down, the knife angled up.

Owen remained still, only his eyes moving.

Brega began moving the knife in his left hand to and fro, allowing it to reflect the light, the movement designed to catch and hold his opponent's attention, and then he began to spin the blade, turning it on his fingers with extraordinary skill until it was spinning at high speed. And then he suddenly thrust with his right hand!

The blow should have taken Owen low in the stomach, the angle of the knife would have brought it up, the heavy Chopt blade easily sundering through the leather jerkin, slashing across muscle and ribs, disemboweling him. But the knife never reached its destination.

Owen's gloved hand closed on the broad spine of the blade just above the hilt, turning it—and Brega's arm with it. The knife in his right hand moved, slashing the exposed flesh, opening the flesh, sundering the veins along the full length of the arm. The blood loss was massive and immediate and dropped the warrior to his knees with the shock. Reaction set in and he began to vomit. Owen pushed the man away from him, shaking his head in disgust. He wiped the knife on his sleeve and slid it back into the sheath sewn inside his boot. "Tend to his arm before he bleeds to death," he said to no one in particular and climbed up out of the pit and moved back to the bar. "You mentioned something about a job," he said to Thome.

19
The Torc Allta

He had enemies aplenty, and they were not always of humankind.

Tales of the Bard

Dawn came suddenly to the Mire and brought with it the unmistakable sounds of pursuit. The sudden crashing, although muted by the fog, brought Buiva and the bard to their feet, eyes and ears alert.

Paedur hopped up onto the tumbled stones of the wall and tilted his head to one side, listening, sorting through the sounds. "Ten men," he said confidently, "armed and wearing mail, and one other, older and wheezing."

"How close?" Buiva asked, turning to awaken the woman warrior, but finding her wide-eyed and listening.

Paedur shook his head. "I'm not sure. The boggy ground and this cursed fog distorts all sound. But close, else we would not have heard them."

Paedur dropped down off the wall. "I'm just wondering how they can follow our trail through this muck," he said.

Buiva strode over and hauled Churon up. "On your feet. We're moving." He glanced at the bard as the sounds shifted, becoming more distinct. "Well, they have our general direction, but either they have a very good tracker or else they're using sorcery."

Paedur looked up sharply. "But I thought few, if any, sorcerers could work here in the Mire, so close to the Planes of Existence, the Shadowland, and the Silent Wood. If it is sorcery, it means a very powerful sorcerer indeed."

Buiva nodded. He roughly spun Churon around and pulled a length of braided cord from his belt. Gripping the Onelord's hands above the wrists he began to tie them up, lacing the cord through the fingers, fashioning a noose around the thumbs. When he pulled the cord tight, Churon's hands were securely locked together, the fingers meshed. Spinning Churon around again, his gauntleted hands tightened into the soft flesh of his cheeks, just below the jaw joint. "Tell me, what sorcerer is powerful enough to work in the Mire?"

The Onelord's eyes remained mocking, and even when the god increased the pressure until the black skin turned purple and he felt the bones beginning to grate together, there was no change in Churon's defiant expression.

"Perhaps if we remove his eyes he'll talk," Katani suggested with a pleasant smile.

Paedur strode cross the clearing. "Look, we have no time for this." He brought his hook up and rested it on the bridge of Churon's nose and then slowly allowed it to fall, the razor-cool metal leaving a burning trail down the Onelord's face and throat. The bard continued to move his hook downwards, until he stopped just below the man's midriff. His flat, dark eyes looked into Churon's, and for the first time in many years, the Onelord felt something like fear touch him with a chill. "You, I think, prided yourself upon your manhood and your ability to sire children in the world of Men. Now, I know you intend to return to the Planes of Existence, and if you intend to keep your manhood you will tell the god what he wants to know." His voice remained low and without inflection, but the Onelord had absolutely no doubt but that he meant it.

"The only magician working in the Mire at the moment is Praetens," he said quickly.

"The Susuru warlock?" Paedur asked.

The Onelord nodded.

Paedur placed his hand in the centre of Churon's chest, and pushed. The man sat down with a thump. "Stay there," he commanded. He inclined his head and Buiva and Katani moved away with him, and the three stood talking quietly together, watching the man on the ground.

"I think I should stay behind and try to kill this Susuru warlock," Paedur said quietly. "If he isn't stopped, he will dog us every step of the way to the Silent Wood and there is no telling what his sorceries or powers are like, but he must be powerful indeed if he is able to operate within the Mire."

"The Susuru are a dangerous race, bard," Buiva said quietly, "and I must say I've never heard of one being killed by any means other than sorcery."

"I have slain one," Paedur said.

"So, what are you suggesting?" Buiva asked.

"You and Katani go ahead with the prisoner. I'll stay here and deal with some of the pursuers and the Susuru if possible."

"And then?"

"I'll catch up with you."

"One man against ten men and a Susuru?" Katani asked in disbelief.

"It's been a long time since I was a man," Paedur said mockingly, glancing sidelong at the god.

The first two warriors cautiously approached the tumbled ruin of stones, nostrils flaring. There was beast blood in them and their features were the flat, broad, snouted masks of boars. Two tusks protruded up from their lower lips and these had been decorated in a twisting, curling caste-mark.

"Humankind," the larger creature said, snouted nostrils wrinkling, "and others, non-human, but not were-folk."

"Two bodies," his companion grunted, "no, three, four?" he asked, looking confused.

The larger creature, wearing a captain's insignia on his helmet, pointed with his short-hafted jabbing spear. "The Onelord here, another humankind here beside him; someone from the Silent Wood by the smell of death about them." He raised his head, eyes and nostrils wide. "There was another creature and something else, something unhuman here." He turned, his spear pointing—and the bard's flashing hook tore into the soft flesh beneath his ear and ripped, neatly severing his throat.

The second creature tuned at the rattling, gurgling sound, and a spear took him through the mouth, pinning him to the trunk of a twisted, blighted tree. He died without a sound.

Shortly afterwards a small group of the boar-creatures approached the ruins, led by a small, frail-seeming white-haired man. Even on the tainted air of the Mire they smelt the metallic odours of blood and death. They stopped in sight of the ruins, and even the bravest of the Torc Allta—the Boar Folk—felt something like fear touch them when they saw the crucified bodies of the two scouts on the walls.

"How many within the walls?" the small man demanded of the huge were-creature towering above him.

"I cannot tell, master. The blood overpowers all else. I

cannot detect anyone, although I know it would have taken many men to do this."

The old man frowned. The Torc Allta were truly terrifying creatures, bloody, merciless warriors without compassion and with one other useful attribute—they ate their victims, even if those victims were of the Torc Allta. He suddenly shivered, conscious only of the cold, the damp, and interminable fatigue. This body was always tired, but when he had been forced to take it, he hadn't much choice at the time. He consoled himself with the thought that soon, soon, he would be able to choose a body more suited to his station.

"Master?" the huge Torc Allta asked.

"Send two warriors in and then two more in directly behind them. I can feel nothing there, but just in case."

The warrior nodded and silently pointed his spear at the two nearest creatures, then waved it towards the ruins. Without hesitation, they moved off towards it. The captain then pointed to a second pair and repeated the gesture, and again they responded without hesitation.

"Those we hunt," the Torc Allta asked, "they are from the Race of Man?"

"Does it matter?" the old man asked, tired, faded eyes looking at the warrior.

The creature shrugged, snout wrinkling. "I am a connoisseur of flesh," he said slowly, "and much of the enjoyment is in the anticipation of the feast."

"You are an animal," the old man smiled.

"I am Torc Allta," the warrior said proudly.

Shaking his head, the old man tuned back to watch the four armoured figures moving in towards the tumbled ruins. "We hunt three," he said slowly. "From the descriptions of those at the monastery and my own little magics, one is from the Silent Wood, another is a god and the third, the third is neither man nor beast, neither living nor dead, but something else, something else." He glanced back over his shoulder at the were-creature. "The Dead and the God are yours, the other is mine—briefly—until I determine what it is, and then its flesh is yours."

Satisfied, the Torc Allta nodded, swallowing saliva. "Dead flesh is interesting, spicy, savoury, but I have never tasted the flesh of a god." He nodded. "I look forward to the feast." His head came up sharply and the short-red-bristled hairs on the backs of his hands rose.

"What is it?" the old man demanded.

"Blood," the Torc Allta said simply. "There has been a killing."

Katani's sword whispered from its scabbard as the two beast-creatures rose in front of her; behind her she heard the rattle of Buiva's mace and she risked a quick glance over her shoulder to find two more of the creatures.

"Torc Allta," she hissed.

Buiva nodded and sighed, glancing longingly at the black line of the River Naman which separated the Mire from the Silent Wood. He had wanted to cross and wait for the bard on the far side, but Katani had been insistent, and so they had sent away the boatman empty-handed and had camped on the filthy, bloody banks of the River of Death waiting for Paedur.

Behind them Churon began to laugh. "You are mine now. They are the Torc Allta. I will have them eat your flesh." The Onelord struggled uselessly against the chains that Buiva had used to bind him to a shattered remnant of a temple column that they had found on the rough beach.

"Where is the bard?" Katani hissed.

The god shook his head. "It is not a good sign..." He stopped as the two creatures before him separated and a small white-haired man stepped out. He ran a speckled, trembling hand through the thinning wiry strands of his hair and smiled on them both. "So we have finally found you." He looked from the man to the woman. "I recognise the armour of course, Katan." A smile wrinkled his face. "I thought they had all been slain on the Sand Plain."

"They were," Katani hissed venomously.

"And not a moment too soon," the old man said simply. "It should have been done much sooner, would have been if Churon had listened to my advice." His eyes flickered in the Onelord's direction. "But, of course, he could never listen to advice."

"Who are you?" Katani whispered. "I never saw you at court." She was aware of the Torc Allta moving in.

"Oh, you saw me," the old man smiled, "but not in this corporeal form."

"He is Praetens, the Susuru," Buiva said quietly.

The old man bowed. "And you are Buiva, God of War of the Pantheon of the Old Faith." He looked back to Katani. "At the precise moment when my body was destroyed during the Battle of the Sand Plain, my essence soared free and lighted upon the nearest weakest essence." His shoulders moved and his hands swept down his body in a quick, almost shy movement. "Unfortunately, this was what I ended up with." And then he laughed, the sound thin and cackling. Wiping tears from his eyes, he continued. "This body once belonged to the slopman, the servant who cleared the foulness and offal from the camp latrines. And now even the mighty Churon bows his head to it."

"I bow to the mind, not the body," Churon said tightly.

"See how he must always have the last word," Praetens said, shaking his head. "But enough of this." He stretched out a wrinkled hand. "You must surrender to us, lay down your weapons and give us Churon. There has been enough killing this day."

"I thought there would be more of you," Buiva said with a sly smile. "The Torc Allta usually travel in groups, do they not, and someone of your station would not travel these dangerous lands so lightly guarded."

"I am too weary to decide whether you are mocking me or attempting to rouse my anger. But I warn you that it is not wise to raise me to anger. Even you, a god, would not stand against me."

"I think if your magic was safe to use you would have used it. But this is the Mire and the laws of Nature and Magic are altered here. Who knows, perhaps you are, like us, bereft of much of your powers and stand before us now as nothing more than an old man."

Praetens turned away. "Take them, their flesh is yours."

"WAIT!"

The voice rang out across the beach, strong enough to set small stones rattling, and rippling the surface of the water. A figure stepped onto a tall flattened boulder at the far end of the beach, a tall, thin figure wrapped in a black furred cloak. The figure pointed with a gleaming sickle-hook that took the place of his left hand, and again the incredibly powerful voice boomed down the beach.

"Are the Torc Allta ordered to their destruction so easily? Are the fabled were-creatures nothing more than *cuine* to be slaughtered? You followed the old man today and you lost six of your brothers, truly lost them now, for their flesh has been taken by the scavengers of the Mire and not by their brothers as is their right. He sends you now against a warrior of the Katan, the same warriors whom even the Onelord surrounded himself with, and Buiva, the God of War, a slayer of Nations. What hope have you against them?" The figure dropped to the pebbles and crunched up the beach to stop before Praetens. "And he sends you against me," he added very softly.

"And who are you?" the magician asked, attempting to sound defiant — but his aged voice trembled and betrayed him.

"I am Paedur, the bard." From beneath his cloak he pulled a large leaf that had been tied into a makeshift pouch with vine. Slicing through the vine with his hook he dropped the leaf on the ground, where it spilled twelve bloody tusks, all worked with the individual caste-marks of the Torc Allta. "I killed your brothers today," he said simply, looking past Praetens to the huge werecreature.

"He lies!" Praetens snapped.

"I do not lie."

"I believe him," the Torc Allta said. He looked at the sharp-faced man with the curious hook, then at his two companions and came to a decision. "We will not fight this day."

"I order you!" Praetens shouted.

"Six of the Torc Allta were taken from us today because of your orders and they were left without the proper rites because of your orders. I will take no further orders from you this day." He jerked his short spear at the trio. "I look at these and I see nothing but destruction. Leave them, master, there will be other times, other places." The Torc Allta nodded to the two creatures standing before Katani and they stepped back and circled around until they were standing behind their leader and the magician. The huge creature moved up beside Praetens and looked at each of the three faces in turn. "I will remember you." he said looking at Katani and Buiva, and then he turned to the bard. "Your flesh is mine."

Paedur bowed slightly. "We will meet again."

The leader of the Torc Allta stooped carefully, his eyes never leaving the bard's face, and he gathered up the twelve caste tusks from the six slain warriors and dropped them into a pouch on his belt.

"You cannot leave me!" Churon suddenly shouted, realising that they were not going to fight for him.

"You are obviously not worth risking destruction for," Paedur said, turning away from the Torc Allta and walking down to the chained warrior.

"I once was."

"That was a long time ago and in a different place." Paedur turned and watched the Torc Allta shoulder their spears and lumber away, moving almost silently for all their great size and apparent clumsiness. Praetens lingered a moment longer, his eyes on the bard's face, and then he too turned away and hurried inelegantly after the were-creatures.

"Perhaps it would have been better if you had given me to them," Churon remarked calmly, watching the figures disappear back into the undergrowth.

"We haven't come all this way just to give you back at the last moment," Katani said, sliding home her sword and smiling with genuine good humour at the bard. "We thought you were dead."

"He only killed six of them," Buiva remarked with a smile. "Not enough to cause Paedur here too much concern."

"Their own fear and expectations killed them," Paedur said. "They were expecting an army, they were looking for an army, and couldn't cope with the idea of a single killer. The hardest part was removing their tusks," he added with a rare smile.

"They will come back for you," Churon said maliciously, "and I hope I'm there to see it."

Buiva nodded in agreement. "They will hunt you, and in force now that they know your capabilities, and you will have to kill them and keep killing them, or be killed. They make bad enemies."

Paedur ran his fingers through his fine hair. "I know. I am a bard, remember. I know the legends of the Torc Allta." He squatted down beside Churon and slipped his hook in under the chains, testing them. He glanced up at the god. "How long have we before the boatman arrives?"

"He only travels during the twilight hours, before sunrise and after sunset."

"We have some time then." He picked up a handful of rough pebbles and tossed them into the blood-black water. "Listen to me then, and I will tell you of the Torc Allta, the Boar-Folk...

In the last days of the Culai before the war with the Humankind, the First Race experimented with the unholy mingling of beast and men, using their magics to delve deep into the bodies of both men and beasts, changing and altering that which differentiates men and beasts, making them unique, and in this way they fashioned the were-folk, that unhappy mingling of beast and man. Of course, there had been creatures that were more beast than man, the true Creatures of the Were, but these were the creations of the gods, and mainly occupied other Planes of Existence than Man.

In the beginning these new were-creatures were merely curiosities, to be looked upon and wondered at and admired, and perhaps that was what caused their downfall, for to possess one of the were-folk became fashionable amongst the Culai, and so their breeding became something of a matter of course rather than a scientific rarity. Soon they became pets and then later, servants, and then of course it became apparent that certain were-creatures, although predominantly human, possessed to a greater degree the attributes of their beast blood, and these talents were seized upon and enhanced, some becoming common labourers, miners, divers, and, of course, warriors. The Torc Allta were of the warrior class. Their antecedents were wild boars and their descendants possessed all the savagery of their distant forebears.

And then, of course, it was discovered that the were-creatures could breed and that their offspring carried tainted were-blood. But the were-folk's breeding cycle was as that of their animal ancestors, and multiple births were commonplace and more than one litter in a season was not unknown. Suddenly, the creatures were no longer a novelty, and very quickly became a threat as their numbers increased dramatically.

The Culai response was simple and effective. In their retreat in the City they worked an incredibly complex magic and one by one, race by race, they banished the were-folk from this plane to inhabit the other Planes of Existence, alongside the true Creatures of the Were. And to their credit they did attempt to suit the creatures to the plane.

And they sent the Torc Allta to one of the planes which borders the Mire, which is, I imagine, how they came to be here. Occasionally one appears in the World of Men, but it is usually considered to be a deformed member of the Chopt race.

Paedur finished.

"I will add a piece to your tale, if you will, bard," Buiva said. Paedur bowed and the god continued. "I was ... acquainted with the Culai and their elite soldiery, the Storm Warriors. I know they used the Torc Allta as trackers, for they possess one extraordinary attribute which astounded even the Culai who created them. They can track across the Planes of Existence, from one to another. Once they make themselves aware of a person's aura, they can track that aura and there is no way to elude them."

"Then that is what the Torc Allta was doing when he was staring at you," Katani said suddenly.

Churon laughed, the sound forced and harsh. "He knows your aura, now. He will track you. There is no place for you to hide and when he finds you, he will consume your flesh. Bard, you are a dead man!"

20
Demon's Law

Chance is the Demon's Law: with it one might change the world, against it the Gods themselves are powerless...

Pantheon of the Old Faith

Libellius, the Lord of Death of the New Religion, differs almost completely from the traditional image of Death personified in that he is always depicted as a fat and jolly man, harvesting souls as another man might harvest fruit...

Balephrenon: the Gods of the New Religion

Geillard XII, Emperor of the Seven Nations, stood in the topmost room of the tallest tower of his palace and looked across his city, out over the walls and into the far distance where the low line of the mountains was barely visible behind a shifting, writhing haze. But at this time of morning, the purple peaks should have been crystal clear, so clear indeed that if he put a glass to his eye he should have been able to see the snow-caps.

Salier, who was standing behind him, leaned forward and said, "You see it?"

"A haze...a fog?"

"Fire," the mage said, coming up to stand beside the Emperor. "Kutor's army is burning the grain fields of Gallowan!"

"Why haven't they been stopped?" Geillard demanded.

"Fodla sent two legions against them yesterday, but there was no battle. Reports are unclear, but it seems Kutor himself went out to speak to the assembled Imperial forces, his voice projected by means of a minor spell, and when he had finished more than half of our legionaries joined his forces."

"And the others?"

"Allowed to go free or fight as they wished. Most chose to go free; some elected to return here; none fought."

"And where are they now?"

"Some are on the road here."

"Stop them!"

"My lord?"

The Emperor rounded on the mage. "They must not reach the capital. Assign them to an outpost and contain them all in one garrison. If they reach here, the effect will be twofold: they'll spread the story like contagion, and what will our troops do when they discover their grain ration has been destroyed?" Imperial troops were paid a portion of their wages in grain and salt.

"I bow to your wisdom," Salier said softly.

"Patronise me and I'll have your head," Geillard snapped icily. "One of these days you'll go too far."

Salier bowed slightly and took a step back. "I will take care of the returning troops, majesty." He paused and then said maliciously, "There is the matter of Prince Kutor."

"Never give him a title in my presence!" Geillard spat.

"I think I have the man to solve our problems," Salier said slowly, watching the Emperor's expression. "He comes from Thome, who recommends him highly."

"I want to see him!"

"Surely that isn't necessary, majesty. I can deal with him."

Geillard shook his head. "No, I want to instruct him personally. My half-brother must suffer before he dies."

"Perhaps it would be better if he did not see you. There could be talk later."

"When he has completed his mission, you will have him slain, of course."

The magus bowed and backed from the tower room.

Tien tZo crouched on the broad rose-coloured steps of the Cathedral, still wrapped in his ragged Andam robes, his wooden bowl between his feet on the smooth stone before him. As was customary with the Andam, he did not beg for charity, merely thanked those who gave. However, because he was a priest of the most primitive form of the Old Faith begging on the steps of the Cathedral to the Gods of the New Religion, his bowl had remained empty thus far, and all he had collected were curses and spittle.

He looked at the sky, gauging the time, wondering how long he would have to wait. But it was of little consequence: he was in no hurry.

The morning was warm and Tien tZo allowed his mind to drift, snatching a few moments of relaxation, though he was not totally unaware of the movement all around him.   He calmed his mind and called upon his own gods and his forefathers, for the Shemmatae honoured their ancestors, worshipping them as minor deities. He called upon the figure of his father, and when he could clearly see the man, then called up his grandfather, and then he worked back through his ancestors until he reached the first Tien tZo, the Destroyer of Cities, the Builder of Tombs. He concentrated upon the shadowy figure, building the image in his mind's eye. He always began with the hands; he knew of others who started with the feet or face, but he began with the hands. The first Tien tZo's hands were small, the fingers blunt, the palms and fingers calloused, the wrists thick. There was a ring on the little finger of his left hand, a small, simple band, bright against his weather-darkened flesh. When he was able to clearly see every detail of the ring on the finger, he knew he had achieved his goal—communion with his ancestor's shade. He framed the first question.

"I must kill this man." He allowed an image of the Hierophant to form in his mind's eye.

"He is deserving of death?" His ancestor's voice was thin and high, not at all what he expected from the squat, bulky warrior-lord.

"He is."

"Must he die publicly?"

"No. But it would be better if his death were seen not to be an accident and could be blamed on a rival faction within his own people."

Tien tZo saw the feral smile that drifted across his ancestor's face. "A ploy I used once." There was a brief moment of waiting, and Tien knew the image in his mind was reading his memories and absorbing what little he knew of the Hierophant. "There are guards," the warlord said finally. "Is your death called for?"

"I would prefer it otherwise."

The mage grunted. "It will not be easy."

"Killing is easy."

"Only dying is easy," the shade said. "Stealth, I think, is out of the question here; it is expected and must therefore be avoided. Approach the man directly, boldly."

"I have assumed the guise of a religious group directly opposed to this man and his beliefs."

"Have you a loyalty to this religion?"

"No!" Tien tZo said, surprised.

"Well then, the answer is simplicity itself." The warlord's laughter echoed through Tien tZo's head. "Defect. Convert to his faith. Surely that in itself would be enough of a coup for him to see you personally, would it not?"

Unconsciously, the man sitting on the steps of the Cathedral nodded, and broke contact with the memory of his infamous ancestor. The butt end of a spear poked at his cloth-wrapped legs.

"On yer way, beggar. These are the cathedral steps. We don't want them sullied by the likes of you."

Tien tZo looked up, squinting against the glare of the sun, and found three of the Cathedral guard standing around him. Their surcoats were spotless and the sunlight burned off the white satin cloth. They were armed with blunted spears and clubs—bloodletting within the boundaries of the cathedral being expressly forbidden.

"That's no beggar," one of the men suddenly said, "it's Andam."

The spear came around again and the broad copper head with its flattened tip touched Tien's chin, raising it. The Shemmat saw their expressions change from dull contempt to open hatred.

"Andam," the largest guard spat. "befouling the very air we breath, soiling the steps of the cathedral…"

"Praying for forgiveness!" Tien said quickly, seeing the man's knuckles tighten around the staff. The warrior knew he could easily defend himself from these three, but that would mean killing one or possibly all three of them, and the last thing he wanted to do now was to attract attention. "I was praying to the New Gods for forgiveness."

The three guards looked at one another. "What do you mean, 'forgiveness?' the largest, the spokesman, said threateningly.

"I have recognised the error of my ways. I wish to convert to the true way, the way of the New Religion."

Their expressions changed to disbelief and distrust, but it was obvious that this was a decision beyond them.

"If you're lying, we'll kill you," the leader threatened.

"I have sat here all morning listening to the voice within, waiting for you to come and take me to enlightenment."

Tien saw the look that passed between them—puzzlement, mingled with a little amusement; they had finally reached the conclusion that he was mad. They herded him off the steps and down an adjoining side street. The alleyway was dark after the sunlight, but remarkably free of the alleyway smells that Tien had grown accustomed to—or perhaps he had just been frequenting the wrong sort of alleyways. He grinned, feeling the rush of exhilaration, suddenly realising that it was going to work. If he got out of this alive, he would sacrifice a whole bothe in his ancestor's memory.

The Cathedral guards stopped outside a door that was guarded by two fully armed Imperial Guards; obviously the edict against spilling blood within the boundaries of the cathedral did not extend to the side streets around it. Their face-shields were down, but Tien could feel their eyes moving across him, and he carefully adjusted his stance, assuming the off-balance, slightly crouching manner of a tired old man. The leader of the Cathedral guards went inside, only to reappear a moment later followed by a second man in the garb of a captain of the Cathedral guard, his rank distinguished by a crimson eye on the shoulder of his satin surcoat.

"You are Andam," he snapped without preamble.

"I am—I was." Tien corrected himself.

"Was?"

"I have seen the true way; I wish to convert to the New Religion, the True Religion."

The man suppressed a quick smile. A converted Andam priest would be quite a coup. "And how long have you been Andam?"

"Twenty summers."

"And why this sudden desire to convert?"

"I have spoken with Trialos!"

In the long shocked silence that followed, Tien tZo knew he had them. Only the Hierophant was supposed to have direct communion with Trialos, the Prime Deity of the New Religion.

"Trialos spoke with you?" the captain asked.

Tien nodded.

"And what did he say?" the man asked, now more curious than demanding.

But Tien shook his head. "I have a message for the Hierophant and it must be for his ears only."

"It could be a trick," the captain said doubtfully.

"But to what end? Why should I deliver myself so readily into your hands if I was not telling you the truth? The force of the lord's message has convinced me, an Andam, to convert to the New Religion and the worship of the Lord Trialos. Where is the trickery in that?"

"But why would the Lord Trialos deliver a message to an Andam?" the man asked, more to himself than to Tien.

"Who are we to question the lord's way?" one of the guards said piously.

"It could be a trick."

"If it's a trick we'll kill him—slowly."

The captain nodded. "Take him to the Gate and deliver him to the guards there. He is to be taken directly to the Hierophant."

In the dim, flickering, candlelit silence of the tiny room, a single figure sat with his back against the chill stone wall. The room was bare and the man was naked; no one, not even his closest friends or lovers, would have recognised Barthus, the Hierophant. His pale flesh was bathed with chill sweat and the muscles and veins were clearly outlined beneath the taut skin. His usually deep-set eyes seemed to have sunk deeper into his skull and his fine hair was plastered against his head. His breathing was ragged and the pounding of his heart was clearly visible against his chest and at his throat and temples.

There were two candles on the bare flagstones before him and another candle in a niche above his head, but the room was not dark. Tiny traceries of red fire darted along the cracks in the stones briefly outlining them, crackling, hissing, spitting slightly as they moved.

But Barthus was unaware of the darting fire; indeed, he was no longer even aware of the room. His whole consciousness was concentrated inwards on the arcane and complicated ritual for calling on the Lord of the Dead.

But like most of the Gods of the New Religion, he had to be paid to attend, and Barthus was paying with his physical body and immortal soul.

The darting, crackling, sparkling lines of red fire began to coalesce on the bare stones beyond the two candles. Their buzzing had become intense, and within the confines of the tiny room they reverberated off the walls so that the naked man felt the sound vibrating deep within his bones, shaking him to his very core. Abruptly, the candle flames began to shiver, and then the candles on the floor trembled and fell over and their flames were extinguished, leaving only the tiny light burning on the wall behind the man's head, throwing the room into deep, menacing shadow.

The buzzing stopped and Barthus opened his eyes.

There was a figure sitting opposite him, shadowy and indistinct in the light, but Barthus recognised him from his bulk and height: Libellius, Lord of the Dead of the New Religion. His memory supplied the description of the god: a short, stout, jovial man, with a thatch of snow-white hair, deep-set twinkling eyes, and a quick and ready smile.

"You called me?" His voice was deep and rich as befitted his appearance.

From a seated position, the Hierophant bowed low, his forehead touching the floor. The God's benign appearance didn't deceive him; he knew how Libellius had become the God of Death of the Religion. "My lord, a humble servant thanks you for your presence here."

Libellius waved stubby beringed fingers. "You called me?" he repeated.

"There is danger, lord. I would not have disturbed you, but the very existence of the Religion is threatened."

The shadowy figure sat forward and Barthus received the vague impression of his pale, round face. "Tell me."

"There is an uprising in the west led by a man called Kutor, halfbrother to the present Emperor. He is an ardent follower of the Faith. If he triumphs, and his defeat is by no means certain, then the Religion will be proscribed and the Faith re-established as the official belief in the Nations."

"If this man Kutor dies, will the rising die with him?"

"If the circumstances of his death are such that he loses all credibility, then I believe so."

"What steps have you taken?"

"Salier has employed a mercenary from one of the many that are flooding into the city at this moment, listening to the distant drums of war. We intend to have him infiltrate Kutor's camp and then kill him."

"I can see no fault in that," Libellius said quickly.

"But I think—no, I know—Kutor is guarded by the forces of the Faith. I have attempted on several occasions to come close to him, but he has, or his guardians have, resisted my best efforts."

"How do you want me to help?" Libellius asked seriously.

"In any way you can."

"I can take some from his army," the fat old man mused. "I can bring in disease and death; there are those would fall easily to my hand. I could assume the guise of Death, the traditional image of death from the legends, and allow myself to be seen walking the camp." He looked up at Barthus. "Well?"

"My lord, any, or indeed all, of these suggestions would be excellent. However, I should add that I do not think you will find the camp unguarded. I have learned that the bard, Paedur, is the prime instigator of this uprising."

Libellius sat back into the shadows, his breath hissing through his teeth. "The bard! In that case, we must assume that the rising is being backed by the Gods of the Old Faith. Interesting." He stopped, shaking his head in puzzlement. "But that doesn't explain what the bard is doing now."

"Where is he now?" Barthus demanded. "I have had my spies watch for him especially."

"They are wasting their time." Libellius grinned. "He is dead at the moment, or more truly, he is within Death's Domain and, saving the Demon's Law of chance, well beyond our sphere of influence for the moment. But we will get him, don't worry. The bard will be ours some day." The god's eyes closed in dreamy reflection of the tortures it would be his pleasure to inflict on the creature when he was finally captured. His eyes snapped open and he sat forward. "So, while I create a distraction within Kutor's army, your mercenary will slay Kutor."

"Will you ensure that Kutor's guards are amongst the first to fall?" Barthus asked.

"I will take as many as I can. And what of Kutor's death itself? How do you wish that to appear?"

The Hierophant shrugged. "It would be to our advantage to discredit the man as much as possible."

"Papers could be left implicating him in an Imperial conspiracy to rid the Nations of the last vestiges of the Faith," Libellius suggested with a chuckle.

"Excellent, lord, excellent!"

"They must appear genuine, mind, for they will be subjected to an intense scrutiny."

"They will be genuine, lord. Geillard himself will sign them."

The Lord of Death sat forward, his eyes glittering in the reflected light. "In the light of this upheaval, this is an auspicious time to further our plans."

Barthus nodded eagerly. "That thought had crossed my mind."

"Then perhaps you should know that the insurgents have infiltrated men into the city." The God raised his hand, the rings on his fingers taking the light. "There are but two, so you must not alarm yourself overmuch. However, they are assassins with orders to slay the Emperor, Salier, Fodla, and, of course, yourself."

"I will have them killed!"

Libellius nodded. "Of course you will, but not immediately." He paused a moment, allowing the message to sink home, and then Barthus suddenly smiled and nodded in understanding.

"We will let them do our killing for us."

Libellius nodded.

"Who are these two? How may I recognise them?"

"One is Owen, a Weapon Master. He was one with our brother Kloor, but the bard released him from his vows and shattered the Iron Band, and now he guides this uprising. He intends to kill Geillard and Fodla. And of course, by the Demon's Law, he is the very man Salier has employed to kill Kutor!" The God smiled broadly. "It has a certain comic rationality to it."

"And the second man?"

"The second is Tien tZo, the slave-companion to Owen. He entered the city disguised as Andam. His task is to kill Salier and you. And even now, he is being escorted into your chambers by the Cathedral guards!"

Barthus surged to his feet, the sudden movement extinguishing the candle above his head, plunging the room into smoky darkness.

"Disguised as Andam, he professes to have seen the true light and wishes to convert to the Religion," Libellius continued evenly. "That is why he has been brought to you. However, play along with the scheme. I would suggest you send him on to Salier, perhaps with a request as to how the greatest use might be made of such a man." He paused and in the darkness, there was the sound of him coming slowly to his feet. "If you take my meaning?"

Barthus bowed. "Of course, my lord." A sudden thought struck him. "But lord, if this mercenary Salier has employed is already working for Kutor, then surely that invalidates the rest of our plan."

Libellius chuckled. "Continue with the plan, but employ a man of your own to do the killing. He will kill Kutor, while Kutor's men will kill Geillard, Salier, and Fodla, leaving you in command."

"It will work out very well," Barthus murmured.

"It is all up to the Demon's Law." Libellius said. "Even the Gods have no say in it now."

21
Churon's Tale

"Death is the last great deceit."

Churon the Onelord

"Welcome back, Churon!" Mannam rubbed clacking hands together and turned from the chained Onelord to Paedur and Katani. "You have done well. And you too, of course," he added, looking at Buiva.

The God of War bowed slightly. "There is nothing to thank me for. As one of the Pantheon, I had my duty to perform." He jerked his grizzled head towards Paedur and the woman. "Their task was much more perilous and their reasons their own, and they went of their own accord. If there is justice, they should be rewarded."

"And so they will," Mannam agreed.

"I want no payment," Paedur said, suddenly feeling utterly weary, "merely the life of my two companions who died in the service of the Pantheon. Their deaths were untimely; return them to life in the World of Men, allow them to act out their allotted span of years."

"Then you are not the paid creature of this, this god?" Churon abruptly demanded, straining forward against his bonds, the wan light from the single window painting his face in a snarl.

"Neither man nor god owns me," the bard said quietly.

"What tale did he tell you?" the Onelord snapped, glaring at Mannam. "What lies?"

"Enough! Silence!" Mannam whirled, his leaved cloak rasping, browned and withered leaves scattering across the darkened room. "Call our brothers," Mannam said to Buiva. "Call Destruction and Madness and let us end this thing now."

The bard stepped up to the Onelord and looked into his sharp blue eyes. "What do you mean?" he asked softly.

"Leave him be, bard!" Mannam demanded, his claw-like hand reaching for the bard's shoulder…only to find itself entrapped within the half circle of his hook. Blue-white fire crackled along the metal and a faint tendril of grey smoke drifted up from between the twisted twigs that served as Mannam's fingers. With an inhuman scream Death fell back, his arm clutched to his body. The bitter odour of scorched wood hung in the air on the still dry air.

"Never touch me!" Paedur said evenly to the fallen figure and then he turned back to the Onelord. "You attempted to usurp Death's position, is that true?"

"It is true I was plotting to overthrow him."

"Why?" Paedur asked simply. "Why did you attempt to destroy him?"

Churon threw back his head and laughed. "Bard, he is Death, the last great deceit. He has misled you. I never attempted to destroy him; quite the contrary, he has constantly sought my death, my complete and absolute destruction, since I left him. That is why I sought to overthrow him."

A branch snapped, silencing Churon. "He lies. Destroy him and be done with it!"

"I want to listen to him," Paedur said mildly.

"And so do I," Buiva added, surprisingly.

Katani folded her arms and said nothing.

The bard turned back to the chained man and slipped the point of his hook into the hasp of one of the huge locks and pulled, snapping the lock open. Churon pulled off the chains and then flung them into a corner. He walked to the window ledge and perched on it, one leg stretched straight out as his stiffened fingers worked on the locked muscles. "Listen to me, then, and I will tell you my tale—or my version of the Dark Lord's tale," he amended. "You may judge for yourselves then."

Paedur glanced quickly at Buiva and Katani and then nodded to Churon. "Speak, then."

The Onelord turned his head slightly, looking out over the silent streets and alleyways of Manach. The light was fading fast and the shadows almost totally consumed him, the darkness swallowing his skin, leaving only his snow-white hair startling against the dusk.

"You must know of my life in the World of Men, you know what I was, what I became," he said suddenly. "But whatever you have heard, and I am sure that much of it is true, you cannot know the reasons for what I did. And to understand that, you would have to understand what it was like to grow up a slave, and a slave with my colouring, only hearing the rumours that spoke of the lady of the house, whose child I later discovered I was. And then she seduced me, coupled with me when I was a youth, and only when she had conceived by me did she tell me her identity. And yes, I slew her, because she was a monster, even more depraved than the creatures she used for her pleasure. I ran away, became a slave again, escaped again, and then became a pirate, a bandit, a warrior, a king..." He shrugged and smiled wanly. "But, of course, you know all that."

Churon looked back into the shadowy darkness of Manach, the City of the Dead. "And then I died. I had never been a very religious man, but when I awoke in the Silent Wood I knew exactly where I was and what to expect. Creatures came for me, the bainte, but they expected me to act as a slave, and that I was not prepared to do. I had been a slave too long in the World of Men; I would not be a slave again in this place. That is how I came to Mannam's attention. I'm not sure what Death expected, or what he was used to with the newly dead, but he certainly never expected resistance.

"Surprisingly, he asked me to return to this place with him; perhaps even more surprisingly I agreed. And that was the start of what I can best describe as a friendship and, if the truth were only known, the first and perhaps the only friendship I had ever experienced in my entire life—or death," he added with a grim smile. "You see, we were equals of sorts. He was dead, he was Death; I could not threaten him, I wanted nothing from him. And he posed no threat to me, there was nothing I could give him. Or so I thought.

"Mannam made me his captain, his second-in-command. I patrolled the outskirts of his kingdom, where it borders some of the less ordered Planes of Existence and places like the Mire, keeping out the vermin and the unacceptable intrusions from those places. It was, I must admit, a very enjoyable phase of my existence. Is that the right word?" he asked, looking at Mannam. Receiving no reply, he shrugged and continued.

"And then I discovered the Dark Lord was plotting against me.

"Don't look so surprised or disbelieving, War God. Are the gods so far above deceit and pettiness?" Churon swung around off the window ledge and looked at the silent group of figures, his gaze coming back to fix on the bard's dark, shadowed eyes. "Perhaps you know, or then again perhaps not, that this Dark Lord, this Mannam, is not the first to wear the Leaved Cloak of the God of

Death." The Onelord's eyes narrowed and his breath hissed through his teeth. "I see you know. But do you know that he cannot just pass the responsibility blithely on to his successor? How many do you know, bard, who would so readily accept the position of Death? Look at him!" His arm swept around in Mannam's direction. "He was a man once—handsome, he told me, strong, proud, and hand-some—and now look at him, withered, a creature of wood and flesh, of rotting bark and mouldering leaves, of dead foul-smelling sap and decay, like a blasted tree that has rotted and wormed. How many, even though they may be dead, would take on that mantle? How many would take it, even though it promises godhood and immortality? And so the only way he could pass the cloak to me was by trickery and treachery. I would become Death and he would assume my body, and who knows, perhaps he would even seek a judgment with Alile, the Judge Impartial, and so legitimately return to the World of Man.

"But at the last moment, I learned of his treachery and fled Manach and made my way into the Mire, where I have—had—successfully avoided the creatures he sent against me."

Paedur turned to look at Mannam, his eyes narrowing. "And what of the attacks against him?" he asked Churon.

"Praetens is in the Mire. He no longer wears the body of a Susuru, but his mind is still as foul and evil. He plots with Libellius, the Deathgod of the New Religion, for the overthrow of Mannam."

"He lies! See how cleverly he weaves his lies!"

"Silence!" Buiva snapped. "Tell me why the Susuru deals with the impostor," he demanded.

"When they overthrow Death, Libellius will replace him, but Praetens can control this new god and so, in effect, the Susuru will be the Lord of the Dead. He intends to raise the dead Susuru race to walk the Planes of Life again, to rule the Sons of Man."

"And your place in this?" Buiva demanded coldly.

"I am—was—a figurehead for the living and dead to rally behind."

"He lies!" Death's voice was high, like wind through a bare branch.

"I believe him," Katani said quietly.

In the long silence that followed, Paedur eventually nodded. "So do I."

Finally Buiva said, "I don't want to believe him, but I'm afraid I have to; I have no alternative."

Churon bowed his head and his shoulders sagged. "Thank you," he said wearily. "I didn't think you would believe me. I didn't think any one of you would believe me."

"Why not?" Buiva asked, sounding surprised.

"Why? Because you and he are Gods of the Pantheon, and this is a bard of the Old Faith, and the warrior...well, she is of the Katan and they have little enough cause to love me."

"Whatever our beliefs and opinions and even loyalties," Buiva replied, "we recognise truth when we hear it. However, there is one thing which still troubles me," he added, turning to face the Dark Lord. "Why did you attempt to kill this man? And don't lie to me," he snapped suddenly, the spiked ball of his mace tapping against the top of his boots.

Mannam had backed up until his cloak was rasping against the chill stone wall and although his face was invisible behind his cowl, his head was turning rapidly from side to side, looking at each figure in turn.

"The Onelord discovered your plan, but surely that is not reason enough for this charade. When he fled Manach," Buiva persisted, "why did you attempt to kill him? And why go to such lengths to bring him back here?"

"He must be destroyed, he is dangerous, evil..."

"How?" the bard hissed. "Tell me how dangerous this man is. Tell me how he could threaten Death."

"He knows too much!" Mannam suddenly spat, branches cracking and snapping.

"Ah," Churon breathed. "I think I am beginning to understand."

"Explain," Buiva said, his eyes never leaving the Lord of the Dead.

The Onelord came and stood between Paedur and Buiva, his hands on his hips, his eyes on Mannam. "For a long time now, the Dark Lord has been taking souls before their time; he has been bringing the living into the Silent Wood!"

Buiva was first to break the horrified silence that followed. "Why—in the name of all the Pantheon, why?" His mace flashed out, the ball smashing into the wall by Mannam's head, showering him in chips of stone and sparks. The Dark Lord dropped to the ground in a shivering, rustling bundle. "WHY?" Buiva screamed, his voice a detonation, and all across the Silent Wood the petrified trees trembled, and boulders cracked and split with the terrifying sound.

Mannam spoke, but the sound was a mere susurration and inaudible.

Buiva's mace flashed out again, the chain entangling itself around the Dark Lord's thin neck, the ball thudding onto his chest. Effortlessly, Buiva hauled Death to his feet and slammed him against the wall, branches snapping and cracking, leaves turning to powder. "Tell me, god, or I will crush you to punk."

"For...for sport," Mannam whispered.

"He hunted them like animals," Churon said quietly.

With a snarl Buiva hurled Death from him, sending him across the room to crash into the wall. He raised the mace again, but the bard's hook captured the chain, staying the blow. The God of War whirled on him, his face contorted, but the bard merely raised his right hand and said, "Wait."

The bard then turned to the Onelord. "Perhaps it would be better if you were to tell us what you know," he suggested.

Churon bobbed his head, suddenly nervous, realising he was standing between the grim-faced god and the hard-eyed bard. "I am as guilty as Death in this respect," he began.

"Explain yourself," Buiva said tightly.

"When I came to this place, I thought it was the accepted practice for Death to hunt in the Silent Wood; I thought he hunted the dead, but it wasn't until much later that I discovered that he was bringing the living into the Silent Wood to hunt them."

"Why the living?" Katani asked, "why did he not make do with the dead?"

"The dead rise again in the Silent Wood," Churon said simply, "and therefore they do not make good quarry; they tend to allow themselves to be killed too easily to end the chase, knowing that they can rise again a little later. No, the living provided far greater sport."

"How did he hunt?" Katani asked.

"He bred some of the bainte especially for this purpose; the talons with which they usually clutch the essence of man were turned into razor-sharp, incredibly long and strong rending claws. He armoured them, putting spikes onto their wing-tips and heads, and once they had a scent—the vibration of a living human aura amongst all the dead—they were able to follow it tirelessly. He, like I, rode one of the Deathhorses, ugly, big-boned, ill-tempered beasts whose stamina and endurance are limitless."

"You don't seem particularly remorseful," Katani remarked.

"I knew no better," Churon said, spreading his hands. "In my defence I should say that when I discovered and protested—violently—that was when Mannam turned against me and I became one of the hunted."

"And how did you end up in the Mire in the company of Praetens?" Buiva asked, his eyes still on the unmoving figure of Mannam.

"Death hunted me all across the Silent Wood and on more than one occasion he almost had me. I had some advantages on my side, however. I knew his ways and I was already dead, so his beasts had difficulty tracking me. I cost him dearly too," he added with a slight smile, "I slew three of his horses and a score of his favourite bainte."

Buiva stepped up to Mannam, the mace and chain in his left hand, the spiked ball of the mace dangling just above Death's head. "Tell me why, Mannam," he whispered.

"I am a god. I am accountable to no-one!"

"You will account to me!" War suddenly roared, raising his hand, the mace ready to crush.

The point of the bard's hook touched the metal ball, blue fire sparking along it. "There is another way, Buiva," he said, his lips moving in a semblance of a smile. He crouched down over the sprawled figure of Death and raised his left arm, his hook glinting balefully in the wan light. "Although my power is negated in this place," he said slowly, his eyes on the shadow that mercifully concealed the god's face, "I have been gifted by C'lte, the Lord of Life, and my hook has burned with the fire of the Lady Dannu." The bard smiled coldly. "And you would not want me to touch you with it."

"Tell me why you did this," Buiva repeated.

Death looked from Buiva to the bard and then back to Buiva again. "Because...because I was bored," he said finally.

22
The Killing

"In every warrior's life, there is a time of killing, and in every warrior's life there is a time to die."

Tien tZo

"To be brief, then, you will infiltrate the Renegade's army and kill this Kutor," Salier said quietly as they crossed the small ornamental bridge and went into the Emperor's private gardens.

"The planning and—if you will pardon the word—the execution, will be left entirely up to you. Do you see any problems with that?"

Owen grunted. "I'd be a fool if I didn't. I'll need a lot more than that before I venture into an enemy camp." He shrugged. "But such things can be thrashed out later; now let us discuss payment. How much?"

Salier's eyes closed in momentary satisfaction and he nodded. He had judged the man correctly; he was a hardened killer, a mercenary in the true sense of the word, worshipping only coin. "The Emperor will reward you well indeed."

Owen stopped on the gravel path, forcing the mage to stop and turn back. "If all you can give me now are the promises of an Emperor then I'm off."

"Name your price," Salier said softly.

"The Province of Lostrice."

Salier, who had been expecting demands of coin or jewels, was momentarily dumbfounded. "Lostrice?"

"I want to be made the Viceroy of Lostrice."

Salier smiled, a curling of the lips, but it never reached his eyes. "A high price indeed."

"I am saving the Emperor's throne," Owen pointed out.

"Indeed you are. Lostrice it is then. Complete this task and it is yours." He made to turn away, but stopped when the mercenary remained still.

"You can make that decision?" Owen demanded. "You have that authority?"

"I am the Emperor's closest friend and adviser. He listens me."

"If you're lying, I'll probably kill you too."

Salier threw back his head and laughed, and then walked on, still laughing.

Owen stood watching him for a few moments, his hands on his hips, absorbing his surroundings. He was all too aware that one of the reasons Salier had agreed to his outrageous demand so easily was that he had no intention of paying. With Kutor dead, his assassin would have to die also. He idly contemplated killing the Emperor now, and Salier also, if the opportunity presented itself, but all his instincts went against it. Although the garden seemed empty, he was uncomfortably aware of the eyes watching him, and he had realised from the first moments Salier had led him across the bridge and into the private garden that the mage was only leading him along selected paths. The garden was trapped, he was sure.

"Warrior?" Salier called.

Owen hitched up his belt and strode down the path after the small, scuttling figure.

The mage led him around a clutch of ornamental trees which had been shaped like warriors locked in battle, and Owen found that the grounds opened out into a perfectly flat lawn that was covered, not with perfectly trimmed grass but rather by ice-smooth sand. In the centre of the lawn was an observatory, a beehive-shaped building of white stone with a long brass looking-tube protruding from a slit and pointing heavenwards.

Salier stopped short of the sand and pointed towards the observatory. "The Emperor awaits you." And then he turned and hurried away.

Owen watched the man walk away and then took a deep breath and held it, suddenly feeling as if he was in a dream. It was unbelievable. It was almost as if he were being offered Geillard's head on a plate. Events were moving too fast for him. He knew now what Kutor had meant: he felt like an actor in a play.

He looked across the grey-gold lawn of sand and wondered why Salier hadn't led him out to the observatory. Unless, of course, this was a test. Owen had been more than surprised when Salier had accepted him merely on Thome's recommendation and hadn't even bothered to have his weapons removed before leading him to the Emperor of the Seven Nations. And now, having led him through the maze of paths, why had he left him here? Accept, then, that everything was not as it seemed; accept, then, that the sand was not merely sand, that the Emperor was now in the observatory and that this was a test, that even now he was being observed and tested. This was a test he needed to pass, and he idly wondered what would happen if he failed.

Owen squatted down and looked closely at the unusual lawn. It certainly looked like sand, except perhaps that the colour was more grey than gold, but that meant little; he had once seen sand the colour of blood. He gripped the hilt of the sword that protruded above his left shoulder with his right hand and pulled, the weapon hissing out of its scabbard, and then he strode back to the ornamental trees and sliced off a long branch that represented a warrior's spear. Cleaning his sword against his leggings he slid it home and returned to the lawn. He probed the sand, almost surprised to find solid ground about a finger-length beneath; he probed again, and was unsurprised when the branch kept going. Returning to his starting point he began probing to determine the width of the path, which was no more than a single pace across, and then he used the length of the branch to determine its direction. It seemed to head straight out towards the observatory, but Owen was too distrustful to depend on that. He snapped the branch across his knee, and using the length of wood as a probe took his first tentative steps out onto the lawn. There was a brief moment of panic as he felt himself sinking, but it was only his weight on the sand. Testing every step he proceeded slowly and cautiously across the lawn.

Halfway over the path disappeared.

Owen stood in the centre of the lawn, feeling slightly ridiculous. Ahead of him there seemed to be nothing, and even when he described an almost complete circle from where he stood with the pole, he struck nothing solid. But if the path ended, he reasoned, it must begin again, and the gap wouldn't be too wide, lest the Emperor himself vanish into whatever terrors lurked beneath the sand. He moved up to the lip of the path he was standing on, and stretching out as far as he could, he continued probing. There was nothing ahead of him. He moved to the left-hand edge of the path and repeated the process, and with similar results. But on the right-hand side he found the path. It was barely a stride away. He stepped cautiously onto it, suddenly fearing that both paths—the one he was on and the one he was about to step onto, would disappear, but it remained firm beneath his feet. The path then continued in a straight line to the observatory.

Owen was about to step up off the sand and onto the gravel that surrounded the white stone building when a figure stepped out of the doorway. Owen's reactions were instinctive. He threw himself forward and down, two handleless throwing knives coming to his hands.

"They will probably kill you before you get close." The voice held just enough amusement in it to infuriate Owen. He came to his feet slowly, looking from the man and back across the sand lawn to the score of crossbowmen who had appeared from the bushes and trees. All the weapons were levelled and pointing at him. He turned back to the tall, thin man and allowed him to see the knife in his left hand. "I could have this in your throat before they even let off one shot. They would be so shocked at seeing you fall that I'd have a chance to get inside."

The man smiled. "And you'll be trapped there, I'm afraid. There is only one way in."

Owen nodded and returned the knives to his belt. "You are Geillard." He made no attempt to bow.

The man nodded, his dark eyes burning deep behind his prominent cheekbones. "And you are the Warrior. No other name?" he queried.

"None that I wish to use."

"That is understandable." He sat down on a slab-like projection of stone that jutted out from the building. Across the lawn the score of crossbowmen kept their positions.

Owen squatted down close enough to the Emperor to use him as a shield if need be. "You are a trustful man," he remarked, nodding at the men.

"They are dedicated to me."

Something in the man's tired voice made Owen look at the crossbowmen again. There was something eerie in their very immobility. "They are *quai?*" he asked.

"Of a sort," Geillard said, smiling, vaguely pleased. The man was intelligent. "They are not true *quai,* but Salier makes them for me. They are all volunteers, of course. All thoughts and images are removed from their minds, leaving just one person in their universe, one being for them to look up to, to adore—and to protect."

"You?"

Geillard nodded. "They are the finest bodyguards. Fearless, untiring, completely dedicated."

"And soulless," Owen spat. He had never been able to overcome his loathing of the *quai*—the soulless warriors he had encountered in his travels—and his one great, and secret, fear was that he would end up like one of them. However, they also introduced a new element into his plan to kill Geillard. It was unlikely he went anywhere without them; they probably even slept in the same room as he.

"Has Salier explained what is needed of you?" Geillard asked, not looking at the man.

"He has. Has he explained my fee?"

"He has not," Geillard replied, enjoying the game that was developing. It would be a shame to have to kill this man.

"For payment I want the Lordship of Lostrice."

"A high price," the Emperor remarked softly, still watching his *quai* bodyguards.

"For a difficult task."

Geillard nodded. "Agreed. I had intended to offer you a high price and a position here at court..."

"Where you could keep an eye on me," Owen finished.

Geillard shrugged. "I won't deny it. But on reflection, it might be useful to have you in a position of power. A man of your talents might prove very useful." Perhaps it would be possible to keep the man alive, Geillard reflected. But no; Salier would insist that he be killed, and he was probably right. A pity.

"Why was it necessary for you to see me? I've done work such as you want for other men and usually they preferred to deal with me through intermediaries."

The Emperor nodded. "Usually the instructions for this work would be handled by Salier, but I wanted to have the opportunity to see you, see what sort of man you were, to speak to you, to give you certain instructions, to make certain suggestions."

"What sort of instructions?" Owen asked bluntly. "To be honest, I'll take no instructions that place my life in danger."

Geillard shook his head. "No, there is nothing of that nature. When you have him—Kutor, I mean—I want him to die slowly. Slow and painful—is that possible?" He turned to look at Owen with such eagerness in his eyes that the hardened warrior was appalled.

To cover his confusion, he looked across at the tireless *quai,* still covering him with their crossbows. "That depends on the circumstances," he said eventually. "It might be necessary for me to slit his throat quickly and then leave."

"Well then, you must bring me back something of his to prove that he is indeed dead."

"What do you want?" Owen asked, although he had already partially guessed.

"His head!"

"No! It's all very well for you to say bring me back his head. But I doubt if you've ever carried a severed head about with you for any length of time. Besides the smell and the flies, they are awkward things to carry and impossible to hide. You can have his ears or his hands or perhaps a strip of flesh if it has some tattoo or birthmark on it. And that's as far as I'm prepared to go."

"His hands, both of them."

Owen sighed. "As you wish."

"And if you have the opportunity to make him suffer?"

"I'll make sure he knows who's killing him. Will that do? I can tell you what he said or what his expression was like as he died."

Geillard nodded happily. "Yes, that will be perfect."

Salier was standing waiting for Owen when he crossed the sand lawn. The *quai* had disappeared, although he knew they were still there, still watching him. The mage turned away as Owen came up onto the track and headed back into the forest, leaving the warrior to follow him.

"What now?" Owen called.

The mage strode on, head bent, his hands tucked into the sleeves of his simple dove-grey robe.

"What do you want me to do?" Owen tried again.

Salier continued to ignore him and, indeed, didn't even seem to hear him.

Owen took two long strides and was actually reaching for Salier's arm when the man's head turned slightly, and Owen recoiled at the look on his face, the look of absolute, chilling evil.

"Never touch me, or even attempt to lay a hand on me," he hissed, his voice scarcely human.

"I was…" Owen began, but Salier continued on in the same measured icy tones, "I tell you this for your own good and not as an idle threat. My art protects me, my aura is charged with power." He smiled, and it was the look of a snarling animal. "And that power would shrivel you."

Unable for the moment to believe or even understand what the magician was saying, Owen contented himself with merely nodding.

"There was a man," Salier continued, looking away, speaking softly, almost to himself, "a man who attempted to kill me. He had been a pupil of mine and he should have known better, but he imagined that by slaying me, he would absorb some of my powers; that can happen when a mage is slain by violence." His steps had slowed and his eyes were almost closed now, mere slits, and his face had settled into a mask of satisfaction; this was clearly a tale he enjoyed. "He had access to my rooms and so one day he took a shortsword and concealed himself there, waiting for me. From the moment I stepped into the room, I knew he was there, but I was confident of my power and did nothing. It was, and is, my custom to bathe every evening—this is a filthy city—and my former pupil knew this. He waited until I was in my bath and then crept up behind me and drove the sword down into my back. But the force that surrounds me snapped the blade and sprayed molten metal fragments back up into his face. Blind and in agony, I was able to kill him at my leisure," he whispered. "He was a long time dying."

"Why have you told me this?" Owen asked quietly, aware of the pounding of his heart. Did Salier know his true purpose?

"Just to warn you never to touch me."

"I wouldn't dream of it."

"Don't." And the warning was implicit.

The two men walked on in silence. Salier seemed to be meandering aimlessly along the gravelled paths, but Owen knew, once they had passed the same spot twice, that he was merely attempting to confuse. Finally, they crossed the small ornamental bridge that led from the private gardens and back into the main palace gardens.

There were two men waiting for them, a servant in white and gold, and a guard wearing the blue and black palace livery; both were clearly in awe of the notorious Salier.

Salier ignored the guard and glared at the servant, who was wearing the colours of the Hierophant, Barthus. "Well?"

"Barthus, Hierophant of the Religion, sends you greetings and trust."

Salier waved his hand impatiently. "The message!" he demanded.

"The Lord Barthus begs your indulgence and assistance in a matter of import. One of the Andam priesthood has come to the lord protesting loyalty to the Religion and claiming to have spoken with the Lord Trialos. The Lord Barthus is convinced that the man's intentions are genuine and wishes your advice as to how this man may be used to the best advantage."

Salier was so shocked at the request that he stared at the man for a few long moments. "And where is this Andam now?" he asked eventually.

The guard spoke up. "He is contained in the anteroom to your chambers, lord."

"Guarded?" Salier snapped.

"By four of my most trusted men."

"That affords me little comfort," Salier remarked and strode past the man, leaving Owen little choice but to follow him.

The mage allowed the mercenary to catch up with him. "Would you be willing to undertake an extra task for me, a personal task?"

"You want someone killed?" Owen asked bluntly.

"You are direct."

"In this profession it is the only honest way."

"Would you slay the Hierophant for me?"

"How much?"

"My loyalty when you have the Lordship of Lostrice."

"Is your loyalty worth so much?" Owen asked, and then he quickly answered his own question. "Do you want him slain before or after I slay Kutor?"

"Before. And I want it to look as if Kutor's men have performed the task."

"When do you want him killed?"

"Soon," Salier hissed, "very soon. You see how bold he grows," he continued, as they strode into the echoing, slightly chilly corridors. "He sends this man to me, testing me."

"Perhaps he lacks your wisdom," Owen suggested, "and is unable to make a decision himself."

Salier's hunched shoulders began to shake and it was a few moments before Owen realised he was laughing. "Oh, foolish man. We are talking about Barthus, a simple priest who fought and schemed and some even say killed to raise himself to the elevated position of Hierophant. A man whose sole ambition seems to be to spread the New Religion all across the known world, by whatever means possible. He is cunning, infinitely cunning, and everything he does, he does with reason. His ambition is to replace me at Geillard's side, and who knows, perhaps even to replace Geillard himself. Even Fodla, who is opposed to me at many points, is in agreement with me on this. He is dangerous."

"Tell me when you want his death," Owen said softly.

They climbed a flight of stairs which led out onto a small landing, which was lined with guards who were standing so rock-still that Owen immediately knew that they must be *quai*, similar to Geillard's bodyguards. At the end of the landing there was a single iron-studded door and there were another two guards outside it. The mage moved silently down the length of the corridor, his head bent, his hands tucked into his sleeves. As he neared the door it abruptly clicked open. Pushing it, he stepped inside and then immediately turned to the right into a small, dimly lit antechamber. The small room was made even smaller by the presence of four guards, all of them fully human and alert and looking almost comically nervous in the presence of Salier. Dwarfed by the men surrounding him was the Andam.

Salier imperiously dismissed the men and then beckoned the Andam forward with a crooked finger.

Tien tZo stepped forward, fingering the tiny throwing spike the guards had missed when they had searched him earlier. His attention shifted from the mage to the tall warrior standing in the shadows behind him; bodyguard, he assumed, or, knowing the rumours that surrounded Salier, a catamite perhaps.

The mage stepped into the main room, fully expecting the priest to follow him, knowing the warrior would take up the rear.

Tien noted that when the warrior came into the large, ornately furnished room, he immediately took up position with his back to the wall beside the door; bodyguard, then, he decided. Salier crossed to a tall, high-backed chair and sank down into it, his hands dangling limply over the edge of the highly polished and ornately worked arms. "Come here. Stand before me," he said simply, the command evident in his voice "You, too," he added, looking at the warrior.

Tien shuffled over to the mage and stood a respectful distance from him. He could feel the man's eyes boring into him, feel his flesh begin to crawl and his scalp to prickle. The warrior walked around the priest and stood by the chair, his arms folded. Tien looked up at the man, seeing him clearly for the first time.

The shock registered in his eyes—disbelief, amazement, horror. Only his eyes betrayed him, his face remained impassive, but slight as the moment of recognition had been, Salier noticed it.

"You know each other!" It was a statement, not a question.

"No," Owen began, shaking his head.

Salier turned to look at the warrior standing beside him, and then he casually lifted his hand and moved it through the air, two fingers extended. Immediately, two lines of red fire crackled across the exposed flesh of his neck, searing the skin black, so fast that he didn't even have time to react or cry out.

Salier's face had turned to stone. "Lie to me and I'll kill you, however useful you think you might be; mercenaries are commonplace. Now, I think an explanation..." he hissed, looking from the Andam to the mercenary. He turned back to Owen. "Tell me!"

"I have never seen this man before in my life. I knew an Andam once, but he was an old man when I was a boy. With the way the light fell, I thought that this was him again." He shrugged. "It's nothing; just chance."

"I do not believe in the Demon's Law," Salier said icily. He was raising his hand again, a ball of red fire already coalescing in the palm of his hand when he caught a glimpse of movement in front of him and turned in time to see the Andam fling a sliver of silver metal towards his face.

"No, Tien!" Owen shouted. The Weapon Master threw himself forward and down, catching Tien across the legs, sending him tumbling across the carpeted floor. They rolled into a polished crystal table, bringing it crashing to the ground, and Owen dragged Tien in behind it.

In the long silence that followed nothing happened.

"I presume you had a reason for that," Tien said, something close to amusement in his voice.

Owen peered through the thick crystal of the table. "He is protected by a spell which turns metal to liquid—or something like that." He could see Salier, warped and twisted by the crystal, still sitting in the chair.

Tien snatched a quick look and then he stood up cautiously, pulling back the cloth hood that covered most of his head. "I don't think his spell worked," he remarked.

Owen came to his feet, automatically righting the table. Salier remained in the chair, an expression of absolute surprise etched on his face, the long throwing spike protruding a finger-length from his left eye. The Weapon Master drummed his fingers on the crystal table in frustration.

"Is something wrong?" Tien asked.

Owen shook his head and grinned. "This was shaping up to be one of the most extraordinary schemes I was ever involved in. I actually thought we might get out of this one easily, but..." He shrugged again.

"The Demon's Law," Tien said. "Chance..."

"Aye," Owen nodded, "but what do we do now?"

There was a sudden pounding on the door.

23
The Court of the Pantheon

Men are but the playthings of the gods.

Death's Law

Without the faith of men there are no gods; the faith of men lends substance to the Pantheon.

Basic tenet of the Old Faith

The Gods of the Pantheon were gathering.

With only the bard and Mannam for company in the long dark library, Buiva had summoned a score of them, calling each by name, and when the shadowy, shimmering, ghostly figures had appeared momentarily on the cool musty air of the room in Manach, he had spoken a single word: "Trial!"

When he finally turned to Paedur, the bard noticed that the god's world-weary, lined face seemed to have aged and the shadows beneath his eyes had deepened. "They will tell the others," he said, his voice barely above a whisper.

"What have you done?" Paedur asked quietly, watching the god intently, although from his lore he had a good idea what Buiva had just set in motion.

"Trial by peer," Buiva said, glancing down at Mannam. "He has betrayed the race of Man."

"I had my reasons," the Dark Lord spat.

"The very race he is oath-bound to protect and serve," Buiva continued, ignoring him. "He seems to have forgotten that without the race of men, the gods themselves cease to exist."

"Faith lends Substance," Paedur murmured the litany.

"Just so," Buiva nodded.

"Then he is to be tried by the Gods of the Faith for his crime?" Paedur asked softly.

"Yes."

Paedur shook his head in disbelief. "But he is Death, one of the most powerful of the gods. Surely he can do what he wishes?"

"He is Death, but in the hierarchy of the Gods he is ranked lowly indeed."

Mannam suddenly struggled to his feet and the very air around him crackled with luminous energy. The dry air was suddenly bitter with soured sap and on the shelves behind him books shivered from their places and tumbled to the floor and rolled parchments snapped open. "I am Death! The gods themselves serve me. You serve me, Buiva, feeding me the carcasses from your many wars. Madness and Destruction both make me offerings. Even the arrogant Lords of Life eventually give me up their subjects. Death is the most powerful of all the gods!"

Buiva's left hand shot out, the spiked pommel of his mace disappearing into the shadows of Mannam's cowl. "You feed on offal, Mannam, on dead things. You cannot bring anything to life; birth and growth are unknown to you. Those who walk your kingdom are little more than quai." He turned away in disgust.

"What happens now?" Paedur asked.

"Now we wait for the Gods of the Pantheon to arrive."

"And then?"

"Trial!"

Katani and Churon had been taken to the library and then locked in, with instructions not to even attempt to break out, no matter what they heard or thought they heard—precautions which, Buiva had assured them both, were for their own safety. Buiva had then taken Paedur to Mannam's huge and sombre throne-room and covered his eyes with layers of thick cloth.

He had waited patiently, only gradually becoming aware of the movement around him, conscious of it at first as the merest disturbance on the chill, dank air.

Paedur's blindfolded head came up suddenly as the Dark Lord began to speak without warning. "You don't know what it's like. None of you can even possibly comprehend what it is like to be trapped in this body, this existence, with no hope of reprieve, no end in sight."

The bard turned his head slightly. The Dark Lord was standing off to his right-hand side and all around him Paedur could now distinguish the softly susurrating movements of the myriad Gods of the Pantheon and smell their perfumes. Someone had moved in front of him moments before, and he had known it was the Lady Adur by the deep, earthy odour of fresh greenery and growth. He felt the itchy crawling of power across his skin, the burning of the radiance of the gods on his face and lips, and he could understand why Buiva had blindfolded him. While the Sons of Man could look upon some of the gods, there were others, like the Lady Dannu, the Mother, or the Lady Lussa, the Goddess of the Moon, who were forbidden to him, lest their radiance shrivel him.

"Continue, Death. Explain." The voice was deep and booming, like rolling thunder on a summer's day. Baistigh, Paedur decided, the Lord of Thunder.

"Acceptance was easy in the beginning, but that was so long ago. I was convinced then that my appearance was nothing more than another part of Death's costume, a means of perpetuating the traditional image of the Dark Lord as somehow being associated with trees and dark forests and the secret places of the woods. It was later, much later, that I discovered that the guise I had adopted from my predecessor had become inseparable from me. And none of you can even begin to understand what it is like to be trapped in the body of a rotting, rotted, foul tree, shunned by both man and god."

The silence that followed was oppressive and the bard turned his head from side to side, listening, feeling the crawling prickle of power on his skin, tasting the sharpness of it on his lips. He didn't know how many of the gods had arrived but he sensed that the room was crowded with silent listeners.

"Continue," Baistigh eventually boomed.

"In the beginning I convinced myself that I was performing a necessary function. After all, Death comes to all men, be they great or small, princes or beggars. Death walked the World of Men more frequently in those days and I personally took many of those destined for the Silent Wood. But I could not take them all, so my bainte took them for me. Eventually the bainte were taking all the essences of those dead people and I was...well, I was almost useless.

"To amuse myself I retired here to my City and populated it with examples of peoples from differing times and places. I indulged myself by insisting that all the writers and artists, poets and sculptors who passed through my kingdom should produce one original work or complete the work they had had in hand before their death. The bard has seen my library, but he has not seen the gallery.

"But eventually even this palled.

"And then one day—accidentally, I swear it—the bainte brought a living soul into the Silent Wood. It was that of a female and she had fallen into a deep sleep in the World of Men, so deep indeed that she was thought to be dead and had been buried with all the ceremony of the Old Faith. As you know, part of that ceremony includes the invocation to Death: 'Come, dread spirit, and take this mortal soul.' And one of my bainte came and took the soul and brought it here. When she awoke in the Silent Wood, the woman's scream ripped through everything, and indeed, I understand that even in the World of Men, a ghostly echo of her scream was heard."

Paedur found himself nodding, remembering an obscure piece of lore, and then Buiva spoke from just behind his head, startling him. "Yes, bard, the Scream from the Void."

Death continued. "When I reached her, her suspicions as to her whereabouts were confirmed and she immediately fled from me. And I gave chase.

"And, do you know, it was an exhilarating experience. She was a thinking human being, clever, terrified, but above all she was alive. And as I chased her, a sudden thought struck me. What would happen if I caught and killed her? Would her body re-appear here in the Silent Wood to continue the chase or...or what?

"So I eventually caught her...and I killed her. And her body vanished. And it wasn't until later, much later, that I discovered that she had re-appeared in the World of Men, whole and alive but in a strange land, many days travel from her own home. When she finally reached her own home—and I followed her progress carefully—the shock of her arrival sent three people to me." Mannam's cracking, snapping laughter filled the silent room.

"And so I went on to deliberately take a live body." A murmur ran around the room, the sound halfway between a moan and a sigh, and even though his eyes were shielded, Paedur knew the intensity of light in the room had increased. He was aware also that the strength of the myriad odours had increased; they had thickened, and he found that his own breathing had become laboured. Fleetingly he remembered that when he had first encountered Death he had been aware of the stench of mould and decay that had hung about him, and later, when he had met C'lte, the Yellow God of Life, he had breathed in the rich odour of spices and herbs the god had exuded.

"And you hunted this Son of Man like an animal." Buiva made the statement into a condemnation.

"I hunted him for sport," Death snapped.

"You condemn yourself out of your own mouth," Buiva said quietly and a quick murmur of assent ran around the room.

"It broke the boredom."

"How many of the Sons of Man have you hunted?" The voice was female this time, but hard and sharp, imperious and commanding. Dannu, Paedur guessed, and Mannam's deferential reply confirmed that it was the Goddess.

"In truth I do not know."

"And it does not seem to concern you overmuch."

"They did not die; they returned to the World of Men again," Mannam said defensively.

"Ah, but many of them came to me." The voice was that of the simpering Nameless God of Madness and Delusion. "The pleasures of your kingdom were just a trifle too much for them. The lucky ones came to me, but the others..." The god giggled, the sound high-pitched and totally insane. "Why, some of them have become killers, bandits, brutes. I know of two that slay only when the Lady Lussa rides the heavens. One has taken to eating human flesh; another has formed a fascination for the myriad forms of fornication with men, women, and beasts." The god giggled again, the sound sending a chill hand creeping up along the bard's spine. "How many souls have you destroyed with your playing, Death? It would have been better if you had taken them properly, instead of leaving them to rot in human shells."

"I didn't know," Mannam whined.

"Your protestations disgust me," the voice Paedur had decided was Dannu's said coldly. "You are no longer fit to hold the place of a god in the Pantheon of the Old Faith. You have destroyed good human essences, threatened the very existence of the Pantheon with your foolish and ill-considered games, and you have failed in the prime function of all the gods, no matter what their faith: you have betrayed your charges."

"They are human!" Mannam spat. "Little better than beasts, they are the playthings of the gods. The Culai had the right idea: they are cattle and should be treated as such!"

The silence that followed was almost physical and Paedur had to resist the almost unendurable urge to scratch where his exposed

flesh burned with the exuded power of the gods. And then, surprisingly, the power began to diminish and the bard had the distinct
impression that the gods were silently leaving one by one. The light
against his blindfold lessened, which only reinforced the idea.

There was movement beside him and he stiffened as a hand
brushed against his head catching the cloth blindfold, and then Buiva
spoke from beside his head. "Don't look at the Goddess; keep
your eyes on Mannam or me. If you value your sanity, you will not
look at the Lady." Paedur nodded and then Buiva twitched the
blindfold away. The bard blinked rapidly, his eyes watering—even
the dim light was blinding—but kept his head ducked.

"Ah, yes, our Champion, the Bard Paedur. What is your part in
this foul affair?"

"I am afraid that, like Churon the Onelord and indeed the Gods
of the Pantheon, I too have been an innocent dupe of Death."

"What brought you to the Silent Wood?"

Paedur kept his eyes fixed on the smooth, black stone of the
bare floor, but from the sound of her voice, he formed the impression of a strong, matronly woman.

"I lost two companions on the Culai Isle when we fought for
the Old Faith. I came here to try and claim them back."

"Death is final," Mannam interrupted. "It is a door which
opens only one way."

"And are there not other doors?" Paedur asked, glancing up at
Mannam, and then stopped in astonishment at the change that had
come over him. The figure of Death had always been tall and thin,
covered in a long, dark cloak of seared and withered leaves, and
with his features hidden beneath the cowl of that cloak. Now he
was bent and twisted, like a tree that had been eaten with disease.
His cloak was frayed and tattered, the leaves scattered around his
feet, and now that the face was partially revealed it was not the
skeletal face Paedur had once glimpsed, but the face of a tired,
incredibly old man, his skin the colour of rotten wood, a web-work
of wrinkles lending his face a gnarled bark-like appearance.

"Your companions are dead," Mannam insisted. "They are beyond Death's aid."

"But you are not Death," the Lady Dannu said coldly.

The bard, whose eyes were on Mannam, saw him look up, saw the
agonised expression appear in his eyes, followed by rage and defiance.

"Then who is Death?" he snarled.

"I am!"

Paedur turned, somehow unsurprised when Churon walked up to stand beside Buiva. He bowed deeply to the woman standing behind the bard.

The twisted figure of Mannam turned, his eyes squinting, attempting to focus, but eventually he gave it up. "And who are you?" he demanded querulously, an old man, squinting, half-blind.

"I am Churon, once Onelord in the World of Men, now Overlord of the Silent Wood."

"And a God of the Old Faith," Paedur added softly.

"Why didn't you accept the position when I offered it to you?" Mannam shouted, his voice cracking and breaking.

"You did not offer, you attempted to trick me into taking it. I liked neither your methods nor your terms," Churon said.

"I hope it twists you as it twisted me," Mannam said venomously.

"I think not. You forget that I knew what it was to rule in the World of Men; I drank deeply of that cup whilst I lived, and it holds no attraction for me now."

"And what of Mannam?" Paedur asked into the silence that followed. He kept his eyes low, looking at the shrunken figure of the Dark Lord. He glanced up as Churon turned to the goddess, "My lady?"

Dannu's voice was hard and cold. "He returns to the World of Men, as he is," she said, "and, Death ..." Both Mannam and Churon looked up, but she had been addressing the Onelord. "You will not take him, not now, not ever, not so long as the Gods of the Pantheon rule and the Old Faith holds sway."

"I don't understand," Churon said slowly, but the bard understood fully, knew what the once-god had been sentenced to.

"He is not to die," Dannu insisted. "You are not to take him. His curse is to wander the Planes of Existence for the rest of eternity..."

"Or until the Old Faith dies," Mannam spat.

Dannu laughed, the sound masculine and totally humourless. "Our Champion here has ensured a revival of interest in the Old Faith; but I forget, you had a hand in that."

The venom behind Mannam's eyes was a physical thing, a leaking foulness. "Then I will work for the downfall of the Gods of the Pantheon and the ending of the Old Faith." He turned, a twisted, vengeful, embittered old man, and stared hard at the bard. "And I will have you slain," he promised. "For all your god-gifted powers, I will destroy you. You brought me to this, and without you the Faith will wither and die!"

"And will you keep Manach?" Paedur asked the new God of Death.

Churon leaned over the battlements of the City of the Dead and looked down over its wide cobbled streets. "Probably. I won't keep the occupants in thrall though, as Mannam did; they will be free to come and go as they please."

"And what of my companions. Did you discover anything about them?"

"I am afraid their essences are beyond me. They both died on the Culai Isle, where, as you know, the laws of the Planes of Existence are negated. And, even if I could discover and reanimate Tuan's existence, the priestess was destroyed when the Chrystallis and the Cords vied for supremacy; her essence was scattered through the void."

"So my journey here was wasted?"

"Not totally," Churon grinned. "Your coming set in motion a train of events that lead to the death of one god and the birthing of another—something not every human can claim."

They walked slowly along the battlements, no longer even conscious of the blood-stench from the Naman. In another time and another place they might have been two old friends strolling companionably together before retiring for the night. When they reached the stairs they stopped and Paedur turned to Churon. "Tell me, why did you accept the position of Death?"

Churon rested a coal-black hand on the equally dark stonework and looked out across his domain towards the shadow that was the Mire, and when he finally turned back to the bard, his blue eyes were sparkling slightly. "To atone, bard. I'm not sure if that makes any sense to you, or if you even can understand it, but just to atone."

The bard paused before replying, and then he finally nodded and turned to climb down the steps. "I understand."

Katani was waiting at the bottom of the stairs. She was sitting with her back to the cold stones, running an oiled cloth along the length of her longsword blade with a monotonous, almost ritual persistence. She came smoothly and silently to her feet as Paedur and Churon descended.

"What now?" she asked simply.

Paedur looked at Churon.

"A time of parting," the new god said quietly. "You, bard, must return to the World of Men; your companions—and the Old Faith—need you and your powers now. And I think you will find your powers enhanced, but use them wisely. Remember the lesson of Mannam: no one is above retribution. And a word of warning: when Mannam went into the World of Men he promptly disappeared, but be assured he will attempt to slay you, and I would imagine he will side with the enemies of the Faith. Be wary of him."

"And what of me?" Katani asked, her voice measured and even, but her eyes troubled.

"You are dead," Churon reminded her.

"Does it have to be so?"

"You are dead," Churon repeated.

"And you are Death."

"Would you return to the World of Men?"

Katani remained silent.

"I have need of a companion, someone to protect me from Mannam," Paedur said, his face expressionless.

The Onelord nodded seriously. "Of course, and there are no finer warriors on the myriad Planes of Existence than the Katan." He looked at the woman again, his expression softening. "It would avail you and I naught, if I were to apologise for what I did those many years ago. What's done is done and cannot be undone. I can send you back into the World of Men again, and this time when you die you can at least die with all the dignity and honour of a Katan warrior. That is all I can give you."

"It is enough."

Churon bowed. "Both of you I shall meet again—but not soon I hope," he added with a smile.

"And I will add a new chapter to my tale of Churon the Onelord," Paedur promised.

24
The Return of the Bard

"The first time I met the bard, I was frightened; the second time, I was terrified."

Tien tZo

There was a long crack and the door split down the centre from top to bottom. Guards both human and *quai* burst into the chamber, squeezing through the shattered doorway. Three died instantly and in the pounding confusion that followed another three went down beneath Owen's sword and Tien tZo's lethal blows.

A gong boomed in the corridor and the guards milling outside the room immediately retreated, giving Owen and Tien a momentary respite. The Shemmat quickly stripped off his Andam robes and began to sift through the armour and weapons of the fallen men, clothing and arming himself, while Owen stood in the doorway, watching the activity in the corridor beyond.

"They're massing for a concerted attack," he said quietly.

Tien glanced up from a warrior whose throat had been opened. "Well, they cannot get more than two or three through the door at any one time, and at that rate we hold this room for an eternity."

Owen smiled tightly. "Much good it will do us."

Tien straightened, tightening the buckles on a jerkin of fine link mail. He pulled on greaves that were a little too big for him and cinched the buckles tight. Into his belt he stuck as many knives as he could comfortably carry, and from the swords he had gathered he picked the two best suited to his height and reach. "I'll check the room; there may be another way out."

The Weapon Master grunted, his attention on the corridor. Something unusual was happening; the *quai* and human guards had massed at the end of the long corridor, obviously preparing for an attack, and yet they hadn't moved. From the way they kept looking around, he guessed that they were waiting for a senior officer, and Owen idly wondered who would have enough authority to order an attack on Salier's own chambers. He smiled at a sudden thought: there was only one person...

"I am Fodla." A huge woman in a simple white woollen shift with a massive sword belt strapped around her waist roughly pushed past the guards and boldly strode down the corridor. She stopped exactly in the centre, her hands on her hips, facing the shattered doorway. "There is no way out of that room. Salier himself designed it that way. The windows are barred and there is a sheer drop to the cobbles below. But to ensure you take no risks, there are archers in the courtyard. The fireplace is barred within the chimney, and even if you manage to bypass that obstacle, there are men on the roof. If you intend to come out, you must come down this corridor." Abruptly, she turned away and walked back to disappear into the growing numbers of palace guards.

"She's right," Tien said, taking up position on Owen's right-hand side. "There are two rooms, this and a bed-chamber which also doubles as a library. All the windows are barred, which, while it keeps us in, also serves to keep them out. There are archers in the courtyard below, but at least the rooms are not overlooked, so we cannot be fired upon. We are trapped," he added unnecessarily.

"Can we dig our way into one of the adjoining rooms?" Owen wondered idly.

"There are only these two chambers in the corridor..." Tien began, and then stopped as a trio of archers took up position at the end of the corridor.

Fodla stepped through the massed ranks again. "You have a chance now to surrender. Your final chance." She waited for a reply, but receiving none, stepped back and nodded once to the archers.

The archers were using screamers, broad, triangular-headed arrows with slits cut into the metal which caused them to emit a high-pitched scream as the air whistled through them. The effect was more than psychological; screamers caused massive wounds and the heads were broad and heavy enough to punch through most layered armours as well as chain and link mails.

Two of the arrows embedded themselves into the broken door, punching entirely through the wood, while the third passed directly through the shattered centre and exploded in a shower of sparks and wood against the wall opposite.

Fodla stepped through the archers and spoke again. "I assume Salier is dead?" Both men instinctively glanced at the still figure in the chair. "But if he isn't, then I would suggest you send him out."

Owen looked at the chair again and then nodded to Tien; the Shemmat nodded in understanding. Leaving his swords by the door, he darted across to the huge fireplace and grabbed the mage by the front of his gown and pulled him up out of the chair. Then, half-lifting, half-dragging the incredibly heavy chair, he hauled it over to the broken door.

Three more arrows screamed in through the opening, only to shatter on the wall opposite.

"Come out now!" Fodla demanded.

Owen nodded and Tien heaved the chair out into the opening, blocking it. The Weapon Master grabbed the opposite arm and dragged it across the gap. They heard the screaming and then the chair shuddered as two more arrows thudded into the back, the tips of their heads actually pricking through the wooden seat. But the gap was now plugged and the only remaining opening was a head-sized triangular split close to the top of the door.

"They can't get in," Tien remarked with a wry smile.

"You cannot get out," Fodla shouted.

"What happens now?" the Shemmat asked, leaning back against the wall, rubbing the flat of the curved swordblade against his sleeve.

"Now we wait."

"They'll fire the rooms," Tien said softly, still rubbing the sword.

Owen nodded.

"We could rush them."

The Weapon Master nodded again.

Tien risked a quick glance out into the corridor. More archers had arrived and two men carrying one of the heavy armour-piercing crossbows were setting up their weapon in the centre of the floor. These crossbows were usually bolted into the ground and used for long-range killing; they were accurate up to a thousand paces, were incredibly powerful, and could punch an iron-tipped, brass-bound shaft through three lines of armoured men. At such close range and in the confines of the corridor, the effect of the heavy man-sized bolts could only be guessed at.

"I think we'd better do something," Tien said dubiously.

There was a creak and a grinding of gears and then the heavy floor-mounted crossbow rocked on its tripod. The enormous bolt punched the heavy chair all the way across the room, literally snapping it in two, splinters and slivers of dark wood hanging in the air like dust. A score of screamers followed, some sinking into the remnants of the door, rocking it on its already torn hinges, others whining around the room to shatter glass and delicate crystal.

Owen readied himself for a suicidal charge down the corridor. "Well, at least we killed Salier," he said philosophically. "Perhaps we might get Fodla also."

"Foolish man! Do you think I am so easily slain?" The voice was a shriek.

Salier was standing by the fire, Tien's throwing spike still protruding from his left eye, a trickle of congealed ichor on his drawn cheeks. His expression was ghastly and the light that burned in this right eye was that of absolute insanity.

Another screamer shattered against the wall, but it was completely ignored. Tien threw a knife underhand, the long, thin, double-edged blade catching the mage low in the throat. The creature—no longer human—staggered, but there was no blood, and Salier plucked it out almost contemptuously from his pale flesh. Turning it in his hand he brought it up to his remaining eye, seemingly captivated by the polished metal, and then he flung it back at the Shemmat. Only Tien's battle-hardened reflexes saved him, the sword coming up automatically, catching and deflecting the thrown knife, sending it ringing against the walls.

Salier raised his left hand and the blood-red glow of fox-fire was already gathering around the fingers when a second heavy crossbow bolt ripped what remained of the door off its hinges. Splinters of wood grazed Tien's cheek and a length of wood almost decapitated Owen, but a flat slab struck Salier flat in the chest, staggering him, sending him toppling backwards. His heels struck the raised marble slabs that surrounded the fire and for a moment he swayed precariously, and then he crashed back into the fire. His robes ignited with a dull explosion.

The scream of the charging guards was drowned by the ghastly ululation from the creature that had once been Salier. A figure, now only vaguely manlike, rose up out of the flames and staggered across the room, its consciousness or dull remembered instinct taking it towards the only exit, the open doorway. Trailing flame and screaming hideously, it staggered out into the corridor, and immediately the guards' shouts changed to screams of terror. Tien and Owen held back undecided, and they watched in horror as the creature staggered down the long corridor, enwrapping everyone it touched in flame. Fodla shouted a command and a score of screamers struck it, sending it staggering, but not knocking it down. The archers on the heavy crossbow were working frantically, cranking the enormous wheel, bending the massive bow.

Owen nodded. "When they fire that, we'll move. Try and take out Fodla before they get you."

"You will remain here!"

The voice from behind them was cool and calmly authoritative, and although they had both only heard it on one previous occasion, it was a voice they would never forget.

"Paedur!"

The bard, standing in the centre of the room, was as they remembered him, tall, thin, dark-clad and forbidding, radiating power and menace. And behind him stood a figure, a creature out of legend, a fantastical creation that it took them both moments to recognise as a human wearing armour. Tien recognised the archaic style first: "The skin of the ice-serpents of Thusal—a Katan warrior!"

The Weapon Master nodded, but his eyes were on the bard. "Where have you been?" he asked softly.

"Later," Paedur said, a smile curling his lips, lending his hard, sharp features character and a touch of humanity. He strode to the door and stared down the fire-streaked and blackened corridor. The heavy crossbow was now wreathed in flames and the two archers nowhere to be seen, although the smouldering pile of filthy ashes on the floor around it might have been the remains of a human. All the guards, both human and *quai,* had vanished also, leaving only a single figure facing the flaming creature that had been Salier the Mage. Fodla pulled the broadsword free of its scabbard, undid the buckler and tossed it to one side before advancing towards the creature, dropping into a fighting crouch.

Paedur pulled his furred cloak tighter around his shoulders and stepped out into the corridor, and although he had moved noiselessly, the creature turned, its hideous screaming ceasing abruptly.

Its face was ghastly. The features had been burned away, leaving only gaping holes where the mouth and nose had been, but the eyes remained, dark and alive and in torment. It stared at the bard and something moved behind the eyes and recognition flared. The mouth worked and a sound that was between a hiss and a word escaped the blackened lips. "Bard!"

Paedur nodded. "I am surprised you still recognise me, mage," he said softly. "It has been a long time."

"Bard!" The creature spat again and raised a flame-wrapped arm. A long spear of white-hot flame lanced from it, but the bard caught it on his hook, wrapping it around the glowing metal like a thread.

While Salier was distracted, Fodla used the opportunity to lunge at the creature with her broadsword. The metal sank deep into its back and then struck something solid and stuck. The creature screamed and spun around, wrenching the sword from her hand, sending her sprawling. Tiny tongues of flame sparkled in the air around the dazed woman, hissing and crackling like insects, floating down to land on her exposed skin, searing the flesh. And then the broadsword began to melt, the metal running liquid down the creature's body to bubble on the scarred stones.

"Why doesn't it die?" Owen whispered.

"Because it is already dead—long dead," Paedur said softly, "and the dead cannot die."

The Katan warrior reached out and almost touched the edge of the bard's cloak. "It will kill the woman," she said evenly, her eyes bright behind the horned demon's mask.

"She is our enemy," Tien said diffidently.

"She is human, and alive; the creature is unhuman and dead," Katani said simply.

Tien nodded and bowed slightly. He looked at Owen, "Master?"

Owen sighed and nodded. He turned to look at the bard. "Can we kill it?"

"It is already dead," Paedur said. But he stepped forward and raised his left arm high, the curved hook glinting in the smoky, sooty air. Something like a smile touched his usually impassive features and he spoke a single word, "Huide!"

The flames rose higher around the creature that had been human, and the heat was strong enough to force Owen and Tien back. Katani's armour protected her somewhat and the bard seemed impervious to the heat, but Fodla, who was barely paces from the creature and clad in nothing more than a torn shift was badly scorched, her skin turning red and cracking before their eyes. Her red hair began to smoke and crinkle.

Tien touched Owen's arm and pointed.

A fine, pale mist had gathered close to the blackened ceiling. As they watched it thickened and darkened, and then it suddenly began to rain down on the creature.

"Huide," Owen gasped, remembering the name, "Huide, the Little God of Summer Rain!"

The creature that had been Salier was now enwrapped in a cloud of hissing steam as the fine mist of rain fell on him. The small flames darting around Fodla were immediately extinguished and slowly, slowly, the raging fire that was burning but not consuming Salier was diminished. There was a dull explosion, as if something had ignited within the mage, and the flames briefly surged again, but the rain intensified and the creature was completely enveloped in a dense cloud of smoke. The fires died and the foul-smelling corridor was suddenly suffused with the fresh odour of damp growth— the smell of a forest after a summer shower.

Without waiting for a command, Owen and Tien ran forward, avoiding the twisting, shifting wreaths of dense white smoke and grabbed Fodla, half-lifting, half-carrying the huge woman back into what had once been Salier's chambers. Paedur remained, watching the greasy pile of charred ashes, before he too turned away, leaving Katani to take up position beside the door.

Owen and Tien had laid Fodla out on the cold marble flagstones before the fire. Her shift had been completely consumed by the flames, leaving her naked except for a simple loin cloth, and all of her exposed skin was red-raw and seeping. Her eyebrows had been burned off and her flaming red hair was crisped and seared, leaving only a thin fuzz close to her skull. And yet she still lived, only her strength and stamina having kept her alive so far.

Paedur knelt beside the woman and touched her with the flat of his hook. The chill of the metal sent a shudder through her body and her cracked lips worked, the skin splitting as she moved them, and while Tien hurried to find liquid to moisten them, she uttered two words: "Kill me."

Without hesitation, Owen unsheathed his knife and placed the tip beneath the woman's breast, preparing to drive it home.

"No," Paedur said simply, his hook lifting the knife.

"She is a warrior and in pain, and there is no cure for this. There is nothing left for her but a lingering, painful death, and she deserves better," Owen said, anger touching his voice. "She would do the same for me. It is part of the warrior's code."

The bard nodded. "And it is also needless."

Tien returned and knelt by the stricken woman with a goblet of pale amber-coloured wine which he placed down beside her. Tearing a strip of cloth from his borrowed shirt, he soaked it in the wine, moistened her lips and allowed a few drops to trickle down the woman's throat.

"Enough," Paedur said. "Now step back."

Tien looked to Owen, and the Weapon Master reluctantly nodded, and both men stood up and moved away from the woman. The bard raised his left arm and allowed his hook to rest barely a hair's breadth above Fodla's body. He moved the hook down to her feet and then bent his head. His lips moved, and abruptly the runes etched into the metal began to sparkle and glow, and then the hook abruptly exuded a pale blue-green light, which seemed to flow from it like liquid and wrap itself around Fodla's burned feet, sinking into the raw flesh. She moaned, shuddering, her eyes opening in shock. The bard slowly moved the hook up the woman's body drawing the blue-green light with it, and leaving in its wake clear, pink, and unblemished skin.

Later Fodla would describe the sensation as that of being rubbed by damp leaves or moss, but even she could only watch awestruck as the seeping skin dried, and the ugly, scorched and hard, burned flesh softened and was absorbed back into the bright, pink, and clean skin of her body. She watched as Paedur moved his hook upwards, saw it clean and cleanse her skin, removing even old scars and weals that had come from a lifetime of battle. She looked at the man's face, saw the concentration, the intentness, recognised the pain in his eyes. And yet she was a stranger to him; why then should he care?

His hook continued upwards, across her stomach and up over her breasts, and she closed her eyes and allowed the cooling, gentle moistness to soothe her wounds. In those moments Fodla decided that there could be nothing evil in a man who was able to heal like this, and who did so for a total stranger. Fodla had experienced mages and magicians, warlocks and wizards in her mercenary trade, but she had only ever known them to be able to kill or harm; none of them were healers. And the few healers she had known were, without exception, gentle, good people, at peace with their world and themselves—as indeed they must be, to be able to heal.

She became aware that the tingling had stopped and there was complete silence in the room. She opened her eyes and looked up into the hard, sharp face of the bard. "Thank you," she said simply.

He smiled and the mask fell away, and for a single heartbeat she glimpsed the man beneath the mask. He reached down with his hand and pulled her to her feet with almost casual ease.

Fodla looked past the bard at the two men standing close to the door—with their backs to the wall, she noted with a wry smile. She turned to Owen, recognising him for what he was, a battle-weary, professional soldier, and smiled a little uneasily. "Thank you."

He returned her smile. "For what?"

"You would have killed me when I was in pain."

"You would have afforded me the same honour," he said, something like shyness touching his voice.

"I hope I would have been able to do so," she said. She looked at Tien. "And you, too, thank you."

"You are a warrior," Tien said simply, as if that explained everything.

"And you, what are you?" Fodla asked him.

"I am merely a servant."

But the Weapon Master shook his head quickly. "He is more than a servant; he is a friend," he said. "I am Owen, Weapon Master, and he is Tien tZo...my companion."

"I have heard of you both," Fodla said. "Indeed, who has not?" She turned to the bard and found he had wandered off and was poking amongst the mage's shelves of scrolls and charts. The Katan warrior was standing by his side as if she were a guard. "And you, who are you both?" Fodla asked.

The woman pulled off her horned helmet and shook loose her bone-white hair. Her amber eyes sparkled with humour and when she spoke her accent sounded quaint and archaic. "I am Katani of the Katan, and this is Paedur."

Paedur turned when he heard his name spoken, and Fodla looked with more interest at the tall, dark man. "Your name is not unfamiliar to me. A fortune awaits the man who kills you."

Paedur shrugged. "I am pleased the Imperials hold me in such high esteem."

"What are you?" Fodla asked quietly.

The bard glanced sidelong at her, something like a smile touching his lips. "I am a bard," he said simply.

"The Prince Kutor's forces are unstoppable. It is said the gods themselves are on their side," Fodla said, lifting the bottle and filling three glasses and then her own; only the bard wasn't drinking.

"When will he enter the city?" Paedur asked, moving away from the shattered door to stand by the table.

"I would imagine there will be one final battle on the plain beyond the gates and that will decide the matter, and that battle will take place within the next three or four days."

"Then we must ensure that it goes in our favour," Owen said. He looked at Fodla. "Are you sure you are with us in this? It will mean betraying everything you have fought for, giving up everything you have achieved, losing what friends, influence, and power you have now."

Fodla bared her teeth in a semblance of a smile. "Like you, I am a mercenary. For all my apparent wealth, I have little coin. As for everything I have achieved, I could leave it without a qualm, and, like most professional warriors, I have taken care to have few friends. Leaving here will be no great loss."

Owen nodded; it was an explanation he could accept. He turned to Katani. "This is not your fight. There is no reason for you to be here."

The warrior-woman ran her long fingers through her white hair, pushing it back off her face, her pointed teeth giving her face a feral appearance. "It is a conflict between Good and Evil…"

"No conflict is ever so sharply defined," Paedur murmured, but Katani continued on.

"I will fight this fight because I want to, because I spent all my life fighting for the Faith and what I believed in. And now that I have a second chance, I see no reason to stop."

"What second chance?" Tien asked, intrigued.

"Now that I am restored to life," the woman said enigmatically.

Tien shook his head in puzzlement and looked at the bard. He smiled. "Katani walked the Silent Wood for a long time, before returning to the Planes of Life with me."

"Do you have the power to restore the dead to life?" Owen asked in astonishment.

Paedur shook his head. "Only a God can restore the dead to Life."

"I thought you were a God," he said.

"Not yet," Katani said with a smile.

Paedur shook his head and returned to the window, looking down over the courtyard, watching the palace guards filing out carrying the bodies of their slain comrades between them. What looked like a whole legion had arrived moments after he had healed Fodla. Their commander had met them and explained that Salier had gone berserk and attempted a coup, using his occult powers to kill and burn all those around him. She explained that he had only been stopped by the people in the room, who had not only killed the mage but also saved her own life. A squadron of her own personal guard took up position along the corridor, occupying the places so recently vacated by Salier's *quai,* while the rest of the men cleared up the dead bodies. For the moment, no one was allowed into the room.

"Where is Barthus the Hierophant?" Paedur asked suddenly.

Fodla shook her head. "No one knows. From what I have been able to put together from my scouts' reports, I understand that following his meeting with the Andam," she smiled at Tien, "he dressed in simple travelling robes and set off for the palace. Last reports place him with the Emperor, but neither man has been seen for a little while."

"Will they have been made aware of what happened here?" Katani asked softly.

"Undoubtedly," Fodla said.

"I would imagine they are attempting to evaluate your position in all this," Owen said slowly. "They will be asking if you are attempting a coup; is Salier really dead and if so, did you kill him? And if you did, do you plan to kill them? Will you side with the rebels? What happened to Geillard's and Salier's hired mercenary— namely me—and what happened to the Andam?"

"What numbers do they control?" Katani asked.

Fodla shook her head. "In this situation it would be difficult to say. The Emperor would control a legion of his personal guard, the Emperor Legion, but they are directly under my command and have all been personally trained by me. They might side with me, and they are a highly skilled fighting force. Barthus would theoretically be able to call upon every able-bodied follower of the New Religion to rally to his flag, but I would imagine he will only call on the temple guard and whatever members of the Iron Band of Kloor are in the capital at the moment."

"We have talked in circles," Tien said softly. "We must return to our original question. What do we do now?"

As one, all the heads turned to the tall figure standing by the window. Without turning, Paedur said, "Fodla will take whatever men she feels will be loyal to our cause and, along with Owen and Tien, return to Prince Kutor and his forces." His voice was soft, each word carefully considered and delivered. "Before going you will attempt to destroy as many of the long-range weapons—the ballistae, the oils, the giant bows—as possible."

"And you?" Owen asked. "What of you?"

"Katani and I will continue with a portion of the original plan; we will attempt to kill Barthus and Geillard."

"Will you succeed?"

Paedur turned from the window and looked at each in turn. "Probably not," he said with a wry smile.

25
Allies

And in his time, Empires rose and fell, and his hand was apparent in it...
Life of Paedur, the Bard

As the afternoon turned, Imperial troops marched into the streets of Karfondal. Although the provinces had seethed in revolution, the capital had remained quiet, with only the additional numbers of soldiers on the streets and the unusual number of mercenaries in the taverns giving any indication that there was in fact a war being fought.

The road to the palace was closed, sealing it off from the rest of the city, with no-one allowed in, but effectively trapping everyone within. Geillard's palace was situated in the precise geographical centre of the city, supposedly following some ancient occult practice, and covered hundreds of thousands of paces in all directions. However, there was only one main thoroughfare that led to the palace—the Royal Way—which in turn led out onto the King Road that bisected the Seven Nations from Thusal to southernmost Lostrice. A squad of the Emperor Legion, augmented by the Imperial Guard, had taken up position across it, behind barricades of metal and stone. Heavy ground-mounted crossbows were bolted into position, and behind them sappers began tearing up the broad marble flags along the tree-lined avenue that led to the palace. The ugly pockmarks they left in their wake were designed to trap and snap a mount's hoof or to render a charge impossible.

Paedur and Katani mingled with the crowd that was growing to watch the proceedings. Both had thrown dusty travelling cloaks over their own clothing to enable them to move through the crowd without attracting undue attention.

Katani nodded at the workmen. "The sign of defeat," she murmured.

"A defeat expected is a defeat accepted," the bard smiled. It was a Katan saying.

There was a sudden commotion and a man wandered out of the crowd, his height and colouring marking him as a mercenary from Thusal, and he was more than a little drunk from his gait. He staggered up to the barricade and demanded to be allowed to pass beyond. The captain of the guard, a slender, dark-skinned woman from Fodla's Emperor Legion, nodded and stepped aside, leaving a space for the leather-clad barbarian to pass through. When he reached the other side he turned to wave at the crowd, and then abruptly disappeared!

"What happened to him?" Katani hissed.

"Someone stuck a knife in his back," Paedur remarked. "Come on." He turned away and made his way through the growing crowd, the people parting almost naturally for the man, although most would have been unaware that they were even doing so.

"Where are we going?" Katani asked.

"There is only one way into the palace," Paedur murmured, ducking past a deserted fruit stall. "We'll try some of the side streets."

There were countless side streets and alleys that led out onto the great open square, but all of these were held by a small group of guards, usually backed up by one of the heavy cross-bows.

The sun was dipping in the heavens by the time the bard was forced to admit defeat. All the routes were held. Paedur walked away from the mouth of an alley shaking his head in disgust. It was so insignificant that he had hoped it would have been overlooked, but two bulky figures in black armour filled the end, chatting softly together, their voices echoing off the grimy stones. Katani was waiting for him by a fruit stall, carefully slicing the hard rind from a green-skinned tropical fruit that grew in Lostrice.

"Well?" She looked up from beneath the cowl of the cloak she was wearing over her armour.

He shook his head.

"But there must be some way in," she insisted, tearing off the last of the skin and turning the pale fruit around and around in her hands, savouring its tart perfume. Since she had returned to the World of Men, she had made a deliberate effort to enjoy every sensation to the utmost, making up for her time spent in Mannam's dark kingdom.

Paedur nodded absently, attempting to recreate the geography of the city from a chart he had seen in Baddalaur's library many years ago and from what he remembered from his stint as Bard to the Imperial Court. There was something at the back of his mind, something from the days of his youth. A smile touched his thin lips, remembering those distant days, the escapades, the pranks, the balls, the women…and the smile broadened as he abruptly remembered a way into the palace.

"Come!"

"Where are we going?" Katani asked, breaking the fruit, popping segments into her mouth, wincing at the sharp, bitter juice.

"There is a way into the palace," Paedur said softly, taking Katani by the arm and leading her through a bewildering maze of mean streets and even meaner alleyways, relying on his visual memory of a single previous visit, of a fog-wrapped night and a wild chase through the backstreets of the capital when he had acted the spy for Geillard.

"How do you know?"

Paedur stopped, hesitating at an intersection. He closed his eyes and then took the street to the right, avoiding a pile of festering refuse. "I was Bard to the Imperial Court a long time ago," he said quietly, almost to himself. "Geillard, who was merely vain and foolish then and not completely insane, suspected his mistress of conducting an affair with a nobleman of the court. He approached me and asked if I would be prepared to follow her when she left the court and report back to him with her eventual destination. The reason why he had chosen me was because, with my infirmity and my unique position at court, I would never be suspected of working for the Emperor. I was a young man then and, like the young, easily flattered, and my expectations and ideals were different. I wanted to be, oh, many things," he smiled almost shyly, "many things."

"And so you followed the woman?"

"I followed her."

"And where did she go?" Katani asked.

"Here!"

The street they had been following had gradually grown meaner, eventually turning into little more than an alleyway, winding down between high-walled foul-smelling tenements.

However, it suddenly opened out into a small enclosed courtyard in the centre of which was a well and pump. Paedur stopped in the mouth of the alley and pointed across the square. "That's where she went."

Katani looked at the four-storied red-brick building, curiously elegant and completely out of place between its shoddy mouldering neighbours. Although the years had not been kind to it, and time and decay had stripped it of much of its grandeur, it still retained enough of the original mouldings and fixtures to give some idea of its former glory. "It's seen better days," she remarked.

"It was the town house of a princeling from one of the provinces in the days when the city was smaller, and although you may find it hard to believe now, it once stood in its own grounds. Then the line died out—the last of them assassinated by one of Geillard's ancestors, or so it is said—and the house passed through several hands before it was gambled away in a very famous game that changed the course of the history of the Nations, which I'll tell you about some time. For the past three generations, however, it has served the same purpose."

"And that is?" Katani asked, although she had already guessed.

"It's a brothel."

Paedur pulled his cloak higher about his shoulders, and with stooped shoulders he walked slowly and carefully across the cracked cobbles. Katani strode along beside him, assuming the role of son to the bard's old man. "You never told me what happened to the woman you were following," she murmured. "Why did she come here?"

"She was the Madam of the house," he whispered. "She disappeared soon afterwards. I suspected Geillard."

They mounted the worn steps that led to the peeling door. Countless feet had worn the stone smooth and glasslike, and to any observers the old man had great difficulty in mounting the steps, gripping the younger man's arm tightly. In reality the bard was issuing last minute instructions to Katani. "Kill anyone who stands against us. For the plan to succeed we must hold this house for almost a whole day, and a life or two counts as little when the fate of every man, woman, and child in Karfondal is at stake."

"How many guards?"

"Unknown, but two or more certainly."

"Women?"

"Again unknown, possibly a dozen or so."

Katani made a face. "Do you think two of us will be enough?"

"Individually, we are greater than two; together, we are an army."

Katani bit down on the inside of her cheeks to suppress a laugh.

The bard raised a hand trembling with age and effort and rapped on the door, twice, and again, and then once more. "I hope they haven't changed the code."

A panel snapped open and hard, dark eyes regarded them suspiciously. "Yes?"

"Reports of the excellent entertainment offered by your house has reached even the provinces," Paedur said, his voice quavering, using the password he had heard all those years ago. He was gambling that it would be unlikely for the brothel to have changed its code or password, if for no other reason than that it would be impossible to acquaint all its customers with the change.

"I don't know you!" the voice said simply, a note of finality in it.

The bard looked up, his eyes catching and holding those of the man behind the door. For a single instant they blazed, burning with an almost visible blue fire, and for a single heartbeat a cold, inhuman creature stared out from behind them. "You know me, don't you?" Paedur suggested, his voice soft, sibilant, like the hiss of a serpent.

"Yes, sir, I know you." The panel snapped shut, there were the sounds of bolts being drawn back, and the door swung open. "Good to see you again, sir." A huge man filled the doorway, and even without his heightened senses Paedur would have been able to tell of the man's mixed non-human ancestry. His features were broad, flat and brutish, and there was Chopt blood in his veins certainly.

The bard and Katani moved into the darkness of the hallway, pushed through a heavy leathern curtain that hung behind the door, and stepped into another world.

From without, the building was shabby and peeling, the woodwork rotten, the stonework crumbling, the metalwork twisting and rusting, but within, it was a palace. Paedur had been expecting it, but to Katani it was a revelation. Deep-piled scented rugs covered the polished wooden floors, exuding scents and odours with every step. The decorated walls were hung with tapestries that glittered and sparkled with rare threads and wools. Many of the interior walls had been removed and scores of floor to ceiling mirrors added to the illusion of space.

The doorman ushered them into a room furnished in the style of the Emperor Geillard VIII, natural woods and polished stone richly decorated and embellished with earthen pigments lending it warmth and character.

The hulking doorman stepped back and closed the door, leaving them alone in the room. Paedur looked at Katani and raised a finger to his lips. She nodded briefly and wandered over to the huge open fireplace, standing with her back to it, warming her hands, her hard eyes assessing the room. Paedur meanwhile crossed to a long couch that had been cut from the bole of an ironwood tree and sank back into its naturally smooth curves. He closed his eyes and allowed his heightened senses to come to the fore. He immediately became aware of the tainted life-aura of Katani: although back in the World of Men, she had not truly shaken off Death's hold. He absorbed that into his consciousness, and then felt the burning glow of life from two other watchers in the room, one off behind a false panel behind him, and another looking out from behind the scrollwork beside the fire. He reached for a goblet of wine, but stopped when his fingers touched the glass: the wine had been treated with some mind-dulling drug—not enough for the ordinary man to notice, but then, he was no ordinary man. He allowed his fingers to move on to the bowl of fruit and discovered that they too had been bathed in the drug, allowing it to seep into their succulent flesh.

He suddenly became aware of a small group gathering in the corridor outside. He recognised the dulled aura of the doorman walking a step or two behind a red-white glow of a person in command, someone large, seething with anger. Behind these two, three more followed, but their auras were the blank white of professional killers or *quai*.

Paedur glanced at Katani, briefly touching her mind. She looked up, startled, and he caught and held her gaze, moving his head slightly towards the door. The warrior-maid nodded slowly, casually. He then allowed the images of a person hiding in the panelling behind him and the second man concealed beside her to drift into her mind. She looked at him sharply, unsure if she were actually seeing a true sending or if it was just her imagination. His lips curled in a slight smile and he nodded.

The double doors of the room had been carved and worked with a frieze of rambling, tumbling flowers from all across the Nations, and a tiny rose cut into the wood suddenly dilated. Although he was sitting across the room, the bard's sensitive hearing caught the tiny rasp of the sliding wood and felt the cold gaze of a woman—he had identified the aura as female—move contemptuously across him. The panel closed silently.

Paedur turned his head slightly to catch the murmur of voices. "I don't know them." Then, obviously to the doorman. "They must have bewitched you." And finally turning to the three cold white auras. "Kill them!"

"Move!" Paedur shouted.

There was a whisper of steel and, without turning, Katani dropped to one knee and plunged her sword through the scroll-work beside the fire, driving the blade in with both hands locked around the long hilt. There was no sound but when she withdrew the sword it was covered in thick blood.

The bard moved like a shadow, coming up and out of the couch in one fluid motion, spinning, the blade of his hook slicing easily through the thin wooden panelling, taking the hidden observer full across the throat, neatly decapitating him. Paedur shrugged off his cloak, wiping his hook clean in the heavy furred material, and then leapt across the couch for the door—just as it opened!

The three guards rushed in on a figure of death. The first died choking on his own blood as the razor edge ripped out his throat, and the second went down with a hammer blow from the bard's open hand to the centre of his forehead. He was dead before he hit the ground, his skull crushed. The third man's charge carried him past the creature in black—straight onto the blade of an ice-haired demon.

Without pausing Paedur raced down the corridor, pursuing the tall, robust woman in red who had actually been casually walking away from the room when her guards were abruptly slaughtered. She attempted to run, but a razor hook encircled her throat, the point pricking the soft skin beneath her right ear. "Move, and I'll rip out your throat. You," he snapped at the doorman, using the Bardic Voice, "return to the room!" Under the influence of the ancient vocal spell, the man obediently turned and walked back into the room where Katani, thinking him another warrior, promptly killed him.

"Who are you?" the woman demanded, desperately attempting to control her trembling voice. "What do you want?" In her youth she would have been a great beauty, but time and excess had taken her beauty and charm, leaving her a foul-eyed, hollow-cheeked harridan who had attempted to disguise her age beneath a layer of paints and coloured powders. She was wearing a gown that would have been outrageous on a woman a third her age and which only served to make her look ridiculous, and she carried enough jewellery about her person to feed most of the capital's poor for the major portion of the year.

"Let me say this once to you," Paedur said, pushing her up against a polished wall, his hand flat against her throat. He raised his left arm, allowed her to see his hook and when he was sure he had her attention, he continued. "I do not need to keep you alive, in fact, you are probably more trouble than you are worth. Answer me truthfully, however, and you will live to see another sunset, but lie to me—and I will know if you even attempt it—and I will kill you. Understand!"

The woman nodded dumbly.

"Where is the tunnel that leads to the palace?"

The madam's eyes widened in surprise and she shook her head, attempting to disguise her shock. "I don't know what you mean," she faltered.

Katani's sword suddenly bit deeply into the wood not a finger's length from her face, severing strands of her grey-brown hair. "Let me kill her," Katani hissed, deliberately accentuating her broad accent.

"I told you not to lie to me," Paedur warned.

"I haven't."

"I know about the tunnel," he said simply.

"The tunnel," she said numbly.

"Let me feed on her," Katani grinned, baring her pointed teeth.

"The tunnel built in the time of Geillard X, the present Emperor's grandfather, and completed by Geillard XI and used most frequently by the present Emperor and his sometime mistress. Now, I don't have much time. Show me the tunnel!"

Something shifted behind the woman's eyes and they suddenly widened in horror. "You're the bard!"

"I am."

"The tunnels are down those stairs, in the second room on the left, behind a pile of disused bedding," she suddenly gushed, certainly terrified now, whatever her feelings had been earlier.

"Thank you." Paedur placed the flat of his hook against her powdered cheek and the woman suddenly slumped.

"Is she dead?" Katani wondered.

"Unconscious."

"What now?"

Paedur looked at the woman, his eyes intense. "You will have to hold this house; business must seem to be continuing as before. Allow everyone into the house, but no-one must leave. However, if you feel the situation is becoming uncontrollable, fire the house and make good your escape."

"And you, what of you?"

"I'm going to visit the palace."

"Imperials coming!"

The rumour moved down the army like wind across a field of wheat, rippling as it went, leaving only stillness in its wake. The rebel army had faced many Imperial assaults over the past days and months, and there was nothing new Geillard's forces could throw against them that they hadn't faced already.

When the first sightings occurred, Keshian rode ahead with one of the scouts in an attempt to determine the Imperials' numbers and deployment. And now, from the concealment of a clump of standing stones, he watched the distant shimmer of metal on the horizon. When the army had approached closely enough for the distant rumble of hooves to sound like thunder, the scout climbed one of the rocks and studied the advancing dust cloud with a glass.

"Well, man, what do you see?" he demanded.

The young man shook his head. "I'm not sure. Imperials certainly, but..."

"But what?"

"But it looks like Owen and Tien leading them!"

"Let me see." He stood in his mount's saddle, his fingers hooking into the jagged rock, and he pulled himself up. The scout passed him the metal-banded leathern tube and Keshian put the glass to his eye, following the scout's pointing arm. For a moment he saw nothing but a shifting, swirling blue, but as he turned the tube, the image leapt into focus. There was a small Imperial army riding towards them—he looked for company or legion flags, but curiously found none—but in the lead, armoured and armed, were Owen, the

Weapon Master, and Tien tZo, his slave-companion. Between them rode a huge female warrior in the armour of an Imperial commander, and the only woman who fitted that description was Fodla, Geillard's commander and sometime body-guard.

He shifted the glass, attempting to concentrate on their expressions. The image was blurred, but he got the impression that they were all laughing.

He concentrated on the approaching army. There were no flags, no pennants, and while the men and women held to a rough formation, there was none of the rigidity that he would have expected of Imperial troops. Also, their armour and weapons were mismatched, almost as if it were personal choice rather than issue.

"Sir?" the scout asked.

"What do you think?" Keshian asked absently, still watching the riders.

The man's thin face broke into a broad smile. "There's not enough for an army. I think they're coming to join us, don't you?"

Keshian looked at the man, his face remaining set in the same grim lines it had worn through all the previous battles, and then he suddenly turned away, unwilling to allow the scout to see the moisture that suddenly blurred his eyes. He strode to the edge of the rock and looked down at his mount. He hesitated for a moment and, glancing back over his shoulder, he said quickly, "I think you're right." And then he dropped down into the saddle with all the agility of a much younger man and, lying low across his mount's neck, he galloped back to the huge rebel camp. There had always been doubts that they could succeed, but whatever doubts he had entertained had vanished now.

The pickets allowed him through. Amongst the mismatched rebel army, Keshian had become something of a legend, and the tale of his defence of the prince against the assassins had grown out of all proportions, until even Keshian himself was unable to tell what had been the original story they had put out.

The battle-captain found Prince Kutor waiting for him in the centre of the huge camp. The prince had stripped to the waist and was assisting the score of blacksmiths and armourers to forge arrow- and spear-heads. His acceptance by the usually dour smiths and his obvious skill in the task had done more to endear him to the army than any amount of speeches and promises, and it had become customary for people to wander in to assist him, working the bellows or holding the metal, while at the same time seeking his advice or requesting favours. The only reminder of his royal blood were the black-armoured guards standing in the shadows beneath the smith's striped awnings.

As Keshian reined in his mount, Kutor looked up, his face open, expectant. "Well?"

"You've heard?"

"Rumours."

Keshian brought his right leg over his mount's head and slid off the sweating beast's back to the ground. A boy hurried over and took the reins from him and another handed him a goblet of warm, thin wine. Keshian strolled under the nearest awning and downed half the goblet in one swallow, while Prince Kutor stood looking at him.

Finally, when he could contain himself no longer, he demanded. "Well, what's happening out there?"

"There's a small army approaching, a single legion or perhaps two legions strong. There are no pennants, no flags or emblems showing, they're not holding to formation, not wearing issue armour, and the weapons are personal. It's being led by both Owen and Tien tZo, and they've another person with them, a woman warrior, a huge creature with flaming red hair."

"Fodla!"

"My thoughts exactly."

"What do you think?"

"I think their mission has been successful, or at least partially successful, and they're returning with deserters from the Imperial forces."

"I can't believe Geillard's dead," Kutor said firmly.

"Neither can I. But something else struck me as I rode in here."

"And what was that?"

"I cannot see Owen and Tien leaving the city together, unless they received orders to do so."

"But who would order?" Kutor asked softly, and then he breathed, "The bard."

Keshian nodded. "I think the bard has returned."

26
The Road to the Throne

"The Road to the Throne is lined with sorrow."
Geillard I, Emperor of the Seven Unified Nations

In the chill darkness of the tunnel Paedur the Bard came up against his first obstacle. The brothel tunnel had begun at the bottom of a flight of steps which had brought him some thirty paces below the level of the streets, and had run arrow-straight for over two thousand paces in the general direction of the palace.

In the pitch blackness of the tunnel, the bard's enhanced sight showed everything in stark shades of black, white, and grey, and initially he had been wary of traps, but strangely the tunnel didn't seem to possess any. It was a beautiful construction, and there was more than a touch of otherworldly power in its making. He touched the walls with his hook, expecting to feel at least some residue of the power that had created them, but the tunnel was so old that all he could feel were the shadows of the emotions of those who had passed down the long corridor in times past. Shuddering, he broke the contact, feeling faintly soiled by the emotions.

The tunnel was an almost perfect circle, with tall, curved ceilings painted a pale blue and touched with white, fleecy clouds which served to disguise the air ducts. The walls were bellied outward, and thin, deep channels ran along the floor, carrying away the water he could hear gurgling all around him. In niches in the wall, statues in poses both erotic and obscene, but with the features of ancient princes and ministers, leered and postured, obviously advertising some of the delights of the house. Further along there were doors, and the bard paused to glance into them. They had been bed-chambers but were now all empty, and they hadn't been used for a long time judging by their general air of decay.

Farther on there was another series of doors, but these were barred and locked with heavy, professionally made locks. He idly contemplated ripping them off, but decided against it, and merely contented himself with allowing his enhanced senses to flare as he moved past the wood—only to recoil in horror. Behind the first door were four mouldering skeletons. With enough remnants of clothing for him to distinguish the male and female and the two small pathetic bundles that lay between them. They had been dead a long time. There was a similar bundle of skeletons behind the next door and the next. From the little he could gather without actually breaking down the doors, from the emotional residue that still clung to the cell doors, he thought he was looking at wealthy families who had been incarcerated and then left to starve to death. From the state of the decomposition and the style of dress, he estimated the deaths had occurred in the time of Geillard VI. He sorted through his lore and then nodded grimly. Geillard the Red-handed's rule had been so merciless that a coup had been planned by several of the noble families. But a spy had betrayed them to the Emperor, and in a single bloody night, they had all mysteriously disappeared, their possessions seized, their servants and slaves butchered. No one knew what had happened to those who had vanished and for a while there had been rumours that they would return, but Paedur fancied he had discovered their whereabouts. As he walked away he vowed that if he survived he would return later and have them buried with all due ceremony.

One hundred paces from the death cells, the corridor curved and he encountered his first obstacle—a dead end.

It was a man-made wall of later construction than the tunnel, rough-hewn square and oblong bricks cemented together to create a crude but effective barrier. It was splashed and streaked with mortar and had all the appearance of hasty work; there was even a space at the top and sides where the mason hadn't allowed for the curvature of the tunnel. Idly wondering why it had been necessary to seal off the tunnel, Paedur placed his hook against the centre of the wall and called upon the Gods of the Pantheon for assistance. There was an immediate sense of disassociation from his body, but he was aware of a growing pressure deep in his skull. Abruptly, his vision doubled and for a moment he saw a constellation of colours shifting and crawling along the walls. He blinked and blinked again, settling the colours into lines and bands that outlined the bricks, and then something hard and bright pulsed through his arm and shimmered along his hook—and the silver-grey metal, sank up to his wrist into the wall! He experienced a brief moment of panic and pulled his arm back—and ripped out the whole centre of the wall. He quickly scrambled through the breech, the wall crumbling around him, fist-sized lumps of stone and brick tumbling around his shoulders but leaving him untouched.

And he remembered then that Churon had promised him that the powers he had grown accustomed to before he had entered the Silent Wood would be enhanced. Now the bard wondered to what extent. He had been able to cut stone before he had gone into Death's Domain—and that was what he had just done—but before it usually left him reeling and exhausted. Now he had ripped a wall apart with no effort and no strain. Paedur couldn't help but wonder what the Pantheon had made him.

Immediately beyond the wall, the floor of the tunnel began to slope upwards, and the bard's ghostly sight began to flicker into colour as light seeped in through frequent ventilation ducts, shafting beams of pale yellow-white light down into the darkness. He walked for another thousand or so paces, stopping only when he reached a staircase. He stood at the bottom of the stairs, looking up, allowing his consciousness to move upwards beyond the heavily barred door at the top and out into the room beyond. It was an antechamber off the library, a seemingly innocent storeroom, holding nothing more than duplicated scrolls and badly copied books. He waited, his head tilted to one side, listening with more than human senses, but the room above seemed to be empty. Finally, he mounted the steps silently and then stopped again before the door, listening, probing the room beyond and the library beyond that again, while he examined the locks and bolts. The antechamber was still empty, but there were two readers in the library itself.

The door had been bolted top, middle and bottom with heavy metal bars and there was a lock of the double key variety dead centre—and they were all on the opposite side of the door. However, the door did not sit flush into its frame and the bard merely slid his hook into the gap, slipped the point under the uppermost bar, and pulled. The hook noiselessly sliced through the metal. He repeated the process with the middle and bottom bars, and then simply hit the door with the palm of his hand just below the lock housing. The lock snapped and the door creaked fractionally open.

Now speed was essential. Even he could not defend himself against a palace full of guards and he had no illusions that once it was known that palace security had been breached it would only be a matter of time before he was captured. But a lot could happen before then.

He placed the flat of his hand against the door and pushed. The door moved slightly and then stopped, and the bard's sensitive hearing caught the grinding of hinges. It had been a long time since the door had been opened. Fully realising the consequences, he put his shoulder to the door and pushed. The warped wood protested, scraping off the ground, and unused hinges screamed but suddenly snapped and gave, tumbling the bard into the small room. He recovered his balance as a man pulled open the leathern curtain that separated the antechamber from the library and strolled into the room, an ancient vellum scroll casually tucked under his arm. He was a small, compact man who had seen service in the Imperial Dragoons, a man who had seen much and heard even more and had long thought himself unshockable, but this creature in black with the terrifying eyes and stone face, wielding an evil-looking hook, stopped him cold in his tracks. And then the hook was at his throat and the creature was leering down at him.

"Where is the Emperor now?" The voice was nothing more than a hiss, cold and compelling.

He started to shake his head, but the creature pressed the point of the hook against the wrinkled skin of his neck, drawing blood. "Don't even think about lying to me now."

The small man started to shake his head again, but stopped when the movement caused the hook to bite more deeply into his flesh.

"Wrong answer."

And then the curtain parted and a second man stepped through. The man was thin and pale, his eyes deep set and squinting, the patches on his breast identifying him as a professional scholar. "Is everything…" he began, and then his weak eyes registered the tableau and widened in horror. He scrabbled for the knife on his belt, his mouth opening to shout—and died when the bard's hook took out his throat.

"Tell me!" Paedur snarled, turning back to the small, quaking man.

"In his personal library," the man quavered. He shifted the chart under his arm. "He sent me down here for this."

Paedur allowed his senses, his intuition, to assess the truthfulness of the statement, and could find no lie in it. Almost as if he was aware of what was happening, the man twisted his head to look up into the flat, merciless eyes. "It's the truth, I swear it."

"How many up there?"

For a single instant the small man thought about defiance, but he was now convinced that the creature was a Duaite—an evil one—and with the scholar's blood still wet and warm on the creature's hook, he wasn't prepared to argue. "The Emperor, Barthus the Hierophant and one other."

"Who?"

"I've never seen him before. A small, stout man."

The bard nodded. "Thank you." And then he allowed unconsciousness to wash over the man and gently lowered him to the floor. He stooped and lifted the scroll from under the man's arm and carefully unrolled it. It was a standard Deed of Covenant, blank and unfilled. "Now, why would Geillard want that," he murmured.

"It is agreed, then?"

Barthus the Hierophant sat forward eagerly, his eyes bright, greedy, fixing themselves on the slender form of Geillard. He glanced quickly at the third man in the room and then turned back to the Emperor. Since the arrival of the renegade army, the tall, thin man had aged almost visibly and now moved with a permanent stoop, and there was a perceptible tremble in his long-fingered hands.

"We must know," the Hierophant persisted. "There is no time now."

"And will this ensure me victory?" the Emperor asked, his voice tired, almost uninterested. Salier's loss had affected him badly: the mage had been more than a counsellor, more than a friend, and Geillard had come to believe him invincible. When he had been told of his loss and then learned of Fodla's treachery, he had begun to suspect that he was not meant to win this battle.

"My lord," the third man spoke, his voice soft, insinuating, like silk on silk. "When I have finished, there will be no army left to face you."

"And in return? What do you want in return?" Geillard demanded, his voice surprisingly bitter. "Death, I have heard, is a treacherous ally."

The short, stout man smiled broadly, his eyes twinkling merrily. "Ah, but Death is also a powerful friend," Libellius said simply. "And as you are already a follower of the Religion, we would be asking nothing untoward of you."

"Then why the Deed of Covenant?" Geillard demanded, turning back to the fire, staring deep into its glowing embers, as if he could read some advice therein.

"Why, merely to ensure that we understand one another," Libellius said softly, looking at Barthus. Now that the Emperor was no longer looking at him, the broad smile had gone from his face and what remained resembled nothing so much as a fleshy skull.

"And payment?" Geillard said without inflection. "What would be the payment?"

The Death Lord of the New Religion waved his hand expansively. "I imagine we would look for certain concessions: the occasional sacrifice, a purge of the followers of the Old Faith, the removal of certain persons in positions of power which we feel might threaten the well-being of the Religion." He shrugged. "Nothing you would not approve of."

"Sacrifices?" Geillard asked tonelessly.

"I think sacrifices might be the wrong word," Barthus said quickly, "begging my lord's pardon," he added quickly to Libellius. "I think perhaps he meant to say that we would look for certain followers of the Religion to volunteer to allow their bodies to become host to the Gods of the Religion."

Libellius nodded quickly, the laughter gone from his dark eyes, leaving them like stones. "That is true. Think of it, Geillard. In your lifetime, during your reign, the Gods of the Religion would assume corporeal form and walk the World of Men. Perhaps even the Lord Trialos himself would walk this Plane again. And what would that make you, oh? What man has yet commanded the gods? What power would you have? Think on that."

Geillard rounded on the stout man. "And what will you do if I say no?"

The smile didn't move on Libellius' face, only the fire behind the eyes died. "Then naturally I would return and leave you to face your enemies." He shrugged. "Then I would attempt to deal with your successor."

"Are you saying I will not survive this battle? Why, don't be preposterous. I have four times the number of men they have; my troops are better armed and we are within a fortified city."

The Lord of the Dead made a face. "Oh, I'm not saying it is a foregone conclusion by any means. They have, however, certain advantages over you." He leaned forward and began ticking off points on his stubby, beringed fingers. "All of their troops are there either by choice or because of coin, and I would imagine that even those who are being paid to fight have already thrown in their lot with Kutor. They firmly believe in what they are doing—namely, overthrowing a cruel and heartless despot. Also, Fodla, the captain of your personal guard and your private bodyguard, has joined them, along with nearly two legions of your best troops. Salier, your mage, is dead; and finally, and perhaps most importantly, the Gods of the Pantheon and their lackey, the Bard Paedur, fight with them."

Geillard's shoulders had slumped during the litany of foes, and when he looked at Libellius, the Death Lord knew he had won. "What will you do?" the Emperor asked wearily.

But it was Barthus who answered. "My Lord Libellius will assume death's most dreaded form and walk through Kutor's army, taking all those who come within his ken."

"Including Kutor?" Geillard said, eagerness showing in his voice for the first time in the conversation.

"Especially Kutor," Barthus continued, "and as many of those close to him as possible: his advisers, Owen, the Weapon Master, his slave Tien tZo, Keshian, his commander, and Fodla, if she is still with them."

"Do it, then," Geillard said, looking at the small, red-clad man, wondering if he indeed had the power to do all he claimed, wondering briefly—but only briefly—if he was indeed Libellius, Lord of the Dead.

And then the man sitting calmly on the chair facing him began to change, a subtle alteration at first, a smudging of the planes of his face, the features softening, melding, the cheekbones and eye-sockets becoming prominent, the line of his jaw becoming more pronounced, the grin becoming permanent as the lips drew back and the flesh tightened, transforming the jowly face into a skull. Only the eyes remained, and where they had once twinkled with merriment, now they glittered with malice. Libellius stood, and now the short, corpulent body was gone and had been replaced by a tall, thin, skeletal creature, still wearing the reds that Libellius favoured. He stretched out an arm and a skeleton's claw appeared, the bones clacking together as the fingers opened and closed. "Such is man's perception of Death, eh?" Libellius asked, and although his soft, cultured voice hadn't changed, coming from those fleshless lips, it sounded obscene.

"Your form is similar to Mannam, the Faith's Lord of the Dead," Geillard said numbly.

"Confusion," Libellius hissed, "confusion." He folded his arms against his sides and simply winked out of existence…

A rebel scout perched in the branches of a tree overlooking the main road into the city was the first to spot the tall figure in red moving slowly and sedately towards them, obviously coming from the city.

"Someone's coming," he called down to the man on the ground.

"Who? How many?"

"Just one," the scout said slowly, attempting to focus on the figure, but his eyes kept blurring. He dug the heels of his hands into his eyes and looked again—and found the figure was standing at the foot of the tree! "Hey you! You!" He struggled to the ground, wondering what had happened to his companion. "Who…who are you?"

The creature in red lifted his head, the white bone of his skull face blotched with red, which dripped from his chin and onto his robe, the blood matching the colour exactly. There was something in the skeletal hand he extended towards the scout. The man looked, drawn against his will, his eyes fixing themselves on the object. For a single pounding heartbeat, his eyes refused to accept what he was seeing, and then he recognised it as a human hand, a bloody hand, bone and tendrils of sinew and flesh still dangling from the stump of the wrist. And then he spotted the small, silver signet ring on the third finger of the shredded hand and recognised it as his friend's. The creature brought the hand to his mouth and bit down on one of the fingers, teeth clacking together over a snapped bone. "I am Death," he hissed, bloody froth bubbling between his lips. "I have come for Kutor's army. Tell him!" And then he turned away.

"What do we do now?" Geillard asked.

"We wait," Barthus said, crossing to a small side-table and examining the selection of wines and liquors.

The Emperor moved from the fire to the window and stood framed against the grey light, looking down over the courtyard, watching the flurry of palace guards preparing the defences that had never actually been used in the eleven generations of his family history.

Barthus poured two glasses of pale wine from the vineyards of Isle of Forme and carried them across to the Emperor. "Where is the man with that Deed of Covenant?" he wondered aloud.

"It's here!"

The two men turned towards the sound and somehow Geillard found he was unsurprised at the dark-clad figure with the hook replacing his left hand standing in the doorway. Something like a smile touched his lips. "Bard?" he breathed.

"I am Paedur, the Bard."

"So we meet again." Geillard stepped forward, his hand extended, palm upwards in the grip of greeting. Paedur ignored him; he was watching the Hierophant.

"You see, you're the cause of all this," Geillard continued, his measured tones beginning to lose something of their calmness. "You incited Kutor to this uprising; you supplied him with his present commander; you freed the Weapon Master from his bondage and sent him to Kutor; you subverted Fodla. It all comes back to you."

"This started with you," Paedur said simply, glancing at the man.

"I remember you from your days here. You could have been great, you could have taken the position Salier or even Barthus here occupied. But you threw it all away."

The Hierophant had regained his composure. When he had turned and found the bard standing framed in the door, his first instinct had been panic. The bard's reputation was fearsome; why, even the Gods of the Religion held him in respect. But then something cold and cunning settled into the Hierophant's brain. After all, if the bard was the creature of the Faith, was not he, Barthus, the creature of the Religion? Had he not the power to call down the gods themselves to serve him? And did that not make him even greater than the bard, Paedur? This was the Hierophant's territory; he was surrounded by all the symbols of the Religion, in a sanctuary of the Religion. Surely all of these would conspire to weaken the bard?

"Have you come to surrender yourself to the mercy of the Religion?" he demanded, his voice harsh, overloud. He stepped past Geillard to face the bard. The glow from the firelight took his metallic vestments and turned them liquid, contrasting with the bard's furred cloak, which seemed to absorb the light, surrounding him in a pool of shifting darkness.

"I have come for Geillard, and you too," Paedur said, matter-of-factly.

"Defeat is upon you and your army," the Hierophant smirked, "but surrender to me now, and I will ensure that your life is spared."

Paedur placed his heel against the door and nudged it shut. "Kutor's army will destroy you," he said simply.

Barthus stepped forward and jabbed a finger towards the bard's face. "Even now, Kutor's army is being destroyed." Seeing the sudden shifting in the bard's eyes, he hurried on. "Even now, even as we speak, Libellius, the Lord of the Dead, walks through your prince's army, plucking their essences like ripe fruit. And be assured, bard, your prince, your Weapon Master, and his companions will be amongst them."

Paedur took a calculated risk and, closing his eyes, shifted his consciousness through the Ghost Worlds and the Void to where he guessed the rebel army would be camped. He could only afford to catch a flicker, but it was enough. A tall figure in red strolled through the camp, leaving a trail of bodies in its wake, and it was heading in the direction of Kutor's tent.

Pain brought him back to his body. Barthus had seized on his momentary absence from his physical body to thrust a small poignard into his chest. His leather jerkin had absorbed much of the blow, but the tip of the dagger had still penetrated the skin, enough to hurt but not to harm. He looked from the ornately hilted dagger to the Hierophant's face, and the look in the bard's eyes was enough to send the man scrambling backwards. Paedur plucked the dagger from his chest and touched the cut with the flat blade of his hook, sealing the wound, and then he flung the dagger at the Hierophant. Barthus flung up his hands and created a reddish-blue film between them; the knife struck the magical shield and careered off to bury itself to the hilt in the window-frame not a finger's length from Geillard s face. The Emperor didn't seem to notice.

Something noisome coiled around the bard's scuffed boots and he found a tentacle of congealed filth taking substance in the air before the Hierophant and drifting across the floor towards him. It abruptly tautened, almost pulling him off balance, but the bard stooped and sliced through the tentacle with his hook. The band of filth recoiled and splattered across the room, daubing it in filth and offal, and the room immediately reeked with the odour of faeces and things long dead. The shock sent Barthus reeling back against the wall. Paedur looked around and then picked up a silver goblet in his right hand and threw it with all his might towards the Hierophant, murmuring one word: "Luid!"

As it spun through the air, the goblet began to alter in shape. It was as if it was being subjected to an intense heat. The metal ran in large silver globules which congealed together, all the while glowing white-hot. Barthus spread his hands and the red-blue film appeared again, but the glowing silverball of molten metal passed clean through it, shredding it as it passed. Barthus managed to scream once and then the ball struck. It exploded against his face and the metal immediately ran, covering his flesh beneath a layer of molten silver. Barthus writhed in agony and attempted to peel off the metal mask, but his fingers came away tipped with silver. He crashed backwards into the fire and hungry little flames—Luid the Firegod's creations—began to devour his heavy vestments. There was a sudden burst of intense blue-white fire and the Hierophant's body was rendered into a fine, ash-like powder, leaving only the smouldering garments and the silver horror-struck mask.

The Emperor looked at the bard, his face expressionless, his eyes dead.

"I will return for you," Paedur promised Geillard, and then he turned and was gone.

27
Death

Death was his ally, his companion, his enemy, his bane...
                                        Life of Paedur, the Bard

Libellius stood in the centre of the field, surrounded on all sides by terrified men wielding pikes and swords. None of them dared approach him. "I am Death," he cried, raising his arms and proceeding to take every third man. The remainder of the men scattered in terror. Libellius rubbed his bony hands together and continued on his slow, casual way towards Kutor's camp.

Paedur burst through the opening into the brothel to find Katani cleaning her swords, a score of bodies scattered around the floor. "Visitors," she said simply.

"We must get to the rebel's camp," he snapped, barely registering the carnage, "Libellius is killing everyone."

"It's half a morning's ride," Katani reminded him.

"I know."

"And there's no way we're even going to get out of the city, even if we could get to them in time."

There was a sudden knock on the door, startling them both, and then the coded sequence was tapped out. Katani smiled tightly without humour. "A popular house." She moved through the leathern curtain and Paedur heard the door open. He didn't need his god-gifted senses to interpret the sounds which followed. Katani reappeared through the curtain and draped the body of the young man across the pile. "Churon will be busy," she said, wiping her knife against the dead man's costly silk surcoat.

And Paedur suddenly had the answer.

The bard moved to the warrior and turned her to face him, his hand on her left shoulder, his hook touching her right. "Do you trust me?" he asked softly, his eyes holding hers.

"You gave me life again," she said simply, as if that explained everything.

"And if I asked you to kill me?"

"To kill you!"

His hand moved across her mouth, silencing her. "Would you do it? Would you kill me if I asked you?"

"But what about Libellius, what about Kutor and his army, what about your friends?" she demanded, suddenly angry. "They are depending on you."

"I am asking you to do it because of them, for them," he explained.

"I don't understand," she said defiantly.

"I need Churon's help to get to the camp."

"Call him, then. He'll come for you."

"There are too many dead and dying out there. He will not heed a call from me."

"So you want me to kill you to send you to him?" she asked.

"Just so."

Katani started to shake her head—and then she plunged her dagger into Paedur's heart.

The archer took careful aim and loosed his arrow. It flew straight and true—and still somehow missed the creature in red. Another fired, and then another, and then on command the line of archers fired together—and they all missed. There was a shouted command and the archers fell back, but every second man was struck dead.

Kutor, surrounded by Keshian, Owen, Tien, and Fodla, watched the steady approach of the figure of Death. Against him they knew there was no escape, no defence.

The bard awoke surrounded by the solidified trees of the Silent Wood, chilled and numb, aching in every muscle—paradoxically human again now that he was dead. He was staggering to his feet when the figure of Katani winked into existence beside him.

The bard attempted to spit the ashes from his mouth, but his mouth was too dry. "How? What happened?" he mumbled.

"I allowed the next person to call at the house to kill me," she said, mouthing the words carefully. "I couldn't let you go alone. But I only hope you know what you're doing."

"So do I!" Churon, the Lord of Death of the Old Faith, stepped out from behind a tree-like chunk of stone and moved silently over to the pair. His coal-black skin shone with an inner luminescence and his blond hair had been cropped close to his skull. He hadn't affected Mannam's garb of the cloak of seared and withered leaves, but had opted instead for a mantle of stone-grey that blended in with the surroundings almost perfectly. Looking at the cloak, Paedur had the distinct impression that it was actually made of stone.

"It is," Churon said, answering his unasked question with a smile.

"You know why we're here?" the bard asked.

Churon nodded. "A desperate measure indeed. No man can ever gainsay your courage," he said. "I presume you want me to resurrect you in the rebel camp?"

Paedur nodded.

"You can do it?" Katani asked uncertainly, unwilling to even consider any other possibility.

"No," Churon whispered sadly. "I am Death; I cannot give you life."

"You gave Katani life," Paedur reminded him.

"That was different."

"In what way?"

"I killed her; I gifted her," he said simply.

Paedur straightened and looked Death in the face. "Libellius is killing the rebel army, and by that action destroying the last chance for the Old Faith to re-establish itself in all its former glory. If you want the Faith to survive, you will think of something. Now, think," he insisted.

"I can shift your corporeal bodies to the battlefield," Churon said slowly. "My *quai* can do that."

"Not much use to us if we're still dead," Katani mumbled. "Can you not breathe some life into us even briefly?"

"I haven't the power."

"Then who has?" she demanded, her voice cracking.

"C'lte," Paedur said slowly, a shadow of a smile touching his lips, "the Yellow God of Life."

"It will never work," Churon said. "The Gods of Life, and the Yellow God in particular, have always been Death's foe."

"Mannam's enemy," Paedur corrected, "but you are now Death. And perhaps he will do it for me—I know C'lte of old—and if not for me, then for the continued existence of the Pantheon."

Churon shook his head doubtfully. "I still don't think it will work."

"It has to," Paedur snapped.

"And if it doesn't?" Katani asked.

"Then we are dead."

The figure in red stopped before the small group. It was impossible to ascribe an expression to its skull-face, but his whole attitude was one of overbearing arrogance. Although they knew it was useless, they had drawn weapons, more for the comfort it gave them than anything else.

"I am Death," Libellius said, his voice susurrating across the distance that separated them, dulling even the screams and panicked shouts from the army beyond. The beasts now had picked up the scent of death and had added their own screams to the general uproar. In contrast, the small area outside Kutor's tent seemed surprisingly quiet and still.

"I have come for you," the figure hissed, raising his arm, pointing at Kutor.

"You are not Death," Owen said abruptly. "Death is dark and wears a cloak of seared and withered leaves."

The skull-face turned. "You are Owen, the Weapon Master. I am Libellius."

"Of the Religion!" Owen gasped.

The creature in red bowed.

Fodla moved a little apart from the group, wondering if she could manage to get around the creature to swing her massive broadsword. The head turned in her direction, "Tell me how the God of Religion can kill the followers of the Faith," she shouted angrily.

"You are Fodla, once commander of the Imperial Army," Libellius said, naming her. "I am Death," he continued, answering her question, "I kill. It is my function. And yes, it is usual for the Death Lords of the various religions to take only their own, but there is no hard and firm law. A balance will be maintained and you may be sure that Mannam will take his quota of the followers of the Religion. At any other time it would mean war, but this suits the Gods of the Religion now, and it is a price we will gladly pay for the defeat of the Faith's army." He took a step forward and reached out with a skeletal hand...

Tien's thrown axe struck the hand and bounced off, leaving it unharmed.

"I am Death," Libellius said simply. "You cannot kill the dead." He looked at the small, wiry man. "You are Tien tZo, the slave-companion to Owen. I will take you too in your turn." He moved forward. "And you are Keshian, once Battle-Captain of Count Karfondal, now Commander of this rabble." The skull turned again. "And you are Kutor, princeling and pretender to the throne." Both skeletal hands opened as the creature fixed on Kutor.

"And I am Paedur the Bard."

Kutor's tent flapped open and Paedur stepped out into the group. There was absolute silence. He moved through them, not acknowledging them, not even looking at them, intent only on the creature in red. And indeed, everyone was so intent on the bard that no-one—except Tien—saw the Katan warrior stagger out of the tent behind him.

Paedur walked up to Death and looked him in the face, much as he had done with Churon earlier, and he found that there was no difference in their eyes; but what was even more disturbing was that their eyes matched his own—they were cold and dead, reflective, like tiny polished mirrors.

"Begone," he said simply.

"You cannot stand against me," Libellius said calmly, but some of the confidence had gone from his voice.

"I have stood against the Gods of the Religion for a long time now," Paedur said with a thin smile. "I have defeated greater gods than you."

"I am Death. There is none greater than me!"

"Take what you have slain this day and go; there is nothing left for you here."

"You are arrogant," Libellius hissed. He stretched out his right arm, his skeletal hand curling into a claw, his pointed nails touching the bard in the chest just below the heart. And then he drew it back with a hiss. Smoke curled from the blackened tips of his fingers and the stench of burning bone was rotten on the air. For a single moment, the image of the figure in red flickered to be replaced by that of a small, stout man with a pale sweating face.

"And you are weak," Paedur smiled. "You have taken many this day; it has left you sated and full—and weak."

"But I have enough left for you, bard," Libellius snapped. The air around the bard was suddenly filled with scores of tiny black motes. They circled around his head, snapping and crackling, and it was only when one moved close to his eye that Paedur realised they were tiny human and demonic heads on bloated bodies, their minute mouths opening and closing, buzzing obscenities, tiny teeth clacking. He had heard about them; they were the Stones of Death. If he was wounded, the motes would dart into the wound and continue eating deep into the flesh, killing him in the most exquisite agony. He lifted his hook and described a circle in the air. The image of the circle hung spinning and silver on the air and then coalesced into a tight ball, and then it darted from face to face, the motes crisping as they came into contact with it or attempted to dart through the circle. Libellius' hand shot out, his claw closing on the circle of light and then he crushed it between forefinger and thumb like a flea, silver light spurting like blood.

"This is for you, bard." He pulled apart his red cloak, and too late the bard realised his mistake as he looked into it—into Nothingness. It was not the soft greyness of the Ghost Worlds, nor the deeper dusky colours of the Void; within Libellius' cloak there was an absence of life, of colour, of sensation. It was more than death; it was desolation and despair. Paedur struggled to escape its dreadful pull. Unconsciously and unwillingly he staggered forward towards Death's clawing grasp. He was blind and deaf, aware only of the need to move deeper into that encompassing blackness. Distantly, dimly, he felt himself moving, something pulling him down, and that part of his mind which remained detached and watching knew that if he fell, then it was all over.

He began to enumerate the Gods of the Pantheon, concentrating all his attention on them. "Hanor and Hara, the First Great Gods; the Lady Dannu; Mannam...no, Churon now; the Lord of the Dead. Churon, aid me now!"

And he fell...

And was caught.

There was a broad black hand in the centre of his chest. It stood out from the blackness of Libellius in that this was a living colour, and as the bard looked, he saw a pair of warm blue eyes staring at him out of the Nothingness.

It was enough. Paedur was back on the plain before Kutor's flapping tent, facing the red-clad God of Death.

Libellius drew back his arm like a swordsman withdrawing his weapon from a shoulder sheath, and then brought it swinging forward again, and as it came round a sword formed in it, a long wavy-edged blade of red-black fire. The first blow seared past the bard's chest, tainting the air with foulness and the stench of burning flesh. Paedur caught the second blow on his hook, blue-white and red-blue sparks coruscating, but the force of it was enough to send the man sprawling. Libellius strode over to him, the sword smoking blue-red fire raised high above his head, a smile tightening his skull-face, his eyes bright and victorious. When he was close enough the bard kicked out, catching his knee, sending him staggering, his mouth working. Paedur scrambled to his feet and faced Death once again.

But the Lord of the Dead hung back now, almost as if he was undecided. And then he abruptly raised his hands. "My children," he called, and throughout the camp an army of dead arose. All those Libellius had claimed took on a brief semblance of life and began to march towards the centre of the camp. "You will all fall to my *quai,*" Libellius boasted as the first appeared.

Owen, Tien, Keshian, Katani, and Fodla formed a protective circle around Prince Kutor as the army of the dead approached. Without any evidence of wounds, they were like sleepwalkers, their movements slow and graceful, their eyes wide but unseeing. They advanced steadily onto the group, intent on overwhelming it, but completely ignoring Paedur and Libellius.

"My *quai* will slay them, and then what will be the point of continuing?" Libellius asked him.

"Even if they all die, even if I die, there will be others; the Religion will never defeat the Faith."

There was a sudden clash of weapons as the first ranks of the quai reached the small group surrounding Kutor.

"Turn and walk from here, bard. Live out the remainder of your days in peace and solitude. You remember how it was before, before Mannam took you."

"He didn't take me; I volunteered."

"He tempted you."

"This is a fruitless discussion," Paedur said wearily. "Only one of us will walk away from here this day."

"Bard," Libellius said in astonishment, "I am a God and you, for all your gifts, are a man. You cannot win this battle, any more than your companions can defend themselves against the *quai.*"

"But they have succeeded so far," Paedur remarked lightly, his eyes never leaving the god, his senses telling him how his companions were faring.

"But for how long?" Libellius hissed. "I took many this day. You cannot hope to defeat them all."

Behind them the bodies were beginning to mount up around the group. There was little skill required. The *quai* lacked the imagination to press home the attack or to use any but the most basic cuts and blows, and it was simple butcher's work, lopping off hands and arms, heads, hacking at spines, cutting open veins, lopping off legs. The *quai,* because they were newly dead, bled and the air stank of blood and offal. The battle was conducted in an eerie silence; there were none of the shouts or cries that had accompanied every conflict since the First Age of Man. The *quai* were unable to speak and the small group too desperate to even try, but what was even more terrifying was that they were butchering warriors whom they had considered companions, some of whom they had broken their fast with that very morning.

"It is time," Libellius said softly, looking at Paedur.

"Time?"

"Time to die!"

Death lunged at Paedur with his sword of red fire. The bard threw himself to one side, but the blade sliced through his cloak, searing it, doing what no mortal weapon had been able to do. The bard dropped to the ground and rolled across and to the right of Libellius, hacking out with his hook as he moved past. The metal sank into Libellius' foot, finding something solid, biting deeply, and when the bard rolled to his feet, flames were licking around the wound. Instead of being a skeletal foot, it was now a soft leather shoe encasing an all too human foot. The two images flickered and were briefly superimposed on one another, and then the image of the skeletal foot reaffirmed itself.

"You cannot harm me, bard."

Paedur cut again, catching the creature low on the arm, just above the wrist, and once again he saw the image of a red-sleeved cloth-covered arm, but this too was only momentary and then it vanished.

There was a sudden cry from behind him and he turned to see that Keshian had gone down, bleeding from a score of wounds, and Kutor had taken his place. Fodla was also bleeding from a bad gash in the thigh, and Tien had been slashed across the forehead, the blood seeping into his eyes, blinding him. Even as he watched, the small Shemmat fell back beneath a flurry of blows.

"They cannot hold out much longer," Libellius hissed, teeth clacking in a grotesque parody of laughter.

Unconsciously Paedur nodded. He knew Death was right this time. There were too many for the small group to stand against, and they were tiring fast. It would end soon. And he was also coming to the realisation that there was no way he could defeat Libellius. Death could not be killed.

"Look, bard, look." Libellius gestured with his sword, and then the *quai* who had already fallen, dismembered or disemboweled, rose again to continue the fight, crawling on shattered limbs, dragging themselves on the stumps of arms over their fallen companions to fight again. "They will fight until they have been hacked to pieces. The battle is ended. You have lost."

Paedur shook his head, "No...no...*NOOOooooo!*"

His terrifying scream stopped the battle. Even the *quai* looked towards the source of the eerie sound. Time wound down and the bard moved towards the red-clad figure of Death with infinite slowness. Libellius brought around his flame blade—and the bard plunged on to it. It erupted from his back, still flaming, but the bard's rush carried him down the blade onto Libellius. His left arm rose and his hook found the god's throat, pressed, sliced through bone, almost— but not quite—decapitating it. Locked together the bodies fell, but before they hit the ground, the bard was holding a small, stout, red-clad man in his arm. When they struck the ground, they simply vanished. And the *quai* fell to the earth, unmoving, truly dead now...

Churon, the Death God, dusted off his hands and watched the figure in black appear on the grey, gritty ground. The man stood up and limped towards the Lord of the Dead. "I thought I had brought you a present," he whispered.

"He has gone to his own place of the dead. It is something of a curiosity, Death as a member of his own kingdom rather than a ruler."

"And what of me?"
"You are dead, bard."
"I have been dead before."
"And will be again, I promise you."

Epilogue

They rode in triumph into the capital and the people lined the streets to hail Kutor, Emperor of the Seven Nations, and his companions: Keshian, his commander; Owen, the Weapon Master; Tien tZo, a Shemmat; Katani, a warrior of the fabled Katan; and Fodla, whom they all knew.

The remnants of their army rode behind them, surprisingly silent for a conquering army, still shocked by what they had witnessed, numb at the loss of so many friends to a foe they couldn't even fight.

Geillard had fled, gone with three trusted guards and as much coin as they could carry. Rumour placed him travelling into the north.

The palace was thrown open for Kutor—there were no attempts at defiance—and he walked the marbled halls in silence, completely numb now that it was actually his, never believing, not even as he rode towards the open city gates, that the seed planted by the bard would flower. His breathing was quick and shallow, and he was almost afraid that he might wake up. But it was no dream, he knew; his wounds and aching muscles reminded him of that.

Fodla and Owen were waiting for him when he reached the throne room. They had gone ahead to ensure there were no traps or assassins lurking in the corridors, while Keshian, Tien, and Katani had accompanied him. The huge doors were closed but not locked, and the two warriors put their shoulders to the polished metal and glowing wood to move them. They swung silently inwards. Fodla and Owen stepped inside, weapons drawn, but the room seemed empty, their footsteps echoing in the vastness of the chamber. Geillard had left in such haste that nothing had been disturbed, its treasures untouched.

Kutor walked into the centre of the room, standing in the pool of coloured light that streamed in through the domed glass roof. The light washed the fatigue from his face, making him seem younger, taller, more of a king, less of a man.

"Was it worth it?" Keshian asked, his voice weak, bitter, his wounds troubling him.

"I'm not sure. Ask me later."

"You will need to move quickly to consolidate your forces," Owen reminded him.

"I know."

"And the people will need to see you," Fodla said.

Kutor nodded.

"And the dead must be buried," Katani added softly.

"Yes," Kutor said, "that first. We will honour our dead." The group moved in around him. "All those who died will be laid to rest with full honours, and then their bodies will be burnt—I don't want the risk of them re-animating as *quai* again." He stopped and looked at each in turn. "And there will be a separate ceremony for the bard, something special—he gave us all this..."

"Honour the dead," Paedur said coldly, stepping out from behind a pillar, "and leave the living in peace. See to your empire, Emperor Kutor. There is much yet to be done!"

DEATH'S LAW

Prologue

Call him Kingmaker...

So Paedur the Bard took a bandit prince and made him an Emperor against all the odds, helping to found the famous and ultimately the infamous line of Kutor.

There have been many accounts of that time and the bard's role in the uprising that followed and, as is usual with partisan histories, they all differ. For history, like truth, is a matter of perspective, politics and religion. What is agreed upon is that the new ruler's early days were not happy ones. Many did not accept the overthrow of the old order, especially the noble houses—the Twelve Families—who rightly felt threatened by the appearance of the Renegade and his rebel army.

To compound the new ruler's troubles, Geillard had escaped and there were rumours of his appearance everywhere, and the most persistent rumour—that he was raising a huge army to overthrow the Usurper—grew in the telling, as did the deposed Emperor's reputation, making him into something of a tragic hero.

Even the very elements—which had been thrown into turmoil by the Cataclysm—seemed to conspire against the new Emperor's rule. After a blistering summer and a mild, mellow autumn, the Cold Months were bitter, and famine and disease walked hand-in-hand with their master, Death. Refugees made their way from all across the devastated nations to the capital, stretching already strained and limited resources to their limits. Stories of rebellion and uprising abounded, and Geillard's followers fomented trouble for their own ends.

Karfondal was a powder-keg awaiting a spark.

There are accounts too which show that the very Planes of Existence were in turmoil. The armies of Faith and Religion had gathered, facing each other across the chequered fields of Ab-Apsalom, awaiting the final call to war. But, mindful of the destruction of previous conflicts, representatives of the two beliefs had met and resolved to set in motion the Death's Law, wherein it is stated that men are but the playthings of the gods, pieces to be moved at will.

And so the Gods looked to their agents and followers, and this was a battle without rules, without codes of conduct or chivalry. But the Gods of the New Religion were fighting for their very existence, and in their last-ditch attempt to secure the belief of Man— and hence increase their strength before the coming battle—they had promised and delivered miracles. And the tide of belief, which had swung back towards the Old Faith with the appearance of Kutor and the bard, Paedur, was now swinging to the Religion once again. A tangible religion, with real gods, promising succour, found belief far more quickly than the Old Faith, with its mysterious and sometimes fickle Pantheon.

And the bard, the one person who could possibly swing that balance back to the Pantheon, had disappeared.

Life of Paedur, the Bard

1
Chopt Moon

*They are the beasts that walk like man; they are the men that act like
beasts; their food of preference is human flesh. They are the Chopt...*
Lilis' Geographica

The beast bared its fangs, threw its shaggy head back and turned
large round eyes to the clear night sky. The moon was full, the Lady
Lussa riding the heavens in all her glory, while the Nightstars wove
their arcane patterns around her. The silver light sparkled on the
snow-covered ground, turning the night into a semblance of day,
but deepening the shadows beneath the trees to pitch.

In the distance, a dog howled, a single cry of absolute loneliness.
It was taken up almost immediately by a second and then a third
dog, baying their hunger and chill to the bitter night.

The beast beneath the tree moved, its tongue clacking against its
teeth in command, and then it was as if every shadow took life as
dozens of the huge creatures moved out from the darkness. The
moonlight shone on matted hair and rusted mail, torn leathers and
scraps of armour culled from a score of lands and a century of
years. Only the weapons, the huge swords, the clubs, and tridents,
and heavy broad-bladed knives, were new and clean.

Without command, without sound, the creatures loped down
towards a long snaking black line that cut through the snow-locked
countryside, north to south, the Mion River. Throughout the day the
guards from the nearby castle had painstakingly kept it unfrozen,
clearing the ice with bonfires and axes, but the bitter night and Snaitle,
the Cold God, were claiming it once again.

The creatures paused on the edge of the sluggish river, watching it, gauging the thickness of the ice, and then looking up at the
Lady Lussa, judging the time. And then they lay down on the
iron-hard ground and rolled in the snow, covering their shaggy
pelts and scraps of clothing with snow, becoming one with the
ground. Even from a short distance, they were invisible. Deep

yellow eyes moved from the river to the moon, watched the Lady Lussa move sedately across the heavens, moving towards the dawn.

But there was time aplenty and they could wait.

Thomas yawned hugely, stretching his arms wide away from his body, feeling his stiffened muscles crack. He glanced into the sky, gauging the time from the moon. A while longer and the Lady Lussa would dip low in the heavens; a little later and the Grey Lights, the precursors of the dawn, would ride across the heavens, and morning would follow.

The slender young man pulled off his thick mittens and dug the heels of his hands into his eyes, rubbing away the grittiness. He had been at his post since midnight and the glare from the moonlight on snow had set his head pounding and he felt vaguely nauseous. He shifted his pike, looking into the polished metal head; his eyes were bloodshot and raw. Well, at least he could report to the physician when he came off duty, and he would be sure to be excused. White-blindness took more warriors in the Northlands than any Chopt blade or bandit arrow. If he was excused sentry duty he would probably be placed on a river watch, ensuring the ice didn't freeze the Mion solid, making a bridge for the beasts to come across.

Thomas shivered in his furs; the night was bitterly cold, and like as not the river had already frozen over. He stamped his feet and poked his head over the edge of the merlons, looking down on the Mion River—and a broad-bladed knife neatly severed his throat...

Solan the Gateman looked up, head tilted to one side, hands automatically reaching for his pike; something had cracked beyond the gates. And Solan, who had watched the gates of Castle Nevin for nearly fifteen cold winters, knew all the sounds of the night. He sat in his tiny hut just inside the gate with a fire going all the year round—and that fire was his companion, his comfort. He needed no-one else, wanted no one, was content with his tiny scrap of flame. He controlled the gate, admitting—or refusing—those who had come after sunset. And in the Northlands, especially in the Cold Months, the castle was always sealed tight as the distant mountains burned red with the last rays of the dying Nusas. And to be locked out meant death.

He heard it again, a click, a crack, a creak; something strange, an odd sound; something he couldn't identify. Reason told him it could be ice falling from the gate, or freezing in the hinges. It could have been a stone shattering with the ice, or the river freezing over, and then breaking again as an undercurrent pulled away the ice-skin... but Solan knew all the sounds of the night and the ice—and this was none of them.

The Gateman shuffled out of his tiny gatehouse and leaned against the tall wooden gates, careful not to touch it with his bare flesh. He heard nothing. Standing well back and using the butt of his pike, he slid back the rectangular viewing slot cut into the right-hand door. He could see nothing. Frowning, Solan shuffled forward, his feet making hardly any sound in the snow-covered courtyard; he should be able to see...

Suddenly the viewing slot was clear, and he realised—too late—that someone had been standing up against it. He opened his mouth to scream—and a slender spear punched through the slot and took him through the mouth...

Count Nevin of Castle Nevin pushed the ornate chart across the polished table towards Aeal, his Captain of Bowmen. The bulky, grey-haired count tapped the vellum with a stubby finger.

"I say we raise an army and carry the fight to them before it's too late. The beasts are becoming bolder, losing what respect and fear we fought so hard to instill. We've had no word out of Thusal for nearly two moons now, and we can only assume that either it is held or the roads are held."

"The roads more like," Aeal said softly. He was a tall slender southerner from Talaria, his pale hair and eyes almost exactly the same colour. He turned the chart of the Northlands with his calloused fingers and touched the hieroglyph for Thusal, the northernmost town of the Seven Nations. "It is a walled town, moated, with its own wells, plentiful supplies of food and grain, with physicians, mages, and priests, as well as one legion of the Northern Guard." He smiled, showing small square teeth. "It cannot be taken."

Count Nevin touched the patch covering his left eye and grinned fiercely. "Of course it can be taken. Every town, every castle can be taken."

Aeal nodded briefly. "But we would have heard, or our mage would have picked up the signs." He chewed on a thumbnail, looking at the chart. "What we need is a Chopt base, a town, a village, caves, whatever...if we had that then I would consider an assault. But without that information..." He shrugged. They both knew what would happen. The weather would claim too many of the men and then the Chopt would complete the decimation. It would be suicide leading an army into the Northlands on a scouting foray.

Count Nevin rested his hands flat on the golden wood of the table, drawing strength from the antique. It had been in his family since Nevin Ironhand had commissioned it on the occasion of his handfasting to Maggan, the daughter of Thurle of the Two Forests. Chriocht the Carpenter, one of the mythical Crinnfaoich, had created the table from a single piece of wood, and invested it with a little of the Old High Magic—which Nevin had learned of only recently. And now, when he was troubled, he drew some consolation—and indeed, seemed to find the strength he sought—from the ancient table. "Have there been more sightings?" he asked.

Aeal nodded. "We sent out three men," he said quietly, "two returned. They both had sighted Chopts, sometimes singly, but also in groups of twos and threes. And you know the saying, "For every one you see..."

Nevin nodded bitterly. For every one you saw there were a dozen you didn't.

"All the outlying farms that are still inhabited reported losses of livestock," Aeal continued slowly, moving his hands slowly across the cracked vellum of the old map, "and there have been some killings." He looked across at the old count. "Without any shadow of a doubt, they are massing for an attack..."

Nevin leaned forward on the polished wood of the table, his face contorted in anger...and then suddenly yelped in pain. He lifted his hands, looking at the palms; both were bright red, as if they had been burned!

Aeal touched the ancient wooden table; the wood felt smooth and cool to his fingers. But when he looked back at the count, he saw sudden panicked comprehension in the old man's single eye. "We're being attacked! The castle is under attack!"

Uncomprehending, Aeal stared at him.

"The castle is under attack," Nevin insisted, "the magic in the wood reacts when the dwelling containing the table is threatened."

Without waiting for anything further, Aeal grabbed his bow, which was propped against a chair, and ran for the door, the count behind him. As they raced out into the corridors, the booming gong of the alarm sounded—only to be abruptly silenced almost immediately.

They looked at one another and then, realising what had happened, they separated, their priorities altered. Their worst fears had been realised—the Chopts were within the castle!

Nevin raced down the deserted corridors, suddenly feeling more frightened than he had been at any time in his life. The Chopts frightened him—they frightened any normal man—but doing battle with them in the snow-covered ice-fields was one thing, fighting a bloody hand-to-hand in the corridors of his own castle was quite another.

He rounded a corner—and ran straight into one of the creatures!

The Chopt was huge. It stood a head and shoulders taller than the count and was broad in proportion. Its face was flat and brutish, with a low sloping forehead and a weak, receding chin. Its nose was flat, with wide flaring nostrils, and its canines were pronounced. Its eyes were deep set and a dark bilious yellow. And it stank.

Nevin hit out on instinct, his left hand slamming into the creature's throat, and as it fell forward and down, he brought his clenched fists down on the base of its neck. The snap of its spine was distinct.

Nevin grabbed the broad-bladed knife from its body and raced for his own chambers. Dimly now he could hear the growing sounds of battle, and then, rising above the din, the terrifying, nerve-shattering battle-howl of a Chopt. It was taken up and repeated again and again until it was a sustained wail of absolute viciousness. The castle walls took the sound and bounced it, until it sounded as if the very stones themselves were crying.

And then rising above the wall came another sound, a sound which twisted the old man's lips into a thin smile: the sound of screamers—broad-headed arrows, grooved and slit so that they whistled as they flew. At a hundred paces they could punch an armoured knight clean from the saddle, and he could only guess what effect they would have on the lightly armoured beasts in the confines of the castle.

The iron-studded door of his chambers was locked. He rattled the handle and called his wife's name softly, unwilling to draw attention to himself. "Nessa...? Nessa...?"

There was no sound from within.

"Nessa...?"

Somewhere further down the corridor he heard a sound that could only be the click of claws on stone.

Nevin rattled the lock. "Nessa!" He knew if he was caught here in the open, he was dead.

"Nessa!"

A Chopt rounded the corner, and stopped, looking at him, its yellow eyes gleaming. It was almost naked, although its matted body hair hid most of its flesh. It carried a wood and bone trident, the tips of which were barbed and were ominously dark stained. Poisoned, Nevin guessed, although that would be unusual, for poison would taint the meat and the beasts preferred their meat fresh. The creature bared its fangs, and a long, sickly red tongue appeared. The Chopt's mouth worked, tendrils of saliva appearing to run down its chin, and then it mouthed a single word. "Nevin!"

"Nessa!" The count pounded on the door. "Nessa, for Faith's sake!"

The Chopt moved the trident in its hand and then slowly, almost deliberately, it moved down the corridor, its mouth twisting, its thick lips moving back from its yellowed teeth in a rictus that might have passed for a smile.

Nevin put his back to the door and lifted the Chopt knife in his hand, weighing it for balance. But against the creature's longer reach and the trident, he had no chance.

And the door opened!

The old man fell through to sprawl on the floor and the door slammed, the bolts ramming home. And from the corridor there was a scream of rage, a solid thump and then the barbed tips of the trident broke through the solid wood.

Nevin scrambled to his feet, grabbed his wife, and pulled her towards the canopied bed. "Use the Hole, quickly. Stay there, whatever happens," he warned ominously. The door shook in its frame as the beast launched itself against it. He took her small face in his hands, brushing the strands of pale red hair from her eyes and kissed her lips gently. "Please," he said, "do this for me." And then he struck the wooden panelling beside the bed with the flat of his hand. Without a sound it swung open, revealing a tall, rectangular-shaped room. Nevin shoved his wife unceremoniously into the opening and then closed the panel silently, listening carefully for the click of the lock.

The door shook again and then a long crack appeared in the wood, running top-to-bottom. Another blow and the door would split. With no time to pull on his armour, the count grabbed his metal gauntlets, and lifted a morningstar off its clips on the wall. Then from beneath the bed he pulled a cocked and loaded cross-bow. He smiled, remembering how his wife had always derided him for his stupidity and foolishness; well, that same stupidity might just save their lives.

The Chopt launched itself against the door again, its calloused feet striking dead centre where it had cracked, all its weight behind it. The door split and was simultaneously ripped from its hinges, cata-pulting the beast into the room…and Nevin nailed it to the floor with a broad-headed bolt.

"Stay where you are," Nevin called to Nessa and then, grabbing a quiver of bolts, he hurried from the room, wondering how the battle went.

Aeal had fought his way out of the confines of the castle and into the courtyard where he, with a trio of his bowmen , were slowly but steadily forcing the Chopts back towards the walls. The beasts had no defence against the archers, and without bows, arbalests, or cata-pults of their own, they couldn't return fire.

But the archers were low—very low—on arrows.

Aeal paused to take stock. A decade of arrows between the four of them, and there were fifteen—no, sixteen—of the beasts left. So, even if they managed to make every arrow count, they were still left with six of the Chopts to face. And the archers were only armed with knives! Aeal drew an arrow, nocked, pulled, and fired all in one smooth movement. It struck a Chopt high in the chest, lifting him off the ground, pushing him backward into the slushy, crimson snow. He pulled another arrow, concentrating solely on choosing a target, holding and firing; he didn't want to think what would happen when they ran out of arrows.

The corridors were like a butcher's slaughtering house, red with blood and meat. A battle-weariness the count had not felt in many years settled over him as he kept stumbling across dead and mutilated servants and old retainers. There was a bitter satisfaction when he occasionally came across a slain Chopt, but these were too few compared with those he had lost.

But where were the guards? Surely he hadn't lost a full century to the creatures?

There was a shouted command and he heard the whine of screamers, the noise surprisingly brief, indicating that the enemy was close. Nevin, following the noise of the screamers, raced down the stairs from the upper floor and out into the courtyard in time to see Aeal draw his last arrow, pull, and release in one smooth movement, dropping another of the creatures with a shot through the eye. Their arrows spent, the archers then threw down their useless bows and drew their knives, forming a simple wedge, with Aeal at the point, awaiting the attack.

With an exultant scream, the six remaining Chopts charged.

Nevin dropped one with a crossbow bolt, but he knew he wouldn't have time to reload before the creatures reached the archers. With a battle cry he hadn't used in a quarter of a century, he raced towards his men…

…And the Lady Lussa disappeared behind the thickening clouds that heralded the dawn, plunging the courtyard into a gritty vague darkness…

There was movement at the rear of the enemy; a shape, black with a thread of silver, darker, more solid than the surrounding night. It appeared briefly behind a Chopt, the silver thread moved blurringly fast to and fro, and then it moved to another—again the silver rose and fell. The shape had moved on to the third creature before the first actually fell to the ground, its spine laid open to the bone. The second fell, a similarly destructive wound opening its back. Another Chopt turned, the shadow shifted, the silver flashed in the wan light, and the creature fell back, its chest opened in a huge x-shaped wound. The two remaining Chopts turned to the shadow maker—and the silver thread rose, moved left to right, and then to the left and right again. The creatures fell, both their chests opened in a huge gaping wound, from waist to shoulder.

In the long silence that followed, the only sound was the trickling of the beast's blood, hissing slightly on the bloody slush.

And then Nevin cranked the crossbow and loaded a quarrel. He pointed it at the vague shadow shape. "Who are you?" he demanded, unable to disguise the tremor in his voice.

Aeal pulled a guttering torch from its bracket and swung it to bring it to blazing life. He lifted it high, throwing milk-yellow light across the courtyard and the bodies.

The shadow shifted and then the silver thread moved again, but slowly this time, a gleaming half-moon of silver appearing, light dancing from the runes etched into it, and before the figure stepped into the light and pushed back the hood of its long travelling cloak, Nevin and Aeal had said the name and title.

"Paedur..."

"...the Bard."

2
Threat

The circle turned. Once again the bard quit the security of the Imperial Court and took to the roads...

Life of Paedur, the Bard

"I've heard tell you're a demon, a Duaiteoiri." Nevin looked up from his hands, which had finally stopped shaking, and stared directly at the bard. The figure was as he remembered him, tall, thin, with sharp, harsh features, and high cheek-bones. Only his eyes had changed. They had once been black, but were now the indeterminate colour of metal—and, like metal, mirror-like and reflective. The metallic eyes robbed his face of all expression, all traces of humanity. He had taken off his long furred cloak, and now wore a vest of fine link-mail over a shirt of purple cotton that had seen much wear. His leggings of deep brown were scuffed and stained almost black, and he wore an ancient pair of high black boots. He looked like any other road-weary traveller, but one had only to look at his face to realise that this was no ordinary tramping bard.

Paedur smiled with what seemed to be genuine amusement. "So I've heard. And before you're much older, you'll hear me called a god, a butcher, a devil, a myth, and even Death himself."

"And what are you?" Aeal asked suddenly, his voice cold. The archer was terrified of the bard and what he represented. He almost preferred the Chopts to this creature; at least he knew them, knew they bled if they were cut, died if the wound were serious enough. He wasn't so sure about the bard.

The bard turned to look at Aeal, sitting across from Nevin, and the smile faded from his thin lips. His eyes—flat and reflective, like polished metal—took the light from the candles and blazed warm gold. "I am a man," he said simply.

Aeal brushed strands of pale hair from his eyes. "No man could have done what you did earlier this day," he remarked, watching the bard's face, but avoiding the mirrored eyes.

"I didn't say I was just a man." The bard tilted his head slightly, considering. "More than a man yes...but less than human," he added, sounding vaguely wistful.

"Aye, well, whatever," Nevin said, becoming uncomfortable with the way the conversation had turned, "we were bloody lucky you came when you did. The beasts very nearly fed well this day." He rubbed his sweating palms on the smooth golden wood of the ancient wooden table, abruptly remembering the previous occasion the bard had been in Castle Nevin—in this very room too. It had been the night of his daughter's handfasting to Adare, the son of Count Adare, their nearest neighbour. Nevin's daughter had taken to the study of the occult and he had prevailed upon the bard to tell his daughter a tale that might frighten her away from her sinister studies. The bard had recounted the ancient tale of Gered and Leal, the Doomed Lovers, but it had had no effect—or if it did, then it was opposite to what Nevin had hoped, and may in fact have driven Suila more deeply into her occult studies. And Adare, her betrothed, never actually became her husband; he was slain—supposedly by the Chopts—while on a hunting expedition in the Northlands. There were, however, those who noticed that Suila was not unduly upset by his death, nor was she seen to use any of her powers to avenge him. She herself had died mysteriously on a night of fire and storm as she practised her craft.

The old man looked up to find the bard's mirrored eyes resting on him; they had now taken the glow from the wooden table and were softer, sympathetic almost. And Nevin instinctively knew that the bard knew.

"Have you lost many?" Paedur asked.

"Not as many as I initially thought," Nevin said, grateful to be back on a subject he could speak about. "When I saw how few guards were about, I thought they had all been slaughtered in their beds, but Aeal found them this morning, safe, still snoring in their bunks..."

Paedur looked at Aeal, his face expressionless.

"Drugged," the Captain of Bowmen continued. "As far as I can determine, their wine last night had been drugged. It was a new shipment; it arrived only yesterday," he added, anticipating the bard's question.

"The supplier would bear investigation," Paedur said softly. Aeal nodded with a grim smile. Both the supplier and the agent who had arranged for the sale of the wine were in chains in Nevin's cellars. They were admitting nothing, but several cases of drugged wine and rofion had been found in the wine merchant's cellars, packed and ready for distribution to some of the other border castles. In all likelihood, the men would be hanged in the next day or two.

"What were your losses?" Paedur asked.

Nevin looked at the bard. "We lost nearly forty people last night; twelve of those were guards, the rest palace staff. But, bard, the beasts have never attacked a castle like this before; when faced with a force of any size they have always elected to fight in the snow-fields. Their targets are isolated farmhouses or small groups of travellers. It's probably significant that we've had no word from Thusal for too long..." he added quietly, his fingers nervously picking at the leather eye-patch. "And now we find the beasts attacking one of the Seven Bastions," he murmured, almost to himself. "But surely the two events cannot be unrelated?"

Paedur nodded. He had turned to face the fire and the warm light had washed his pale features a saffron colour, and his reflective eyes danced with the flames. He lifted his left arm and rested the hook, that took the place of his left hand, down on the wooden table. Both Nevin and Aeal clearly heard the snap of power and a pale blue spark leapt from the ancient table and crackled on the rune-incised half circle.

"What is going on in the ice-fields?" Nevin demanded. "Do you know?"

Paedur paused a moment before replying, and then he turned his head slightly, looking at the two men. "You've heard of the recent events in the Southlands, in and around the capital?" he asked, seemingly ignoring the question.

Nevin glanced at Aeal before turning back to the bard. "We've heard rumours of course. But a change at court has no effect upon us in any way. Our task is to keep the Chopts from the Southlands."

The bard nodded briefly. "But you do know that Geillard is no longer Emperor?"

The two men nodded. "We heard you deposed him," Aeal muttered.

"People and rumour have a habit of ascribing victory—or defeat—to one person or thing," Paedur said, with a ghost of a smile. "With some little assistance from those who had elected to follow him, and the help of the Pantheon, I put Kutor on the throne," he continued, studying their faces carefully, wondering how they would react. Even with his god-enhanced senses, he sometimes found it difficult to gauge a person's snap judgement or reaction.

"It doesn't sit well with me to acknowledge a bandit my Emperor," Nevin grumbled.

"There is royal blood in him," Paedur said, "albeit on the wrong side of the blanket."

"The Gods of the Pantheon approve this choice?" Nevin asked.

"They do. He is a good man. Honest after a fashion, strong, not so easily led, but willing to follow advice, and loyal to the Faith. Because he was a Wasteland bandit, he realised the danger of the beast-folk, so one of his first acts was to begin preparations for the building of a series of defensive forts on the far side of the Mion River in the blind-spots between the Seven Bastions on this side."

"I've been advising that for years," Nevin grunted.

"Well, it will happen soon."

"Is that why you're here?" Aeal asked.

Paedur shook his head, but said nothing.

When the silence had lengthened, Nevin asked quietly, "Well, why are you here? Who sent you?"

"No one knows I'm here, and that is the way I would like it kept." The bard turned back to the fire and settled into his chair, suddenly—foolishly—wishing he could sleep again. The Gods of the Pantheon had granted him many gifts—immortality, almost complete invulnerability, the ability to divine men's thoughts, to perceive the aura of all living things, to call down Power—but the cost had been high, and he had lost much of his humanity. The bard was seldom seen to eat, neither did he drink anything except water, and he was never known to sleep. He regretted that loss most of all. "What I tell you now is no great secret, but equally, it is not common knowledge. So perhaps it would be better if you were not to discuss it with others, even with the other holders of the Bastions." He looked quickly at the two men. "Well?"

"Yes…"

"Of course…"

Paedur looked back to the fire, staring deep into the flames, his eyes flickering in unison with their movements. "Kutor's great victory at Karfondal was not as decisive as perhaps it should have been, and certainly not as decisive as he would have wanted. It was practically bloodless for a start, and whilst that was no bad thing, there can be no denial that blood is an excellent purge; it allows demons to be exorcised, old angers, ancient enmities to be washed away, and when the killing is done, there is a sense of relief that it is over, and a resolution that it must never happen again. Much can be achieved in such an atmosphere." He lifted his left arm, allowing his hook to ring off the table. "But that didn't happen.

"And of course, Geillard escaped.

"But his private circle of counsellors had been destroyed. Salier had been slain, as was Barthus the Hierophant, although because his corpse wasn't found, it has been assumed that he fled with the Emperor; and Fodla shifted her allegiance over to the new ruler. Their position has now been taken by Owen, the infamous Weapon Master, and Keshian, formerly Kutor's Commander but now the new Emperor's Chief Counsellor. Fodla has retained her position as Commander of the Emperor Legion and the Imperial Army, but her reputation has suffered somewhat because she shifted sides just before the decisive moment.

"Kutor left the old ruling clans—the Twelve Families—of Karfondal intact; it would have been suicidal to attempt to oust them now, and indeed he has left everything much as it was except that he has installed the Old Faith as the official belief in the Nations." Paedur shrugged. "I had insisted on it; it was part of the price of my aid. However, Geillard was a convert to the Religion, and the New Religion had gained many converts during the deposed Emperor's reign and the Hierophant's excellent missionary work. The Religion is a belief which appeals to the wealthy and those in power, and nearly all the ruling families in the capital follow the Religion; naturally, these people were reluctant to accept a new ruler—especially a new ruler who followed the Faith.

"And lest you think that all of this had left the Gods unscathed and untouched, both the Faith and the Religion had lost their Deathgods!" Paedur smiled grimly; both 'deaths'—if the figure of Death could truly 'die'—were attributable to him. "But Kutor's accession to the throne made the Religion step up its campaign to win converts. Miracle cures, sudden growth in desolate places, unseasonal flowering and fruiting of trees and bushes have drawn many to the New Religion. Of course the Old Gods retaliated, but slowly, slowly, and even now the battle rages." He paused and added softly, "And then of course the rumours began."

"What rumours?" Nevin interrupted.

Paedur seemed almost startled by the man's abrupt question. "Why, that Geillard is plotting to overthrow the Usurper from a base in the Northlands, with a Chopt army at his back."

Nevin grunted derisively, but stopped suddenly. "It might explain the beasts' sudden activity and boldness," he said, almost to himself.

"How much credence do you put in that rumour?" Aeal asked the bard.

"Enough to come into the Northlands looking for him," he said, turning back to the fire and closing his eyes, terminating the conversation. What he didn't tell them was that the rumour had been confirmed by an impeccable source.

Death had come for the bard in the last muggy days of summer.

Paedur had been deep in the bowels of the Imperial Library at Karfondal, sitting in a darkened corner with his back against the cool stone, reading a slab of waxed wood which had been inscribed with the fine curling script of the Susurun. It told the legend of the Lady Esanne who had loved one of the dark ancient folk and who had borne the only known child of mixed blood, the Magus Narre.

The bard turned the tablet of wood and placed it face down in its cloth-lined protective box and was reaching for the fourteenth and final slab of wood when he experienced the unmistakable tingle of power along the curve of his hook. The curling runes sparkled briefly and then died, drawing into themselves all traces of the power that still lingered in the long darkened room. Paedur rested his head against the stone wall and allowed his consciousness to expand and his enhanced senses to come to the fore, questing the darkness and his surroundings. He was alone on this, the deepest of the library's four basement floors. On the floor above him was the librarian, an old man who had seen three—now four—Emperors take the throne, and he had watched them come without interest or even care. But he had never been so frightened in all his life as on the day the bard

had descended on the library like some Duaiteoiri, and proceeded
to scour the shelves, delving deep into portions of the great library
that had remained untouched in centuries. Even now, Paedur could
sense his fear and vague resentment of the strange unhuman creature in his domain. On the floor above the librarian were two scholars, monks of the Order of Ectoraige, the God of Learning and
Knowledge, and they were deep in their studies, one reading Cambris'
Heraldic Genealogies, the other—Paedur suppressed a smile—making
notes on the *Life of Paedur, the Bard.* Other than these the library was
empty, the cramped, book- scroll- chart- ledger- wood- stone- and
skin-filled rooms proving too hot and uncomfortable in the op-
pressively humid weather.

But what had fired his hook? Paedur touched the incised metal
with his fingertips; it was now cool to his touch, which usually indicated that no danger threatened.

Usually.

Paedur stood, coming fluidly and silently to his feet, but he
didn't step out of the niche holding the Susurun writings. He looked
out across the floor. This portion of the library had originally
been a wine cellar, and it showed in the construction and layout of
the floor. A series of arched niches ran along both walls, and
whereas they had once contained wines of different vintages, times,
and origins, they now held writings from different eras, schools of
thought, or writers. Down the centre of the floor ran a series of
low chart-chests, holding sea-charts and maps not only of this
place but of most of the Planes of Existence. The only entrance
to the cellar was by the stairs at the far end of the long room; there
were no windows, and no light. The bard had been reading in
total darkness.

Paedur looked from niche to niche, his enhanced sight bringing
the room to a dull amber, speckled with shifting, twisting lines and
spots of brighter, harder colours. When the colour obscured the
object, he interpreted the shifting patterns of colour as books or
scrolls, manuscripts or rune-etched wood or stone, the natural materials still retaining a little of their original auras. But all these niches
seemed to be empty.

Perhaps he had been imagining it. Shaking his head, he turned
away, about to return to his reading when a hand reached out and
touched his face just below the eye!

Abruptly terrified—both by the presence and the failure of his powers—he reacted instinctively, his left arm snapping up, the curve of his hook aiming to take the person low in the body and then rip upwards, opening a huge wound from stomach to chest.

His arm struck stone—unnatural stone too, for his blade was capable of sundering stone. The shock sent him reeling, his arm and chest instantly, totally numb. He staggered back, crashing into the piles of ancient wooden tablets, scattering them to the ground.

Death stepped into the niche. "Slow and hasty, bard, if that is not a contradiction."

Paedur looked up into the night-black face of Churon, once the infamous Onelord and now the Deathgod of the Old Faith. The god's bright blue eyes were sparkling with humour. The bard sat up, rubbing his aching shoulder, moving his elbow, loosening the stiffness, and then he examined his hook. He had struck Death's cloak; although it was as supple as cloth, it was actually made of stone from the Silent Wood, the domain of the Dead. The bard's own furred cloak had similar properties. His hook seemed to be undamaged, the magical blade surprisingly unmarked, unchipped.

"You've grown strong," Paedur grunted, coming to his feet, "or perhaps I'm losing my powers. Usually I can detect the presence of a god...indeed, magical forces of any kind."

Churon smiled broadly, his teeth startlingly white against his ebon skin, matching in colour his closely-cropped hair. "You've become over-familiar with my presence," Death said. "And then again, perhaps I have come into my full powers. My predecessor, for all his bluster, was content to use barely a fraction of the position's full authority. Of course, he may have been unaware of the forces Death can command."

Paedur brushed past Churon, his hook blazing cold blue light with the proximity to the god, and stepped out into the cellar. He strode over to a map-case and then turned to look back at the god. "What do you want with me now? I've given the Pantheon what they wanted; I put a follower of the Faith on the throne."

Churon grinned, but without humour. "And now I'm afraid you must work to keep him there."

"My part is done," Paedur said firmly.

"You are still the Champion of the Faith," Churon reminded him, a chill note entering his voice, his smile now nothing more than a twisting of his thin lips. "You knew that was something you could not leave off when you were tired of it, like a worn cloak."

The bard nodded, almost wearily. "I know. But there seems to be no end to it."

"There will never be an end to it—not while we have two prime religious systems vying for the belief of a limited number of followers." Churon moved over to the bard, his footsteps sounding vaguely gritty although the floor was clean, almost as if he were walking on gravel. Paedur was briefly reminded of the time he had walked Death's Domain, the Silent Wood: it too was covered in a fine gritty gravel. Death stooped and pulled a long linen chart from beneath the table. Moving the bard gently to one side, he rolled open the chart, Paedur automatically holding down one edge with the flat of his hook.

It was the Scalae map—an original—and the most perfect representation of the geography of the Seven Nations, from Thusaland in the north to Lostrice in the south, and even showed the fabled Southern Continent in outline. It back dated before the Cataclysm, which had changed the face of the entire Plane of Existence, especially along the coast.

Churon tapped the top left-hand corner of the map, in the trackless white ice-fields beyond Thusal, the northernmost town. "Geillard is in the Northlands in one of the hidden Chopt towns, probably in the capital. He has a score of Gallowglas mercenaries by his side, as well as some of the Torc Allta, the Boar-Folk, a dozen priests of the New Religion, about two hundred of his own followers, those who either fled with him or went to him later…plus nearly three thousand Chopts."

"I didn't think there were three thousand in the whole of the Northlands," Paedur murmured.

"They are usually a solitary people, but they have been brought together by the presence of Geillard, who has made many promises, especially of land and title in the Southlands. More importantly, though, they have been drawn together by the twelve priests of the Religion: they have promised—and delivered—miracles. The Chopts now worship the gods of the New Religion, and when they kill, they kill in their name!"

"Blood sacrifice!"

Churon nodded. "Blood sacrifice of the most powerful kind. Whatever victory we gained when Kutor took the throne has been negated—possibly we are even worse off than before. Our plan, successful though it seemed, has actually worked against us. Is there a lesson in that for us, I wonder?" he asked. "Those whose allegiance to the Religion was never firm, have suddenly become fanatical, and the followers of the Faith have become...well, shall we say lazy in their devotions? The Faith has become complacent, while the Religion has been forced to work all the harder for converts—and they are reaping that reward now."

Paedur looked at the chart, remembering the last time he had walked the King Road to the North. That had been...how long ago now? It would have been shortly—no, immediately—after he had been gifted by C'lte the Yellow God...and that had been the beginning of it all. On that road he had met the Weapon Master, Tien tZo, Keshian...and Kutor. He shivered suddenly; had the wheel turned? "What do you want me to do?" he asked tiredly.

"Go north," Death said decisively, "as swiftly and as secretly as you can. Go north...and destroy this conspiracy!"

"You mean kill Geillard?" Paedur asked cynically.

"Kill Geillard, the priests of the Religion, and whatever leaders hold the Chopt clans together. Without them, the Chopt army will disintegrate into individual warring clans, and the threat will be negated." Churon shrugged.

"And if I fail?" Paedur wondered.

"Then the Chopts will come streaming out of the Northlands, and in the resultant butchery—and every death a sacrifice to the Religion, remember—their gods will grow too powerful for the Pantheon to contend with. They will destroy us, and you, of course. Yes, they will have something special in mind for you."

Paedur smiled humourlessly. "Is that supposed to frighten me?"

Churon showed his teeth in a mirthless smile. "Bard, if the Gods of Faith and Religion go to war, then the resultant destruction will wipe the myriad planes of life clean of all life, possibly for ever."

"And I must do it alone, I suppose?"

"Do it whatever way you can, bard, but do it soon," Death said, and merged back into the stone walls, and was gone.

3
The Assassin

And in the early days there were several attempts on the Emperor's life...
The Warrior, the Life of Owen, Weapon Master

In a matter of moons, the price on Kutor's head doubled and then redoubled...
Tien tZo

The assassin was small and slight and female.

She had boldly walked in with the evening staff as they were coming on duty. She carried a coloured chip which proclaimed her a rooms-maid, the irregular edge of which matched a similar chip in the guard's possession. There was no admittance without the chip. The assassin made her way through the servants' quarters and up various back stairs and servants' corridors, taking to the palace corridors only when absolutely necessary, and then moving swiftly and in absolute silence. She was challenged only once, and the guard had been more curious than alarmed at finding a small, young-looking woman marching boldly down the centre of the corridor. When he called her, she had turned, smiled, and walked up to him without hesitation. She was still smiling as she drove the slim poisoned spike up through his eye into his brain, and the same smile only wavered slightly as his blood spattered across her patterned rust-coloured gown. But it mattered little; when the blood dried it would fade into the pattern and become indistinguishable.

Two floors further up the assassin stopped to orient herself, vividly recalling the plans her employers had provided. The corridor here divided and divided again, each one leading to the office of one of the many Imperial functionaries. Her decision made, she took off down an insignificant side corridor, moving swiftly now, keeping to the wall, a slender handleless throwing dagger resting lightly in her cupped palm. She would not be so lucky to be challenged on this floor. Standing orders called for an intruder to be slain without question, without hesitation. There had been a previous attempt on the Emperor's life, and it had been a close enough thing, she had heard.

The young woman stopped at the second door from the end of the corridor, her every sense tingling. There was no light coming from beneath the door and she gently pressed her sensitive fingers against the wood, listening with them, but there were no vibrations, no sounds from within. She moved her hand, pressing just above the lock, and pushed, but the door didn't move. Removing a flat finger-length piece of metal from her sleeve, she slid it into the jamb of the door and pushed upwards, lifting the simple bar, and she was in.

She had been provided plans of this room also, charts which her employers had drawn from memory and she hoped that memory hadn't been playing them false. Moving slowly and in complete darkness, she made her way across to the bed, which was against the left hand wall. She reached out and up with her right hand and touched heavy, hanging cloth, and then slowly, infinitely slowly, she pulled the curtain back to admit a wan night light. It was enough for her to make out the vague shape of someone sleeping in the bed. Taking the covers between forefinger and thumb she carefully peeled them back, ensuring that it was the person she wanted. Lying curled up in a ball on the bed was a naked female. Satisfied, the assassin killed her swiftly and noiselessly with a blow to the throat.

Turning back to the window, she pulled the heavy curtains fully open and looked out. Beyond and below her Karfondal lay spread out in all its capital splendour, but the assassin had no eyes for it. She had been raised in the tenements of the Lower City: she knew its every sight and smell; she knew the rot that lurked beneath the paint; she knew the unmarked but clearly demarcated line that separated the Lower from the Upper City. Karfondal might be the capital, but two wildly differing cities existed within the boundary walls.

Shaking her head slightly, she turned away from the vista and looked up; she was pleased to find that there was no light from the room above. The man she had come to kill, the Emperor Kutor, had obviously retired for the night.

The assassin moved back into the room and pulled off her rust-red gown. Beneath, she was wearing a simple leather jerkin over leather breeks, and strapped around her waist were two knives, one broad and heavy, the other a slim stiletto. Around her wrist, secured by studded leather bands, were a dozen throwing spikes, and there were two matched throwing knives strapped low on her calves. Pulling on a pair of fingerless leather gloves, she touched her weapons, checking them, and then moved back to the window. She pulled herself up easily and without apparent effort so that she was standing on the window ledge. Her fingers sought—and found—holds and she levered herself out of the room and up onto the wall.

The climb up the wall proved to be surprisingly easy. The palace was one of the oldest buildings in an already ancient city. It had originally been built by the Culai, the First Race, but had been added onto by successive generations. The walls were pitted by time and the elements; at one time a tenacious creeping vine had covered most of the wall, and although a drought had taken it, it had left the wall scarred in a score of places.

The assassin continued climbing until she was level with the balcony of the room above, and then she waited; clinging to the wall, her every sense alert, listening, watching, even smelling, but there were no noises, no signs or sounds of movement from the room within—and the only smell was the bitter-sweet smell of a quenched candle.

Satisfied, the assassin moved over onto the balcony and dropped down, and once again she waited patiently. She had nearly two hundred kills to her credit, and she owed them all to the extraordinary degree of care and planning she undertook before their execution, and then the caution she used while actually making the kills. An assassin usually only made one mistake—and that was the fatal one. She stilled her breathing and waited until her pounding heartbeat had slowed, listening, listening all the time. And only when she was completely satisfied that there was no one awake within, did she draw her heavy-bladed knife and enter through the open shutters.

With her eyes now fully adjusted to the light, she spotted the Emperor's bed immediately. The gods were with her; he slept alone tonight, although he occasionally took one of the females to his bed with him, and while she had no compunction about killing the Emperor and his bed-partner, she was only being paid for one. Well, this was going to be easier than she had thought. Where was the Emperor's much vaunted security? Where were the dreaded Emperor Legion, each one sworn to give her life for his?

The assassin moved over to the edge of the bed and raised her knife, adopting a two-handed chopping hold. Using the weight of the blade, she was going to remove his head.

Ice-cold steel touched her throat. "Move and I will cripple you!"

And then the light hit her like a blow.

When her eyes had cleared and she could see again, she found that the room had filled with people, and all of them were armed and armoured. She had either been expected or she had tripped an alarm along the way. She recognised some of the people in the room. Facing her was Fodla, the Weapons Maid, Commander of the Emperor Legion, formerly Geillard's personal bodyguard and now providing the new ruler with the same service. She was a tall, broad woman with flaming red hair and green eyes that had much the same glitter as broken glass. There was a savage grin on her face, her teeth bared in something that could never have been mistaken for a smile.

Beside her stood the legendary Weapon Master, Owen. He was as tall as Fodla, although not so broad, and his rough handsome features bore the scars of a lifetime of campaigning. His close-cropped hair, recently iron-grey, was now turning white. Owen's face was stone and completely expressionless.

The assassin moved her head slightly, drawing blood where the curved sword scraped the flesh of her throat, but she confirmed her suspicion: the Shemmat, Tien tZo, stood behind her.

In the long silence that followed no one spoke, no one even moved, until there was a noise in the hallway beyond and then Kutor, once bandit, now Emperor, followed by the short, stout figure of Keshian, strode into the room.

He stepped up until he was almost touching her, and the assassin was surprised to find that they were of a height, and somehow that robbed him of his dignity. "Well, an assassin." The Emperor's voice was surprisingly neutral, but his broad features were set in ugly lines. "I have two dead people below, a guard and a serving girl. The girl, I presume, was killed because her room lay directly below mine."

The assassin remained silent. She was assessing her chances of making a break for the window; if she could throw herself out... catch the balcony below...

"You are a professional," Kutor said suddenly, startling her, "a paid killer. I will double whatever price is on me and allow you to go free if you give me the names of your employers."

The woman continued to look at him. There was a curious tone in his voice, one almost of pleading. She looked closely at his face for the first time, and found it softer than she had expected, the

wrinkles around his eyes and mouth making it seem vaguely feminine—but it only confirmed the rumours she had beard that he was
indeed a puppet, and that his spectacular campaign through the
Outlands and on into the Nations had been little of his doing. She
decided he was a weak man—and weak men were usually squea-
mish, and easily manipulated. And here he was offering to double
her payment for information she would freely give. She was not
paid to endure torture; she felt no obligation to her employers.

Kutor—who had watched greed in men's eyes for too long—
recognised the change in her expression, and knew what her answer would be. But for good measure, he added smoothly, "If
you do not feel like selling me the names," he continued, "I will
walk out of this room and leave you to these people. You know
Fodla; you are aware of her reputation. And perhaps the Weapon
Master's reputation is known to you also. However, you will not
be so familiar with the Shemmat, Tien tZo. He is reputed to be
able to extract information from a stone. He enjoys it." Kutor's
lips curled in a thin, cruel smile. "Why, I remember the last
person...he cut them up, but slowly, slowly, keeping them alive
and in their senses and then he ate their flesh before their eyes—
while they still had eyes, that is. How would you like to see the
Shemmat consume you piece by piece?"

"I have no loyalty to my employers," the assassin said suddenly.

"I didn't think you would have," Kutor observed.

"But I don't know their names," the assassin continued quickly.
"I only met their representative."

"Where?" Fodla growled.

"A tavern in the Lower City. I don't know its name, I'm not
even sure it has one, but it's off Shop Street, close to the spice
merchant's. I've lived there all my life and yet I've never known the
name of that tavern; it has a blue door..."

Fodla nodded. "I know it."

"A man called Stinger is their agent. He contacted the Guild of
Assassins, asking for me particularly. I met him in the tavern where
he outlined the mission, giving me to understand that he had backing
from those closest to the throne. When we agreed on the price he
provided me with the plans of the palace defences and the room
layouts which he had obtained from his employers..."

"What am I worth?" Kutor asked with a slight smile.

The assassin smiled, but it lent her pinched, sharp face no humanity. "The highest price on the market at the moment is a standing reward offered by the New Religion for the bard Paedur—a thousand thousand pieces of fist-weight gold."

Kutor gasped. A thousand pieces of fist-weight gold would keep a whole kingdom in grain and fuels for a year. A thousand thousand pieces was an incredible price; why, when he had been running in the Outlands as a bandit, the highest price on his head was around one hundred silver pieces, or the equivalent of ten gold pieces.

"But there is a price of one thousand pieces on your head," the assassin continued.

"A king's ransom indeed," Owen said softly.

"And you have promised me twice that," the assassin reminded the Emperor.

"I haven't forgotten. But tell me more about this Stinger and the people he represents."

"I know very little about him," she said, attempting to shake her head, and then remembering the blade at her throat. "He is well known in the Lower City as an arranger, a fixer. He deals in whatever will yield a profit: contraband, weapons, slaves, information. He has contacts at court and in the church and he often arranges assassinations or abductions for them. I don't know who he is working for, but that shouldn't be difficult for you to discover. You made many enemies when you took the throne from Geillard."

Kutor grinned broadly. "The Twelve Families have made their feelings clear."

"It is common knowledge that they wish to overthrow you, and return Geillard to the throne. Even now an army is supposed to be gathering in the north which will sweep down to oust you and restore the old order. You must have heard the rumours."

"I've heard them."

"That is all I know," the assassin finished. "Now you must pay me."

Kutor nodded slowly. He looked into the woman's hard, dead eyes, and smiled. "Could I pay you to kill this Stinger for me?"

She nodded quickly. This would be a profitable night. She had already received half the payment due on Kutor's death, which was five hundred pieces...and she had been promised double the full price...two thousand pieces...and now a quick and easy kill...and possibly the man Stinger would be carrying the second half of the payment on him. It was time she retired anyway…headed south, made for the islands…and with two and a half or three thousand fist-weight pieces of gold to spend, she could live out the rest of her days in absolute luxury.

"How much?" Kutor asked.

"One hundred gold pieces, fist-weight."

Kutor began to nod and then stopped and seemed to be considering. "But if I pay you, how do I know you will not betray me as you have betrayed your present employers?"

The assassin frowned, unsure what he meant…

Kutor turned away. "Kill her."

"You promised!" she screamed, and then Tien tZo snapped her neck with a single blow of his fist.

Fodla stood looking down at the body, her huge hands on her hips. "Sometimes," she said to no one in particular, "I forget that he was a bandit before he became Emperor."

"Do you place so much faith in his word, then?" Owen asked quietly.

"But he promised her money and freedom, and if he breaks his promise to her, what will he do to us when the time comes, eh?" she demanded fiercely.

Owen shook his head. "I've never trusted him. 'Beware the word of a prince or a god,'" he quoted and turned away.

Keshian followed the Emperor into the tiny room he was now using as a bed chamber, and had been since he had first taken the throne; the Imperial bed-chamber was nothing more than a carefully laid trap. Keshian was now the closest person Kutor had to a friend, and one of the very few he actually trusted.

He came straight to the point. "I suggest we move on this inn, take this Stinger and extract the names of his employers. If we don't stop this now…well, the gods alone only know where it may end."

Kutor turned up the oil lamp; the room had no windows, no skylights and only one door, and that had been magically keyed to Kutor's touch alone—only he could open it. The room itself was tiny, and had once been used as a storage cupboard. It held a bed, an old wooden table and two chairs, and there was a large wooden chest at the foot of the bed. Propped up against one wall was a crossbow and a sword. The room was a cell—but at least Kutor could sleep secure at night. "What do we do if this man doesn't know the names of his employers?" The pale yellow light from the lamp washed his features, deepening the shadows under his eyes, aging him.

"He had to have a contact; we'll find that contact and work back from that..."

Kutor nodded wearily, pulling off his sword belt, tossing it onto the table and then dropping down onto his bed still fully clothed. "It was easier when I was a bandit," he said, looking at the high ceiling. "You knew who your friends were; you knew who to trust..."

The short stout man nodded. Recalling his own days as a battle-captain with one of the minor lords, he could sympathise; it had been easier then, much easier than his present position as the Commander of the Imperial Army.

"Do what you have to do," Kutor said finally. "Find this Stinger, and discover what he knows. And then I want you to take this city apart, find those who oppose me, and exterminate them. We'll stop this now. You're right: if it continues, it'll start a rot that will threaten everything the bard has worked for, and I think I owe him enough to make some attempts to protect it."

"There's no word," Keshian said quickly, anticipating the Emperor's next question. "We have news of him heading north, and then he vanishes. Perhaps he has moved on to one of the other Planes of Existence; perhaps he has gone back to the Silent Wood again, or to the Lands of Life Eternal—we just don't know." He paused and added quietly, "Oh, and Katani has disappeared, also."

The Emperor sat up quickly. "Where? When?"

"It was only confirmed earlier this evening, but she has not been seen since early morning, and she didn't appear for her meals all day. So I sent a guard to her rooms just before twilight, but he found the door open and the room empty. If you want my opinion, she's headed north after the bard."

"There is a spot in that iron-hard killer's heart of hers for him," Kutor grinned.

"You think so? I think she'd have a better chance with a Chopt than with the bard; whatever was human in him is long gone now."

The Emperor nodded. "Aye; we all lost something when we took this road, eh, Keshian? But the bard, I fancy, lost most of all."

The man called Stinger sat in a corner in the nameless tavern on Shop Street, his eyes on the shadow thrown by the rising sun that was slowly shifting across his much-scarred table. It was well past dawn and the assassin should have been here by now. What in the name of all the gods was keeping her?

He was a tall, thin, hard-faced man, whose pale grey eyes betrayed something of his furtive character: they were constantly moving, never resting long enough on anyone or anything. His clothing was nondescript and of poor quality, and he could have passed unnoticed in any crowd—which was exactly what he intended.

Although not usually a nervous man, he found his palms were sweating this morning, but he put it down to the five hundred pieces of fist-weight gold around his waist—it was as heavy as a suit of full battle-armour. He would give her another few moments and then he would go; there was an alternative meeting place they had arranged for noon, but he knew if he hadn't heard from her by noon, then she was dead and the mission failed. In fact, he had half a suspicion that something was badly wrong—the woman had never failed before. The only thing which kept him in his seat was that he had heard nothing from his sources at the palace, and surely if an attempt had been made on the Emperor's life he would have heard something...unless...unless of course the Emperor was already dead and the palace had been sealed! If that was so, then the palace would be in an uproar while Kutor's friends frantically attempted to regain control, perhaps even arranging to place a figurehead on the throne...

Then again, if the Emperor was dead, perhaps they were gathering their belongings and as much coin, metal, or precious stones as they could carry. In any case they would seal the palace tight. Of course, that must be it! In better spirits now, he raised his arm to order another drink...

...and a pike burst through the thin shell window beside him, the barbed head touching the soft flesh just beneath his ear!

Simultaneously, doors to two of the rooms upstairs burst open and archers appeared, the weapons levelled at his chest. A crossbowman appeared in the kitchen doorway, followed by two pikemen.

Finally the inn door opened and Fodla tramped in. The Commander of the Legion was wearing full armour and the colours of the Emperor Legion, and in that moment, Stinger realised he was a dead man. The huge woman crossed the floor in two long strides, hooked her foot into a chair and spun it around towards her. Then she sat and stared at the terrified man for what seemed like an eternity.

Stinger's thin face was ashen, his slightly protruding eyes bulbous and darting. He kept licking his thin lips.

Finally Fodla spoke. "An employee of yours gave us your name before she met with a fatal accident."

For a brief moment Stinger thought about denying it, but as his eyes drifted across Fodla's face, he realised the Commander would just as likely kill him out of hand if he made some excuse.

"You have some information which is of interest to me," the woman continued, her huge hands resting lightly on the wooden table between them. Stinger looked at the hands, immediately re-calling the story about the time an island wildcat had come ashore from a boat in the harbour. The creature had killed three men and badly mauled two others, before Fodla had grabbed the creature in her huge hands and snapped its spine across her knee. His darting eyes moved across her face again, and he realised she would kill or cripple him with just as much compassion.

Stinger swallowed hard. "How can I help?"

"Names." Fodla looked around. "Drinks here, innkeeper... rofion." She looked back at the shivering man. "Now, you can give me the name of the person or persons who contacted you and arranged for you to organise an assassination, and you can give me these names here, or we can go to the palace and talk there. But I'm afraid the Emperor is not in good humour at the moment, and I think your reception would be anything but pleasant."

"I know noth..." Stinger began.

"And if you were to say that you knew nothing, then I'm afraid all this will have been wasted, and if you are of no further use, then I'll just have to kill you."

Stinger nodded. "I'll tell you." His face took on a slightly shifty, cunning look, and his eyes settled on her face. "But would I be recompensed for this information?"

Fodla's urbane mask vanished, and she struck him backhanded across the table. Her metal-plated glove tore the flesh from his cheekbones and broke teeth, sending him sprawling against the wall.

"You want payment for telling us what you did?" she snarled. "You want payment because you arranged an assassination…well, then of course we'll arrange payment—in kind. Names!" she roared.

As Stinger struggled to his feet, his right hand found the stiletto hidden in his left sleeve. His fingers curled around the smooth bone handle; if he was going to die now he would at least take this ruthless…

Fodla's right hand moved—and a knife that was more like a short sword pinned the cloth of his sleeve to the table. The woman's face was set into hard, cruel lines, and when she smiled, it was nothing more than the drawing back of her lips over her teeth, much as an animal does before it feeds. "I know why you're called Stinger, but you won't use your little toy on me. Now I asked you a question. Answer me!"

"You can rot!" Stinger spluttered, blood dripping down his chin.

"You're going to tell me…sooner or later you're going to tell me. But do you think those you've been defending will appreciate what you've done for them, eh? All you'll have done is to buy them time—time to make good their escape, and continue on with their plans, with another messenger boy, another Stinger, or perhaps you'll have bought them time to arrange an assassination, eh? After all, they can't afford to allow you to live, can they?"

Stinger turned away and looked out through the shattered window. What the woman said was true: he owed his employers no loyalty, and they would have no hesitation about ordering his death, they had too much to lose…something on a nearby roof caught his attention, distracting him, but his vision was still blurred from where the woman had hit him, and he couldn't focus properly on it…

So he never saw the crossbow bolt that took him through the eye, killing him instantly.

Fodla tossed the stained crossbow bolt onto the polished table later that afternoon. "We scoured the area as thoroughly as we could, but you know the Lower City; it's a warren. An army could hide out there…" she began and then, realising what she was saying, shut up and sat down.

"So you discovered nothing," Kutor said softly. The late afternoon sunlight slanting in through the window washed around him in a dusky halo, lending him a slightly mystical air. This was the chamber formerly used by Geillard, where he had held all his conferences with his most trusted advisors. The new Emperor had continued to use it for that function, enjoying its warm, wood-panelled silence.

Kutor, Fodla, Keshian, and Owen were seated around the circular table, while Tien tZo stood perfectly at ease beside the door, the fingers of his left hand resting lightly on the wood, reading the activity in the corridor outside by the vibrations.

"I don't think we've learned *nothing,*" Owen said quietly, rubbing his hands through his thinning hair. "We know there is a definite conspiracy to oust you, probably headed by one or all of the Twelve Families; we know that Stinger knew the identity of one of the organisers, who was obviously someone of importance and probably someone close to you—otherwise why should this person bother to kill him? Now, what else do we know?" He touched the crossbow bolt with his forefinger. It was a black shaft of wood as long as a man's forearm, from elbow to little finger, and tipped with a broad-headed pyramid of metal. "This is a handmade piece—no common or soldier's shaft; it's probably even grooved and fitted for a particular weapon."

"An assassin's tool?" Fodla asked, reaching for the shaft and examining it again. The fletching was also black.

"Not especially, but a hunting tool, certainly. Now think, do you know of a lord here at court who uses black bolts, or has a black crossbow, or whose colours are black?"

"All of the nobility know how to use a crossbow of course..." Fodla said slowly.

"But with such skill?" Owen persisted. "We're talking about a shot of about five hundred paces, with the target below the bowman, in shadow, and behind glass—albeit broken glass. A difficult—nay, an almost impossible—shot to achieve."

"I know of no one at court using that colour bow or shafts," Keshian said, "and while some of the younger people adopt black dress, it is not the official colours of any of the nobility."

Owen gripped the bolt in his fist, his knuckles tightening around it. "This is our only lead."

"There must be an armourer in the city," Tien tZo suggested softly, "someone who deals with the nobility."

Owen grinned triumphantly. "Of course, of course! Someone who specialises..."

"I have just remembered something," Fodla said. "As Commander of the Imperial Army, I recently signed an order for several hundred thousand crossbow bolts and arrows to be made by various armourers across the city, and it occurs to me that each of these must have a distinctive style all of their own. Surely all we have to do is to bring the bolt to one of these armourers—and I think there is one in the palace at the moment—and ask them who they think made it?"

"The other thing we might do," Keshian, the Chief Counsellor, added with a grin, "is to put out the rumour that Stinger spoke before he was killed, and that even now we're putting together a case against his employers…It might be interesting to see who panics."

"You'd probably find yourself without a court in the morning," Fodla smiled.

Kutor raised his hand. "I think both ideas have merit. However, let us try and identify the bolt first, and then we'll think about Keshian's suggestion. I'm not sure anyone will fall for it, however," he added. "They know that if we had a name we would act immediately." He shrugged and looked at Fodla. "But try to get me a name. I want to know for whom that bolt was made." He stood up, abruptly ending the meeting. "Until later, then…"

Night had fallen before the huge Commander returned. Messengers brought Owen and Tien tZo and Keshian to Kutor's official bedchamber, where they found the Emperor, leaning against the window, looking out across the city. Fodla was standing to attention at the side of the huge bed, her strong face grim, but her green eyes sparkling with triumph. Tien closed the door and stood against it, and Kutor turned. His face was stone and there were shadows under his eyes. In his hand he held the crossbow bolt. He tossed the bolt onto the floor between Owen and Keshian, where it rolled around in a circle, its metal head clicking on the polished stones.

"Pick it up," Kutor said quietly, his voice unnaturally calm. "Hold it to the light, and look at the underside of the head."

Owen stopped, caught the bolt and brought it over to a smoking oil-lamp, where he and Keshian leaned over the light, turning the bolt to catch the light. There was a shape cut into the underside of the head…the familiar shape of a half moon…

Fodla looked straight ahead. "I was told that the bolt had been made for the one-handed storyteller, Paedur the Bard!"

4
The Survivor

North of the River Mion is an icy wasteland, inhabited by beasts and bandits. The next town of any note is Thusal, an important, but lawless trading town. Once one ventures onto the north side of the river one is beyond the law, beyond all retribution except that of the gods...

Lilis' Geographica

The creature was squatting on top of a tall pillar of stone on the hill above Castle Nevin on the wrong side—the northern side—of the Mion River.

Paedur had crossed the river with first light, walking across the frozen surface of the Mion's black water. When he reached the bank, he had turned and raised his hook to Nevin and Aeal, who were standing, watching him, while behind them smoke from the great funeral pyre of the slain Chopts hung almost completely motionless in the still early morning air. Burning the corpses had been the bard's idea; the beast-folk believed that a Chopt whose corpse was consumed by the flame and not by the members of his own clan would never reach his gods to find immortality. The pyre would have the effect not only of enraging the creatures but would also make them realise what would happen to their bodies if they were slain fighting along the Mion. The bard had also showed Nevin how the attack might be used to his advantage—and to that of all the Bastions along the river. This was the first time the beasts had actually attacked one of the ancient forts, and if reports of the numbers of beasts were exaggerated, it would almost certainly bring Imperial troops, and that would allow Nevin to place the district under the Rule of War. The Rules, which had been drawn up nearly two centuries previously, placed the control of the entire region in the hands of the most senior or experienced noble actually present. Amongst its many powers, it enabled this noble (in other words Nevin) to conscript every able-bodied man between the ages of fifteen and fifty summers, and call in all available food and weapons. As the bard had walked away, his footsteps barely creaking on the ice, Nevin had promised to call the Lords of the Seven Bastions together, and between them, they would raise the largest army the Northlands had ever seen to guard the Mion.

The bard walked up the hill, a tall, shapeless figure, enveloped in a hooded travelling cloak, noiseless after the recent light snowfall, making for a pillar he remembered from the previous occasion he had been here. When he crested the hill, he spotted the creature crouched atop it. It swivelled its horned head to look at him, the lacquered plates on its arms and legs rasping slightly.

"I'm freezing up here!"

"How did you find me?" he asked, his voice neutral.

"I am Katan." The voice, although distorted, was recognisably female; she unfolded her legs and dropped lightly to the ground. She then bent her head and twisted off the hideous helmet to reveal a broad square face, pleasant but not pretty, and a pair of hard amber-coloured eyes. Her hair was the colour of snow. She smiled humourlessly. "You don't seem overjoyed to see me."

"It concerns me that if you could find me then so could others…"

"I shouldn't think so."

"Then how did you know where I was?" Paedur demanded.

The woman didn't answer immediately, but hooked her helmet to her belt and settled the two swords she carried on either side of her waist. She glanced sidelong at the bard, but he was still looking at her, awaiting an answer. She sighed, knowing she couldn't try his patience; his appreciation of time differed to most other humans'. "I had help," she confessed eventually.

"Churon?"

"How did you know?"

Paedur shrugged and walked past the standing stone and the woman. Without looking over his shoulder, he said, "Only he knew where I was going. Did he tell you why?"

"He only told me I would find you at Castle Nevin," she said, hurrying to catch up with him. "My relationship with Death is still a little strained," she added with a wry smile.

The bard nodded, but said nothing.

The woman was Katani, a warrior-maid of the fabled female warriors, the Katan. Betrayed and murdered, she had spent many years in Death's Domain before finally encountering the bard on his travels through the Silent Wood. She had travelled with him through Death's Domain, and had helped him bring down Mannam, the renegade god. Partially as a gift for this service, and also through the bard's assistance, she had been able to return to the World of Men. But there was little love lost between her and Churon, the man who had originally killed her, and who now held the position as Deathgod of the Faith.

"How long have you been waiting?" Paedur asked abruptly.

"I saw you battle—or should I say butcher?—the Chopts yesterday morn. I was on the wall directly behind and to your left; I'm surprised you didn't sense me," she added.

"So am I," Paedur murmured. "Perhaps in the heat of battle..."

"So you were never in any great danger," she continued.

"That's comforting," he said, his voice and face neutral.

They continued on, comfortable enough in each other's company to walk in silence. The sky, which had been threatening all morning, grew darker around noon and it began to snow, great, soft, silent flakes that quickly blanketed the ground, obscuring even the vaguest traces of a path.

Katani pulled on her horned helmet and unrolled a thick travelling cloak from her pack and swung it around her shoulders. She pulled up the deep hood and shivered in her fleece-lined leather and metal armour. She was bitterly cold; she glanced sidelong at the bard, but as usual he seemed unaffected by the elements, and not for the first time she found herself undecided as to whether he was still of humankind or not.

She touched the bard's arm, and then drew her gauntleted fingers back with a yelp; something had stung, and when she looked at the fingertips of her gauntlets, she found they were scorched and blackened. "We had better seek shelter; it looks like it's down for the rest of the day."

Paedur nodded, the movement dislodging some of the heavy covering of snow that clung to the fine hairs of his cloak. He pointed with his hook. "Beyond the rise there is a fishing village, and a Monastery of Ectoraige; we're sure to find shelter there."

Katani nodded gratefully; her teeth were chattering together so loudly she couldn't talk. Paedur suddenly reached out and wrapped the curve of his hook around her armoured shoulder, the metal scraping on the lacquer. Katani watched the runes which were incised into the hook sparkle with a vague blue light and then warmth flowed through her shoulder and down into her body. This was no brief warming spell; this was a deep satisfying heat that seemed to come from within. Not for the first time, the Katan wondered what powers the bard possessed—and then she wondered, did he even know the half of them himself? Without saying a word, the bard turned away.

As they crested the hill, Katani realised that they had now reached the coast, and the breeze coming in off the stone-coloured sea was laced with sleet and ice, and drove the snow in almost horizontally. Even with the bard's warming strength within her, Katani knew they couldn't survive a night in this weather. "How much further to this village?" she called.

"It should be down..." Paedur began, then stopped suddenly, and even though the temperature was freezing, Katani felt the sudden chill that wafted from him. A tiny thread of blue fire crackled along the coarse hairs of his cloak.

Katani's hand immediately moved to her sword. "What's wrong?"

Paedur shook his head quickly, silencing her. The snow was now a blizzard, and visibility was almost down to nil. The only discernible features were the grey-black body of the ocean in the distance, and the indeterminate bulk of a building stuck high on the cliffs to her right.

"What's wrong?" she demanded, drawing her short sword.

"The village...the Monastery..."

"What about them?"

"They're dead"

The Monastery of Ectoraige was ancient. It perched atop the cliffs like a hulking beast left over from the dawn of the Planes of Existence. It was Culai built, and while its original purpose was obscure, it seemed more than likely that it had served wilder gods and demons than either the Faith or Religion, before the blue-robed followers of Ectoraige, the God of Learning and Knowledge, had converted the desolated building. It was of typical Culai construction: massively hewn stones that were not native to this plain, set one atop the other, perfectly joined without the aid of mortar. The gates were solid brukwood, the usually unworkable wood, smoothed and shaped by a craft or magic that had died with the Culai, and were bolted through with fist-sized square-headed rivets. There was a school at the foot of the cliffs, build around the crudely cut staircase that was the only entrance to the Monastery. The building had commenced nearly two hundred years previously, and successive generations had added to it as occasion and opportunity demanded. The school was constructed simply but solidly of cordwood which had been coated in what the fishermen called boat-paint, a distillation of various seaweeds which produced a thick, greenish tar which prevented boards from warping. During the summer months it stank, and even in the depths of the Cold Months it remained tacky. Young men interested in a life in the Brotherhood usually spent anything from three to five years in the school before climbing the thousand steps to the Monastery. But only a tiny proportion climbed the steps. The Monastery itself never held more than a hundred monks at any one time, but the School would usually have had up to five hundred young men studying in its long halls.

They had both been decimated.

Paedur and Katani moved swiftly and silently through the rambling school. It had obviously been attacked by what must have been a sizeable army of Chopts; their prints and their animal stench remained, their odours strong enough to overlay the marine smell of the tar paint and the sickly-sweetness of blood. The building had been surrounded by a palisade wall of sharpened stakes, more to keep marauding beasts out and wayward pupils in, than to repel a determined assault. The palisade had literally been torn apart in several places and the poles then used as a ram to shatter the main doors. Every door in the school had been shattered, the windows of horn and parchment paper torn or pulled out and the white-sanded floors scored with the marks of claws and bloody feet.

There was blood everywhere.

The sleeping chambers looked like an abattoir. Every bed was splashed with thick rust-brown stains and there was blood spattered all across the floor and in long speckled tracks up along the white-washed walls; even the low beamed ceiling hadn't escaped the spurting blood. Both Paedur and Katani knew the signs; the sleepers had had their throats cut, hence the spattered blood, which indicated a huge force, working together and in absolute silence. And that was most unusual, for the beasts, although clannish by nature, preferred to kill in private, and even then they usually proclaimed the death-blow with a triumphant warcry.

The bard and the warrior made their way to the heart of the school—the chapel. The long chapel to the Faith had been desecrated. Every statue had been destroyed, and the pews crushed and splintered. The holy books had been torn apart, their gilded leaves scattered across the room; the scrolls had been piled in the centre of the floor and fired; the prayer rugs had been rent in pieces and befouled. Someone had even pounded upon the marble floor in a score of places, sending a spider-web of cracks across the white stone.

Paedur spoke for the first time since entering the school. "This is not true Chopt work—they kill for flesh and sport, not for religion, and they care nothing for objects. They wouldn't have caused such wanton destruction."

"Unless they had been incited," Katani added quietly, glancing up at him. His sharp face was set in hard lines, and his eyes had taken the whiteness of the marble floor, turning them to stone.

"You can wait here while I go up," he said suddenly, startling her. He raised his head slightly, and she knew he meant the Monastery on the cliffs above.

"I think I'd rather go with you," the Katan said without hesitation.

Paedur nodded and abruptly turned away; Katani took one last look around and hurried after him, shaking her head, wondering what they were going to find in the building above.

The bard and the warrior-maid climbed the long, flight of stone steps that led up to the Monastery. It was long slow work, even for the bard; the steps were piled deep with snow above a sheathing of ice, each one having to be cleared before a foothold could be found, and with every step the icy wind threatened to hurl them down to the school building below. It was exhausting, both physically and mentally, and Katani found the very presence of the sheer drop on her right-hand side an additional drain on her energy. Before they were half way up, the bard was half-carrying an exhausted Katani, dragging her from step to step, his voice knifing deep into the lethal doze she had slipped into, dragging her back to consciousness, urging her on. By the time they reached the top of the steps he was bearing all the weight of her body clad in its ornate and heavy armour with no apparent effort. He put her down in the lee of a large

standing stone incised with the glyphs "Learning leads to Knowledge, Knowledge leads to Power—" and allowed a trickle of his
own strength to flow through his hook into her exhausted body.

The solid brukwood gates of the Monastery were still closed
and for a moment the bard allowed himself the brief fantasy that
the blue-robed monks were still alive and safe behind the walls, even
though his enhanced senses told him otherwise. But if the gates
were closed, then how had the creatures got inside?

He found the breach in the wall less than a hundred paces from
the gates; there was a huge gaping hole in the stone wall, and the
ground around the hole was littered with chunks of rock. It looked
as if a levin bolt had struck the stone, destroying it. Paedur knelt and
touched the wall with his hook, but the metal remained cold, the
runes dull, giving him no indication how the hole had been made.
But if it was magic—and it surely looked that way—then it was fire-
magic of sorts...and the Chopts abhorred fire. It was beginning to
look as if more than just the beasts had been in on the attack.

Paedur crawled through the opening, which sliced right through
the massive wall as thick as he was tall, and found himself in a tiny
courtyard which, although he had never seen one before, he immediately realised was the brothers' cemetery. The bodies of the monks
were usually burned and their ashes stored in tiny philtres of glass in
niches in the walls. If a monk had achieved special greatness or advanced either the cause of Learning or the Old Faith in general, then
the philtre might be made of crystal or even precious stone. A simple
plaque on the wall gave the Brother's name and age; if he had been
martyred then that was noted by the single word. But here the small
plaques had been ripped from the walls, the ground was littered with
shards of blue glass and covered in a layer of a fine grey-brown dust.

Paedur muttered a benediction as he stepped across the ashes
of generations of monks, and experienced a sudden burst of an
emotion—the first real emotion he had felt in a long time—an emotion which approached anger. This needless, senseless destruction
appalled him; there was no reason for this, no excuse, and again it
was completely out of character for the creatures. There was something more to this, something sinister.

Beyond the tiny courtyard lay a long, high hall, the intricate stonework and corbelling the hallmarks of the Culai master-builders. The
windows, set high in the walls to admit the wan northern light, had

once been glazed with delicate coloured glass depicting the Gods of the Pantheon, but each one had been systematically broken, which, the bard noted, had taken both time and effort. All the doors had been shattered, hacked with axes or swords, and the older doors, where the hinges had been of leather, had been completely removed.

This had all been done to a deliberate cold-blooded plan; only its purpose eluded him.

When Paedur flung open the Monastery's great brukwood gates, Katani immediately stepped back, both swords coming almost naturally to her hands. With the light behind him, and his eyes reflecting the snow, the bard was a black demon-shape with glowing silver eyes. He turned away without a word, and crossed the courtyard into the huge church building.

Katani hurried through the gates, suddenly reluctant to be alone on the wind-swept ledge before the gates. She slid her swords back into their sheaths, and put her back to one of the doors, unsurprised when it closed easily and noiselessly. Closing the second gate, she lifted the bar and dropped it into place, and then cranked the chains that locked the enormous metal hinges into position, rendering them immovable. The gates were locked for the night. She turned and hurried after the bard, feeling foolishly like a child, conscious of the creeping shadows around her.

Paedur was standing just inside the chapel doors, unmoving. His very stillness warned Katani and she slid her shortsword free and immediately moved to the right hand side of the door, stepping quickly inside, her back to the cold stone. Without looking at her, the bard pointed upwards with his fore and little fingers. She squinted up into the dimness, but could see nothing except the barest outline of the time-darkened rafter beams.

Paedur moved his right arm, urging her out into the aisle, towards the simple stone altar-piece which now lay shattered across the cracked marbled steps. He pointed to her sword and then to her belt, his instructions plain. Reluctantly, Katani sheathed her sword and, with a steadying breath, walked slowly and steadily out into the open...and immediately heard the sound. There was someone—or something—in the rafters. Her fingers touched the throwing spikes in her sleeves, and curled around the deadly slivers of metal. She needed another sound—another sound to identify the location of the creature—and then she would drop to the ground, roll, and throw...

"NOOOoooo...!"

The bard's command was ice-cold fire in her brain, stopping her in her tracks, almost sending her to her knees with its power. She half-turned—but found the bard had vanished. Throwing caution aside, she drew her swords and launched herself forward, moving across to a small side altar, and rolling through the arched entrance. Here at least she couldn't be seen from above. Crouching, she peered out into the chapel, looking for the bard; she eventually spotted him crawling up the wall like some hugely deformed spider, moving swiftly, scuttling sideways, then throwing himself away from the wall to catch his hook on a beam, and finally swinging himself around and up onto the beam, to stand unmoving on it. She became aware of other sounds on the beam, a squeal of—terror?—followed by the patter of feet across the wood. Speckles of dust drifted down from the rafters onto her face, making her blink, and turn away.

There was a sudden rasp of steel, and then she saw something small and pale move towards the still figure of the bard. The creature was carrying a long curved sabre that seemed far too large for it. The scream began then, a high-pitched wail of absolute terror and rage, coupled with a deep and terrible anger. The sabre fell, the bard's hook catching and entangling the blade, turning, twisting it, wrenching it from the creature's grasp, sending it whirling out off the beam. It plunged point first into a wooden pew and remained there, thrumming.

Katani stepped from the side chapel, a throwing spike aligned along her index finger...and then something launched itself at the bard, something small and white and blue.

Abruptly, all sound ceased.

Paedur stepped off the rafter...to land lightly on his feet before the startled woman. In his arms was a pale bundle.

Katani approached, trying to make sense of the white cloth-wrapped shape. "What is it?" she asked quietly, pointing with her sword.

Paedur gently lifted a long strip of dirty blue cloth, revealing a boy's filthy face. "It's a survivor," he said, with a humourless smile.

They camped that night in the ruins of the church, sheltering in one of the small side chapels. While Katani tended to the boy, Paedur dragged in some of the broken pews, chopping them up for firewood with his hook, using his hook again to strike sparks from the stones. When the wood was burning strongly, he went in search of water, returning a few moments late with a much-dented altar vessel piled high with crushed snow.

He crouched down beside Katani and looked at the still figure of the boy, now sleeping peacefully beneath the warrior-maid's heavy furred cloak.

"I can find no injuries," Katani said, glancing at the bard; in the firelight her amber-coloured eyes burned a deep red and her ice-white hair was burnished copper. "He is remarkably well, with the exception of some cuts, bruises, and scrapes, and from the condition of his fingers and toes, some mild frostbite. He hasn't eaten for a time, and I dare say hasn't slept well either."

Paedur nodded. He lifted the ragged blue robe which Katani had cut off the boy, turning it in his hand. "An acolyte of the Order; I wonder how he escaped." He stood up—and Katani abruptly noticed he cast no dancing shadow on the wall. "He will not awake until close to midnight. If you remain with him, I'll go and find you something to eat."

The warrior-maid sat back against the cold stone wall, her longsword unsheathed and lying across her knees; her shortsword by her side. Her armour, which had been crafted from the cast-off skin of the extinct ice-serpents of Thusal, protected her somewhat from the bitter cold, but she was still chilled, a deep internal feeling she hadn't been able to shake off since she had left Death's Domain. She reached out and touched the boy; he seemed surprisingly warm, and she wondered if the bard had any hand in that.

She looked at the boy, surprised by her own mixed emotions and the depth of her feelings of pity and sorrow at his plight and suffering. She had never felt the slightest maternal urge during her previous brief life in the World of Men, and she had died before she had gifted her clan with a child. The Katan were warriors; they fought and died without time for husband or family, without ties that might lessen their effectiveness as warriors. However, each woman was expected to bear at least one child for the Katan tribe. Usually the most auspicious time for conception was chosen by one of the Craft Women, which almost always ensured that the child was a girl, and the fathers were usually taken from the freelance male warriors who often accompanied the Katan. For the Katan walked with War, as the saying went, and a mercenary—male or female—might become wealthy fighting with the Katan allies. But Katani had never contributed her child to the warriors; she had never felt the urge, nor found a male warrior she respected enough. It had never bothered her before. She had never even thought about it until now...

When she had accompanied the bard from the Silent Wood back into the Planes of Existence she had resolved to do all the things she hadn't done in her previous life: to live her life to the full, to broaden her interests, and even to give up the sword. And of course she had done none of them. She had fallen all so easily back into the life of a warrior; killing was her only trade—and it was something at which she was a perfectionist. She knew a thousand ways to take a life...She looked down at the sleeping boy and wondered what it would be like to create a life.

She reached out, brushing a length of cobweb from his face, wondering about him. Who was he, and where had he come from and, more importantly, how had he escaped the slaughter? He was small and slender, with fine smooth skin, which was a light tan colour beneath the dirt and bruises. His face was small, almost round, and although his head had been shaved bald recently, a thin black fuzz had appeared. She found it difficult to guess his age, but his face was smooth, and there was no evidence that he shaved.

She moved his top lip slightly; his teeth were all intact, and reasonably clean. She then lifted his hand, looking at it. The skin was soft, the nails, although broken and cracked now, had once been smooth and even, and there was no evidence of welts or callouses either on his palms or fingers. He was from a family of wealth, and had obviously only lately come to the order. She knew it was customary for third or later sons of a lesser noble to be sent to the school for an education, but this boy had obviously been intended for the brotherhood—otherwise why had he been in the Monastery?

When she looked up, she found the boy had opened his eyes and was looking at her. His eyes were a deep, almost chestnut brown, and looked huge in the gauntness of his face. She gently laid his hand down, and then patted it, smiling in what she hoped was an encouraging manner, careful not to expose her pointed incisor teeth.

"I am Katani," she said slowly and clearly.

The boy nodded, attempting a smile. He opened his mouth—and screamed, his eyes wide with terror!

Katani whirled, her sword moving up and back in a back handed slash, her left hand drawing her shortsword as she was coming to her feet.

Her sword struck metal and then the long blade was caught in metallic half circle and twisted from her grasp. "Paedur," she breathed, and then realised what had frightened the boy: the figure standing in the doorway looked the very essence of evil, a shadowless black shape, eyes blazing red fire.

She sheathed her swords and knelt by the boy's side and wrapped her arms around him. He was gasping for breath, shivering uncontrollably. "SSShhh, ssshh now. It's all right. He's a friend. He will not harm you." His face was a rigid mask, his eyes squeezed shut, and she wasn't even sure if the boy could hear her. She looked up at the bard. "Help him, please."

Paedur stepped into the tiny chamber, the light flowing from his cloak like oil off water, and suddenly—swiftly—reached out and touched the boy lightly in the centre of the chest. He immediately slumped in Katani's arms, his features lax and at peace. He was breathing deeply, evenly. Katani then settled him back beneath the covers, and wiped the long trails of spittle from his chin and the tears from his cheeks.

Paedur tossed a pair of small birds into the corner beside the woman. "Will you prepare these?" he asked abruptly.

Katani nodded.

"The boy hungers; it would be better to have food prepared for him; it will help ease his fear. In the meantime, perhaps I can ease his troubled mind."

"How?"

The bard turned to look at the boy; he was sleeping easily now, his thin chest rising and falling beneath Katani's cloak, his features smooth and untroubled. Paedur reached out and, with the point of his hook, carefully pulled back the cloak from the boy's chest. He was naked beneath, the Katan having removed his soiled and damp clothing earlier; then the bard laid the flat of his hook across the boy's body. The metal glowed warmly red in the firelight, the twisting runes coming to a brief sparkling life, and the boy twisted his head, mumbling in his sleep. Beneath his closed eyelids his eyes darted.

"Who are you?" Paedur asked suddenly.

The boy's lips moved, moved again before they formed the single word, "Gire," he said, pronouncing it to rhyme with "fire."

"That's a Talarian name," Katani said quickly. "In my day there was a warrior in the Katan who bore the feminine version, Gireer."

Paedur lifted his hand, silencing her. "Where are you from?" he asked, his voice soft and gentle...and insistent.

"Talaria," the boy said quietly. His voice had grown stronger, and he now lay still and restful; only his eyes, behind his closed eyelids, were active.

"And what are you doing here?

"I am to be a monk in the Order of Ectoraige."

"And you are long here?"

"Less than one moon."

Katani, who had begun to pluck the two small birds the bard had brought, looked up and grunted. "Welcome to the Northlands."

"Gire, listen to me very carefully. I want you to open your eyes and look around you. You will see two people: a man and a woman. They are your friends: they mean you no harm. Now open your eyes, and look to your right..."

Gire's deep brown eyes snapped open, and settled on the woman. "This is Katani, a warrior of the fabled Katan. You have nothing to fear from her; she is a friend to the Faith. Now, look at me..."

Even in his enchanted state the boy's dulled eyes widened in shock...horror...recognition?

"Do you know me?" Paedur asked curiously. "Have we met?

"I have never met you before."

"But you know me?" Paedur persisted.

"I have heard tell of a man with a hook in place of his left hand."

"And who is that?"

"He is legend; he is the Bard Paedur."

"I am the Bard Paedur." He pulled back his cloak to reveal the bardic sigil high on his left shoulder. "Now, when I touch you, this enchantment will end, and you will awaken fully, and you will remember everything that has gone before. You will know us, and you will know you have nothing to fear." He lifted his hook off the boy's chest and touched him lightly with the fingers of his right hand.

Gire's eyes cleared, and it was as if life had flowed back into his face, animating it, bringing it alive. He sat up suddenly and looked from the bard to Katani and then back to the tall shadowed figure. "You really are the bard," he breathed. It was more a statement than a question.

Paedur nodded silently, his face expressionless.

"I know all about you; even in Talaria, you are legend—of course they don't believe you are real. But the monks taught us about you. I've always wanted to meet you…" The words tumbled over themselves in his excitement.

Paedur raised his hand, shaking his head to stop the flow of questions. "Later, all this can come later," he said softly. "Now you must rest and eat. Later, we will talk and decide your future."

"I'm going with you," the boy said impulsively.

Paedur shook his head. "You cannot go where I'm going."

"Is it true you're immortal, that you were gifted by C'lte, the Lord of Life, with Life Immortal?"

"I am long-lived," Paedur murmured.

"You cannot die?" the boy whispered in amazement.

"Oh, I can die," Paedur's lips curled in a smile, "but it seems I cannot stay dead. Now rest," he commanded. "We will talk later." His index finger touched the boy's forehead; the deep brown eyes immediately rolled upwards and the boy dropped back onto the makeshift pillow, asleep.

"What are we going to do with him?" Katani asked. She had plucked the birds and was now cleaning them out with a tiny knife.

"He cannot come with us." Paedur settled back against the cold stones, stretching out his long legs. He adjusted his cloak about his body and tilted his head back, closing his eyes. With the light gone from his eyes, and his pale expressionless face reflecting the flickering reddish-yellow light, he looked as if he had been carved from stone.

"What are we going to do with him?" Katani repeated.

"We will leave him in Thusal—there is a bardhouse there."

"Thusal is hardly the safest of places now, is it?"

"Safer than travelling on the road with us," the bard said quietly.

Katani contented herself with wrapping the birds into balls of soft clay and then pushing them deep into the fire with the point of her knife.

She looked up at the bard, and it took an almost deliberate effort of will to separate him from the shadows flickering across the wall. "Leaving the problem of the boy aside for the moment, have you decided what we are going to do?"

He shook his head briefly.

"Do you know where we're going, then?"

"Thusal," he said shortly.

"And then?"

"In search of Geillard if he is here in the Northlands, and in search of the intelligence behind these Chopt raids."

"And?"

"Kill them both."

Katani looked at him. "Why?"

"Because…" he began.

"Because the Pantheon, through Churon, ordered you," the woman interrupted.

Paedur nodded. "Perhaps not in so many words…"

"And you're not going to question that?"

The bard's eyes opened, the firelight blazing in them, reflecting back at Katani. She looked away quickly and concentrated on the fire, rolling the hardened balls of mud around with a twig. Without looking up, she said. "They've made you into their creature…"

"I know that. They paid me well for it, though," the bard said quickly, almost defensively.

"Did you ever have a choice? While I was in Karfondal, I heard the story of how you became the Champion of the Gods. They tricked you, and then used you, first to save themselves from the Religion and the Sealed Vessel of the Chrystallis, and then they used you to put Kutor on the throne and further the cause of the Faith, and now they're using you again. You've killed for them in the past and now you're planning to kill again—and all without question. You've become a *quai!*"

From the corner of her eye, Katani saw the bard's head coming up. "Even the Katan," she hurried on, "the finest killers on all the Planes of Existence, never killed without reason or just cause; it is the *reason* which differentiates simple murder from killing."

"Warrior," Paedur said, his voice almost cold, "I am a follower of the Old Faith. It is the One True Belief, and I am honoured to be its Champion. I will die—and kill—in its defence."

"Without question?"

The bard didn't reply.

"If you kill without question, you become little better than those you are killing."

Paedur closed his eyes without replying and bent his head, effectively ending the conversation.

Katani woke Gire a little later. She fed him water in sips, and then rolled one of the balls of fire-hardened mud from the fire. With the metal sleeve on her forearm she cracked it open, and the delicious aroma of roasted fowl wafted around the tiny broken chapel. Gire's stomach rumbled loudly. Katani peeled off the solid mud covering, the bird's wrinkled skin pulling away with it, and she passed the bird to Gire on the end of one of her knives. "Carefully, now; it's hot. Take small bites and chew thoroughly, otherwise you'll end up with a stomach-ache that not even the bard can cure." She cracked open the second bird for herself, impaling it on two knives.

Gire, his mouth bright with grease, looked at the apparently sleeping bard. "What about Paedur?"

Katani grunted around a mouthful of hot flesh. "Paedur does not eat, he does not drink and, despite appearances, he does not sleep."

The boy nodded, seemingly unsurprised. "Have you known him long?"

"Long enough," Katani grinned. "We spent some time dead together." She laughed at Gire's expression. "Eat your food. I'll explain later."

They continued eating in silence, Katani watching in amusement as he picked the bones clean. When he was finished, she passed him the remnants of the water the bard had brought earlier and a rag to clean his face and hands. He sat back, his spine against the stone and rested both hands on his stomach. "I feel human again."

Katani couldn't resist a smile. "Well, you're probably the only one of this company who is."

"I haven't eaten so well for...well...not since..." his eyes clouded.

"Do you want to tell me what happened?" Katani asked.

The boy shook his head slightly.

"It would help—both you and us," she said. "In my land there was a saying, 'Telling eases the trouble.'"

Gire looked at Paedur. "He can hear us," Katani assured him. "We need to know who attacked you, how many, what they were like…"

Gire nodded. He shivered suddenly and drew Katani's cloak tighter around his body, and then he looked into the fire, his eyes sparkling brilliantly with unshed tears. He took a deep sobbing breath and began…

"They came five—no six—nights ago. Hundreds of them.

"The evening meal was long over, and the mid-evening bell had rung, so it would have been sometime before the midnight bell, and most of the brothers by that time would have gone to their beds. The brothers disdain the use of artificial light, for they say it destroys the eyes and that knowledge should only be sought and absorbed in the pure light of day. So most retire to bed early, rising again just before the dawn.

"I was not abed, however, for I had received a summons earlier that day to attend the Master directly after the evening meal. I had been expecting the call for days, for I was new to the Order and had not yet had the opportunity to discuss my future with him, and it was said that he prided himself that he knew every man and boy's name, his family, country, and ambitions.

"But when I climbed the steps and was admitted into the Monastery I learned that the Master and the Teachers were all in conference together, and would in all likelihood be there for some portion of the evening.

"I didn't know what to do. Should I wait, or would it be better if I were to return on the morrow? But there was no one to advise me, and then I suddenly thought that this might be one of those tests the Teachers sometimes set a pupil: setting him a strange or difficult task, and then judging his performance. I decided to stay—at least for a little time. So, I sat down in the shadow of a statue of the Lord Ectoraige in the main hall, where I could see the conference room—and there I promptly fell asleep.

"I don't know how long I slept—not long I think, but I awoke suddenly, bitterly cold, and feeling strangely numb. I recall rubbing my eyes, which felt sore and gritty, and watching, almost stupidly, as a fog—a pale yellowish, dirty fog—rolled down the corridor. It piled up around the doors to the conference room, like waves washing around a stone, until it had almost reached the handles—and then it was as if it had been suddenly sucked in under the door.

"I tried to move, but I couldn't; I couldn't even shout.

"I heard screams from within, deep, racking coughs, furniture falling—and then there was nothing, no sound, no sound at all.

"And then the beasts came.

"They were Chopts. I had never seen one before, but they had been described to me often. They walked like men, and they were filthy, their long hair matted to their bodies. Their speech was like the sound of animals. Their weapons were new—I remember that clearly—they were bright and sparkling, clean almost.

"There were others with them, and these were men. They were wild folk, tall, with dark weathered skins, and beards and hair that looked as if they were wet, and the beards divided down the middle and were plaited. They carried swords that were almost as tall as themselves. They looked like warriors.

"They walked past me, and although they were no farther away from me than I am from you, they didn't seem to see me, but perhaps that was because they were intent on the conference room. They opened the doors and went inside, and I caught a brief glimpse of the Master and Teachers slumped, some over the table, others on the floor, their skins the same yellowish colour as the fog.

"And then…and then…and then the beasts and the men killed them…

"And then they fed…

"Later, much later, I don't know how long, but it was long enough for them to have fed well, another man appeared. He was alone, and although he was smaller and thinner than any of the others, they all bowed to him, and seemed almost terrified of him.

"And I'll tell you true, when I first saw the bard, I thought it was him again. But I think he was smaller, but that might have been the only difference; he wore a dark cloak in the same fashion as the bard, and moved just as smoothly and swiftly. I didn't see his face, but as he passed me, I caught a glimpse of one of his hands, and it looked like a twisted piece of rotten wood. There were two guards with him, and they were like nothing I have ever seen before: they were neither man nor beast. They weren't tall, but they were broad and looked incredibly powerful; they had two long tusks curling up from their lower lips, and these looked as if they had been painted in a twisting, curling design, and their bodies were covered in short bristling hair.

"The small man stood in the doorway of the conference room and then I clearly heard him say, 'Excellent. This will bring him like a moth to a flame, and like the flame to the moth, it will destroy him!'"

5

Sacrifice

What evil is committed and condoned in the name of religion?
The Warrior, the Life of Owen, Weapon Master

Owen stepped into the shop and immediately stood to one side and paused, allowing his eyes to adjust to the relative dimness of the interior before moving. It smelled of leather and metal, of polish and grit, a smell which the Weapon Master over his long years of campaigning had come to associate with death.

The shop was an Armoury, the finest in the Nations.

The shop was situated in a side street just off the quays, a tall, thin, high building, that contained some of the most lethal weaponry the Weapon Master had ever seen. Most were imports, strange creations from each of the Seven Nations, others from the outlying provinces, and even some from the Island Kingdoms. The majority of them he knew and had used; of the few he didn't, he could at least guess at their function, but that still left one or two that were a complete mystery to him.

The proprietor of the Armoury looked very much like his shop and its lethal contents; he was tall and thin, sharp-featured, with perhaps a touch of Shemmatae blood in him, lending him a curiously sinister appearance. He was wearing a long, loose-sleeved merchant's robe of the newly-fashionable metallic cloth, and his hands were buried in the drooping sleeves. He bowed deeply.

"I am honoured, sir."

Owen nodded slightly, his eyes moving, his senses alert, absorbing his surroundings. There was a third person in the shop, he was sure of it: the small hairs on the back of his neck had risen, a primitive warning signal that he had learned never to ignore.

"It is a pleasure to be in the company of a professional," the merchant continued, the smile on his face fixed and unmoving, his black eyes expressionless. "I am the Warlord..." his smile deepened at Owen's change of expression. "You will pardon my little joke, but my name was—is—Wasloden, and its singularity and my singular occupation have encouraged the populace to address me by the title, 'Warlord.' I adhere to it out of a sense of amusement."

"It is apt," Owen said softly, his eyes moving over the man, probing the dimness behind him. There! He fixed the position of the third man behind and to the left of the Warlord, in the shadows behind a display of chain and linked mail shirts.

"And you are Owen, the Weapon Master of course," the Warlord said, his smile deepening even further at Owen's obvious surprise. "Oh, please do not look so alarmed; modesty would be false and unbecoming. I am aware—as I am sure is everyone in Karfondal—of your identity, and those of us with sources of information are also aware just who was the engineer of our present Emperor's sudden elevation to the throne."

Owen silently worked out the details of the Warlord's sentence, and when he had finally got it right, he said, "I am but a mercenary..."

"Nay, nay, more than a mercenary. The Defender of Car'an'tual, the Weapon Master, the Killer, Wandering Death, and now Kingmaker."

"You seem remarkably well informed," Owen said; and then added dryly, "If you have any affection for the person lurking in the shadows, you will tell them to go, lest I am forced to kill them— merely for my continued peace of mind, of course."

The Warlord bowed again, the smile tightening on his thin lips, and then, without turning around he said, "Go, go." There was a movement behind him and a broad, stocky young man carrying a cocked and loaded crossbow moved from the shadows and hurried back down the shop. "He is there for *my* continued peace of mind," the Warlord said. "And now, you will join me in a cup before we conduct some business?"

Owen nodded, and followed the Warlord back through the long dark shop and out into a surprisingly large courtyard. The courtyard was closed in by a high spike-topped wall on two sides, and although the third side was open to the river, it was protected by a deep ditch which was lined with spikes whose barbs were suspiciously discoloured. To one side of the courtyard was a series of man-tall straw poles. There was a simple red and white patch about chest height on each.

As they came out into the courtyard, the young man Owen had seen earlier was firing, reloading, and firing his crossbow with surprising swiftness and equally surprising accuracy.

The Warlord stopped behind the young man and Owen, watching him, and seeing them together, noticed the resemblance between the two men.

"This is my son," the Warlord said, deliberately not naming the boy.

The boy turned to the Weapon Master and bowed deeply, his eyes chill and sullen.

"Your speed and accuracy with that weapon are extraordinary," Owen said, bowing slightly.

The boy bowed again, his expression unchanged.

The Warlord's face creased into the first genuine smile Owen had seen on it. "My son has mastered the various types of crossbows, both hunting and target, and has even designed two versions of his own, which we should be marketing shortly. Perhaps they might interest you, Weapon Master; one is a bow shooting multiple bolts—a dozen would seem to be the best figure—and the other is a completely silent weapon, no noise, no snap of prod or twang of cord; it would be suitable for…night work…"

"An assassin's tool," Owen said flatly.

"Ah, well, yes, yes, of course it could be used for that, I suppose," the Warlord said softly, as if the idea had only just occurred to him. He turned away from his son and crossed the courtyard to a tall, slender doorway that was cut flush into the wall and without surround, lintel, or step; it was so smooth and featureless that it might easily be passed over—especially in the dark. As Owen followed the man through the door, he noticed the heavy iron grill that was now fixed open against the wall directly behind the door. At night it would be locked in place, making access through the door—which was a handspan thick—almost certainly impossible. He suddenly wondered why the Warlord was allowing him to see all this.

As if reading his thoughts the Warlord said, "My security must be tight. There have been several attempted break-ins, all of which have, of course, failed. Men seeking weapons either for themselves or resale, I suppose. This is the finest collection in the Nations," he added proudly.

"I've heard you also deal in precious metals," Owen said quietly, following the man up a flight of narrow, uneven stairs.

The Warlord paused with his hand on the handle of a solid-looking brukwood door. He glanced back over his shoulder and smiled thinly at the hard-faced man. "And who would have told you that, eh?"

"I've heard that because your security is so good various merchants have asked you to hold their metal, jewels, or coin in safe-keeping for them. I've also heard that you're prepared to finance certain individuals or projects—for a consideration, of course."

The Warlord turned away, his face a stone mask, and threw open the door and walked into a long white room. It was tall and thin, more like a hallway than a room, and barely wide enough to accommodate the two chairs positioned on opposite sides of a square table at the far end of the long room. Light, streaming in through the rectangular window above the table, burned off the white walls, ceilings, and floor, giving the room a vaguely threatening, oppressive atmosphere.

The Warlord strode to the end of the room and sank down into the padded seat of the tall-backed wooden chair, resting both arms on the table.

And the Weapon Master suddenly realised that the man had no hands. Two spikes of metal protruded from the stumps of his wrists.

Owen sat down opposite him, and immediately checked the window, but it was canted in such a way that although he could see out and the slightly stale breeze off the river wafted in, the room wasn't overlooked by any other building. He turned back to the man, his features assuming their usual impassive mask, carefully avoiding looking at the spiked arms. But the Warlord deliberately raised his hands. "You may have heard about these—I can tell you the tale that I lost them experimenting with explosive powders, or I can tell you how they were severed in an accident aboard ship where they were caught in the ropes, or I can even tell you the tale how they were badly mangled as I fought off some wild animal. But the truth is they were chopped off by order of a court in Lostrice when I was a boy, as punishment for stealing."

"A barbarous thing..." Owen remarked, looking at the spikes, considering them as weapons; although the body of the spike was round, the tips had been flattened slightly to give them a pyramidal shape and then sharpened to give four—albeit small—obviously razor-sharp edges and a point. "Why did you tell me?" he suddenly asked. "Why didn't you tell me one of your stories?"

The Warlord smiled, and perhaps there was some genuine emotion in it now. "Because you must have done some research before you came to me—and if you've come to me you must want something, something important, I'll wager, to bring you here yourself rather than sending a servant to summon me to the palace. Suffice it to say that I don't want to risk lying to you at this early stage in our relationship."

"I admire honesty in a man."

"Perhaps you would care to reciprocate," the Warlord suggested.

The Weapon Master smiled thinly and, pulling out a black crossbow bolt, laid it carefully on the table between them. For a moment, it rocked back and forth on its black feathers, the tiny ticking noise loud in the warm silence of the room.

"I won't ask if it is yours," Owen said watching the Warlord's eyes. "The workmanship speaks for that, but let me tell you something of its recent history. It was pulled out of the eye socket of a man named Stinger this morning. He had been shot from quite a distance by someone of great skill. Stinger was a link in a chain which leads back to the conspirators who are plotting against the throne, and the Imperials are actively pursuing that link at the moment; indeed they are currently looking for the maker of this bolt..."

"They have already been here," the Warlord interrupted, "and I told them it had been made for a one-handed bard..."

"...named Paedur, I know. I also happen to know that that isn't true; which immediately made me wonder why you should lie, and there is no reason for you to lie—unless of course you had something to hide. I think you have, and that makes me think you might be the next link in the chain."

"I don't think..." the Warlord began, beginning to rise to his feet.

Owen raised his hand. "Listen. This is not, perhaps, what you think. If need be I could have come here with a full squadron of the Emperor Legion and had them beat down the door and tear this place apart, and then think of the fun Fodla would have had extracting information from you and your son..." He shook his head, smiling slightly at the thought. "No, I came to you because I want you to put me in touch with the opposition leaders."

"And why should I want to do that…assuming I could, of course?" the Warlord asked curiously.

"I have a proposition for them."

"What sort of proposition?"

"I made this Emperor—I can break him also, and just as easily."

"And why would you want to do that?" the Warlord asked very softly, leaning across the table.

"For several reasons…"

"Such as?"

"Because although I am first and foremost a mercenary, I do have principles—principles which are very important to me. I defended Car'an'tual because of those principles. I made Kutor Emperor because I believed his claim to the throne to be a just one and also because I believed that Geillard's reign had degenerated into a useless mockery."

"And now?" the Warlord asked, when Owen paused.

"And now I believe I was wrong. Kutor is no better than Geillard; perhaps he'll be even worse. Already he has diverted vital funds from the army to aid the refugees coming in from the devastated coastal regions. I learned this morning that there are reports of more coming up from the Southlands which have been hit by drought, and still more coming down from the north where the weather has turned unseasonably cold. Karfondal cannot cope with this sudden influx of people; it has neither the resources nor the space to contain them. Kutor, however, is planning new towns, new roads, and he intends to pay for them with a major reorganisation of the taxes. One of the more interesting bits of this new legislation will be to levy a substantially heavier tax on items which he will deem to be not of an essential nature—and you will find weapons amongst that class."

"That is madness!"

"His long-term plan is to take the weapons away from the common people, but leave them in the hands of his chosen few, his army, his militia—therefore making it all the easier to control the people."

"I've heard nothing about this," the Warlord said quietly, turning to stare at the pale blue sky through the window.

"It is hardly the sort of thing he will announce in a proclamation, now is it?" Owen asked dryly. "But there will be an announcement about the refugee aid programme soon, I should imagine. You can judge the truth of what I am saying then."

The Warlord waved an arm, his spike glittering in the light. "Oh, I have no reason to doubt you…"

"But this could be a devious ploy…" Owen suggested, with a wry smile.

The Warlord smiled thinly. "I don't think so. It is too cumbersome and crudely contrived to be a ploy. I'm sure Kutor and his cronies could have thought up something more interesting, something original. And of course, I am a very good judge of men," he added. "I believe you."

Owen looked at him without saying anything.

"Would you be prepared to kill Kutor?"

"I am a mercenary, not an assassin," the Weapon Master said immediately.

"A mercenary is a paid warrior, an assassin is a paid killer—the roles are not so different," the Warlord said. "If the price was right, would you kill him?"

"No." And before the Warlord could say anything, Owen continued, "However, I would deliver him into the hands of…well, shall we say of those who have Karfondal's best interests at heart."

"With what preconditions?"

"The only precondition would be the price, and that it would be paid in full up front."

"That is unusual," the Warlord said, looking at the table, touching the tips of his spikes together. "The usual agreement is for half on agreement, half on completion."

"But I am a man of principle; I would not attempt to cheat you."

The Warlord bowed. "I know that, but I cannot say yea or nay on this; I have not the authority. I will need to bring it before my principals. Come to my shop three days hence. I will know then."

Owen nodded. "Good enough." He stood up, looking at the thin man expectantly.

The Warlord rapped one of his metal spikes against the wooden table, making the metal sing. The door immediately opened and the armourer's son stepped into the room. He was still carrying the cocked and loaded crossbow. "Our visitor is leaving; please take him down." He looked up at the Weapon Master. "In three days."

Owen nodded and stepped away from the table; then he stopped and looked back. "Tell me, why did you tell the Imperials that the black crossbow bolt had been made for the bard?"

"Imagine the consternation it must have caused at court!" The Warlord grinned.

Owen shook his head slightly and walked away without another word.

The Warlord waited until he heard the door below shut solidly, and then he stretched to his full height and looked through the window, watching his son lead the Weapon Master across the courtyard towards the shop, and only when he was satisfied that the warrior was gone, did he turn back to the room. "Well, lady?"

A section of the bone-white wall swung open and a tiny, old woman stepped into the room. Although she had always been small in stature, the years had withered her even further, twisting her frail body into a mockery of its former shape. Her features were seamed with age, giving her an almost simian or mummified appearance, but her eyes were sharp, as hard as glass, and the colour of a winter's sky.

She was the Lady Esse, a sorceress of almost legendary power, once Geillard's teacher, but long since gone into retirement to pursue her occult studies. When Geillard had been dethroned, she had immediately returned to the capital to organise the resistance against the usurper, and she was using the Warlord's armoury as her base.

"Is he genuine?" the Warlord asked, deferentially.

The tiny woman limped down the length of the room and sank into the chair the Weapon Master had vacated. "What do you think?" she asked venomously. "This is the man who fought with the Band of Kloor, and then forsook it—the only man ever to do so—with the assistance of the cursed bard. This is the man the bard sent to the Outlands to aid the outlaw chief; this is the man who organised Kutor's army; this is the man who came to the city during the height of the battle with the intention of assassinating the Emperor; this is the man who is responsible for the death of Salier. Because of this man, a usurper sits upon the throne of the Seven Nations while the rightful Emperor lurks in the Choptlands. And you ask me if he is genuine?" she spat.

"Then it is a ploy to discover the identities of those plotting against Kutor?" the Warlord suggested, but here the old woman didn't look quite so certain.

"Possibly, possibly. But I feel sure that the usurper knows, or at the very least has a very good idea of those who are against him. Indeed, this may be nothing more than a crude ploy to establish the names of the individuals or families who are actively plotting against him, rather than those who merely oppose him on principle. However, the man, this Owen, is interesting." Her pale eyes closed into slits. "I sense confusion within him, almost as if he himself were experiencing doubts about the new ruler—and these are doubts that might be capitalised upon later. This is no crude brigand, no simple mercenary. This is a man with principles, a proud man, a man of honour. And they are often the easiest to bend and use."

"We could kill him," the Warlord suggested.

"Aye—and bring the wrath of Kutor and his army down upon us, and if they don't get you, then that savage Shemmat servant of his will." Her eyes snapped open, catching and holding the armourer's black eyes. "At the moment, you are the link, Warlord; you are the only clue they have..." Her voice fell, and the Warlord felt something cold and chill walk up his spine. "Remove you and we remove the link," she said speculatively.

"Lady, you cannot..."

The Lady Esse shook her head slightly. "I was merely thinking aloud. You may rest easy for the moment—you are truly useful to me, and Geillard's cause."

"There is no stauncher supporter," the Warlord said fervently, realising how close to death he had come. He had seen the old woman kill without a second thought or qualm, merely because she had assumed there might be a threat in the future or because someone's present use was limited or finished. Working with the Lady Esse was a gamble. If her plans succeeded and Geillard returned to the throne, then those who had helped her would be placed in positions of extraordinary power. But there were risks, and besides the risks of failure, there was the prime risk of either her anger or her disinterest. Both were lethal. "What should I do regarding the Weapon Master, Lady?" he asked diffidently.

"Bring him back. Tell him you need proof of his support for your cause, and in return give him...give him de Courtney's name..."

"But, Lady, he is one of us..."

"If the Weapon Master is on our side, then de Courtney will be safe, but if not...de Courtney's services are dispensable. His support is not perhaps as staunch as it should be, and those not fully with us are against us. He has contributed nothing in the past few moons, and he will run at the first sign of trouble. He will be no loss. There is also the problem that they suspect him because of his closeness to Geillard, so his name will be neither a surprise nor a revelation. And by giving it, we lose nothing."

"But if he should talk?"

Lady Esse grinned mirthlessly. "He will not talk!"

The Warlord closed up shop late in the afternoon, just as the sun was beginning to dip below the city walls, lengthening the shadows, allowing the first chill of evening to settle in. He had pulled on a travelling cloak over his merchant's robe and pulled up the hood, perhaps against the chill, but more likely to conceal his features.

Tien tZo waited until he was sure the Warlord was on the move before stepping out of the shadows and hurrying after him. The small Shemmat had once again donned the guise of a holy man, an Andam, one of those blessed—or cursed—with the wasting sickness associated with their faith. Completely swathed in the torn grey robes, with only his eyes uncovered, Tien had no difficulty in following the Warlord, his great height alone making him stand out from the crowd, and most of these people parted for the diseased holy man following behind.

The arms merchant took a circuitous route through the Lower City and then moved on through the banking district into the more prosperous trading section.

The perfumery was an ornately decorated establishment backing onto the main thoroughfare, a small shop rich in odours and essences which contrasted sharply with the distinctive sweet-sour scent of the city in general. Tien tZo watched from across the street while the Warlord spoke briefly to the short, foppish owner, who accompanied him to the door. The perfumery owner allowed the tall, angular figure to continue his route up the street, before checking the street in both directions and then closing the door and pulling down the embroidered blind to indicate that the shop was closed. The Warlord stopped again, this time at a shop that was decorated in beaten brass and metal, and with a sign that proclaimed its tenant a blacksmith. The Shemmat squatted in the street opposite the shop, his head bent, his eyes lost in the shadow of his cowl. He immediately decided that this was no common blacksmith, this was no maker of shoes, no hammerer of bars; this man created tiny, delicate artifacts from glowing metal, turning a simple torch or even a doorhandle into something of beauty. Again, the Warlord spoke to him briefly and hurried on, and when he had gone the blacksmith too closed up shop.

In all the Warlord spoke to a dozen merchants, all of them wealthy men, with fine addresses in the best districts. Tien tZo had the distinct impression that he was arranging a meeting or gathering of some sort.

Hurrying now—as if he had lingered too long—the Warlord made his way to the Cathedral of the Religion which stood in the main square, and which had once been dedicated to the Old Faith. When Kutor had taken power—and against the bard's wishes—the new Emperor had refused to rededicate the old temple to the Faith, and had merely had it closed and sealed, banning all worship in it. He had sworn that as a token of his thanks to the Gods of the Pantheon, he would build the finest cathedral in all the Planes of Existence to the Faith. But that had been before the realities of the situation had sunk in—and Karfondal had been flooded with refugees. Now only the promise remained.

When he had turned into the main square, Tien tZo immediately thought that the Warlord was going to pray before the sealed and chained doors of the cathedral, but the merchant had hurried on up the rose-coloured marble steps and, ignoring the main doors, slipped in behind one of the supporting pillars—and didn't reappear. It took Tien a few moments to realise that the man must have gone inside somehow. From his position in the shadow of an alley, the Shemmat studied the occupants of the square—and immediately spotted three watchers, or guards. Although they were dressed as common fruit sellers, Tien recognised by the way they walked and moved that they were armed and alert.

But he needed to get inside...

And then he remembered the last time he had visited the cathedral. It had been in the last days of the battle, before Kutor had ascended the throne, when he and Owen had come to Karfondal in an attempt to kill Geillard and as many of his advisers as possible. That had been the first time he had worn the Andam disguise; he had sat on those rose-marbled steps and prayed to his ancestor, and the Cathedral Guards had come and taken him around the side of the cathedral into a tiny side street... The Shemmat's dour face broke into a rare smile: he had his way in.

The smell hit him as soon as he forced open the lock. The Shemmat had lived with the smell of death for almost all his life, and he knew the stink of it, and its attendant odours of blood and faeces, sweat and urine. Something—no, many things—had died here!

Tien waited until his eyes adjusted to the gloom and then slowly and quietly stripped off the Andam robes; beneath he was wearing a simple cotton shirt over cotton breeks tucked into his old boots. In his belt were two hand axes, and there was a long, slim-bladed knife in a sheath sewn into his right boot. Drawing the knife, he padded softly down the corridor, following the death-smell.

In a tiny room at the end of the corridor he found seven dead bodies. They were all female, all young—the eldest around seventeen or so—and in every case their chest had been opened and their hearts torn out. They had been sacrificed!

The Shemmat closed the door and had begun to silently re-trace his steps when another door opened and a short, stout, young man wearing a heavy black robe stepped out into the corridor. The hood of his robe was thrown back on his bald head and his pale face was glistening with sweat. His eyes were glazed and there was a curiously vacant smile fixed to his lips. He was carrying another corpse over his shoulder, the dead girl's blood seeping into his heavy robe.

The young man stopped, his eyes beginning to blink rapidly. In the single moment it took him to come out of his trance Tien tZo killed him with a single blow above the lip that drove slivers of shattered bone into the brain. He was dead before he hit the ground.

Quietly, furiously angry with himself, Tien tZo dragged the two bodies to the small reeking room and tossed them in on top of the piled corpses.

He had reacted instinctively, killing the man—and now those who congregated here would know that their sanctuary had been discovered. So he had but one chance to find out as much as he could...

Settling his weapons, Tien stripped off the dead youth's heavy black cloak and pulled it over his own head. Moving quietly to the door the youth had come through, Tien pulled up the hood—and stepped out into the cathedral. He was standing behind and to the left of the altar, facing a surprisingly large congregation of a little more than a hundred people, and even as he was walking up to stand behind the altar-stone, his hands buried in his sleeves, copying a similarly dressed man opposite him, two things were immediately apparent: the congregation were all male, and all from the nobility or wealthy merchant classes.

The Cathedral of the New Religion—because of its original use as a temple of the Old Faith—was a curious mixture of styles. There were empty spaces where statuary of the Pantheon had stood, and blank—scrubbed or painted-over—inscriptions on the walls. The new statues of the Religion's gods were crude and looked almost unfinished, while the invocations to the gods of the Religion looked like graffiti on the elegant walls.

And the congregation was lost within the vastness of the building. They were gathered in the long pews directly before the altar, serious men, for the most part soberly dressed, but it was their expressions that interested Tien. He had seen that look before, the glazed, fixed stare, the mouth slightly open, tongues moving frequently across dry lips. It was the same expression he had seen in the arena, or on those ghouls who wandered a battlefield following an engagement. It was the blood-look. They had come to see a sacrifice.

Tien had discovered seven bodies in the room below, and then there was the one the smiling thug had brought down, which made eight, and there were four girls sitting on a bench before him—four to be butchered. Twelve young women, and he had no doubt that they were virgins. What he did find surprising, however, was that the four remaining girls were sitting quite still, unshackled and un-bound. Tien looked at their eyes for signs of drugging, but they were bright and alert; which meant that they were giving themselves freely for sacrifice. He looked at the congregation again, concentrating now on the first two rows, and immediately spotted the like-nesses between at least two of the girls and two of the men there.

There was movement and a small wizened woman limped down from the altar throne. In her brown, seamed face only her eyes—

which were a pale watery blue—seemed alive. She didn't have to speak: without a word the next girl stood up and shrugged off her simple robe, and then, naked, she climbed the steps to the altar, bowed to the old woman, climbed up onto the bloodstained stone, and closed her eyes.

The old woman reached out and touched her lightly on the face, and the girl's whole body twitched. "Fear not," the woman hissed, "your gift to your god will be rewarded a thousandfold."

The girl nodded jerkily. "Forgive my transgressions," she said quickly.

"Your presence here forgives them." The old woman reached down by her side and lifted a slightly curved butchering knife. Although it had been plated in silver and the hilt inset with gemstones, Tien tZo still recognised the basic shape—it was designed to cut flesh and bone with the least resistance.

"Lord Trialos," the old woman said suddenly, "we call upon you again in the name of these here present to accept this virgin bride as a token of our allegiance and devotion to you. And if you find this body acceptable, then take it as your own and walk amongst us. But thy will be done, and we dedicate the body's essence to your cause to use as you so wish."

And she plunged the knife down, driving it in below the young woman's breast.

Tien tZo heard bone pop and crack, and the woman convulsed once and died. The old woman turned the knife, cutting through flesh and bone, opening the chest, and then she reached into the bloody mess and pulled out something which filled her hand, something darkly reddish-purple, veined—and pulsating!

"Accept this body, accept this escaping life essence, accept this death," the old woman screamed. And then she tossed the heart into a burning brazier. It spat and hissed and added its own horrible odour to the many others in the room. "Her heart is yours…"

And the corpse, its chest torn open, its heart consumed by the flames, sat up!

6
Gire

And he was the Champion of the Old Faith, and his enemies were many...
Life of Paedur, the Bard

"Mannam!" Paedur breathed. "It can only be Mannam."

"The once-lord of the Dead? But he is human now and lost on the Planes of Existence," Katani said quickly, feeling something cold settle against her spine.

"Not lost, merely missing. Until now. It can only be Mannam," Paedur insisted. "He swore vengeance when the Pantheon stripped him of his godhood, not only on me but on them also. Obviously, he is exacting that vengeance now through the Chopts."

"And his guards?"

"The Torc Allta, the Boar-Folk," Paedur said quickly.

"And the sword-bearers are Gallowglas, professional mercenaries..."

The bard nodded. "Aye, and related to the Chopt tribes. Interesting that they are all—Chopt, Torc Allta and Gallowglas—cannibals and flesh-eaters." He stopped suddenly, realising the boy was still there, staring open-mouthed at him. "Is that all they said; nothing more?" he asked gently.

Gire shook his head. "Nothing else. The small dark man turned away, followed by his two beast-guards...the...the Torc Allta?"

Paedur nodded absently. "Why weren't you killed?" he asked suddenly.

Gire shook his head, looking quickly from the bard to Katani, his eyes sparkling with moisture. This was the first real emotion he had shown during the telling of his tale and Katani couldn't help but wonder if the bard had somehow dulled his senses a little to allow him to relate the events with no outburst of emotion. "I don't know why I wasn't killed. I've gone back to the spot again and again. I can only think that I was sitting in the shadow of the God of Learning, and behind the statue is a small ventilation grille—perhaps that prevented the yellow gas from taking hold of me. But I still don't know why they passed me over."

The warrior nodded. "But where are the bodies of the slain? There must have been hundreds of bodies?"

"They took them away with them!" He saw Katani's startled look and nodded quickly. "The beasts came back with carts—large-wheeled wooden carts—and piled them high with bodies and parts of bodies and took them away with them. When I wandered the Monastery halls and down through the School later, I found no bodies at all. All that remained were the deep track marks in the snow, all heading back into the Northlands. They had taken away all the bodies!"

"Why?" Katani whispered, aghast.

"Food," Paedur said shortly. "It's a hard winter in the Northlands; they're bringing food home to their families, much as any human hunter would."

Gire drew up his knees and leaned forwards, wrapping his arms around them. "But why did they do it; why did they attack the Monastery and school? Why did they deliberately destroy all the holy relics and books? Why? And what did the little man mean when he said that it would 'bring him.' Bring whom?"

The bard's lips curled into something like a smile. "You belong in the Order of Ectoraige if you question everything like that," he said. "And you probably deserve answers," he added. "The small dark man was undoubtedly Mannam, once the God of Death, the Lord of the Silent Wood. But god no longer. He was tried by his peers—the Pantheon of the Old Faith—found guilty of crimes against the dead, stripped of his godhood and returned to the World of Men as his punishment. He blames me for that. The creatures with him, the beasts with tusks, were the Torc Allta. When I walked the Silent Wood, I killed several of their number and they swore an oath to slay me; obviously they have joined forces with Mannam.

"And this was a trap, a lure as it were, to draw me. By killing the followers of the Old Faith in this bloody fashion—sacrificing them almost—the Gods of the Religion grow stronger, and a welcome bonus of course is that by doing this terrible deed, they knew I would come to investigate."

"All the Brothers, the monks, the students...they were all killed just to draw you here?" Gire whispered, his eyes, which had been wide and round, now settling into slits. His face tightened into a mask of contempt. "You are responsible for their deaths—all their deaths!"

"Stop that!" Katani snapped. "The bard was no more responsible than you were. If there is any blame, then let it lie with the Gods of the Old Faith, who didn't warn their followers that death in this terrible fashion was stalking them."

"Perhaps they did," Paedur said quietly. "Remember the Brothers were meeting in conclave when death struck."

"A late warning is no warning," Katani muttered. "But what do we do now?"

"This place is undoubtedly watched—although whether by magical wards or by distant watchers, I'm not sure. However, I've felt no presences, either occult or human," he added, by way of reassurance.

Katani leaned forward. "Bard, hundreds of men and boys— all staunch followers of the Faith—were butchered here in the name of the New Religion; the very stones have been bathed in their blood. The gods and followers of the Religion will need no watchers to know that one of the Faith is here."

"You're right, of course." Paedur stood up, flowing silently to his feet, his cloak settling around him like a shadow. "Get dressed, boy. You're coming with us."

"Where are we going?" Gire asked, something of the bard's seeming nervousness conducting itself to him.

"Out of this place first; we'll decide our destination later." The bard pulled his hood around his head and then, having become one with the night, slipped out into the ruins of the chapel. He allowed his enhanced senses to flare and immediately the pitch-black night flared to light as the bard became aware of the aura of life that every living creature exuded. He was surrounded in a shifting mass of colour, and he stood still for a moment, absorbing the colours, identifying and sorting them. Katani was behind him, vibrant colours surrounding her stark whiteness—the aura of one dead—obviously the legacy of time in the Silent Wood. Beside her the boy radiated fear and exhaustion, and his aura was curiously overlain with a pale blue tinge the bard had never encountered before. Paedur blanked these from his consciousness and concentrated on the area within the chapel, and found it deserted save for the usual night creatures. Expanding his consciousness he quested beyond the Monastery walls, slowly and methodically blanking

out the life-auras of the myriad creatures that inhabited the secret places of any ancient building, gradually turning the night
to black once again.

He found them on the steps beyond the gate.

The colours were strange, they were mixed and distorted
and tainted with a gritty greyness. It took him a moment to
resolve the coloured shapes into—Torc Allta! The auras were
alien to this Plane of Existence, and the greyness was the grey of
the Ghost Worlds between the planes, through which the Boar-
Folk had the ability to travel at will.

He sorted through the auras, counting. There were certainly
four, and possibly one other, but the colours were so broken and
distorted that he was unable to tell. Two were on either side of
the gate, and the other two—or three—were grouped on the steps.
He—and Katani and the boy—were trapped, then. There was no
way past them—the steps were the only entrance to the Monastery
of Ectoraige. In the past this had proved the monks' salvation,
for a single man could easily hold the steps against an army. It was
now likely to prove his bane.

There was movement behind him and the bard spun around;
Katani and Gire had emerged from the small chapel. Behind them
a curl of grey smoke twisted in the darkness, and the odour of
doused wood was bitter on the air. The warrior was in her full
armour, with both swords in her hands. Gire was wearing his tattered blue robe and had Katani's travelling cloak tied around him.
He was carrying one of the Katan's throwing knives.

"There are Torc Allta beyond the gates and on the steps,"
Paedur said shortly.

"Is there any other way out?" Katani asked.

"None that I know of." He stooped down and looked into
Gire's eyes. "Do you know of any other way out of this building?"

Gire shook his almost bald head. "None."

"So we fight," Katani said, almost tiredly. She had had one
lifetime of killing, and had endured countless years in the timeless world of the Silent Wood, slaying—butchering—the dead,
and now, back again in the World of Men, she was once again
killing.

"We fight on our terms," Paedur said quickly.

The Torc Allta waited with all the patience of beasts. Their prey was close now, very close. They had tracked him from the Mire that bordered Death's Kingdom, across the myriad Planes of Existence to this place, seeking vengeance on the brothers he had so foully killed and mutilated.

And if they took the Katan warrior, then that would be a bonus. Her flesh they would feast upon immediately—soft, succulent, woman-flesh. The bard they must deliver alive to the rest of their company, so he could be ritually slain and his flesh distributed in the proper fashion.

With the bard dead and their mission complete, they could plan their future, and those plans did not include returning to their own desolate plane.

They had fed well since they had come through to this Plane of Existence. They had slain many and eaten well, and if their compan-ions, the Chopts, had too much beast blood in them for their liking, and if the Gallowglas were too human for them to be truly com-fortable with, then when the time came, they too would feed the Torc Allta…

The two guards at the gate stiffened, and the three lurking on the steps heard the sudden sound also—it was the chink of metal, brittle and sharp on the chill air. Then their sensitive sense of smell caught the odours of burning wood and turf. Fire had been lit inside the Monastery—which probably meant that the bard was going to stay the night. The guards on either side of the gate looked back down the steps for directions, but their instructions had been clear: under no circumstances were they to enter the Monastery. Although the butchery they had wrought in the hallowed halls would have washed the Old Faith Magic from the stones and coated the whole building in a miasma of blood and death, there was still every chance that the bard, the Champion of the Old Faith, would be instantly aware of their presence. They were counting on the fact that expo-sure to the atmosphere of the Monastery would dull his senses, and render him vulnerable, so that when he left the Monastery they would be able to take him.

The fire inside the Monastery had obviously been fuelled: sparks and large black cinders began spiralling to the heavens and a pale glow suffused the night sky. The Torc Allta were both puzzled and alarmed now. Surely these were not the actions of a nervous man, nor those of someone who wished to travel quietly?

One of the Torc Allta darted out of the shadow of the door and crouched on the top step, looking down at his three companions. "Let us leave now; this noise, this display, bodes ill for us..."

"We wait—he must leave eventually," a voice snarled from below him. "Return to your post."

The first guard nodded and walked slowly back to the huge locked doors, rubbing his curling tusks in frustration. His every sense told him something was wrong, that they should leave now...

Something cold and wet moved across his chest. His hand came up, expecting to find water, rain...but came away warmly sticky. He lifted his hand and held it to his snout, and then his tongue darted out, tasting it—blood. The noises in his head increased, and as he opened his mouth to shout a warning, the noise overwhelmed him.

The second guard saw the first fall to the ground, a vague shape in the dimness. He stepped away from the door, wondering if he had tripped and fallen, when he was abruptly deluged in liquid. It was bitterly cold and the sudden chill drove the air from his lungs. He opened his mouth to scream—when the smell hit him. It was fish oil. There was a shape in front of him; tall, black, with a silver hook where his left hand should have been. The hook darted out, and the guard reacted, bringing up his short-hafted jabbing spear; the hook slid down along the haft, striking sparks from the metal hand-guard...

The explosion lifted the Torc Allta off his feet and threw him against the wall. Completely wrapped in flame, he staggered to his feet and wove his unsteady way past the still, silent shape of the bard, instinct alone guiding him towards the steps and his own kind. He teetered on the top step, and then staggered forward—straight into the arms of his companions. In a screaming, bellowing, squealing heap, the four bodies, one aflame, tumbled down the hundreds of steps to the School below. All noise had ceased long before they hit the bottom.

Paedur turned his head to look up to where Katani and Gire were standing on the battlements above the door. "We fight on our terms."

In the icy fastness of a buried cave in the heart of the Northlands, beyond Thusal, a tall, twisted creature watched the bard in a block of smoothly polished ice, which he had turned into a scrying stone with the assistance of Hirwas, God of Far Seeing, one of the twelve Trialdone of the New Religion.

He watched impassively as the bard and his two companions climbed down the uncounted steps from the Monastery to the School below. Even without his powers of godhood, and even from this distance, he could feel the approach of the bard, feel the power he radiated...and once again experienced the fear. He had some protection though; in return for his allegiance to the New Religion, he had extricated several promises from the new gods, and they included both patronage and protection. There was something else in his favour at the moment—the bard was unaware of the mutated nature of his own powers since he had returned from the Silent Wood. It might be possible to use that ignorance for his destruction.

The bard would be destroyed, and without him the Old Faith would wither and die and its Pantheon of Gods with it, and then he would have his vengeance, sweet, sweet vengeance.

And Mannam, once-lord of the Silent Wood, the abode of the Dead, smiled involuntarily, his seamed face cracking, tiny runnels of clear fluid running from the wounds, like sap leaking from a wounded bark.

"Thusal is the next town," Gire said, as they climbed the score of steps that led off the side road onto the impressive width of the King Road.

Paedur nodded impassively.

"And Thusal has been cut off; there has been no word out of it for the past several moons. The Brothers thought it might be besieged by the Chopts and their allies, or perhaps that it had already fallen," Gire continued, looking at Katani.

"Perhaps the road is blocked," she said, her voice sounding faintly muffled inside her horned, demon-mask helmet. She was wearing her full armour, more for protection from the elements than any attacker. It was bitterly cold, and there were banks of hard-packed snow on either side of the road, although the centre of the road was still relatively clear. Thus far in the season, there had been no heavy snowfalls.

"In the olden days," the boy continued eagerly, his nervousness making him talk, "there were pipes running under the King Road, which carried water from the hot springs of the Northlands, and which served to keep the road free of ice and snow."

Paedur glanced at the boy. "And who told you that?"

"I read it in a book in the library at Ectoraige."

"You read?"

Gire nodded proudly. "Four languages, and I can read Culai script."

The bard turned to look at the boy, his reflective eyes taking the white of the snow, making him look blind. "You didn't learn that from the Brothers." There was a note of genuine respect in his voice.

"My mother taught me."

"A learned woman."

"It was said she knew everything," Gire said simply. "She was the Lady Sophia..."

"The Teacher?" Paedur said abruptly.

Gire nodded. "She was called that."

"A tall, elegant woman, with deeply black hair, and deep chestnut-coloured eyes?"

Gire nodded.

The bard smiled, one of his rare genuine smiles, which lit up his face, lending it a human cast once again. "I studied under the Lady Sophia at Baddalaur, the College of Bards. She was an almost legendary figure when I was there as a young man. And truly, I've heard it said that she knew everything. There were stories that she had done a deal with one of the Duaite or Auithe for a perfect memory, but whatever, it is true that she had only to look at a scroll, or a page of manuscript, once to have it word for word. She was a very fine lady," he added fondly, shaking his head, "and I've often wondered what happened to her. When I went back to Baddalaur some time ago, I asked after her, but she had left then, and no one knew where she had gone." He suddenly reached out his hand and the boy tentatively took it, and Katani, walking behind them allowed herself a smile; it was difficult to reconcile the often terrifying, sometimes god-like bard with the occasional human touches which showed through the armour. And she wondered what he had been like before he had become the Champion of the Old Faith.

"My mother delighted in telling me that she created the single greatest scandal at Baddalaur since Arin the Bard Master was stabbed by one of his pupils because of an affair of the heart..." Gire said quickly, and added, "but she never told me what the first scandal was..."

Paedur smiled, remembering. "It was before my time, but it was the talk of the college for seasons afterwards; Arin was a man of strange tastes, and he developed an affection for a young boy from one of the western families. When he made his advances—at the dead of night too—the boy was so angered that he picked up a stool and cracked Arin over the head with it. In a rage, Arin pulled a knife, which the boy—who stood taller than the Bard Master, and was broad on proportion—promptly took away from him and stabbed him in...stabbed him with it. The man conducted his classes for the rest of that season standing up."

Gire laughed, his laughter ringing flatly across the ice-locked landscape. As far as the eye could see, there was nothing but the blasted whiteness of a snowscape, unrelieved by any vegetation or habitation.

"I often wondered," Gire said, "but Mama would never tell me."

"And what was her scandal?" Paedur wondered.

"She married one of her students!"

The bard blinked, but said nothing.

Gire grinned. "And to make matters worse, he was much younger than she."

"What is so strange about that?" Katani asked. "In my time, it was accepted that the wife should be older than the man; experience being necessary to curb the impetuousness of youth."

"Times and mores change, Katani," Paedur said, "but in the Outland tribes that custom persists. Here, however, the wife is usually of an age, if not younger than the husband."

"Foolishness," Katani grunted, turning her attention back to the landscape. Although it looked deserted, she couldn't shake the feeling that they were being watched.

Paedur looked down at Gire. "And your mother left Baddalaur?"

"She never spoke about her reasons for leaving, but I suspect that she was forced to leave. And I know that when she returned to Talaria with her new husband—my father—she was not well

received by my father's family. Apparently, they were in the process of arranging a suitable marriage for him—something political, no doubt. But my mother vindicated herself when she designed a drainage system that ensured that the borderlands would
never again suffer drought, and when the Taourg Pirates raided
the coastal villages, my mother designed the ballista which sank
four of the pirate ships the first time it was used and ensured that
they never again raided Talaria's coasts. In my land she is worshipped almost as a goddess."

"Did she decide to send you to the College of Ectoraige?"

"I am the youngest," Gire answered, "and my two brothers and
two sisters all have their appointed careers. My mother prevailed
upon my father to send me to college; she said I would find my
destiny there."

Paedur looked at him curiously, but said nothing. The Lady
Sophia's precognitive talent was well-known, and there was a single
volume devoted to her successful predictions in the College Library.
The bard wondered what destiny she had seen for her son.

7
Andam

I often knew fear before I encountered the bard, but after him, and the events
he set in motion, I learned the true meaning of terror...
                                    Tien tZo, biographer of Owen, the Weapon Master

"There was panic when the corpse sat up," Tien tZo said quietly, his
voice even, his hands still on the table before him, and yet everyone
present could sense the tension within him. "They were hoping for
it, perhaps some of them were even expecting it, but when it happened, they ran terrified. And I ran with them."

"You're sure the body was dead?" Keshian asked quietly. "I've
seen too many men with fatal wounds, killing wounds, death
wounds, continue to fight on long after they should have died, the
physical body moving even though the essence had left it. I once
saw a man with an arrow in his heart fight on to kill the archer who
had 'killed' him."

"I know, I know," Tien tZo said quickly. "I've seen that happen,
but this was not like that. The woman was dead: the old woman
had cut her open like any other butchered beast, a long cut beneath
the breast, and then up along the breastbone, opening the chest like
the door to a cage. I saw her tear out the heart, rip it, tubes and
veins, from the chest, saw her hold it aloft while it still pulsed and
trembled, before finally throwing it into the fire. The heart was
consumed—I almost threw up when the stink hit me."

Owen reached over and placed his hand on his friend's shoulder
in a rare gesture of physical affection. "Gently, gently, now." He
looked around at the three people in the room, Kutor, Keshian, and
Fodla, and shook his head slightly. "If Tien says the corpse rose up,
then it rose, and we must consider the possibility that the body has
been inhabited by something from the void or the Ghost Lands."

"So it is a *quai?*" Fodla said.

The Weapon Master shook his head. "More than a *quai*, I
think. A *quai* is a dead body controlled by someone living, but
what we have here is a dead body occupied by something which

was deliberately called down. This girl was sacrificed with the sole intention of providing a habitable shell for her god."

"They were calling down Trialos," Tien reminded them. "Could not the god have heeded that call?"

"I hope not," Fodla said, feelingly.

Owen turned back to Tien. "What happened when the corpse rose?"

"There was panic…"

"I know there was panic," Owen said gently, "but what did the thing—this corpse—do? Did it speak, did it raise a hand, turn…? I want to know what it did."

The Shemmat shrugged. "It did…nothing. It merely sat up on the bloody table and looked around, its head moving, slowly, its eyes wide and unblinking—like a serpent," he said suddenly. "That's what it brought to mind—a serpent."

"In the panic that followed, did anyone remain behind?" Keshian asked.

"The woman, the old woman, the one who killed the girls and called down the god, she remained, and so did the Warlord," he added quickly. "He was at the back of the cathedral as I passed him, but he had stepped out of the milling throng, and seemed to be waiting."

"How did he look?" Keshian asked.

"I didn't stop to find out," Tien snapped. "I was too busy getting out."

"You did well," the Emperor said quietly. "Thanks to you we now have some indication of the old royalists' plans. We know the Warlord is involved, and this withered old woman should be easily identifiable…"

"She is the Lady Esse," Fodla said, the surprise in her voice evident. "I thought you knew."

"I am a bandit from the Outlands; my friends are mercenaries, thieves, and brigands; I'm afraid I am not well-used to who's who in the old Imperial Court," Kutor said sarcastically.

Fodla grinned good-humouredly. "You'll find there's little difference—they're barbarians all. The woman Tien described could only be the Lady Esse. When I first came to court many years ago, she was the real power behind Geillard's father, and even when Geillard, the deposed Emperor, took the throne, she was still active, her hand evident in every major policy decision. Salier, Geillard's late unlamented chief counsellor, magician, and personal attendant, was her student and some said, her son, but I personally think that is unlikely."

"And what was this woman, this Lady Esse?" Kutor asked.

"She was a sorceress, a sorceress of incredible power, who had once staunchly upheld the Old Faith, but for some reason which no-one knows, changed her allegiance to the New Religion. She is an evil woman—and I use the term very carefully—embittered by her stature and her looks, detesting the Faith and everything connected with it, and loyal to only one thing, and that is Geillard and the power he wields—or perhaps it is just the power."

"And she is a follower of the Religion?" Owen asked.

"Personally, I always believed that she followed older, wilder gods, for her power was phenomenal. But yes, she professes to adhere to the Religion and from what Tien has just described, she obviously has been working on its behalf."

"Could she be working with them solely to oust me?" Kutor asked.

"Very possibly."

Tien tZo coughed softly. "If I may be allowed to say something…" he said diffidently. When he had their attention he continued, choosing his words carefully: "We really need the bard now; his knowledge of these people, the gods they worship, and the powers they wield would be invaluable. But we don't have the bard, and we're the poorer for it. Since none of us here has that knowledge—that specialised lore—may I suggest that we find someone who has?"

"It is an excellent idea," Kutor said eventually, when the Shemmat's words had sunk in. He looked at the faces around him. "Another bard, perhaps?"

"I was thinking of someone else," Tien continued.

"Who?"

"The Andam!"

Deep in the heart of the Southern Marshes was a temple, a simple honeycombed artificial mountain that had been old when the Culai had first walked the World of Men. Its builders had not been of human kind, and the building was constructed with curiously shaped windows, strangely low doors, and no stairs; low, gently sloping ramps curved up to the topmost floors. There was nothing else like it in all the Planes of Existence.

It had lain neglected and forgotten for many generations until a warrior, the last of a massacred unit, wandering lost in the treacherous marshes, discovered the ruin. Seeking shelter in the building, he had undergone a terrifying visionary experience wherein he had travelled back through the lines of time to the First Age of Man, when the gods walked the World of Men, and it was during this vision—and because of it—that he formulated the *Epistles of the Andam*. This was the Old Faith in its purest form, a stark, harsh belief, adhering strictly to the principles laid down by the First Gods, but believing only in a single supreme deity rather than a pantheon of gods. And although the belief differed from the Old Faith in several other major respects, its priests and followers were regarded with a certain amount of awe by the believers of the Faith.

The wandering priests were a familiar and generally welcome sight on the roads of the Nations. They were gifted with the power of healing, and exercised their powers without regard for a patient's religion or belief. It was also said that they were powerful magicians.

But the Andam had paid a price for their belief and their gifts; four out of five of the priests who went to study in the temple in the Southern Marshes where the Andam belief had originated, contracted a terrifying wasting disease, which ate into the flesh and drew the skin so taut on the bones that it eventually cracked and split, leaving long open gashes on the flesh. To hide the shocking effects of the disease, the Andam priests wrapped themselves in robes of grey, usually leaving only their eyes free.

When Tien tZo had entered Karfondal before the fall of Geillard, he had come disguised as one of the Andam. While queuing for admittance to the city he had been drawn into conversation with another of the Andam. Although the man had seen through the Shemmat's disguise, he had nevertheless vouched for him with the city guards, allowing him access to the city. Once through the gates, the Andam had blessed him and gone on his way, and Tien had never seen him again.

Tien made his way down to the older part of the city. Karfondal, like most cities, had grown up on the ruins of an earlier settlement, and time and growing prosperity had moved the grander houses away from the stink of the quayside. And the waterfront—like the waterfronts of so many cities—quickly gained an infamous reputation.

In the past few moons, following the Cataclysm when the very fabric of the Planes of Existence had been rent, Karfondal had been flooded with refugees. And the vast majority of them had settled in rough shanty towns on the banks of the River Dal. Some of the dwellings—which were little more than scraps of cloth and baked mud tied onto a wooden framework—were actually built on the foul ooze of the Dal. There was no water, no sanitation, and the stench was incredible. The dwellings—if they could be called that—were built one on top of the other, and the partition between them was sometimes nothing more than a scrap of cloth. Whole families occupied a room no bigger than a large box. A thin passageway separated one side of the "street" from the other; it was nothing more than a stinking quagmire of ankle-deep filth at the best of times, which occasionally dipped into a shallow basin that could swallow a child.

For once, the Shemmat didn't feel out of place. There were representatives of nearly every nation in the known world; from Thusal at the top of the world, to the Dark Continent at the bottom, and all the Island Kingdoms, City States, and Nations in between.

The smell of death overlay the expected smells of humanity, with its cooking and excrement, and the ever-present stench of the river. This was the perfect breeding ground for revolution.

This hadn't existed before Kutor came to power—and although he was not the cause of it, people had short memories; the city dwellers would only remember that the refugees had come in with the bandit-chief, and the refugees would only remember that they had a better life before Kutor had taken the throne. Either way he would lose—and the Religion would be quick to step in and capitalise on that loss.

Tien found the Andam shelter deep in the heart of the shantytown, in the centre of a dingy square that opened out onto the docks. It consisted of a score of tents made of grubby grey canvas that had been stitched together and then pegged out on a wooden platform. A long line of refugees ran from the tent's opening, across the square and back through the dingy streets; there were men with slumped shoulders, women with babes in arms, and dull-eyed children standing patiently for the loaf of hard bread and the satchel of sour wine or milk that the priests distributed without asking for payment. Tien wondered briefly where they got the food and wine.

The Shemmat walked across the street, bypassing the silent line of people, and hopped up onto the wooden platform. Immediately the crowd came to dull, angry life, a buzz rippling down the line like a swarm of approaching insects. There was movement in the mouth of the tent and four of the Andam appeared. They were unlike any of the other priests Tien had seen in the past; these were tall, broad men, their grey robes doing little to disguise their muscular build. They were carrying metal-tipped staffs and the look in their eyes and the hard set to their faces was anything but priestly.

The priest nearest Tien lifted his staff, holding it in both hands and spun it once, the movement smooth and practised; then he pointed to the throng. "Join the queue, brother, there is food and drink enough for all," he said pleasantly. Again, unlike any of the Andam the Shemmat had seen, this man had the hood of his robes thrown back, revealing a broad, slightly flat-featured face—which showed no signs of the Andam disease. Tien tZo wondered if the four men were merely hired muscle brought in to ensure order.

The four were now crowding around him, and Tien knew if it came to a fight, their own positioning would hinder them, preventing them from using their staffs effectively, and he had no doubts that he could dispose of them easily enough. However, what about the crowd—how would they react? They had fallen silent now with the appearance of the Andam, watching, enjoying the entertainment, wondering what was going to happen, but Tien didn't want to think what might occur if he tossed the four priests into the mud at their feet.

"I have not come seeking alms," he said slowly, keeping his voice measured and reasoned, looking at each in turn, trying to decide which was the leader, and who would make the first move.

"I thought you looked a little too plump, a little too well-dressed to seek alms at our shelter," the first man spoke again. "But we'll feed all, irrespective of appearances." He looked at Tien again, noting the axes in the small yellow-skinned man's belt. "What do you want, brother?"

"I wish to speak to one of the Andam."

"We are Andam," the man said.

Tien said nothing, but the slight shifting of his expression betrayed his suspicions.

"Truly we are; not all of us contract the holy sickness."

"My business is…is not to be discussed in the open," Tien said. He made to take a step forward—and the four staves came down, barring his path. "My business concerns a certain hook-handed bard," he said softly.

Suddenly indecisive at the mention of the bard's, the four men looked at one another, and then one slipped away and ducked back into the grey tent. He appeared a moment later, and nodded, and the three remaining guards stepped aside, allowing Tien to enter.

The interior of the tent was dim and dusky, with the only illumination coming from a brazier on a tall stand in the centre of the surprisingly large open space. The flame was guttering, dancing blue-green across curling pieces of wood, emitting a pale white smoke, and the tent was heavy with a sharp, slightly acrid odour of herbs and spices which served to disguise the smells of the people, the river, and the city. Otherwise the tent was bare except for half a dozen huge baskets and a simple wooden bench.

There were four more Andam in the tent. One was tall and broad, like the brothers outside, two were typical Andam priests, small and frail, completely swathed in their robes and heavy grey bandages. The fourth man was also robed in the Andam fashion, but he was tall and thin, towering over the two smaller men. He was sitting behind the wooden bench, his bandaged hands wrapped around a much-travelled staff.

"So we meet again, Tien tZo, of the Shemmatae," the Andam said, coming slowly to his feet, leaning heavily on his staff.

Tien was completely taken by surprise. "My lord…"

The Andam smiled, his teeth white and strong in the shadow of his cowl. "There are no lords here, only brothers of the One."

"You're the Andam I met…" Tien said suddenly.

The priest nodded. "We have met before."

"I came looking for you—but if the truth be told, I never expected to find you."

"But you did. And what brings you in search of the Andam? Salvation, perhaps?" Again the quick smile.

"I fear I am past salvation," Tien said with a wry smile, "but I am in need of help."

"How may I help, brother?"

Tien looked around the tent, at the other Andam and the guards who were within earshot. "Can we talk elsewhere? I have no wish to cast doubts on your brothers' honour or trustworthiness, but I fear we may be overheard by those not of the Faith, and what I have to say to you is too sensitive to be lost to the enemy yet. And if we talk elsewhere," he added, "then the people outside will not have to wait."

The Andam nodded. "Of course. We will walk." He glanced down at the two seated priests. "I will return shortly; continue feeding the people." He looked at Tien again. "This way, please; we will go out the back way."

As Tien hurried past the table, he glanced down into the baskets that surrounded it and found them to be full of bread—long dark loaves—small caskets of milk or wine, and one was filled with fruit. "Tell me," he said, when they stepped off the wooden platform onto the muddy ground, "how do you manage to feed so many, with never a shortage, nor any turned away empty-handed? Is your supply so inexhaustible?"

"It is a simple spell—well, perhaps not so simple," the Andam amended, "but it is nothing more than a spell of multiplication, creating two from one, and then four from two, and so on. As long as we retain the original object, we can create as many as we need."

"What do I call you?" Tien said, glancing up at the tall priest.

"How many Andam do you know?"

"Just you," Tien said with a smile.

"Then call me Andam," the priest said. "It will suffice." He jerked his head back in the direction of the tent and the long line of silent people. "If you or the bard have any influence at court, then you might use it to see if you can do something to alleviate this situation. There is genuine suffering here: people are dying and diseased. It's only a matter of time before plague takes over, and when it does, then it will be something like Yellow Sickness or Water Fever, and it will not just be contained in the Lower City, or on the docks, it will spread throughout the entire capital."

"I was thinking much the same myself earlier as I was looking for you," Tien said. "I didn't realise things were so bad there, and

I truly don't think Kutor knows either. He has allotted certain funds for the refugees but obviously not enough. Don't worry, I'll tell him—or perhaps you could even tell him yourself," he said suddenly.

Andam glanced sidelong at him, but said nothing. He walked on and turned down a side street that led directly onto the wooden pilings of the docks, before asking, "What do you mean?"

"I mean I could arrange for you to meet the Emperor."

"Why would you want to do that? What would be the price?"

"There would be no price—except perhaps a little advice."

The Andam smiled quickly again. "Perhaps you should start at the beginning and tell your tale…" he suggested.

Kutor fixed the bolt in the door and then turned and leaned back against the polished wood to survey the small room that had become his prison; he might be Emperor of the Seven Nations, but everything he could call his own was in this room.

He stripped off his swordbelt and tossed it onto his bed, and then pulled his surcoat over his head to get at his link-mail shirt—nowadays he went nowhere without the metal shirt and without carrying arms of some description. At least when he'd been a bandit in the Outlands, he had been able to relax once in a while, and there he had been surrounded by his friends. It was something he had been thinking about a lot recently, turning it around in his head, trying to discover a solution, but all it did was to turn circle after circle and get him nowhere—he was stuck with it. He couldn't abdicate—not just yet in any case—and besides he owed it to those who had given so much to make him ruler, especially to the memory of those who had given their lives.

Keshian kept telling him everything would be fine when they broke the conspiracy, but Kutor knew that when—if—the conspiracy was broken, there would be something else that would keep him a prisoner in this tiny cell.

He had entertained the vague fantasy of just upping and leaving. He could slip out one night, take a horse from the stables and ride off with as much money as he could manage. He'd do it, too—except that he would probably have the cursed bard arrive after him—or more likely, have him there waiting for him when he arrived.

And where was the bard now? Where had he gone when they most needed him? North most likely, but what was north, except cold and Chopts, and both were deadly?

What was he to do? People were coming to him daily with questions, things to do, deeds to sign, decisions to be made, always decisions. When he'd been a bandit chief, things had been easier; he had been making decisions for only ten, fifteen, sometimes twenty people; now, his decisions affected thousands, if not tens of thousands of people.

And was he taking the right decision in agreeing to support the Old Faith? Could he in all honesty say he approved of the Faith with its rigid insistences and observations upon law and devotion to a Pantheon that rarely—if ever—demonstrated its power? The Religion, on the other hand, was a modern, accessible belief, with a small but seemingly powerful pantheon of gods who almost daily appeared to demonstrate some aspect of their power.

If the truth be told, Kutor, Emperor of the Seven Nations, supported the New Religion. And perhaps the time was drawing near for him to admit it.

The old woman slumped in her chair. "There, 'tis done. The room is warded, cleverly too, but not cleverly enough. The thought is planted..."

"And now what?" the Warlord asked eagerly.

"Now, we wait. On no account can this be hurried. He must think this is his own idea. The conclusion must be his and his alone." She smiled, her face dissolving into a spiderweb of wrinkles. "If we cannot break him, we will surely bend him..."

"It is not Trialos," the Andam said quickly, when Tien tZo finished his tale.

"How can you be sure?"

"Because if Trialos walked this plane, then I—and every other sensitive or part-sensitive on this Plane of Existence—would know. I would imagine it's just a loose presence from the Ghost World, some cursed thing which heard the call and latched onto an empty body. It happens."

"Are they dangerous?"

"They are savage creatures usually, some of them with a taste for human blood because it contains a part of the essence of life, and by drinking the blood they are taking that person's essence into themselves."

"Vampir!" Tien breathed, suddenly chilled.

Andam shook his head slightly. "Not exactly; the vampir sustains its life by drinking the blood of the living, while this is a dead creature seeking to restore itself to a semblance of life by drinking blood."

"Vampir!" Tien stressed savagely. "Can they be destroyed?"

"The host body must be completely consumed by fire."

Tien grinned. "That can be arranged."

"Perhaps not," Andam said. "You don't know the identity of the creature that is now inhabiting that poor girl's body. It need not even be of human kind. But you can be sure that now it has got a foothold in the World of Men it is not going to relinquish it so easily. It will be strong, and it will also have access to some small magics—whatever lore it absorbed in the Ghost Worlds."

"Can it be controlled?"

The Andam shrugged. He walked to the end of a rotten wooden pier and looked down into the scummed water. "I certainly wouldn't like to try and control it. But this Lady Esse should have some measure of control over it—but for how long, I don't know." He turned and looked at Tien, his metal-grey eyes glittering beneath his hood. "You should also know that it will have the power to call others of its kind to this Plane of Existence, and you can be sure they will not side with the Old Faith!"

8
Conspiracy

Man is unique amongst the beasts in that he will betray his own kind...
The Warrior, the Life of Owen, Weapon Master

The howl ripped through the Lower City, a terrifying, terrible cry of hunger.

The howl shattered the night silence again, rising now to an eerie wail that brought the shanty town to life—but no one ventured out into the open. In the squalid tents children cried, but were swiftly quietened, and both men and women stifled their moans. The wealthier merchants checked the bars on their windows, called out tentatively for their guards, while the poorer shopkeepers checked weapons, and the few people still unlucky to be on the streets—the late revellers and the women of the night—scurried for shelter.

The third cry was all the more horrific because the note of triumph in it was clearly audible!

And then there was silence.

The vampir had awoken at twilight. This was its first sign of "life" since it had sat up in the girl's body on the bloody altar stone two days previously. Then it had merely looked around, and after the panicked exit of the congregation, it had slumped into a deep, trance-like slumber. But in that time the huge wound in the body had healed, until all that remained was a thin white scar beneath her breast and up along her breastbone.

Just when the Warlord had thought the girl was dead—truly dead now—he had noticed the fluttering of her eyes beneath the closed eyelids; whatever had taken up residence in her torn corpse remained.

It was too late now, but he was bitterly regretting that he had allowed the Lady Esse to bring the creature to the Armoury. She had argued that the cells were the safest place for it; the three cells were buried deep beneath the building, the walls, floor, and ceiling as thick as a man's body and sheathed in metal. The bars on the door were each the thickness of a man's arm; there were no windows. The cells were usually used for holding precious metal, script, or coin, or sometimes special consignments of weapons, and were virtually impregnable.

On the Lady Esse's instructions, the Warlord had sent his son out earlier that evening to find one of the women of the night; with the huge increase in refugees in the city, the numbers of women walking the streets, trying to find the price of a meal for themselves or their families had increased dramatically, and the Warlord's son was careful to make his choice from this group. He had returned just before twilight, with a tall, blond-haired, pale-eyed woman from the Northlands. The woman had been given a heavily drugged wine and when she collapsed she had been dragged down the stairs to the cellar and thrown into the cell with the creature. The Warlord had then sent his son away, and he and the Lady Esse had remained behind to await the awakening of the creature.

This new presence in the cell seemed to stir the creature, and her muscles began to ripple and her fingers and toes to twitch and curl. In the world above as the light faded and the sun dipped below the horizon, the creature's eyes snapped open—and it was like looking into two pits. At a cursory glance she was a reasonably pretty young woman, newly come to womanhood, with pale close-cropped blond hair. But her eyes and her movements betrayed her—for both pupil and white were completely black, and seemed to have hardened, giving them a slightly metallic sheen, and she moved with all the fluidity of a hunting animal.

The Lady Esse sighed and nodded her head; it was as she suspected—it was a vampir, a presence from the Ghost World who had battened onto the newly-dead body.

"It is...is it the Lord Trialos?" the Warlord asked tentatively.

"Vampir," the Lady Esse said.

"Ah," he breathed.

"It is still useful," the twisted old woman said. She nodded, murmuring softly to herself, "Yes, the vampir have their uses..."

And then the creature howled!

Within the confines of the cell the noise was incredible. It sat forward, its head thrown back, its neck taut, mouth open, teeth bared, the sound issuing out from it in a single, breathless scream. The Warlord pressed his arms to his ears and staggered back, terrified that the sound would be heard in the streets above, and immediately realising that the scream could probably be heard all across the city.

The vampir came slowly, shakily, to its feet—and screamed again.

The Warlord sank slowly to his knees at the incredible noise. He tasted salt and copper on his lips and realised that his nose was bleeding, there was a rushing roaring sound in his ears, and he was afraid lest his eardrums burst. Through a red haze he saw the creature—the vampir—take a step across the cell in the direction of the drugged woman, who was already stirring, the noise having penetrated to her subconscious. The vampir's head was thrust forward, its teeth bared, its hands stiff, the fingers hooked inwards like claws, and the Warlord had a brief momentary flash of a bear-like creature, and wondered if this was what now inhabited the woman's body. And then the vampir fell upon the stirring woman. Its teeth closed around the soft flesh of the neck, tearing into it—not the image the Warlord had of a vampir delicately sucking blood—this was a beast feeding.

And then the creature threw back its head and screamed again, screaming triumphantly, then bent its head and buried its face in the torn neck. The sounds of feeding disgusted even the hardened warmerchant.

The Warlord turned away from the cell door, pale-faced and sweating. He leaned back against the wall, and the two spikes that replaced his hands rattled slightly off the stone with the trembling of his body. Beside him the Lady Esse looked through the reinforced bars of the cell, watching impassively as the creature fed.

She turned to the Warlord, her eyes triumphant. "Soon, we will have two…"

In the Andam mission deep in the shanty town on the banks of the Dal, the Andam priest sat up; he was shivering even though the night was muggy and close. He touched his face, feeling the bones through the parchment-like skin, and his fingers came away bloody. It could have been the sudden splitting of his skin which had awoken him, but he doubted it—he had lived with it for most of his adult life. There was movement at the far end of the tent, a hiss of cloth on cloth, and the Andam reached for his staff. Pointing it in the direction of the noise, the priest fired the staff, bringing it to a pale green light, but nothing was revealed in the trembling glow. However, his wounds were aching—a sure sign that something was amiss...

He was moving before he realised what was happening, throwing himself forward and down, hitting the wooden boards with a thump. Every joint in his body cracked and popped and scores of old wounds reopened as the skin was stretched by the sudden exertion. But Andam kept rolling, ignoring the flaring pain, rising to his feet, his staff coming around, swinging up and across his body, a hard emerald light streaming from it. Caught in the green light was a short, squat, bald man, with a deeply curved scimitar held in both hands. The would-be assassin hesitated, trying to decide whether it was worth attacking the priest again. His decision made, he had actually started moving towards Andam when the tent flap was thrown back and four of the large, undiseased brothers ran in, attracted by the green light that was flooding from the tent. The bald man spat something at Andam, then turned and fled through a slit in the tent. Two of the brothers followed him, while the other two remained with the priest.

"Holy Father, are you all right?"

"You're hurt..."

Andam raised both hands. "I am unhurt; the blood you see is merely the result of old wounds reopening. Bring me some warm water if you will. I will bathe them."

One of the men hurried away immediately. "Did you recognise the man, Holy Father?" the remaining brother asked.

"No; I hadn't seen him before. He was an assassin of sorts, not a very good one, I should think."

"But who would want to attack you, Holy Father?"

"I'm sure many people would, but you need not concern yourself with that at the moment. When I have bathed and rested a little, two of you may accompany me to the palace. I think it is time I spoke to the Emperor."

"I heard there was trouble around here last night." Owen had his back to the Warlord as he spoke, but he was watching the man's reflection in a highly-polished shield.

"Indeed, so my son told me this morning." The man's thin face remained a mask, although Owen thought he saw something move behind his dark eyes.

"You heard nothing?" Owen turned around and deliberately walked past the war-merchant to examine a display of knives mounted on a board behind him.

"I sleep deeply," he said suavely.

The Weapon Master laughed. "You must sleep like one of the dead in that case—I heard the screams, and I was in my room in the palace. What is so special about this?" he asked, changing the subject, and pointing to one of the knives.

"Aaah," the Warlord said, grateful for the change of subject, "you have an eye for the unusual." He skilfully lifted the knife from its pegs on the board, using his two spikes, and presented it to the Weapon Master. "You will notice the rigid spine of the blade, and its thickness too—that is to lend it strength—and you will also notice the one-piece construction. Blade and handle are both of one piece, with the handle wrapped around with strips of leather and cloth. But the unusual feature of this blade is the way the underside of the blade curves gently away from the point."

The Weapon Master balanced the knife in his hand. "It's unwieldy and point heavy…"

"It will also pierce chain mail and some plate armour!"

Owen looked at the blade more appreciatively. Armour-piercing knives were not unknown, but they were usually huge, bulky things, more akin to swords than knives. "Where did you get it?"

"There are a lot of fine weapons coming out of the north these days," the Warlord said quickly, and then turned away, abruptly finishing the conversation: "I have discussed your offer with my principals and they have accepted…tentatively. You will, of course, understand their reluctance to accept this about-face by one of the chief architects in the removal of Geillard from the throne?"

Owen nodded. He continued turning the blade over and over in his hands, but his eyes were on the merchant's sallow face.

"You will go to the Duke de Courtney where you will receive your instructions, and he will make the necessary arrangements."

"Arrangements for what?"

"Why, for the removal of Kutor, of course!"

De Courtney was a small, slightly foppish young man, with a sharp, hard face, a too-quick smile and eyes that never looked a person in the face. Owen distrusted and disliked him on sight, and his instincts

told him that whatever else this young man was, he was no conspirator. He also realised that this man was expendable—which was why
he had been given his name.

"I understand you are with us," de Courtney said, immediately
the servant had closed the doors on the large, glass-roofed chamber.

Owen looked around the room before replying. The glass roof
made it surprisingly bright, and the lightness was accentuated by the
white marble walls and pale blue marble floor. An ornately carved
and decorated white crystal fountain spat scented water in the centre
of the room, the effect spoiled slightly because the water pressure
was low and the water came in spurts rather than a smooth arc.
Otherwise the room was bare, devoid of all furniture, pictures, tapestries, or ornaments. And against it the Duke de Courtney was a
gaudy splash of colour, wines, reds, and purples, robes in the latest
fashions, matching the paint on his lips and cheeks, highlighting his
rather pale complexion. The Weapon Master walked around the
edge of the chamber, while the gaudy young man stood in the centre of the room, nervously watching him.

"You are with us?" de Courtney asked again, and this time the
doubt was clear in his voice.

"It depends what I'm supposed to be with you in," Owen said
quietly. The room made him feel dirty, unwashed, and unkempt—
although in the last few moons he had never dressed so well, washed
so often, nor ate so frequently.

"We are to topple the renegade." The young man smiled delightedly.

"And who are we?" Owen asked suddenly.

"The Twelve..." de Courtney began and then smiled self-consciously. "Aaah, I'm not supposed to tell you that until you have
proved yourself."

In the huge cellars beneath the Warlord's Armoury, representatives
of the Twelve Families, Karfondal's ruling clans, were gathering,
summoned by the Lady Esse. They had come, some reluctantly,
others eagerly, but they had all come; they knew how destructively
virulent the woman's wrath could be. They had come to see the
creatures they had all heard about, the creatures that would aid them
in their struggle against the renegade. They had come to see the
vampir.

Owen had refused an offer of drink, and watched in silence while the young man nervously swallowed his own drink and then immediately started in on the second. "I understand there is some difficulty in you actually killing the usurper yourself," de Courtney asked, his eyes dancing across the Weapon Master's face.

"I am no assassin," Owen stated flatly.

De Courtney said nothing, but his eyes betrayed him. "Disbelieve me you may," Owen said softly, "but call me a liar and I'll butcher you here and now in your pristine hall, and stain these white walls red with your blood."

"I didn't...I never..."

"You doubted my word!" Owen snapped.

De Courtney swallowed hard. Unconsciously, his hand drifted down to his belt, close to the ivory-hilted dagger.

"And so much as touch that knife and I'll take off your hand!" The duke's hand moved away from the dagger as if it were red-hot. "Now, tell me what you want of me?" Owen snarled, deliberately adopting the guise of the savage bloody-handed killer. De Courtney was so obviously not a conspirator that Owen wondered what game the Warlord was playing in using the young man. He had half-expected to be attacked once he was in the duke's presence, but whatever he had been expecting it was not to be met by this frightened creature.

"Kutor has announced that he intends to visit each of the Seven Nations very shortly, survey the damage caused by the Cataclysm, and meet with the Viceroys. We need an itinerary of the usurper's travels over the next moon; we need to know where he's going and when, how many men he'll be taking with him, and where they're passing the night."

"Is that all?" Owen asked sarcastically, but it was a wasted effort, the duke was too frightened to recognise sarcasm.

De Courtney suddenly shook his head. "No, not quite. If it's at all possible, we would like to know the actual room he'll be sleeping in." He paused and added. "Can you do it?"

Owen nodded. "Some of it I can get immediately, the rest will come a little later, but yes, you'll get your information."

De Courtney rubbed his hands together. "With it we can kill the usurper..."

"With these we can kill the usurper," the Lady Esse said proudly, twitching back the curtain the Warlord had drawn across the cell doors.

"What are they?" a woman breathed, the loathing in her voice belying the fascination in her face.

"They are vampir: dead bodies inhabited by creatures from the Ghost World..."

The two vampir had come close to the cell's bars. On the surface, they were two naked young women, one bearing a slight scar beneath her breasts and in the centre of her chest, the other with heavy bruising around her throat. Only the metallic coal-black spaces where their eyes should have been betrayed their inhuman occupants.

"I thought the Lord Trialos had come..." the young woman continued, and then fell abruptly silent under the Lady Esse's grim stare.

"These are his gifts," the ancient sorceress snarled. "They have been sent to us by the Lord Trialos to further his—and our—ends."

A white-haired man, with the pale blue eyes of an innocent, touched the young woman who had spoken, drawing her back from the Lady Esse's wrath. "And how can we achieve this end?" he asked quietly, respectfully. "How can we best use these creatures? What is your advice?"

The Lord Rocque was the last representative of one of the most ancient ruling families in the Seven Nations. The Rocques had seen Emperors come and go, yet, surprisingly, they had never attempted to take the crown for themselves. The Rocques were administrators always, yet wielding as much power as any King or Emperor. Lord Rocque had been treasurer to both Geillard XI and his son, and he had continued in the position when the renegade Kutor came to power solely because there was no one to replace him.

The Lady Esse walked away from the cells and limped down the corridor into one of the Warlord's huge storerooms. The centre of the floor had been cleared, and a single ornately carved onyx chair placed on a beautiful Talarian rug. The sorceress sank down onto the cushioned seat of the chair, and the Warlord immediately draped a heavy woollen blanket around her legs. The nobles found themselves seats on wooden boxes or remained standing, facing the old woman. The Warlord stood behind the Lady Esse.

From down the hallway came the muffled whimper of one of the vampir.

The Warlord looked around the room. The representatives of the Twelve Families had been meeting here since the usurper first seized power, and it amused him slightly to see how they resumed the seats and positions they had taken up on the first time they had met here. However, of the twelve present, only four were of any consequence, and their decisions would decide the other eight.

There was the Lord Rocque, now Kutor's treasurer, a man of extraordinary cunning and with a fortune that was reputed to rival Geillard's during the height of his power. He was an indifferent devotee of the New Religion, but recognised it as an interesting and successful way of gaining and wielding power. He was also aware, however, that Kutor would not—could not—afford to leave him in his position much longer, and that alone provided enough of a spur to encourage him to remove the usurper.

Standing to one side, his arms folded across an enormous stomach, was the Lord Bleau. A great personal friend of the deposed Emperor, his vast estates and holdings bordered and surrounded Karfondal and the approaches to the capital. The Bleau family had built up their huge fortune from the slave trade, and the present holder of the title had supplemented it with the production of exotics: highly-trained, single-skilled slaves who performed but one function—and performed it to perfection. A man of immense wealth, he had a nightmare vision of his lands being forfeited and his private wealth confiscated...and Kutor's feelings about slavery were well-known. A deeply religious man, however, he had been a long-time follower of the Religion, and had provided a major portion of the funds and nearly all the slaves and craftsmen which had gone into the building of the cathedral in the centre of the city. The fat man seemed unusually nervous tonight, the Warlord thought, but that might have been just from his proximity to the vampir.

The woman sitting in front of him, however, showed no signs of nervousness. Rumour had it that the Lady d'Homana had a heart of stone, and in truth, in all the years the Warlord had known her, he had never once seen the slightest trace of anything that even vaguely resembled the gentler emotions cross her hatchet face. Her age was indeterminate, although the merchant would have placed it somewhere around his own for she still dressed in a style that had been fashionable for young women at the time of his youth, a fashion which left her shoulders, upper arms, and most of her breasts bare. Despite her age, her skin was still flawless, and the Warlord wondered if there was any truth in the rumour that she bathed in fresh blood every day to keep it that way. He could well believe it. She derived much of her wealth from the Northlands, since her estates bordered the mineral-rich ice-fields, and she took a bounty on every animal trapped within her domain. She also kept a Gallowglas mercenary as a bodyguard, and the rumour was that he was more than just a mere bodyguard; those who crossed her were apt to come to particularly bloody ends. Her attraction to the Religion—like Rocque's—was mainly the power and the opportunities for power which it offered.

As the Lady Esse looked up, preparing to speak, the Warlord glanced over at the fourth influential member of the twelve, Boazio, Master of the Fleet.

For generations, the Boazios had captained the Imperial Fleet, ruling the sea as others had ruled the land. The Boazio fortune had been originally made by piracy and the present holder of the title was still not adverse to lowering the Imperial colours on occasion and running up his own. His reputation with his mariners was impeccable, and he treated them with the utmost respect and fairness; they in return adored him almost to the point of godhood; and yet the Warlord knew that the tall, blond, ruddy-faced man, now into middle-age, had killed at least a score of servants at his palace, and when in his cups—and he only drank on dry land—had an evil temper. Surprisingly, his devotion to the Religion seemed a genuine belief, and he was a staunch devotee of Aiaida, the Lord of the Sea Wind. He abhorred Kutor for no other reason than he had usurped the Imperial Throne and followed the Old Faith.

"There is a way for us to kill this usurper," the Lady Esse said suddenly, her voice rasping. "We can do it in such a way that no blame will fall to us, so that it will appear to have been an act of the gods—a sign of their displeasure, as it were. Already, I have put about the rumour that the gods—both Religion and Pantheon—are angry with Kutor for usurping the throne of his half-brother…"

"Should we highlight that?" Lord Rocque said suddenly.

The Lady Esse's eyes flashed angrily at the interruption. "Every man fears having his inheritance snatched from him by a greedy relative; that is how I am portraying Kutor."

The Lord Rocque bowed, a smile playing across his thin lips.

"Later, when our plans are at a more advanced stage, I will have it put abroad that the gods—of either belief, whichever suits our purpose—have decided that Kutor must pay the price for his greed. And then the vampir will slay him." She paused, looking at the faces for reaction, reading the different expressions, and then using her occult skills to probe below the surface, reading their deeper thoughts. Their fear of her brought a ghost of a smile to her twisted lips.

"I thought there should be at least six vampir," she added.

"Why so many?" the Lord Bleau asked quickly, mopping his brow; he thought two of the creatures were two too many. He had seen many creatures that were neither man nor beast, he had observed creatures from other Planes of Existence, and had once even seen one of the fabulous frai-forde, the Star Lorn, but never had he been so frightened as when he looked, first at the naked female bodies, seeing those only, and then into the depthless black pits that took the place of their eyes.

"There will be six," the Lady Esse said firmly. "One each for Keshian, Owen, his servant, and Fodla, and two for Kutor—of his death we must be assured."

The Lady d'Homana leaned forward. "And the resurrected warrior-bitch?"

"The Katan warrior has followed her bard into the Northlands." The Lady Esse's lips curled. "Steps are being taken to ensure that neither of them return."

"The bard is a dangerous and powerful enemy," Boazio said suddenly from the corner of the room.

"But this time he doesn't know what he's up against!"

"When will we strike?" Boazio asked.

"Soon. Kutor plans to visit the capitals of the nations. He will be on the road for three or more moons; there will be plenty of opportunity then."

The Lady d'Homana sat forward. "Even with the vampir, we will still need additional information on the usurper's movements," she said quickly. "Obviously the information we supplied the last assassin was incorrect in some way. My informants in the palace tell me she got nowhere near the bed chamber."

"We have a new agent in the palace, someone close to the throne.

We are testing his reliability at the moment, and I am somewhat encouraged. He will supply us with the usurper's itinerary."

"There is also the matter of the Andam..." the Lord Rocque said. "The High Priest must be removed from the picture before we act."

"That should be taken care of this very night," she snapped. She glared around the room, almost as if daring anyone to question her further. "So, if there are no further questions and no objections to my plan...?"

There were none.

9
The God-Touched

Thusal is the northernmost town of the Seven Nations, a disreputable den of every vice imaginable...

Lilis' Geographica

Thusal is the northernmost town, and is a valuable link between the barbarian Northlands and the civilised Southern Nations. What little law there is in this otherwise lawless land is to be found in Thusal...

Lilis' Geographica (Revised Edition)

This day came to us a brother, by name Paedur, called the Hookhand, with two companions—a female warrior in the armour of a Katan and a boy, late of the Monastery of Ectoraige...

Register of the Thusal Bardhouse

"I don't know how you got through," the man said bluntly, putting a platter of still smoking bread onto the white-sanded table. "You're the first—the only—travellers to make it across the Wastelands this season. Of course," he added, smiling a gap-toothed smile, "I realise you're no ordinary traveller."

Paedur turned from the fire and looked at the man wearing the brown and gold robes of a Bard-Master. "You're suggesting we were let through?"

Eiron, Bard-Master of the Thusal Bardhouse, eased his tall, spare frame into a chair and broke the crumbling bread for the woman and boy, passing it to them on simple wooden plates. He glanced up at the bard—the "infamous" Paedur Shanaqui—and grinned again. "Bard, Thusal is surrounded—it may not be evident, but it is surrounded, and this place is doubly watched. You reached here because they wanted you to reach here."

Paedur looked at the old man, and for a single moment, that tiny part of him which was still human felt a pang of envy; if things had been otherwise, he might have lived out the remainder of his days in peace and simplicity like Eiron, continuing his research, writing, teaching perhaps. He had never asked to be the Champion of the Old Gods—but he hadn't refused it, either. "Perhaps you had better prepare for an attack, then," he said finally.

But the Bard-Master shook his head. "If they were going to attack you, they could have done so on the King Road, or at any other point on your journey. No," he shook his balding head, "it is my belief that you are being drawn deeper and deeper into the Northlands for some reason." He sat back for a moment and watched the woman and the boy devouring the steaming herb-bread, and then he stood up, his eyes on the bard's sharp face. "Perhaps we will leave your companions to eat in peace and we will walk awhile in the corridors; the air is cooler there—our thoughts will be clearer."

Katani went to stand up but the bard, in a rare moment of physical contact, rested his hand on her shoulder. "No, stay, please. Eat and rest. Only the Gods know when you will be able to do either again." Surprised, the woman looked up, and found that his eyes had taken the warm white gold of the table, giving his face an almost human appearance.

Eiron and Paedur stepped silently into the corridor and immediately turned to the left, heading down into the courtyard. They were almost of a height, although the bard was perhaps fractionally taller, but the Bard Master's rather chubby, red-checked face and his almost perpetual smile made him something the bard could never be again—it made him human.

Now that they were alone, they automatically fell into the respective attitudes of master and pupil, even though Paedur had far surpassed Eiron, and both knew it; but old ingrained habits were difficult to break.

"How did you get past the guards on the city gates?" Eiron asked softly, stopping to look out through the open doorway into the enclosed courtyard beyond.

"A simple glamour," Paedur replied, puffing up his hood as they stepped out into the uncovered courtyard, more by habit than from any feeling of chill. Since he had been gifted by the gods he had become inured to extremes of heat and cold.

Eiron frowned. "But if you could do that, then so could the beasts…"

"With respect, Master, my powers are somewhat beyond theirs."

Eiron pulled up his own hood and grinned hugely. "So I've heard. Tell me, brother, are half the stories they tell about you true?"

Paedur's eyes, white and grey from the snow on the cobbled stones, crinkled in a brief smile. "Half are."

"You are aware that the Council of Bards are trying to decide whether to venerate you or to strip you of your rank?" the older man asked very softly.

The bard stopped in shock. Eiron walked on a few steps and then turned and said, "You have broken the basic precepts of a bard; you have interfered in politics; you have used your tales for ends other than teaching and the furtherance of knowledge; you have consorted with magicians, and have taken to using their arts…" Eiron shrugged. "The list of charges grows daily. It need not worry you at the moment, but there will come a time when it should. You made enemies at Baddalaur."

"Tell me what bard has not used his tales to influence people and events? Surely that is the main function of a bard, and my use of the arts is not entirely of my doing…"

Eiron raised both hands. "I know, I know. You need not argue with me; at the last Council meeting when it was put to the vote whether to recall you for trial, I voted in your favour, if that is any consolation."

"Thank you…" Paedur murmured.

They walked around the statue of Ectoraige, the God of Learning and Knowledge, one of the gods whom the monks, scribes, and bards had in common. "You know how they fear change, and anything which threatens the old Order, and by association, their rule. I suppose they're frightened that if the old Emperor regains his throne, he will begin a campaign against the bards solely because of you…"

"If Geillard regains the throne, he will begin a pogrom against all the followers of the Old Faith, not just the bards. This time they mean to destroy the Faith completely."

"And that is why you are in the north?" Eiron asked shrewdly. They had crossed the courtyard and were standing before a tall, arched door. There was no lock, but the Bard-Master touched four of the decorative studs in a certain order and then pushed the door open.

The library of the Thusal Bardhouse was small—and the shelves were completely bare.

"What happened?"

"When I learned what had happened at the Monastery of Ectoraige, I had the library stripped, the books, manuscripts, scrolls, and charts sealed in waxed containers and then buried."

"Why?" Paedur walked into the centre of the room, the empty shelves echoing slightly as Eiron moved to join him.

"It is my belief that the beasts—or whoever controls them now, for they have never been like this before—seem intent on destroying all knowledge. In the last few moons, whenever the farmhouses or isolated crofts or keeps were raided, the Chopts have ensured that all signs of learning, the books, the scrolls, the maps, have been destroyed. They have never done that before—for what interest have they in books and lore? And then when I learned what they had done to the Ectoraige library, I knew what their plan was." He looked up at the bard but in the dimness of the small room, his features were almost unreadable. "They have set out to destroy all knowledge...or more likely they have been instructed to do this. Without knowledge there is no progress—only ignorance and regression. And an ignorant people are ripe for the wiles of priests and gods. Unlearned folk believe with a far stronger will than educated people."

The bard was nodding slowly. "You are close enough to the truth. I think they have been instructed to destroy all the evidence of the Old Faith, wiping this plane free of everything pertaining to the Pantheon and the Old Gods. Without knowledge, there will be no belief, and without belief, there will be no gods." Paedur looked around the empty shelves again, deciding that there was no lonelier sight than bare library shelves. "Have you advised Baddalaur of your suspicions?"

"I sent a messenger bird, but I've received no reply. They'll probably dismiss it as just another stupid idea."

The bard grimaced; the Council's stupidity would prove their downfall.

They left the bare library and returned to the courtyard. Eiron led Paedur to a stairway that was almost hidden behind a species of wild northern creeper, and together they climbed the worn stone steps to stand on the top of the open watchtower, looking down over the town of Thusal. Although it was still early forenoon, the lights were burning brightly in the town, and the sounds of early revelry were brittle and sharply distinct on the bitter air.

"Thusal, the last bastion of civilisation..." Eiron sounded almost disgusted.

"Compared to what lurks in the snow-fields, it is," Paedur remarked.

Surprisingly, Eiron shook his head in disagreement. "The beasts have a code of sorts—a savage, brutal code admittedly—but they live by it. Here in this supposedly civilised town there is no law but the blade and cunning." He shook his head savagely. "Aaah, but I'm getting too old for this. The Cold Months make me morbid. It's not a bad place really, once you get to know the rules. But the hard part is just learning those rules."

"And what are the rules?" Paedur asked, leaning forward, his eyes sparkling with the glow of the distant lights.

"To mind your own business." The Bard-Master looked at the bard. "And speaking of business, what brings you to the Northlands?" he asked quietly.

"I thought I came looking for Geillard, but now I find I'm chasing Mannam, once-lord of the Dead."

"I heard a tale that you were personally responsible for his demise as the Lord of the Dead..."

"How did you know?" Paedur asked quickly

"I too am a follower of the Faith, remember. I have walked the myriad Planes of Existence. I have contact with the Ghost World..."

"It is true," Paedur nodded, and turned back to the town.

"And when you find Geillard and Mannam—what then?"

"I'd like to tell you I'd kill them—but somehow I'm not sure any more. I'll certainly try to stop them if I can—and without bloodshed if that's possible. Although," he added very quietly, "I'm not sure that that is possible."

Eiron nodded. "It would be preferable; there is already too much blood on your head and hands. They are with the Chopts, you think?" he asked, continuing on in a brisker tone.

"I can only assume so."

"Then you'll need someone who can lead you to the Chopt encampments and caves."

"Is there such a guide?" Paedur asked, surprised. "I didn't think there was any dealing with the beasts."

Eiron grinned hugely. "Of course there are dealings. The beasts bring furs and precious stones and herbs from the Northlands; in

return they get blankets and food and unofficially, of course, weapons. However the trade in weapons seems to have died down—
recently they've been carrying new weapons of their own, fine workmanship, too. Perhaps they've finally trained a proper weapon-smith."

"And where would I find such a guide?" Paedur asked patiently, aware that Eiron would receive few visitors in the course of
the seasons, and therefore could be excused if he tended to ramble
from the point.

"You'll find him at the Tavern of the Blasted Tree. His name is
Bastion...he is called the Marked Man!"

The Tavern of the Blasted Tree had once been a church to one of
the wilder northern gods and was so ancient that even its name and
the name of its deity had been forgotten now. When its followers
had died out, then so too had the god. The gods thrive on the faith
of Man and without faith there is no substance.

Paedur pushed open the tall double doors of the church and
stepped into the murky interior. The air was foetid, rank with odours,
mainly human, and principally those of excrement and sour wine,
tainted with the sharp stench of urine. Little of the church's earlier
decorations remained, with the exception of a series of particularly
well-done frescoes high on the walls, but these were so begrimed
now that only small portions gave a hint of their former excellence.
The tall-sided, almost box-like pews remained, still in their original
positions, and the bar was now where the altar had once been. Paedur
found the whole arrangement vaguely obscene.

He walked down the centre aisle, aware of the stares he was
attracting, although no-one made a move to challenge him. Thusal,
like many towns on the outskirts of civilisation, had its share of
drifters, and questions could often be answered with a knife or sword
in the belly. Nevertheless, Paedur's height and bearing marked him
apart from ordinary men, and even though he had kept his hood
pulled forward over his face, his eyes had taken the light from the
smoky torches and occasionally glinted gold or bronze from beneath his cowl.

The bar keeper didn't even look up at the new arrival, merely set
up a glass of murky rofion and pushed it towards him. "I'll take
whatever coin you got."

"I'm looking for Bastion."

"Don't serve that here," the bar keeper began with a gap-toothed smile, looking into the bard's shadowed cowl. But his eyes remained pitiless, and his left hand moved down to the edge of the bar.

Paedur tilted his head back and allowed the light from the trio of torches behind the bar to turn his eyes to brass. "Touch the club under the bar and I'll take your hand off at the wrist," he hissed. He moved his left arm, allowing the curve of his etched hook to appear from beneath his cloak.

Colour drained from the bar keeper's face. "You're Paedur the Bard!"

"Bastion!"

The man started to shake his head, but Paedur moved his own head slightly "Tell me," he mouthed, "which do you fear more, Bastion or me?"

The man's bloodless lips formed the single word, "Bastion."

The bard smiled, his face stone, and the bar keeper thought it was the most terrifying thing he had ever seen. "A pity. You should fear me. Bastion can only kill you, but I...well, you don't know what I can do to you, now do you? Bastion?" he asked again, beginning to lift his hook, blue-green fire writhing across the etched blade.

And this time the man's eyes flickered across the bard's left shoulder into a corner.

Paedur turned, slowly and casually, allowing his eyes to adjust to the dimness and then allowing his enhanced senses to flare as he probed the darkness. There was a figure sitting in the furthest corner of a pew, in the shadow of a pillar. The bard glanced back at the bar keeper, his eyebrows raised in a question. The man's head moved fractionally.

Paedur took the drink and walked across to the darkened corner, sitting down directly opposite the still-shadowed figure. He pushed the drink across the scarred wood. "You're Bastion?"

The figure didn't reply, but something hard and metallic clicked twice in the dimness.

"I don't recognise the weapon," Paedur said casually.

"You wouldn't, but does a man need to know what kills him?" The voice was soft, very soft and yet slightly rasping, as if the speaker's throat had once been damaged.

Paedur allowed his enhanced sight to come to the fore as he looked at the figure—and was shocked when he found it had no effect. He turned his head slightly, looking at the other patrons of the bar, seeing them as splashes of colour, mainly muted and dulled now with drunkenness and livid with disease. But turning back to the mysterious Bastion he found he could still see nothing except the vaguest outline.

"You are not of humankind," Paedur said.

"Nor you, it seems," the man hissed.

"Bard-Master Eiron sent me here to look for Bastion."

"And you have found me."

Again Paedur attempted to detect either an accent or inflection in the soft voice, but found it strangely neutral.

"Why?" the man asked simply.

"I need a guide into the Northlands. I need to find the Chopt encampments."

"Why?"

"There is a war brewing—and the beasts are being used as pieces in the game. I must speak to them, try to stop this war, before they are butchered," the bard said carefully, unsure where this strange man's loyalties lay.

There was a long silence, and then came the same metallic double click the bard had heard before. "We will talk, then. Upstairs. You first."

Paedur looked for the stairs and found them behind and to his right. Coming slowly to his feet, he deliberately turned his back on the man and took the curving wooden steps up to the balcony that ran round the building. He stood with his hand and hook curving around the rail, looking down over the crowd, shutting off his sense of smell, and dulling his senses back to normal.

Bastion joined him at the rail. "Look at them—animals, stinking animals! And they hunt the Chopts as beasts."

Paedur turned to look at Bastion, and only his bard's training kept his face expressionless. Bastion was diseased. Great weeping sores had turned his face into an open wound, and his eyes, tiny behind swollen cheekbones, were hard and small and black. He was tall, almost as tall as the bard, but broad where the bard was thin. He was completely hairless and the bard no longer wondered at his hoarse voice.

"I am Bastion." He said it proudly, almost defying reaction. He was wearing a simple merchant's robe of a dark, intermediate colour, belted around the middle with a broadsword belt, on which hung a short cutlass, a broad-bladed Chopt knife and a long rectangular-shaped pouch.

"Who are you?" Bastion asked softly.

"I am Paedur…"

"…the Bard," Bastion finished, nodding. "Yes, I have heard of you."

Paedur, anticipating his next question, lifted his left arm, showing his hook. Bastion examined it closely, turning his head to study it from all angles, but not touching the blade. "Toriocht's work," he said eventually.

Surprised, Paedur nodded. "So I believe."

"It is," Bastion said assuredly. "I've viewed his work before." He looked up at Paedur, his lips drawing back from his teeth in a smile. "Tell me about this forthcoming war."

"There is little enough to tell. I believe that the Chopts are being used by Geillard, once-Emperor, aided by Mannam, once-God, to mount an attack on the Southlands in an attempt to overthrow Kutor, the new Emperor, and to destroy the Old Faith in the process. And who knows, perhaps Geillard and his followers will be successful— but the Chopts will suffer the heaviest casualties."

"Promises have been made to the Chopts," Bastion said, turning away, leaning his broad arms across the balcony rail and looking down onto what would have been the central aisle of the old church. Paedur noted that he wore black gloves, and that his bare forearms were also scarred with the open sores.

"Promises that will not be kept. Neither Geillard's nor Mannam's words can be counted on."

"The Chopts have eaten well these last moons. And that is a persuasive argument."

"Human flesh, killed in the name of the New Religion!" Paedur said savagely.

"The Chopts have their own gods. And if they pay lip service to other gods then that is all it is."

"But the deaths are perceived and accepted as sacrifices to the Religion," the bard argued.

Bastion nodded. "I accept your point." He grunted in amusement as two men below started an argument over a slattern. While they were fighting, she wandered off with another man. Then he turned to look at the bard, his scarred face expressionless. "What you've told me bears out certain rumours that have come down from the north in the past few moons. There is war brewing, the clans are gathering and weapons are plentiful, and, for all the beast-folk's reputation, they are not usually wanton killers." He nodded, as if coming to a decision. "I'll take you into the Northlands if you give me your word not to harm any of the beast-folk."

"I cannot do that. I can only swear not to attack them, but if I am attacked, then I will defend myself."

Bastion nodded. "That is good enough. Know this, bard: I am risking much by taking you north with me. The Chopts know me, trust me, and in their own fashion they are an honest race, loyal and true. They make good friends, but cross one and you are a dead man. Cross me, bard—betray me—and, for all your god-given powers, I will kill you."

Paedur nodded. "What are you, Bastion?"

The man grinned. "I am nothing, bard." He turned away and moved silently to the stairs but stopped on the top step. "Meet me at the north gate at dawn."

"I'll be there."

"You know nothing about this man," Katani argued, stamping her feet against the bitter cold. It was the still silent hour before dawn. "By your own admission, he is not of humankind, and you cannot read him."

"I trust him. Eiron trusts him."

"And if he is of the Religion?"

"I would know…"

"I am not of the Religion. Nor am I of the Faith." The wheezing, gasping voice was so close that it startled them both. Katani's swords whispered from their scabbards as she spun towards the speaker.

"Who are your gods, then?" Paedur asked, without turning, aware only that he hadn't sensed the approach of the man, aware of the pounding of his heart, suddenly feeling terribly vulnerable, feeling, for a single moment, human again.

"My gods are…my gods," Bastion said, "and my own affair." He deliberately turned to look at the woman warrior in the early morning light, pushing the furred hood of his bulky white and grey quilted jacket off his head, and in the grey light of dawn his ruptured skin looked even more hideous. Perhaps he intended it to shock, but Katani had been trained to school her features to betray none of her feelings, and her face remained impassive. Bastion stared at her for a few moments before speaking. "You are Katani of the Katan, companion of the bard. You came with him out of the Silent Wood. You also have with you a boy, by name Gire, a survivor of the Chopt attack on the Monastery and School of Ectoraige."

The bard turned, his expression stone, his eyes reflecting the purple-grey light of the morning. "And how do you know all this?

"I have survived so long in this wild land because I make it my business to know. I have learned a lot about you, bard, since we last spoke."

"And does it alter your decision to guide me?"

"On the contrary; you are a man of honour—rare in these times—and dedicated to your cause, which would seem to be the upholding of the Old Faith. And I have since discovered certain information, shall we say, which bears out what you told me. I will guide you."

"Paedur, I must accompany you..." Katani began, but the bard raised his hook, the metal glistening with the dawn chill.

"No. You will accompany Gire back to the capital, and wait for me there. Stay at Kutor's side at all times; an attack on him is inevitable..."

"There have been two assassination attempts on the new Emperor," Bastion wheezed. "Both have failed."

"But the next may not." The bard turned to the warrior. "Kutor must be kept alive. He is the figurehead, the rallying point, the symbol of the Old Faith. Protect him."

Katani nodded. "And the boy?"

"Keep him in Karfondal for the moment. When this is over I will take him south to Talaria myself."

"Dawn," Bastion said. "Time."

Paedur reached out and touched Katani on the shoulder. "If there is trouble, I will contact you."

"How?"

But the bard only smiled and turned away. With Bastion by his side, he walked forward without once glancing back.

Katani turned away, slamming her swords into their sheaths and walked back through the north gate and into Thusal, heading back towards the bardhouse. The bard was dismissing her—Katani, one of the finest warriors from the greatest warrior class ever to walk this Plane of Existence—to the status of a simple bodyguard, first of a boy and then of a man. Well, she would do it this time, but when this was all over, she had plans of her own. A highly skilled mercenary could command quite respectable fees, and when she had enough money she could retire, head south into warmer climes, or perhaps open a school, a training school catering to the sons and daughters of the nobility...

She glanced back over her shoulder, but already Paedur and Bastion had disappeared from view in the dim grey early morning light. Well, they were welcome to one another; they were two of a kind...

"How far?" Paedur asked eventually when they had walked several thousand paces in silence.

"The nearest camp is about a day's march; the nearest settlement, perhaps a day beyond that, and the capital—if you want to call it such—half a day beyond that."

"Two and a half days' march, then," Paedur murmured. "And have you any word of the men I'm looking for?"

"There are said to be strangers in the capital," Bastion whispered, "some of humankind, others Chopt-kindred."

"Gallowglas and Torc Allta," Paedur said.

Bastion glanced sidelong at the bard but said nothing.

They continued on in silence, into a dreary and blasted landscape. Although every outline had been softened or obscured by the blanket of snow, the effect only served to highlight the absence of life. Every tree and bush was bare, and in some cases the branches were snapped off neatly when the weight of the snow had crushed them. The rivers were frozen solid, and once they passed close to a frozen waterfall, where the bard paused in wonder, looking at the wan sunlight reflecting through the frozen droplets.

Close to midmorning, Bastion turned off the barely perceptible track they had been following and found his way down to a small hollow in the centre of which was a frozen pool. Tucked away in one corner of the hollow were the remains of a single-roomed dwelling; snow and frost had conspired to reduce it to a pile of tumbled stones. "We'll stop here awhile. Unlike you, I need to rest and I need food," he whispered.

"You seem to know a lot about me," Paedur murmured, walking around the pool to examine the remains of the building.

"I like to know with whom I'm travelling."

"Your sources are what interest me."

Bastion grinned. "My sources are impeccable." He sorted through the satchel he had been carrying on his back and produced a small metal pot. Walking over to the edge of the pool, he stamped through the ice with the heel of his boot, and then scooped chill water into the pot. With flint and tinder he fired a few dry twigs and scraps of fluffy cloth which he had also taken from his satchel and set the pot to boil. He then broke some bread that was so hard it snapped with a resounding crack like stone, and dropped it into the pot of water to soften.

"Why do you prefer the Chopts to humankind?" Paedur asked suddenly.

Bastion looked up from the pot. "Because they are an honest folk; because they do not judge by appearance." He smiled ruefully. "Humankind are not well-disposed to those who have been god-touched."

"God-touched?" Paedur whispered.

Bastion's blighted hands rose to briefly touch his face. "This. In the Northlands, it is called god-touched."

"It is like no other disease I've seen before."

"It is not a disease, bard," Bastion said, sounding surprised at the bard's ignorance. "I angered the gods, and this was their punishment."

"Which gods?" Paedur whispered.

Bastion shrugged. "Does it matter? I broke the cardinal rule, the Death's Law—Men are but the playthings of the gods. I was a piece on their gameboard which refused to play. They could not slay me, but with this they gifted me."

Paedur walked around the pool and sank to his knees beside Bastion, looking into his wounded face. "The gods did this?"

The water began to bubble in the pot. "Listen to me, then, bard, and I will tell you how I was god-touched..." He added a thick granulated powder to the water and began to stir, immediately forming a pale, watery soup.

"I was...a successful man. Not wealthy, but not poor. I dealt in furs, rare and otherwise, ice-spices, exotic stones and woods, all the produce of the Northlands.

"I was recently married, a northern girl naturally, a beauty who had, I am convinced, a touch of beast blood in her, for she was an exotic rare creature herself, passionate and exciting.

"I followed my gods, she followed hers, and if they were not the same, then there was no argument, no dissent, and it mattered little to us, for we were in love. I was active in my church and with every possibility of becoming an elder when the time was opportune.

"And then one day I received a visitor, an elder of the church, a man I respected. He suggested that I should bring my new wife to the church to bless our marriage vows—for we had been married in a private civil ceremony—and that perhaps she should be introduced into the congregation as a new member of the faith.

"I explained to him that she followed her own gods, and I would not interfere with them, but he insisted that it was my duty as a follower of the...of my belief that I should encourage her to shift her allegiance.

"I listened and, perhaps because I respected the man, or perhaps because I was in awe of him, I agreed. That night I spoke to my wife, and that night we had our first argument.

"It passed, as all such arguments do, but it was not forgotten. When I left for worship on the Sabbath, I could see the anger or resentment in her eyes, and when she disappeared every month when the moon was full, I was curious and perhaps slightly jealous, for I had heard tales of the wild Sabbaths to honour the hard northern gods.

"I was often away for long periods of time in those days; it was around the time I was beginning to trade with the Chopts. The risk was high, but so was the profit. It was nerve-wracking work. When I camped with them, I rarely slept, and expected to receive a knife in the back at any hour of the night or day. To bolster my courage I often spoke to my gods—and, do you know, in my arrogance I imagined they replied.

"And then one day a deal went wrong—I insulted a chief's daughter—I'm still not sure how, but I think I refused a piece of clothwork she had executed. The Chopts were enraged, and I was forced to flee, with the beasts howling behind me.

"I took shelter in a cave in the Thusal Mountains, a tiny opening in the sheer rockface where they could only come at me one at a time and I could defend myself relatively easily—until my strength and stamina gave out, that is.

"I prayed then—I prayed to my gods as I had never prayed before. And even as the Chopts were coming at me, even as I was defending myself from their blows, I prayed. I promised my gods anything; I promised them everything. I promised to serve them to the end of my days without hesitation, without question.

"And my prayers were answered.

"There was a low roll of thunder across the clear sky and then lightning cracked across the heavens. The levin bolt struck the rockface almost directly below me—and the whole cliff gave way, wiping out the beasts.

"And then deep, deep in my skull, I heard the voice, booming like the thunder, sharp, painful like the lightning: 'You are ours; you are our servant, now in this and in all things.'

"And I bowed my head and agreed. 'I am your servant.'

"When I returned to my town, there was another shock awaiting me: my wife had been taken for questioning by the Inquisition. She had been put to the Question and found to be an enemy of— of our belief. She had been tried and sentenced, and her sentence was death.

"I was enraged beyond belief. I railed against the inquisitors, the town fathers, the elders of...our belief, but all to no avail. I prayed to the gods—the gods who had so recently saved me—but they wouldn't answer me.

"So I resolved to free my wife. Indeed, what other choice had I?

"On the eve of her execution, I made ready to break her free, when once again the booming, ice-sharp voice spoke deep in my head. 'You must not do this. She has been condemned to death. Leave her to die.'"

"'No,' I screamed.

"'You must,' the voice commanded. 'You are our creature now; sworn and oath-bound to us. You must obey us.'

"And I refused, laughing my defiance at the gods.

"Freeing my wife proved to be almost remarkably easy. I had come prepared to kill, but the guards were absent from their posts, and the keys to her cell were hung within easy reach. But all the time, I could hear the voice, muted now, but still present, commanding me not to do this, that I was the creature of the gods.

"I ignored it.

"I opened her cell and unchained her, and together we raced through the silent deserted corridors heading for the horses I had hidden beyond the postern gate. But as we ran the voice grew louder and louder, commanding and then threatening...

"And still I managed to ignore it, although it now threatened to burst my skull.

"As we slipped through the postern gate, there was the low booming of thunder, ominously familiar, and suddenly I could feel my heart beginning to pound as the thunder rumbled closer and closer. I knew something was terribly wrong, that something was going to happen.

"I got my wife into the saddle and slapped her mount into motion. I was just reaching for the bridle of my own mount when the voice in my ear erupted into laughter, sharp, piercing, hideous laughter—and the lightning bolt struck!

"I remember the pain. The intense, cold, sharp, piercing, terrible pain...

"And the laughter, I remember the laughter.

"When I awoke I was in Thusal, with my wife and some of the healers of her people tending me. I had been burned, terribly burned, and it was not expected that I would live. But I lived, for the gods did not want me for themselves yet. My skin should have healed, scarred certainly, but healed. But it never healed; this is what you see.

"I had been god-touched. I am one of those who inhabit the Shadowland between the Kingdoms of Life and Death, belonging to neither, part of neither. That is why your god-enhanced senses are blind to me, bard. I am like you."

Bastion turned away suddenly, abruptly finishing the conversation. Paedur watched him for a few moments, and then he too turned away, walking back around the small frozen lake, sorting the man's tale into his ordered bardic lore.

What Bastion had said, though, was disturbing, incredibly disturbing, for it shed a new light on the Old Faith. Paedur had been aware that Bastion had been very careful to mention neither the Faith nor the Religion, but the bard knew the Old Faith had used the Inquisition in the past and that those who failed the Question were deemed to threaten the Faith and often executed. It was glossed over now, ignored in the modern history texts, but the Faith had once been as repressive as the New Religion.

But what disturbed the bard most of all was the Pantheon's treatment of the man Bastion. And Paedur couldn't help wondering what would happen to him if he ever refused to obey the

Old Faith or decided that he no longer wished to be the Champion of the Old Faith.

Gire was finishing off a bowl of hot salted gruel when Katani returned to the Bardhouse. He looked up as she quietly entered the long dining hall. "Where's Paedur?"

She placed her horned helmet on the smooth wooden boards and dropped her gauntlets on top of it. She pulled out a chair halfway down the table and sank into it, resting both hands flat on the table top. Finally, she looked up at Gire, and said, "He's gone into the Northlands."

The boy looked at her open-mouthed. "Without us?"

Katani smiled. "You didn't think he was going to take you with him, now did you?"

"But he has to!"

Katani smiled. "The bard does only what he wants to..."

"He has to take me! He has to! He has to!" Gire's voice, which had grown shrill, suddenly cracked and broke, and Katani, who was watching the boy's face, saw his deep brown eyes turn small and hard and black, and then something flickered behind them, and he slowly closed his eyes. When he opened them again, his eyes were clear stone grey!

Katani's swords whispered from their scabbards. "Who are you—what are you?" she demanded, surging to her feet. Behind her the door clicked open and reflected in the shining length of her longsword she saw Eiron. "Don't come any closer; something has taken possession of the boy."

"I know," Eiron said quietly, almost sadly.

Katani risked a quick glance over her shoulder. The Bard-Master closed the door without turning and walked down the room to stand directly across from Katani. "You need not fear," he said.

"Who is it? What spirit controls the boy?" she demanded, looking at Gire, noting how the planes of his face had almost imperceptibly shifted, becoming harder, sharper, lending his face a certain adult solidity.

The voice, when it came, was deep and resounding, the tones calm and measured, like those of an old man. But they issued from the boy's throat. "I am Ectoraige of the Pantheon, the God of Learning and Knowledge!"

10
The Tempting of Kutor

I discovered more about myself in the first few moons of my rule than I had in all my years in the Outlands...

Kutor, Emperor of the Seven Nations

Kutor had discovered he was a gardener.

He had never had a garden, nor shown the slightest interest in gardening, yet when he had first come to the palace at Karfondal and Fodla had shown him around the grounds, he had immediately fallen in love with Geillard's private garden—a small square patch of cultivated ground, completely walled in and roofed with crystal to allow the sunlight in and to intensify the heat. It had been the deposed Emperor's private plot, and none of the royal gardeners were allowed admittance. Perhaps it was its very neglected appearance, while surrounded on all sides by perfectly cultivated lawns, that had attracted him to it. It reminded him a little of his present situation—a rough bandit surrounded by the fops and ceremony of the Imperial Court. He had started work in it almost immediately and hadn't missed a day since.

Another part of the garden's attraction, he suspected, was because he lost his guards when he was within the confines of the walled garden. With the exception of his tiny cell-like bedroom, it was the one place where he was truly alone. Although both Fodla and Owen had argued with him, he had insisted that the two guards who had been permanently assigned to him would remain outside the garden. The only concession he had made was that the garden would be searched every day before he entered, and he would only be allowed admittance when it had been pronounced safe.

But it still didn't stop him from feeling trapped...Trapped not only by those who followed Geillard and who were actively plotting against him, even while they smiled and bowed in his court every day, but he was also trapped by his own people, by those who had followed him in from the Outlands, flocking to his banner. He found he owed so many people so much. They had made him

Emperor—for their own ends, admittedly—but hadn't that been what he had wanted all along? He certainly hadn't resisted. And so now, here he was with the world at his feet—and no way out...

Suicide!

The idea came to him suddenly, and he straightened, pressing his hand to the small of his back. Suicide. He grinned. Now wouldn't that upset all their plans, friends and foes alike? He could come into the garden, sit over there by the fountain, pop his arm into the chill waters and slit his wrists—completely painless...indeed, almost a pleasant way to die.

He wondered what they would all do without him. Carry on as usual, he conceded bitterly. They didn't need him; he was a figure-head, a totem, nothing more. Why, he hadn't been seen by the public for...for how long now? He had his daily reports; he knew that Owen had contacted de Courtney and that that foolish young man had let slip that it was the Twelve Families who were arranged against him. He was also receiving reports of the situation in the north; along with the flood of refugees and a bitter spell of cold weather, there was increased Chopt activity, which could very easily escalate into a bloodbath if it wasn't stopped quickly. And there were the plans for him to tour the capitals of the Nations...and to marry— Keshian had been talking of a arranged marriage recently—and there were orders to be signed...and roads to be approved...and the refugee problem needed to be looked at closely...and...and...and...

So, suicide...it came back to suicide again.

The Emperor wandered down the gravel path to the plain fountain in the centre of the garden and sat down on the low wall surrounding it. He looked into the clear waters, dipping his fingers into the chill liquid, bringing them to his lips; they tasted tart and bitter. Well, suicide would solve all his problems; no more worries, no more decisions, no more pain...no more regrets. For Kutor bitterly regretted having accepted the bard's invitation to become Emperor, and Kutor was rapidly coming to hate the Bard Paedur and all he stood for. The bard had used him. And where was he now? Where was he when he was most needed? Where was he with his heroic tales that would inspire and uplift men's hearts? Where was he?

Wood snapped and Kutor looked up, his hand falling to his waist, but he wore no weapon now. There was a figure standing over against the wall, amongst the trailing vines. He opened his mouth to call out—a word would bring the guards running, but something stopped him.

He looked at the shape amongst the vines and trailing creepers again. It was tall, and vaguely man-shaped, but the sunlight, already distorted by the crystal roof of the small garden, shining through the leaves, dappled across the figure in a camouflaged pattern, rendering it virtually impossible to distinguish any of its features.

"Who are you?" Kutor demanded quietly.

"You do not want to know." The voice was soft, a whisper, a rasp like that of grasses blowing in the wind, of leaves hissing against bark.

"What do you want, then? Speak now, lest I call in the guards and have them butcher you where you stand."

"I mean you no harm, *Emperor.*" The emphasis was placed on the last word, making it sound like an insult. "If I wanted you dead, then you would be lying at my feet."

"Brave words," Kutor mocked.

The figure stepped away from the concealment of the vines, and the Emperor felt something cold and solid settle into the pit of his stomach. He was looking at Death. He was looking at Mannam of the Silent Wood.

The tall, twisted figure in the cloak of seared and withered leaves stretched out a hand that was gnarled and twisted like the branch of a tree, and a twiglike finger hooked in Kutor's direction. "Do you want me to call you to me now?" the voice hissed.

And Kutor, who had been contemplating suicide barely moments before, shook his head. Faced with the immediate prospect of death, he found he wanted to live. "What do you want of me?" he asked quietly.

"Your faith," Mannam hissed, "and the faith of your subjects." Kutor frowned and started to shake his head—and then he suddenly realised that the bard had been instrumental in having Mannam deposed. "You're not Death," he gasped.

Wood snapped with the sound of Mannam's anger. "But I can still slay you. I was a god for generations—that cannot be taken away from me, nor the knowledge I gained in that time. I may have been stripped of my godhood, but my powers are of the most extraordinary kind."

"And you want my...faith?" Kutor asked, intrigued now. He looked down into the waters of the fountain and found that Mannam cast no reflection.

"Faith lends Substance," Mannam said, quoting the ancient proverb. "I intend to retake my throne in the Silent Wood, but before I do that I need the belief of the people on this Plane of Existence. I want you to believe in me, and to promote the belief in me throughout the Seven Nations..." The creature stopped; Kutor was shaking his head and smiling. "There is something wrong?"

"Tell me why I should do this?"

"In return for my help."

"And how can a deposed god help me?" Kutor asked.

"There are formidable forces gathering against you, enemies both on this plane and in the Realm of the Gods. The Twelve Families stand ready to move; Karfondal is a thunderstorm ready to burst; there are vampir abroad with your destruction—your personal destruction—in their black hearts; there is an army growing in the north, an army of humankind: Torc Allta, Gallowglas and the Chopts have agreed to lend their weight to Geillard's army."

"I know all this."

"But I can remove some of these obstacles," Mannam whispered. "In return you will build a fane to Mannam, the Dark Lord, and make worship there mandatory."

"But the bard..."

"The bard cannot help you now. Soon he will be unable to help anyone—even himself. He has overstepped himself this time."

The Emperor moved his hand to and fro in the chill water, creating reflections which sparkled in rainbow colours against the stone. "There is more to this, I fancy. Tell me why you haven't approached the Twelve Families, for example?"

Kutor felt Mannam's gaze bore into him for several long moments, before he finally said, "The Religion has its Deathgod—or Goddess, rather. The bard slew Libellius, the Religion's Lord of the Dead, and to fill the void left by his departure, the Lady Asherat, the Taker of Souls, came to the fore. She is young and vicious, and she will not give up her post so easily."

"And Churon is the Lord of the Dead of the Faith—what is to say that he will abdicate?" Kutor asked.

There was a hiss like that of a leaf being torn in two. "I did not say that you would build a fane to the Faith, but only to me. Also, an important part of our bargain would be that you let the Old Faith die out, while encouraging devotion to me…"

"You would grow stronger while the rest of the gods of the Pantheon weaken," Kutor said slowly, nodding. "But it would mean betraying the Old Faith, the bard, and those who put me on this throne."

"And have they not betrayed you?" Mannam snapped. "Have they not used you, abandoned you, made you a prisoner here? You owe them nothing," the creature insisted. "Where is the bandit prince who ruled the Outlands with a hand of iron, beholden to no one, answerable to no man?"

Leaves suddenly blew up all around Mannam and Kutor, hissing, sizzling, rattling and clacking in from all sides. When the dust had settled, Mannam, once-god, was gone.

The Lady Esse sat back from the ornately carved scrying mirror and watched its reflective surface turn to black. She was well pleased; a few more pushes and Kutor might very well be theirs—without actually knowing it.

And even if the ploy failed, well, then the vampir would feast.

Tien tZo introduced Owen to the Andam priest. They had met in the midst of the vast Market Square, close to the fountain of Geillard I, the Emperor who had helped unite the Seven Nations, taking over where Churon the Onelord had left off—or so history said. Perhaps it was significant that the fountain hadn't worked for many years and the statue was chipped and worn, stained white by the passage of many birds.

Both Owen and Tien had pulled long travelling cloaks over their usual clothes, and had ensured that they weren't being followed. In the past few days the Weapon Master had been shadowed by two disreputable characters he had picked up on his second visit to the Warlord's Armoury. He had no doubts but that they had been assigned by either the Warlord or his employers to keep track of his movements.

They had arrived at the fountain well before noon, wending their way through the crowds that thronged the square. Tien noticed that while the food stalls had proliferated, the quality of the food—baked breads, stuffed vegetables, sticky sweetmeats—seemed to have deteriorated, and once he passed a stall that was selling what it called slivers of bird's flesh cooked in herbs, but the Shemmat's sensitive nose recognised the meat as being nothing more than vermin.

There was no fruit on sale, and spices were fetching exorbitant prices since the Cataclysm had struck in the middle of the growing season, destroying much of the present season's crops, and had wiped out the trade routes and many of the trading ports.

They passed clothes stalls, where many of the articles offered were suspiciously patched and stained, and on the shoe and boot stands, even the best item on sale had seen much usage. Weapon stands were more numerous now, and they were offering a surprisingly large display of used weapons—most of it picked up off the battlefields after Kutor's rebel army had rolled over the Imperial forces. The Weapon Master picked through it with a professional interest, but there was nothing he hadn't already seen, and most of what was available hadn't been cleaned after its last usage and the blades were already beginning to rust.

Owen and Tien walked past the fountain twice; the first time there was no sign of the priest, but he was there the second time they came around. Even so, they continued on their way, and then separated, giving a final check that they weren't being observed before making their way back through the crowd to sit down on either side of the grey-clad priest.

"This is Owen, my Master," Tien said softly, without moving his lips, his eyes on the crowd.

"I have heard of the Weapon Master," Andam said quietly, glancing sidelong at Owen. "Indeed, who has not?"

"We should be brief," Owen warned quietly.

The Andam nodded. "There was an attack on my life last night."

Startled, Tien glanced around. "You are unhurt?"

"By the grace of the One."

"How many?" Owen asked, not looking at the priest, watching the crowds milling around, watching their faces, their eyes, their movements, looking for someone paying more than casual attention to the three men sitting on the low wall.

"There was one man."

"Have you ever seen him before? Would you perhaps have encountered him in your congregation?" the Weapon Master continued.

"I did not know him then, but I have since discovered that he is in the employ of the Lady Esse."

"Was this a Gallowglas?" Tien asked quickly.

"If it was I would be dead," the Andam said, the amusement plain in his voice. "I tried to contact you last night," he said then, in a different tone of voice. Both Owen and Tien turned to look at him. "I went to the palace immediately…"

"Why?" Owen interrupted.

"I decided I needed your protection…"

"You think they will try again?" Tien asked.

"I am sure of it. I am the only reasonably powerful representative of a branch of the Old Faith in Karfondal, even though I am of the Andam branch. But the Faith itself has no High Priest here at present, and although it has many adherents, the few priests here are weak, untried men—boys, some of them. I think if the Religion suddenly wants me dead then there is indeed something powerful afoot. I think they intend to work some great magic, perhaps call something else from the Ghost Worlds, perhaps even Trialos himself. If that is so then I would be able to detect and—in some small way—combat it."

Owen nodded. "Of course. And you think they were attempting to put you out of the way before they worked this magic?"

"I think so."

"We didn't know you had come to the palace," Tien said.

"I was refused admission!"

"Impossible!" Tien snapped.

The Andam shook his head slightly. "No, not impossible. I presented myself at the gate, and the guards, recognising my status, allowed me into the inner vestibule. I asked to see you, Tien, but I was told that you were not available, nor was the Weapon Master, when I asked for him…"

"We were patrolling the streets, hunting the vampir…" Tien murmured.

"I then requested to see the Emperor himself—a bold enough request as you might think, but nevertheless, I made it."

"And what happened?" Owen asked automatically. He was watching a figure standing over by one of the weapons-stands, a tall, thin man, with a long travelling cloak on his shoulders, tied at the neck, with the hood back. The Weapon Master noted that the cloak's ties were undone and that the man's hands were nowhere to be seen. He could easily be nothing more than a thief, a common pick-pocket, but...the Weapon Master had learned never to ignore his hunches. He looked up and found Tien regarding him quizzically, the Shemmat sensing something amiss; Owen deliberately shifted his gaze until it rested on the figure he had been watching. Tien looked at the man for a moment and then nodded slightly.

"The Emperor refused to see me!"

"Why?" Owen demanded.

"I was given no reason. But his Counsellor Keshian came to me and apologised, saying that the Emperor had had a busy and troubled day and was receiving no more visitors. I explained that I had something of importance to tell the Emperor and, although I think the man himself was troubled, he said that Kutor had refused to see me under any circumstances. Keshian did say that if I was to return today, he would do his utmost to ensure that the Emperor saw me."

"I'll see that he does," Owen muttered.

"I left the message with the guards at the gate that I would like to meet you here today, and I left."

"Kutor has been somewhat distracted of late..." Owen began...

...And then he saw the thin man at the weapons-stand raise his hands from beneath his cloak...he was holding a cocked and loaded crossbow. He saw his knuckles whiten as they tightened on the trigger...saw the bow snap and the bolt leap from the bow...

He was aware that Tien was reaching over for the Andam, saw his hands close over the grey robes, but realised that he would never pull him out of the way in time...

His shortsword cleared its sheath, coming up around and down—and cleaved the bolt in two! His sword continued moving, describing an almost complete circle, and when it had reached the horizontal, Owen released it. It took the assassin—who still hadn't moved—directly through the centre of the chest, punching him across a table of swords, knives, axes and maces, knocking out the stand's supports, pulling the awning in on top of him. Tearing off his cloak, and drawing his longsword, Owen darted after his weapon.

Tien grabbed Andam and turned—and found himself facing two black-clad figures, male and female. They were both unarmed but they moved like assassins. The male, tall, broad, and battle-scarred, moved in on the Shemmat, while the masked female positioned herself before the priest.

The man moved, pulling a long thin chain from his sleeve and snapping it at Tien's face. Instinct dictated that he grab for the weighted end of the chain, but the Shemmat knew that that was all the assassin was waiting for—while he was distracted, another weapon, knife, shortsword, throwing spike, would take him in the throat. He shifted his weight slightly, allowing the metal to buzz past his ear—and then his own throwing axe snapped out on the end of its leather thong. It took the assassin high on the thigh, opening the major veins down the inside of the leg, bringing the man to his knees. He opened his mouth to scream—and Tien's second axe took his head off at the shoulders!

He spun around, his right arm already drawing back, ready to launch his remaining axe—and found the female assassin lying shivering at the Andam's feet.

Owen came running up. He had been recognised and his name was now buzzing around the gathering crowd.

"Weapon Master...Weapon Master...Master...Weapon Master..."

He hooked his foot in under the shivering woman and turned her over. Beneath her full face mask, her eyes were hard and staring. Owen knelt and pulled off her mask, and then passed his hand over her ashen face; there was no reaction, and her breathing was laboured. He placed his hand below her breast and felt her heart pounding rapidly. Owen looked up at Andam. "What did you do to her?"

"Merely let her see her true self."

"She must have seen something terrifying," Tien murmured.

"Few men ever examine themselves—their true selves—closely. Instinctively, they know they will not like what they find."

"Will she recover? Can you bring her back?" Owen demanded.

"Of course."

The Weapon Master looked at Tien. "We'll take her with us; perhaps she might be persuaded to tell us who hired her."

Tien nodded doubtfully. He bent and lifted the woman off the ground—and a crossbow bolt snatched her from his hands!

The bolt was completely black, from pyramidal head to ebon feathers.

Kutor listened to the story of events and then lightly touched the bloody crossbow bolt with the tips of his fingers. "It matches the bolt that killed the man Stinger?"

Owen nodded. "Exactly."

"And they can only be manufactured by this man, this Warlord?"

Owen nodded again. "And probably fired by his son who is a more than accomplished archer. The shot that killed the woman was fired from at least three hundred paces away, from the opposite side of the square."

Kutor looked up at the Weapon Master. The Emperor's face was almost unreadable, and his eyes were distant, as if he wasn't truly concerned with what had occurred. "Perhaps the archer was aiming at someone else?" He looked at the far end of the room where the Andam priest stood, still and silent.

"It took the woman through the throat," the Weapon Master said. "The first attack was against the Andam, but then, when the tide turned against the attackers, she was killed to ensure that she didn't talk."

Kutor sighed deeply. "So we are blocked again. At every turn there is an enemy, a knife in every shadow, poison in every cup. It was easier before; life was simpler then. We cannot win; we cannot hold this position. Geillard will return. He has too many people working for him—and, you know, I think I would welcome his return. If he were to walk in now I might just give him back his cursed throne! This is getting too...much." He shook his head and turned his back on the warrior. "Too much. Too much!"

"Kutor?" Owen asked, but the Emperor had already walked away and had climbed the steps to his huge throne and slumped down in it. His lips were moving and he was talking softly to himself. The Weapon Master turned, and was startled to find that the Andam had come up silently behind him. "Something's wrong. He is unwell..."

"Leave us," the Andam said very softly, his grey eyes concerned. "Leave us be. I am a healer; I may be able to help."

Owen looked at Kutor, but the Emperor was lost in his own world, and the Weapon Master doubted that he was even aware that there were people still in the room. He turned and nodded to Tien and then left the throne room, pulling the huge wooden doors shut behind them, joining Fodla and Keshian who were waiting in the hallway outside. Briefly Owen explained what had happened.

"Possession," the huge Commander of the Legion hissed.

Keshian nodded slowly. "It would seem so...but who?" he asked. "Possession takes power."

"The only person in Karfondal with that sort of power is the Lady Esse," Fodla said softly.

The short stout man nodded. "Then this changes everything. We should attack now—hard and fast. Destroy them now..." Both Fodla and Owen were nodding, when Tien said:

"It is too soon."

"If we leave it any longer, Kutor will be their creature and we will have lost everything we fought to achieve," Keshian protested.

"Let us wait and see what the Andam says," the Shemmat insisted.

The Andam walked slowly around the base of the throne, looking at the Emperor. The Andam priests were reputed to possess certain magical powers, but in truth, with the exception of healing, the majority of them were unskilled. However, the higher echelons of the priesthood had access to extraordinary power, drawing it as needed from its source, deep in the Southern Marshes. Usually a long period of preparation and ritual was required to ensure that it was used for the good of the Andam and the existence of the Planes of Existence. But there were occasions when the merest shadow of the power could be called up at a moment's notice—as when the Andam had stopped the female assassin in her tracks. And the Andam called upon that power now, pouring strength into the Emperor, chipping away at the accumulated detritus the Lady Esse and Mannam had laid on him.

"There is a stink of Death about you," the Andam said quietly, walking up the steps to stand before Kutor, "a stink of old gods, of promises, and self-pity."

Kutor raised his head to look at him.

"Your aura has been muddled by power and minor magics. You have been troubled, set upon, attacked, if you will..." He pitched his voice carefully, using something similar to the Bardic Voice, attempting to break through the Emperor's daze. "The followers of the Religion have been working on you. Doubts have been planted like evil seeds, to grow and seem insurmountable, while promises have been made to you, promises which seem to hold the answers to your problems."

"Mannam," Kutor mumbled, "there was Mannam."

"A deposed god, who has cast in his lot with the Religion solely to gain vengeance on the bard and the Pantheon of the Faith. You have been used, Emperor..."

"But by my own people!" Kutor suddenly protested, and the Andam suppressed a smile; it was the first sign of interest the Emperor had shown.

"You were perfectly willing to allow them to make the decisions for you!" Andam snapped. "The bandit prince of the Outlands could have been Emperor long ago if he had merely chosen to pursue his claim to the throne through the legitimate means. But fear and laziness prevented him. And when his hand was forced, he sat back content and allowed others to carry him along, and when he was handed the Kingship of the Nations he continued to allow others to make the decisions and rule through him." The Andam turned and walked down the steps, pausing on the bottom step to look up. "And that weakness was spotted and preyed upon by the Religion." The Andam walked down the long marbled floor towards the doors. "You are a fool, Kutor, and worse, you are a weak fool. You are a coward, for all your vaunted bravery. If you wear a crown, then act the part of a king!" He walked out of the chamber and closed the door behind him.

When the power left him the Andam sagged against the doors and Tien hurried to catch him before he fell.

"Well?" Owen asked.

"I tried to shake him out of his lethargy, while pouring power into him, strengthening his will, his self-respect, stripping off the layers of the Religion's magic."

"Did it work?"

The doors were suddenly flung open and Kutor strode out. Physically, the man hadn't changed, but gone was the short, soft stocky man, running to fat, and now Kutor, bandit prince of the Outlands, was back. He looked around at the five anxious faces, and he smiled broadly.

"It is time to act!"

11
Ectoraige

Ectoraige is the God of Learning and Knowledge. He rarely appears but prefers to speak through the medium of his followers. Traditionally, his appearance is that of a man wise in years but still sturdy, and he affects the blue teaching robe of one of the ancient Lore Lords...

Pantheon of the Old Faith

Born of Ice and Snow in the Winter of the World...

Chopt Proverb

"He is Ectoraige, I can assure you," Eiron said quietly.

The creature that was both Gire and Ectoraige looked at Katani and she felt a sudden chill run icy fingers down her spine as the clear grey eyes settled onto her face.

The voice was strong, powerful and assured. "Without me the bard dies—a true and final death also—and without me the Seven Nations will go down in flames, and with them the believers of the Old Faith, and thus will die the gods of the Pantheon. And without the Pantheon to counter the excesses of the Religion, the balance will tip and the Planes of Existence will drift back into the void from whence they came."

Katani sank back into her seat, her swords clattering onto the wooden table. The creature had made the statement clearly and simply and she found herself believing him.

"I am Ectoraige. This boy is my tool, receptive to my thoughts, strong in body and mind, courageous, with an enquiring curiosity and an excellent pedigree for learning. He will make a good monk."

"Why have you taken over this boy's mind, turning him into a *quai,* a mindless thing?" Katani hissed. When she had guarded the approaches to the Silent Wood, she had known many of the *quai*—the mindless creatures—and had come to fear and loathe them.

"He is not *quai*—not permanently at any rate. He is merely useful at this time as a mouthpiece. Were another tool avail-able, then I would use that." Although the boy's face remained expressionless, his eyes were darting, flashing, conveying a wealth of nuance and energy.

Katani looked over at Eiron. The Bard-Master caught her despairing gaze and smiled reassuringly. "Trust him; he is a God of the Faith."

"Do you believe that? Truly believe that?" she asked.

"I do."

"And it is his faith, his belief that lends me the strength to be here," Ectoraige said through Gire's mouth. "And now, Katan warrior, you must listen to me, if not for your sake, then for the sake of the bard, and if not for his then for the continued existence of this entire plane of life."

Katani dismissed him with a wave of her hand. "Just tell me what needs to be done," she snapped.

"Follow the bard into the Northlands. He will need your assistance, for he will be betrayed and will be in sore need…"

"I told him not to trust Bastion!"

"And take care lest you judge too quickly," Ectoraige advised, and the woman warrior had a brief and momentary glimpse of an old man with snow-white hair and the faintest of beards, smiling benignly at her. "I must speak to the bard through the medium of this boy."

"So I must take Gire with me?"

"I am afraid so. And you must ensure his safety at all costs. Without him, I might find it difficult to find another suitable mouthpiece in the Northlands."

"I'll keep him alive," Katani growled, her expression sour. "But would it not be better for you to tell me what is so important now, lest anything happen to him?"

"But if you were taken and tortured…?" Ectoraige asked.

"I am Katan!" the warrior snarled, affronted.

"But you are also humankind." Ectoraige shook his head. "No, what I say is for the bard alone. Now I will rest this body, for it is debilitating both for me and the boy. Leave him, he will rest peacefully. But we will speak again, warrior." The eyes closed and a shudder rippled through the boy's body. His eyes flickered open and they were deep chestnut brown. He looked confusedly at Katani and Eiron. "I feel so tired…" and then he rested his head on his arms and immediately fell asleep.

Katani looked over at Eiron. She stood up and sheathed both swords. "Let us talk, you and I, about this God of Learning and Knowledge."

The Bard-Master of Thusal and the Katan Warrior walked the small enclosed courtyard beneath a leaden sky. The morning's snow had been brushed off the smooth rounded cobbles, and the statues dusted clean, leaving the area looking oddly out of place with the rest of the snow-covered building.

Eiron had pulled on his brown and gold cloak, dragged the hood up over his head, and tucked his hands into his deep sleeves. Katani was wearing her armour and gauntlets, but had left off her helmet, preferring a broad brimmed conical hat.

"What do you know of Ectoraige, the God of Learning and Knowledge?" Eiron asked.

"I know nothing. When I first left the World of Men, he was unknown."

"And you left—you died—on the Sand Plain?"

Katani nodded.

Eiron's head moved slightly beneath the enveloping hood. "The worship of Ectoraige was just beginning then. It started in the Northlands, but quickly spread south, aided, I should add, by your old employer, Churon the Onelord. He was a great believer in knowledge."

Katani grunted at the mention of Churon's name. "Tell me about Ectoraige."

Eiron nodded. "Listen then, and I will tell you how a man became a god..."

The old man stood on the banks of the rushing river measuring the depth of the water by gauging its height against the bank. He turned to the short stout man standing by his side. "It has risen again. By sunrise, it will have reached the top of the banks, by mid-morning..." He left the sentence unfinished, but they both knew the consequences if the river overflowed.

Mansen, Burgomaster of the City of Palentian, the seat of Count Palent, rubbed his hands nervously together. "It's too late now to evacuate the city..."

"You should have listened to me," the old man snapped.

"I did, but the Count…well, you know what the Count is like."

Ectoraige, the Lore Lord, nodded wearily and turned away from the River Seme, swollen now by the unseasonal snow high in the mountains behind them.

"Is there anything you can do?" Mansen asked.

Ectoraige turned to look back up into the snowcapped mountains. He shook his head, his eyes darkening. "I'm not sure; I don't think so."

"But you have to," Mansen protested. "The people are counting on you. You saved us from the wolves, defended us from the bandits, even defeated the plague. The people trust you. I asked my servants to flee, but they refused. They said, 'The Lore Lord will save us.'"

Ectoraige ran a long-fingered hand through his fine white hair. "But not this time, I think," he said softly.

"But you'll try?" the Burgomaster asked eagerly.

Ectoraige smiled. "Of course, I'll try." He turned away and walked back to his horse. "Will Palent give me any men?" he called back.

"As many as you need."

"Send me as many as he can spare—the more the better—to the Seme Falls, as quickly as possible. I'll need digging equipment and a reasonably competent magician with knowledge of fire."

Mansen nodded and hurried off for his own horse, looking nervously into the lowering skies, with their promise of snow and rain. The gods were in cruel form these days. The war with the Demons was obviously not progressing well. And then he reflected that perhaps the recent harsh and unseasonal weather was precisely because the war with the Demon-kind was not progressing well. The gods needed their prayers—and so did Ectoraige.

The Lore Lord rode into the mountains feeling the chill bite into his bones; he was getting far too old for this foolishness. At his age he should be sitting by some king's side, dispensing wisdom and advice, with certainly one, and possibly more, wives to tend to his needs.

Well, this would be the last time, he promised himself. His knowledge, his lore, had surely not been collected and garnered from every land in the known world and from several Planes of Existence only to be frittered away on stupid schemes.

And what else could he be using his knowledge for? He wondered. Telling tales like some itinerant bard at some king's court? What use was knowledge if it was not used, not shared? Surely he had a duty to put his knowledge to good use—and what better use for knowledge than for the saving of humankind?

He reined in his mount in sight of the Seme Falls. At this time of year—the season had turned towards high summer—they should have been little more than a trickle. But the falls were in full flood, the river arching far out over the lip about five hundred lengths over his head. Even from this distance the mist and spray dampened his face.

Ectoraige urged his mount forward, and when the path forked, he took the right-hand path which led up along the edge of the falls, turning and switching back through a forest grown wild with the constant moisture. Eventually he had to dismount and lead his horse upwards because of the amount of moss and treacherous slime underfoot. When he reached the top of the falls he moved out to the edge of the foaming river and looked down—and then wished he hadn't. Shrugging his shoulders, he moved back from the water's edge and attempted to find a relatively sheltered and dry spot.

Count Palent's warrior's arrived later that afternoon; a century of men with three wagonloads of equipment. However, there was no mage with them, the Count preferring to keep his magician with him.

Masking his disgust and disappointment, the old Lore Lord mounted his horse again and rode slowly upriver, looking for a spot suitable for his purposes. Every hundred paces or so he would stop and consult his chart of the region.

Finally, as the dusk was rolling in and the first stars were beginning to glitter in the clear sky, he reined in his mount for a final time and dismounted. He waited until the Captain of the Guard rode up to join him, and then he pointed to the river. "I'll want the bank built up on that side...the beginnings of a channel gouged out along here...and then I'll need the river dammed across there."

The young captain, clearly in awe of the famous Lore Lord, had merely nodded. "It will be done as you say. We will need your assistance."

Ectoraige smiled at the young man's unquestioning obedience. "Of course."

"When do we start?" the captain had asked.

Ectoraige had grinned humourlessly. "If it is not completed by morning, then Palentian will be flooded and the sown fields swept away. You remember the harshness of the last winter and the amount of stores of food and fuel and city used? You remember the rationing and the threat of famine? If the fields are destroyed now then that famine will become a reality this winter, and those who survive the flood will surely perish."

Ectoraige divided the men up into two groups of fifty, one raising the bank on the right-hand side of the river, the other cutting away a track on the left-hand side, but keeping the bank intact for the moment. When the time was right, the bank would be knocked away and simultaneously the river would be dammed. In theory, the river should turn and flow down through the forest into the plain below, bypassing the city.

They worked on through the night, working in shifts, and when they slowed down, or slackened, Ectoraige would simply say to them, "Think of your families in Palentian."

And all the time the river rose.

As morning approached and the work neared completion, the captain approached Ectoraige, who was sitting slumped against a tree, his robes filthy, his clear grey eyes dulled.

"My lord, we have a problem."

Ectoraige looked up and nodded. "I know. How do we dam the river and how do we break down the bank on this side?"

The captain nodded wordlessly.

"I wanted a magician," Ectoraige explained, "someone who could destroy the bank and then shift that pile of rocks up there"— he pointed to the hillside up above the river—"and bring it down to block the channel. A good magician could have done that—why, even a poor magician could have done that!" He shook his head bitterly. "But I'm sorry, I can think of no way of doing both together. I've ransacked my lore, but I can think of nothing…"

The captain had smiled. He walked away and rummaged through the carts, returning moments later with a satchel filled with a coarse brownish powder. "This explodes when set alight," he said. "Watch." He took a fistful of powder and allowed some to trickle from his hand into a neat pile on the ground, and then he used the rest of the powder to draw a small trail away from the pile. With flint and tinder he dropped a spark onto the first of the brown grains. The powder fizzled, sparked, and then erupted into a sputtering flame. The flame writhed along the ground and when it reached the pile it exploded in a shower of sparking cinders.

Ectoraige's face was like that of a child. "How much do you have?"

The captain lifted the satchel.

"Leave me some—enough to tear a hole in that bank, and then you take the rest. Use it to bring down that rock pile."

The captain poured enough of the brown powder to fill a flask and then saluted and hurried off, calling his men. Ectoraige watched them go, and then he looked back at the flask. When the captain had demonstrated the powder's capabilities, he had immediately grasped the single remaining practical problem of exploding the powder beside the river. The damp...

"... his body was never found," Eiron finished. "He knew he would never be able to light the powder in the damp air, so he apparently dug a hole in the bank, crouched down over it, shielding it with his body and set the fuse alight." The Bard-Master shook his head. "Such a loss."

"And Palentian?"

"Saved, of course. That was when the devotion to him began. And almost immediately he began speaking through suitable mediums. It was assumed that he never appeared in any other way because his body had been completely destroyed, but I'm sure that's not the case. He laid down the rules for the foundation of his colleges and schools, and of course as soon as the young men and women began to learn in his schools, veneration to Ectoraige increased, very quickly turning him into a powerful god."

"And is he still so powerful?"

"Not as powerful as he once was. Now men worship power, not learning, but his time will come again; I've seen several such cycles swing from might to lore and back to might again. Usually in times of tribulation it swings to might."

"Do you believe him when he says that only he can save the bard and the Nations?" Katani asked seriously.

The Bard-Master stopped and turned to look into the warrior's amber eyes. "Without Ectoraige's help, I am convinced the bard will die."

Bastion moved the snow-laden branch away from his face and pointed down into the hollow with a black-gloved hand. "Chopt camp," he said shortly.

Paedur, who had been standing with his back to the man, turned round, his thin face pinched in a frown, his eyes reflecting the silver-white of the snow and ice.

"Something troubles you?"

Paedur shook his head. "Something…but I'm not sure what. I thought something was following us, but if there is anything it is well-shielded." He shook his head abruptly. "I don't know…it might be nothing…"

Bastion nodded. He reached into his loose coat and pulled out a short, stubby-handled tube. He pulled back an ornate spur on the back of the tube and the bard heard again the double click he had heard in the Tavern of the Blasted Tree. "It is a projectile weapon," Bastion explained, "shooting a dart as far as a crossbow can fire a bolt."

The bard nodded briefly and immediately lost interest. He looked down on the Chopt encampment. His knowledge of the beasts was surprisingly limited; most of what he knew was culled from the archives of the Bardic Library at Baddalaur, the repository of all the knowledge in the known world. That knowledge was being constantly updated, but even so, the most recent records of the Chopts had been nearly three generations old.

Well, if he survived this, he would be able to add to that knowledge.

The Chopt village was not dissimilar to the more primitive villages of humankind. Behind a sturdy palisade of sharpened stakes was a village of simple square wooden huts surrounding a longer, larger hut from which issued a thin stream of grey smoke. The ground between the huts and around the larger hut had been churned to mud, and in one corner of the village a score of hogs rooted noisily. Other than that, there was no visible sign of activity in the village.

"It looks like any other human village," Paedur said without turning around.

"Why, what did you expect?" Bastion wheezed.

"I'm not sure," Paedur said, turning, and suddenly stopping. Less than a hundred paces away, directly across the snow-covered clearing were two of the Torc Allta, the Boar-Folk. Their beast-like heads were raised to the heavens, wet snouts tasting the air, their upcurved tusks gleaming yellow in the light.

"I know," Bastion said softly, his voice barely above a whisper.

"How did I not know they were there?" Paedur demanded in a harsh whisper.

"Like me they are not fully of this world, but rather inhabit the Shadowland between. You are blind to those too like yourself, bard."

One of the Torc Allta pointed towards the trees where the bard and Bastion were standing, and the beasts shifted the long tridents in their hands and moved towards them.

Bastion lifted the small tubed weapon and rested it on a branch. He ducked his head and looked down the length of the barrel, and then he pressed on a stud set into the back of the handle.

The weapon clicked loudly, and they both clearly heard something ping off the nearest Torc Allta's breastplate. The creature stopped to look down at the long scratch mark across the metal. It turned to its companion...and Bastion's second shot hit it in the side of the throat. It fell as if it had been struck with an axe.

"Poisoned," Bastion murmured, pulling back the lever and when the stud popped out of the handle, firing again. This time the second creature's paw went to its face and touched the long sliver of wood that protruded from its eye. It opened its mouth to scream and Bastion's next shot took it through the mouth, killing it instantly.

"An interesting weapon," Paedur murmured.

Bastion smiled. "A gift from...from a weaponmaker I did a favour for. It is the only one like it on this Plane of Existence."

"The legends speak of similar weapons," Paedur said, ducking beneath a branch and walking slowly towards the still bodies of the Torc Allta. "Some were reputed to be capable of killing from over a thousand paces; others could destroy whole armies at a time."

"Myth!" Bastion snorted.

The bard smiled coldly. "You're holding a myth in your hand." He knelt beside the body of the first of the Boar-Folk. He could smell the rank beast odour from the creature, but only with what would have been normal human senses; with his enhanced god-given senses the creature was invisible. He turned the beast's head, examining the curling caste marks cut into the yellow tusks that protruded from the bottom lip. "Warrior-hunter class," he murmured. "I'm afraid I lack the knowledge to interpret the clan and familial marks."

Bastion nudged the second beast with his foot. "They're dead—that's all that's important." He paused and added with a smile wide enough to open the wounds on his face. "And more importantly, we have some gifts for our friends below."

Paedur looked up quickly, his eyebrows raised in a question.

Bastion kicked the Torc Allta again. "Food for our hosts. The Chopts like fresh meat."

Paedur stood back and watched Bastion deal with the beasts. They obviously knew the man, but even without his enhanced senses Paedur could feel their mistrust. He was the object of much curiosity and from the shifting patterns of the beasts' auras, they obviously regarded him as something fearful.

He remained still and unmoving, his arms folded into his sleeves, his hood over his face, listening, trying to place the language. It was familiar, hauntingly so, but with nuances and sounds that were totally alien to his ears, sounds that could or should only have been made by beasts. But the Chopts were more than beasts, he reminded himself. Remove the over-abundance of hair and dress them in civilised clothes and most of them could have passed unnoticed in any of the cities of the Nations.

He sorted through his huge store of knowledge, slowly and meticulously matching the language—and came to a simple, startling conclusion. With very minor alterations, and some accentual differences, they were speaking almost pure Culai—a language dead to all but the most dedicated scholar.

Bastion's haggling with the Chopt leader was obviously drawing to a close, and two of the creatures came forward, took up the two bodies of the slain Boar-Folk and carried them on their shoulders into the Chopt encampment. Most of the onlookers immediately drifted away after them, leaving only Bastion, the Chopt leader, and a single guard facing Paedur.

Bastion raised his arm and called the bard forward; his scarred face was tight and his small dark eyes were unreadable, but the bard could sense his tension. Paedur stopped a score of paces from the trio, and raised his head slightly, allowing the snow to turn his eyes white and blind-seeming. The two Chopts moved uneasily.

"This is Paedur, a bard. There is no harm in him. He is wise in lore and legends and he has taken the hard road into the Northlands to prepare the legends of the Chopt so that the humankind may know the greatness of the People of the Ice." He turned from the bard to the older of the two Chopts. "This is Icewalker, Datar of this clan," he said, using the Chief's given-name rather than his personal name, and being careful not to name the clan. Paedur also noticed that he had called him 'Datar,' the ancient respectful term for father, usually applied to a holy man.

The Chopt, a huge creature a head and more taller than the bard, and broad in proportion, bowed slightly, his eyes never leaving the bard's face. The only obvious signs of his age were the streaks of white running through the hair on his face and body and that he was almost completely toothless.

"And this is Ironwinter."

The second Chopt bowed quickly and briefly, his eyes on the bard's, his right hand resting on the gleaming new hilt of a Chopt knife in his belt. He was smaller than the older beast, though still taller than the bard, and whereas the former Chopt was bulky, the younger Chopt was almost slender. His features were typically Chopt: flat, with a broad, receding forehead and a similarly receding jaw, leaving his long canine teeth protruding slightly over his lip. His eyes were small and black, sunk deep behind high cheek-bones. His hair was long, black and coarse, and kept away from his eyes with a leather thong, and from what the bard could see of his body, he was covered in short, bristling hair.

Both men were dressed alike in ancient worn leathers and scraps of furs. They were both barefoot, and both of them carried long broad-bladed knives, the traditional Chopt knife—and, curiously, the knives were new.

The two men were looking at the bard expectantly, and he glanced at Bastion for instruction, but the man remained unmoving. Finally, Paedur raised his right hand and pushed back his hood, revealing his face.

The elder Chopt, Icewalker, stepped forward to stare into the bard's eyes, and then grunted with fright as he saw himself reflected in the perfect mirrors. He reached out with his left hand, the fingers curved slightly, the nails long, slab-like, and filthy. He was about to touch the bard in the centre of the chest when Paedur pulled back, his left arm came up, his hook encircling the Chopt's wrist.

Ironwinter hissed with shock and his knife came out of its sheath in one quick movement.

"The Law of the Bards does not allow them to be touched by any man, lest it...lest it taint their knowledge," Bastion said quickly. "That is why they enjoy the ancient King Privilege."

Icewalker nodded, but Ironwinter was less easily convinced. The older beast withdrew his hand slowly from the sparkling half-circle of the bard's hook, and only when Paedur dropped his arm did the younger Chopt sheath his knife.

Icewalker grinned at the bard, revealing his discoloured gums, still studded with the remaining shards of teeth, and wafted fetid breath in his direction. "You are fast, humankind, fast, as fast as I've seen." His accent was thick and slurred, but completely distinguishable, and the bard immediately wrote off another myth about the beast folk—that they could not speak any of the tongues of humankind. "You will share our table."

Paedur saw Bastion nod quickly, and he immediately inclined his head. "I would be honoured," he said slowly and clearly.

The Chopt grinned again, and turned away, his hand closing on his guard's shoulder, forcibly spinning him around, and almost pushing him ahead.

"Someone doesn't like us," Paedur said, as Bastion joined him.

"Ironwinter's parents were slain by humankind; he has no cause to love them."

"Love them?" Paedur asked. "You speak of the humankind as if they were a race foreign to you. Do you no longer think of yourself as humankind, then?"

Bastion smiled tightly. "Do you?"

The meal was a long, slow and tense affair, with the Chopts wary of the two strangers, and both Bastion and Paedur as cautious of their hosts.

The whole Chopt tribe of about twenty adults and roughly the same number of children had gathered to enjoy the feast. The Torc Allta had been treated as any other animal, gutted, cleaned, and then stuffed before cooking on a spit over an open fire. All the major organs had been removed and these were cooked separately, with the choicest pieces saved for the Datar and the other elders of the tribe.

Icewalker sat at the head of the long table. On his right-hand side sat two other beasts, both of them showing similar signs of age, and opposite these sat Bastion and the bard. Behind them stood what were obviously guards, while behind the two elders crouched two plump females, their task to masticate the tough boar-flesh before passing it on for them to chew in their toothless mouths. Behind Icewalker stood Ironwinter.

The room was dark, illuminated only by wicks floating in bowls of stinking oil, but the main illumination came from the roaring fire at the end of the long room. Most of the tribe were crouched around it, both for heat and to watch the two Torc Allta roast. The stench in the room was incredible.

"The Marked Man says you want to be taken to the Source," Icewalker said suddenly, turning to the bard, a large earthen goblet in his hand.

Paedur glanced quickly at Bastion, and the man nodded. "I am the Marked Man; the Source is their capital."

The bard turned back to the Chopt leader. "That is correct."

"Why?" Ironwinter suddenly snarled. "There is a stink of Death about you, you are not of humankind, you carry the destruction of the People of the Ice within you."

Paedur looked at the young Chopt with more interest. His diction was perfect and completely without accent; this was no ordinary beast, and he obviously had some degree of Sight. "Every man dies, every man carries his destruction within him," he said softly.

Ironwinter leaned across Icewalker and rammed his knife into the wooden table before the bard. "I do not trust you. I think you should die, bard," he spat.

Paedur looked at the knife vibrating in the table, and then he slowly reached out and encircled it within his hook. His lips moved slightly. The hook glowed with a cool pale blue light, and then the burnished metal of the knife began to run in sluggish liquid, pooling on the wooden table, scorching the wood, the stink of burning metal and wood overlain with the acrid odour of power.

Behind his covering of hair, Ironwinter had paled, and his small dark eyes were now clearly encircled with white.

"And will you kill me?" Paedur whispered, his voice cold, lifting his face so his eyes burned with the light from the fire, turning them gold and flickering bronze.

Icewalker deliberately poured his drink over the sizzling remains of the knife. "The boy is headstrong, but means well. He has reason enough to hate the humankind. You will forgive him."

Paedur was unsure whether the last had been a request or a statement, but he slowly nodded. "There is nothing to forgive; words spoken in haste…"

"I meant them!" Ironwinter said defiantly.

Icewalker suddenly struck upwards with his goblet, the earthen bowl shattering against the Chopt's chest, sending him staggering back. Before he could recover, the old beast swept his legs from under him, sending him crashing to the ground, and his own knife was resting against the younger creature's throat. "You insult my guest; you invite bloodshed; you summon death," Icewalker snarled. "This man, this bard, is not humankind. He will kill you without thinking, without trying and with no effort. So if you wish to die then at least let it be by my hand." Although he had been speaking in the Chopt dialect, Paedur had caught most of it, but he still turned to Bastion for a translation, deciding not to betray his knowledge of the language just yet.

"Icewalker says you are not of humankind and could kill the boy," the guide said shortly.

"Tell them if my presence here causes them upset, I will leave."

"Don't be a fool," Bastion said quickly. "You're in the Northlands now—the customs are different, the manners changed. You have accepted Icewalker's hospitality for the night, and you must stay the night. To leave before the dawn is the action of a thief or an assassin, and is extremely discourteous—and dangerous. If you even suggest it, Icewalker himself will probably use that nice new knife on you."

The bard nodded. "I'll abide by what you say. But you might compliment him on the knife, you'll notice all the creatures are carrying new weapons."

"I noticed."

Icewalker had resumed his seat. He slapped both gnarled hands down on the table and glared at the bard. "You have brought dissent to my table…"

Paedur looked at the creature and allowed a little of his trained Bardic Voice to project. "I brought meat to your table; I brought respect. I was met with threats and insults. I came to honour the Chopt Lore, but perhaps the Chopt Lore is not worthy of saving."

Icewalker's lips pulled back from his gums in a broad smile. "A threat unworthy of one who wears the cloak and device of a bard."

Paedur bowed slightly, acknowledging his mistake; he was beginning to realise that he had badly misjudged these people. They might look like beasts, they might live and eat and even smell like beasts, but these were no unthinking animals.

"If you have travelled this far for our lore then you are not going to be so easily turned back," Icewalker continued, picking up a second goblet which one of the females had placed before him. "Tell me first what you want to know."

"I would like to travel to your capital—the Source—and learn from any records that have been kept."

"The People of the Ice keep no records in script or stone." He tapped his head with a blunt nail. "Here is where we record the history of our race. There are few skills amongst us, but our memories are prodigious."

"You have the skill of metal work," Bastion remarked. "The new knives are a marvel."

Something shifted behind the beast's eyes, and he looked uncomfortable. "The knives were...a gift from the Source."

The guide grinned. "I thought the People of the Ice accepted no gift save the gift of the gods."

"The knives are a gift of the gods," Icewalker said shortly.

Paedur, sensing the way the conversation had shifted, changed the subject quickly. "Can you tell me then the History of the People of the Ice?" he asked.

The Chopt looked surprised. "You would listen to it?"

"I am a bard—my first and last delight is in the telling and hearing of tales."

"Datar!" Ironwinter said warningly, but Icewalker ignored him.

"Can you tell me how the People of the Ice came to the Northlands?" Paedur asked.

Surprisingly, Icewalker shook his head. "That is not my tale. Each clan of the People has a tale to tell; some tell of the creation of the People, others of their coming to the Northlands, others of their growth to Empire, and still others—and this is my tale—tell of their fall from power. I will tell you, bard, how the Chopt race became little more than beasts."

As he had been speaking, the rest of his clan had gathered around to listen, their faces and mouths slick with grease from the boar meat. Paedur closed his eyes and allowed his senses to expand, taking in the room, reading the coloured auras, most of them reflecting something close to contentment, a simple people satisfied with simple pleasures. Ironwinter was still seething with rage, his aura flickering red and white, and Icewalker to his right was glowing with a soft satisfaction; obviously he wasn't often asked to tell his clan's tale.

The bard then allowed his consciousness to move beyond the long hall and out into the camp beyond. He picked up the sentries patrolling the walls, and then beyond them the stillness of the forest. A pack of wolves slunk by beneath the trees, radiating animal rage and hunger; there was a snowbear hunting on the banks of a frozen river; and to the north a pack of ice-cats had killed and were eating, but then beyond them there was no living thing, no movement.

Reasonably satisfied, Paedur opened his eyes, and found both Bastion and Icewalker looking at him. He smiled an apology, and the Chopt began...

This was the last days of the Shining Folk, the First Race; this was the time when the worlds were in turmoil and the Planes of Existence seethed and shifted. This was the Time of Ending.

The Shining Folk were hunted then, hunted by their own creations, by those who had sworn to protect them, hunted by their children. They retreated to the Outlands, the hidden places, secret groves and concealed valleys wherein to continue their works and magics. And so they moved north, driven away from the civilised world by the newly civilised peoples, and eventually they settled in a secret hidden valley deep in the Land of Ice and Fire. But the borderland between the Northlands and the newly-established Southern Kingdoms was guarded, and often the southerners sent forays into the bitter Northlands seeking their old masters and, if they were found, subjecting them to the most barbaric tortures before putting them to death.

So in their desperation the Shining Folk brought forth the People of the Ice, the Chopt. They were the last creations of the

Shining Folk, and the First Race used the sum total of their knowledge and lore to create a people beautiful, strong and wise. They
created creatures that were in their own likeness, but stronger and
with a warlike barbarity that was unknown to the Shining Folk.

But this is not my tale; others have the telling of it. My tale is
later, when the seasons have passed, and the Shining Folk have left
this world for ever, leaving their sons, the People of the Ice, alone.

The Chopt race had created an Empire in the Northlands for
the Shining Ones, using the last of their magic, working with their
tools, following their advice, but when the First Race went, the
Empire of Ice and Snow collapsed, crumbled in on itself, dissolved
in turmoil, bickering, and revolution. The Empire fell and the race
of humankind added its weight to its dissolution, and attacked its
borders.

The humankind moreover, retained a little of the Shining One's
magic and used this against the People of the Ice, and death and
disease walked amongst the clans of the Northlands. The peoples
separated, seeking safety in solitude, and to this end sought the ice
caves and secret places, much as their creators had done in previous
generations.

And then it was as if the very elements conspired against the
Chopt race. The seasons turned, and although the Northlands had
always been a land of ice and snow, in the Turnings of the Year it
was as pleasant as any other southern land, but now this too
changed, and the ice and snow closed in on it, sealing it in an iron
claw, creating the harsh and bitter land it is today. And it was said at
the time that the weather had been influenced by the magic of the
humankind, but there is no one alive now to say the truth in this.

However, the bitter weather proved to be both the blessing
and the bane of the People of the Ice.

The humankind had their own problems; their gods warred
both with others like themselves and with the demon-kind and
their troubles were reflected on the World of Men. The humankind—excepting those living on the borders of the Northlands—
soon forgot about the Chopts, for their own troubles were many
and manifold.

But the bitter weather that sealed off the Northlands, enclosed
the small scattered tribes within tiny encampments and caves. And
you must remember that this was still in the days when the People

of the Ice were akin to humankind, soft of skin, though strong of heart; this was the time before the People of the Ice learned to survive in the Northlands.

Trapped as they were, they broke the First Rule of the Shining Folk—they bred with themselves.

The Shining Folk had left their children the Rules, seven guides for the continuance of their existence. Some are meaningless now, their content lost with the passage of the Seasons; only two remain relevant, not to breed with one's own clan, and not to eat of the flesh of one's own race.

The First Rule was broken, the Second never so.

The first generation—the result of such inbreeding—was much as their parents, the only noticeable difference being the quality and quantity of their hair which, it is remembered, was strong and coarse and covered much of their bodies. And in the bitter Northlands, this was no small advantage. So the elders of the clan examined the children and found them to be strong and hale and pronounced it safe for the clan to breed within itself.

The next generation was also hale. They too were covered in hair, and as they grew towards maturity it was found that they were stronger than the previous generation.

But their taste for blood was strong too.

The next generation saw the beginnings of the fall. Their children were ugly—not all of them, but enough for the chiefs to recognise that here was the result of breaking the First Rule. The children were not monsters: their limbs and senses were correct, but their features were misshapen, and they were no longer in the image of the Shining Ones. They too were strong, and their taste for blood and flesh equally so.

Successive generations produced children that were more and more unlike the Shining Ones, but although their appearance became more and more savage—almost beast-like—their intellect did not change at first; but later, as the old learning was no longer recited and remembered, the Chopt lost the last of their gifts from the Shining Ones, the gift of knowledge.

What remained were much as you see the People today, strong in body, hardy, but lacking in knowledge and hungry for flesh. How the People discovered the flesh of humankind is another tale, but that was the beginning of the war with the soft-skinned ones.

These were the People of the Ice who first brought terror to the fields of Men and caused the building of the Seven Bastions of the North along the banks of the Seme.

The humankind warred with the People, and the Chopts gathered together the last army ever to be seen in the Northlands and moved south on the soft-skinned ones. And in a battle that lasted seven days and seven nights they were driven back at the Seme by the very things they had once cast aside—the knowledge of the Elder Race.

The humankind employed their magic and knowledge to break the Chopts forever. No more would they be a force to threaten the Southern Nations; now they were only bands of savage marauders, attacking isolated villages and farms, taking human flesh where they could.

All that remained to them was the promise, the promise that they would one day arise again as a Nation and carry fire and destruction into the Southlands under the leadership of a mighty Datar.

The People of the Ice await that day.

And it nears...

12
Confrontation

*The nobles were growing confident, and with that confidence came a certain
amount of arrogance; Kutor realised he must act soon, lest the usurper be
usurped!*
           The Turbulent Years: a History of the Seven Nations

There was revolution in the air.

In the Lower City there were riots as more and more refugees
poured into the city, stretching the new Emperor's aid to the limits.
Shops and warehouses were raided for food and clothing, and the
larger public buildings—theatres, arenas, auction houses, and even
churches and temples—were taken over by the homeless. Whole
sections of the Lower City became refugee enclaves, where the only
law was that of might and the sword.

Death, both violent and bloody, was commonplace and there
were fires in the ancient wooden buildings every day; it was only a
matter of time before there was a major fire that would gut the
Lower City.

And through it all wandered the priests of the Religion, spreading rumours, creating dissent—it was a dangerous and foolish job,
and several paid the price of that foolishness—but the Religion
claimed these as martyrs to their cause.

In the confusion, the vampir were born.

Under the Lady Esse's direction, the two vampir walked the
streets at night—and fed, taking their victims in the darkness from
amongst the women of the street. They took only females, and
most of them were pretty and young. Three of these women—
coal-eyed and already inhabited by the creatures from the Ghost
World—that staggered back to the Warlord's dungeon were just
that, but the fourth was a stout, ugly woman from the Northlands,
her skin weathered and hard, her hair bleached brittle white. The
Lady Esse immediately locked up the shambling creature and then
had the Warlord's son go back into the streets to find one of the
type of women she desired.

While she was waiting for the boy to return with a suitable woman, the sorceress had chained the ugly vampir to the floor and doused her in oil. When the boy returned with his unconscious victim, she was chained to the floor beside the creature and then the Lady Esse set the vampir alight. The creature's howls ripped through the night, and then one by one, the five other vampir joined in the chorus, until it seemed as if the very gods themselves cried in pain. When the body was completely wreathed in flame, the sorceress plunged her dagger into the body of the young woman on the floor. She bucked and heaved, her mouth opening in a scream that never materialised, and suddenly she opened her eyes—and they were coal black. The Lady Esse had her sixth vampir.

The following morning, the Emperor Legion marched into the Lower City in a display of strength.

The Emperor Legion enjoyed a terrifying reputation. It was the creation of one woman, and was composed entirely of women, all of them hand-picked and trained to an extraordinary degree of weaponship by the Commander of the Legion, Fodla. Indeed, such was its association with her that the legion was sometimes called Fodla's Own.

The very presence of the Legion was enough to quell some of the rioting immediately, and streets that had been bloodied and violent grew deserted and silent as the Legion in the Imperial colours of blue and black marched through.

A fragile, brittle calm returned.

In the palace, Kutor sat opposite the Weapons Master, while Tien lurked in the shadows behind his master. The change that had come over the Emperor was extraordinary; his newfound energy was infectious and almost exhausting, and Owen privately wondered if he didn't prefer the old Kutor.

The table between them was strewn with maps of the city, which had been marked and coloured to show the disposition of the Imperial Legion and the trouble spots. They were receiving reports at regular intervals and—on the charts in any case—the Imperial Legion had taken control of most of the Lower City. The gates to Karfondal had been locked, and the guards doubled and redoubled, and the Way Stations along the roads had been alerted to stop and hold any travellers.

Owen pushed the charts aside and looked at Kutor. "So what do you want us to do?" he asked, although he already had a very good idea.

Kutor smiled, showing his teeth in a feral smile. "All eyes are on Fodla now; they are expecting—perhaps they are even hoping for—a bloodbath in the Lower City. But she has her instructions and there will be no killing unless absolutely necessary. It is not the refugees' fault there is not enough food and blankets, no shelter and no water available. It is not their fault that they have been driven from their homes by the elements, and in many cases it is not their fault they have been stirred up into this frenzy. The Andam has told me that the Religion's priests are working against them, raising passions." Kutor's fingers toyed with a piece of coloured wax with which he had been marking the charts. He looked at his hands and then deliberately placed the stick down. "Did you know that the Andam Brothers working the mission on the docks were slaughtered?" he asked softly. "No? It has been assumed that it was the mob, but Andam tells me that it was the work of a Gallowglas and a band of hired thugs who killed the Brothers in cold blood and then wrecked the mission to make it look as if a mob had stormed through." The Emperor leaned forward. "And that is your first mission. I want that Gallowglas—and the mercenaries who were with him, if possible."

Owen nodded. "That should be easy enough."

"Perhaps not," Kutor smiled grimly. "The Gallowglas is in the employ of the Lady Esse—he is her personal guard. The same lady has just overseen the creation of four more vampir. They are being kept in the cellars beneath the Warlord's Armoury. And that is your second mission. I want those vampir dead or destroyed, or whatever it is you do with the creatures. Perhaps the Andam can help?"

"They will have to be taken during the day when they are sleeping," Owen mused. "But how do you know where they are?"

"Since his brothers were slain, the Andam has apparently been drawing on some sort of occult power—it's almost as if their deaths provided him with the power—which makes him even more powerful than the Lady Esse."

"Then why doesn't he use his power against the sorceress?"

"To do so would be to taint it," Kutor said, "or so he told me. So I am afraid you will have to kill her yourselves without aid of any description."

Owen looked uncomfortable; this sounded too close to assassination for his liking.

Kutor shuffled the maps together on the table. "Now let us consider the Twelve Families. Of the twelve only four are of any consequence: the Lords Rocque and Bleau; Boazio, the Master of the Fleet; and the Lady d'Homana, who also has a Gallowglas bodyguard. I want them all removed."

"I am not an assassin," Owen said softly.

The Emperor looked surprised. "You are…a warrior."

"A warrior is not an assassin."

"You are a mercenary in my employ," Kutor reminded him coldly, "and if I tell you to kill, then you will kill!"

"You forget yourself, Kutor," Owen blazed. "You forget who put you on this throne; you forget whose presence here keeps you on it. Who do you think would support you if I or even Fodla left you?"

"I am the Emperor…"

"You are a bandit, a usurper, nothing more. Without me, without the bard, without our support you would still be a bandit."

Kutor surged to his feet. "And what am I now? I am a prisoner, a puppet to be moved to your will. And if all of this is with your support—then perhaps I would be better off without it!"

The two men glared at one another and Tien, recognising the very real threat of violence, began to move towards them, when the Andam swept into the room. "Enough! Enough of this squabbling. You remind me of children in the market, fighting over scraps." He looked at the two men, noting Kutor's angry flush, and the Weapon Master's set expression. The Andam's harsh, whispering voice was almost raw with emotion. "Save your anger for your enemies. Accept that you need one another; Kutor would not have become Emperor without the Weapon Master's aid and experience, but Owen would still be nothing more than a penniless mercenary wandering the fringes of the Nations. Accept that. And also accept that the bard brought you together in the name of the Pantheon. Remember that. And when you speak of making and breaking, remember that the Gods of the Old Faith can make or break at will."

"They are not your gods," Kutor said sullenly.

"But they are yours," the Andam hissed. "And while you sit here squabbling together, your enemies conspire and act." Within the grey cowl, the priest's head turned to Owen. "Go, slay these vampir if you can—they present the greatest threat. Let the humankind wait for the present."

Owen stood up, grateful to be doing something that didn't go against what little conscience he lived by. "How may I destroy these creatures?" he asked.

"Fire," the Andam hissed, "only fire."

When Owen, followed by Tien had left the room, the Andam priest turned back to Kutor. "And now you must prepare yourself; a delegation from the Twelve Families awaits..." And Owen could have sworn the Andam was smiling.

The Warlord turned as the door to the Armoury opened and a small figure stepped in, and then stood there, fully illuminated by the light and outlined against the door. The Warlord grinned; this was no professional. Sliding the spikes that took the place of his hands into his sleeves, he hurried down the long shop, his face settling itself into its customary mask. His steps faltered but otherwise he showed no surprise when he saw the figure standing in the light; it was a Shemmat. He recognised the distinctive skin and eyes, but he couldn't remember when he had last had a Shemmat in the shop.

"You're looking for a weapon?" he inquired.

The man grunted.

He had the look of a warrior, the Warlord mused, but he might be nothing more than a servant—many of the Shemmat in the Nations were in service, a relic of the days when their ancestors had been defeated on the Sand Plain and the survivors sold into servitude. If he was a Shemmat servant—especially from a family of servants— then there was a possibility that he was tongueless, the custom persisting in some of the households which followed the traditional ways.

"Is this something for battle or for more personal protection?"

"To kill..." the Shemmat muttered indistinctly.

"A battlefield weapon, then," the Warlord said, turning away. He suddenly felt uncomfortable. There was something about this man...

He had dealt with warriors of all types in his long career as armourer and weapons-merchant to the Imperial and mercenary armies. There had been men he had liked, others he had positively loathed; some had amused him, others had made him angry, but only a few—a very few—had actually made him nervous. He glanced around at the Shemmat again, and found the man staring at him, his green eyes glittering slightly in the light reflected from the piled weapons. His expression was like that of a serpent, poised about to strike.

The Warlord turned, and indicated a display of maces, war hammers, morningstars, clubs, and short pikes. "For someone of your stature, I would suggest something which would give you a little extra reach, but not a long pike or spear which would be too heavy, and too unwieldy for your size. A mace perhaps: either this type, which is nothing more than a spiked ball on a long shaft, or this type, where the spiked ball is attached to the shaft by a chain." He looked back at the Shemmat, and once again found the small man staring intently at him. The Warlord was suddenly grateful for the knowledge that his son was at his back, hiding amongst the weapons and armour, his crossbow levelled at the customer's throat.

"Axe," the Shemmat said.

The Warlord started to shake his head. "An axe requires great skill and dexterity…"

"And there is no one with greater skill than my servant, Tien tZo," Owen said very softly, coming out from behind the Warlord, a stiletto pressed to his son's throat.

Too late, the Warlord realised what it was about the Shemmat that had been bothering him; the way he moved, his stance, all indicated confidence, self-assurance, even arrogance—qualities few servants would have possessed. Also, he should have recognised the Shemmat as being the Weapon Master's servant—but who looked for servants? He turned back to Owen, his usually sallow complexion now ashen. "What is wrong? I thought you were with us?"

"Vampir," Owen breathed the word. "Tell me where I will find vampir."

"I don't know what…" the Warlord began.

"You son lives and breathes; the vampir are dead things." Tien said suddenly, pitching his voice low, turning it into a menacing hiss. "Is your son's life worth that of the dead things?"

"I cannot," the Warlord said, shaking his head.

"Perhaps you should remove the boy's ear," Tien suggested, glancing at Owen.

The Weapon Master nodded and raised his knife…

"In the cellar. They're in the cellar. Four of them; the Lady Esse has taken the other two away with her…"

Owen nodded and then looked at Tien, his mouth open to say something...when the Warlord moved! The spikes that took the place of his hands flashed out towards Owen's face. Owen reacted instinctively, jerking back, using the young man as a shield—and one of the spikes took the youth through the throat! The boy's eyes opened wide in surprise and he died without a sound.

Tien rapped the Warlord across the back of the head with the flat of an axe, and his senseless body dropped to the floor on top of his son's corpse. Tien looked across at Owen, but the Weapon Master's face was set in an expressionless mask, a mask Tien knew well; the body at his feet was already forgotten, and would never be mourned over. Now the Master was composing himself to kill— and to die too, if necessary.

They smelt the creatures and their lair long before they found them. There was the rank, foul odour of something long dead, mingled with the sharp, acrid, salty smell of fresh blood, overlain with other, less readily recognisable smells, not least of which was the odour of rotting flesh.

"I'm surprised the entire street doesn't smell this," Tien said softly, as they stood on the top of the stairs looking down into the cellars.

"We're close to the docks," Owen said shortly. Drawing his short sword, and pressing his back to the left-hand wall, he began to descend the steps. Tien waited until he was four steps down before drawing his left-hand axe and pressing himself to the right-hand wall, and then following the master, step for step down into the darkened cellars.

There was a door at the base of the stairs, a thick, solid brukwood door, reinforced with strips of iron and studded with round-headed bolts. But any door is only as strong as its lock, and Tien had once served a brief apprenticeship to a locksmith. He worked on the lock with a pair of slender metal probes, and the lock clicked open almost immediately.

The cellars were vast, far bigger than the shop above, and consisted of scores of rooms on either side of a long, broad corridor. The storerooms were filled with weaponry from just about every Plane of Existence, each piece wrapped and carefully oiled and neatly stacked; there were also stores of non-lethal military equipment from blankets to sandals. One of the largest rooms was almost empty, but it had obviously been used for meetings; all the boxes had been pushed to the walls, and there was a large ornate chair in the centre of the room.

And at the end of the long corridor they found the cells. Four pretty young women slept naked in one cell. They were filthy, their hair matted and unkempt, their bodies smeared with feces and blood—and there was blood everywhere—splashed high on the walls, on the floor, even speckled across the ceiling.

Owen looked at Tien. "Are these the vampir?"

The Shemmat nodded. "The first vampir was called to the body of a young woman; this cursed sorceress has obviously continued to do that for some reason."

"I find it difficult to accept," Owen murmured, drawing right up to the thick cell bars, finding that they too were smeared with blood.

"Look at their wounds," Tien hissed.

"I don't see any wounds."

"Then look at their scars!"

The Weapon Master looked beneath the filth and dried blood, and found that two of the women were carrying terrible scars across their throats, as if they had once been torn out. There was another whose abdomen was streaked with what looked like claw marks, and a fourth, whose scars were still purpling across her chest. He shuddered and turned away in disgust. "Find something that burns," he hissed, swallowing hard.

"I saw some oil..." Tien said, and disappeared down the corridor.

"Owen?" The voice was soft and feminine—and familiar!

The Weapon Master froze, not truly believing what he had heard, unwilling to turn 'round.

"Owen, it is I."

The Weapon Master started to shake his head, his mouth opening, silently forming the single word, "N-n-n-o."

"Owen, look at me?"

Owen brought his sword up before his eyes, and looked at the mirror-bright blade. In the reflection was the face of Lisse, his sister. His long-dead sister.

"Look at me, Owen. It is I, it is Lisse, your own baby sister." And when Owen didn't turn, the voice changed, becoming harsh, "The sister you killed!"

Owen turned—and found himself staring into the coal black eyes of one of the vampir. The black ovals expanded, swallowing him, drawing him forward, pulling him in, drowning him...

There was a sound, the sound of his own heart pounding, pounding, pounding, his blood surging through his veins, the roaring of that blood in his ears, and running through it, keeping time with the pounding, his sister's vaguely mocking voice...

"Remember me, Owen? Remember little Lisse? Remember how you betrayed me, and not only me, but the whole family? Remember how you cursed us, condemning us all to death, calling on your new-found gods to bear witness to you..."

Owen staggered forward another step, the automatic step of a sleepwalker. His eyes were glazed and his face expressionless.

"And remember how we died, struck down by the plague you had conjured? Do you remember all that? And did you think we would forget? Did you think we would forgive? What you did was unforgettable, unforgivable.

"And do you know what I want now?

"You took my life—as surely as if you had struck me down with your sword, so now I want you to give me yours. I want you to give me your blood..."

Owen stepped up to the bars, and filthy clawed hands reached for him, drawing him in closer. His head was turned, exposing his neck, and the vampir bent her head down, her mouth open, exposing teeth, ready to rend and tear—and a thrown axe struck her high in the chest, lifting her clear off the floor, punching her back against the wall. She screamed, a screeching cry of rage and anger rather than pain, and one by one the other vampir's eyes opened.

Tien grabbed Owen, dragging him away from the bars, spinning him across the room, and then he smashed a jar of oil across the bars of the cell. The rancid, slightly sour odour of fish-oil filled the cells, and the stench seemed to send the vampir wild. They attacked the bars, arms and legs flailing, their blackened nails tearing at the thick metal, teeth rasping on the bars. Tien darted back to the door where he had dropped the box containing the jars of oil. He threw two more, smashing one to the floor around the vampir's feet, the second breaking high on the wall behind the creatures. He placed his next shots carefully, ensuring that each of the creatures was doused in the thick, foul-smelling oil.

The vampir who had enticed Owen staggered forward, pulling the axe from her pallid flesh. She swung it once and then launched it with savage fury through the bars of the cells. The leather thong on its handle caught in the bars, dropping it sharply to the ground. The metal head struck sparks off the stones...

The explosion lifted Tien clean off his feet, sending him tumbling down the corridor, a solid sheet of flame licking down along the walls, scorching the air, lapping against the door at the far end of the corridor.

The Shemmat staggered to his feet and dashed back into the room—and blundered into Owen who was staggering out. The Weapon Master was a ball of flame, having absorbed the full force of the blast, and it was nothing more than blind instinct that had brought him out.

Tien tripped him, bringing him to the floor, rolling him over, smothering the flames. He pulled off his own smouldering jacket and beat at the tiny blue flames licking at his master's clothing, dragging him away from the inferno that still raged in the cells.

Tien looked back into the room once—and froze in horror. It was sheathed in flame, and the four figures of the vampir writhed in their cells, one of them wrapped around the bars, arms outstretched. Their mouths were open as if they were screaming, but Tien heard nothing. He watched as the dead flesh blackened and then curled and crisped, exposing the muscles beneath, and then this too fell away, the fatty flesh boiling and hissing, spitting like cooking meat. Soon there was nothing left but the skeletons—and the eyes. The black eyes, deep as night, cold as ice, the eyes remained in the white skulls. The skeletons continued to flail against the flames, but they were weaker now, the bones themselves turning brown, then black, then crumbling into filthy powder as the intense heat ate into them. Tien deliberately threw the remainder of the jars at the skeleton creatures, watching in satisfaction as the flames, renewed, ate into the remaining slivers of bone and scattered the dust.

The Shemmat turned back to his master. Owen was semiconscious, most of the skin on his face gone, all his hair burned away, his head almost seared to the skull. However, his leathers seemed to have taken most of the burns, though it was burned through to the flesh in some places.

"It's over," Tien whispered. "It's over." He dragged Owen to his feet and carried him down the corridor and up the steps leading off the burning cellar. The door at the top was hot to the touch—and it was locked!

Tien eased Owen gently to the steps and pushed against it, thinking that perhaps the heat had swelled it in its frame, but there was slight play at the top and bottom. Stooping, he put his eye to the large keyhole—just as a large spike punched its way through! Tien staggered backwards, almost tumbling down the steps, his right eye watering: the spike had brushed his eyelashes.

Keeping well back, he bent and looked through the keyhole again—and once again the spike was jabbed through the keyhole and immediately withdrawn. The Warlord was waiting...

Drawing his remaining battle-axe, Tien once again peered through the keyhole. The spike appeared immediately—and Tien hammered down on the projecting end of the spike with the blunt end of his axe, bending the metal at an acute angle. The spike was now trapped. But so were they—and the flames were spreading. When they reached the storerooms the whole building would go up; the Shemmat had seen enough explosives and oils to outfit the Imperial Army...and a smile touched his normally impassive features. Leaving the Weapon Master lying semi-conscious on the steps, he raced back down into the flames which had now found supplies of blankets and furs and were eating through them, belching acrid grey smoke into the cellars. If the fire didn't get them, the smoke would.

Tien found what he was looking for in the first storeroom. Luid-dust, named after Luid, the Fire Sprite, was a gritty, slightly pebbly, brown powder which ignited with an impressive explosion. He grabbed the nearest bag and hauled it back up the steps to the door. Without even pausing to check on Owen, he tied the bag around the Warlord's hook which was still stuck through the keyhole. Moving quickly now, he dragged Owen back down the steps into the first storeroom and propped him up against a wall. Next, he punched a hole in a wooden box and snapped out a spar, and then he raced down the corridor to where the flames were licking around the entrance to the largest storeroom, the one in which the Lady Esse had plotted with the Twelve Families. Tien plunged the wood into the fire and held it there

until it was burning furiously, the dry wood splintering and crackling. Turning, he ran back down the corridor to the foot of the
steps. Judging the distance carefully, his eyes watering from the
smoke, he swung the burning spar of wood underarm and then
threw it towards the bag of Luid-dust...

The explosion blew out the door and most of the wall surrounding it, punching a hole clean through the opposite wall, and
out onto the Armoury's rear courtyard.

No trace of the Warlord was ever discovered.

13
The Henge

And treat only with respect what the past yields, lest your disrespect destroy you...

> *Proverb, common to most of the Seven Nations*

Katani's amber eyes snapped open, and she remained still and unmoving, wondering what had awakened her. Around her the night was silent and chill, and her blanket was dusted with a light covering of snow. Above the trees she could see the Lady Lussa riding proud and full across a cloud-streaked sky, turning the snowscape into sharp bands of black and white.

She had dozed off, sitting up against a tree, and directly across from her, in the shadow of a bush, she could see the small bundle that was Gire, almost lost beneath the furs Eiron had forced on them when they had finally left the Bardhouse three days previously.

A clump of ice fell to the ground at her feet from the trees above.

The woman relaxed; her warrior senses were so finely attuned that she awoke for the slightest reason, and then was unable to return to sleep until she had discovered what had alerted her. It was not, however, a trait she regretted—it had saved her life on far too many occasions.

She settled back into her armour, shifting her spine away from the rough gnarled tree trunk and was about to close her eyes again when a second jagged piece of frozen snow fell to the ground. This piece was a little further away, closer to Gire.

Without moving her head, Katani looked up. The trees were coal-black shapes against the purple of the sky. With the light from the Lady Lussa slanting through them, distorting their shapes, adding depth to them, it was impossible to make out if anything was lurking up there. A bird probably, Katani thought, or a small rodent. Another clump of ice fell to the ground, almost at Gire's feet...

Katani was moving even as the creature dropped out of the branches, her sword whining in the chill air. The Chopt turned at the sound, his own knife coming up automatically. Katani's sword sheared through the metal, and continued on to take off the Chopt's head in one long smooth stroke.

Katani kicked the body aside, wrinkling her nose at the copper-tart stench of fresh blood on the sharp night air. She was about to shake Gire awake when the boy sat up. His eyes were stone grey. "Look to yourself, warrior," Ectoraige said crisply.

Katani whirled to find that four of the beasts had materialised out of the shadows of the trees. Two were armed with barbed tridents, one had a sword and the fourth was carrying two of the long Chopt knives. Their lips had drawn back from their teeth and saliva shone wetly on their receding chins. In the moonlight their eyes were tiny and black.

The two beasts with the tridents moved apart from the others and Katani realised that they were going to try and take her from all sides at once. The swordsman and the knifeman were directly in front of her, standing a little apart, watching her eagerly, hungrily.

Katani screamed! The keening death psalm rent the brittle night air, shocking the beasts. And the warrior moved, her second sword coming free as she launched herself forward, then down, rolling between the two beasts before her, her swords slashing out, taking the creatures behind the knee, crippling them both. Still moving, she rolled to her feet, turned, cut and cut again, her sword finding throat and face. Two were dead, and it had taken less than a handful of heartbeats to do it.

The two remaining Chopts charged, the short stabbing tridents held before them in both hands. The nearest one jabbed—and Katani's shortsword took the head off the weapon. Her long-sword sliced out, opening a long gash in the beast's chest, sending him reeling back, both paws clutching the gaping wound.

The second beast attacked then, and Katani barely turned her body in time; the barbed prongs screamed off her armour, and the beast lunged forward off-balance. The warrior cracked downwards with her mailed fist and the knurled pommel of her shortsword snapped into his skull, driving him to the ground. Spinning on her heel, Katani's longsword tore out the wounded beast's throat; continuing to spin, she came down on one knee, plunging her shortsword down through the other's throat as he attempted to rise.

"Truly you are Katan." The boy stepped out from beneath the trees, and Katani had to wait for the light to fall on his face to see whether it was the boy or the god talking. His eyes were their usual warm chestnut brown once again.

Katani stooped down and methodically cleaned her weapons in the rags of the Chopts' clothing. "Why, did you think I was otherwise?" she asked, looking up.

Gire shook his head, his expression serious. "But the Katan are legend; my mother spoke to me of their exploits, and she also told me that the last of them died at the Battle of the Sand Plain, many generations ago."

"The last of them did," the warrior said quietly, coming to her feet, sheathing her swords. "I was the last of the Katan Warriors to die on the Sand Plain."

Gire's face twisted in puzzlement. "I don't think I understand." Katani shook her head. "Oh, the reasons are easy enough. I died, and walked the Silent Wood, guarding the approaches to Death's Kingdom for...for many seasons. And then Paedur the Bard appeared..."

"He was dead?" Gire asked, astonished.

"Not then," Katani smiled, gathering up her blanket and retrieving their bags from a niche in the branches of the trees. "No, he came to the Silent Wood in search of two companions who had given their lives in the service of the Pantheon. We...met and I travelled with him for a while, and then we did a service for the Gods of the Pantheon, and created a new Deathgod. In return, I was allowed to return to the World of Men once again. I am the last of the Katan Warriors." She slung her bundle over her shoulder. "We had better move, as the blood will bring predators of all sorts, and I don't want to be here when they arrive."

The boy nodded. He was quiet and obedient, and although he was aware in a vague way that God Ectoraige was speaking through him, he accepted it without question or comment. He followed Katani, aware only that she was chasing the bard because of something which the God of Learning had passed on to her. He had no knowledge of what the god was saying, and he experienced the times of possession as a dream-like state. When he awoke, however, he found he had absorbed a little of the god's knowledge—odd, scattered fragments, which he carefully filed away for future use.

They had left Thusal three days previously, and had made surprisingly good time along the tracks that led into the north. The smooth width of the King Road officially ended in Thusal and beyond it there was nothing but a series of tracks worn by centuries of travellers, trappers, and traders, as they headed out into the ice-fields to ply their dangerous trade with the beasts. One in four never returned.

Three days out of Thusal and this had been the first attack. They had been lucky. Katani had been expecting one much sooner, and the previous day, when they had been trailed by a dozen huge ice wolves, she had been sure they were going to die beneath scores of finger-length claws and teeth that supposedly could shear through a solid slab of frozen meat. The wolves had been shadowing their trail since noon and as the evening had drawn in, she had begun to seek a defensible position. But in the undulating barren landscape there had been nothing. Abruptly, however, the wolves had vanished, and later that night she had heard them howling in the distance. She didn't know what had happened, but she suspected that Ectoraige had something to do with it—after all, it wouldn't do for his mouthpiece to get eaten, now, would it?

Morning found them close to the ruins of a fort, a simple beehive-shape construction of crude unpolished stone. There were gaping holes in the rounded roof and part of one wall had collapsed.

"Chopt handiwork?" Katani asked, slowing down, wondering what might dwell in the ruins.

"I think not," Gire said, and Katani had to glance at him to make sure it was the boy and not the god talking. "It's an old trading station—the round shape is traditional—but I fancy the elements have wrought this destruction."

"Is that possible?" Katani asked.

"Bitter cold can snap metal," the boy said, "or so I was taught."

Katani nodded. "I believe you. Now, I wonder if yon ruin is occupied?"

"Why?" the boy asked, his voice suddenly deepening, becoming even more authoritative. "There is distance to travel, and even the gods themselves hold no sway over time." The boy turned to look at Katani and she found herself staring at the cold hard eyes of the god.

"The boy, or his body, at least—and I—need hot food," Katani snapped. "And you could have warned me last night," she accused. "The beasts could have slain us."

"There were only four of them," Ectoraige said mildly. "And in any case I wanted you to fight and slay them!"

"Why? In the name of all the gods such a risk is uncalled for! We're running enough risks without you calling down others on us."

"There were wolves on your trail," Ectoraige said, as if that explained everything.

"So?" Katani demanded.

"So, had you not given them something to eat—then they would have eaten you. As it was they were satisfied with the slain Chopts."

"You are a god," Katani said, rounding on the slight figure of the boy, "And a powerful one, I understand. Can you not render us some more substantial assistance? We are going to need all the help we can get if we're to complete this mission and reach the bard in time to warn him."

"I don't have the power," the god said simply. "My followers, the monks, were butchered; their students, my future generation of believers, dead also. Without their worship, my power wanes daily. The few who still believe and still pray to me are not enough and are just not strong enough to enable me to do all you wish. I am dying, warrior, slowly but surely dying. Without faith there is no substance," he quoted. "Without the belief of Man, the gods have no power."

Katani nodded. "I see. I did not know." She breathed deeply, abruptly conscious of how exposed they were out on this snow-covered plain. She looked at the ruin again. "Can you tell me if anything lives within?"

The boy looked at the ruin of a trading station. "It is empty now," he said, "but snow bears sometimes seek shelter within if the night is exceptionally bitter." His voice changed and when he looked back at Katani, his eyes were brown. "I'm cold and hungry."

Katani put her arm around his thin shoulders. "Come on, we'll shelter in the ruins and get something to eat..."

"Our companion here means to kill us." Paedur's voice suddenly echoed ice-cold, knife-sharp within Bastion's head.

Without breaking stride, the guide nodded slightly.

Paedur continued looking at the Chopt, Ironwinter, who had been chosen to lead them to the Source, the Chopt capital. "Could you find the Source without this creature?" the chilling voice continued.

Bastion shook his head almost imperceptibly.

"He will try to kill us, although whether he means to do it now or when we reach the Source is not entirely clear. At the moment he is radiating hate and rage."

It had only been with the greatest reluctance that the elders of the Chopt clan had agreed to allow the two outsiders to be taken to the Source. However, under no circumstances would they provide directions or a map, not even to the Marked Man, whom they trusted after a fashion. A guide would be provided—and Ironwinter had been chosen. The bard had been looking at the Chopt when Icewalker had called out his name, and even without his enhanced powers he had been able to read the satisfaction on the beast's face. Given the opportunity, Ironwinter would kill them, and feast on their flesh.

They had started the following morning, rising just before the night birds had winged their way home; in the northern climes time was measured by the passage of the creatures, since the elements were not to be trusted, and no satisfactory method of measuring time had yet been discovered that would survive the rigours of the bitter weather.

Although the beasts were up and about early, Paedur had been waiting for them in the long hall when they arrived to break their fast. Ironwinter arrived first; he was dressed as if for battle, with a sword slung over his back, two Chopt knives in his belt, and carrying a trident. The bard noted that all the weapons seemed to be new and displayed a curiously fine degree of workmanship.

Bastion arrived a little later; there was a Chopt woman on his arm, the same woman he had left with the previous night, and the look of disgust on Ironwinter's face was almost palpable. The bard read his aura, and it was white and blank, the aura of a killer.

Breakfast was a gruel that looked surprisingly bloody and the bard didn't care to guess what had gone into its making, glad that he only had to make a show of eating to please his hosts. He noticed that the two dead Torc Allta whom the beasts had feasted off the previous night had disappeared from the cooking spits, although there had still been some flesh on their bones when the Chopts had retired for the night. Later, he would learn that they were used much as any other beasts the Chopts killed: the flesh eaten, the muscles used for thread, the skins tanned for clothing, the bones used to make pins, needles, and trident heads.

They had left immediately after breakfast, following a silent Ironwinter who had set a stiff pace, obviously hoping to upset his unwanted charges. However, Bastion was an accomplished and experienced trapper and the pace presented him with no problems, and the bard felt neither exhaustion nor pain.

They walked on through the day, stopping for neither food nor rest. As the evening drew in and the wind changed direction for the night, Ironwinter abruptly diverged from the track he had been following—which was, in effect, nothing more than a long narrow depression in the snow—and headed down towards a clump of standing stones.

As soon as they had turned off the track and approached the stones, Paedur felt the immediate tingle of ancient power. The runes incised into his hook began to sparkle and glitter, and he thought he saw a similar glitter on the nearest stone.

"Ancient," Bastion said shortly.

"And powerful," Paedur added, "but not harmful."

"Not to our friend, in any case," Bastion nodded at Ironwinter who had stepped into the centre of the standing stones and laid his two hands flat on what might have once been an altar stone.

A thin line of white fire crackled around the stones, sparking from one to another.

The stones had been arranged in a perfect triangle, three stones to a side, each stone taller than a tall man and broader than two men standing side by side. In the centre was another triangular-shaped piece of stone, but this was laid flat on the ground. This was the stone the Chopt had touched.

"I've never heard of this," Bastion murmured, "nor anything like it."

Paedur stopped before stepping between the two stones. He lifted his left arm and brought it close to the stone; the hook blazed with a cold blue-white light. Paedur brought his hook closer to the stone before finally resting it against the gritty surface. When metal touched stone, the entire slab of stone pulsed with a chill white light, and then slowly and in sequence, each stone pulsed into a trembling light.

Smiling with a certain grim satisfaction Paedur stepped through the opening between the stones and the light died. Bastion followed him. "What was that for?" he murmured.

Paedur nodded towards the Chopt; Ironwinter was staring at him, his eyes wide, his expression almost one of horror. *"Just a demonstration,"* the bard whispered into Bastion's skull.

Later, much later, when the Lady Lussa rode high in the heavens, and the Sceptre and Orb had risen to join her, Ironwinter came to stand before the bard.

Paedur, who was sitting with his back to one of the stones, looked up at the Chopt, his eyes taking the sparkling brilliance of the night stars.

The Chopt radiated confusion and fear. "Will you speak to me of these stones, Datar?" The term of respect did not come easily to him.

"Tell me what you know of them," Paedur said softly.

Ironwinter squatted down before him. "They are relics of the past, relics of the Shining Ones."

"And?"

"We are taught that if we are ever forced to spend the night in the ice-fields, then we should always attempt to find one of the stone clusters to shelter within; no harm comes to those within the protection of the clusters."

Paedur nodded. "Beasts would be sensitive to the lingering aura of power resonating from the stones; they would be loath to approach. Can you not feel anything?"

"A tingling, a warm prickling sensation, not unpleasant."

"Are there many such clusters in the Northlands?"

"I know of half a score intact, and perhaps the same number again which have tumbled and are reputed to be useless and worse than useless—they are reputed to be haunted."

The bard nodded. "That would be true after a fashion. Once the henges are disturbed, their energies are released into themselves, and yes, if you were to stand close enough to them, you would hear voices and see strange and wondrous things."

Ironwinter nodded. "I have seen and heard them. I fled lest my essence be stolen by the spirits of the stone."

Paedur shook his head. "There are no spirits within these stones." He touched the stone behind him ringingly with his hook, and both stone and metal sparked. "There are stones like these in the Southlands, they are called Henges there, and the ancients used them for several purposes, but principally as a means of travel."

Bastion, who was sitting across from the bard, moved closer. "I thought that was myth."

"There is often more than a grain of truth in a myth. No, I assure you it is true. The Great Henges were linked, and a man might travel either from place to place upon his own plane or from plane to plane, instantaneously."

The Chopt shook his head, his black eyes narrowed to slits.

"This is too much; explain."

Paedur smiled. He briefly read the beast's aura, noting the murderous white blankness was gone and had been replaced by a genuine curiosity, interest, and something else, something approaching awe.

"The Culai, the race you call the Shining Ones..."

Bastion interrupted. "The Culai were the Shining Ones?"

The bard nodded.

"Then the Chopt race was created by the Culai?"

Paedur nodded again. "Aye, much in the same way that they created some of the other races that walk this and the other Planes of Existence, much in the same way that they created the human-kind and the beast-folk. Not all of their experiments were success-ful—consider the Chopt race for example. But unlike many of the other races which died out or reverted to their animal form, the Chopts reverted to a primitive form of the humankind—probably the same basic stock the Culai had used when they were working on the humankind. The Chopts have survived because successive gen-erations adapted themselves to their environment."

"And the stones?" Ironwinter persisted.

The bard turned back to the Chopt. "In the ancient past, and up to relatively recently too, it was possible for a man to step through a similar arrangement of stones—except that it was a circle rather than a triangle—and then, by the process of a fixed spell, emerge a league or a thousand leagues distant."

Ironwinter nodded, his eyes wide.

"And some of these henges allowed travel between the planes..." He saw the Chopt's blank expression and looked at Bastion, who shook his head. "The People of the Ice have no concept of the multiple worlds," the Marked Man said quickly.

Paedur turned back to the beast. "There is more than one world," he explained simply. "There are a myriad worlds, a myriad Planes of Existence. Some are like this place and others completely different, so strange that you would not recognise it as a place fit for life." He raised his hand and pointed to a standing stone. "Imagine that to be a world, and then that next stone to be another, and the next stone a third world. Don't look so doubtful, I have travelled between the Planes of Existence. Nowadays to pass from stone to stone, to cross that gap between the worlds, requires a magician or sorcerer of great power, but in times past, it was possible to cross by stepping through the stone Henges."

"And has this cluster—this Henge—that power?" Bastion wondered softly, looking around.

"There is still power within it; every time a Chopt comes here and lays his hand on the centre stone he is imparting some of his nervous or psychic energy into it. You saw how the Henge glowed with power when I touched it. So, yes," he nodded with a slight smile. "If you're asking me can this Henge still be used then the answer is yes. The only question is: where does it lead?"

"There is a similar cluster in the Source," Ironwinter said quietly.

"Aaah," Paedur breathed.

"What are you thinking?" Bastion asked.

Paedur stood up suddenly. "The shape of this Henge is wrong; only a circle can generate great amounts of power, so as these are different, I would imagine they are of limited power." He glanced over at Ironwinter. "What do the Chopt legends say of these stone clusters? Think…think carefully, now, the exact phrasing."

"When in danger or lost seek the sanctuary of the stones; it will succour you," the Chopt said slowly, mouthing the phrase carefully.

Paedur smiled, and it changed his features, making them softer, almost human. "I think perhaps that in times past these Henges were automatically triggered if a Chopt was in danger—possibly it operated off the life-aura which changes in colour and intensity with emotion." He shrugged. "It's only a guess. But these are limited Henges—they have a single use only, and a very short range." He turned to the Chopt again. "How far are we from the Source now?"

"A day, a night and a day's travel."

Paedur nodded. "We will try it. Here; stand with your toes touching the centre stone." He shoved Bastion up against the centre stone, moving the bulky man with ease. "Now you, Ironwinter." The Chopt took up position facing Bastion, and Paedur stood up against the third side of the triangular stone. The bard then stooped and struck his hook ringingly against the stone.

For a single moment the thin high note hung vibrating on the still night air, then it disappeared. And then Bastion swore softly, and Ironwinter whimpered deep in his throat like an animal. The stone at their feet was changing colour, the plain grey granite was suffused with a pale bluish colour. The lighter covering of snowflakes that had lain over it vanished in a hiss of steam, and the scattered few flakes that drifted onto it now hissed as they touched it. The blue light deepened, becoming stronger, more intense, and then suddenly a solid triangular shaft of light shot upwards into the night sky, blinding them.

And then it winked out.

Paedur bent his head and massaged the throbbing pupils with his single hand, blinking away the blue after-image. The chill within him told him that something had happened, although he wasn't sure what. He tilted his head back and opened his eyes—and discovered they were in a high-roofed cave, but the blue explosions on his retina prevented him from picking out details.

He heard Bastion on his left sit down suddenly. "Curse you, bard, you've opened all my wounds." The pain in the man's hoarse voice was clearly audible. And then on his right hand-side he heard Ironwinter's excited voice. "You did it, bard, you've taken us to the Source!"

And then another voice spoke from behind the bard. It was soft and susurrant, chillingly, terrifyingly familiar. It sounded like the rasp of wind-blown leaves.

"Welcome to the Source, bard!"

Paedur whirled, falling into a fighting crouch. Beyond the triangular Henge stood a shape, a vaguely human shape but twisted, like a bent and withered tree. The figure shuffled forward, its every movement accompanied by a sound like leaves crisping underfoot—and Mannam, once-lord of the Dead stepped up to the Henge stones.

Branches snapped, and there was the obscene sound of the creature's laughter. "Now, I will destroy you!" Mannam hissed.

Cold, blue-white light wound around the bard's hook and darted out towards the figure in the cloak of seared and withered leaves. But the levin bolt didn't pass out of the triangle of stones. It twisted visibly in mid-air and arced onto the nearest stone and then it flashed from stone to stone bringing them each to a brief incandescent life.

Paedur used his power again, drawing on a different source now, and the ball of sizzling energy that formed on the tip of his hook was a pale green colour, the essence of the warm earth. The bard tossed it, much as a man would toss a ball underhand, and it floated slowly—almost lazily—through the air towards the shadowy figure of the once-god.

And once again it shifted, moving in mid-air to fall onto the nearest stone, where it exploded in a wash of crackling, sparkling green light, which flowed down the stone like liquid.

And then from behind Paedur came a rapid clicking sound. Paedur clearly saw the poisoned slivers of wood from Bastion's weapon shoot past his face—and saw them shatter against the stones.

"You are trapped, bard," Mannam hissed, "trapped within the cluster of stones, trapped by your own stupidity, your own ignorance and your own arrogance." Wood snapped as the once-god laughed again. "You couldn't resist demonstrating your knowledge, your power, could you? And see where it has led you now. You are dead, bard!"

"I have been dead before," Paedur said coldly.

"I will destroy you!"

"If you had the power, you would have done so already," Paedur said, glancing around at Bastion and Ironwinter. "But in the same way that we cannot get out, I don't think you can get in."

A second figure loomed up out of the shadows. "You are correct of course, bard. But I think the advantage is ours."

Paedur heard Ironwinter's sudden intake of breath as the figure stepped up to the edge of the triangle of stones. The creature rested a large, blunt-nailed paw on the stone and opened its mouth in what might have passed for a smile. Its features were flat and bestial, its eyes small and deepset above a rounded flaring snout. From its mouth two tusks jutted upwards, each one intricately decorated in clan and caste marks.

"I am Fenar na Torc Allta," the huge beast said. "I am the lord of the Torc Allta, the Boar-Folk." Its huge head turned slightly, looking at each of the three figures in turn, before its gaze returned to settle on the bard. And then Paedur clearly saw the short coarse hair on the back of its hands rise. "I have come for you, bard. I have tracked you across the Planes of Existence to avenge my people."

"You seem to be a very popular person," Bastion murmured from behind the bard. "Two dangerous enemies."

"I'm not sure which is the more dangerous," Paedur admitted. "The Torc Allta is a dangerous beast, strong and vicious in battle but he lacks magical power, while Mannam, for all his apparent frailty, is possibly even stronger, and I'm unsure what power he still retains from his days of godhood—some, certainly."

"If we survive you can tell me how you managed to upset them both."

Paedur smiled one of his rare smiles. "They are only two of many, I'm afraid." He looked out at the two figures standing beyond the stones. "What happens now?"

"Now we kill you!" Mannam hissed gleefully.

Paedur nodded almost impatiently. "Yes, yes, I know that. But I mean this instant. What do you plan to do with us now?"

The huge Torc Allta looked at Mannam, obviously at a loss. Whatever they had been expecting of the bard, it was obviously not this slightly impatient, argumentative attitude.

There was movement in the shadows behind the pair and two more figures stepped into the cave, and although they were both humankind, the once-god and the Lord of the Torc Allta bowed to them. They stood beside the once-god and the beast looking only at the bard, looking almost surprised that he had been captured so easily.

"This is a day for reunions," Paedur said softly. "Geillard XII, deposed Emperor of the Seven Nations, and Praetens, once Susuru warlock to Churon the Onelord."

"A better class of enemy," Bastion murmured.

"They are united in many things," Paedur said quietly, "but principally they all want my destruction, and with my death, they hope the destruction of the followers of the Old Faith will follow and without them the end of the Gods of the Pantheon."

Praetens stepped up to the stones. The small, frail-seeming, white-haired old man smiled toothlessly. "No, nothing so simple now, bard. We have concocted a much grander plan in which your death will be but a small and pleasant interlude."

The bard walked forward to the edge of the stones and looked out at the old man. "I see you still inhabit the body of a slopman; is your power so weakened now that the infamous Susuru warlock cannot perform a simple essence transference?"

Praetens' face twisted in rage and his left hand moved, his fingers hooked. Thin streaks of intense red-black light lanced out from his fingernails like claws—only to be twisted onto the stones and broken.

The bard nodded and stepped back, satisfied. He had proven his point; although his power couldn't extend beyond the stones, neither could they be attacked from the other side. The triangle of stones attracted power to them, probably absorbing it for their own continuance. Many of the ancient objects were self-perpetuating in this manner.

Paedur turned back to the four figures beyond the stones. "You have captured me, but you have no use for those who accompanied me: they were merely guides. Bastion is well known to the Chopts as the Marked Man; they will vouch for him. And Ironwinter is a clansman—you can have no use for them."

Mannam shuffled forward, his cloak rasping against the stones. "Bastion is known to me; he is remarkable because I once refused his essence. The Chopt is nothing. But, in any case, they are both tainted by your presence. They will die with you."

Ironwinter suddenly moved, his knife coming up to slash at Mannam's hooded face—only to have his knife bounce off an invisible curtain between them. "I am Chopt," he growled. "I demand to see Stonehand, Lord of the People of the Ice."

Fenar's tusks clicked tightly shut. "That is impossible."

Ironwinter threw back his head and suddenly howled, the sound echoing and re-echoing off the cave walls, bouncing, magnifying until it had become a blood-curdling, ear-shattering wail. The bard, the once-god and the Torc Allta were unaffected but Geillard, Praetens and Bastion were forced to the ground, their heads buried in their hands, faces locked in pain. Bastion's facial wounds split and reopened until his features were a mass of blood and liquid.

Paedur touched Ironwinter on the shoulder and the beast reluctantly stopped. "I imagine it is a wasted effort," he said, his voice sounding unnaturally loud in the sudden silence. "No one can hear you. I think we are deep underground, in an unused part of the Source...?" he raised an eyebrow and looked at Fenar.

The Torc Allta nodded. "This is the Closed City; the beasts imagine it to be inhabited only by dangerous and blood-thirsty spirits, and they never come here. This cave is one of several

Henge-rooms which are in the very deepest sections, and there are a series of doors between here and the upper caves. These doors are soundproofed and incredibly solid in the manner of all Culai creations. Perhaps they had occasionally unwelcome visitors through the Henges from the outside world; perhaps that is why they turned their gates into prisons. And the gates are one-way bard, lest you get any ideas; if you try to go back there will be nothing but a huge surge of power that will leave you nothing but a husk."

"What are you going to do with us?" Paedur asked reasonably. The Torc Allta opened his mouth in a smile. "Nothing has been decided yet; I admit that, although your capture was carefully planned, only Mannam was certain he could lure you here. I would imagine there will be a trial; not for you—too many people want you dead— but a trial to decide who gets you. Your companions will be passed to either the Chopts or the Torc Allta for consumption. I would imagine they will be saved until the feast at which we will all gather to watch your destruction." The Torc Allta's mouth opened, displaying his sharpened teeth behind the two curved tusks. "Not even your gods can help you now, bard, they hold no sway in this forsaken place. Soon we will destroy you!"

"Why is it called the Source?" Katani asked, lying flat and peering over the edge of the sunken valley, down onto the cluster of wood and stone buildings below.

"Because this is where the Culai created the Chopts, the People of the Ice." Katani didn't even have to turn round to know that the God Ectoraige had taken possession of the boy again. "When the First Race fled north in their final days on this plane, they sought shelter in those caves." He pointed down to where the cliff face opposite was dotted with caves; the largest of them even had huge, typically Culai-wrought doors. "Deep in the mountains they worked their magics to create the Chopts, and later the Chopts ventured out of the caves and built their own dwellings, first in the valley and then on throughout the Northlands." He indicated the primitive huts. "These are their first buildings, this is the Source, the Chopt Capital."

"And the bard is here?" Katani asked, glancing around at the god.

Ectoraige nodded. "Deep within the old caves, in part of what is now known as the Closed City, I can sense an aura of immense power. But it is muted, dulled, as if something is sapping that power, draining it."

"But it is the bard?" Katani insisted. Ectoraige nodded. "I'm sure of it."

"Well, what do we do now?"

"Now, we wait until nightfall; we can move freely then."

Katani raised an eyebrow. "How?"

"There is no moon this night, and the beasts are loath to walk the night when there is no Lady to light their way; they fear if they die they will not find their way to the Otherworld. And besides," he added with a sly grin, "the Chopts do not post guards here at the Source; no one knows the location of this place."

Katani sighed. "So, we wait."

Behind her the boy's eyes changed colour, turning from stone grey to deep brown. And then he rested his head on his hands and immediately fell asleep.

The warrior shook her head and turned back to the valley below, wondering how they were going to get down to the caves on the far side of the cliffs. Directly below her the ground fell sharply away for about five hundred paces. At the bottom there was a patch of what she at first took to be shrub, but later realised must be small stunted trees. Running down the centre of the valley and bisecting the almost circular Chopt camp was a rapidly flowing river— and then she realised something else: there was no snow in the valley. Where she was lying was covered in a thick and permanent snowfall, but although she could see the odd flake drifting down into the valley itself, there was no snow on the valley floor, and the river was unfrozen.

The Chopt camp was in the centre of the valley, a huge collection of wood and stone huts of various shapes and sizes, the method of construction obviously crude and primitive. There were signs of activity in the valley below, and there were enough of the creatures moving in and around the caves for her to guess that at least some of the caves were still inhabited—and probably a damn sight warmer than the stone huts, too!

She contented herself with plotting a course down the cliff face and across the Source and up into the caves on the far side where Ectoraige had determined the bard was being held. Once inside the caves her plans became somewhat hazy—free the bard certainly, kill anyone who got in her way, and then...well then, the bard would know what to do. He knew everything.

"I don't know what to do," Paedur said evenly, walking withershins around the triangle of stones. "This device, this cluster, swallows my power, and even now I can feel it drawing on my energy, draining me."

Bastion dabbed at his bloody face with a cloth. "My wounds have opened and remain open, and they only do that in the presence of power."

"If Stonehand, my lord, were here, he would not allow me to be kept in this place," Ironwinter growled.

Bastion grunted. "Chopt, I doubt if your lord could do anything to get us out of here. If a Susuru magician, a deposed god, a dethroned emperor, and a vengeful Torc Allta cannot get us out then no one can."

"But there has to be a way out," Ironwinter protested.

Paedur nodded, agreeing. "There has to be. I would imagine this trapping function was to allow either the Culai or the early Chopts to monitor who and what came through here. But there must be a key to this cell."

Bastion stood up slowly and limped over to the edge of the stones, peering into the darkness beyond. "Are we looking for a physical device, or would a spell have been used?"

"A physical device, I would imagine: something to shut off the power even momentarily."

"But obviously not something immediately recognisable," Bastion continued. "Something in plain sight, but something which might easily have been passed over in time."

And they both found they were looking at the ornate frieze of tiles that had been laid on the floor directly beyond the standing stones. Ironwinter followed their gaze.

"They tell the tale of the creation of the Chopt race," he said slowly, "but the order is wrong. See," he pointed with a hairy paw, "that scene should come first, and then that, rather than that scene..."

Paedur looked at Bastion and nodded. They had the key, all they needed now was to work out how to use it.

Katani's fears about descending the cliff face in the dark proved to be ill-founded. When night came on, the boy had awoken, but his eyes had been those of the god. He stood up and without a word had led her off to the right to where a tiny staircase, each step barely as wide as her foot, had been cut into the stone. Still without speaking, he led her down the countless hundred steps to the valley floor below. At the bottom of the stairs there was a tiny hut, a simple one-roomed round stone shape, almost lost against the cliff face. From inside they both clearly heard the rasping, buzzing snore of a beast asleep.

"Well-room," Ectoraige said softly, "one of a dozen in the valley, but with one distinct difference—its waters are hot!"

Katani nodded; she could feel the heat seeping up through the ground into her feet.

They entered a forest of small, stunted trees which she at first did not recognise but which she later realised were common toor trees, which had obviously been warped by the unnatural temperature of the place. And immediately beyond the forest the first of the buildings began. The huts were crude, far cruder than Katani had expected, and it was only as she neared them that she realised that they were, in fact, ancient. All of the buildings were dark, but there were sounds from some indicating that they were at least inhabited. Strangely there was no light seeping out into the night.

Ectoraige led her through the scattered buildings keeping to the shadows, moving so swiftly and silently that even Katani, who had been trained since birth to such skills, found herself losing sight of him occasionally.

The first obstacle they encountered was the bridge across the river that bisected the town. The bridge had been built in three sections, the two end pieces fixed and rooted solidly on dry land but the middle piece which joined the two halves was missing—obviously it was removed at night.

Ectoraige stopped in the shadow of a tumbled building and waited for Katani to join him. He pointed towards the bridge. "The gap is approximately two man lengths—can you jump it?"

The woman-warrior squinted into the night. Two man lengths, six double-steps carrying weapons and wearing full armour and all of this over a rushing river! "What's the alternative if I can't?"

"You stay here and I'll go on alone, and rejoin you later if I can."

"I'll jump."

"If you fall you're dead."

"I'll jump," she said decisively.

Ectoraige nodded. And then he moved, running lightly across the ground. His feet made no sound on the bridge's wooden spars; he leapt at the very edge of the bridge, his legs bunching, pushing him up and over—and Katani could have sworn that he hung in the air a fraction longer than was natural. He landed lightly on the far side and immediately darted away into the shadows.

With a brief prayer for protection Katani settled her weapons around her and after a final look around, darted towards the bridge. She had paced it out mentally, attempting to gauge her steps, working out where exactly she would be when she hit the edge.

She had misjudged.

Katani knew at the final moment, just before she launched herself out across the void—which looked enormous now—that she was not going to make it. She had jumped high—too high—and slightly wide, which meant that even if she did come down within reach of the edge, she would only be able to grasp it with one hand.

"Paedur, help me now!" she gasped as she sailed through the air.

The gust of warm air from below struck her like a blow, spinning her around, pushing her forwards and over. It was enough. She hit the far side of the bridge in a clatter of armour and weapons. She was up and running before the first shaft of light darted out from the nearest Chopt dwelling. And then a small hand grabbed her, pulling her into the concealing shadows.

"Nicely done," Ectoraige said evenly, and Katani was unable to work out whether he was being sarcastic or not.

Light was appearing from buildings all over the Source, and Katani was able to see that the interiors of the crude dwellings had been covered with beautifully woven rugs, piled one overlapping the other. Some were simple geometrical designs, others were ornate and intricate Chopt hunting scenes. That was why no light had seeped out, and within the buildings it looked warm and comfortable. She revised her opinion of the inhabitants.

"Will they investigate?" she hissed.

"They cannot. The middle section of the bridge is kept on this side."

Behind them, some of the cave doors opened, sending long shafts of light down onto the bridge. Armed shadows moved in the light.

Mannam had come to gloat. He shuffled around the triangle of stones, his cloak hissing, crackling together, the sound like that of swept leaves.

"You cannot know how long I have waited for this," he clacked. "You cannot know how many times I have dreamt of this scene. It has kept me from despair."

"I am glad I did something to help you," Paedur said evenly. He was sitting cross-legged in the centre of the stones, facing the apex of the triangle, sorting through his lore, checking the legends, seeking a way out of the trap.

"You present us with a problem, do you know that, bard?" Mannam continued. "Because you are virtually immortal, we cannot just leave you to die here of hunger or thirst, so you must be slain. And you see, so many of us want you dead. Do you know the price the Gods of the New Religion have offered for you? Fenar of the Torc Allta wants you, Geillard wants you, and even Praetens wants you—although his case is weakest of all, for he plans to occupy your body.

"No, I think we will end up flaying you—that is a spectacle we can all watch. We will give your skin to the Torc Allta—they can probably eat it or something. And then we will dismember you, but slowly...oh, so slowly. The Torc Allta and the Chopts who are masters of this torture have devised a plan that will keep you alive for many seasons—long enough for you to see the death of the Old Faith."

"That is a song I have heard before," Paedur said almost tiredly.

"But this time it is different; this time it is real; this time it will happen," Mannam snarled. "Even now the Gods of the New Religion are gathering to plan the destruction of the Pantheon of the Old Faith. And, bard, because of all the pain you have caused them, they will ensure that you remain alive to witness the destruction of everything you loved!"

14
The Gods of the New Religion

The Gods of the New Religion fear not these petty godlets and spirits of the Old Faith, for the Gods of the New Religion are strong...
Epistle of the Religion

The Gods of the New Religion were gathering.

In a vast empty cave deep in the heart of the series of caves called the Closed City, Mannam, once-lord of the Dead, presided over the Calling of the Gods, a ritual older than the race of human-kind.

The dark twisted figure stood in the centre of the dusty floor and raised his arms high; his cloak slipping down his arms, revealing skin that resembled a dun gnarled bark, and hands that were little more than knots of twisted wood, his fingers curled twigs. He raised his head, and his eyes blazed red in the shadow of his cowl.

In the gloom in the furthest corner of the cave, Praetens stretched out his quavering left hand and pointed it towards the once-god, while Geillard and Fenar each placed their hands over the magician's upraised right hand. A tracery of red fire wound its way around their hands, tying them together, allowing the magician to suck strength from them and direct it towards Mannam.

"Come, Gods of Light and Dark, Gods of Night and Day, Gods of Fire and Ice..."

The cave took the once-god's voice and sent it trembling around the room, echoing and re-echoing, building in volume and power.

"Trialos, come to us. We call you in the name of belief, in the name of faith, in the name of trust..."

A pale mist gathered high in the cave, almost as if a cloud had formed and the dry, slightly musty air of the long-disused cave was suddenly tainted by something foul and rancid. The mist thickened and as it did the foul odours were almost lost beneath the suddenly cloying scent of flowers.

"Come to us now, lord," Mannam commanded, the strain show-ing in his voice.

The mist thickened to an almost solid waxen ball close to the ceiling. It throbbed, slowly, with an almost heartbeat-like intensity, and its waxy pallor was shot through with tiny red tendrils that looked suspiciously like veins.

Mannam's whispering voice had risen to a shriek. "Come to us, come to us now. Come—we so command it!"

And the ball suddenly fell.

It plummeted from the ceiling to stop, quivering, above the once-god's head. It was throbbing violently now, pulsing deeply, like a huge heart. And then a segment broke away, falling to the dirty floor to pulse and twitch like a giant slug. A second segment detached itself and fell to the ground, followed by a third. What was left of the cloud—a vague gaseous shape—seemed to draw in on itself and then it flowed down into Mannam's outstretched hands. The once-god stiffened, and then fell, shuddering, to his knees.

The three slugs thrashed around on the ground, lengthening as they moved, their waxy, greasy covering sloughing off, like a serpent's skin. Patches of what looked like pale flesh appeared.

Praetens had broken contact with Geillard and Fenar when the last of the cloud had been absorbed into Mannam. He darted forward and knelt by the shuddering figure. And both Geillard and the Torc Allta heard the magician's sudden sharp intake of breath. Mannam had raised both arms and held his hands out-stretched before him—and what had once been a twisted knot of twigs was coated in a thin covering of pale flesh, and now recognisable fingers and hands had appeared, thick veins visible beneath waxen flesh.

"The Gods of the New Religion have gifted you," Praetens said. "Another gift like this and your features will be of flesh and blood again."

The Torc Allta suddenly spat an oath as one of the writhing slugs split from top to bottom, and out from the sticky white mass appeared a human arm. A second arm appeared, then a body rose up out of the fluid, a tall, dark, naked figure that was unmistakably female. Her hair was long and a deep lustrous black, but was plastered to her back with the liquid, and her features, though of humankind, seemed slightly distorted, although not in any immediately recognisable way.

She looked over to the second shell, which had also cracked, and the figure that sat up from the milky fluid was male, and like

his female counterpart, dark complexioned and of humankind—
although there was certainly beast blood in him. The third slug
cracked open and the figure that rose smoothly to his feet was
taller than the once-god, and yet as broad as the Torc Allta. He ran
his hands through his wet hair, brushing the white fluid away from
his face and then abruptly opened his eyes. They were the colour
of blood.

He looked at the four figures and smiled hugely. "The Lords
of the New Religion thank you. You shall be rewarded to your
heart's desire, as has the once-god." His huge head moved slowly,
his blood-red eyes lingering on each face in turn, and each of them—
even the fearless Torc Allta, even the once-god—shivered; for what
looked at them was powerful even beyond imagining.

"I am Sheesarak, the Destroyer." His voice had a slightly echoing quality to it which was amplified by the cave.

The female had stepped out of the remains of the slug, and
glutinous white fluid dripped from her body. She brought her hands
together and her dark skin suddenly glowed with an intense white
light, which vaporised the fluids, leaving her skin glowing softly in
the dim light. Her mane of hair crackled with power, flowing around
her like a cloak.

Her voice was soft, slightly sibilant, and she spoke slowly and
distinctly, as if the language of humankind was alien to her. "I am
the Lady Asherat. I am the Taker of Souls."

The third creature came to his feet; his resemblance to the Lady
Asherat was pronounced, but his features were distinctively marked
with traces of beast blood, especially around the eyes which were
slit-pupilled, like a cat's. "I am Ghede, Lord of the Beasts." His
voice was a deep growl, like a mountain-cat's snarl.

Sheesarak looked around, his blood-red eyes blinking slowly,
and then he was joined by the Lady Asherat and Ghede. He stretched
out both hands and they placed both their hands in his and bowed
their heads in respect. The gods' lips moved and the trio were
abruptly clothed in simple robes of a metallic red-black cloth.

Sheesarak looked up and his eyes found Mannam. "We have
been sent by the Lord Trialos to prepare the way for him. We are
of the Trialdone, the Companions of the Lord."

Mannam bowed slightly. "We have heard of the Twelve
Trialdone."

"The Lord Trialos decided that our respective and combined talents should be sufficient to destroy the Old Faith. Now we must prepare."

Mannam bowed again. "There is a room set aside for your use."

The Lady Asherat spoke. "And when we have planned the destruction of the Faith, let us amuse ourselves with their creature, the Bard Paedur."

Fenar, the Torc Allta, laughed. "I doubt if there's enough of him to go around."

"We shall each have a piece," the Lady Asherat said without humour.

"Bard, if you do not get us out of here we are dead." Ironwinter crouched before the bard, staring into his face, seeing himself reflected in the mirror eyes.

Paedur nodded abstractedly. He was kneeling on the floor, scratching on the stones with the point of his hook, while Bastion stood behind him, looking over his shoulder.

"We will get out," the Marked Man said to the Chopt. "The bard has a plan."

Although Ironwinter said nothing and his expression didn't change, he still managed to look unconvinced. Bastion motioned him to his feet and then led him over to the edge of the standing stones. He pointed to the decorative tiles that ran around the outer rim of the cluster. "As you said, they tell of the creation of the Chopt race…"

"But they're in the wrong order," Ironwinter protested.

Bastion nodded impatiently. "We know, we know. But we think—we are convinced—that if the tiles are touched in the correct order then the stones' power will die, allowing us to escape."

The Chopt considered this and then he finally nodded. "That may be so, but there is a slight problem…"

Bastion smiled tightly, careful not to split any further the already-open wounds on his face. "I know—how do we touch the tiles?" He looked back at the bard. "That is what Paedur is working on now."

The bard came smoothly to his feet, a rare smile on his face. "I think I have it—I hope so, because we will only get one chance…"

"This way—quickly!" Katani shoved the boy in through an opening, her sensitive battle-trained hearing catching the almost silent pad of bare feet closing in on them. She was still unsure whether the beasts had actually caught sight of them on the bridge, but, although there had been no outcry, scores of the creatures were still roaming around, the only sound the pad of their feet and the occasional clink of metal on stone.

Katani followed the boy, still possessed by the essence of Ectoraige, down through what was obviously nothing more than an air duct or chimney in the cave system. The interior was coated in a vaguely luminescent fungus, which, while not lighting the tunnel, meant that they were not moving in total darkness. The tunnel was surprisingly smooth and regular, although in her bulky armour it was more than a tight fit for Katani, and on two occasions, Ectoraige had to return to unbuckle greaves or breastplate to allow her to squeeze through.

Light appeared, a vague, slightly sulphurous glow far ahead of them. Katani looked at Ectoraige, the boy's face a vaguely pale glow in the wan light, and he nodded without hesitation and set off towards it. Shaking her heard, Katani followed. If only the bard knew what she was doing for him.

As they neared the light, they heard the voices—a group of people chatting together, differing accents, differing sounds, and one more powerful than the rest booming out regularly.

The light was coming through a grille set high in the wall of what was obviously a long disused cave. Even the burnt herbs and the odours of food couldn't dispel the rank cloying odour of mildew and decay, and the air-duct was clogged with dirt and thick trailing webs.

Katani and Ectoraige lay flat in the tunnel and peered through the filthy grille. The cave beyond had once been a grand hall—a king's throne-room perhaps, a ballroom—but the ornate wood-panelling on the walls had rotted away and now hung in tattered strips from the original stone. If there had been curtains, and the metal hangers seemed to indicate that there had been, they had long since disintegrated, and whatever colours the room had been decorated in had been long hidden beneath a thick layer of grime.

Only the table in the centre of the room and the eight chairs positioned round it were new.

But neither Katani nor Ectoraige had time to study the cave; all they could see were the eight creatures—humankind and otherwise—that sat around the highly-polished table.

The table was circular and in its centre was an ancient but beautifully wrought candelabra, holding the traditional twelve candles. Ectoraige slid across to Katani and named the eight sitters. "The three to the side, in the metallic robes, are Trialdone, Trialos's creatures, Gods of the New Religion." He sounded slightly awed at the sight. "Sheesarak the Destroyer sits in the centre, with the Lady Asherat on his left hand side, and Ghede, Lord of the Beasts, on his right. Asherat was a very minor spirit until the bard killed Libellius, the Death Lord of the Religion. She is now the closest the Religion has to a Deathgod." Ectoraige shifted slightly, "The creature in black..." he began.

"...is Mannam," Katani spat. "I know him, and I know Geillard, once Emperor of the Nations, and the old man there is Praetens, the Susuru magician. Who are the beasts?" she hissed.

"The Chopt is Stonehand, Lord of the People of the Ice, but he is thoroughly under Praetens' control; he is—in every sense of the word—a puppet. The Torc Allta is Fenar, the Lord of the Boar-Folk. He has come to avenge his brethren's death in the Mire."

"As evil a gathering as you're ever likely to find," Katani murmured.

"And they all want the bard dead," Ectoraige reminded her.

"We all want the bard dead," Mannam said suddenly. "All that remains to be decided is how he should die."

"His death will be a symbol of the fall of the Old Faith," Ghede said suddenly, his voice harsh, his lips drawing back from his flat, slab-like teeth.

"His death is secondary," Sheesarak said slowly, his booming voice echoing in the confines of the cave. "Let us first decide upon the complete and absolute destruction of the Faith. You—" he pointed a long-nailed finger at Geillard, "do you support the cause of the Religion without question, without hesitation?"

The tall, thin man nodded quickly. The harsh conditions and long moons of travel had taken their toll and his usually thin features were now skeletal. "I support the Religion. It was on account of the Faith and the bard that I was deposed."

"Do you have support still?"

Geillard nodded. "My following in Karfondal is still strong amongst the nobility. They fear this new Emperor, this Kutor, they fear what he is, what he has done, and they fear what he might do in the future. They will have no hesitation in rallying their forces and rising up against him."

The god smiled, displaying teeth that matched his eyes and fingernails—they were blood red. He shifted his massive head and looked at Mannam. "And you?"

"I was a god before the bard took that away from me. My vengeance is on him. I was a god before my brothers and sisters cast me out into the World of Men. My vengeance is on them also. You need neither fear nor doubt my loyalty."

Sheesarak nodded and then turned to look at Praetens. "You are known to us. What is the price for your support?"

"A body," the magician said without hesitation. "A young body, strong and male. That is all I ask."

"And you, Torc Allta, where do your loyalties lie?"

Fenar grinned, displaying his sharpened teeth. "My loyalty is with the Boar-Folk; I care nothing for your squabble. I have travelled across the Planes of Existence in search of this bard. And I will have his flesh," he added ominously. "Deny me that and you will have cause to regret it."

The Lady Asherat hissed and turned to look at Fenar, her dark eyes clouding with blood, turning them a deep baleful red.

"There are many here with a claim on the bard. But you shall have a part of him," Sheesarak promised. "What is the price of your support?"

"We are not mercenaries—we are not Chopts!"

"You would be honoured supporters. Name your price," the god insisted.

"Flesh without question—you would allow us to kill and eat and never question the why or where of it?"

Sheesarak nodded.

"And a place in this world."

"Explain."

"My people—the Boar-Folk—are now few in numbers, and there has not been a birthing in the Mire for nigh on two generations. We are a dying breed. I am looking for a nation, a land, an island kingdom particularly, where the Torc Allta could live without hindrance or let, and be allowed to pursue their own culture."

"And if we gave you this we would have your support in return?"

"Our absolute and unquestioning support."

"I give to you—on behalf of the God Trialos, and in the name of the Twelve Trialdone, of which we are a part—any of the outlying provinces or island kingdoms that you find suited to your needs."

"Then you have our support."

Sheesarak finally turned to the still silent figure of Stonehand, the Chopt King. "And what of him?"

"He is under my thrall," Praetens said. "He will do what I command him to do, say what I tell him to say."

"And what promises have you—through him—made to the People of the Ice?"

The old man laughed breathlessly. "I have promised them land and flesh—humankind flesh. It will fulfil an ancient prophecy, and they found it to their liking. The Chopts will follow Stonehand's words without question. So, they are mine, and through me, they are yours to use as you will."

Sheesarak threw back his head and laughed and the walls took the sound and threw it back until it was a cacophony, hideous and wailing. "Then there is no way that victory can elude us. This, then, is the plan devised by the Lord Trialos for the destruction of the Faith..."

Paedur stood with his hook pointing towards the stones. He was still and his face was expressionless.

Ironwinter lay on the ground with his head at the edge of the stones, as close as he could possibly get to the invisible line of power that surrounded the Henge; his task was to watch the ornate tiles.

Bastion stood behind the bard. He was holding the short-barrelled tubed weapon in both hands, holding it as steadily as possible, pointing it at a spot the bard had shown him on the ceiling high above. In the hollow handle of the weapon there were eight of the poison-tipped slivers of wood.

"Ironwinter?" Paedur asked. The beast grunted without looking up. "Bastion?" His reply was the double click of the weapon being readied.

Paedur breathed a sigh and then suddenly unleashed a thin intense stream of white fire towards the nearest stone. All the stones lit up with power as they drank in the raw energy, and the air was abruptly filled with the harsh metallic stink of it.

Bastion breathed a sigh also and pressed the stud on the handle of the weapon. There was a click and a sliver of wood snapped through the thinned shell of power surrounding the cluster of stones, ricocheted off the stone ceiling and snapped onto the ground, just clipping the edge of a tile.

"Too low," Ironwinter growled.

Bastion fired again. Again the sliver broke through the thinned barrier and bounced off the ceiling—and this time it struck the tile dead centre. With the faintest of clicks, the tile sank into the ground.

"That's it, that's it," the Chopt said excitedly. "But hurry, hurry, the bard cannot last." Paedur was sagging visibly, his usually pale features now ashen, and the reflective glow gone from his eyes, leaving them like soiled and spotted mirrors.

Bastion fired again—and missed. His fourth shot struck the low ceiling at the correct angle and cracked perfectly into the second tile. Again, it sank slightly.

The bard's stream of power was weakening now; the light was no longer so intense, and whereas before the light had been without heat, now the temperature had risen dramatically.

"Again, again!"

The Marked Man fired again—and missed. He corrected the angle and fired again—and missed.

"Bastion..." Ironwinter warned.

Bastion fired just as the bard's power died and he crumpled. The Chopt rolled over and caught him as he fell—and didn't even see the sliver strike the third tile dead centre. It sank with the faintest of clicks.

Abruptly the cluster of stones turned black.

Bastion looked at Ironwinter in astonishment, and then they both grabbed the bard and dragged him out of the triangle of standing stones. They had barely passed over the ornate tiles when the three key tiles rose again with a series of laboured clicks, and the stones resumed their usual granite appearance.

"Now what?" Ironwinter asked with a smile.

Bastion grinned. His face was a mass of blood since his concentration had opened the wounds on his face. "Now we get out of here!"

Sheesarak the Destroyer concluded, "…and so we have decided that since the Old Faith can only be rekindled by the existence of some sort of records of the observances and teachings, every teacher, every priest, every scribe, every monk and every bard should be put to death as a first priority. The Lady Asharet will see to that."

"But first we must destroy the source of all this knowledge about the Faith. We must destroy the great Bardic Library at Baddalaur. Without it, the Faith dies!"

"I think he's dead," Ironwinter gasped.

"He's immortal, he cannot die—I think," Bastion grunted.

They were standing in the corridor outside the cave which held the cluster of stones, wondering which direction to take. The Chopt was carrying the bard slung over one shoulder, while the Marked Man paced ahead, his cutlass and almost empty weapon in his hands.

"I cannot hear a lifebeat," Ironwinter hissed, turning his head slightly to press his ear to the bard's chest.

"He's immortal—he doesn't have one."

"Only the dead don't have one."

"I don't have one," Bastion grinned. "Now, which way?"

The Chopt shook his head. "I don't know. This is the Closed City; no one has ventured here in a thousand seasons."

Bastion shook his head in frustration. He expected Mannam and his unlovely companions to appear at any moment; the bard's use of power wouldn't—couldn't—have gone unnoticed. But which way? The walls of the tunnel had been painted in a thick luminescent paint—an old Culai trick—made from a natural phosphorescent fungi that grew in most cave systems. They had refined it to provide a solid, if dim, source of light. The tunnel stretched in a straight line in both directions until it faded into shadows. It was lined with dark openings, which obviously led into other caves, but these were all dark, and looked likely to be disused. Finally, the Marked Man dropped to his hands and knees, examining the lie of the ground—and immediately discovered that the floor to the left-hand side of the tunnel was coated in a fine layer of dust—undisturbed dust. He stood up and set off in the opposite direction without a word.

With a grunt, Ironwinter settled the unconscious bard onto his shoulder and set off after him, hoping the Marked Man knew what he was doing.

"We've got to warn the bard," Katani hissed desperately.

Ectoraige shook his head. "I know. Be still, they're leaving…"
In the room there was movement as the gods, beasts, and men
abruptly came to their feet, with Praetens pulling the enchanted
Stonehand up with him. They moved away towards the door, chatting quietly together, small, inconsequential things, like a merchants'
guild meeting discussing the price of grain and carriage and the
weather. When the room was empty, Ectoraige suddenly gripped
Katani's arm, making her jump.

"We must hurry."

"The bard, where's the bard?"

"Come on. We've got to get away from here." The god in the
body of the boy brushed past the warrior and raced back down the
tunnel, and his sudden sense of urgency touched Katani with a strange
fear. Something was wrong, desperately wrong. Whatever the god
had come to the Source for, whatever information he had possessed, had been changed or altered in some way by the gathering
they had just witnessed. He had brought her to the Source to free
the bard—or so she thought—but now here he was fleeing the Source
and without even looking for Paedur.

Katani caught up with him as he was preparing to crawl through
a low archway. Her longsword whispered from its sheath to touch
his throat, just beneath his left ear. "Wait…wait a moment, now.
Where is the bard? I'm not leaving here without him."

The god's stone-grey eyes blazed and Katani clearly saw the
hardened features of the man through the softer flesh of the boys'
face. "I am Learning and Knowledge. I know where the bard is. I
am going to him now."

"Something you learned in the cave disturbed you…"

"Foolish child! The Pantheon was aware that the Religion was
planning something like this. That is why the bard was sent here;
that is why I was sent here. My chief concern now is the bard; he
is in mortal danger, and needs our help—that is the cause of my
haste."

Katani reluctantly sheathed her sword. "I thought…"

"What you thought is of no consequence at the moment. The
bard needs us now." He dropped to the ground and wriggled
through the archway.

"You sound as if he might actually die," Katani called after him.

"The bard is immortal," Ectoraige's hollow voice echoed back. "He cannot die, but in his present weakened state he is susceptible."

"Susceptible to what?"

"Possession!"

The old man walked into the chill night air and breathed deeply, sucking the raw chill into his lungs and then abruptly doubling as a coughing fit wracked his body. For the thousandth-thousandth time since he had occupied this aged and enfeebled body, Praetens, once of the Susuru and then magician to the Onelord, cursed his blighted luck that day of the Battle of the Sand Plain. He had died that day, died as the Shemmatae magicians attacked, and only a last desperate effort of his will had sent his essence into the nearest weakened body—that of a nameless slopman, the lowest and foulest of occupations.

He had worn that body of the slopman for so long now that he had almost forgotten what it was like to be strong again, what it was like to be able to run, to lift weights, to see and hear clearly, but most of all what it was like to eat. He was toothless now—having removed the slopman's few remaining original teeth to prevent poisoning himself—and he was forced to take his food like a child, mashed into a paste. For a while he had experimented with providing himself with a set of teeth, but his heritage and magic was Susuru, and the Susuru were not of humankind, so the few teeth that had grown had been exercises in agony, as fangs that the Torc Allta would have been proud of filled his small human mouth.

But soon...soon he would take on a new body. He had no real hope of taking the bard's body—too many others had claims on it. But there would be a body—humankind certainly, a man, young, tall, and broad, handsome, hopefully, and when the magician inhabited the body, it would remain in that state for ever, never aging, never dying. But he only had one chance, and that was why he had to make his choice carefully. A man could shift his essence only twice; the first and second time weakened the body's essence to a certain extent, but the third ruptured it entirely, and what took up residence in the host body was never sane, and sometimes, as the weakened essence passed through the Shadowland, it picked up an unwelcome passenger or two.

But in the coming war there were sure to be hundreds, thousands, of suitable candidates. And now that the Gods of the Religion had manifested themselves and the Torc Allta had thrown in their lot with them, was there any way they could lose?

He stretched, looking up into the night sky, his dimmed eyes seeking the brighter stars, gauging the time by their position—and then he smelt it, the tell-tale stink of power, raw, magical power! But here—in the Closed City!

Praetens turned—in time to spot the two figures stagger out from a cave mouth lower down. He looked again, and immediately realised that what he had taken for a large second figure was actually a Chopt carrying a body—and then he recognised the Marked Man, and Ironwinter...carrying what could only be the bard.

He had actually turned to sound the alarm when a sudden thought struck him, and he turned back to look at the escaping prisoners, a smile twisting his thin lips.

The bard was unconscious—obviously drained by his use of power, and that power must have been incredible to escape the pull of the cluster. That was of no importance. They had escaped; it was enough. The magician's weak eyes narrowed. Was there a better host, a more fitting host than the body of the creature that had caused so much sorrow to the Religion? What a huge joke it would be on the Gods of the Pantheon to see their creature now serving the Religion. And in that single moment, he decided that the bard would be his new body!

The ritual was surprisingly easy, requiring no preparation and no special invocations. Taking his knife from his belt and holding it in his left hand he pointed the blade downwards, and placed his right hand across his heart. Then he began the ritual known as Casting the Net. In his mind's eye he visualised a net in the air above the bard, a thin, silver spider's web creation floating on an ethereal breeze, rippling slightly. When he could clearly visualise the web, he coloured it red and black, the colours swallowing the silver like fire.

And then within the net he set the beast.

The beast was a product of his own imagination, and every magician used his own particular version of the beast. Praeten's image was squat and foul, with too many legs, a head that had too many eyes, and a body that was bloated and obscene. When his visualisation of the beast was complete he allowed himself a brief smile of satisfaction—rarely had the ritual of visualisation come so easily and never with such spectacularly clear results. Why, he could almost reach out and touch...

He allowed the web to drift lower, until it was moving above the head of the Chopt carrying the unconscious bard. Praetens brought the beast out from the centre of the web to crouch at the spot where he would touch the bard—and then he allowed the web to drop!

It wrapped itself around the Chopt, bringing him crashing to the ground—and although he couldn't see it, Ironwinter could clearly feel the metal-strong strands of the web—and then he felt something warm and loathsome brush past his fingertips.

And only Praetens saw the beast crouch over the sprawled body of the bard, and only Praetens saw that a vaguely milky substance had begun to gather in the beast's jaws...but Praetens never even heard the whistling longsword that took his head off at the shoulders!

Bastion whirled at the sound, and spotted the round white object bouncing down the stones to come to a stop at his feet. He turned it with his foot, and found himself looking down on the staring eyes of Praetens, with more life and humanity in them now than they ever had while he breathed. There was a smile frozen on the magician's lips.

Ironwinter came surging to his feet, slapping at the invisible bonds that had only moments before bound him. At his feet the bard groaned, and shifted in his sleep.

Bastion raised his weapon as two figures appeared like smoke out of the night, and lowered it again when he recognised the ornate Katan armour of the bard's companion. The longsword in her hand was still thick with gore. She passed by him without a word and knelt by the bard's side.

"Does he live?" She looked up, looking beyond Bastion to the slight figure of a boy who stood still in shadow, but although the silhouette was that of a boy, the voice's cadence was that of an aged man.

"He lives."

And then from the caves in the cliffs behind them, echoed and magnified to a terrible crescendo, came a scream of absolute rage.

Bastion smiled tightly. "I think they know we have gone."

Sheesarak's rage was awesome to behold—and almost comical in its childishness. Along with Mannam, Fenar, and Geillard, he had come down to the cave in the Closed City to see for himself this terrifying creature, the bard Paedur. Both Ghede and the Lady Asherat had declined the invitation—they were taking to their chambers to enjoy the sensations of possessing a physical body once again.

As they walked down the long corridor that led to the cave, Mannam had suggested to Sheesarak that perhaps it would be possible for him to use his power to destroy the stones and allow them access to the bard and his companions.

Fenar na Torc Allta had been looking at the god when Mannam had put the suggestion. Sheesarak had nodded his broad head, but a little doubtfully, Fenar thought. Privately the Torc Allta thought that if the bard had not been able to break out, then neither would this New Religion usurper be able to break in. Becoming tired of the once-god's prattle, he had gone on ahead of the other three, and so was the first to spot the empty triangle of stones—and somehow he wasn't entirely surprised.

Mannam stopped and began to choke, and then Sheesarak screamed. The sound started low, but grew from a bass rumble to a shrill piercing sound, and the cave took it and amplified it, sending it pounding, throbbing, shrieking out into the chill night air. Walls cracked, floors split, and blocks that had stood for centuries tumbled from the ceilings.

Fenar turned and calmly walked from the chamber, followed a moment later by Geillard. Behind them, Mannam and Sheesarak were beginning to argue while the cave tumbled in around them, seemingly unconcerned—perhaps even unaware—of what was happening.

"I sometimes think," Geillard said tiredly, "that I may be worshipping the wrong gods."

Sheesarak's howl had ripped through the Source, blasting houses, tumbling fences, barns, totems, even uprooting small trees. The Chopts, terrified by the sudden signs of life from the haunted Closed City, turned and fled to the concealed entrances that led to the underground caves; and later when Katani and Ectoraige, with Bastion in the lead and Ironwinter still carrying the bard, marched through the devastated Chopt capital they found nothing moving, nothing stirring in the ruins.

15
The Armourer

The Armourer is the Maker of Weapons, a mythical figure who brought the killing tools to the World of Men...

Tales of the Bard

The three Trialdone, the Gods of Trialos, called upon their brother, Kishar Stormbrother, the God of Storms, to find and take the escaped prisoners. Gone were the plans for lingering torture—all they wanted now were the deaths of the bard and his companions. And just as Bastion and Katani, Ectoraige and Ironwinter were beginning to think that they had made their escape, the storm came rolling in over the flat undulating ice-fields...

Later the Chopts would come to call that particular storm the Taker of Souls. It scoured through the Northlands like Death incarnate, and whole villages, Chopt and humankind, were lost beneath its howling fury. The King Road—which had remained clear since it had first been laid down generations past—was lost beneath a blanket of snow as high as a tall man's head; bridges cracked and snapped beneath the weight of snow and ice; rivers turned into solid sheets of ice; every living tree and bush was flattened by the weight of snow or ripped up by the wind's fury. The creatures—whether they walked on two legs or four—that didn't find shelter immediately were buried, and perished in the bitter conditions; their carcasses—whole and frozen solid—were to surface over the next three generations of the Chopt, their flesh still edible.

Ironwinter had sensed the coming of the storm first. He had stopped, his broad flat head turned towards the heavens, his beast's snout damp and trembling. Bastion felt it next: the sudden stinging in his wounds, the touch of fluid as the old scars cracked, warned of the foul weather coming. And then Ectoraige, who had been watching the movements of the clouds above the mountains and the sudden shifting of the wind, knew what the signs heralded. Katani only realised that something was amiss when Bastion, who was in the lead, suddenly left the road and began to run towards a nearby outcropping of rock.

"What's wrong?"

"Rockscourer coming!" he whispered hoarsely, dabbing at a cut above his eye.

"What's a rockscourer?" Katani demanded, imagining a serpent or northern ice-beast, but the Marked Man had hurried on towards the rocks. She looked down at the boy, who was still inhabited by the spirit of the god.

"A rockscourer is a particular type of northern storm, with high winds, heavy snowfall, and a sharp drop in temperature. The Chopt call it a rockscourer because it cleans the rocks and stones of lichens and mosses, scouring them of all signs of growth," he said seriously, and then he added with a slight smile. "And if it catches us in the open we're dead!"

"There are times when I think I was better off dead," Katani murmured.

"You probably were," Ectoraige grinned, and set off at a run for the rocks. Katani sighed and followed him.

As they neared the stones, Katani realised that they had once formed the walls of a building, probably a Way Station, but the weather, combined with the local Chopts' depredation of the stones for their own dwellings had reduced it to a heap of rubble, the remaining walls moulded together by the elements into a solid lump. Bastion, who had disappeared into the midst of the stones, re-appeared as the remainder of the group hurried up. The Marked Man's face was covered in blood and his expression was that of pure disgust. "Nothing, there's no shelter, we'll have to go on." He looked at Ironwinter. "This is your land—where's the nearest shelter?"

Ironwinter suddenly looked evasive. He shrugged his broad shoulders, almost dropping the bard to the ground. "There's nothing really..." he began.

"There must be something," Bastion snapped. He glanced up into the lowering skies. Clouds were visibly scudding across the heavens, and the clouds themselves were the colour of metal, dark and brilliant.

"The Armoury," Ectoraige said softly. "Are you not forgetting the Armoury?"

The Chopt snarled, his lips drawing back from his tusks in a savage grimace. "What do you know of that?"

"The body may be that of a boy, but I am Ectoraige, the God of Learning and Knowledge. Nothing of your lore is hidden from me. Now, I suggest you take us to the Armoury lest we are caught by the rockscourer."

"But the *geasa*..." Ironwinter mumbled.

"Does the *geasa*—the forbidding spell—call for you to lay down your life for the People of the Ice and their secret? Does it call for you to die for a king who is under the thrall of the Chopts' enemies?"

Bastion climbed up out of the stones. "But the Armoury is a myth," he said, "and the Armourer nothing but legend."

Ectoraige grinned. "Well, this legend, this myth, might just save your life." He turned back to Ironwinter. "Will you lead them or shall I?"

"I'll take them." The Chopt whirled away, doubling back on the path and striking out across the flat plain. Flurries of snow whirled around their heads, slivers of ice in their midst, and the Chopt suddenly increased his pace. Less than a thousand paces from the tumbled stones he suddenly took a path that led down into a hollow. Running through the hollow was a thin rushing stream, crossed at its narrowest point by a simple stone bridge. But instead of taking the worn track to the bridge, Ironwinter led them down towards the river. At the water's edge he turned and followed a thread of a path under the bridge. The noise under the arch of the bridge was incredible, the rushing water foaming and booming, echoing and re-echoing off the stones.

And then Ironwinter, who was in the lead, vanished.

Katani, who was walking behind him, was looking at him one moment, and then she turned to check on the boy behind her, and when she looked back he was gone. She stopped in shock; from the rear, she heard Bastion swear, his hoarse voice echoing slightly.

Allowing her shortsword to come to her hand she moved forward, her right hand pressed against the slimy stones—and suddenly she was touching nothing. She turned and found she was looking into a tall, slim opening—a doorway—in the stones. There was movement within the opening and her sword came up, and then light sparked and flared and a torch flickered into life. "This way," Ironwinter grunted and turned away, taking the light with him. There was nothing left to do but to follow him.

The Chopt led them down a long almost perfectly straight tunnel that was obviously ancient, and almost certainly created by some magical power. It was as if a levin bolt had sliced through the earth, fusing the stones into polished, molten slag, leaving the tunnel walls, ceiling and floor with a black, mirror-like coating. Ironwinter's torch danced and flickered along the polished surfaces, illuminating it in places to an almost painful brilliance. After the noise beneath the bridge, it was surprisingly quiet within the tunnel, the rocks seeming to absorb sound. Nevertheless, they all clearly heard the sounds of the storm breaking outside, an ominous rumbling, like the growl of a hungry beast.

At the bottom of the tunnel was a gate of iron bars, and beyond that a second door that looked to be made of stone.

Ironwinter stopped before the gate and rattled the huge chain that held it closed. He stuck his torch in a bracket on the wall, bent over and laid the bard on the ground and then settled himself on the floor beside the unconscious figure.

"What now?" Bastion demanded, his whisper hissing around the corridor.

"Now we wait."

"For how long?"

"As long as it takes. If the Armourer is occupied then it could take some time, a day, two days, perhaps longer, but if not—well, we might get in soon."

"It had better be very soon," Ectoraige murmured, "otherwise we might just freeze to death down here."

"Are we not safe?" Katani asked.

The boy shook his head. "The tunnel is straight, the wind and cold will just roll straight in. If the tunnel had been curved or twisting we might have stood a chance."

Even as he was speaking, they could feel the chill creep in, and now that they had finally stopped moving, the cold began to seep through their clothing into their bones.

"That is no natural storm," Ironwinter grunted.

Ectoraige nodded. "Aye, a product of Kishar Stormbrother, I shouldn't wonder."

"They must want you badly," the beast said.

"They want us all badly," Ectoraige said. "No matter where your loyalties once lay, you are associated with us now—if they catch you, they will kill you, make no mistake about that."

Ironwinter nodded. "I know." He was about to say more when the stone door suddenly rumbled open, flooding the tunnel with warm golden light and the combined heat and smell of burning metal.

One of the People of the Ice stood in the doorway. He was old and stooped and certainly one of the oldest Chopts Bastion had ever seen, since the beasts did not tend to live much beyond their middle years, but this man had all the appearance of being a century or more. He shuffled up to the metal gate and stared out through the bars. His eyes lingered on the comatose figure of the bard and then turned to the boy, and surprisingly he bowed. "We welcome one of the Pantheon."

Ectoraige bowed in turn. "I give you thanks on behalf of my companions and myself. We seek shelter from the wrath of the followers of the New Religion and the evil weather wrought by Kishar Stormbrother."

The ancient Chopt touched the chain, and the bar, as thick as a man's thumb, slid back of its own accord. "You are freely welcomed." He raised his arm and pointed through the stone door. "Enter, you are expected."

Ironwinter picked up the bard and was the first through the door, followed by Bastion, then Katani, both swords in her hands now, and finally Ectoraige. He paused and spoke briefly to the Chopt, chatting as if they were old friends, before moving inside.

The inner room was an armoury.

The cave was huge, stretching perhaps a thousand paces in every direction. Against the nearest wall was a monstrous forge, while all around, strewn over every available space were weapons, some finished, others in various degrees of completion. They hung on the walls, were piled in corners, spilled from chests and a few—a very few—lay neatly shelved and catalogued. Every available weapon seemed to be represented, from every time and nation, from the crudest club to the most fabulous crossbow. There were even examples of Bastion's dart-thrower. But mostly there were the Chopt knives, the broad-bladed, drop-pointed knives that were the favoured weapon of the People of the Ice, and the weapon which most of humankind had come to associate with them. There were thousands of them, hundreds of thousands, some larger than usual, others slightly smaller, some drop-pointed, others spear-pointed, single and double-edged, some curved, others straight-bladed.

And all of them sparkling new.

The light from countless candles spilled across the metal, burnishing it to bronze, sparkling, glittering, glinting, turning the cave into a constellation of golden light. A figure stepped out from the midst of the weaponry and the light, a tall, slightly stout woman. She was naked, except for a long blacksmith's leather apron and a pair of high leather gauntlets, and she was completely hairless. She made straight for Ectoraige and stopped before him. She was holding a long-handled blacksmith's hammer in her left hand and she kept patting it into the palm of her right hand. Although she was naked and unarmed save for the hammer, there was something so threatening about her that Katani moved around behind the woman, ready to strike. The woman stood as tall and as broad as Bastion, her muscles rigid and defined clearly beneath deep bronze skin. Her features, while those of humankind, were slightly mismatched; her eyes were bright, bright blue and set wide apart, giving her a vaguely guileless expression; her nose was small and slightly off-centre; and her mouth was a thin narrow line set above a strong jaw.

The woman bowed quickly, jerkily, before Ectoraige, and her mouth moved several times before she actually spoke, as it speech were something she was unused to.

"Is it time?" Her voice was surprisingly soft for so large a woman.

Ectoraige shook his head almost sadly. "Not yet, lady, not yet."

"But soon. It will be soon," she said, a statement rather than a question. "I have awoken. There will be war."

"Soon," Ectoraige agreed.

"Tell the woman warrior to put away her toys lest I shatter them and her," the huge blacksmith said suddenly.

Ectoraige looked at Katani and shook his small head slightly. The warrior stepped back and sheathed her swords. "This is the Armourer," he said, introducing the woman. "She is legend." He then introduced his companions one by one to the Armourer.

"Bastion, the Marked Man."

The Armourer nodded. "He is known to me."

"Ironwinter."

"He too is known to me."

"Katani, once of the Katan, now the last of their number, the sole survivor of the Battle of the Sand Plain."

The Armourer smiled, her face shifting, giving it a somewhat distorted cast. "I made weapons for that war."

"And the one on the floor is the bard, Paedur. He is the Champion of the Old Faith."

The woman grunted in surprise and knelt beside Paedur; she lifted his left arm, examining his hook. Then she touched it and the runes incised into the metal came to a sparkling, glittering life. "Toriocht's work?" she asked, looking up at Ectoraige.

The boy's face shadowed briefly. "Aye, the Smith made it."

"I know his work."

"What are you?" Katani suddenly asked. "And where are we?"

"This is the Armourer," Ectoraige said quietly, "and this is the Armoury where the Chopt weapons are made."

"But tell them the why of it," Paedur said abruptly, coming smoothly and silently to his feet. His usually thin features were now gaunt and he was ashen-faced, his eyes nothing more than black stones in his head—even the reflective glare had gone from them.

The Armourer stood up and walked away, muttering distractedly to herself, heading back towards her forge. Moments later the air was split by the clanging of metal on metal.

"Aaah, you are with us once again, bard," Ectoraige said smoothly. "Come, let us find a place to sit and warm ourselves. Are you aware of what has happened?"

Surprisingly, Paedur nodded. "I was aware; it was only my physical body that was exhausted. My spirit rested in the Ghost Worlds." He nodded at the Armourer, now bathed in the ruddy glow of the fire. "But I'll admit, I thought that woman legend."

"She is, but she exists," Ectoraige said. "And her function remains the same. She is cursed to follow her old traits."

Bastion cleared a table of short throwing darts and heaved his bulk up onto it. "And what were her traits?"

"She brought the gift of weapons to the humankind."

"She is not of this plane, then?" Paedur asked.

"She is not, but she is trapped here now for an eternity. There is a *geasa* on her chaining her to this Plane of Existence until a Belief—a Faith—dies. When a system of belief dies, she will be free again, and so, when there is a war brewing, involving deities, she awakes from her slumbers and sets about forging her weapons of destruction. She takes no sides; she merely wishes to be free of her curse. She has slept these five hundred years, and she awoke but recently."

"That is why the People of the Ice are all carrying new knives," Bastion said suddenly.

"So there is a full-scale war between the Faith and the Religion coming?" Paedur said, looking directly at the god.

"There is. The Gods of Faith and Religion go to war once again—and for the last time, I think."

"They intend to destroy the Library at Baddalaur," Katani broke in.

Paedur turned to look at her in disbelief, and the woman clearly saw his eyes turn to mirrors once again.

Ectoraige nodded. "I think this will be the Last Battle. The Armourer is awake and working, and already in some of the outlying reaches of this place the borders between this world and the next are breaking down. A combined army of the Chopts, assisted by the Torc Allta and the humankind who accompanied Geillard, will sweep down out of the Ice-fields taking all before it, heading for Karfondal. Supposedly the army is under Geillard's command, but we know he is but the puppet of the Religion. Three of the Trialdone now accompany the deposed Emperor, as well as Mannam the once-god. They are throwing everything into this effort. We overheard them planning, and as Katani said, they intend to destroy the Library of Baddalaur on the grounds that if all knowledge of the rituals and observances of the Old Faith are destroyed, it can never be recreated, and thus the Gods of the Faith will die."

"Will that happen?"

Ectoraige shrugged. "It could. And they have forgotten the Magician's Law, the Force of Equals. Because the Faith and Religion exist, a balance of sorts is maintained; but take away one of those and the balance tips. Without the Faith, the Religion will continue unchecked, sliding this Plane of Existence into Chaos. Unable to maintain control, the borders between this and the Shadowlands will crumble and this plane will be overwhelmed and eventually destroyed: and with its destruction, then the other Planes of Existence will decay into a collapse."

Paedur nodded wearily. It all sounded so familiar.

"You must stop them, bard," Ectoraige said softly.

"And what about the Gods?" Paedur demanded.

"Even now the Gods prepare to do battle on the chequered fields of Ab-Apsalom. You cannot count on them for help."

"When will the army march?" He looked at Ectoraige and then turned to Ironwinter.

The Chopt shrugged. "Soon, soon, I think. Preparations are almost complete."

"What do you know?" Paedur snapped.

"Only that we are to carry a war into the Southlands, taking advantage of the recent turmoil, both political and geographical. We are to march on the capital, destroying everything in our paths. Thusal will fall first and then Baddalaur—or so I have been told," he added quickly.

Paedur shook his head slightly, and he looked over at Katani. "Perhaps you should have stayed dead," he smiled.

She nodded. "I know. And what now?"

He settled his cloak over his shoulders and shrugged. "The only route to Karfondal is through Badaur, the town surrounding Baddalaur, the Bardic College. That is where we shall stop them— or die in the attempt."

"I think you'll probably die," Ironwinter said softly.

So do I, Katani silently agreed.

16
Desertion

We fought for many causes—most of them were lost!
Tien tZo, Shemmat servant of Owen, Weapon Master

The explosion ripped out almost an entire section of the quayside, devastating the Lower City and killing more than a hundred men, women, and children. But it did have one positive effect: it immediately quelled the riots that had raged through the Lower City, and every able-bodied person was pressed into service to prevent the fire from sweeping throughout the slum and tenement quarters, much of which was constructed from wood.

Tien dragged Owen out of the burning building, across the filthy, foul-smelling square and into the large tenement opposite. He kicked open the first door he came to and found himself facing a startled couple who were finishing a meagre meal. The man opened his mouth to protest, but the look on Tien's face and the sight of Owen's tattered and bloody flesh silenced him.

"You," Tien glanced at the man, "find Fodla, the Commander of the Emperor Legion. Tell her the Weapon Master is hurt, and bring her here. Hurry!" The man took a quick look at Owen and then hurried out into the street which was already beginning to fill with smoke and foul-smelling fumes. "And you," he turned to look at the woman, "can bring me some hot water."

"I've no hot…"

"Then boil some!" the Shemmat snapped. "I'm sorry," he immediately apologised, "but my master is hurt…"

The woman pushed a blackened kettle over a small bed of glowing coals and then knelt beside the two men, touching small fingers to Owen's blistered cheeks. "Burnt?" she whispered, and looking questioningly at Tien.

Then the building across the street exploded. The fire had finally reached the Warlord's supplies of Luid-dust, fire-works, marker flares, cinder-blocks, and fire-wood. Streamers of fire erupted high into the sky, some falling to splash onto the surrounding buildings, starting more fires.

The woman fell onto the floor with a startled cry. She was about to turn and crawl under the table when Tien touched her arm, gently, his calloused fingers like harsh sand. "There is no danger, I think. But you must help my master. The water?"

"Your master?" the woman asked, frightened eyes going from Tien to Owen.

"I've told you; he is Owen, the Weapon Master," Tien said proudly.

Realisation dawned in the woman's eyes. She stood quickly and looked through the shattered window at the building opposite. "The Warlord!" she gasped.

"Is dead. And the water is boiled."

While the woman brought the water, Tien carefully peeled off Owen's scorched leathers, cutting away the skin where it had become fused with the cloth. With the hot water he gently sponged the wounds clear.

"Will he live?" the woman asked.

Tien placed his hand flat against his master's chest. "He is strong," he said confidently, although his eyes betrayed his concern. "He has survived worse wounds." He looked up. "Why hasn't Fodla come?" he demanded.

"Here I am."

The Commander of the Legion strode into the small room, immediately seeming to fill it, followed by the Andam priest; in the background the woman's husband lurked, still bemused by the speed at which events had occurred.

Fodla knelt by Owen, her broad face creasing in concern, her fingers seeking a pulse at his throat. "How?" she asked.

"He destroyed four of the vampir—and the Warlord," Tien said softly.

"And most of the Lower City too, if we're not lucky," Fodla said sourly.

"It very nearly cost him his life!" Tien blazed.

The huge woman nodded. "I know, I know," she said gently. Her experienced eyes took in the Shemmat, noting his single battle-axe and the scorchmarks on his sleeves and boots, and she fancied he had played more of a part in the vampir's destruction than he was telling. "I'll get some transport, and in the meantime, if you would see what you can do," she said, looking up at the Andam.

The grey-robed priest nodded. "Go, then, try to contain the fire," he said, his voice a strained whisper. Fodla stood and hurried from the room without another word. The Andam turned to look at Tien. "And now you must trust me—as you did once before, if I recall. I want you to leave us—assist Fodla if you will—but leave us alone for some time."

"But Owen…"

"I will not harm him," the Andam said.

Tien looked at the priest, seeing only his eyes in his enveloping robes, and those eyes burned with something which the Shemmat decided could only be raw power. He nodded once and then walked from the room.

The Andam turned to look at the young woman who was standing still and silent in a corner. "If you too could leave us for a little while…?" he said gently.

She nodded, and scurried around the priest, her eyes never leaving him, regarding him with a superstitious awe, her fingers automatically making the Sign of Protection.

Alone now with the unconscious man, the Andam sank down onto his knees and stared at the Weapon Master's bloodied and blackened face. The burns were serious enough, and would leave his face a mass of scar tissue unless…unless he drew upon his power to heal him. Since his brothers had been slain, the Andam had communed with the Andam Source, made himself one with the ancient power that was at the heart of the Andam belief. All those who followed the Andam way used the power of their Source at some time during their lives, but only a few ever took the path of communion, becoming part of it, submerging themselves in the raw power. The Andam Source consumed, consumed utterly and completely, and so to become one with the Source was to die.

But the Andam priesthood had some measure of the Sight, especially those touched with the disease that destroyed the flesh, and on the night that his brothers had been taken, Andam had looked into the probable future—and found it terrifying. There had been images, many terrifying and bloody images, there had been death and torture, war, beasts, and destruction. On the chequered fields of Ab-Apsalom he had seen the Gods of the Pantheon sorely pressed by the combined forces of the Demons and the Gods of the New Religion. Every shred of his power, his magic, would be needed then. So should he, could he afford to use it—to waste it?—now on the Weapon Master?

But had he the right to make that decision? Surely the decision had already been made for him; he had been with Fodla when the man had come to the Commander of the Legion with the tale of the wounded warrior...and he alone had the power to heal.

Sighing slightly, the Andam reached out and touched the Weapon Master's face.

There was pain and there were memories, and perhaps that had been another reason why he had been reluctant to heal Owen, for to heal meant he had to touch, and the Andam priesthood was particularly receptive to the emotions and thoughts of others. And before he could begin the healing process the emotional turmoil would have to be soothed, the thoughts settled so that they did not intrude.

The Weapon Master's memories were of the events in the Warlord's cellars. There was a face, a girl's face, his sister's face, drawing him, pulling him, trapping him, and the Andam's eyes hardened, recognising what had happened. The vampir deceived by illusion, fastening on memories, using them to create an image and then using that image to lure its victim within striking distance. Through Owen's eyes the Andam saw the creature who wore two faces, the dead face of the vampir and the heart-shaped face of his long-dead sister. He saw it lure Owen, saw the hands reach out... And then he saw the creature struck down with the thrown axe, saw the oil and the flames—and the Andam realised then who had destroyed the vampir.

There was pain and confusion, and in the confusion there were disjointed images from the Weapon Master's life, most of them from the past, some from the possible future. There was death—death always—past and future, and there was fear. Beneath the seemingly imperturbable killer lurked a deeply fearful man, a coward almost.

But the Andam was no judge. When Alile, the Judge Impartial, eventually came to weigh Owen's fate, he would consider the deeds as well as the intent.

Closing his eyes, the Andam reached out his hands and touched the burnt body...and called upon his Source...then the priest stiffened as the power—white-hot, ice-cold—lanced through his body, opening every wound on his flesh, turning his body into a mass of agony. The skin split on his fingertips and where he touched the Weapon Master, he left trails of blood. And there was life in the blood. He moved his hands across the wounds, touching the scorched and blackened skin, brushing over the blisters—and leaving in his wake, clear, clean skin...

Moving from head to foot, the Andam covered Owen with his blood, and as the blood seeped out of the Andam, life flowed into the warrior...

The Andam slumped exhausted, and Owen sat up. He was aware, on a deep almost unconscious level, of what had occurred, but like a dream the events were rapidly fading. He stood stiffly, his joints popping and cracking, and looked at himself in the bowl of water Tien had used earlier for cleaning his wounds. His face was a bloody mask, but beneath the blood, which was drying to a crusty flake, he was healed and whole again. He plunged his face into the tepid water, washing away the blood and the memories. He knelt beside the slumped Andam and touched him gently on the shoulder.

"Datar?" he whispered, using the ancient term for father, for holy man. "Datar?"

The Andam reached out and Owen caught his arm, lifting him gently to his feet. The renewed contact sparked the dregs of power within the priest which sent echoes deep into Owen's brain, bringing with them the vaguest of memories. "Datar, what have you done?"

"I've done what is necessary; what I feel to be necessary," he corrected weakly.

"And how long have you left on this Plane of Existence?"

The Andam shrugged, and then winced as torn and aching muscles protested. "Only the God knows. But long enough, I suspect." The priest turned to look at Owen and his usually sharp grey eyes were dulled and pained. "Time is running out for Kutor and his followers, and with their destruction will come the destruction of the Old Faith. It is time to act!"

The guard turned as the door opened, tensing, and then relaxing as the young woman walked boldly down the centre of the corridor, a large tray in her hands balanced precariously before her. The tray was easily one of the largest the guard had ever seen, and she noted the five crystal goblets and the ancient stone crock of what must surely be a fine vintage. She experienced a brief twinge of envy, but decided that after today's events, she'd rather be a simple guard in the Emperor Legion, than one of the five people in the room behind her.

She looked at the servant, wondering just who she was, but her face was concealed behind the glasses and the stone crock. She allowed her eyes to wander down the girl's body, almost completely visible beneath the light robes. There was a scar running down between her breasts...

The guard swung her short stabbing spear around—just as the sharpened edge of the tray sliced through her throat!

The Andam was moving and Owen's sword was in his hand even before the sound of breaking glass beyond the locked door had settled. Tien and Fodla bustled Kutor over to the far side of the room and positioned themselves before him.

"Unhuman..." The word formed on the Andam's lips—and then the door was struck a blow that actually ripped the lock from the wood, and the vampir strode in. It might have looked incongruous, one nearly naked young woman facing six people, all of them, with one exception, armed—but no one was laughing. The vampir's eyes were blank, empty, cold, and lifeless. It turned its head, almost as if it were an animal seeking a scent; perhaps the number of warm bodies in the room confused it, Owen thought, abruptly chilled with the memory of what a creature like this had done to him.

"It will concentrate on Kutor," the Andam said softly, and the creature's head snapped in his direction, "but it will destroy anything that comes in its way."

"Divide," Owen said, drawing its attention to him.

Tien tZo moved, and the vampir edged closer to him.

Then a thrown knife bit deeply into the creature's throat. It didn't even flinch, perhaps it didn't even notice. Fodla pulled a second knife from her sleeve and snapped it towards the creature's face. It sliced through the flesh, just below the eye, but it drew no blood, and didn't even slow the vampir's slow, tentative steps towards Kutor.

"On my command," Owen whispered, readying his sword and knife. Tien settled his remaining axe in his hand, and slipped a long slim knife from his right boot, while Fodla moved her matching swords before her in tight circles.

They all clearly saw the muscles in the vampir's thighs tense and stiffen as she prepared to jump—and then the creature burst into flame! The intense cold-white light ate through the body, turning it into an almost solid pile of filthy grey ash. It crumpled to the ground, Fodla's knife in its midst.

"She would have slain you all," the Andam said weakly, turning away.

The Lady Esse stared deeply into the coal black eyes of the vampir, her gnarled hands resting lightly on its shoulders. Looking into the eyes of this vampir, she saw through the eyes of its unholy sister.

She saw the female guard standing outside the door, saw the way her eyes moved speculatively up and down the vampir's body, saw the sharpened edge of the metal tray bite deeply into the woman's throat, nearly severing the head from the body. She saw a foot rise, snapping its heel into the wood of the door just above the lock, breaking the doors open, and then she found the vampir facing the usurper and his minions.

The ancient sorceress' lips tightened as the vampir looked from face to face. She saw their mouths working as they talked, and then she saw the large woman—Fodla—throw a knife. Slowly...slowly, infinitely slowly, the throwing dagger arched through the air, and the Lady Esse blinked as it thudded home below her range of vision. There was movement—the Weapon Master and his servant preparing weapons—and then a second thrown dagger moved slowly through the air, and even the hardened sorceress flinched as the dagger touched the vampir's face. Well, no matter, the vampir were impervious to pain, and Fodla would pay, as they all would pay...

And then there was fire!

The vampir before her—through whose eyes she was seeing the events—staggered back, her mouth open, and the scream which bubbled through her lips was that of pure and absolute agony. The sorceress's hands tightened on the vampir's shoulders, but the creature fell away, her wails increasing in intensity as her eyes—no longer black now, but red and flame—reflected the fire that was consuming her sister on the other side of the city. The Lady Esse broke the contact between the two creatures and then dropped the last remaining vampir into a trance-like state. One left, just one, and this one would not—could not—fail.

The small stunted woman walked slowly across the room and tugged on the slender bell rope; a servant immediately appeared at the door. "We are moving. Is all in order?" she snapped.

"Everything is packed and awaiting your order and directions," the servant bowed.

"Send the wagons out, then—send them north to Baddalaur. They will be met on the road by one of my agents."

"My lady." The man bowed, and backed from the room.

"Rom!" the Lady Esse called.

The door opened and a hugely tall man stepped into the room, his features and colouring typical of the Gallowglas tribe.

"We are for the north," the woman snapped. "Baddalaur first, and then Thusal if necessary. The creature failed," she added, more quietly now, "and now the usurper and his people will move against us. They have no other alternative. Send the knife to the Twelve."

And that night, the heads of the Twelve Families of Karfondal each received a tiny ornate dagger.

The raids came in the still silent hour before the dawn. The raiding parties were composed principally of the Emperor Legion, backed up by the troops hand-picked by Fodla and Keshian, all seasoned and experienced warriors—and all of them unquestionably loyal to either Kutor or Fodla. They raided the palaces and town houses of the heads of the Twelve Families, with orders, signed by Kutor and bearing the Imperial Seal, to arrest them for treason.

But the raiding parties found nothing. The heads of the households, along with their wives and children, mistresses, lovers, personal servants and guards, were gone, leaving only the regular servants behind to tend hastily vacated houses. They all told stories of a rider coming late in the night, speaking briefly with the master of the house and then moving on. As preparations for an immediate departure had already begun, by the time Kutor's troops arrived the Twelve Families were long gone.

The dawn brought with it several other surprises. There had been desertions from the Imperial Army—and on an unprecedented scale. Several thousand men had vanished overnight—in some cases whole battalions, from cooks to captains had disappeared, taking with them not only their kit, including weapons and rations, but also wagons filled with supplies of food, clothing, blankets, and weapons.

"We've lost just over one-third of the army," Keshian said sombrely.

"And these would have been men loyal to Geillard?" Kutor asked, his longer stride easily outpacing the smaller, stouter man as they strode down the corridor towards the Lord Rocque's suite in the palace.

"Not necessarily," Keshian panted. "It's difficult at the moment, with so many men missing, to form any sort of picture about those who've gone, and the remaining troops are understandably reticent. They would certainly seem to have been men who were traditionalists, loyal to the old ways, perhaps even followers of the Religion, rather than the Faith, and some of course were troops who were loyal to the Twelve Families and went with them."

They turned left down a brightly-lit corridor where Owen and Fodla could be seen deep in conversation outside the Treasurer's door. They both turned as Kutor, with Keshian in tow, came hurrying up.

"Later," Kutor snapped as they both opened their mouths to speak. He pushed his way into the room—and found himself standing in the midst of chaos. The usually pristine chambers of the Lord Rocque were covered with papers, parchments, charts and rolls. Every drawer had been emptied and the enormous fireplace at the far end of the room was piled high with smouldering ashes. The Andam was on his knees before the fire, sifting through the ashes with a poker.

"What happened?" Kutor asked in astonishment.

The Andam gestured with a cloth-wrapped hand. "Every record had been destroyed: every note, every tally book, every tax account burnt. The fifedom records, tax districts, genealogies, even the charts and maps which were redrawn after the Cataclysm have all been destroyed. It seems the Lord Rocque was determined to leave nothing useful behind." The Andam looked up at the Emperor, his grey eyes piercing. "You know what this means, don't you?"

"I'm not sure..." Kutor said hesitantly.

"They do not intend to return—or if they do return," he amended, "they will not be re-establishing the old Order. They're wiping the slate clear, preparing to start afresh."

"Andam's right," Owen said softly. "Those troops who deserted could have simply risen against you; an uprising would have drawn many to its banner, and there are enough disaffected parties in the city at the moment to lend them support, or who would simply have joined in for the booty."

"What are they doing, then?"

"It is my guess that they're heading north to join forces with Geillard's troops, and then the combined forces will deal us a solid, crushing blow."

"Geillard hasn't the forces," Kutor protested.

"You've seen the reports," Keshian interrupted. "We're talking about a combined army of Chopts, Gallowglas, and humankind, which will at least equal our members, if not surpass it."

"It will also have the advantage of fighting for a cause it believes in," Owen said quietly. "Much as our army did when it took Karfondal."

"The deserters can't have gone too far; we could follow and attack them."

Fodla shook her massive head. "It wouldn't work; our troops would be fighting men they know, men they would have drunk with, gambled with, sung with perhaps only the previous night. They would have no heart for it."

"We could use some of the mercenary forces to harry them," Kutor suggested.

"No! How do you think the men will feel if they see the mercenary forces attacking their old friends? We've worked too long and too hard to have them fight as a unit and consider themselves one unit—Kutor's army—rather than the Imperial forces and the mercenaries. Something like this could wipe out all that work. No," she shook her head, "far better for us to allow them to join up with the northern army and be absorbed into it. At that stage, the deserters will have visibly aligned themselves with the enemy; we can fight them then."

"All we have from the north are rumours," Kutor said quickly, looking around at the faces.

"The reports..." Keshian began.

"There are no rumours," the Andam said quickly. He touched the fire and immediately the ashes flared into incandescent light. "Look." For a moment they saw nothing, and then, within the flames, images formed, tiny pictures of a huge seething shape crawling across something white, like a mass of insects across a blanket.

But then the image changed, becoming larger, clearer, and the mass resolved itself into an army, a Chopt army, and moving through the army were the Gallowglas, cousins to the Chopts, professional mercenaries, and alongside them were creatures only the Andam recognised. "Torc Allta," he whispered, and they all knew the name. The pictures changed, now showing a huge human army that was part of, and yet separate from the Chopts and the beasts. The humans were a mixture, some of them soldiers, others obviously mercenaries, others who looked as if they might be trappers, hunters, or farmers, and then the image changed, the swirling flames seeming to pick out a face, a single human face, a face they all recognised: "Geillard!"

The flames died, leaving only ashes in their wake, but a picture remained in those ashes, a picture of a devastated landscape, whole villages wiped out, towns decimated, the land laid waste. The Andam looked up, his eyes cold and dead in his head. "They intend to destroy this world, Kutor; they intend to destroy it and then have their gods recreate it afresh."

"Can they do that?" Kutor asked, wrenching his gaze away from the ashes.

The Andam stood. "No," he said, his voice wooden. "There is a balance that must be maintained, both on the spiritual and physical plane. Disturb that balance and Chaos reigns. They intend to destroy the Old Faith totally; they intend to ensure that it will never revive. They are killing every follower of the Faith they can find: every priest, every teacher, every monk, scribe, and bard. The churches and fanes are being torn down stone by stone, the statues pulverised. The College of Ectoraige has been decimated, the monks and students massacred. They intend to destroy the Library and College of Baddalaur. If that happens, then the Old Faith will have been dealt a mortal blow. And when the Old Faith dies—as it surely will if the College is destroyed—then the balance will tip and this plane and every other Plane of Existence will be annihilated."

"So, what do we do?" Kutor asked, looking at the Andam, but it was Owen who answered.

"We make our stand at Baddalaur!"

Three days later, the remnants of the Imperial Army set out on the long road for the College of Bards.

17
The Return to Baddalaur

This day returned to us a brother, by name Paedur, called the Hookhand,
who has achieved certain fame and notoriety, and some say has brought the
brotherhood into disrepute...

Register of Baddalaur, the College of Bards

Five travellers made their way into Badaur, the town that lay at the
base of Baddalaur, the College of Bards.

The town had grown up around the College and had only one
function—to service the largest college of learning and the finest
library in all the Planes of Existence. Students from every nation
came to study in Baddalaur's Culai-built halls, and Badaur provided
them with lodgings, food, and entertainment. At any season it might
be expected to be full, but now, with the land locked in a bitter chill,
the town was filled to overflowing, with few of the students or
scholars willing to venture out onto the roads. Daily, stragglers were
trickling in from the Outlands or the Northlands and no one paid
them any attention—except the guards on the gates who were running a lucrative little operation on the side...

Neer was on duty when he spotted the five figures out in the
snow-fields, and he immediately began assessing their worth. His
experience as a professional soldier had given him an excellent eye
for the relative values of things, and over the past couple of moons
he had been practising—daily. No one entered Badaur without first
having to pay a fee—a Chill Fee, Neer jokingly called it, and the
name had stuck. The fee varied according to the wealth of those
seeking admittance, and the last couple of moons had made him
and the others guards very wealthy men indeed.

The grizzled veteran squinted out into the ice-fields. The five
figures were coming in along the barely outlined track that had once
been the King Road, coming from the north—which could only
mean Thusal. Trappers almost certainly—most of those who lived
in the northern town trapped the ice-beasts for a living, but they
could also be farmers, fishers, miners...anyway, they were sure to

have wealth, either in the form of scrip money, metal coinage or plates, furs or weapons. There were some nice weapons coming out of the north these days; he absently patted the new Chopt knife that hung on his belt.

Four adults and a child, which probably meant that one of the adults was a woman, but nevertheless that still left five separate payments. He stepped out of his shelter beside the gate and raised a gloved hand. "Halt."

Three of the adults and the child stopped, but one, tall and thin, kept moving as if he hadn't heard the guard. Neer dropped his spear across the man's path. "Halt, I said. Where are you coming from? Where are you going?"

The man Neer had stopped didn't move or speak, but a bulky man in a furred cloak stepped forward and whispered, his voice obviously raw with the intense chill, "We've walked from Thusal, fleeing the weather. We seek shelter in Badaur."

"Many people seek shelter in Badaur at the moment; why should you be admitted?" Neer said, lowering his voice. It was subtle enough and yet most people got the hint, but this crowd were obviously too numbed by the cold to even think—or else they were incredibly stupid.

"We seek admittance," the bulky man whispered again. "Let us through."

Neer shook his head slowly, his eyes small and dark and amused. He took a certain pleasure in toying with the travellers, exercising what little power he imagined he possessed. "There are certain formalities to be..."

"Let us through!" The voice was as chill as the ice, and Neer jumped with fright. He stepped away from the man who had spoken and brought up his spear, levelling it at the man's shadowed face.

"I think the town is full," he said venomously. "There is no admittance."

Metal winked on the chill air, and suddenly a curved hook wrapped itself around the barbed head of his spear. With a twist and wrench, the spearhead was sheared clean off. The cowled man raised his hand, pushing back his hood: and even before the eyes— mirrored, reflective eyes, now the colour of snow—turned on him, Neer knew the identity of the traveller.

"I am Paedur, the Bard."

In a town where hierarchy and power were measured by knowledge, and knowledge was a closely-guarded secret available only for a price, news of the bard's arrival travelled through the streets with extraordinary speed.

The bard's reputation had preceded him; in parts of the Nations he was already considered as a legend, and stories of sightings of him were universal. So as he walked through Badaur, heading up the Avenue of a Thousand Steps to the College of Bards, a still, silent crowd gathered. They lined the Avenue, watching, looking only at him, almost completely ignoring the four figures that walked behind him. They had come expecting to see someone—something—remarkable. Most of them were disappointed. His legendary hook was hidden beneath his snow-covered cloak, and he stared straight ahead, looking neither right nor left, denying them the opportunity to see his mirror-bright eyes.

When he had passed by, most people turned away, some of them embarrassed or even annoyed that they had left what they had been doing to see...well...to see a man.

One of the watchers, however, didn't turn away. He kept pace with the small group and only when the College's Culai-built gates swung open and the bard and his companions disappeared inside, did he turn back, heading for the outskirts of the town. Moments later, a snow-eagle lifted to the iron-grey skies; it immediately winged its way northwards.

The bard had come home.

By the time the afternoon had faded into evening, Mannam and the Trialdone were aware of the fact.

The guest chambers in the College of Bards were spectacular, more like a royal bedchamber than a guestroom in a school. The rooms— a connecting suite comprised of bedchambers, a deep-sunk ornate marbled bath, and a large central conference room complete with long table and a dozen chairs—were luxurious. The floors were covered in beautifully worked carpets, deep-piled and warm to the touch where they covered the hot-water pipes sunk into the floor. The bare stone walls had been covered with tapestries and decorative furs, and one wall of the conference chamber was covered in books, all bound in warm reds and browns, golds and bronzes which immediately lent warmth to the large circular room. Gire—abruptly abandoned now by the god—walked around the rooms, touching the furnishings and finally ending up in the bath chamber. His cry of delight brought Katani and Bastion running.

"Not even in Talaria do we have this."

Bastion smiled. "In very few courts would you find this, I'll wager." He touched a spigot and steaming hot water hissed out. "It might be nice to try…" he said longingly.

There was a shadow in the doorway. "Try it, we'll be here for a while." Paedur stepped into the room. "I have to see the Council of Bards and…" he shrugged, "well, there are certain formalities to be observed. We'll certainly be here for two, possibly three days."

Bastion looked at Katani; they both knew the bard didn't intend to leave Baddalaur.

Katani, who was slowly removing her armour a piece at a time, piling them up on a broad bench beside the bath, looked up. "What is this council for?"

"I will warn them of the approaching army, and the Religion's threat. They can decide what to do," Paedur said, not answering her question.

"Can the Library be moved?"

He shook his head. "Impossible."

Bastion looked around. "What about the important pieces?"

Paedur smiled wistfully. "There are just too many of them. Now, bathe and eat, drink, sleep, enjoy all the comforts of this place—they'll be the last you'll have for a long time, I'll wager."

Paedur turned and walked back into the conference chamber. Ironwinter was sitting in the centre of the floor, rubbing his long-nailed paws against a snowcat's spotted pelt.

"What of me, bard?" he asked, without looking up. "What will happen to me?"

"You are under my protection," Paedur said quietly, pulling the door to the bath chamber closed behind him. "Nothing will happen to you."

The beast shook his head. "That is not what I meant. I am Chopt first and last. I belong in the ice-fields with my people."

"Your people have been tricked. They are being led by a king who is in thrall to the Religion. They are being led to their destruction."

"Are they, bard? Are they? How can you be so sure?" Ironwinter surged to his feet, facing the bard. He was taller than Paedur, and although slender by Chopt standards, was still far more powerful than the bard. "The prophecy is being fulfilled: 'When the Weapon Maker wakes, and the gods war, then will come the time of the Chopt.' The Armourer has awoken. There is war coming. And how can you be so sure your gods and your people will triumph? Times change, bard. The seasons turn. Perhaps the Season of Humankind is drawing to a close and the Season of the People of the Ice is dawning."

"If it is then it is a blighted season," Paedur said, and made to walk past the beast, but Ironwinter stretched out his arm, almost—but not quite—touching the bard.

"I would rather die with my people, then."

Paedur shook his head. "The Gods—all of them—move and weave us at their will and whim. Do you know the Death's Law: 'Men are but the playthings of the Gods?' The Gods, yours and mine, placed us together at a certain place in a certain time. Your destiny is now irrevocably woven with mine. For better or ill, you are seen by your people as having chosen to accompany me; they see you as a traitor. If you return they will kill you."

"What am I to do?" Ironwinter asked, the anguish plain in his voice.

Gently, very gently, Paedur reached out and touched the beast's bare arm with his fingertips. "I have no Sight. I cannot see into the future. But I think it is inconceivable that the Gods—yours and mine—would have thrown us together for no purpose. All we have to do is to divine that purpose." He was about to turn away, when he added, "I think the People of the Ice will be in need of a king when this is ended."

"This is not a trial," the voice from the shadows said as soon as the bard had closed the door behind him.

"A trial presupposes a crime," Paedur said, turning and walking forward into the circle of light in the centre of the floor. There was a low three-legged stool in the centre of the circle, but the bard ignored it, preferring to stand.

This was the council chamber of the College of Bards, and Paedur knew that in the darkness beyond the light there sat three hundred bards, all of them full professed, many of them Bard- Masters, but no apprentices. Immediately before him, almost visible in the light, sat Seon, Master Bard of Baddalaur, whose word was absolute and who had ruled the College and dictated the Bardic Law as he saw it for well on three generations. There was unhuman blood in him, and it was even rumoured that he was alien to this Plane of Existence. Immediately to Paedur's left and right sat two Bard-Masters, and if the trial—and he had no illusions that that was what it was— were to follow the traditional cause, one would speak in his defence, the other speak against him, with the Master Bard having the deciding vote.

Paedur, who had been deliberately suppressing his enhanced senses since he had entered the College, now allowed them to come to the fore—and immediately the huge chamber burst into incandescent light. The bard rapidly sorted through the myriad auras, reading the colours, and was surprised to find that most of these were various hues of red—the predominant mood of the assembled bards was anger! On his right-hand side—as his advocate—he was surprised to find his old companion Gwion. Although he would have been of an age with Paedur, he had grown old in the service of the College and his hair and beard were now streaked with grey, and the lines around his eyes and forehead told of weakening eyes. His aura spoke of confusion, frustration and something else, something the bard couldn't quite define, but something that looked suspiciously like fear.

To his left sat a surprising figure, another figure from the bard's past, and someone with no love for Paedur. As the bard stripped away his aura—which was one of anger and self-satisfaction—Paedur realised that time had done little to change him. Urien's thin features had been handsome in his youth, but now that age had touched him, they were merely cruel.

Theirs had been an inexplicable rivalry; they had taken an instant dislike to one another, and on several occasions it had come to blows. Once Paedur had cut the young Urien quite badly with his hook and whatever chance there had been of the rift mending had been forever lost, for what had been a simple dislike had then turned to hatred. Gwion had once said that he thought it was because they were so alike, so chill, so aloof, so confident.

"This has all the trappings of a trial," Paedur said loudly, addressing the Master.

"We are here to judge a bard," Seon said coldly, his usually clipped accent now sounding almost staccato. But the bard's sensitive hearing caught the nervousness in the man's voice.

"And what has this bard done to deserve being tried before the Council of Bards?"

Urien spoke suddenly, and the harsh, slightly mocking tones he had often adopted deliberately in his youth, had remained with him, making him sound sour and bitter. "The Bard Paedur is charged with having brought the bardic vocation into disrepute, with deliberate and exaggerated misuse of his lore, and with having taken a prominent part in politics."

"These are serious charges," Seon snapped. "How do you answer them?"

"I thought this was no trial?" Paedur smiled.

"Answer the charges and state your case. Later there will be a trial—if it is deemed necessary."

The bard's expression hardened. "You are playing with words. This is a trial. But I will play along with your game. With the exception of bringing the bardic vocation into disrepute I accept that the charges levelled at me are true..." He paused while the assembly murmured amongst themselves, and then added. "But I was acting under instructions, and cannot be held accountable for my acts."

Gwion spoke quickly. "There are tales that the Bard Paedur has been chosen as the Champion of the Faith..."

"Tales...gossip!" Urien spat.

"I am the Champion of the Old Faith," Paedur said loudly, and then he slipped into the Bardic Voice, a method of voice projection, coupled with a touch of the Old Magic that resulted in catching and holding the listener's attention—sometimes against his will.

"I am the Champion of the Old Faith; I am the God-Sought, God-Taught; I am the Teller of Tales, the Weaver of Lies, the Bringer of Faith.

"I have walked C'lte's Kingdom of Life; I have sailed the Sea of Galae, the Haunted Sea; I have walked the Culai Isle, and seen the last of the First Race go down in destruction that threatened the fabric of the Planes of Existence; I have walked Mannam's Silent Woods; I have deposed a god and put a new god in his place.

"I am Paedur the Bard."

The echoes rolled round and around the huge hall and when they had died, there was complete and utter silence.

Paedur raised his left arm and allowed the light to sparkle off his hook, and then, calling upon the Fire Sprite to help him, he fired it, calling up an intense blue-white flame. Moving his wrist slightly, he spun the flame into a ball, which he then tossed up towards the ceiling. When it had almost reached the blackened spars it burst, flooding the chamber in a warm blue light.

"You have interfered in politics," Urien said into the absolute silence.

"I have told my tales to renew belief in the Old Faith," he said simply. "I put Kutor on the throne at Karfondal only because the Pantheon instructed me to do so. I travelled north to Thusal and the Ice-fields beyond because the Pantheon—the same Pantheon you all worship—instructed me."

He turned his head to look at Urien and the man recoiled at the bard's expression, for it was as cold and as lifeless as that of a statue. "And I deny I brought the bardic vocation into disrepute—if anything I have demonstrated the power of the bard and what we can achieve when we set our minds to it." He turned back to Seon, the Master. "For too long the bards have stagnated and merely contented themselves with being collectors and tellers of tales; we have squandered our talents. Our forefathers—the same bards who first set up the Bardic College here—were always a force to be reckoned with. They sat with kings and princes. They walked with gods and demons. They helped shape the world—all we shape now are scats."

"Bard, you go too far," Seon warned.

"No, I don't think I go far enough! But what matter? Soon, it will be too late…"

"What do you mean?" Gwion asked quietly.

"There is a war brewing in the Northlands, a war organised by Geillard and the remnants of his followers, supported by the Chopts and some of the Torc Allta. Three of the Trialdone have taken corporeal form: Sheesarak the Destroyer, the Lady Asherat, the Taker of Souls, and Ghede, the Lord of Beasts; and Mannam, once-god of the Faith, sides with them. Even the Armourer has awoken."

"They will be defeated." Urien said shakily. "We have nothing to fear."

"No. No," Paedur hissed, "not this time. This time the first target of this huge cannibal army will be the literature and learning of the Old Faith. Every book, every scroll, tablet, chart, page, and parchment will be destroyed. Without the observances of the Law, the Faith will die—or so they believe. They intend to butcher—and probably eat—every monk, scribe, and bard they find. They have destroyed the Monastery of Ectoraige—and they intend to raze Baddalaur to the ground!"

Paedur waited until the tumult had subsided. "And they are already moving against us. And since we cannot move the Library before they arrive, that leaves us but one course of action. We fight!"

"We'll die," Urien said savagely, his voice close to hysteria. "This is madness."

"And if we die, we will die fighting for what we believe in!"

"So they called you to trial, and you turned the tables on them?" Katani raised her glass of clear northern wine and toasted the bard.

"He was magnificent," Gwion said, lifting his glass also. They had all gathered in the conference chamber of the large suite, Katani and Bastion, Gire, Ironwinter, and Gwion. The meal had been magnificent, although Paedur had eaten nothing and Ironwinter had taken the tiny slivers of spiced meat, carried them to the fire and scorched them thoroughly until they were to his liking.

"Will they fight?" Bastion asked. Now that he was relaxed and away from the bitter cold, the wounds on his face had healed and only in a certain light did the scars show.

"Bards—with the possible exception of Paedur, here—don't fight," Gwion said with a grin. He was a short stout man, of the bard's age, although he looked much older, and with a tiny spill of jet black hair across the top of his head and large round eyes that seemed to be of deepest black. He obviously enjoyed his food and drink.

"They'll fight to protect the lore," Paedur said. "Even now, they are shifting the more valuable materials into the vaults buried deep, deep underground. Even if the entire building is razed to the ground, they will survive."

"Except that they will be underground, buried beneath a pile of stone," Katani observed with a wry smile.

"And even if we could clear the Library, where would we take it? In this weather the roads are barely passable," Gwion continued. "And people make the mistake of thinking that the Library is just one building, while in effect it is over a hundred buildings, not counting the single rooms, the vaults, the cellars, the attics, and the outhouses, all of which are full of material. Even the entire College of Bards, with all its apprentices, couldn't clear the place in a season."

"You could if you decided what was junk and could therefore be disposed of," Paedur grunted.

"Yes, like the *Tales of the Shanaqui,*" Gwion said innocently.

Paedur threw back his head and laughed, the first time any of the company had ever seen him do it. "Yes, yes, exactly," he said, and then, seeing Katani's puzzled frown, he added, "My tales are recorded here under the sigil of the hook, the Shanaqui."

Ironwinter grunted to attract their attention. He was squatting before the open fire, tearing at his strips of meat with drooling fangs. "And what now, bard?"

"Now we wait."

"For what?"

"There has been a revolt of some sort in the capital—the reports are sketchy and incomplete, but it seems that a major portion of the army has deserted to Geillard's cause. They were last seen heading north, followed a few days later by the Imperial Army under Kutor himself. Nothing has been heard from Thusal for the past few days, no report from Eiron, and the assumption here is that Thusal has fallen..."

Katani bowed her head and muttered a brief prayer for the Bard-Master of Thusal, who had remained even though he knew what might be the eventual consequences.

"You could go," Paedur suggested, looking at each one in turn. "Head east or west, wait until the fighting has died down..."

One by one, they all shook their heads, and Bastion spoke for all of them. "Sure, where would we go?"

"So, here we stay; we have nowhere else to go. There is a Chopt army and their allies coming down from the north, and reinforcements coming up from the south, with our own troops somewhere behind them."

"Can we win?" Bastion asked.

Paedur smiled, a movement of his lips only, it never reached his eyes. "We can fight!"

18
Death's Law

The dream ends at Baddalaur...

Paedur, the Bard

Men are but the playthings of the gods, pieces to be moved to their will; this is Death's Law...

Grimoire Magnum

The board was set, the pieces gathered and ready. The game was about to begin...

Tales of the Bard

The sun was still a vague glow below the horizon when the bard climbed to the top of Baddalaur's highest tower and looked to the north. The battlements were coated in a thin layer of ice, and the breeze coming in from the north was bitter. Here, above the College and the town, there was no sound, and in the silence, the shrill voice of a solitary bird sounded very loud and lost. And suddenly for some unknown reason—and for the first time in as long as he could remember—Paedur felt very lonely indeed.

There were those whom he could call friends, but how much of their purported friendship was made up of fear or loathing? How easy was it to befriend one of the unhumans? That was another "gift" he owed the Gods of the Pantheon; when they had made him Champion of the Old Faith, they had neglected to inform him that it would cost him everything, from his friends to his humanity.

But too late now...far too late...

He looked back into the north. As far as the eye could see the landscape was blanketed in white, nothing moving, nothing disturbing the pristine cover, the unseasonal weather having closed in—permanently it seemed—turning the fields into a close approximation of the Northlands. Paedur smiled thinly. Mannam's and the Trialdone's work, but while the bitter weather worked to the Chopts' advantage, he couldn't help wondering how the rest of the beasts' allies were faring in the intense chill—especially the Torc Allta, whose homeland was warm and moist.

He wondered if the snowscape before him was as empty as it seemed. Allowing his enhanced senses to come to the fore, he quested out into the wasteland, and was immediately struck by its emptiness—there were no birds, no beasts, either large or small, roaming around. Obviously the sudden cold weather had caught them by surprise and unprepared. He moved further out into the snowfields—and discovered three Chopts lurking in the snow, watching the College, their auras dirty splashes of colour on the whiteness of the snow. These were mature, seasoned warriors, their auras tainted by the colour of the New Religion, radiating distrust for the huge stone buildings and simple blood-lust, mingled with a little hunger. The beasts had not eaten for some time and they hungered for the flesh of humankind. They were scouts for the army, and that meant that the army itself was no more than two or three days behind.

They would have to be killed eventually, Paedur decided, if for no other reason than to cause confusion or delay reports to the Chopt camp. At the moment any delay—no matter how small or insignificant—was welcome, since it allowed the Imperial troops under Kutor to draw nearer. He toyed with the idea of slaying the beasts himself—but then realised that it would expose his position to the Trialdone and weaken him fractionally. Far better to allow Katani to slay them.

Reverting to his normal human senses, he leaned his arms on the cold stone wall and stared vacantly into the north, his reflective eyes half-closed against the wind, reviewing the events of the last few days.

The numbers of refugees flooding into Badaur had increased, and the town which usually held around three hundred souls, now hosted close to two thousand. Every spare room, cellar, and attic in the town was being used, and already food and fuel were running short, and all attempts at rationing had failed. Badaur was nothing more than a town servicing a college—it had no need for troops or officials necessary to enforce such regulations. Some of the Bard-Masters had attempted to enforce some authority—but authority tends to wither in the face of fear—and they had either been ignored or mocked.

The town was rife with rumours, and stories about the size and ferocity of the Chopt army grew daily, until it had assumed gigantic proportions. There had been calls for the women and children to be sent to the south, but these had ceased swiftly when the College had announced that there was a renegade army already on the King Road, fleeing Karfondal, hoping to meet up with the Chopts around Badaur. They were trapped.

Fear walked the narrow streets and winding lanes, keeping many indoors, huddled behind barred doors—as if that would do them any good. But in the Wall Streets—those abutting onto the town's high walls, containing the bars and brothels—an almost carnival air prevailed. Here, the priests, the bars, and the whores were doing an excellent trade, but the atmosphere was brittle, close to hysteria, and the bard knew it would take very little to send it over the edge.

He was familiar with the reports that were coming in regularly from the Seven Bastions. The main body of the Chopt army had bypassed the Seven Bastions, leaving only small contingents—each one heavily armed and battle-trained—to besiege the castles. Their purpose was obviously not to attack, merely to keep the garrisons inside. All sorties from the Bastions had been beaten back with heavy losses, but the Chopts had been careful not to engage in any protracted fight. Paedur assumed that later, when Baddalaur had fallen, the Chopts would either fall back and destroy the Bastions or simply starve them out; either way, they couldn't afford to have them at their backs while they pressed on towards the capital.

And what if Baddalaur fell? What if the bards were butchered and all the knowledge held within these hallowed halls was destroyed—what would happen to the World of Men then? Would it go down in flames as Ectoraige claimed?

And if Baddalaur was destroyed in the name of the Religion and the power generated by that destruction transferred to its gods, how powerful would that make the Gods of the New Religion? Strong enough to defeat the Pantheon of the Old Faith?

The bard had tried contacting his own gods, but with no response; they, too, were preparing for war.

And if the gods were unable or unwilling to assist him, then he would have to fight the approaching army some other way—or at least hold them until Kutor and his army arrived, but that was still some four days away. And what hope had a single man against an army of thousands?

Katani's plan was simple and direct. "The town is indefensible; its walls are too low, its gates too many and too flimsy—it is wide open. But Baddalaur itself is a different matter. It is Culai-built; its walls are thicker than a tall man, and it has but one gate, and that is solid teel-wood." She looked at the faces around the table, Bastion and Ectoraige on her left, Ironwinter on her right. Sitting directly across from her was Seon, Master Bard of Baddalaur, and standing behind him, looking deep into the blazing fire was Paedur the Bard.

She took a deep breath and continued slowly. "I suggest we evacuate the town to the College and then booby-trap the empty buildings, the walls, the gates, even the alley-ways. The Chopts will take Badaur—we know that—but at least we can make them pay dearly for it."

"The College is already full..." Seon said stiffly.

"Nonsense," Ectoraige said. "You could easily double or treble the numbers here without too much trouble. I think the plan has merit. Paedur?" he asked.

"I think it is an excellent suggestion," he said, and then paused. "There are two possible problems, however," he said slowly, glancing sidelong at the group around the table. Firelight and shadow took his face, painting it red and black. "You must first convince the townspeople to move—and secondly, I think we are forgetting the Trialdone."

Ectoraige smiled, his boyish smile completely in contrast with his deep voice. "This is a college of storytellers and myth-makers, surely some of these professional storytellers could go down into the town and frighten the people up here." The smile faded and the god's stone-grey eyes looked directly into the bard's reflective gaze. "But you must face the Trialdone yourself. If the People of the Ice were to lose the Trialdone, then it would be a bitter blow to them. The seasons would immediately begin to return to normal and without the Trialdone, the killings committed in the Religion's name would take longer to be absorbed by the new gods. Their deaths would not only weaken the Chopts, but also all the gods of the Religion. But only you can face the Trialdone, bard, and you must do it in the Ghost World."

"They are gods and I am but a man," Paedur said into the deathly silence.

"They are not gods, bard, and you are more than a man!"

"Could we turn the Chopts back?" Seon asked, fear making his clipped accent sound harsh.

"No." All heads turned to Ironwinter. The beast shook his head. "Not now; it is too late and they are too far down this road to be turned aside now."

"Who commands them?" Seon demanded. "Could he not be prevailed upon...?"

"They follow Stonehand, Lord of the People of the Ice; his word is law."

"But you said he was in thrall to Praetens," Seon said, turning to Ectoraige.

"He was," the god said, "but Praetens is dead now, and Mannam, the once-god, has taken over the spell."

Bastion cleared his throat. "What would it take to lift that spell?"

"The death of Mannam," Ectoraige said. "Or if not his death, then he would have to be wounded, hurt or threatened—something that would call upon all his power. At the moment, a tiny fraction of power is all that holds the king in thrall."

"And if the spell was lifted or broken," Bastion asked hoarsely, "how do you think Stonehand would react? Would he be aware of what had been happening? Would he know he had been used?"

Ectoraige nodded. "I'm sure of it."

"Then let me slay this Mannam," Ironwinter said quickly. "I am Chopt. I can pass through their ranks..."

"It would need two," Paedur said quietly. "One to distract or wound Mannam—and I would suggest fire as the most likely method—the other to assist Stonehand. When the spell is broken he will be disorientated and confused, but susceptible. If some-one was to suggest to him that the Chopts were to retreat, there is every possibility that he would agree to it."

"I will go with Ironwinter," Bastion said.

"So it is settled..." Ectoraige coughed, and the cough broke, changing in timbre to become high-pitched and shrill. "I must leave you now," the God of Learning and Knowledge said quickly. "I can do no more. I have lingered too long in this body as it is. I go now to fight with my brothers on the chequered fields of

Ab-Apsalom." He turned to look at Paedur, and even as he spoke, his eyes visibly changed from grey to brown. "So it comes back down to you again, bard. Should you fail then we all go down with you. Look to your lore, bard, look to your lore…"

…Deep-brown eyes blinked around the room, and the boy Gire said simply, "I feel so tired now."

Paedur walked with Katani along one of the galleries that looked down into Baddalaur's main library. The huge three-storeyed building was deserted and completely silent, the huge walls and cushioned doors blocking out all sound, and the Katan found it difficult to believe that there were whole families sleeping in the corridors outside.

Badaur's inhabitants had moved up from the town with surprising speed and with very little reluctance; the threat of the Chopts was enough for them to leave their flimsy dwellings for the comparative safety of Baddalaur's Culai-built walls. Now, every room— with the exception of the main library—was occupied, from the attics to the cellars. All the old wells—and there were more than a score—were uncovered and cleaned, and after some threats, all the resources and supplies from the town had been pooled and passed onto the bards for eventual distribution in the coming siege. A few had resisted this sharing of wealth, but usually a visit from Paedur— or the threat of a visit—was enough to make them change their minds. When the town was completely emptied, Katani, Bastion, and Ironwinter had moved in, and turned every street, door, window, cellar, and well into a devastating booby-trap. The first wave of Chopts that swept through Badaur would be cut to pieces, but enough of the traps were within the buildings, and these would only be triggered at a later stage.

"Can we win this conflict?" Katani asked quietly, not looking at the bard, but concentrating on row upon row of polished brown, ochre, bronze, and gold leather bindings, each one embossed with the eye and triangle sigil of the College.

"That depends how you define 'win,'" the bard murmured, not looking at her.

"Will we survive?"

"The beasts are many and we are few."

"That is not an answer to my question."

Paedur bowed his head slightly. "It isn't, but I don't have an answer to your question. I do not know. All we can do is fight, but remembering that if we fail then this Plane of Existence and all the others go down into Chaos."

"Truly?" she asked.

"Truly," he nodded.

They continued on in silence, until eventually Katani asked, "So what happens now?"

"Now we wait. The beasts approach from the north, the rebel army from the south. Our own army also approaches from the south, but it is too far away to help us. All we can do is to try and ensure that the Chopt numbers have been reduced considerably by the time they arrive."

They had reached the end of the gallery. Above, around and below them lay the library. The cool, pale northern light lanced in through the tall, high windows, washing the books, scrolls, charts, and maps in wan ghostly light. Dust motes swam in the slanting rays; giving the place an almost timeless character—as if this was how it had been since the dawn of the world, and this was how it would be when all the Planes of Existence aligned and the worlds collapsed onto one another and ended. Paedur gestured down with his hook to the main floor, with its long reading tables, some still piled high with books and charts. The walls were lined with books. "With this I could create a world, give it a history, past and present, a geography, a pantheon of gods, a technology and a future. Knowledge is power— and this is the greatest collection of knowledge in any one place…"

"And yet it is all too vulnerable to destruction by beasts who can barely speak, let alone read," the Katan murmured.

"Ignorance always tries to tear down knowledge." His eyes blinked soft and golden in the light for a few moments, but then he turned back to Katani, and they took the whiteness of her hair, making him look blind. "I go to fight the Trialdone this night…" He paused, and then reached beneath his cloak and handed Katani a short tube of time-yellowed ivory, stopped at both ends with gold. "When all else seems lost, you may use this; open it and read the scroll within. Ectoraige told me to look to my lore as if an answer lay therein. I've looked, but I discovered nothing…however, I remembered this." He tapped the tube with the flat of his hook, and Katani saw a blue spark wind around the tube and leap onto the metal.

"What is it?" she asked, turning it over in her hands.

"Something...Something I won a long time ago. It may even be the solution." He shook his head. "I don't know."

"You sound as if you don't expect to return..." Katani said very softly.

The bard smiled slightly. "I didn't say that."

"I know you didn't."

He turned away abruptly and strode down the gallery towards the stairs. Caught by surprise, Katani hurried to catch up with him. "There are three Chopt scouts to the north of here. They are watching our every movement and reporting back to the army by means of messenger birds. I was unsure whether to kill them or not, but now with Bastion and Ironwinter about to set off for the Chopt camp, it becomes necessary."

Katani smiled hugely. "I will see to it personally."

Mannam consulted his charts and then turned to Geillard. "At this rate another two days travel should see us pounding on Baddalaur's gates."

The deposed Emperor's long-fingered hands closed into fists. "Then everything will be as it was," he said softly.

Within his cowl of seared and withered leaves, Mannam, the once-god, smiled deeply.

Owen the Weapon Master pushed away the charts and looked across the table at Fodla and Kutor. "At this rate, we've another four days ahead of us at least."

The Commander of the Legion shook her head. "Geillard's forces will be there in two, and the deserting soldiers in or around the same time. We're going to arrive too late."

"But a small party riding hard could be there in two days," Tien tZo suggested quietly.

Kutor looked at him. "What would that achieve?"

The Shemmat shrugged. "Only the Gods know—but it might be enough to tilt the balance. Wars are not won by huge armies, but by the actions of single men."

"How small a party?" Keshian asked.

"Three, possibly four men."

"Make it three men and leave before sunset," Kutor said tightly. He was all too aware that this campaign was balanced on a knife edge, on decisions made, on immediate action and incisive decisions. He didn't even want to stop to think whether those decisions were the right ones.

The Lady Esse took the deeply curved, black-handled knife and approached Rom, her Gallowglas bodyguard. The red-eyed creature that was the vampir followed her silently, like an obedient pet.

She looked up into the Gallowglas's impassive face. "Stretch out your hand," she commanded.

The huge warrior immediately stretched out his left hand. The twisted old woman took the knife and quickly slashed open the man's palm. His face and eyes remained expressionless, betraying nothing. The Lady Esse then turned to the vampir and, wrapping her hand in the creature's greasy hair, shoved her face onto the man's bloody hand. The creature began to drink. "Obey this man whose life's blood you have sipped," she commanded, lifting the blood-smeared face off his hand and staring into its crimson eyes. "Obey him!" And then she shoved the face back to the palm. "She will follow you, do as you command," the old woman said to Rom. "But ensure that she is fed—otherwise her craving for blood will be such that she will feed off you."

The Gallowglas bowed deeply.

The Lady Esse spread an ancient chart on the table before her. Her long-nailed finger tapped it. "This is Baddalaur before the town grew up around it. These lines represent air ducts into the lower cellars and ventilation shafts to regulate the library rooms. Some of them must still exist." She allowed the chart to snap closed. "Find one and you have your way into the College. I want you both to leave now. I want you to reach Baddalaur before the army—and I want you to slay the bard. No-one else matters now. Just the bard. Paedur the Bard must die!"

The bard couldn't remember the last time he had slept. He wondered, as he lay down on the cold stones on the top floor of the tower, what it would be like to close his eyes and drift off into dreamless sleep. Since he had become one of the God-Sought, God-Taught, and the Champion of the Old Faith, he had lost much of the simple pleasures of humankind; he ate but rarely, drank only water, and never seemed to sleep. The closest he came to sleep was when he shut down all his senses one by one, cutting off the exterior world and retreating into himself—and even then he was still always aware of his surroundings.

Composing himself, he prepared to enter the Ghost World. Every human entered the Ghost World while they slept; while the physical body rested, the essence—the soul—wandered through the formless space of the Ghost World, the grey void between the Planes of Existence. Mystics claimed that dreams were a fragmentary re-membrance of the soul's experiences within the Ghost World.

But the bard knew that the Ghost World was much more. To those with power, it was a place where thought could become fact, a place where dreams and nightmares walked hand in hand, moving at the whim of their creator. It could be a place of great beauty—or one of absolute terror.

And the bard who went to do battle with the Trialdone had no doubt which it would be.

The Chopt stretched his stiffened legs and eased back his cramped shoulders. He had been lying in the snow for most of the day, watching the distant College of Bards, observing the movements in and out—and now, with the sun beginning to sink down in the west, he was as convinced as he had been at sunrise that it was all a total and absolute waste of time. The town around the College was sealed tighter than an ice-locked lake, and he and his two compan-ions were too far away from the building to make out the numbers and disposition of the guards on the battlements. So far all he had to report was that no-one had entered or left the town all day, and that was poor return for a day spent freezing in the snow. Well, he'd wait until the sun sank and then he would join his brothers...

He closed his eyes and rolled over in the snow—and Katani's longsword removed his head from his shoulders!

The warrior had left the town through one of the postern gates as dusk was seeping in across the ice-fields. She had daubed her armour with whitewash, left off her helmet, and powdered her face to match her ice-white hair, so that even Bastion and Ironwinter, who were watching her as she moved through the banks of snow, could barely pick her out from her surroundings.

She had found the first beast by the simple expedient of fol-lowing her nose. The creature might be perfectly disguised in the ice-fields, but he stank—a rich, musky animal odour, combined with the stench of raw flesh, that stood out like a beacon on the cold sharp air.

She found the second beast by the same method, and killed him while he still slept.

Night had fallen by the time she approached the third beast, but this time he was prepared. Something—perhaps the stench of blood on the air—had alerted him. He had turned in time to see the creature in white glide through the bushes towards him, and for a moment his heart almost stopped in his chest as he imagined that the Lady Lussa—the White Goddess—was coming for him. But then the fading light had glinted on the creature's sword and he realised that this was no Goddess or Duaiteoiri—this was a mere human, and the humankind were easy prey.

The beast lunged with a trident as soon as the creature came within reach—and Katani deftly sliced the head off the weapon, and then her second sword licked out and tore through the creature's throat. While he gagged in surprise, she removed his head.

By the time the Lady Lussa had risen much higher in the heavens, Katani had returned to the town, and Bastion and Ironwinter had left by the same gate to set out on their own mission.

No one, especially Bastion and Ironwinter, expected them to return.

The vampir suddenly picked up her head, her nostrils flaring like a hunting animal's having found the scent. The red-eyed creature in the body of the woman stopped and silently pointed out across the ice-fields, away from the town and College. Her pointing fingers moved twice more, and the Gallowglas by her side got the impression that she had scented three fresh corpses in the snow. He was tempted to investigate. What had died in this desolate landscape so close to Baddalaur?

The vampir made a sound deep in her throat—the vampir had not the power of speech—but the Gallowglas recognised the query in her voice. He shook his head and pointed towards the shadowed bulk of Badaur with Baddalaur rising massive and ominous above it. "The Lady Esse would not permit it," he said roughly. He was unsure how much the creature understood. Sometimes he imagined it was nothing more than an animal in a human body—an animal with a taste for human blood—but there were times when he looked at her and he thought he discerned a gleam of intelligence in her eyes. "There will be blood within the College—including the ichor of the bard, and that should be a rich feast indeed."

The Gallowglas settled his huge sword on his back and then continued his search through the gnarled clump of bushes that grew in the lee of an ancient outcropping of weathered stone. He was working mainly by touch, for although the Lady Lussa provided ample light, it still left the interior of the stone in deep shadow, and he was loath to strike a light which would only betray his position, but if needs be...

He discovered the grille close to the ground, a rusted rectangle set into the stone outcropping, completely concealed by the bush. He wrapped a large hand around the grille and pulled. Nothing happened. Gripping it in both hands he leaned back, exerting his full weight on the grille but it still didn't move. And then a small pale hand—its nails were long and filthy, he suddenly noticed—wrapped itself around one of the rusted bars and ripped it clean out of the wall.

Rom lay on the snow-covered ground and peered into the darkness of the tunnel. He could see nothing, but musty, cold air wafted past his face. If it had originally been part of the air-shafts that honeycombed Baddalaur, then it ran directly into the lower cellars of the College.

The Gallowglas smiled grimly. He had his way into the College of Bards. He glanced at his pale-skinned, red-eyed companion— and had no doubt but that she could kill the bard.

Owen the Weapon Master reined his mount and pointed to the distant shape on the skyline. Behind him Tien tZo and Fodla halted their own labouring mounts. With the Lady Lussa rising almost directly overhead, it looked like an image—a faery image of a castle— towers and turrets spiking the night sky.

"Baddalaur," Owen panted. "We should be there by dawn."

The grey void of the Ghost World was bright with shifting, twisting lights, tiny sparkling balls that spun and sizzled against the vaguely damp texture of the place between the planes.

The bard could taste the power, the raw energy that strode through the Ghost World. The expanse, which was usually inhabited by the

shadowy essences of those who slept in the myriad Worlds of Men,
was empty, and the bard guessed that there would be many nightmares in the World of the Humankind that night.

He turned around and looked back, seeing his own body lying
on the simple bed in the tower in the College of Bards. It was
possible for him to bring his physical body through into the Ghost
World, but it took energy and power, and Paedur knew he would
need all his power to survive this encounter with the Trialdone.

If they attacked him, taking him by surprise, there was no way
he could survive, so he would have to carry the fight to them. Willing himself higher, the bard moved straight up through the shifting
grey mass, which allowed him an overview of the patterns of power
and light that were forming and reforming in its misty heart.

The bard spotted several areas of power in the Ghost World
below, but there were three distinct spots that were positioned close
together, and all of them tinged with the vaguely reddish-black glow
of the Religion.

The bard drifted lower...

The Trialdone had created a garden for themselves out of the
stuff of the Ghost World. A simple garden of stunted trees and
low shrubs, surrounding a green-scummed pond whose waters were
solid with the detritus of the forest. Vaguely wondering why they
had expended energy in the creation of the image, the bard stepped
onto the rotten mulch. By accepting the creation and entering into it,
he had also accepted its reality. Now the trees, the bushes, the foul
weeds, the odours of wood and rot, the bitter-sweet smell of pu-
trefaction were all real.

Paedur waited patiently, his senses alert, watching, listening.

There was no sound in this creation, no birds sang in the trees,
nothing moved through the undergrowth. It might look like a forest dell, but it was still a dead place.

And then there was a scream.

High-pitched and agonised, it echoed through the creation. A
cold knot settled in the bard's stomach, for the scream had been
familiar, hauntingly familiar. Although he knew it was a trap, the
sound drew him. Ducking beneath an overhanging branch, he set
off through the trees towards the sound. The Gods alone knew
what the Trialdone had brought into the Ghost World, but whatever
it was, it was obviously something the bard knew...

The trees ended abruptly, and across a small almost circular clearing he spotted the cell, a simple construction of stone, daubed with mud, and then—suddenly, terrifyingly—he realised where he was. He was back in the Forest of Euarthe, back where it had all started, back where Mannam had first come for him.

The scream rent the fetid air once again—and then he knew why it had been so familiar. He was hearing his own voice.

His first thoughts were to blast the cell, call down his power and unleash it in a levin bolt that would rip through the stone cell and whatever—or whoever—lurked inside.

But his own voice? Why his own voice? And this was no magical imitation, he knew that much. This was the voice of Paedur the Bard.

Touching the knife in his boot, a weapon he had not used for a long time, he crossed the clearing in four quick strides. He called upon his enhanced senses just before he burst through the opening. There were three of power and one of humankind within…

In the still quiet hour before the dawn, Bastion and Ironwinter came upon the Chopt army. They immediately realised that their intelligence reports had been wrong on two accounts—it was far larger than they had suspected, and it was also far closer to Baddalaur!

The Chopt and the Marked Man lay in the snow and looked down over the edge of the bluff onto an army that stretched almost as far as the eye could see. It was a huge chaotic mess, with absolutely no order or pattern to it—but this, combined with its size, only rendered it more intimidating. Abruptly, both Bastion and Ironwinter had absolutely no doubts that this army could indeed take and destroy Baddalaur.

"Where would you expect to find Stonehand's camp?" Bastion hissed.

The Chopt shrugged. "It could be anywhere."

Bastion ground his teeth in frustration. Time was against them; they needed to find the king's tent now.

Ironwinter suddenly pointed. "There; that tent is not unlike the king's tent, and it is alongside other tents of quality. That one is certainly of Torc Allta design, and that one off to the left is Gallowglas, I'm sure of it."

Bastion followed the Chopt's pointing arm, and slowly nodded in agreement—but the king's tent was on the other side of the camp. To reach it they would have to walk right through the huge army.

But moving through the army proved to be surprisingly easy. There was such a racial mixture of humankind, the various Chopt tribes, as well as Torc Allta and Gallowglas, that no one paid any attention to the cowled man and the Chopt as they made their way through the churned mud and slush towards the tents of the leaders.

As they drew near the tents, they separated. Their plan was simple; Ironwinter would walk past the guards and into the tent while Bastion would attempt to gain entry through the rear. They would take Mannam first; both man and beast were carrying small pots of Luid-dust and oil. They would break the pots on Mannam and then push him into the fire...after that their plan got hazy.

"You! You're Ironwinter!" One of the Chopts standing guard before the tent suddenly shouted, fumbling with his trident.

Ironwinter hit the beast just below the snout, shattering the jaw bone, teeth, and neck in one blow. Continuing to move, he smashed the hilt of his knife up between the second guard's eyes, sending him crashing back into the tent...

Time slowed...

Ironwinter raced into the tent, and found himself facing a huge Torc Allta. His knife lifted, slashed, slashed again and the Torc Allta was down, his throat open from ear to ear. Behind him, but seated at a table was another of the Boar-Folk, the one called Fenar, and beside him sat Stonehand and Geillard. Mannam stood behind the Chopt king.

Ignoring the others, Ironwinter grabbed the pot of Luid-dust and oil from his belt and threw it left-handed at the once-god. It fell short and shattered on the ground, soaking his feet. The Chopt smelt the sweet sharp scent of the oil and then the Torc Allta was before him, his left arm extended—and Ironwinter felt the pain in his chest then...

Time slowed...

Dimly he saw the back of the tent split apart and Bastion's scarred face appear behind Mannam. He saw the man's arm go up and fall ...dimly heard the breaking of the pot, distantly smelt the oil.

The pain became agony as the Torc Allta ripped the sword from his chest and turned, and in the last few heartbeats of clarity that remained to him, he saw the spark—and felt the heat and clearly heard the explosion. His eyes fluttered, and his last image was of the once-god burning in a solid pillar of flame.

Time stopped.

The pillar of flame sliced through the night sky, a roaring crackling, thunderous column that looked curiously like a huge tree. And Katani, standing alone in the tower in Baddalaur, bent her head and wept for the first time ever. Her wish was that her companions' passing had been swift and painless.

The blast that destroyed Mannam badly burned Stonehand and Geillard, but curiously both Bastion and Fenar were barely scorched. Both man and beast had been thrown clear by the explosion, and later, when Bastion was brought before the Torc Allta, their conversation had been brief and civilised.

"I admire bravery," Fenar na Torc Allta said, blinking at the Marked Man through singed eyes, his hands rubbing at flame-yellowed tusks. "But I deplore stupidity."

"The line between the two is very fine," Bastion said very softly. All his wounds had opened and he was in great pain.

"What did you hope to gain?"

Bastion shrugged and then winced as torn flesh and muscles protested. "Ultimately a little time, I think. We had some plan about releasing Stonehand from Mannam's spell, but it was a vague, formless plan. We knew if we slew Mannam, we would have struck a great blow for our cause."

"You have seen the size of our army; how can you doubt that we will succeed?" Fenar asked.

"But you have seen what two determined men can do. And you are facing a host of determined men."

"I still think you will lose."

"So do I," Bastion agreed, very quietly.

Fenar stood. "Because you are a brave man, I will do you the honour of killing you myself, and your meat will honour my table."

Bastion bowed to hide his smile—and Fenar na Torc Allta took off his head with a single blow of his sword.

Later, the leaders of the Torc Allta were joined by the Gallowglas leaders as well as some of the elders of the Chopts, to enjoy the flesh of the would-be assassin. The meat—served raw or cooked according to taste—was consumed with all the ceremony and respect due to a brave man.

Later still, the guards standing outside the tent would investigate the curious silence within. They would find the diners dead—all dead; they had been poisoned by the meat. Bastion had been a walking dead man for far too long; his flesh had been rotten.

Within the stone cell, the Trialdone were torturing the figure of a man. Ghede had wrapped his beast-like arms around his body, while the Lady Asherat held the figure's left arm out from his body. Her eyes were bright, even in the darkness, and her tongue was like a serpent's, flicking wetly across her lips. Sheesarak the Destroyer stood before the figure, both his hands closed tightly around the man's wrist. He twisted—and the man threw back his head and screamed again...

And the face and body were those of Paedur the bard...

There was a sickening crack and blood splashed across the trio. Sheesarak lifted his hands; he was holding a curved rune-etched silver hook, tendrils of flesh and muscle still attached to the end.

Even as he attacked, Paedur knew what they were doing. He could feel the agony already beginning low in his left arm, just above where his hook joined the bone of his wrist. They had created a simulacrum—a likeness—and by destroying it they were hoping to destroy him. Indeed, they would destroy him unless...

His hook opened the copper-colour flesh of Sheesarak's back from shoulder to base of spine, and as the god spun around, the bard's hook cut at his face, opening a second wound from jaw to eye, sending him reeling away, his face a mask of reddish-blue blood.

Paedur continued moving, his hook punching into Ghede's shoulder, sinking into the flesh, twisting, tearing away a huge chunk of muscle...

And then the Lady Asherat was behind him. Her hair wrapped itself around him like coiled ropes, sliding off his cloak, the fur sizzling. It touched his flesh—and burned red weals into the skin. He felt her long nails sinking to her fingertips into the flesh of his back, and knew if she closed her hands, she would literally tear away gobbets of flesh. He reversed the knife in his right hand, striking backwards blindly, feeling the blade meet brief resistance and then

sink home. Her grip on his flesh loosened. He turned the knife in
the wound, wrenching it upwards...and then dropped to the floor
as Ghede lurched for him. He slashed at the creature's face as he
went down, sending him stumbling into the Lady Asherat. Her
hair—like a nest of serpents—coiled around the Trialdone's bare
flesh, hissing, sizzling, burning through to the bone. Strands touched
his eyes, his mouth...panicking, the huge beast struck at her, its great
claws battering the fine features, cracking her skull. Her blade-like
fingernails sank into his chest just below his heart...

The bard used the opportunity to open both their throats with
his hook.

Now only the Destroyer remained.

Tien spotted the disturbance in the snow in the pale dawn light.
"This way. Here!" He reined in his mount and dropped from the
saddle, examining the marks around the opening in the outcropping
of stone. Owen and Fodla remained on their mounts, watching
him, not wishing to disturb the ground with their own tracks.

"A man, tall, heavy, armoured...and a woman, small, light, bare-
footed. Together they pulled this grille from the wall and went
inside..." He stood and looked towards the College. "It leads to
Baddalaur."

Owen and Fodla both dropped from their saddles. Without a
word, they followed Tien into the tunnel.

There were people everywhere.

It took the Gallowglas a few moments to realise what had happened; the townspeople had been taken into the College, which meant
that there were several floors and the Gods alone knew how many
people between him and the bard.

Rom stepped back into the cellar and pulled the door closed,
wedging it shut with a length of wood. The vampir stood on
the stairs behind him, her pale face and red eyes mask-like in the
vague light that filtered down to the disused cellar. He was unsure how much the vampir understood, so he kept his commands simple and direct. "There are people outside. Many
people. Too many to kill. We must have a distraction—something that will draw the people away from here. Do you know
where the bard is now?"

The creature's face remained expressionless but she nodded once. "Are you sure?"

Again the single nod. And then the vampir pointed, her arm raising up, her fingers curling, pointing with index and little finger.

Rom nodded. He lifted his long two-handed sword which was as tall as he, and pulled it slowly and lovingly from its leather sheath. He dropped the sheath—he wouldn't be needing it again—and pulled off his cloak so as to leave his arms unencumbered. He was going out to die—but he would take many of the enemy with him. Death held no fears for him—the Lady Esse had promised to return him to this world when the Religion's Gods had triumphed. And what honour would be his then? He would have been instrumental in the destruction of the ultimate symbol of the Faith—the cursed bard, Paedur.

He looked at the vampir for a final time. "I will draw the enemy away from here. You must kill the bard. Do not fail us now!"

And the Gallowglas stepped out into the crowded hall…

Three bards were standing directly in front of the door, talking to a baker from the town. They had almost convinced the man to assist in the College kitchens when his eyes suddenly widened in shock as he looked past them. They turned slowly, curiously—and the Gallowglas's huge blade scythed through the three of them. The Gallowglas allowed the terrified baker to scream once before he killed him also.

There was a single shocked moment of silence and immobility, and then everyone turned and fled down the corridor, while the Gallowglas stood and laughed.

Rom strode down the hall, using his huge sword selectively, killing some, wounding others. He favoured those wearing the colours of the College. He always allowed them to scream before killing them, smiling as their cries brought others to the corridor, to his sword.

He glanced behind only once, and that was to see the vampir dart out of the dark cellar opening and move swiftly and silently in the opposite direction.

Time, all he needed now was time. Time to allow the vampir to slay the bard.

"Vampir," Tien breathed, throwing back his head and breathing in the dry atmosphere of the tunnel.

"What?" Fodla demanded.

"I can smell vampir on the air; can you not smell it?"

The Commander of the Legion breathed deeply, and then nodded. "Blood and dead meat."

"The bard!" Owen snapped. "It must be after the bard."

"But who is with the creature?" Fodla asked. "You said there were two…"

"A large, heavy man…" Tien mused.

"Gallowglas—the Lady Esse's guard," Owen said quickly. "We've got to get to the bard."

Katani was standing in the tower, looking out over the walls, watching the line of the Chopt army march across the snow-fields, when she heard the screams from below. She looked down in time to see a huge warrior, wielding a sword as tall as himself, come marching out into the courtyard, wreaking slaughter. She saw guards running at him—only to be cut down by the fearsome sword.

She turned and looked into the room behind her where the bard still slept, wondering what to do. He had left instructions that on no account—no matter what happened—was he to be disturbed. His breathing was rapid, his long thin hair was plastered to his head and his pale face was sheened in sweat. Beneath his closed eyelids, his eyes were darting.

Another chorus of screams brought her back to the parapet, but still she lingered a moment longer, loath to leave the bard's side. Was this just a single warrior on a suicide mission, or had more of the Gallowglas managed to breach the College's defences? But if there were more, well, then, where were they? Convinced that this was a single warrior, she turned and raced down the stairs to do battle with it—and ran headlong into the vampir!

The vampir screamed—a blood-chilling sound that was designed to freeze its victims immobile—but the sound was cut short as Katani's gauntleted fists closed around its throat. Off-balance, the vampir staggered backwards and then fell, dragging the warrior down the stairs with her. Even as they were falling, bouncing off the stone steps, crashing into the walls, the vampir's fangs were slashing at Katani, rasping along her link-mail, and her fists were hammering at the Katan's body armour. All Katani could do was to hold on, her hands locked around the creature's throat, blanking her mind to the agony of snapping bones and torn flesh, concentrating on the creature in her hands, forcing the head back, her thumbs in the soft flesh of the jaw, pressing...

It was two hundred and twenty steps to the bottom of the tower...

They burst out of the tunnel following the screams. In the corridor they found the first of the bodies and it was then a simple matter of following the trail of death and destruction.

They found the Gallowglas standing in the centre of the courtyard, surrounded by the dead and dying. The huge warrior was splashed with blood, but none of it seemed to be his. He turned slowly towards the three—now the only people moving in the courtyard—and his eyes brightened.

"The Weapon Master and Kutor's Commander. I am pleased that I warrant such attention. Will you come at me together, or will you do me honour in single combat?"

"Kill him now," Tien advised. "A thrown knife..."

Owen stepped forward. "Single combat." He glanced back over his shoulder at Tien and Fodla. "Find the bard," he said, "I'll take care of this." He was slowly walking across the courtyard to the Gallowglas when the huge warrior attacked. For all his size, and the weight of his sword, he moved surprisingly swiftly, using the longsword as if it weighed no more than a knife.

Even though he was unprepared for the sudden assault, Owen was already moving as the sword came whistling in, but the blade still caught him low on the side, the blow cracking his armour, but not cutting through to the skin, spinning him away, half a dozen ribs cracked or broken. Ignoring the wounded man, the Gallowglas advanced on Fodla, his sword scything from side to side, its length giving him a decided advantage.

Fodla attacked with two swords, wielding them in a blinding intricate pattern, a move designed to confuse—but the Gallowglas's longsword simply swept through them both, shattering one and spinning the second from her grasp, snapping her wrist in the process.

Tien's thrown axe took the creature through the throat, stopping it in its tracks, and then the small Shemmat was alongside it, his knife licking out, slicing tendons and muscles, bringing the creature to its knees. In a last desperate movement Rom struck out blindly, the flat of his sword striking Fodla across her left knee, shattering it. And then Tien killed him.

A rib had punctured Owen's lung and he was spitting blood. "Find the bard," he hissed desperately.

And then from beyond the walls came the distant, but distinct savage howling of the Chopt army.

Tien found Katani first. She was lying at the bottom of the stairs that led to the highest tower in the College; she was unmoving and her legs were twisted at awkward angles. And it was only when he knelt beside her that he discovered that she was lying on top of a bloody rag that had once been a woman...a vampir, he corrected himself, seeing the creature's teeth. The Katan's hands were still locked around the creature's throat, but the top of its head was missing, where it had repeatedly struck the stones on the way down.

Tien gently touched Katani, brushing strands of her white hair from her face—and her amber eyes snapped open!

"Vampir," her mouth formed the word.

"I know." Tien nodded. "The bard?"

Katani's eyes moved upwards. "He...he does battle with the Trialdone...he cannot be woken..."

"The Chopts are close."

Katani's mouth worked, and blood began to trickle from her lips. "My belt pouch..."

Tien carefully, gently, lifted the woman's broken body and pulled off her belt pouch. Inside he found an ivory tube. It was cracked now and inside he could see a sheaf of ancient parchment.

Katani nodded when he showed it to her. "The bard gave it to me. Carry me to the battlements..." She saw the hesitation in his eyes. "Do it!"

Tien nodded and began to unbuckle Katani's weapons and heavier armour. It looked as if she had broken every bone in her body; there was surprisingly little blood, but she would be bleeding inside, he knew. She was surprisingly light when he lifted her and she made no sound, although he knew she must be in agony. "The bard?" he asked.

"The bard fights his own battle. He is beyond our help, and we beyond his."

Sheesarak the Destroyer touched his face with his right hand, his fingers coming away sticky with his own blood. The bard's hook had opened a wound from the point of his jaw to just below his left eye. A fraction to the right and he would have lost the eye. He could also feel his blood trickling down his back where the bard had first slashed him. "You have wounded me," he said, his voice astonished.

"Have you never been cut before?" Paedur asked, concentrating intently on the god, unwilling even to devote a fraction of his power to heal the wounds in his back from the Lady Asherat's claws. He remembered then that when she had walked the World of Men, she had slain women—always young, always virginal—using her nails, and then had bathed in their blood in an attempt to retain her youth. He wondered vaguely if her nails had been poisoned.

"I will cut you, bard," Sheesarak lifted the simulacrum's hook in his right hand. It was identical to the bard's, even down to the runes etched in the metal; in every respect it was the bard's hook. The Trialdone had obviously prepared their creature very carefully indeed; the closer it resembled its victim the more effective the magic—and this one looked identical! "What will happen if I cut you with your own hook, eh?"

"It is not my hook," Paedur said, glancing into the shadows behind the god to where the figure of the simulacrum sat rocking slowly to and fro, cradling its wrist.

The god smiled, exposing his long red teeth, and his voice regained some of its echoing quality. "Oh, but it is, bard. This is no simulacrum…this is no mud doll, no golem, no magical construct. This is Paedur the Bard!" The god stepped back and sank his long fingers into the creature's hair and pulled him to his feet, dragging him forward.

"Look—judge for yourself."

And the bard found himself looking into his own long, thin face. There were differences, of course. The simulacrum's face was slightly plumper, the eyes were dark, the mouth not so cruel, but it was still unmistakably his face.

"This is how you might have been, bard. This is you had you not accepted Mannam's quest. We plucked this bard from one of the closer Planes of Existence, indeed, one so close that it almost mirrors this one, but with minor—very minor—differences, of course. On that other plane, the bard Paedur didn't accept Mannam's quest, and the train of events that were set in motion then which lead up to this present situation, never occurred. On that neighbouring Plane of Existence, this creature, this shadow-you, is aware of your activities only as nightmares." Blood trickled into the god's mouth, making him grimace. "But do you know, bard, he is inextricably linked to you…" Slowly, the god drew the hook in his hand up along the man's back, opening the flesh in a huge wound…

And both the bard and the man screamed!

"You see, bard, you are linked. And if he dies, then so do you."

Paedur rubbed a shaking hand across his face. He tasted salt. "But you removed the hook, and I felt only the vaguest discomfort."

Sheesarak shrugged, and then winced as the pain of his back wound bit through him. "The hook is a magical construct, and not truly part of you." He cut the man again and again, and each time Paedur felt the wounds. He moved his right hand around and felt the blood on his back.

"Oh, yes," the Trialdone continued, "you will bleed. And you will die." The god laughed, the sound rising to boom around the small stone cell. "Do you know what is happening on the World of Men, bard? Even now the Chopt are preparing to attack the College of Bards; your servants are all wounded or dying. We have won, bard." He raised the hook high, and then brought it down and around, resting it against the man's throat. "It is time to die…"

Paedur moved. Calling down his power, he lunged forward, his left arm extended, his hook punching through the man in the god's arms, sundering the heart, bursting through his back—and then plunging into Sheesarak's heart! The god's howl sundered the fabric of the Ghost World, catapulting the three figures into the grey void. The hook in the god's hand rose and fell spasmodically— striking Paedur at the base of the skull, plunging deep into the spine! With his strength flowing out of him, Paedur drifted away from the god, one arm locked around the man Paedur, the other still buried in his chest…

The Chopts flowed across the plain in a vast undulating wave, the howls and cries suddenly joined by the throbbing of giant war drums from the south; the Lady Esse and her forces had arrived.

Luid-dust destroyed the gates of Badaur, and then the army—of humankind, Gallowglas, Torc Allta, and Chopts—swarmed through the town. Many died in the traps that Katani, Bastion and Ironwinter had laid, plunging into cellars set with spikes, opening booby-trapped doors, dying beneath hails of poisoned darts, setting off explosions. But the booby traps were finite in number, whereas the army seemed infinite.

Baddalaur's defenders—and they seemed pitifully few—lined the walls and attempted to keep the attackers away from the gates. The Chopts launched attack after attack, firing casks and satchels of Luid-dust against the huge iron-studded doors. Many fell short, but enough struck home or fell close enough to coat the base of the door and the ground around it in a fine layer of brown dust.

Now it was only a matter of time—a very short time—before it was set alight and the doors were breached. And when that happened it would all be over.

Katani appeared on the battlements directly above the gates. Tien stood behind her, physically holding her upright. With numb and broken fingers she pulled the single sheet of parchment from the ivory tube and unfolded it.

The words swam before her eyes, moving, twisting, changing symbols—until suddenly they were in a language she understood—Ko-eche, the dead language of the Katan Warriors. As she looked down the words, she felt a slow strength burn into her fingers and down through her body, and Tien suddenly felt the woman straighten and stand tall and erect—although both her legs were broken.

And Katani began to recite the Lament of Lugas.

Her first words were lost in the roar of battle—and then her voice suddenly gained in power—until it was booming across the ice-fields. The noise, the roars, cries, and screams all died, as everyone—man and beast—stopped, somehow compelled to listen to the ancient magical Lament.

But the Lament of Lugas had been created by the Old High Magic, and that magic drew its energy directly from its user. The flames began. Tiny at first, they lapped blue-white around Katani's feet, like miniature waves. But the heat was intense, strong enough to drive Tien back.

The Katan's voice thundered out, the sound high and eerie, the magical symbols woven into the words soothing, calming, dulling battle-incensed men and beasts. Weapons dropped from numbed fingers as, enwrapped in the spell, they all watched the slight figure on the battlements, seeing the blue flames wrap themselves around her and grow higher.

The Katan was burning, the intense heat melting away her mail shirt, turning the metal to liquid. The pain ate through the euphoria that had taken her and her voice faltered...

...And the Lament was taken up by a second voice, a strong, powerful trained voice.

Paedur the Bard gently lifted Katani out of the flames and handed her to Tien, and he took the scroll of parchment into his right hand. His eyes—no longer reflective now, merely dark and pained—looked across the courtyard and lingered briefly on Fodla and Owen, and then he turned back to the confused army. He took up the Lament again, reciting it without looking at the scroll, and the flames of the Old High Magic rose higher, consuming him, drawing its energy from him, sending it out into the massed armies below.

And the army turned away, single men at first, and then in greater and greater numbers, the men and beasts wandered away, each one wrapped up within his own thoughts, their task forgotten, hatred and enmities wiped clean by the Lament of Lugas.

The blue flames flared higher into a magnificent leaf shape— and then vanished. There was no sign of Paedur the Bard.

It was later, much, much later, that Tien tZo remembered that the man who had lifted Katani out of the flames and continued the Lament of Lugas had no hook...

Epilogue

So the wheel turned.

The Lament of Lugas, the Dove's Cry, that had set the bard out on his quest, now finished it. Lugas the Bard had invested the Lament with the last of the Old High Magic, imbuing it with the power to quieten even the most maddened of warriors. Even as the last words were hanging on the air, the army was disbanding, all thoughts of battle forgotten. And those who heard the Lament were never the same again.

When Kutor and his army rode into Baddalaur two days later, they found the fields deserted, the bodies of the dead smouldering on a huge funeral pyre. The dead included the remains of an old woman who had been found in one of the deserted wagons of the renegade army. Her corpse had been in an advanced state of decay and identification was impossible, but it was speculated that she had been the Lady Esse, perhaps slain by the power of the High Magic.

With the sudden loss of their followers, the Gods of the New Religion suffered a crushing defeat on the chequered fields of Ab-Apsalom, and when Kutor instituted the Faith as the official religion of his Empire, he effectively ended any real threat by the Religion. His reign was long and remarkably peaceful. Many said he had the blessing of the Gods.

Fodla and Owen recovered from their wounds and were eventually wed—much to everyone's surprise, even their own.

Tien requested and was given his freedom by Owen and joined the Order of Bards. He created a huge body of work, including the definitive biographies of both the Bard and the Weapon Master.

Gire went on to re-establish the Order of Ectoraige. He dedicated it not only to teaching but also to medicine and healing. Geillard, who never recovered from the burns he received when Mannam was destroyed, was one of his long-term patients. Towards the end of his life the old man embraced the Faith, and he is buried in the grounds of the Monastery.

The Katan Warrior never fully recovered from her wounds. Her broken bones never set properly, and her mind had been disturbed by the Old High Magic that fed off her essence. She never fought again, and one night she simply walked out of Karfondal and disappeared.

Katani was never seen again, although rumour and later legend placed her in the Northlands in the company of a tall, dark-eyed man with one hand...

Life of Paedur, the Bard